THE GUERMANTES WAY

THE GUERMANTES WAY

Marcel Proust

TRANSLATED
FROM THE FRENCH BY
C. K. Scott Moncrieff

Vintage Books
A DIVISION OF RANDOM HOUSE
NEW YORK

To

Mrs. H——,

on her Birthday

Oberon, in the Athenian glade,
Reduced by deft Titania's power,
Invented arts for Nature's aid
And from a snowflake shaped a flower:
Nature, to outdo him, wrought of human clay
A fairy blossom, which we acclaim to-day.

Hebe, to high Olympus borne,
Undoomed to death, by age uncurst,
Xeres and Porto, night and morn,
Let flow, to appease celestial thirst:
Ev'n so, untouched by years that envious pass
Youth greets the guests to-night and fills the glass.

Hesione, for monstrous feast,
Against a rock was chained, to die;
Young Hercles came, he slew the beast,
Nor won the award of chivalry:
E. S. P. H., whom monsters hold in awe,
Shield thee from injury, and enforce the law!

                                        C. K. S. M.

CONTENTS

Part I

Part II

The French text of Le Côté de Guermantes *being extremely inaccurate, every
care has been taken to correct it in the
process of translation. In three places
in this volume the sequence of para-
graphs has been altered, as the reader
may discover by comparing the French
and English texts.*

THE
GUERMANTES WAY

PART I

CHAPTER ONE

THE DUCHESSE DE GUERMANTES

THE twittering of the birds at daybreak sounded insipid to Françoise. Every word uttered by the maids upstairs made her jump; disturbed by all their running about, she kept asking herself what they could be doing. In other words, we had moved. Certainly the servants had made no less noise in the attics of our old home; but she knew them, she had made of their comings and goings familiar events. Now she faced even silence with a strained attention. And as our new neighbourhood appeared to be as quiet as the boulevard on to which we had hitherto looked had been noisy, the song (distinct at a distance, when it was still quite faint, like an orchestral *motif*) of a passer-by brought tears to the eyes of a Françoise in exile. And so if I had been tempted to laugh at her in her misery at having to leave a house in which she was 'so well respected on all sides' and had packed her trunks with tears, according to the Use of Combray, declaring superior to all possible houses that which had been ours, on the other hand I, who found it as hard to assimilate new as I found it easy to abandon old conditions, I felt myself drawn towards our old servant when I saw that this installation of herself in a building where she had not received from the hall-porter, who did not yet know us, the marks of respect necessary to her moral wellbeing, had brought her positively to the verge of dissolution. She alone could understand what I was feeling; certainly her young footman was not the person to do so; for him, who was as unlike the Combray type as it was possible to conceive, packing up, moving, living in another district, were all like taking a holiday in which the novelty of one's surroundings gave one the same sense of refreshment as if one had actually travelled; he thought he was in the country; and a cold in the head afforded him, as though he had been sitting in a draughty railway carriage, the delicious sensation of having seen the world; at each fresh sneeze he rejoiced that he had found so smart a place, having always longed to be with people who travelled a lot. And so, without giving him a thought, I went straight to Françoise, who, in return for my having

laughed at her tears over a removal which had left me cold, now shewed
an icy indifference to my sorrow, but because she shared it. The 'sensibility'
claimed by neurotic people is matched by their egotism; they cannot abide
the flaunting by others of the sufferings to which they pay an ever increasing attention in themselves. Françoise, who would not allow the least of
her own ailments to pass unnoticed, if I were in pain would turn her head
from me so that I should not have the satisfaction of seeing my sufferings
pitied, or so much as observed. It was the same as soon as I tried to speak
to her about our new house. Moreover, having been obliged, a day or two
later, to return to the house we had just left, to retrieve some clothes
which had been overlooked in our removal, while I, as a result of it, had
still a 'temperature,' and like a boa constrictor that has just swallowed
an ox felt myself painfully distended by the sight of a long trunk which
my eyes had still to digest, Françoise, with true feminine inconstancy,
came back saying that she had really thought she would stifle on our old
boulevard, it was so stuffy, that she had found it quite a day's journey to
get there, that never had she seen such stairs, that she would not go back
to live there for a king's ransom, not if you were to offer her millions—a
pure hypothesis—and that everything (everything, that is to say, to do
with the kitchen and 'usual offices') was much better fitted up in the new
house. Which, it is high time now that the reader should be told—and told
also that we had moved into it because my grandmother, not having been
at all well (though we took care to keep this reason from her), was in
need of better air—was a flat forming part of the Hôtel de Guermantes.

At the age when a Name, offering us an image of the unknowable which
we have poured into its mould, while at the same moment it connotes for
us also an existing place, forces us accordingly to identify one with the
other to such a point that we set out to seek in a city for a soul which it
cannot embody but which we have no longer the power to expel from the
sound of its name, it is not only to towns and rivers that names give an
individuality, as do allegorical paintings, it is not only the physical universe which they pattern with differences, people with marvels, there is
the social universe also; and so every historic house, in town or country,
has its lady or its fairy, as every forest has its spirit, as there is a nymph
for every stream. Sometimes, hidden in the heart of its name, the fairy is
transformed to suit the life of our imagination by which she lives; thus it
was that the atmosphere in which Mme. de Guermantes existed in me,
after having been for years no more than the shadow cast by a magic lantern
slide or the light falling through a painted window, began to let its colours
fade when quite other dreams impregnated it with the bubbling coolness
of her flowing streams.

And yet the fairy must perish if we come in contact with the real person
to whom her name corresponds, for that person the name then begins to
reflect, and she has in her nothing of the fairy; the fairy may revive if we
remove ourself from the person, but if we remain in her presence the fairy
definitely dies and with her the name, as happened to the family of
Lusignan, which was fated to become extinct on the day when the fairy
Mélusine should disappear. Then the Name, beneath our successive 'res-

torations' of which we may end by finding, as their original, the beautiful portrait of a strange lady whom we are never to meet, is nothing more than the mere photograph, for identification, to which we refer in order to decide whether we know, whether or not we ought to bow to a person who passes us in the street. But let a sensation from a bygone year—like those recording instruments which preserve the sound and the manner of the various artists who have sung or played into them—enable our memory to make us hear that name with the particular ring with which it then sounded in our ears, then, while the name itself has apparently not changed, we feel the distance that separates the dreams which at different times its same syllables have meant to us. For a moment, from the clear echo of its warbling in some distant spring, we can extract, as from the little tubes which we use in painting, the exact, forgotten, mysterious, fresh tint of the days which we had believed ourself to be recalling, when, like a bad painter, we were giving to the whole of our past, spread out on the same canvas, the tones, conventional and all alike, of our unprompted memory. Whereas on the contrary, each of the moments that composed it employed, for an original creation, in a matchless harmony, the colour of those days which we no longer know, and which, for that matter, will still suddenly enrapture me if by any chance the name 'Guermantes,' resuming for a moment, after all these years, the sound, so different from its sound to-day, which it had for me on the day of Mlle. Percepied's marriage, brings back to me that mauve—so delicate, almost too bright, too new—with which the billowy scarf of the young Duchess glowed, and, like two periwinkle flowers, growing beyond reach and blossoming now again, her two eyes, sunlit with an azure smile. And the name Guermantes of those days is also like one of those little balloons which have been filled with oxygen, or some such gas; when I come to explode it, to make it emit what it contains, I breathe the air of the Combray of that year, of that day, mingled with a fragrance of hawthorn blossom blown by the wind from the corner of the square, harbinger of rain, which now sent the sun packing, now let him spread himself over the red woollen carpet to the sacristy, steeping it in a bright geranium scarlet, with that, so to speak, Wagnerian harmony in its gaiety which makes the wedding service always impressive. But even apart from rare moments such as these, in which suddenly we feel the original entity quiver and resume its form, carve itself out of the syllables now soundless, dead; if, in the giddy rush of daily life, in which they serve only the most practical purposes, names have lost all their colour, like a prismatic top that spins too quickly and seems only grey, when, on the other hand, in our musings we reflect, we seek, so as to return to the past, to slacken, to suspend the perpetual motion by which we are borne along, gradually we see once more appear, side by side, but entirely distinct from one another, the tints which in the course of our existence have been successively presented to us by a single name.

What form was assumed in my mind by this name Guermantes when my first nurse—knowing no more, probably, than I know to-day in whose honour it had been composed—sang me to sleep with that old ditty, *Gloire à la Marquise de Guermantes,* or when, some years later, the veteran

Maréchal de Guermantes, making my nursery-maid's bosom swell with
pride, stopped in the Champs-Elysées to remark: "A fine child, that!" and
gave me a chocolate drop from his comfit-box, I cannot, of course, now
say. Those years of my earliest childhood are no longer a part of myself;
they are external to me; I can learn nothing of them save—as we learn
things that happened before we were born—from the accounts given me
by other people. But more recently I find in the period of that name's
occupation of me seven or eight different shapes which it has successively
assumed; the earliest were the most beautiful; gradually my musings,
forced by reality to abandon a position that was no longer tenable, established themselves anew in one slightly less advanced until they were
obliged to retire still farther. And, with Mme. de Guermantes, was transformed simultaneously her dwelling, itself also the offspring of that name,
fertilised from year to year by some word or other that came to my ears
and modulated the tone of my musings; that dwelling of hers reflected
them in its very stones, which had turned to mirrors, like the surface of a
cloud or of a lake. A dungeon keep without mass, no more indeed than
a band of orange light from the summit of which the lord and his lady
dealt out life and death to their vassals, had given place—right at the end
of that 'Guermantes way' along which, on so many summer afternoons, I
retraced with my parents the course of the Vivonne—to that land of bubbling streams where the Duchess taught me to fish for trout and to know
the names of the flowers whose red and purple clusters adorned the walls
of the neighbouring gardens; then it had been the ancient heritage, famous
in song and story, from which the proud race of Guermantes, like a carved
and mellow tower that traverses the ages, had risen already over France
when the sky was still empty at those points where, later, were to rise
Notre Dame of Paris and Notre Dame of Chartres, when on the summit
of the hill of Laon the nave of its cathedral had not yet been poised, like
the Ark of the Deluge on the summit of Mount Ararat, crowded with
Patriarchs and Judges anxiously leaning from its windows to see whether
the wrath of God were yet appeased, carrying with it the types of the
vegetation that was to multiply on the earth, brimming over with animals
which have escaped even by the towers, where oxen grazing calmly upon
the roof look down over the plains of Champagne; when the traveller who
left Beauvais at the close of day did not yet see, following him and
turning with his road, outspread against the gilded screen of the western
sky, the black, ribbed wings of the cathedral. It was, this 'Guermantes,'
like the scene of a novel, an imaginary landscape which I could with difficulty picture to myself and longed all the more to discover, set in the midst
of real lands and roads which all of a sudden would become alive with
heraldic details, within a few miles of a railway station; I recalled the
names of the places round it as if they had been situated at the foot of
Parnassus or of Helicon, and they seemed precious to me, as the physical
conditions—in the realm of topographical science—required for the production of an unaccountable phenomenon. I saw again the escutcheons
blazoned beneath the windows of Combray church; their quarters filled,
century after century, with all the lordships which, by marriage or con-

quest, this illustrious house had brought flying to it from all the corners of Germany, Italy and France; vast territories in the North, strong cities in the South, assembled there to group themselves in Guermantes, and, losing their material quality, to inscribe allegorically their dungeon vert, or castle triple-towered argent upon its azure field. I had heard of the famous tapestries of Guermantes, I could see them, mediaeval and blue, a trifle coarse, detach themselves like a floating cloud from the legendary, amaranthine name at the foot of the ancient forest in which Childebert went so often hunting; and this delicate, mysterious background of their lands, this vista of the ages, it seemed to me that, as effectively as by journeying to see them, I might penetrate all their secrets simply by coming in contact for a moment in Paris with Mme. de Guermantes, the princess paramount of the place and lady of the lake, as if her face, her speech must possess the local charm of forest groves and streams, and the same secular peculiarities as the old customs recorded in her archives. But then I had met Saint-Loup; he had told me that the castle had borne the name of Guermantes only since the seventeenth century, when that family had acquired it. They had lived, until then, in the neighbourhood, but their title was not taken from those parts. The village of Guermantes had received its name from the castle round which it had been built, and so that it should not destroy the view from the castle, a servitude, still in force, traced the line of its streets and limited the height of its houses. As for the tapestries, they were by Boucher, bought in the nineteenth century by a Guermantes with a taste for the arts, and hung, interspersed with a number of sporting pictures of no merit which he himself had painted, in a hideous drawing-room upholstered in 'adrianople' and plush. By these revelations Saint-Loup had introduced into the castle elements foreign to the name of Guermantes which made it impossible for me to continue to extract solely from the resonance of the syllables the stone and mortar of its walls. And so, in the heart of the name, was effaced the castle mirrored in its lake, and what now became apparent to me, surrounding Mme. de Guermantes as her dwelling, had been her house in Paris, the Hôtel de Guermantes, limpid like its name, for no material and opaque element intervened to interrupt and blind its transparence. As the word church signifies not only the temple but the assembly of the faithful also, this Hôtel de Guermantes comprised all those who shared the life of the Duchess, but these intimates on whom I had never set eyes were for me only famous and poetic names, and knowing exclusively persons who themselves also were names only, did but enhance and protect the mystery of the Duchess by extending all round her a vast halo which at the most declined in brilliance as its circumference increased.

In the parties which she gave, since I could not imagine the guests as having any bodies, any moustaches, any boots, as making any utterances that were commonplace, or even original in a human and rational way, this whirlpool of names, introducing less material substance than would a phantom banquet or a spectral ball, round that statuette in Dresden china which was Madame de Guermantes, kept for her palace of glass the transparence of a showcase. Then, after Saint-Loup had told me various anecdotes about his cousin's chaplain, her gardener, and the rest, the Hôtel de Guermantes had become—as the Louvre might have been in days gone by—a kind of castle, surrounded, in the very heart of Paris, by its own domains, acquired by inheritance, by virtue of an ancient right that had quaintly survived, over which she still enjoyed feudal privileges. But this last dwelling itself vanished when we had come to live beside Mme. de Villeparisis in one of the flats adjoining that occupied by Mme. de Guermantes in a wing of the Hôtel. It was one of those old town houses, a few of which are perhaps still to be found, in which the court of honour— whether they were alluvial deposits washed there by the rising tide of democracy, or a legacy from a more primitive time when the different trades were clustered round the overlord—is flanked by little shops and workrooms, a shoemaker's, for instance, or a tailor's, such as we see nestling between the buttresses of those cathedrals which the aesthetic zeal of the restorer has not swept clear of such accretions; a porter who also does cobbling, keeps hens, grows flowers, and, at the far end, in the main building, a 'Comtesse' who, when she drives out in her old carriage and pair, flaunting on her hat a few nasturtiums which seem to have escaped from the plot by the porter's lodge (with, by the coachman's side on the box, a footman who gets down to leave cards at every aristocratic mansion in the neighbourhood), scatters vague little smiles and waves her hand in greeting to the porter's children and to such of her respectable fellow-tenants as may happen to be passing, who, to her contemptuous affability and levelling pride, seem all the same.

In the house in which we had now come to live, the great lady at the end of the courtyard was a Duchess, smart and still quite young. She was, in fact, Mme. de Guermantes and, thanks to Françoise, I soon came to know all about her household. For the Guermantes (to whom Françoise regularly alluded as the people 'below,' or 'downstairs') were her constant preoccupation from the first thing in the morning when, as she did Mamma's hair, casting a forbidden, irresistible, furtive glance down into the courtyard, she would say: "Look at that, now; a pair of holy Sisters; that'll be for downstairs, surely;" or, "Oh! just look at the fine pheasants in the kitchen window; no need to ask where they came from, the Duke will have been out with his gun!"—until the last thing at night when, if her ear, while she was putting out my night-things, caught a few notes of a song, she would conclude: "They're having company down below; gay doings, I'll be bound;" whereupon, in her symmetrical face, beneath the arch of her now snow-white hair, a smile from her young days, sprightly but proper, would for a moment set each of her features in its place, arranging them in an intricate and special order, as though for a country-dance.

But the moment in the life of the Guermantes which excited the keenest interest in Françoise, gave her the most complete satisfaction and at the same time the sharpest annoyance was that at which, the two halves of the great gate having been thrust apart, the Duchess stepped into her carriage. It was generally a little while after our servants had finished the celebration of that sort of solemn passover which none might disturb, called their midday dinner, during which they were so far taboo that my father himself was not allowed to ring for them, knowing moreover that none of them would have paid any more attention to the fifth peal than to the first, and that the discourtesy would therefore have been a pure waste of time and trouble, though not without trouble in store for himself. For Françoise (who, in her old age, lost no opportunity of standing upon her dignity) would without fail have presented him, for the rest of the day, with a face covered with the tiny red cuneiform hieroglyphs by which she made visible—though by no means legible—to the outer world the long tale of her griefs and the profound reasons for her dissatisfactions. She would enlarge upon them, too, in a running 'aside,' but not so that we could catch her words. She called this practice—which, she imagined, must be infuriating, 'mortifying' as she herself put it, 'vexing' to us—'saying low masses all the blessed day.'

The last rites accomplished, Françoise, who was at one and the same time, as in the primitive church, the celebrant and one of the faithful, helped herself to a final glass, undid the napkin from her throat, folded it after wiping from her lips a stain of watered wine and coffee, slipped it into its ring, turned a doleful eye to thank 'her' young footman who, to shew his zeal in her service, was saying: "Come, ma'am, a drop more of the grape; it's d'licious to-day," and went straight across to the window, which she flung open, protesting that it was too hot to breathe in 'this wretched kitchen.' Dexterously casting, as she turned the latch and let in the fresh air, a glance of studied indifference into the courtyard below, she furtively elicited the conclusion that the Duchess was not ready yet to start, brooded for a moment with contemptuous, impassioned eyes over the waiting carriage, and, this meed of attention once paid to the things of the earth, raised them towards the heavens, whose purity she had already divined from the sweetness of the air and the warmth of the sun; and let them rest on a corner of the roof, at the place where, every spring, there came and built, immediately over the chimney of my bedroom, a pair of pigeons like those she used to hear cooing from her kitchen at Combray.

"Ah! Combray, Combray!" she cried. And the almost singing tone in which she declaimed this invocation might, taken with the Arlesian purity of her features, have made the onlooker suspect her of a Southern origin and that the lost land which she was lamenting was no more, really, than a land of adoption. If so, he would have been wrong, for it seems that there is no province that has not its own South-country; do we not indeed constantly meet Savoyards and Bretons in whose speech we find all those pleasing transpositions of longs and shorts that are characteristic of the Southerner? "Ah, Combray, when shall I look on thee again, poor land! When shall I pass the blessed day among thy hawthorns, under our own poor lily-oaks, hearing the grasshoppers sing, and the Vivonne making a little noise like someone whispering, instead of that wretched bell from our young master, who can never stay still for half an hour on end without having me run the length of that wicked corridor. And even then he makes out I don't come quick enough; you'd need to hear the bell ring before he has pulled it, and if you're a minute late, away he flies into the most towering rage. Alas, poor Combray; maybe I shall see thee only in death, when they drop me like a stone into the hollow of the tomb. And so, never-more shall I smell thy lovely hawthorns, so white and all. But in the sleep of death I dare say I shall still hear those three peals of the bell which will have driven me to damnation in this world."

Her soliloquy was interrupted by the voice of the waistcoat-maker downstairs, the same who had so delighted my grandmother once, long ago, when she had gone to pay a call on Mme. de Villeparisis, and now occupied no less exalted a place in Françoise's affections. Having raised his head when he heard our window open, he had already been trying for some time to attract his neighbour's attention, in order to bid her good day. The coquetry of the young girl that Françoise had once been softened and refined for M. Jupien the querulous face of our old cook, dulled by age, ill-temper and the heat of the kitchen fire, and it was with a charming blend of reserve, familiarity and modesty that she bestowed a gracious salutation on the waistcoat-maker, but without making any audible re-sponse, for if she did infringe Mamma's orders by looking into the court-yard, she would never have dared to go the length of talking from the window, which would have been quite enough (according to her) to bring down on her 'a whole chapter' from the Mistress. She pointed to the wait-ing carriage, as who should say: "A fine pair, eh!" though what she actually muttered was: "What an old rattle-trap!" but principally because she knew that he would be bound to answer, putting his hand to his lips so as to be audible without having to shout:

"*You* could have one too if you liked, as good as they have and better, I dare say, only you don't care for that sort of thing."

And Franoise, after a modest, evasive signal of delight, the meaning of which was, more or less: "Tastes differ, you know; simplicity's the rule in this house," shut the window again in case Mamma should come in. These 'you' who might have had more horses than the Guermantes were ourselves, but Jupien was right in saying 'you' since, except for a few purely personal gratifications, such as, when she coughed all day long without ceasing and everyone in the house was afraid of catching her cold, that of pretending, with an irritating little titter, that she had not got a cold, like those plants that an animal to which they are wholly attached keeps alive with food which it catches, eats and digests for them and of which it offers them the ultimate and easily assimilable residue, Françoise lived with us in full community; it was we who, with our virtues, our wealth, our style of living, must take on ourselves the task of concocting those little sops to her vanity out of which was formed—with the addition of the recognised rights of freely practising the cult of the midday dinner according to the traditional custom, which included a mouthful of air at the window when the meal was finished, a certain amount of loitering in the street when she went out to do her marketing, and a holiday on Sundays when she paid a visit to her niece—the portion of happiness indispensable to her existence. And so it can be understood that Françoise might well have suc-cumbed in those first days of our migration, a victim, in a house where my father's claims to distinction were not yet known, to a malady which she herself called 'wearying,' wearying in the active sense in which the word *ennui* is employed by Corneille, or in the last letters of soldiers who end by taking their own lives because they are wearying for their girls or for their native villages. Françoise's wearying had soon been cured by none other than Jupien, for he at once procured her a pleasure no less keen, indeed more refined than she would have felt if we had decided to keep a carriage. "Very good class, those Juliens," (for Françoise readily assimilated new names to those with which she was already familiar) "very worthy people; you can see it written on their faces." Jupien was in fact able to understand, and to inform the world that if we did not keep a carriage it was because we had no wish for one. This new friend of Françoise was very little at home, having obtained a post in one of the Government offices. A waistcoat-maker first of all, with the 'chit of a girl' whom my grandmother had taken for his daughter, he had lost all interest in the exercise of that calling after his assistant (who, when still little more than a child, had shewn great skill in darning a torn skirt, that day when my grandmother had gone to call on Mme. de Villeparisis) had turned to ladies' fashions and become a seamstress. A prentice hand, to begin with, in a dressmaker's workroom, set to stitch a seam, to fasten a flounce, to sew on a button or to press a crease, to fix a waistband with hooks and eyes, she had quickly risen to be second and then chief assistant, and having formed a connexion of her own among ladies of fashion now worked at home, that is to say in our courtyard, generally with one or two of her young friends from the workroom, whom she had taken on as apprentices. After this, Jupien's presence in the place had ceased to matter. No doubt the little girl (a big girl by this time) had often to cut out waistcoats still. But with her friends to assist her she needed no one besides. And so Jupien, her uncle, had sought employment outside. He was free at first to return home at midday, then, when he had definitely succeeded the man whose substitute only he had begun by being, not before dinner-time. His appointment to the 'regular establishment' was, fortunately, not announced until some weeks after our arrival, so that his courtesy could be brought to bear on her long enough to help Françoise to pass through the first, most difficult phase without undue suffering. At the same time, and without underrating his value to Françoise as, so to speak, a sedative during the period of transition, I am bound to say that my first impression of Jupien had been far from favourable. At a little distance, entirely ruining the effect that his plump cheeks and vivid colouring would otherwise have produced, his eyes, brimming with a compassionate, mournful, dreamy gaze, led one to suppose that he was seriously ill or had just suffered a great bereavement. Not only was he nothing of the sort, but as soon as he opened his mouth (and his speech, by the way, was perfect) he was quite markedly cynical and cold. There resulted from this discord between eyes and lips a certain falsity which was not attractive, and by which he had himself the air of being made as uncomfortable as a guest who arrives in morning dress at a party where everyone else is in evening dress, or as a commoner who having to speak to a Royal Personage does not know exactly how he ought to address him and gets round the difficulty by cutting down his remarks to almost nothing. Jupien's (here the comparison ends) were, on the contrary, charming. Indeed, corresponding possibly to this overflowing of his face by his eyes (which one ceased to notice when one came to know him), I soon discerned in him a rare intellect, and one of the most spontaneously literary that it has been my privilege to come across, in the sense that, probably without education, he possessed or had assimilated, with the help only of a few books skimmed in early life, the most ingenious turns of speech. The most gifted people that I had known had died young. And so I was convinced that Jupien's life would soon be cut short. Kindness was among his qualities, and pity, the most delicate and the most generous feelings for others. But his part in the life of Françoise had soon ceased to be indispensable. She had learned to put up with understudies.

Indeed, when a tradesman or servant came to our door with a parcel or message, while seeming to pay no attention and merely pointing vaguely to an empty chair, Françoise so skilfully put to the best advantage the few seconds that he spent in the kitchen, while he waited for Mamma's answer, that it was very seldom that the stranger went away without having ineradicably engraved upon his memory the conviction that, if we 'did not have' any particular thing, it was because we had 'no wish' for it. If she made such a point of other people's knowing that we 'had money' (for she knew nothing of what Saint-Loup used to call partitive articles, and said simply 'have money,' 'fetch water'), of their realising that we were rich, it was not because riches with nothing else besides, riches without virtue, were in her eyes the supreme good in life; but virtue without riches was not her ideal either. Riches were for her, so to speak, a necessary condition of virtue, failing which virtue itself would lack both merit and charm. She distinguished so little between them that she had come in time to invest each with the other's attributes, to expect some material comfort from virtue, to discover something edifying in riches.

As soon as she had shut the window again, which she did quickly—otherwise Mamma would, it appeared, have heaped on her 'every conceivable insult'—Françoise began with many groans and sighs to put straight the kitchen table.

"There are some Guermantes who stay in the Rue de la Chaise," began my father's valet; "I had a friend who used to be with them; he was their second coachman. And I know a fellow, not my old pal, but his brother-in-law, who did his time in the Army with one of the Baron de Guermantes's stud grooms. Does your mother know you're out?" added the valet, who was in the habit, just as he used to hum the popular airs of the season, of peppering his conversation with all the latest witticisms.

Françoise, with the tired eyes of an ageing woman, eyes which moreover saw everything from Combray, in a hazy distance, made out not the witticism that underlay the words, but that there must be something witty in them since they bore no relation to the rest of his speech and had been uttered with considerable emphasis by one whom she knew to be a joker. She smiled at him, therefore, with an air of benevolent bewilderment, as who should say: "Always the same, that Victor!" And she was genuinely pleased, knowing that listening to smart sayings of this sort was akin—if remotely—to those reputable social pleasures for which, in every class of society, people make haste to dress themselves in their best and run the risk of catching cold. Furthermore, she believed the valet to be a friend after her own heart, for he never left off denouncing, with fierce indignation, the appalling measures which the Republic was about to enforce against the clergy. Françoise had not yet learned that our cruellest adversaries are not those who contradict and try to convince us, but those who magnify or invent reports which may make us unhappy, taking care not to include any appearance of justification, which might lessen our discomfort, and perhaps give us some slight regard for a party which they make a point of displaying to us, to complete our torment, as being at once terrible and triumphant.

"The Duchess must be connected with all that lot," said Françoise, bringing the conversation back to the Guermantes of the Rue de la Chaise, as one plays a piece over again from the andante. "I can't recall who it was told me that one of them had married a cousin of the Duke. It's the same kindred, anyway. Ay, they're a great family, the Guermantes!" she added, in a tone of respect founding the greatness of the family at once on the number of its branches and the brilliance of its connexions, as Pascal founds the truth of Religion on Reason and on the Authority of the Scriptures. For since there was but the single word 'great' to express both meanings, it seemed to her that they formed a single idea, her vocabulary, like cut stones sometimes, shewing thus on certain of its facets a flaw which projected a ray of darkness into the recesses of her mind. "I wonder now if it wouldn't be them that have their castle at Guermantes, not a score of miles from Combray; then they must be kin to their cousin at Algiers, too." My mother and I long asked ourselves who this cousin at Algiers could be until finally we discovered that Françoise meant by the name 'Algiers' the town of Angers. What is far off may be more familiar to us than what is quite near. Françoise, who knew the name 'Algiers' from some particularly unpleasant dates that used to be given us at the New Year, had never heard of Angers. Her language, like the French language itself, and especially that of place-names, was thickly strewn with errors. "I meant to talk to their butler about it. What is it again you call him?" she interrupted herself as though putting a formal question as to the correct procedure, which she went on to answer with: "Oh, of course, it's Antoine you call him!" as though Antoine had been a title. "He's the one who could tell me, but he's quite the gentleman, he is, a great scholar, you'd say they'd cut his tongue out, or that he'd forgotten to learn to speak. He makes no response when you talk to him," went on Françoise, who used 'make response' in the same sense as Mme. de Sévigné. "But," she added, quite untruthfully, "so long as I know what's boiling in my pot, I don't bother my head about what's in other people's. Whatever he is, he's not a Catholic. Besides, he's not a courageous man." (This criticism might have led one to suppose that Françoise had changed her mind about physical bravery which, according to her, in Combray days, lowered men to the level of wild beasts. But it was not so. 'Courageous' meant simply a hard worker.) "They do say, too, that he's thievish as a magpie, but it doesn't do to believe all one hears. The servants never stay long there because of the lodge; the porters are jealous and set the Duchess against them. But it's safe to say that he's a real twister, that Antoine, and his Antoinesse is no better," concluded Françoise, who, in furnishing the name 'Antoine' with a feminine ending that would designate the butler's wife, was inspired, no doubt, in her act of word-formation by an unconscious memory of the words *chanoine* and *chanoinesse*. If so, she was not far wrong. There is still a street near Notre-Dame called Rue Chanoinesse, a name which must have been given to it (since it was never inhabited by any but male Canons) by those Frenchmen of olden days of whom Françoise was, properly speaking, the contemporary. She proceeded, moreover, at once to furnish another example of this way of forming feminine endings, for she went on: "But one thing sure and certain is that it's the Duchess that has Guermantes Castle. And it's she that is the Lady Mayoress down in those parts. That's always something."

"I can well believe that it is something," came with conviction from the footman, who had not detected the irony.

"You think so, do you, my boy, you think it's something? Why, for folk like them to be Mayor and Mayoress, it's just thank you for nothing. Ah, if it was mine, that Guermantes Castle, you wouldn't see me setting foot in Paris, I can tell you. I'm sure a family who've got something to go on with, like Monsieur and Madame here, must have queer ideas to stay on in this wretched town rather than get away down to Combray the moment they're free to start, and no one hindering them. Why do they put off retiring? They've got everything they want. Why wait till they're dead? Ah, if I had only a crust of dry bread to eat and a faggot to keep me warm in winter, a fine time I'd have of it at home in my brother's poor old house at Combray. Down there you do feel you're alive; you haven't all these houses stuck up in front of you, there is so little noise at night-time, you can hear the frogs singing five miles off and more."

"That must indeed be fine!" exclaimed the young footman with enthusiasm, as though this last attraction had been as peculiar to Combray as the gondola is to Venice. A more recent arrival in the household than my father's valet, he used to talk to Françoise about things which might interest not himself so much as her. And Françoise, whose face wrinkled up in disgust when she was treated as a mere cook, had for the young footman, who referred to her always as the 'housekeeper,' that peculiar tenderness which Princes not of the blood royal feel towards the well-meaning young men who dignify them with a 'Highness.'

"At any rate one knows what one's about, there, and what time of year it is. It isn't like here where you won't find one wretched buttercup flowering at holy Easter any more than you would at Christmas, and I can't hear so much as the tiniest angelus ring when I lift my old bones out of bed in the morning. Down there, you can hear every hour; there's only the one poor bell, but you say to yourself: 'My brother will be coming in from the field now,' and you watch the daylight fade, and the bell rings to bless the fruits of the earth, and you have time to take a turn before you light the lamp. But here it's daytime and it's nighttime, and you go to bed, and you can't say any more than the dumb beasts what you've been about all day."

"I gather Méséglise is a fine place, too, Madame," broke in the young footman, who found that the conversation was becoming a little too abstract for his liking, and happened to remember having heard us, at table, mention Méséglise.

"Oh! Méséglise, is it?" said Françoise with the broad smile which one could always bring to her lips by uttering any of those names—Méséglise, Combray, Tansonville. They were so intimate a part of her life that she felt, on meeting them outside it, on hearing them used in conversation, a hilarity more or less akin to that which a professor excites in his class by making an allusion to some contemporary personage whose name the students had never supposed could possibly greet their ears from the height of the academic chair. Her pleasure arose also from the feeling that these places were something to her which they were not for the rest of the world, old companions with whom one has shared many delights; and she smiled at them as if she found in them something witty, because she did find there a great part of herself.

"Yes, you may well say so, son, it is a pretty enough place is Méséglise;" she went on with a tinkling laugh, "but how did you ever come to hear tell of Méséglise?"

"How did I hear of Méséglise? But it's a well-known place; people have told me about it—yes, over and over again," he assured her with that criminal inexactitude of the informer who, whenever we attempt to form an impartial estimate of the importance that a thing which matters to us may have for other people, makes it impossible for us to succeed.

"I can tell you, it's better down there, under the cherry trees, than standing before the fire all day."

She spoke to them even of Eulalie as a good person. For since Eulalie's death Françoise had completely forgotten that she had loved her as little in her lifetime as she loved every one whose cupboard was bare, who was dying of hunger, and after that came, like a good for nothing, thanks to the bounty of the rich, to 'put on airs.' It no longer pained her that Eulalie had so skilfully managed, Sunday after Sunday, to secure her 'trifle' from my aunt. As for the latter, Françoise never left off singing her praises.

"But it was at Combray, surely, that you used to be, with a cousin of Madame?" asked the young footman.

"Yes, with Mme. Octave—oh, a dear, good, holy woman, my poor friends, and a house where there was always enough and to spare, and all of the very best, a good woman, you may well say, who had no pity on the partridges, or the pheasants, or anything; you might turn up five to dinner or six, it was never the meat that was lacking, and of the first quality too, and white wine, and red wine, and everything you could wish." (Françoise used the word 'pity' in the sense given it by Labruyère.) "It was she that paid the damages, always, even if the family stayed for months and years." (This reflection was not really a slur upon us, for Françoise belonged to an epoch when the words 'damages' was not restricted to a legal use and meant simply expense.) "Ah, I can tell you, people didn't go empty away from that house. As his reverence the Curé has told us, many's the time, if there ever was a woman who could count on going straight before the Throne of God, it was she. Poor Madame, I can hear her saying now, in the little voice she had: 'You know, Françoise, I can eat nothing myself, but I want it all to be just as nice for the others as if I could.' They weren't for her, the victuals, you may be quite sure. If you'd only seen her, she weighed no more than a bag of cherries; there wasn't that much of her. She would never listen to a word I said, she would never send for the doctor. Ah, it wasn't in that house that you'd have to gobble down your dinner. She liked her servants to be fed properly. Here, it's been just the same again to-day; we haven't had time for so much as to break a crust of bread; everything goes like ducks and drakes."

What annoyed her more than anything were the rusks of pulled bread that my father used to eat. She was convinced that he had them simply to give himself airs and to keep her 'dancing.' "I can tell you frankly," the young footman assured her, "that I never saw the like." He said it as if he had seen everything, and as if in him the range of a millennial experience extended over all countries and their customs, among which was not anywhere to be found a custom of eating pulled bread. "Yes, yes," the butler muttered, "but that will all be changed; the mén are going on strike in Canada, and the Minister told Monsieur the other evening that he's clearing two hundred thousand francs out of it." There was no note of censure in his tone, not that he was not himself entirely honest, but since he regarded all politicians as unsound the crime of peculation seemed to him less serious than the pettiest larceny. He did not even stop to ask himself whether he had heard this historic utterance aright, and was not struck by the improbability that such a thing would have been admitted by the guilty party himself to my father without my father's immediately turning him out of the house. But the philosophy of Combray made it impossible for Françoise to expect that the strikes in Canada could have any repercussion on the use of pulled bread. "So long as the world goes round, look, there'll be masters to keep us on the trot, and servants to do their bidding." In disproof of this theory of perpetual motion, for the last quarter of an hour my mother (who probably did not employ the same measures of time as Françoise in reckoning the duration of the latter's dinner) had been saying:

"What on earth can they be doing? They've been at least two hours at their dinner."

And she rang timidly three or four times. Françoise, 'her' footman, the butler, heard the bell ring, not as a summons to themselves, and with no thought of answering it, but rather like the first sounds of the instruments being tuned when the next part of a concert is just going to begin, and one knows that there will be only a few minutes more of interval. And so, when the peals were repeated and became more urgent, our servants began to pay attention, and, judging that they had not much time left and that the resumption of work was at hand, at a peal somewhat louder than the rest gave a collective sigh and went their several ways, the footman slipping downstairs to smoke a cigarette outside the door, Françoise, after a string of reflexions on ourselves, such as: "They've got the jumps to-day, surely,"

going up to put her things tidy in her attic, while the butler, having supplied himself first with note-paper from my bedroom, polished off the
arrears of his private correspondence.

Despite the apparent stiffness of their butler, Françoise had been in a
position, from the first, to inform me that the Guermantes occupied their
mansion by virtue not of an immemorial right but of a quite recent ten-
ancy, and that the garden over which it looked on the side that I did not
know was quite small and just like all the gardens along the street; and
I realised at length that there were not to be seen there pit and gallows
or fortified mill, secret chamber, pillared dovecot, manorial bakehouse or
tithe-barn, dungeon or drawbridge, or fixed bridge either for that matter,
any more than toll-houses or pinnacles, charters, muniments, ramparts or
commemorative mounds. But just as Elstir, when the bay of Balbec, losing
its mystery, had become for me simply a portion, interchangeable with any
other, of the total quantity of salt water distributed over the earth's surface, had suddenly restored to it a personality of its own by telling me that
it was the gulf of opal painted by Whistler in his 'Harmonies in Blue and
Silver,' so the name Guermantes had seen perish under the strokes of
Françoise's hammer the last of the dwellings that had issued from its
syllables when one day an old friend of my father said to us, speaking of
the Duchess: "She is the first lady in the Faubourg Saint-Germain; hers
is the leading house in the Faubourg Saint-Germain." No doubt the most
exclusive drawing-room, the leading house in the Faubourg Saint-Germain
was little or nothing after all those other mansions of which in turn I had
dreamed. And yet in this one too (and it was to be the last of the series),
there was something, however humble, quite apart from its material com-
ponents, a secret differentiation.

And it became all the more essential that I should be able to explore in
the drawing-room of Mme. de Guermantes, among her friends, the mystery
of her name, since I did not find it in her person when I saw her leave the
house in the morning on foot, or in the afternoon in her carriage. Once
before, indeed, in the church at Combray, she had appeared to me in the
blinding flash of a transfiguration, with cheeks irreducible to, impenetrable
by, the colour of the name Guermantes and of afternoons on the banks of
the Vivonne, taking the place of my shattered dream like a swan or willow
into which has been changed a god or nymph, and which henceforward,
subjected to natural laws, will glide over the water or be shaken by the
wind. And yet, when that radiance had vanished, hardly had I lost sight
of it before it formed itself again, like the green and rosy afterglow of
sunset after the sweep of the oar has broken it, and in the solitude of
my thoughts the name had quickly appropriated to itself my impression of
the face. But now, frequently, I saw her at her window, in the courtyard,
in the street, and for myself at least if I did not succeed in integrating in
her the name Guermantes, I cast the blame on the impotence of my mind
to accomplish the whole act that I demanded of it; but she, our neighbour,
she seemed to make the same error, nay more to make it without discomfiture, without any of my scruples, without even suspecting that it was
an error. Thus Mme. de Guermantes shewed in her dresses the same

anxiety to follow the fashions as if, believing herself to have become simply
a woman like all the rest, she had aspired to that elegance in her attire in
which other ordinary women might equal and perhaps surpass her; I had
seen her in the street gaze admiringly at a well-dressed actress; and in the
morning, before she sallied forth on foot, as if the opinion of the passers-
by, whose vulgarity she accentuated by parading familiarly through their
midst her inaccessible life, could be a tribunal competent to judge her, I
would see her before the glass playing, with a conviction free from all
pretence or irony, with passion, with ill-humour, with conceit, like a queen
who has consented to appear as a servant-girl in theatricals at court, this
part, so unworthy of her, of a fashionable woman; and in this mythological oblivion of her natural grandeur, she looked to see whether her veil
was hanging properly, smoothed her cuffs, straightened her cloak, as the
celestial swan performs all the movements natural to his animal species,
keeps his eyes painted on either side of his beak without putting into them
any glint of life, and darts suddenly after a bud or an umbrella, as a swan
would, without remembering that he is a god. But as the traveller, disappointed by the first appearance of a strange town, reminds himself that he
will doubtless succeed in penetrating its charm if he visits its museums and
galleries, so I assured myself that, had I been given the right of entry into
Mme. de Guermantes's house, were I one of her friends, were I to penetrate
into her life, I should then know what, within its glowing orange-tawny
envelope, her name did really, objectively enclose for other people, since,
after all, my father's friend had said that the Guermantes set was something quite by itself in the Faubourg Saint-Germain.

The life which I supposed them to lead there flowed from a source so
different from anything in my experience, and must, I felt, be so indissolubly associated with that particular house that I could not have imagined the presence, at the Duchess's parties, of people in whose company I
myself had already been, of people who really existed. For not being able
suddenly to change their nature, they would have carried on conversations there of the sort that I knew; their partners would perhaps have
stooped to reply to them in the same human speech; and, in the course of
an evening spent in the leading house in the Faubourg Saint-Germain,
there would have been moments identical with moments that I had already
lived. Which was impossible. It was thus that my mind was embarrassed
by certain difficulties, and the Presence of Our Lord's Body in the Host
seemed to me no more obscure a mystery than this leading house in the
Faubourg, situated here, on the right bank of the river, and so near that
from my bed, in the morning, I could hear its carpets being beaten. But
the line of demarcation that separated me from the Faubourg Saint-Germain seemed to me all the more real because it was purely ideal. I felt
clearly that it was already part of the Faubourg, when I saw the Guermantes doormat, spread out beyond that intangible Equator, of which my
mother had made bold to say, having like myself caught a glimpse of it
one day when their door stood open, that it was a shocking state. For the
rest, how could their dining-room, their dim gallery upholstered in red
plush, into which I could see sometimes from our kitchen window, have

failed to possess in my eyes the mysterious charm of the Faubourg Saint-Germain, to form part of it in an essential fashion, to be geographically situated within it, since to have been entertained to dinner in that room was to have gone into the Faubourg Saint-Germain, to have breathed its atmosphere, since the people who, before going to table, sat down by the side of Mme. de Guermantes on the leather-covered sofa in that gallery were all of the Faubourg Saint-Germain. No doubt elsewhere than in the Faubourg, at certain parties, one might see now and then, majestically enthroned amid the vulgar herd of fashion, one of those men who were mere names and varyingly assumed, when one tried to form a picture of them, the aspect of a tournament or of a royal forest. But here, in the leading house in the Faubourg Saint-German, in the drawing-room, in the dim gallery, there were only they. They were wrought of precious materials, the columns that upheld the temple. Indeed for quiet family parties it was from among them only that Mme. de Guermantes might select her guests, and in the dinners for twelve, gathered around the dazzling napery and plate, they were like the golden statues of the Apostles in the Sainte-Chapelle, symbolic, consecrative pillars before the Holy Table. As for the tiny strip of garden that stretched between high walls at the back of the house, where on summer evenings Mme. de Guermantes had liqueurs and orangeade brought out after dinner, how could I not have felt that to sit there of an evening, between nine and eleven, on its iron chairs—endowed with a magic as potent as the leathern sofa—without inhaling the breezes peculiar to the Faubourg Saint-Germain was as impossible as to take a siesta in the oasis of Figuig without thereby being necessarily in Africa. Only imagination and belief can differentiate from the rest certain objects, certain people, and can create an atmosphere. Alas, those picturesque sites, those natural accidents, those local curiosities, those works of art of the Faubourg Saint-Germain, never probably should I be permitted to set my feet among them. And I must content myself with a shiver of excitement as I sighted, from the deep sea (and without the least hope of ever landing there) like an outstanding minaret, like the first palm, like the first signs of some exotic industry or vegetation, the well-trodden doormat of its shore.

But if the Hôtel de Guermantes began for me at its hall-door, its dependencies must be regarded as extending a long way farther, according to the Duke, who, looking on all the other tenants as farmers, peasants, purchasers of forfeited estates, whose opinion was of no account, shaved himself every morning in his nightshirt at the window, came down into the courtyard, according to the warmth or coldness of the day, in his shirt-sleeves, in pyjamas, in a plaid coat of startling colours, with a shaggy nap, in little light-coloured coats shorter than the jackets beneath, and made one of his grooms lead past him at a trot some horse that he had just been buying. More than once, indeed, the horse broke the window of Jupien's shop, whereupon Jupien, to the Duke's indignation, demanded compensation. "If it were only in consideration of all the good that Madame la Duchesse does in the house, here, and in the parish," said M. de Guermantes, "it is an outrage on this fellow's part to claim a penny from us."

But Jupien had stuck to his point, apparently not having the faintest idea what 'good' the Duchess had ever done. And yet she did do good, but—since one cannot do good to everybody at once—the memory of the benefits that we have heaped on one person is a valid reason for our abstaining from helping another, whose discontent we thereby make all the stronger. From other points of view than that of charity the quarter appeared to the Duke —and this over a considerable area—to be only an extension of his court-yard, a longer track for his horses. After seeing how a new acquisition trotted by itself he would have it harnessed and taken through all the neighbouring streets, the groom running beside the carriage holding the reins, making it pass to and fro before the Duke who stood on the pave-ment, erect, gigantic, enormous in his vivid clothes, a cigar between his teeth, his head in the air, his eyeglass scrutinous, until the moment when he sprang on the box, drove the horse up and down for a little to try it, then set off with his new turn-out to pick up his mistress in the Champs-Elysées. M. de Guermantes bade good day, before leaving the courtyard, to two couples who belonged more or less to his world; the first, some cousins of his who, like working-class parents, were never at home to look after their children, since every morning the wife went off to the Schola to study counterpoint and fugue, and the husband to his studio to carve wood and beat leather; and after them the Baron and Baronne de Norpois, always dressed in black, she like a pew-opener and he like a mute at a funeral, who emerged several times daily on their way to church. They were the nephew and niece of the old Ambassador who was our friend, and whom my father had, in fact, met at the foot of the staircase without realising from where he came; for my father supposed that so important a personage, one who had come in contact with the most eminent men in Europe and was probably quite indifferent to the empty distinctions of rank, was hardly likely to frequent the society of these obscure, clerical and narrow-minded nobles. They had not been long in the place; Jupien, who had come out into the courtyard to say a word to the husband just as he was greeting M. de Guermantes, called him 'M. Norpois,' not being certain of his name.

"Monsieur Norpois, indeed! Oh, that really is good! Just wait a little! This individual will be calling you Comrade Norpois next!" exclaimed M. de Guermantes, turning to the Baron. He was at last able to vent his spleen against Jupien who addressed him as 'Monsieur,' instead of 'Monsieur le Duc."

One day when M. de Guermantes required some information upon a matter of which my father had professional knowledge, he had intro-duced himself to him with great courtesy. After that, he had often some neighbourly service to ask of my father and, as soon as he saw him begin to come downstairs, his mind occupied with his work and anxious to avoid any interruption, the Duke, leaving his stable-boys, would come up to him in the courtyard, straighten the collar of his great-coat, with the serviceable deftness inherited from a line of royal body-servants in days gone by, take him by the hand, and, holding it in his own, patting it even to prove to my father, with a courtesan's or courtier's shamelessness, that he, the Duc de

Guermantes, made no bargain about my father's right to the privilege of contact with the ducal flesh, lead him, so to speak, on leash, extremely annoyed and thinking only how he might escape, through the carriage entrance out into the street. He had given us a sweeping bow one day when we had come in just as he was going out in the carriage with his wife; he was bound to have told her my name; but what likelihood was there of her remembering it, or my face either? And besides, what a feeble recommendation to be pointed out simply as being one of her tenants! Another, more valuable, would have been my meeting the Duchess in the drawing-room of Mme. de Villeparisis, who, as it happened, had just sent word by my grandmother that I was to go and see her, and, remembering that I had been intending to go in for literature, had added that I should meet several authors there. But my father felt that I was still a little young to go into society, and as the state of my health continued to give him uneasiness he did not see the use of establishing precedents that would do me no good.

As one of Mme. de Guermantes's footmen was in the habit of talking to Françoise, I picked up the names of several of the houses which she frequented, but formed no impression of any of them; from the moment in which they were a part of her life, of that life which I saw only through the veil of her name, were they not inconceivable?

"To-night there's a big party with a Chinese shadow show at the Princesse de Parme's," said the footman, "but we shan't be going, because at five o'clock Madame is taking the train to Chantilly, to spend a few days with the Duc d'Aumale; but it'll be the lady's maid and valet that are going with her. I'm to stay here. She won't be at all pleased, the Princesse de Parme won't, that's four times already she's written to Madame la Duchesse."

"Then you won't be going down to Guermantes Castle this year?"

"It's the first time we shan't be going there: it's because of the Duke's rheumatics, the doctor says he's not to go there till the hot pipes are in, but we've been there every year till now, right on to January. If the hot pipes aren't ready, perhaps Madame will go for a few days to Cannes, to the Duchesse de Guise, but nothing's settled yet."

"And to the theatre, do you go, sometimes?"

"We go now and then to the Opéra, usually on the evenings when the Princesse de Parme has her box, that's once a week; it seems it's a fine show they give there, plays, operas, everything. Madame refused to subscribe to it herself, but we go all the same to the boxes Madame's friends take, one one night, another another, often with the Princesse de Guermantes, the Duke's cousin's lady. She's sister to the Duke of Bavaria. And so you've got to run upstairs again now, have you?" went on the footman, who, albeit identified with the Guermantes, looked upon masters in general as a political estate, a view which allowed him to treat Françoise with as much respect as if she too were in service with a duchess. "You enjoy good health, ma'am."

"Oh, if it wasn't for these cursed legs of mine! On the plain I can still get along" ('on the plain' meant in the courtyard or in the streets, where

Françoise had no objection to walking, in other words 'on a plane surface') "but it's these stairs that do me in, devil take them. Good day to you,
sir, see you again, perhaps, this evening."

She was all the more anxious to continue her conversations with the
footman after he mentioned to her that the sons of dukes often bore a
princely title which they retained until their fathers were dead. Evidently
the cult of the nobility, blended with and accommodating itself to a certain spirit of revolt against it, must, springing hereditarily from the soil of
France, be very strongly implanted still in her people. For Françoise, to
whom you might speak of the genius of Napoleon or of wireless telegraphy
without succeeding in attracting her attention, and without her slackening
for an instant the movements with which she was scraping the ashes from
the grate or laying the table, if she were simply to be told these idiosyncrasies of nomenclature, and that the younger son of the Duc de Guermantes was generally called Prince d'Oléron, would at once exclaim:
"That's fine, that is!" and stand there dazed, as though in contemplation
of a stained window in church.

Françoise learned also from the Prince d'Agrigente's valet, who had
become friends with her by coming often to the house with notes for the
Duchess, that he had been hearing a great deal of talk in society about the
marriage of the Marquis de Saint-Loup to Mlle. d'Ambresac, and that it
was practically settled.

That villa, that opera-box, into which Mme. de Guermantes transfused
the current of her life, must, it seemed to me, be places no less fairylike
than her home. The names of Guise, of Parme, of Guermantes-Bavière,
differentiated from all possible others the holiday places to which the
Duchess resorted, the daily festivities which the track of her bowling
wheels bound, as with ribbons, to her mansion. If they told me that in
those holidays, in those festivities, consisted serially the life of Mme. de
Guermantes, they brought no further light to bear on it. Each of them
gave to the life of the Duchess a different determination, but succeeded
only in changing the mystery of it, without allowing to escape any of its
own mystery which simply floated, protected by a covering, enclosed in
a bell, through the tide of the life of all the world. The Duchess might take
her luncheon on the shore of the Mediterranean at Carnival time, but, in
the villa of Mme. de Guise, where the queen of Parisian society was nothing more, in her white linen dress, among numberless princesses, than a
guest like any of the rest, and on that account more moving still to me,
more herself by being thus made new, like a star of the ballet who in the
fantastic course of a figure takes the place of each of her humbler sisters in
succession; she might look at Chinese shadow shows, but at a party given
by the Princesse de Parme, listen to tragedy or opera, but from the box of
the Princesse de Guermantes.

As we localise in the body of a person all the potentialities of that person's life, our recollections of the people he knows and has just left or is
on his way to meet, if, having learned from Françoise that Mme. de Guermantes was going on foot to luncheon with the Princesse de Parme, I saw
her, about midday, emerge from her house in a gown of flesh-coloured

satin over which her face was of the same shade, like a cloud that rises above
the setting sun, it was all the pleasures of the Faubourg Saint-Germain
that I saw before me, contained in that small compass, as in a shell, between
its twin valves that glowed with roseate nacre.

My father had a friend at the Ministry, one A. J. Moreau, who, to distinguish him from the other Moreaus, took care always to prefix both ini-
tials to his name, with the result that people called him, for short, 'A.J.'
Well, somehow or other, this A. J. found himself entitled to a stall at the
Opéra-Comique on a gala night, he sent the ticket to my father, and as
Berma, whom I had not been again to see since my first disappointment,
was to give an act of *Phèdre*, my grandmother persuaded my father to pass
it on to me.

To tell the truth, I attached no importance to this possibility of hearing
Berma which, a few years earlier, had plunged me in such a state of agitation. And it was not without a sense of melancholy that I realized the
fact of my indifference to what at one time I had put before health, comfort, everything. It was not that there had been any slackening of my
desire for an opportunity to contemplate close at hand the precious particles
of reality of which my imagination caught a broken glimpse. But my imagination no longer placed these in the diction of a great actress; since my
visits to Elstir, it was on certain tapestries, certain modern paintings that
I had brought to bear the inner faith I had once had in this acting, in this
tragic art of Berma; my faith, my desire, no longer coming forward to pay
incessant worship to the diction, the attitudes of Berma, the counterpart
that I possessed of them in my heart had gradually perished, like those
other counterparts of the dead in ancient Egypt which had to be fed continually in order to maintain their originals in eternal life. This art had
become a feeble, tawdry thing. No deep-lying soul inhabited it any more.

That evening, as, armed with the ticket my father had received from his
friend, I was climbing the grand staircase of the Opera, I saw in front of
me a man whom I took at first for M. de Charlus, whose bearing he had;
when he turned his head to ask some question of one of the staff I saw that
I had been mistaken, but I had no hesitation in placing the stranger in the
same class of society, from the way not only in which he was dressed but
in which he spoke to the man who took the tickets and to the box-openers
who were keeping him waiting. For, apart from personal details of similarity, there was still at this period between any smart and wealthy man
of that section of the nobility and any smart and wealthy man of the world
of finance or 'big business' a strongly marked difference. Where one of the
latter would have thought he was giving proof of his exclusiveness by
adopting a sharp, haughty tone in speaking to an inferior, the great gentleman, affable, pleasant, smiling, had the air of considering, practising an
affectation of humility and patience, a pretence of being just one of the
audience, as a privilege of his good breeding. It is quite likely that, on
seeing him thus dissemble behind a smile overflowing with good nature the
barred threshold of the little world apart which he carried in his person,
more than one wealthy banker's son, entering the theatre at that moment,
would have taken this great gentleman for a person of no importance if he

had not remarked in him an astonishing resemblance to the portrait that
had recently appeared in the illustrated papers of a nephew of the Austrian Emperor, the Prince of Saxony, who happened to be in Paris at the
time. I knew him to be a great friend of the Guermantes. As I reached the
attendant I heard the Prince of Saxony (or his double) say with a smile:
"I don't know the number; it was my cousin who·told me I had only to
ask for her box."

He may well have been the Prince of Saxony; it was perhaps of the
Duchesse de Guermantes (whom, in that event, I should be able to watch
in the process of living one of those moments of her unimaginable life in
her cousin's box) that his eyes formed a mental picture when he referred
to 'my cousin who told me I had only to ask for her box,' so much so that
that smiling gaze peculiar to himself, those so simple words caressed my
heart (far more gently than would any abstract meditation) with the
alternative feelers of a possible happiness and a vague distinction. Whatever he was, in uttering this sentence to the attendant he grafted upon a
commonplace evening in my everyday life a potential outlet into a new
world; the passage to which he was directed after mentioning the word
'box' and along which he now proceeded was moist and mildewed and
seemed to lead to subaqueous grottoes, to the mythical kingdom of the
water-nymphs. I had before me a gentleman in evening dress who was
walking away from me, but I kept playing upon and round him, as with
a badly fitting reflector on a lamp, and without ever succeeding in making
it actually coincide with him, the idea that he was the Prince of Saxony
and was on his way to join the Duchesse de Guermantes. And, for all
that he was alone, that idea, external to himself, impalpable, immense, unstable as the shadow projected by a magic lantern, seemed to precede and
guide him like that deity, invisible to the rest of mankind, who stands
beside the Greek warrior in the hour of battle.

I took my seat, striving all the time to recapture a line from *Phèdre*
which I could not quite remember. In the form in which I repeated it to
myself it had not the right number of feet, but as I made no attempt to
count them, between its unwieldiness and a classical line of poetry it seemed
as though no common measure could exist. It would not have surprised me
to learn that I must subtract at least half a dozen syllables from that por-
tentous phrase to reduce it to alexandrine dimensions. But suddenly I
remembered it, the irremediable asperities of an inhuman world vanished
as if by magic; the syllables of the line at once filled up the requisite
measure, what there was in excess floated off with the ease, the dexterity
of a bubble of air that rises to burst on the water's brink. And, after all,
this excrescence with which I had been struggling consisted of but a single
foot.

A certain number of orchestra stalls had been offered for sale at the
box office and bought, out of snobbishness or curiosity, by such as wished
to study the appearance of people whom they might not have another
opportunity of seeing at close quarters. And it was indeed a fragment of
their true social life, ordinarily kept secret, that one could examine here
in public, for, the Princesse de Parme having herself distributed among

her friends the seats in stalls, balconies and boxes, the house was like a drawing-room in which everyone changed his place, went to sit here or there wherever he caught sight of a woman whom he knew.

Next to me were some common people who, not knowing the regular subscribers, were anxious to shew that they were capable of identifying them and named them aloud. They went on to remark that these subscribers behaved there as though they were in their own drawing-rooms, meaning that they paid no attention to what was being played. Which was the exact opposite of what did happen. A budding genius who had taken a stall in order to hear Berma thinks only of not soiling his gloves, of not disturbing, of making friends with the neighbour whom chance has put beside him, of pursuing with an intermittent smile the fugitive—avoiding with apparent want of politeness the intercepted gaze of a person of his acquaintance whom he has discovered in the audience and to whom, after a thousand indecisions, he makes up his mind to go and talk just as the three hammer-blows from the stage, sounding before he has had time to reach his friend, force him to take flight, like the Hebrews in the Red Sea, through a heaving tide of spectators and spectatresses whom he has obliged to rise and whose dresses he tears as he passes, or tramples on their boots. On the other hand it was because the society people sat in their boxes (behind the general terrace of the balcony, as in so many little drawing-rooms, the fourth walls of which had been removed, or in so many little cafés, to which one might go for refreshment, without letting oneself be intimidated by the mirrors in gilt frames or the red plush seats, in the Neapolitan style, of the establishment), it was because they rested an indifferent hand on the gilded shafts of the columns which upheld this temple of the lyric art, it was because they remained unmoved by the extravagant honours which seemed to be being paid them by a pair of carved figures which held out towards the boxes branches of palm and laurel, that they and they only would have had minds free to listen to the play, if only they had had minds.

At first there was nothing visible but vague shadows, in which one suddenly struck—like the gleam of a precious stone which one cannot see—the phosphorescence of a pair of famous eyes, or, like a medallion of Henri IV on a dark background, the bent profile of the Duc d'Aumale, to whom an invisible lady was exclaiming "Monseigneur must allow me to take his coat," to which the Prince replied, "Oh, come, come! Really, Madame d'Ambresac." She took it, in spite of this vague prohibition, and was envied by all the rest her being thus honoured.

But in the other boxes, everywhere almost, the white deities who inhabited those sombre abodes had flown for shelter against their shadowy walls and remained invisible. Gradually, however, as the performance went on, their vaguely human forms detached themselves, one by one, from the shades of night which they patterned, and, raising themselves towards the light, allowed their semi-nude bodies to emerge, and rose, and stopped at the limit of their course, at the luminous, shaded surface on which their brilliant faces appeared behind the gaily breaking foam of the feather fans they unfurled and lightly waved, beneath their hya-

cinthine locks begemmed with pearls, which the flow of the tide seemed to
have caught and drawn with it; this side of them, began the orchestra
stalls, abode of mortals for ever separated from the transparent, shadowy
realm to which, at points here and there, served as boundaries, on its
brimming surface, the limpid, mirroring eyes of the water-nymphs. For the
folding seats on its shore, the forms of the monsters in the stalls were
painted upon the surface of those eyes in simple obedience to the laws of
optics and according to their angle of incidence, as happens with those
two sections of external reality to which, knowing that they do not possess
any soul, however rudimentary, that can be considered as analogous to our
own, we should think ourselves mad if we addressed a smile or a glance of
recognition: namely, minerals and people to whom we have not been introduced. Beyond this boundary, withdrawing from the limit of their domain,
the radiant daughters of the sea kept turning at every moment to smile up
at the bearded tritons who clung to the anfractuosities of the cliff, or towards some aquatic demi-god, whose head was a polished stone to which
the tides had borne a smooth covering of seaweed, and his gaze a disc of
rock crystal. They leaned towards these creatures, offering them sweetmeats; sometimes the flood parted to admit a fresh Nereid who, belated,
smiling, apologetic, had just floated into blossom out of the shadowy
depths; then, the act ended, having no further hope of hearing the melodious sounds of earth which had drawn them to the surface, plunging back
all in a moment the several sisters vanished into the night. But of all these
retreats, to the thresholds of which their mild desire to behold the works
of man brought the curious goddesses who let none approach them, the
most famous was the cube of semi-darkness known to the world as the
stage box of the Princesse de Guermantes.

Like a mighty goddess who presides from far aloft over the sports of
lesser deities, the Princess had deliberately remained a little way back on
a sofa placed sideways in the box, red as a reef of coral, beside a big, glassy
splash of reflexion which was probably a mirror and made one think of
the section cut by a ray of sunlight, vertical, clear, liquid, through the
flashing crystal of the sea. At once plume and blossom, like certain subaqueous growths, a great white flower, downy as the wing of a bird, fell
from the brow of the Princess along one of her cheeks, the curve of which
it followed with a pliancy, coquettish, amorous, alive, and seemed almost
to enfold it like a rosy egg in the softness of a halcyon's nest. Over her hair,
reaching in front to her eyebrows and caught back lower down at the level
of her throat, was spread a net upon which those little white shells which
are gathered on some shore of the South Seas alternated with pearls, a
marine mosaic barely emerging from the waves and at every moment
plunged back again into a darkness in the depths of which even then a
human presence was revealed by the ubiquitous flashing of the Princess's
eyes. The beauty which set her far above all the other fabulous daughters
of the dusk was not altogether materially and comprehensively inscribed
on her neck, her shoulders, her arms, her figure. But the exquisite, unfinished line of the last was the exact starting point, the inevitable focus of
invisible lines which the eye could not help prolonging, marvellous lines,

springing into life round the woman like the spectrum of an ideal form projected upon the screen of darkness.

"That's the Princesse de Guermantes," said my neighbour to the gentleman beside her, taking care to begin the word 'Princesse' with a string of P's, to shew that a title like that was absurd. "She hasn't been sparing with her pearls. I'm sure, if I had as many as that, I wouldn't make such a display of them; it doesn't look at all well, not to my mind."

And yet, when they caught sight of the Princess, all those who were looking round to see who was in the audience felt springing up for her in their hearts the rightful throne of beauty. Indeed, with the Duchesse de Luxembourg, with Mme. de Morienval, with Mme. de Saint-Euverte, and any number of others, what enabled one to identify their faces would be the juxtaposition of a big red nose to a hare-lip, or of a pair of wrinkled cheeks to a faint moustache. These features were nevertheless sufficient in themselves to attract the eye, since having merely the conventional value of a written document they gave one to read a famous and impressive name; but also they gave one, cumulatively, the idea that ugliness had about it something aristocratic, and that it was unnecessary that the face of a great lady, provided it was distinguished, should be beautiful as well. But like certain artists who, instead of the letters of their names, set at the foot of their canvas a form that is beautiful in itself, a butterfly, a lizard, a flower, so it was the form of a delicious face and figure that the Princess had put in the corner of her box, thereby shewing that beauty can be the noblest of signatures; for the presence there of Mme. de Guermantes-Bavière, who brought to the theatre only such persons as at other times formed part of her intimate circle, was in the eyes of specialists in aristocracy the best possible certificate of the authenticity of the picture which her box presented, a sort of evocation of a scene in the ordinary private life of the Princess in her palaces in Munich and in Paris.

Our imagination being like a barrel organ out of order, which always plays some other tune than that shewn on its card, every time that I had heard any mention of the Princesse de Guermantes-Bavière, a recollection of certain sixteenth-century masterpieces had begun singing in my brain. I was obliged to rid myself quickly of this association, now that I saw her engaged in offering crystallised fruit to a stout gentleman in a swallow-tail coat. Certainly I was very far from the conclusion that she and her guests were mere human beings like the rest of the audience. I understood that what they were doing there was all only a game, and that as a prelude to the acts of their real life (of which, presumably, this was not where they spent the important part) they had arranged, in obedience to a ritual unknown to me, they were feigning to offer and decline sweetmeats, a gesture robbed of its ordinary significance and regulated beforehand like the step of a dancer who alternately raises herself on her toes and circles about an upheld scarf. For all I knew, perhaps at the moment of offering him her sweetmeats the goddess was saying, with that note of irony in her voice (for I saw her smile): "Do have one, won't you?" What mattered that to me? I should have found a delicious refinement in the deliberate dryness, in the style of Mérimée or Meilhac, of such words addressed by a goddess to a demi-god who, conscious himself what were the sublime thoughts which they both had in their minds, in reserve, doubtless, until the moment when they would begin again to live their true life, consenting to join in the game, was answering with the same mysterious bitterness: "Thanks; I should like a cherry." And I should have listened to this dialogue with the same avidity as to a scene from *Le Mari de la Débutante*, where the absence of poetry, of lofty thoughts, things so familiar to me which, I suppose, Meilhac could easily, had he chosen, have put into it a thousand times over, seemed to me in itself a refinement, a conventional refinement and therefore all the more mysterious and instructive.

"That fat fellow is the Marquis de Ganançay," came in a knowing tone from the man next to me, who had not quite caught the name whispered in the row behind.

The Marquis de Palancy, his face bent downwards at the end of his long neck, his round bulging eye glued to the glass of his monocle, was moving with a leisurely displacement through the transparent shade and appeared no more to see the public in the stalls than a fish that drifts past, unconscious of the press of curious gazers, behind the glass wall of an aquarium. Now and again he paused, a venerable, wheezing monument, and the audience could not have told whether he was in pain, asleep, swimming, about to spawn, or merely taking breath. No one else aroused in me so much envy as he, on account of his apparent familiarity with this box and the indifference with which he allowed the Princess to hold out to him her box of sweetmeats; throwing him, at the same time, a glance from her fine eyes, cut in a pair of diamonds which at such moments wit and friendliness seemed to liquefy, whereas, when they were at rest, reduced to their purely material beauty, to their mineral brilliance alone, if the least reflected flash disturbed them ever so slightly, they set the darkness ablaze with inhuman horizontal splendid fires. But now, because the act of *Phèdre* in which Berma was playing was due to start, the Princess came to the front of the box; whereupon, as if she herself were a theatrical production, in the zone of light which she traversed, I saw not only the colour but the material of her adornments change. And in the box, dry now, emerging, a part no longer of the watery realm, the Princess, ceasing to be a Nereid, appeared turbanned in white and blue like some marvellous tragic actress dressed for the part of Zaïre, or perhaps of Orosmane; finally, when she had taken her place in the front row I saw that the soft halcyon's nest which tenderly shielded the rosy nacre of her cheeks was—downy, dazzling, velvety, an immense bird of paradise.

But now my gaze was diverted from the Princesse de Guermantes's box by a little woman who came in, ill-dressed, plain, her eyes ablaze with indignation, followed by two young men, and sat down a few places from me. At length the curtain went up. I could not help being saddened by the reflexion that there remained now no trace of my old disposition, at the period when, so as to miss nothing of the extraordinary phenomenon which I would have gone to the ends of the earth to see, I kept my mind prepared, like the sensitive plates which astronomers take out to Africa, to the West Indies, to make and record an exact observation of a comet or an eclipse; when I trembled for fear lest some cloud (a fit of ill humour on the artist's part or an incident in the audience) should prevent the spectacle from presenting itself with the maximum of intensity; when I should not have believed that I was watching it in the most perfect conditions had I not gone to the very theatre which was consecrated to it like an altar, in which I then felt to be still a part of it, though an accessory part only, the officials with their white carnations, appointed by her, the vaulted balcony covering a pit filled with a shabbily dressed crowd, the women selling programmes that had her photograph, the chestnut trees in the square outside, all those companions, those confidants of my impressions of those days which seemed to me to be inseparable from them. *Phèdre,* the 'Declaration Scene,' Berma, had had then for me a sort of absolute existence. Standing aloof from the world of current experience they existed by themselves, I must go to meet them, I should penetrate what I could of them, and if I opened my eyes and soul to their fullest extent I should still absorb but a very little of them. But how pleasant life seemed to me: the triviality of the form of it that I myself was leading mattered nothing, no more than the time we spend on dressing, on getting ready to go out, since, transcending it, there existed in an absolute form, good and difficult to approach, impossible to possess in their entirety, those more solid realities, *Phèdre* and the way in which Berma spoke her part. Steeped in these dreams of perfection in the dramatic art (a strong dose of which anyone who had at that time subjected my mind to analysis at any moment of the day or even the night would have been able to prepare from it), I was like a battery that accumulates and stores up electricity. And a time had come when, ill as I was, even if I had believed that I should die of it, I should still have been compelled to go and hear Berma. But now, like a hill which from a distance seems a patch of azure sky, but, as we draw nearer, returns to its place in our ordinary field of vision, all this had left the world of the absolute and was no more than a thing like other things, of which I took cognisance because I was there, the actors were people of the same substance as the people I knew, trying to speak in the best possible way these lines of *Phèdre,* which themselves no longer formed a sublime and individual essence, distinct from everything else, but were simply more or less effective lines ready to slip back into the vast corpus of French poetry, of which they were merely a part. I felt a discouragement that was all the more profound in that, if the object of my headstrong and active desire no longer existed, the same tendencies, on the other hand, to indulge in a perpetual dream, which varied from year to year but led me always to sudden impulses, regardless of danger, still persisted. The day on which I rose from my bed of sickness and set out to see, in some country house or other, a picture by Elstir or a mediaeval tapestry, was so like the day on which I ought to have started for Venice, or that on which I did go to hear Berma, or start for Balbec, that I felt before going that the immediate object of my sacrifice would, after a little while, leave me cold, that then I might pass close by the place without stopping even to look at that picture, those tapestries for which I would at this moment risk so many sleepless nights, so many hours of pain. I discerned in the insta-

bility of its object the vanity of my effort, and at the same time its vast-
ness, which I had not before noticed, like a neurasthenic whose exhaustion
we double by pointing out to him that he is exhausted. In the meantime
my musings gave a distinction to everything that had any connexion with
them. And even in my most carnal desires, magnetised always in a certain
direction, concentrated about a single dream, I might have recognised as
their primary motive an idea, an idea for which I would have laid down
my life, at the innermost core of which, as in my day dreams while I sat
reading all afternoon in the garden at Combray, lay the thought of perfection.

I no longer felt the same indulgence as on the former occasion towards
the deliberate expressions of affection or anger which I had then remarked
in the delivery and gestures of Aricie, Ismène and Hippolyte. It was not
that the players—they were the same, by the way—did not still seek, with
the same intelligent application, to impart now a caressing inflexion, or a
calculated ambiguity to their voices, now a tragic amplitude, or a suppliant
meekness to their movements. Their intonations bade the voice: "Be
gentle, sing like a nightingale, caress and woo"; or else, "now wax furious,"
and then hurled themselves upon it, trying to carry it off with them in
their frenzied rush. But it, mutinous, independent of their diction, remained unalterably their natural voice with its material defects or charms,
its everyday vulgarity or affectation, and thus presented a sum-total of
acoustic or social phenomena which the sentiment contained in the lines
they were repeating was powerless to alter.

Similarly the gestures of the players said to their arms, to their garments: "Be majestic." But each of these unsubmissive members allowed
to flaunt itself between shoulder and elbow a biceps which knew nothing
of the part; they continued to express the triviality of everyday life and
to bring into prominence, instead of fine shades of Racinian meaning, mere
muscular attachments; and the draperies which they held up fell back
again along vertical lines in which the natural law that governs falling
bodies was challenged only by an insipid textile pliancy. At this point the
little woman who was sitting near me exclaimed:

"Not a hand! Did you ever see such a get-up? She's too old; she can't
play the part; she ought to have retired ages ago."

Amid a sibilant protest from their neighbours the two young men with
her succeeded in making her keep quiet and her fury raged now only in
her eyes. This fury could, moreover, be prompted only by the thought of
success, of fame, for Berma, who had earned so much money, was overwhelmed with debts. Since she was always making business or social appointments which she was prevented from keeping, she had messengers
flying with apologies along every street in Paris, and what with rooms in
hotels which she would never occupy engaged in advance, oceans of scent
to bathe her dogs, heavy penalties for breaches of contract with all her
managers, failing any more serious expense and being not so voluptuous
as Cleopatra, she would have found the means of squandering on telegrams
and jobmasters provinces and kingdoms. But the little woman was an
actress who had never tasted success, and had vowed a deadly hatred

against Berma. The latter had just come on to the stage. And then—oh, the miracle—like those lessons which we laboured in vain to learn overnight, and find intact, got by heart, on waking up next morning, like, too, those faces of dead friends which the impassioned efforts of our memory pursue without recapturing them, and which, when we are no longer thinking of them, are there before our eyes just as they were in life—the talent of Berma, which had evaded me when I sought so greedily to seize its essential quality, now, after these years of oblivion, in this hour of indifference, imposed itself, with all the force of a thing directly seen, on my admiration. Formerly, in my attempts to isolate the talent, I deducted, so to speak, from what I heard the part itself, a part common to all the actresses who appeared as Phèdre, which I had myself studied beforehand so that I might be capable of subtracting it, of receiving in the strained residue only the talent of Mme. Berma. But this talent which I sought to discover outside the part itself was indissolubly one with it. So with a great musician (it appears that this was the case with Vinteuil when he played the piano), his playing is that of so fine a pianist that one cannot even be certain whether the performer is a pianist at all, since (not interposing all that mechanism of muscular effort, crowned here and there with brilliant effects, all that spattering shower of notes in which at least the listener who does not quite know where he is thinks that he can discern talent in its material, tangible objectivity) his playing is become so transparent, so full of what he is interpreting, that himself one no longer sees and he is nothing now but a window opening upon a great work of art. The intentions which surrounded, like a majestic or delicate border, the voice and mimicry of Aricie, Ismène or Hippolyte I had been able to distinguish, but Phèdre had taken hers into herself, and my mind had not succeeded in wresting from her diction and attitudes, in apprehending in the miserly simplicity of their unbroken surfaces those treasures, those effects of which no sign emerged, so completely had they been absorbed. Berma's voice, in which not one atom of lifeless matter refractory to the mind remained undissolved, did not allow any sign to be discernible around it of that overflow of tears which one could feel, because they had not been able to absorb it in themselves, trickling over the marble voice of Aricie or Ismène, but had been brought to an exquisite perfection in each of its tiniest cells like the instrument of a master violinist, in whom one means, when one says that his music has a fine sound, to praise not a physical peculiarity but a superiority of soul; and, as in the classical landscape where in the place of a vanished nymph there is an inanimate waterspring, a clear and concrete intention had been transformed into a certain quality of tone, strangely, appropriately, coldly limpid. Berma's arms, which the lines themselves, by the same dynamic force that made the words issue from her lips, seemed to raise on to her bosom like leaves disturbed by a gush of water; her attitude, on the stage, which she had gradually built up, which she was to modify yet further, and which was based upon reasonings of a different profundity from those of which traces might be seen in the gestures of her fellow-actors, but of reasonings that had lost their original deliberation, and had melted into a sort of radiance in which they sent throbbing, round the person of the heroine, elements rich and complex, but which the fascinated spectator took not as an artistic triumph but as a natural gift; those white veils themselves, which, tenuous and clinging, seemed to be of a living substance and to have been woven by the suffering, half-pagan, half-Jansenist, around which they drew close like a frail, shrinking chrysalis; all of them, voice, attitude, gestures, veils, were nothing more, round this embodiment of an idea, which a line of poetry is (an embodiment that, unlike our human bodies, covers the soul not with an opaque screen which prevents us from seeing it, but with a purified, a quickened garment through which the soul is diffused and we discover it), than additional envelopes which instead of concealing shewed up in greater splendour the soul that had assimilated them to itself and had spread itself through them, than layers of different substances, grown translucent, the interpolation of which has the effect only of causing a richer refraction of the imprisoned, central ray that pierces through them, and of making more extensive, more precious and more fair the matter purified by fire in which it is enshrined. So Berma's interpretation was, around Racine's work, a second work, quickened also by the breath of genius.

My own impression, to tell the truth, though more pleasant than on the earlier occasion, was not really different. Only, I no longer put it to the test of a pre-existent, abstract and false idea of dramatic genius, and I understood now that dramatic genius was precisely this. It had just occurred to me that if I had not derived any pleasure from my first hearing of Berma, it was because, as earlier still when I used to meet Gilberte in the Champs-Elysées, I had come to her with too strong a desire. Between my two disappointments there was perhaps not only this resemblance, but another more profound. The impression given us by a person or a work (or a rendering, for that matter) of marked individuality is peculiar to that person or work. We have brought to it the ideas of 'beauty,' 'breadth of style,' 'pathos' and so forth which we might, failing anything better, have had the illusion of discovering in the commonplace show of a 'correct' face or talent, but our critical spirit has before it the insistent challenge of a form of which it possesses no intellectual equivalent, in which it must detect and isolate the unknown element. It hears a shrill sound, an oddly interrogative intonation. It asks itself: "Is that good? Is what I am feeling just now admiration? Is that richness of colouring, nobility, strength?" And what answers it again is a shrill voice, a curiously questioning tone, the despotic impression caused by a person whom one does not know, wholly material, in which there is no room left for 'breadth of interpretation.' And for this reason it is the really beautiful works that, if we listen to them with sincerity, must disappoint us most keenly, because in the storehouse of our ideas there is none that corresponds to an individual impression.

This was precisely what Berma's acting shewed me. This was what was meant by nobility, by intelligence of diction. Now I could appreciate the worth of a broad, poetical, powerful interpretation, or rather it was to this that those epithets were conventionally applied, but only as we give the names of Mars, Venus, Saturn to planets which have no place in classical mythology. We feel in one world, we think, we give names to things in another; between the two we can establish a certain correspondence, but not bridge the interval. It was quite narrow, this interval, this fault that I had had to cross when, that afternoon on which I went first to hear Berma, having strained my ears to catch every word, I had found some difficulty in correlating my ideas of 'nobility of interpretation,' of 'originality,' and had broken out in applause only after a moment of unconsciousness and as if my applause sprang not from my actual impression but was connected in some way with my preconceived ideas, with the pleasure that I found in saying to myself: "At last I am listening to Berma." And the difference that there is between a person, or a work of art which is markedly individual and the idea of beauty, exists just as much between what they make us feel and the idea of love, or of admiration. Wherefore we fail to recognise them. I had found no pleasure in listening to Berma (any more than, earlier still, in seeing Gilberte). I had said to myself: "Well, I do not admire this." But then I was thinking only of mastering the secret of Berma's acting, I was preoccupied with that alone, I was trying to open my mind as wide as possible to receive all that her acting contained. I understood now that all this amounted to nothing more nor less than admiration.

This genius of which Berma's rendering of the part was only the revelation, was it indeed the genius of Racine and nothing more?

I thought so at first. I was soon to be undeceived when the curtain fell on the act from *Phèdre,* amid enthusiastic recalls from the audience, through which the old actress, beside herself with rage, drawing her little body up to its full height, turning sideways in her seat, stiffened the muscles of her face and folded her arms on her bosom to shew that she was not joining the others in their applause, and to make more noticeable a protest which to her appeared sensational though it passed unperceived. The piece that followed was one of those novelties which at one time I had expected, since they were not famous, to be inevitably trivial and of no general application, devoid as they were of any existence outside the performance that was being given of them at the moment. But I had not with them as with a classic the disappointment of seeing the infinity and eternity of a masterpiece occupy no more space or time than the width of the footlights and the length of a performance which would finish it as effectively as a piece written for the occasion. Besides, at every fresh passage which, I felt, had appealed to the audience and would one day be famous, in place of the fame which it was prevented from having won in the past I added that which it would enjoy in the future, by a mental process the converse of that which consists in imagining masterpieces on the day of their first thin performance, when it seemed inconceivable that a title which no one had ever heard before could one day be set, bathed in the same mellow light, beside those of the author's other works. And this part would be set one day in the list of her finest impersonations, next to that of Phèdre. Not that in itself it was not destitute of all literary merit. But Berma was as sublime in one as in the other. I realised then that the work of the playwright was for the actress no more than the material, the nature of which was comparatively unimportant, for the creation of her masterpiece of interpretation, just as the great painter whom I had met at Balbec, Elstir, had found the inspiration for two pictures of equal merit in a school building without any character and a cathedral which was in itself a work of art. And as the painter dissolves houses, carts, people, in some broad effect of light which makes them all alike, so Berma spread out great sheets of terror or tenderness over words that were all melted together in a common mould, lowered or raised to one level, which a lesser artist would have carefully detached from one another. No doubt each of them had an inflexion of its own, and Berma's diction did not prevent one from catching the rhythm of the verse. Is it not already a first element of ordered complexity, of beauty, when, on hearing a rhyme, that is to say something which is at once similar to and different from the preceding rhyme, which was prompted by it, but introduces the variety of a new idea, one is conscious of two systems overlapping each other, one intellectual, the other prosodic? But Berma at the same time made her words, her lines, her whole speeches even, flow into lakes of sound vaster than themselves, at the margins of which it was a joy to see them obliged to stop, to break off; thus it is that a poet takes pleasure in making hesitate for a moment at the rhyming point the word which is about to spring forth, and a composer in merging the various words of his libretto in a single rhythm which contradicts, captures and controls them. Thus into the prose sentences of the modern playwright as into the poetry of Racine Berma managed to introduce those vast images of grief, nobility, passion, which were the masterpieces of her own personal art, and in which she could be recognised as, in the portraits which he has made of different sitters, we recognise a painter.

I had no longer any desire, as on the former occasion, to be able to arrest and perpetuate Berma's attitudes, the fine colour effect which she gave for a moment only in a beam of limelight which at once faded never to reappear, nor to make her repeat a single line a hundred times over. I realised that my original desire had been more exacting than the intentions of the poet, the actress, the great decorative artist who supervised her productions, and that that charm which floated over a line as it was spoken, those unstable poses perpetually transformed into others, those successive pictures were the transient result, the momentary object, the changing masterpiece which the art of the theatre undertook to create and which would perish were an attempt made to fix it for all time by a too much enraptured listener. I did not even make a resolution to come back another day and hear Berma again. I was satisfied with her; it was when I admired too keenly not to be disappointed by the object of my admiration, whether that object were Gilberte or Berma, that I demanded in advance, of the impression to be received on the morrow, the pleasure that yesterday's impression had refused to afford me. Without seeking to analyse the joy which I had begun now to feel, and might perhaps have been turning to some more profitable use, I said to myself, as in the old days I might have said to one of my schoolfellows: "Certainly, I put Berma first!" not without a confused feeling that Berma's genius was not, perhaps, very accurately represented by this affirmation of my preference, or this award to her of a 'first' place, whatever the peace of mind that it might incidentally restore to me.

Just as the curtain was rising on this second play I looked up at Mme. de Guermantes's box. The Princess was in the act—by a movement that called into being an exquisite line which my mind pursued into the void—of turning her head towards the back of the box; her party were all standing, and also turning towards the back, and between the double hedge which they thus formed, with all the assurance, the grandeur of the goddess that she was, but with a strange meekness which so late an arrival, making every one else get up in the middle of the performance, blended with the white muslin in which she was attired, just as an adroitly compounded air of simplicity, shyness and confusion tempered her triumphant smile, the Duchesse de Guermantes, who had at that moment entered the box, came towards her cousin, made a profound obeisance to a young man with fair hair who was seated in the front row, and turning again towards the amphibian monsters who were floating in the recesses of the cavern, gave to these demi-gods of the Jockey Club—who at that moment, and among them all M. de Palancy in particular, were the men whom I should most have liked to be—the familiar 'good evening' of an old and intimate friend, an allusion to the daily sequence of her relations with them during the last fifteen years. I felt the mystery, but could not solve the riddle of that smiling gaze which she addressed to her friends, in the azure brilliance with which it glowed while she surrendered her hand to one and then to another, a gaze which, could I have broken up its prism, analysed its crystallisation, might perhaps have revealed to me the essential quality of the unknown form of life which became apparent in it at that moment. The Duc de Guermantes followed his wife, the flash of his monocle, the gleam of his teeth, the whiteness of his carnation or of his pleated shirt-front scattering, to make room for their light, the darkness of his eyebrows, lips and coat; with a wave of his outstretched hand which he let drop on to their shoulders, vertically, without moving his head, he commanded the inferior monsters, who were making way for him, to resume their seats, and made a profound bow to the fair young man. One would have said that the Duchess had guessed that her cousin, of whom, it was rumoured, she was inclined to make fun for what she called her 'exaggerations' (a name which, from her own point of view, so typically French and restrained, would naturally be applied to the poetry and enthusiasm of the Teuton), would be wearing this evening one of those costumes in which the Duchess thought of her as 'dressed up,' and that she had decided to give her a lesson in good taste. Instead of the wonderful downy plumage which, from the crown of the Princess's head, fell and swept her throat, instead of her net of shells and pearls, the Duchess wore in her hair only a simple aigrette, which, rising above her arched nose and level eyes, reminded one of the crest on the head of a bird. Her neck and shoulders emerged from a drift of snow-white muslin, against which fluttered a swansdown fan, but below this her gown, the bodice of which had for its sole ornament innumerable spangles (either little sticks and beads of metal, or possibly brilliants), moulded her figure with a precision that was positively British. But different as their two costumes were, after the Princess had given her cousin the chair in which she herself had previously been sitting, they could be seen turning to gaze at one another in mutual appreciation.

Possibly a smile would curve the lips of Mme. de Guermantes when next day she referred to the headdress, a little too complicated, which the Princess had worn, but certainly she would declare that it had been, all the same, quite lovely, and marvellously arranged; and the Princess, whose own tastes found something a little cold, a little austere, a little 'tailor-made' in her cousin's way of dressing, would discover in this rigid sobriety an exquisite refinement. Moreover the harmony that existed between them, the universal and pre-established gravitation exercised by their upbringing, neutralised the contrasts not only in their apparel but in their attitude. By those invisible magnetic longitudes which the refinement of their manners traced between them the expansive nature of the Princess was stopped short, while on the other side the formal correctness of the Duchess allowed itself to be attracted and relaxed, turned to sweetness and charm. As, in the play which was now being performed, to realise how much personal poetry Berma extracted from it one had only to entrust the part which she was playing, which she alone could play, to no matter what other actress, so the spectator who should raise his eyes to the balcony might see in two smaller boxes there how an 'arrangement' supposed to suggest that of the Princesse de Guermantes simply made the Baronne de Morienval appear eccentric, pretentious and ill-bred, while an effort, as painstaking as it must have been costly, to imitate the clothes and style of the Duchesse de Guermantes only made Mme. de Cambremer look like some provincial schoolgirl, mounted on wires, rigid, erect, dry, angular, with a plume of raven's feathers stuck vertically in her hair. Perhaps the proper place for this lady was not a theatre in which it was only with the brightest stars of the season that the boxes (even those in the highest tier, which from below seemed like great hampers brimming with human flowers and fastened to the gallery on which they stood by the red cords of their plush-covered partitions) composed a panorama which deaths, scandals, illnesses, quarrels would soon alter, but which this evening was held motionless by attention, heat, giddiness, dust, smartness or boredom, in that so to speak everlasting moment of unconscious waiting and calm torpor which, in retrospect, seems always to have preceded the explosion of a bomb or the first flicker of a fire.

The explanation of Mme. de Cambremer's presence on this occasion was that the Princesse de Parme, devoid of snobbishness as are most truly royal personages, and to make up for this devoured by a pride in and passion for charity which held an equal place in her heart with her taste for what she believed to be the Arts, had bestowed a few boxes here and there upon women like Mme. de Cambremer who were not numbered among the highest aristocratic society but with whom she was connected in various charitable undertakings. Mme. de Cambremer never took her eyes off the Duchesse and Princesse de Guermantes, which was all the simpler for her since, not being actually acquainted with either, she could not be suspected of angling for recognition. Inclusion in the visiting lists of these two great ladies was nevertheless the goal towards which she had been marching for the last ten years with untiring patience. She had calculated that she might reach it, possibly, in five years more. But having been smitten by a relentless malady, the inexorable character of which—for she prided herself upon her medical knowledge—she thought she knew, she was afraid that she might not live so long. This evening she was happy at least in the thought that all these women whom she barely knew would see in her company a man who was one of their own set, the young Marquis de Beausergent, Mme. d'Argencourt's brother, who moved impartially in both worlds and with whom the women of the second were greatly delighted to bedizen themselves before the eyes of those of the first. He was seated behind Mme. de Cambremer on a chair placed at an angle, so that he might rake the other boxes with his glasses. He knew everyone in the house, and, to greet his friends, with the irresistible charm of his beautifully curved figure, and fine fair head, he half rose from his seat, stiffening his body, a smile brightening his blue eyes, with a blend of deference and detachment, a picture delicately engraved, in its rectangular frame, and placed at an angle to the wall, like one of those old prints which portray a great nobleman in his courtly pride. He often accepted these invitations to go with Mme. de Cambremer to the play. In the theatre itself, and on their way out, in the lobby, he stood gallantly by her side in the thick of the throng of more brilliant friends whom he saw about him, and to whom he refrained from speaking, to avoid any awkwardness, just as though he had been in doubtful company. If at such moments there swept by him the Princesse de Guermantes, lightfoot and fair as Diana, letting trail behind her the folds of an incomparable cloak, turning after her every head and followed by every eye (and, most of all, by Mme. de Cambremer's), M. de Beausergent would become absorbed in conversation with his companion, acknowledging the friendly and dazzling smile of the Princess only with constraint, under compulsion, and with the well-bred reserve, the considerate coldness of a person whose friendliness might at the moment have been inconvenient.

Had not Mme. de Cambremer known already that the box belonged to the Princess, she could still have told that the Duchesse de Guermantes was the guest from the air of keener interest with which she was survey-ing the spectacle of stage and stalls, out of politeness to her hostess. But simultaneously with this centrifugal force, an equal and opposite force generated by the same desire to be sociable drew her attention back to her own attire, her plume, her necklace, her bodice and also to that of the Princess, whose subject, whose slave her cousin seemed thus to proclaim herself, come thither solely to see her, ready to follow her elsewhere should it have taken the fancy of the official occupant of the box to rise and leave, and regarding as composed merely of strangers, worth looking at simply as curiosities, the rest of the house, in which, nevertheless, she numbered many friends to whose boxes she regularly repaired on other evenings and with regard to whom she never failed on those occasions to demonstrate a similar loyalism, exclusive, conditional and hebdomadary. Mme. de Cambremer was surprised to see her there that evening. She knew that the Duchess was staying on very late at Guermantes, and had supposed her to be there still. But she had been told, also, that sometimes, when there was some special function in Paris which she considered it worth her while to attend, Mme. de Guermantes would order one of her carriages to be brought round as soon as she had taken tea with the guns, and, as the sun was setting, start out at a spanking pace through the gathering darkness of the forest, then over the high road, to join the train at Combray and so be in Paris the same evening. "Perhaps she has come up from Guermantes on purpose to hear Berma," thought Mme. de Cambremer, and marvelled at the thought. And she remembered having heard Swann say in that ambiguous jargon which he used in common with M. de Charlus: "The Duchess is one of the noblest souls in Paris, the cream of the most refined, the choicest society." For myself, who derived from the names Guermantes, Bavaria and Condé what I imagined to be the life, the thoughts of the two cousins (I could no longer so ascribe their faces, having seen them), I would rather have had their opinion of *Phèdre* than that of the greatest critic in the world. For in his I should have found merely intellect, an intellect superior to my own but similar in kind. But what the Duchesse and Princesse de Guermantes might think, an opinion which would have furnished me with an invaluable clue to the nature of these two poetic creatures, I imagined with the aid of their names, I endowed with an irrational charm, and, with the thirst, the longing of a fever-stricken wretch, what I demanded that their opinion of *Phèdre* should yield to me was the charm of the summer afternoons that I had spent in wandering along the Guermantes way.

Mme. de Cambremer was trying to make out how exactly the cousins were dressed. For my own part, I never doubted that their garments were peculiar to themselves, not merely in the sense in which the livery with red collar or blue facings had belonged once exclusively to the houses of Guermantes and Condé, but rather as is peculiar to a bird the plumage which, as well as being a heightening of its beauty, is an extension of its body. The toilet of these two ladies seemed to me like a materialisation, snow-white or patterned with colour, of their internal activity, and, like the gestures which I had seen the Princesse de Guermantes make, with no doubt in my own mind that they corresponded to some idea latent in hers, the plumes which swept downward from her brow, and her cousin's glittering spangled bodice seemed each to have a special meaning, to be to one or the other lady an attribute which was hers and hers alone, the significance of which I would eagerly have learned; the bird of paradise seemed inseparable from its wearer as her peacock is from Juno, and I did not believe that any other woman could usurp that spangled bodice, any more than the fringed and flashing aegis of Minerva. And when I turned my eyes to their box, far more than on the ceiling of the theatre, painted with cold and lifeless allegories, it was as though I had seen, thanks to a miraculous rending of the clouds that ordinarily veiled it, the Assembly of the Gods in the act of contemplating the spectacle of mankind, beneath a crimson canopy, in a clear lighted space, between two pillars of Heaven. I gazed on this brief transfiguration with a disturbance which was partly soothed by the feeling that I myself was unknown to these Immortals; the Duchess had indeed seen me once with her husband, but could surely have kept no memory of that, and it gave me no pain that she found herself, owing to the place that she occupied in the box, in a position to gaze down upon the nameless, collective madrepores of the public in the stalls, for I had the happy sense that my own personality had been dissolved in theirs, when, at the moment in which, by the force of certain optical laws, there must, I suppose, have come to paint itself on the impassive current of those blue eyes the blurred outline of the protozoon, devoid of any individual existence, which was myself, I saw a ray illumine them; the Duchess, goddess turned woman, and appearing in that moment a thousand times more lovely, raised, pointed in my direction the white-gloved hand which had been resting on the balustrade of the box, waved it at me in token of friendship; my gaze felt itself trapped in the spontaneous incandescence of the flashing eyes of the Princess, who had unconsciously set them ablaze merely by turning her head to see who it might be that her cousin was thus greeting, while the Duchess, who had remembered me, showered upon me the sparkling and celestial torrent of her smile.

And now every morning, long before the hour at which she would appear, I went by a devious course to post myself at the corner of the street along which she generally came, and, when the moment of her arrival seemed imminent, strolled homewards with an air of being absorbed in something else, looking the other way and raising my eyes to her face as I drew level with her, but as though I had not in the least expected to see her. Indeed, for the first few mornings, so as to be sure of not missing her, I waited opposite the house. And every time that the carriage gate opened (letting out one after another so many people who were none of them she for whom I was waiting) its grinding rattle continued in my heart in a series of oscillations which it took me a long time to subdue. For never was devotee of a famous actress whom he did not know, posting himself and patrolling the pavement outside the stage door, never was angry or idolatrous crowd, gathered to insult or to carry in triumph through the streets the condemned assassin or the national hero whom it believes to be on the point of coming whenever a sound is heard from the inside of the prison or the palace, never were these so stirred by their emotion as I was, awaiting the emergence of this great lady who in her simple attire was able, by the grace of her movements (quite different from the gait she affected on entering a drawing-room or a box), to make of her morning walk—and for me there was no one in the world but herself out walking—a whole poem of elegant refinement and the finest ornament, the most curious flower of the season. But after the third day, so that the porter should not discover my stratagem, I betook myself much farther afield, to some point upon the Duchess's usual route. Often before that evening at the theatre I had made similar little excursions before luncheon when the weather was fine; if it had been raining, at the first gleam of sunshine I would hasten downstairs to take a turn, and if, suddenly, coming towards me, on the still wet pavement changed by the sun into a golden lacquer, in the transformation scene of a crossroads dusty with a grey mist which the sun tanned and gilded, I caught sight of a schoolgirl followed by her governess or of a dairy-maid with her white sleeves, I stood motionless, my hand pressed to my heart which was already leaping towards an unexplored form of life; I tried to bear in mind the street, the time, the number of the door through which the girl (whom I followed sometimes) had vanished and failed to reappear. Fortunately the fleeting nature of these cherished images, which I promised myself that I would make an effort to see again, prevented them from fixing themselves with any vividness in my memory. No matter, I was less sad now at the thought of my own ill health, of my never having summoned up courage to set to work, to begin a book, the world appeared to me now a pleasanter place to live in, life a more interesting experience now that I had learned that the streets of Paris, like the roads round Balbec, were aflower with those unknown beauties whom I had so often sought to evoke from the woods of Méséglise, each one of whom aroused a sensual longing which she alone appeared capable of assuaging.

On coming home from the Opéra-Comique I had added for next morning to the list of those which for some days past I had been hoping to meet again the form of Mme. de Guermantes, tall, with her high-piled crown of silky, golden hair; with the kindness promised me in the smile which she had directed at me from her cousin's box. I would follow the course which Françoise had told me that the Duchess generally took, and I would try at the same time, in the hope of meeting two girls whom I had seen a few days earlier, not to miss the break-up of their respective class and catechism. But in the mean time, ever and again, the scintillating smile of Mme. de Guermantes, the pleasant sensation it had given me, returned. And without exactly knowing what I was doing, I tried to find a place for them (as a woman studies the possible effect on her dress of some set of jewelled buttons that have just been given her) beside the romantic ideas which I had long held and which Albertine's coldness, Gisèle's premature departure, and before them my deliberate and too long sustained separation from Gilberte, had set free (the idea, for instance of being loved by a woman, of having a life in common with her); next, it had been the image of one or other of the two girls seen in the street that I brought into relation with those ideas, to which immediately afterwards I was trying to adapt my memory of the Duchess. Compared with those ideas my memory of Mme. de Guermantes at the Opéra-Comique was a very little thing, a tiny star twinkling beside the long tail of a blazing comet; moreover I had been quite familiar with the ideas long before I came to know Mme. de Guermantes; my memory of her, on the contrary, I possessed but imperfectly; every now and then it escaped me; it was during the hours when, from floating vaguely in my mind in the same way as the images of various other pretty women, it passed gradually into a unique and definite association —exclusive of every other feminine form—with those romantic ideas of so much longer standing than itself, it was during those few hours in which I remembered it most clearly that I ought to have taken steps to find out exactly what it was; but I did not then know the importance which it was to assume for me; it was pleasant merely as a first private meeting with Mme. de Guermantes inside myself, it was the first, the only accurate sketch, the only one taken from life, the only one that was really Mme.

de Guermantes; during the few hours in which I was fortunate enough to retain it without having the sense to pay it any attention, it must all the same have been charming, that memory, since it was always to it, and quite freely moreover, to that moment, without haste, without strain, without the slightest compulsion or anxiety, that my ideas of love returned; then, as gradually those ideas fixed it more definitely, it acquired from them a proportionately greater strength but itself became more vague; presently I could no longer recapture it; and in my dreams I probably altered it completely, for whenever I saw Mme. de Guermantes I realised the difference —never twice, as it happened, the same—between what I had imagined and what I saw. And now every morning, certainly at the moment when Mme. de Guermantes emerged from her gateway at the top of the street I saw again her tall figure, her face with its bright eyes and crown of silken hair—all the things for which I was there waiting; but, on the other hand, a minute or two later, when, having first turned my eyes away so as to appear not to be waiting for this encounter which I had come out to seek, I raised them to look at the Duchess at the moment in which we converged, what I saw then were red patches (as to which I knew not whether they were due to the fresh air or to a faulty complexion) on a sullen face which with the curtest of nods, a long way removed from the affability of the *Phèdre* evening, acknowledged my salute, which I addressed to her daily with an air of surprise, and which did not seem to please her. And yet, after a few days, during which the memory of the two girls fought against heavy odds for the mastery of my amorous feelings against that of Mme. de Guermantes, it was in the end the latter which, as though of its own accord, generally prevailed while its competitors withdrew; it was to it that I finally found myself, deliberately moreover, and as though by preference and for my own pleasure, to have transferred all my thoughts of love. I had ceased to dream of the little girls coming from their catechism, or of a certain dairy-maid; and yet I had also lost all hope of encountering in the street what I had come out to seek, either the affection promised to me, at the theatre, in a smile, or the profile, the bright face beneath its pile of golden hair which were so only when seen from afar. Now I should not even have been able to say what Mme. de Guermantes was like, by what I recognised her, for every day, in the picture which she presented as a whole, the face was different, as were the dress and the hat.

Why did I one morning, when I saw bearing down on me beneath a violet hood a sweet, smooth face whose charms were symmetrically arranged about a pair of blue eyes, a face in which the curve of the nose seemed to have been absorbed, gauge from a joyous commotion in my bosom that I was not going to return home without having caught a glimpse of Mme. de Guermantes; and on the next feel the same disturbance, affect the same indifference, turn away my eyes in the same careless manner as on the day before, on the apparition, seen in profile as she crossed from a side street and crowned by a navy-blue toque, of a beak-like nose bounding a flushed cheek chequered with a piercing eye, like some Egyptian deity? Once it was not merely a woman with a bird's beak that I saw but almost the bird itself; the outer garments, even the toque of Mme. de Guermantes

were of fur, and since she thus left no cloth visible, she seemed naturally
furred, like certain vultures whose thick, smooth, dusky, downy plumage
suggests rather the skin of a wild beast. From the midst of this natural
plumage, the tiny head arched out its beak and the two eyes on its surface were piercing-keen and blue.

One day I had been pacing up and down the street for hours on end
without a vestige of Mme. de Guermantes when suddenly, inside a pastry-
cook's shop tucked in between two of the mansions of this aristocratic
and plebeian quarter, there appeared, took shape the vague and unfamiliar
face of a fashionably dressed woman who was asking to see some little
cakes, and, before I had had time to make her out, there shot forth at
me like a lightning flash, reaching me sooner than its accompaniment of
thunder, the glance of the Duchess; another time, having failed to meet
her and hearing twelve strike, I realised that it was not worth my
while to wait for her any longer, I was sorrowfully making my way homewards; and, absorbed in my own disappointment, looking absently after
and not seeing a carriage that had overtaken me, I realised suddenly that
the movement of her head which I saw a lady make through the carriage
window was meant for me, and that this lady, whose features, relaxed
and pale, or it might equally be tense and vivid, composed, beneath a round
hat which nestled at the foot of a towering plume, the face of a stranger
whom I had supposed that I did not know, was Mme. de Guermantes, by
whom I had let myself be greeted without so much as acknowledging her
bow. And sometimes I came upon her as I entered the gate, standing outside the lodge where the detestable porter whose scrutinous eye I loathed
and dreaded was in the act of making her a profound obeisance and also,
no doubt, his daily report. For the entire staff of the Guermantes household, hidden behind the window curtains, were trembling as they watched
a conversation which they were unable to overhear, but which meant as
they very well knew that one or other of them would certainly have his
'day out' stopped by the Duchess to whom this Cerberus was betraying
him. In view of the whole series of different faces which Mme. Guermantes
displayed thus one after another, faces that occupied a relative and varying extent, contracted one day, vast the next, in her person and attire as
a whole, my love was not attached to any one of those changeable and
ever-changing elements of flesh and fabric which replaced one another as
day followed day, and which she could modify, could almost entirely
reconstruct without altering my disturbance because beneath them, beneath the new collar and the strange cheek, I felt that it was still Mme.
de Guermantes. What I loved was the invisible person who set all this
outward show in motion, her whose hostility so distressed me, whose approach set me trembling, whose life I would fain have made my own and
driven out of it her friends. She might flaunt a blue feather or shew a
fiery cheek without her actions' losing their importance for me.

I should not myself have felt that Mme. de Guermantes was tired of
meeting me day after day, had I not learned it indirectly by reading it
on the face, stiff with coldness, disapproval and pity which Françoise
shewed when she was helping me to get ready for these morning walks.

The moment I asked her for my outdoor things I felt a contrary wind arise in her worn and battered features. I made no attempt to win her confidence, for I knew that I should not succeed. She had, for at once discovering any unpleasant thing that might have happened to my parents or myself, a power the nature of which I have never been able to fathom. Perhaps it was not supernatural, but was to be explained by sources of information that were open to her alone: as it may happen that the news which often reaches a savage tribe several days before the post has brought it to the European colony has really been transmitted to them not by telepathy but from hill-top to hill-top by a chain of beacon fires. So, in the particular instance of my morning walks, possibly Mme. de Guermantes's servants had heard their mistress say how tired she was of running into me every day without fail wherever she went, and had repeated her remarks to Françoise. My parents might, it is true, have attached some servant other than Françoise to my person, still I should have been no better off. Françoise was in a sense less of a servant than the others. In her way of feeling things, of being kind and pitiful, hard and distant, superior and narrow, of combining a white skin with red hands, she was still the village maiden whose parents had had 'a place of their own' but having come to grief had been obliged to put her into service. Her presence in our household was the country air, the social life of a farm of fifty years ago wafted to us by a sort of reversal of the normal order of travel whereby it is the place that comes to visit the person. As the glass cases in a local museum are filled with specimens of the curious handiwork which the peasants still carve or embroider or whatever it may be in certain parts of the country, so our flat in Paris was decorated with the words of Françoise, inspired by a traditional local sentiment and governed by extremely ancient laws. And she could in Paris find her way back as though by clues of coloured thread to the songbirds and cherry trees of her childhood, to her mother's death-bed, which she still vividly saw. But in spite of all this wealth of background, once she had come to Paris and had entered our service she had acquired—as, obviously, anyone else coming there in her place would have acquired—the ideas, the system of interpretation used by the servants on the other floors, compensating for the respect which she was obliged to shew to us by repeating the rude words that the cook on the fourth floor had used to her mistress, with a servile gratification so intense that, for the first time in our lives, feeling a sort of solidarity between ourselves and the detestable occupant of the fourth floor flat, we said to ourselves that possibly we too were 'employers' after all. This alteration in Françoise's character was perhaps inevitable. Certain forms of existence are so abnormal that they are bound to produce certain characteristic faults; such was the life led by the King at Versailles among his courtiers, a life as strange as that of a Pharaoh or a Doge—and, far more even than his, the life of his courtiers. The life led by our servants is probably of an even more monstrous abnormality, which only its familiarity can prevent us from seeing. But it was actually in details more intimate still that I should have been obliged, if I had dismissed Françoise, to keep the same servant. For various others might, in years to come, enter my service; already furnished with the defects common to all servants, they underwent never-theless a rapid transformation with me. As, in the rules of tactics, an attack in one sector compels a counter-attack in another, so as not to be hurt by the asperities of my nature, all of them effected in their own an identical resilience, always at the same points, and to make up for this took advantage of the gaps in my line to thrust out advanced posts. Of these gaps I knew nothing, any more than of the salients to which they gave rise, precisely because they were gaps. But my servants, by gradually becoming spoiled, taught me of their existence. It was from the defects which they invariably acquired that I learned what were my own natural and invariable short-comings; their character offered me a sort of negative plate of my own. We had always laughed, my mother and I, at Mme. Sazerat, who used, in speaking of her servants, expressions like 'the lower orders' or 'the servant class.' But I am bound to admit that what made it useless to think of replacing Françoise by anyone else was that her successor would in-evitably have belonged just as much to the race of servants in general and to the class of my servants in particular.

To return to Françoise, I never in my life experienced any humiliation without having seen beforehand on her face a store of condolences pre-pared and waiting; and if then in my anger at the thought of being pitied by her I tried to pretend that on the contrary I had scored a distinct suc-cess, my lies broke feebly on the wall of her respectful but obvious unbelief and the consciousness that she enjoyed of her own infallibility. For she knew the truth. She refrained from uttering it, and made only a slight movement with her lips as if she still had her mouth full and was finishing a tasty morsel. She refrained from uttering it, or so at least I long believed, for at that time I still supposed that it was by means of words that one communicated the truth to others. Indeed the words that people used to me recorded their meaning so unalterably on the sensitive plate of my mind that I could no more believe it to be possible that anyone who had professed to love me did not love me than Françoise herself could have doubted when she had read it in a newspaper that some clergyman or gen-tleman was prepared, on receipt of a stamped envelope, to furnish us free of charge with an infallible remedy for every known complaint or with the means of multiplying our income an hundredfold. (If, on the other hand, our doctor were to prescribe for her the simplest ointment to cure a cold in the head, she, so stubborn to endure the keenest suffering, would complain bitterly of what she had been made to sniff, insisting that it tickled her nose and that life was not worth living.) But she was the first person to prove to me by her example (which I was not to understand until, long afterwards, when it was given me afresh and to my greater dis-comfort, as will be found in the later volumes of this work, by a person who was dearer to me than Françoise) that the truth has no need to be uttered to be made apparent, and that one may perhaps gather it with more certainty, without waiting for words, without even bothering one's head about them, from a thousand outward signs, even from certain in-visible phenomena, analogous in the sphere of human character to what in nature are atmospheric changes. I might perhaps have suspected this, since to myself at that time it frequently occurred that I said things in which there was no vestige of truth, while I made the real truth plain by all manner of involuntary confidences expressed by my body and in my actions (which were at once interpreted by Françoise); I ought perhaps to have suspected it, but to do so I should first have had to be conscious that I myself was occasionally untruthful and dishonest. Now untruthfulness and dishonesty were with me, as with most people, called into being in so immediate, so contingent a fashion, and in self-defence, by some particular interest, that my mind, fixed on some lofty ideal, allowed my character, in the darkness below, to set about those urgent, sordid tasks, and did not look down to observe them. When Françoise, in the evening, was polite to me, and asked my permission before sitting down in my room, it seemed as though her face became transparent and I could see the goodness and honesty that lay beneath. But Jupien, who had lapses into indiscretion of which I learned only later, revealed afterwards that she had told him that I was not worth the price of a rope to hang me, and that I had tried to insult her in every possible way. These words of Jupien set up at once before my eyes, in new and strange colours, a print of the picture of my relations with Françoise so different from that on which I used to like letting my eyes rest, and in which, without the least possibility of doubt, Françoise adored me and lost no opportunity of singing my praises, that I realised that it is not only the material world that is different from the aspect in which we see it; that all reality is perhaps equally dissimilar from what we think ourselves to be directly perceiving; that the trees, the sun and the sky would not be the same as what we see if they were apprehended by creatures having eyes differently constituted from ours, or, better still, endowed for that purpose with organs other than eyes which would furnish trees and sky and sun with equivalents, though not visual. However that might be, this sudden outlet which Jupien threw open for me upon the real world appalled me. So far it was only Françoise that was revealed, and of her I barely thought. Was it the same with all one's social relations? And in what depths of despair might this not some day plunge me, if it were the same with love? That was the future's secret. For the present only Françoise was concerned. Did she sincerely believe what she had said to Jupien? Had she said it to embroil Jupien with me, possibly so that we should not appoint Jupien's girl as her successor? At any rate I realised the impossibility of obtaining any direct and certain knowledge of whether Françoise loved or lothed me. And thus it was she who first gave me the idea that a person does not (as I had imagined) stand motionless and clear before our eyes with his merits, his defects, his plans, his intentions with regard to ourself exposed on his surface, like a garden at which, with all its borders spread out before us, we gaze through a railing, but is a shadow which we can never succeed in penetrating, of which there can be no such thing as direct knowledge, with respect to which we form countless beliefs, based upon his words and sometimes upon his actions, though neither words nor actions can give us anything but inadequate and as it proves contradictory information—a shadow behind which we can alternately imagine, with equal-justification, that there burns the flame of hatred and of love.

I was genuinely in love with Mme. de Guermantes. The greatest happiness that I could have asked of God would have been that He should overwhelm her under every imaginable calamity, and that ruined, despised, stripped of all the privileges that divided her from me, having no longer any home of her own or people who would condescend to speak to her, she should come to me for refuge. I imagined her doing so. And indeed on those evenings when some change in the atmosphere or in my own condition brought to the surface of my consciousness some forgotten scroll on which were recorded impressions of other days, instead of profiting by the refreshing strength that had been generated in me, instead of employing it to decipher in my own mind thoughts which as a rule escaped me, instead of setting myself at last to work, I preferred to relate aloud, to plan out in the third person, with a flow of invention as useless as was my declamation of it, a whole novel crammed with adventure, in which the Duchess, fallen upon misfortune, came to implore assistance from me—me who had become, by a converse change of circumstances, rich and powerful. And when I had let myself thus for hours on end imagine the circumstances, rehearse the sentences with which I should welcome the Duchess beneath my roof, the situation remained unaltered; I had, alas, in reality, chosen to love the very woman who, in her own person, combined perhaps the greatest possible number of different advantages; in whose eyes, accordingly, I could not hope, myself, ever to cut any figure; for she was as rich as the richest commoner—and noble also; without reckoning that personal charm which set her at the pinnacle of fashion, made her among the rest a sort of queen.

I felt that I was annoying her by crossing her path in this way every morning; but even if I had had the courage to refrain, for two or three days consecutively, from doing so, perhaps that abstention, which would have represented so great a sacrifice on my part, Mme. de Guermantes would not have noticed, or would have set it down to some obstacle beyond my control. And indeed I could not have succeeded in making myself cease to track her down except by arranging that it should be impossible for me to do so, for the need incessantly reviving in me to meet her, to be for a moment the object of her attention, the person to whom her bow was addressed, was stronger than my fear of arousing her displeasure. I should have had to go away for some time; and for that I had not the heart. I did think of it more than once. I would then tell Françoise to pack my boxes, and immediately afterwards to unpack them. And as the spirit of imitation, the desire not to appear behind the times, alters the most natural and most positive form of oneself, Françoise, borrowing the expression from her daughter's vocabulary, used to remark that I was 'dippy.' She did not approve of this; she said that I was always 'balancing,' for she made use, when she was not aspiring to rival the moderns, of the language of Saint-Simon. It is true that she liked it still less when I spoke to her as master to servant. She knew that this was not natural to me, and did not suit me, a condition which she rendered in words as 'where there isn't a will.' I should never have had the heart to leave Paris except in a direction that would bring me closer to Mme. de Guermantes. This was by no means an impossibility. Should I not indeed find myself nearer to her than I was in the morning, in the street, solitary, abashed, feeling that not a single one of the thoughts which I should have liked to convey to her ever reached her, in that weary patrolling up and down of walks which might be continued, day after day, for ever without the slightest advantage to myself, if I were to go miles away from Mme. de Guermantes, but go to some one of her acquaintance, some one whom she knew to be particular in the choice of his friends and who would appreciate my good qualities, would be able to speak to her about me, and if not to obtain it from her at least to make her know what I wanted, some one by means of whom, in any event, simply because I should discuss with him whether or not it would be possible for him to convey this or that message to her, I should give to my solitary and silent meditations a new form, spoken, active, which would seem an advance, almost a realisation. What she did during the mysterious daily life of the 'Guermantes' that she was—this was the constant object of my thoughts; and to break through the mystery, even by indirect means, as with a lever, by employing the services of a person to whom were not forbidden the town house of the Duchess, her parties, unrestricted conversation with her, would not that be a contact more distant but at the same time more effective than my contemplation of her every morning in the street?

The friendship, the admiration that Saint-Loup felt for me seemed to me undeserved and had hitherto left me unmoved. All at once I attached a value to them, I would have liked him to disclose them to Mme. de Guermantes, I was quite prepared even to ask him to do so. For when we are in love, all the trifling little privileges that we enjoy we would like to be able to divulge to the woman we love, as people who have been disinherited and bores of other kinds do to us in everyday life. We are distressed by her ignorance of them; we seek consolation in the thought that just because they are never visible she has perhaps added to the opinion which she already had of us this possibility of further advantages that must remain unknown.

Saint-Loup had not for a long time been able to come to Paris, whether, as he himself explained, on account of his military duties, or, as was more likely, on account of the trouble that he was having with his mistress, with whom he had twice now been on the point of breaking off relations. He had often told me what a pleasure it would be to him if I came to visit him at that garrison town, the name of which, a couple of days after his leaving Balbec, had caused me so much joy when I had read it on the envelope of the first letter I received from my friend. It was (not so far from Balbec as its wholly inland surroundings might have led one to think) one of those little fortified towns, aristocratic and military, set in a broad expanse of country over which on fine days there floats so often into the distance a sort of intermittent haze of sound which—as a screen of poplars by its sinuosities outlines the course of a river which one cannot see—indicates the movements of a regiment on parade, so that the very atmosphere of its streets, avenues and squares has been gradually tuned to a sort of perpetual vibration, musical and martial, while the most ordinary note of cartwheel or tramway is prolonged in vague trumpet calls, indefinitely repeated, to the hallucinated ear, by the silence. It was not too far away from Paris for me to be able, if I took the express, to return, join my mother and grandmother and sleep in my own bed. As soon as I realised this, troubled by a painful longing, I had too little will power to decide not to return to Paris but rather to stay in this town; but also too little to prevent a porter from carrying my luggage to a cab and not to adopt, as I walked behind him, the unburdened mind of a traveller who is looking after his luggage and for whom no grandmother is waiting anywhere at home, to get into the carriage with the complete detachment of a person who, having ceased to think of what it is that he wants, has the air of knowing what he wants, and to give the driver the address of the cavalry barracks. I thought that Saint-Loup might come to sleep that night at the hotel at which I should be staying, so as to make less painful for me the first shock of contact with this strange town. One of the guard went to find him, and I waited at the barrack gate, before that huge ship of stone, booming with the November wind, out of which, every moment, for it was now six o'clock, men were emerging in pairs into the street, staggering as if they were coming ashore in some foreign port in which they found themselves temporarily anchored.

Saint-Loup appeared, moving like a whirlwind, his eyeglass spinning in the air before him; I had not given my name, I was eager to enjoy his surprise and delight. "Oh! What a bore!" he exclaimed, suddenly catching sight of me, and blushing to the tips of his ears. "I have just had a week's leave, and I shan't be off duty again for another week."

And, preoccupied by the thought of my having to spend this first night alone, for he knew better than anyone my bed-time agonies, which he had often remarked and soothed at Balbec, he broke off his lamentation to turn and look at me, coax me with little smiles, with tender though unsymmetrical glances, half of them coming directly from his eye, the other half through his eyeglass, but both sorts alike an allusion to the emotion that he felt on seeing me again, an allusion also to that important matter which I did not always understand but which concerned me now vitally, our friendship.

"I say! Where are you going to sleep? Really, I can't recommend the hotel where we mess; it is next to the Exhibition ground, where there's a show just starting; you'll find it beastly crowded. No, you'd better go to the Hôtel de Flandre; it is a little eighteenth-century palace with old tapestries. It 'makes' quite an 'old-world residence.' "

Saint-Loup employed in every connexion the word 'makes' for 'has the air of,' because the spoken language, like the written, feels from time to time the need of these alterations in the meanings of words, these refinements of expression. And just as journalists often have not the least idea from what school of literature come the 'turns of speech' that they borrow, so the vocabulary, the very diction of Saint-Loup were formed in imitation of three different aesthetes, none of whom he knew personally but whose way of speaking had been indirectly instilled into him. "Besides," he concluded, "the hotel I mean is more or less adapted to your supersensitiveness of hearing. You will have no neighbours. I quite see that it is a slender advantage, and as, after all, another visitor may arrive to-morrow, it would not be worth your while to choose that particular hotel with so precarious an object in view. No, it is for its appeal to the eye that I recommend it. The rooms are quite attractive, all the furniture is old and comfortable; there is something reassuring about that." But to me, less of an artist than Saint-Loup, the pleasure that an attractive house could give was superficial, almost non-existent, and could not calm my growing anguish, as painful as that which I used to feel long ago at Combray when my mother did not come upstairs to say good night, or that which I felt on the evening of my arrival at Balbec in the room with the unnaturally high ceiling, which smelt of flowering grasses. Saint-Loup read all this in my fixed gaze.

"A lot you care, though, about this charming palace, my poor fellow; you're quite pale; and here am I like a great brute talking to you about tapestries which you won't have the heart to look at, even. I know the room they'll put you in; personally I find it most enlivening, but I can quite understand that it won't have the same effect on you with your sensitive nature. You mustn't think I don't understand; I don't feel the same myself, but I can put myself in your place."

At that moment a serjeant who was exercising a horse on the square, entirely absorbed in making the animal jump, disregarding the salutes of passing troopers, but hurling volleys of oaths at such as got in his way, turned with a smile to Saint-Loup and, seeing that he had a friend with him, saluted us. But his horse at once reared. Saint-Loup flung himself at its head, caught it by the bridle, succeeded in quieting it and returned to my side.

"Yes," he resumed; "I assure you that I fully understand; I feel for you as keenly as you do yourself. I am wretched," he went on, laying his hand lovingly on my shoulder, "when I think that if I could have stayed with you to-night, I might have been able, if we talked till morning, to relieve you of a little of your unhappiness. I can lend you any number of books, but you won't want to read if you're feeling like that. And I shan't be able to get anyone else to take my duty here; I've been off now twice running because my girl came down to see me."

And he knitted his brows partly with vexation and also in the effort to decide, like a doctor, what remedy he might best apply to my disease.

"Run along and light the fire in my quarters," he called to a trooper who passed us. "Hurry up; get a move on!"

After which he turned once more to me, and his eyeglass and his peering, myopic gaze hinted an allusion to our great friendship.

"No! To see you here, in these barracks where I have spent so much time thinking about you, I can scarcely believe my eyes. I must be dreaming. And how are you? Better, I hope. You must tell me all about yourself presently. We'll go up to my room; we mustn't hang about too long on the square, there's the devil of a draught; I don't feel it now myself, but you aren't accustomed to it, I'm afraid of your catching cold. And what

about your work; have you started yet? No? You are a quaint fellow! If
I had your talent I'm sure I should be writing morning, noon and night.
It amuses you more to do nothing? What a pity it is that it's the useless
fellows like me who are always ready to work, and the ones who could if
they wanted to, won't. There, and I've clean forgotten to ask you how
your grandmother is. Her Proudhons are in safe keeping. I never part from
them."

An officer, tall, handsome, majestic, emerged with slow and solemn gait
from the foot of a staircase. Saint-Loup saluted him and arrested the perpetual instability of his body for the moment occupied in holding his hand
against the peak of his cap. But he had flung himself into the action with
so much force, straightening himself with so sharp a movement, and, the
salute ended, let his hand fall with so abrupt a relaxation, altering all the
positions of shoulder, leg, and eyeglass, that this moment was one not so
much of immobility as of a throbbing tension in which were neutralised
the excessive movements which he had just made and those on which he
was about to embark. Meanwhile the officer, without coming any nearer
us, calm, benevolent, dignified, imperial, representing, in short, the direct
opposite of Saint-Loup, himself also, but without haste, raised his hand to
the peak of his cap.

"I must just say a word to the Captain," whispered Saint-Loup. "Be a
good fellow, and go and wait for me in my room. It's the second on the
right, on the third floor; I'll be with you in a minute."

And setting off at the double, preceded by his eyeglass which fluttered
in every direction, he made straight for the slow and stately Captain whose
horse had just been brought round and who, before preparing to mount,
was giving orders with a studied nobility of gesture as in some historical
painting, and as though he were setting forth to take part in some battle of
the First Empire, whereas he was simply going to ride home, to the house
which he had taken for the period of his service at Doncières, and which
stood in a Square that was named, as though in an ironical anticipation
of the arrival of this Napoleonid, Place de la République. I started to climb
the staircase, nearly slipping on each of its nail-studded steps, catching
glimpses of barrack-rooms, their bare walls edged with a double line of
beds and kits. I was shewn Saint-Loup's room. I stood for a moment outside
its closed door, for I could hear some one stirring; he moved something,
let fall something else; I felt that the room was not empty, that there must
be somebody there. But it was only the freshly lighted fire beginning to
burn. It could not keep quiet, it kept shifting its faggots about, and very
clumsily. I entered the room; it let one roll into the fender and set another
smoking. And even when it was not moving, like an ill-bred person it made
noises all the time, which, from the moment I saw the flames rising, revealed
themselves to me as noises made by a fire, although if I had been on the
other side of a wall I should have thought that they came from some one
who was blowing his nose and walking about. I sat down in the room and
waited. Liberty hangings and old German stuffs of the eighteenth century
managed to rid it of the smell that was exhaled by the rest of the building,
a coarse, insipid, mouldy smell like that of stale toast. It was here, in this

charming room, that I could have dined and slept with a calm and happy mind. Saint-Loup seemed almost to be present by reason of the text-books which littered his table, between his photographs, among which I could make out my own and that of the Duchesse de Guermantes, by the light of the fire which had at length grown accustomed to the grate, and, like an animal crouching in an ardent, noiseless, faithful watchfulness, let fall only now and then a smouldering log which crumbled into sparks, or licked with a tongue of flame the sides of the chimney. I heard the tick of Saint-Loup's watch, which could not be far away. This tick changed its place every moment, for I could not see the watch; it seemed to come from behind, from in front of me, from my right, from my left, sometimes to die away as though at a great distance. Suddenly I caught sight of the watch on the table. Then I heard the tick in a fixed place from which it did not move again. That is to say, I thought I heard it at this place; I did not hear it there; I saw it there, for sounds have no position in space. Or rather we associate them with movements, and in that way they serve the purpose of warning us of those movements, of appearing to make them necessary and natural. Certainly it happens commonly enough that a sick man whose ears have been stopped with cotton-wool ceases to hear the noise of a fire such as was crackling at that moment in Saint-Loup's fireplace, labouring at the formation of brands and cinders, which it then lets fall into the fender, nor would he hear the passage of the tramway-cars whose music took its flight, at regular intervals, over the Grand'place of Doncières. Let the sick man then read a book, and the pages will turn silently before him, as though they were moved by the fingers of a god. The dull thunder of a bath which is being filled becomes thin, faint and distant as the twittering of birds in the sky. The withdrawal of sound, its dilution, take from it all its power to hurt us; driven mad a moment ago by hammer-blows which seemed to be shattering the ceiling above our head, it is with a quiet delight that we now gather in their sound, light, caressing, distant, like the murmur of leaves playing by the roadside with the passing breeze. We play games of patience with cards which we do not hear, until we imagine that we have not touched them, that they are moving of their own accord, and, anticipating our desire to play with them, have begun to play with us. And in this connexion we may ask ourselves whether, in the case of love (to which indeed we may add the love of life and the love of fame, since there are, it appears, persons who are acquainted with these latter sentiments), we ought not to act like those who, when a noise disturbs them, instead of praying that it may cease, stop their ears; and, with them for our pattern, bring our attention, our defensive strength to bear on ourselves, give ourselves as an objective to capture not the 'other person' with whom we are in love but our capacity for suffering at that person's hands.

To return to the problem of sounds, we have only to thicken the wads which close the aural passages, and they confine to a pianissimo the girl who has just been playing a boisterous tune overhead; if we go farther, and steep the wad in grease, at once the whole household must obey its despotic rule; its laws extend even beyond our portals. Pianissimo is not enough; the wad instantly orders the piano to be shut, and the music lesson is abruptly ended; the gentleman who was walking up and down in the room above breaks off in the middle of his beat; the movement of carriages and tramways is interrupted as though a Sovereign were expected to pass. And indeed this attenuation of sounds sometimes disturbs our slumbers instead of guarding them. Only yesterday the incessant noise in our ears, by describing to us in a continuous narrative all that was happening in the street and in the house, succeeded at length in making us sleep, like a boring book; to-night, through the sheet of silence that is spread over our sleep a shock, louder than the rest, manages to make itself heard, gentle as a sigh, unrelated to any other sound, mysterious; and the call for an explanation which it emits is sufficient to awaken us. Take away for a moment from the sick man the cotton-wool that has been stopping his ears and in a flash the full daylight, the sun of sound dawns afresh, dazzling him, is born again in his universe; in all haste returns the multitude of exiled sounds; we are present, as though it were the chanting of choirs of angels, at the resurrection of the voice. The empty streets are filled for a moment with the whirr of the swift, consecutive wings of the singing tramway-cars. In the bedroom itself, the sick man has created, not, like Prometheus, fire, but the sound of fire. And when we increase or reduce the wads of cotton-wool, it is as though we were pressing alternately one and the other of the two pedals with which we have extended the resonant compass of the outer world.

Only there are also suppressions of sound which are not temporary. The man who has grown completely deaf cannot even heat a pan of milk by his bedside, but he must keep an eye open to watch, on the tilted lid, for the white, arctic reflexion, like that of a coming snowstorm, which is the warning sign which he is wise to obey, by cutting off (as Our Lord bade the waves be still) the electric current; for already the swelling, jerkily climbing egg of boiling milk-film is reaching its climax in a series of side-long movements, has filled and set bellying the drooping sails with which the cream has skimmed its surface, sends in a sudden storm a scud of pearly substance flying overboard—sails which the cutting off of the current, if the electric storm is hushed in time, will fold back upon themselves and let fall with the ebbing tide, changed now to magnolia petals. But if the sick man should not be quick enough in taking the necessary precautions, presently, when his drowned books and watch are seen barely emerging from the milky tide, he will be obliged to call the old nurse who, though he be himself an eminent statesman or a famous writer, will tell him that he has no more sense than a child of five. At other times in the magic chamber, between us and the closed door, a person who was not there a moment ago makes his appearance; it is a visitor whom we did not hear coming in, and who merely gesticulates, like a figure in one of those little puppet theatres, so restful for those who have taken a dislike to the spoken tongue. And for this totally deaf man, since the loss of a sense adds as much beauty to the world as its acquisition, it is with ecstasy that he walks now upon an earth grown almost an Eden, in which sound has not yet been created. The highest waterfalls unfold for his eyes alone their ribbons of crystal, stiller than the glassy sea, like the cascades of Paradise. As sound was for

him before his deafness the perceptible form in which the cause of a movement was draped, objects moved without sound seemed to be being moved
also without cause; deprived of all resonant quality, they shew a spontaneous activity, seem to be alive. They move, halt, become alight of their
own accord. Of their own accord they vanish in the air like the winged
monsters of prehistoric days. In the solitary and unneighboured home of
the deaf man the service which, before his infirmity was complete, was
already shewing an increased discretion, was being carried on in silence,
is now assured him with a sort of surreptitious deftness, by mutes, as at
the court of a fairy-tale king. And, as upon the stage, the building on which
the deaf man looks from his window—be it barracks, church, or town hall
—is only so much scenery. If one day it should fall to the ground, it may
emit a cloud of dust and leave visible ruins; but, less material even than
a palace on the stage, though it has not the same exiguity, it will subside
in the magic universe without letting the fall of its heavy blocks of stone
tarnish, with anything so vulgar as sound, the chastity of the prevailing
silence.

The silence, though only relative, which reigned in the little barrack-
room where I sat waiting was now broken. The door opened and Saint-Loup,
dropping his eyeglass, dashed in.

"Ah, my dear Robert, you make yourself very comfortable here," I said
to him; "how jolly it would be if one were allowed to dine and sleep here."

And to be sure, had it not been against the regulations, what repose
untinged by sadness I could have tasted there, guarded by that atmosphere
of tranquillity, vigilance and gaiety which was maintained by a thousand
wills controlled and free from care, a thousand heedless spirits, in that
great community called a barracks where, time having taken the form of
action, the sad bell that tolled the hours outside was replaced by the same
joyous clarion of those martial calls, the ringing memory of which was kept
perpetually alive in the paved streets of the town, like the dust that floats
in a sunbeam;—a voice sure of being heard, and musical because it was
the command not only of authority to obedience but of wisdom to happiness.

"So you'd rather stay with me and sleep here, would you, than to go
the hotel by yourself?" Saint-Loup asked me, smiling.

"Oh, Robert, it is cruel of you to be sarcastic about it," I pleaded; "you
know it's not possible, and you know how wretched I shall be over there."

"Good! You flatter me!" he replied. "It occurred to me just now that
you would rather stay here to-night. And that is precisely what I stopped
to ask the Captain."

"And he has given you leave?" I cried.

"He hadn't the slightest objection."

"Oh! I adore him!"

"No; that would be going too far. But now, let me just get hold of my
batman and tell him to see about our dinner," he went on, while I turned
away so as to hide my tears.

We were several times interrupted by one or other of Saint-Loup's friends'
coming in. He drove them all out again.

"Get out of here. Buzz off!"

I begged him to let them stay.

"No, really; they would bore you stiff; they are absolutely uncultured; all they can talk about is racing, or stables shop. Besides, I don't want them here either; they would spoil these precious moments I've been looking forward to. But you mustn't think, when I tell you that these fellows are brainless, that everything military is devoid of intellectuality. Far from it. We have a major here who is a splendid chap. He's given us a course in which military history is treated like a demonstration, like a problem in algebra. Even from the aesthetic point of view there is a curious beauty, alternately inductive and deductive, about it which you couldn't fail to appreciate."

"That's not the officer who's given me leave to stay here to-night?"

"No; thank God! The man you 'adore' for so very trifling a service is the biggest fool that ever walked the face of the earth. He is perfect at looking after messing, and at kit inspections; he spends hours with the serjeant major and the master tailor. There you have his mentality. Apart from that he has a vast contempt, like everyone here, for the excellent major I was telling you about. No one will speak to him because he's a freemason and doesn't go to confession. The Prince de Borodino would never have an outsider like that in his house. Which is pretty fair cheek, when all's said and done, from a man whose great-grandfather was a small farmer, and who would probably be a small farmer himself if it hadn't been for the Napoleonic wars. Not that he hasn't a lurking sense of his own rather ambiguous position in society, where he's neither flesh nor fowl. He hardly ever shews his face at the Jockey, it makes him feel so deuced awkward, this so-called Prince," added Robert, who, having been led by the same spirit of imitation to adopt the social theories of his teachers and the worldly prejudices of his relatives, had unconsciously wedded the democratic love of humanity to a contempt for the nobility of the Empire.

I was looking at the photograph of his aunt, and the thought that, since Saint-Loup had this photograph in his possession, he might perhaps give it to me, made me feel all the fonder of him and hope to do him a thousand services, which seemed to me a very small exchange for it. For this photograph was like one encounter more, added to all those that I had already had, with Mme. de Guermantes; better still, a prolonged encounter, as if, by some sudden stride forward in our relations, she had stopped beside me, in a garden hat, and had allowed me for the first time to gaze at my leisure at that plump cheek, that arched neck, that tapering eyebrow (veiled from me hitherto by the swiftness of her passage, the bewilderment of my impressions, the imperfection of memory); and the contemplation of them, as well as of the bare bosom and arms of a woman whom I had never seen save in a high-necked and long-sleeved bodice, was to me a voluptuous discovery, a priceless favour. Those lines, which had seemed to me almost a forbidden spectacle, I could study there, as in a text-book of the only geometry that had any value for me. Later on, when I looked at Robert, I noticed that he too was a little like the photograph of his aunt, and by a mysterious process which I found almost as moving, since, if his face had not been directly created by hers, the two had nevertheless a common origin. The features of the Duchesse de Guermantes, which were pinned to my vision of Combray, the nose like a falcon's beak, the piercing eyes, seemed to have served also as a pattern for the cutting out—in another copy analogous and slender, with too delicate a skin—of Robert's face, which might almost be superimposed upon his aunt's. I saw in him, with a keen longing, those features characteristic of the Guermantes, of that race which had remained so individual in the midst of a world with which it was not confounded, in which it remained isolated in the glory of an ornitho-morphic divinity, for it seemed to have been the issue, in the age of mythology, of the union of a goddess with a bird.

Robert, without being aware of its cause, was touched by my evident affection. This was moreover increased by the sense of comfort inspired in me by the heat of the fire and by the champagne which bedewed at the same time my brow with beads of sweat and my cheeks with tears; it washed down the partridges; I ate mine with the dumb wonder of a profane mortal of any sort when he finds in a form of life with which he is not familiar what he has supposed that form of life to exclude—the wonder, for instance, of an atheist who sits down to an exquisitely cooked dinner in a presbytery. And next morning, when I awoke, I rose and went to cast from Saint-Loup's window, which being at a great height overlooked the whole countryside, a curious scrutiny to make the acquaintance of my new neighbour, the landscape which I had not been able to distinguish the day before, having arrived too late, at an hour when it was already sleeping beneath the outspread cloak of night. And yet, early as it had awoken from its sleep, I could see the ground, when I opened the window and looked out, only as one sees it from the window of a country house, overlooking the lake, shrouded still in its soft white morning gown of mist which scarcely allowed me to make out anything at all. But I knew that, before the troopers who were busy with their horses in the square had finished grooming them, it would have cast its gown aside. In the meantime, I could see only a meagre hill, rearing close up against the side of the barracks a back already swept clear of darkness, rough and wrinkled. Through the transparent cur-tain of frost I could not take my eyes from this stranger who, too, was looking at me for the first time. But when I had formed the habit of com-ing to the barracks, my consciousness that the hill was there, more real, consequently, even when I did not see it, than the hotel at Balbec, than our house in Paris, of which I thought as of absent—or dead—friends, that is to say without any strong belief in their existence, brought it about that, even although I was not aware of it myself, its reflected shape outlined itself on the slightest impressions that I formed at Doncières, and among them, to begin with this first morning, on the pleasing impression of warmth given me by the cup of chocolate prepared by Saint-Loup's batman in this comfortable room, which had the effect of being an optical centre from which to look out at the hill—the idea of there being anything else to do but just gaze at it, the idea of actually climbing it, being rendered impos-sible by this same mist. Imbibing the shape of the hill, associated with the taste of hot chocolate and with the whole web of my fancies at that par-ticular time, this mist, without my having thought at all about it, succeeded in moistening all my subsequent thoughts about that period, just as a massive and unmelting lump of gold had remained allied to my impressions of Balbec, or as the proximity of the outside stairs of blackish sandstone gave a grey background to my impressions of Combray. It did not, however, persist late into the day; the sun began by hurling at it, in vain, a few darts which sprinkled it with brilliants before they finally overcame it. The hill might expose its grizzled rump to the sun's rays, which, an hour later, when I went down to the town, gave to the russet tints of the autumn leaves, to the reds and blues of the election posters pasted on the walls, an exaltation which raised my spirits also and made me stamp, singing as I went, on the pavements from which I could hardly keep myself from jumping in the air for joy.

But after that first night I had to sleep at the hotel. And I knew beforehand that I was doomed to find sorrow there. It was like an unbreathable aroma which all my life long had been exhaled for me by every new bedroom, that is to say by every bedroom; in the one which I usually occupied I was not present, my mind remained elsewhere, and in its place sent only the sense of familiarity. But I could not employ this servant, less sensitive than myself, to look after things for me in a new place, where I preceded him, where I arrived by myself, where I must bring into contact with its environment that 'Self' which I rediscovered only at year-long intervals, but always the same, having not grown at all since Combray, since my first arrival at Balbec, weeping, without any possibility of consolation, on the edge of an unpacked trunk.

As it happened, I was mistaken. I had no time to be sad, for I was not left alone for an instant. The fact of the matter was that there remained of the old palace a superfluous refinement of structure and decoration, out of place in a modern hotel, which, released from the service of any practical purpose, had in its long spell of leisure acquired a sort of life: passages winding about in all directions, which one was continually crossing in their aimless wanderings, lobbies as long as corridors and as ornate as drawing-rooms, which had the air rather of being dwellers there themselves than of forming part of a dwelling, which could not be induced to enter and settle down in any of the rooms but wandered about outside mine and came up at once to offer me their company—neighbours of a sort, idle but never noisy, menial ghosts of the past who had been granted the privilege of staying, provided they kept quiet, by the doors of the rooms which were let to visitors, and who, every time that I came across them, greeted me with a silent deference. In short, the idea of a lodging, of simply a case for our existence from day to day which shields us only from the cold and from being overlooked by other people, was absolutely inapplicable to this house, an assembly of rooms as real as a colony of people, living, it was true, in silence, but things which one was obliged to meet, to avoid, to appreciate, as one came in. One tried not to disturb them, and one could not look without respect at the great drawing-room which had formed, far back in the eighteenth century, the habit of stretching itself at its ease, among its hangings of old gold and beneath the clouds of its painted ceiling. And one was seized with a more personal curiosity as to the smaller rooms which, without any regard for symmetry, ran all round it, innumerable, startled, fleeing in disorder as far as the garden, to which they had so easy an access down three broken steps.

If I wished to go out or to come in without taking the lift or being seen from the main staircase, a smaller private staircase, no longer in use, offered me its steps so skilfully arranged, one close above another, that there seemed to exist in their gradation a perfect proportion of the same kind as those which, in colours, scents, savours, often arouse in us a peculiar, sensuous pleasure. But the pleasure to be found in going up and down-stairs I had had to come here to learn, as once before to a health resort in the Alps to find that the act—as a rule not noticed—of drawing breath could be a perpetual delight. I received that dispensation from effort which is granted to us only by the things to which long use has accustomed us, when I set my feet for the first time on those steps, familiar before ever I knew them, as if they possessed, deposited on them, perhaps, embodied in them by the masters of long ago whom they used to welcome every day, the prospective charm of habits which I had not yet contracted and which indeed could only grow weaker once they had become my own. I looked into a room; the double doors closed themselves behind me, the hangings let in a silence in which I felt myself invested with a sort of exhilarating royalty; a marble mantelpiece with ornaments of wrought brass—of which one would have been wrong to think that its sole idea was to represent the art of the Directory—offered me a fire, and a little easy chair on short legs helped me to warm myself as comfortably as if I had been sitting on the hearthrug. The walls held the room in a close embrace, separating it from the rest of the world and, to let in, to enclose what made it complete, parted to make way for the bookcase, reserved a place for the bed, on either side of which a column airily upheld the raised ceiling of the alcove. And the room was prolonged in depth by two closets as large as itself, the latter of which had hanging from its wall, to scent the occasion on which one had recourse to it, a voluptuous rosary of orris-roots; the doors, if I left them open when I withdrew into this innermost retreat, were not content with tripling its dimensions without its ceasing to be well-proportioned, and not only allowed my eyes to enjoy the delights of extension after those of con-centration, but added further to the pleasure of my solitude, which, while still inviolable, was no longer shut in, the sense of liberty. This closet looked out upon a courtyard, a fair solitary stranger whom I was glad to have for a neighbour when next morning my eyes fell on her, a captive between her high walls in which no other window opened, with nothing but two yellowing trees which were enough to give a pinkish softness to the pure sky above.

Before going to bed I decided to leave the room in order to explore the whole of my fairy kingdom. I walked down a long gallery which did me homage successively with all that it had to offer me if I could not sleep, an armchair placed waiting in a corner, a spinet, on a table against the wall, a bowl of blue crockery filled with cinerarias, and, in an old frame, the phantom of a lady of long ago whose powdered hair was starred with blue flowers, holding in her hand a bunch of carnations. When I came to the end, the bare wall in which no door opened said to me simply "Now you must turn and go back, but, you see, you are at home here, the house is yours," while the soft carpet, not to be left out, added that if I did not sleep that night I could easily come in barefoot, and the unshuttered windows, looking out over the open country, assured me that they would hold a sleepless vigil and that, at whatever hour I chose to come in, I need not be afraid of disturbing anyone. And behind a hanging curtain I surprised only a little closet which, stopped by the wall and unable to escape any farther, had hidden itself there with a guilty conscience and gave me a frightened stare from its little round window, glowing blue in the moonlight. I went to bed, but the presence of the eiderdown quilt, of the pillars, of the neat fireplace, by straining my attention to a pitch beyond that of Paris, prevented me from letting myself go upon my habitual train of fancies. And as it is this particular state of strained attention that enfolds our slumbers, acts upon them, modifies them, brings them into line with this or that series of past impressions, the images that filled my dreams that first night were borrowed from a memory entirely distinct from that on which I was in the habit of drawing. If I had been tempted while asleep to let myself be swept back upon my ordinary current of remembrance, the bed to which I was not accustomed, the comfortable attention which I was obliged to pay to the position of my various limbs when I turned over, were sufficient to correct my error, to disentangle and to keep running the new thread of my dreams. It is the same with sleep as with our perception of the external world. It needs only a modification in our habits to make it poetic, it is enough that while undressing we should have dozed off unconsciously upon the bed, for the dimensions of our dream-world to be altered and its beauty felt. We awake, look at our watch, see 'four o'clock'; it is only four o'clock in the morning, but we imagine that the whole day has gone by, so vividly does this nap of a few minutes, unsought by us, appear to have come down to us from the skies, by virtue of some divine right, full-bodied, vast, like an Emperor's orb of gold. In the morning, while worrying over the thought that my grandfather was ready, and was waiting for me to start on our walk along the Méséglise way, I was awakened by the blare of a regimental band which passed every day beneath my windows. But on several occasions—and I mention these because one cannot properly describe human life unless one shews it soaked in the sleep in which it plunges, which, night after night, sweeps round it as a promontory is encircled by the sea—the intervening layer of sleep was strong enough to bear the shock of the music and I heard nothing. On the other mornings it gave way for a moment; but, still velvety with the refreshment of having slept, my consciousness (like those organs by which, after a local anaesthetic, a cauterisation, not perceived at first, is felt only at the very end and then as a faint burning smart) was touched only gently by the shrill points of the fifes which caressed it with a vague, cool, matutinal warbling; and after this brief interruption in which the silence had turned to music it relapsed into my slumber before even the dragoons had finished passing, depriving me of the latest opening buds of the sparkling clangorous nosegay. And the zone of my consciousness which its springing stems had brushed was so narrow, so circumscribed with sleep that later on, when Saint-Loup asked me whether I had heard the band, I was no longer certain that the sound of its brasses had not been as imaginary as that which I heard during the day echo, after the slightest noise, from the paved streets of the town. Perhaps I had heard it only in a dream, prompted by my fear of being awakened, or else of not being awakened and so not seeing the regiment march past. For often, when I was still asleep at the moment when, on the contrary, I had supposed that the noise would awaken me, for the next hour I imagined that I was awake, while still drowsing, and I enacted to myself with tenuous shadow-shapes on the screen of my slumber the various scenes of which it deprived me but at which I had the illusion of looking on.

What one has meant to do during the day, as it turns out, sleep intervening, one accomplishes only in one's dreams, that is to say after it has been distorted by sleep into following another line than one would have chosen when awake. The same story branches off and has a different ending. When all is said, the world in which we live when we are asleep is so different that people who have difficulty in going to sleep seek first of all to escape from the waking world. After having desperately, for hours on end, with shut eyes, revolved in their minds thoughts similar to those which they would have had with their eyes open, they take heart again on noticing that the last minute has been crawling under the weight of an argument in formal contradiction of the laws of thought, and their realisation of this, and the brief 'absence' to which it points, indicate that the door is now open through which they will perhaps be able, presently, to escape from the perception of the real, to advance to a resting-place more or less remote on the other side, which will mean their having a more or less 'good' night. But already a great stride has been made when we turn our back on the real, when we reach the cave in which 'auto-suggestions' prepare—like witches—the hell-broth of imaginary maladies or of the recurrence of nervous disorders, and watch for the hour at which the storm that has been gathering during our unconscious sleep will break with sufficient force to make sleep cease.

Not far thence is the secret garden in which grow like strange flowers the kinds of sleep, so different one from another, the sleep induced by datura, by the multiple extracts of ether, the sleep of belladonna, of opium, of valerian, flowers whose petals remain shut until the day when the pre-destined visitor shall come and, touching them, bid them open, and for long hours inhale the aroma of their peculiar dreams into a marvelling and bewildered being. At the end of the garden stands the convent with open windows through which we hear voices repeating the lessons learned before we went to sleep, which we shall know only at the moment of awakening; while, a presage of that moment, sounds the resonant tick of that inward alarum which our preoccupation has so effectively regulated that when our housekeeper comes in with the warning: "It is seven o'clock," she will find us awake and ready. On the dim walls of that chamber which opens upon our dreams, within which toils without ceasing that oblivion of the sorrows of love whose task, interrupted and brought to nought at

times by a nightmare big with reminiscence, is ever speedily resumed, hang,
even after we are awake, the memories of our dreams, but so overshadowed
that often we catch sight of them for the first time only in the broad light
of the afternoon when the ray of a similar idea happens by chance to strike
them; some of them brilliant and harmonious while we slept, but already
so distorted that, having failed to recognise them, we can but hasten to lay
them in the earth like dead bodies too quickly decomposed or relics so
seriously damaged, so nearly crumbling into dust that the most skilful
restorer could not bring them back to their true form or make anything
of them. Near the gate is the quarry to which our heavier slumbers repair
in search of substances which coat the brain with so unbreakable a glaze
that, to awaken the sleeper, his own will is obliged, even on a golden
morning, to smite him with mighty blows like a young Siegfried. Beyond
this, again, are the nightmares of which the doctors foolishly assert that
they tire us more than does insomnia, whereas on the contrary they enable
the thinker to escape from the strain of thought; those nightmares with
their fantastic picture-books in which our relatives who are dead are
shewn meeting with a serious accident which at the same time does not
preclude their speedy recovery. Until then we keep them in a little rat-cage,
in which they are smaller than white mice and, covered with big red spots,
out of each of which a feather sprouts, engage us in Ciceronian dialogues.
Next to this picture-book is the revolving disc of awakening, by virtue
of which we submit for a moment to the tedium of having to return at
once to a house which was pulled down fifty years ago, the memory of
which is gradually effaced as sleep grows more distant by a number of
others, until we arrive at that memory which the disc presents only when
it has ceased to revolve and which coincides with what we shall see with
opened eyes.

Sometimes I had heard nothing, being in one of those slumbers into
which we fall as into a pit from which we are heartily glad to be drawn up
a little later, heavy, overfed, digesting all that has been brought to us (as
by the nymphs who fed the infant Hercules) by those agile, vegetative
powers whose activity is doubled while we sleep.

That kind of sleep is called 'sleeping like lead,' and it seems as though
one has become, oneself, and remains for a few moments after such a sleep
is ended, simply a leaden image. One is no longer a person. How then,
seeking for one's mind, one's personality, as one seeks for a thing that is
lost, does one recover one's own self rather than any other? Why, when
one begins again to think, is it not another personality than yesterday's
that is incarnate in one? One fails to see what can dictate the choice, or
why, among the millions of human beings any one of whom one might be,
it is on him who one was overnight that unerringly one lays one's hand?
What is it that guides us, when there has been an actual interruption—
whether it be that our unconsciousness has been complete or our dreams
entirely different from ourselves? There has indeed been death, as when the
heart has ceased to beat and a rhythmical friction of the tongue revives us.
No doubt the room, even if we have seen it only once before, awakens
memories to which other, older memories cling. Or were some memories

also asleep in us of which we now become conscious? The resurrection at our awakening—after that healing attack of mental alienation which is sleep—must after all be similar to what occurs when we recapture a name, a line, a refrain that we had forgotten. And perhaps the resurrection of the soul after death is to be conceived as a phenomenon of memory.

When I had finished sleeping, tempted by the sunlit sky—but discouraged by the chill—of those last autumn mornings, so luminous and so cold, in which winter begins, to get up and look at the trees on which the leaves were indicated now only by a few strokes, golden or rosy, which seemed to have been left in the air, on an invisible web, I raised my head from the pillow and stretched my neck, keeping my body still hidden beneath the bedclothes; like a chrysalis in the process of change I was a dual creature, with the different parts of which a single environment did not agree; for my eyes colour was sufficient, without warmth; my chest on the other hand was anxious for warmth and not for colour. I rose only after my fire had been lighted, and studied the picture, so delicate and transparent, of the pink and golden morning, to which I had now added by artificial means the element of warmth that it lacked, poking my fire which burned and smoked like a good pipe and gave me, as a pipe would have given me, a pleasure at once coarse because it was based upon a material comfort and delicate because beyond it was printed a pure vision. The walls of my dressing-room were covered with a paper on which a violent red background was patterned with black and white flowers, to which it seemed that I should have some difficulty in growing accustomed. But they succeeded only in striking me as novel, in forcing me to enter not into conflict but into contact with them, in modulating the gaiety, the songs of my morning toilet, they succeeded only in imprisoning me in the heart of a sort of poppy, out of which to look at a world which I saw quite differently from in Paris, from the gay screen which was this new dwelling-place, of a different aspect from the house of my parents, and into which flowed a purer air. On certain days, I was agitated by the desire to see my grandmother again, or by the fear that she might be ill, or else it was the memory of some undertaking which I had left half-finished in Paris, and which seemed to have made no progress; sometimes again it was some difficulty in which, even here, I had managed to become involved. One or other of these anxieties had kept me from sleeping, and I was without strength to face my sorrow which in a moment grew to fill the whole of my existence. Then from the hotel I sent a messenger to the barracks, with a line to Saint-Loup: I told him that, should it be materially possible—I knew that it was extremely difficult for him—I should be most grateful if he would look in for a minute. An hour later he arrived; and on hearing his ring at the door I felt myself liberated from my obsessions. I knew that, if they were stronger than I, he was stronger than they, and my attention was diverted from them and concentrated on him who would have to settle them. He had come into the room, and already he had enveloped me in the gust of fresh air in which from before dawn he had been displaying so much activity, a vital atmosphere very different from that of my room, to which I at once adapted myself by appropriate reactions.

"I hope you weren't angry with me for bothering you; there is something that is worrying me, as you probably guessed."

"Not at all; I just supposed you wanted to see me, and I thought it very nice of you. I was delighted that you should have sent for me. But what is the trouble? Things not going well? What can I do to help?"

He listened to my explanations, and gave careful answers; but before he had uttered a word he had transformed me to his own likeness; compared with the important occupations which kept him so busy, so alert, so happy, the worries which, a moment ago, I had been unable to endure for another instant seemed to me as to him negligible; I was like a man who, not having been able to open his eyes for some days, sends for a doctor, who neatly and gently raises his eyelid, removes from beneath it and shews him a grain of sand; the sufferer is healed and comforted. All my cares resolved themselves into a telegram which Saint-Loup undertook to dispatch. Life seemed to me so different, so delightful; I was flooded with such a surfeit of strength that I longed for action.

"What are you doing now?" I asked him.

"I must leave you, I'm afraid; we're going on a route march in three quarters of an hour, and I have to be on parade."

"Then it's been a great bother to you, coming here?"

"No, no bother at all, the Captain was very good about it; he told me that if it was for you I must go at once; but you understand, I don't like to seem to be abusing the privilege."

"But if I got up and dressed quickly and went by myself to the place where you'll be training, it would interest me immensely, and I could perhaps talk to you during the breaks."

"I shouldn't advise you to do that; you have been lying awake, racking your brains over a thing which, I assure you, is not of the slightest importance, but now that it has ceased to worry you, lay your head down on the pillow and go to sleep, which you will find an excellent antidote to the demineralisation of your nerve-cells; only you mustn't go to sleep too soon, because our band-boys will be coming along under your windows; but as soon as they've passed I think you'll be left in peace, and we shall meet again this evening, at dinner."

But soon I was constantly going to see the regiment being trained in field operations, when I began to take an interest in the military theories which Saint-Loup's friends used to expound over the dinner-table, and when it had become the chief desire of my life to see at close quarters their various leaders, just as a person who makes music his principal study and spends his life in the concert halls finds pleasure in frequenting the cafés in which one mingles with the life of the members of the orchestra. To reach the training ground I used to have to take tremendously long walks. In the evening after dinner the longing for sleep made my head drop every now and then as in a swoon. Next morning I realised that I had no more heard the band than, at Balbec, after the evenings on which Saint-Loup had taken me to dinner at Rivebelle, I used to hear the concert on the beach. And at the moment when I wished to rise I had a delicious feeling of incapacity; I felt myself fastened to a deep, invisible ground

by the articulations (of which my tiredness made me conscious) of muscular and nutritious roots. I felt myself full of strength; life seemed to
extend more amply before me; this was because I had reverted to the
good tiredness of my childhood at Combray on the mornings following
days on which we had taken the Guermantes walk. Poets make out that
we recapture for a moment the self that we were long ago when we enter
some house or garden in which we used to live in our youth. But these
are most hazardous pilgrimages, which end as often in disappointment as
in success. The fixed places, contemporary with different years, it is in
ourselves that we should rather seek to find them. This is where the advantage comes in, to a certain extent, of great exhaustion followed by a
good night's rest. Good nights, to make us descend into the most subter-
ranean galleries of sleep, where no reflexion from overnight, no gleam of
memory comes to lighten the inward monologue (if so be that it cease
not also), turn so effectively the soil and break through the surface stone
of our body that we discover there, where our muscles dive down and
throw out their twisted roots and breathe the air of the new life, the garden
in which as a child we used to play. There is no need to travel in order to
see it again; we must dig down inwardly to discover it. What once covered
the earth is no longer upon it but beneath; a mere excursion does not suffice for a visit to the dead city, excavation is necessary also. But we shall
see how certain impressions, fugitive and fortuitous, carry us back even
more effectively to the past, with a more delicate precision, with a flight
more light-winged, more immaterial, more headlong, more unerring, more
immortal than these organic dislocations.

Sometimes my exhaustion was greater still; I had, without any opportunity of going to bed, been following the operations for several days on
end. How blessed then was my return to the hotel! As I got into bed I
seemed to have escaped at last from the hands of enchanters, sorcerers
like those who people the 'romances' beloved of our forebears in the seventeenth century. My sleep that night and the lazy morning that followed
it were no more than a charming fairy tale. Charming; beneficent perhaps
also. I reminded myself that the keenest sufferings have their place of
sanctuary, that one can always, when all else fails, find repose. These
thoughts carried me far.

On days when, although there was no parade, Saint-Loup had to stay in
barracks, I used often to go and visit him there. It was a long way; I had to
leave the town and cross the viaduct, from either side of which I had an
immense view. A strong breeze blew almost always over this high ground,
and filled all the buildings erected on three sides of the barrack-square,
which howled incessantly like a cave of the winds. While I waited for
Robert—he being engaged on some duty or other—outside the door of his
room or in the mess, talking to some of his friends to whom he had introduced me (and whom later on I came now and then to see, even when he
was not to be there), looking down from the window three hundred feet
to the country below, bare now except where recently sown fields, often
still soaked with rain and glittering in the sun, shewed a few stripes of
green, of the brilliance and translucent limpidity of enamel, I could hear

him discussed by the others, and I soon learned what a popular favourite he was. Among many of the volunteers, belonging to other squadrons, sons of rich business or professional men who looked at the higher aristocratic society only from outside and without penetrating its enclosure, the at-traction which they naturally felt towards what they knew of Saint-Loup's character was reinforced by the distinction that attached in their eyes to the young man whom, on Saturday evenings, when they went on pass to Paris, they had seen supping in the Café de la Paix with the Duc d'Uzès and the Prince d'Orléans. And on that account, into his handsome face, his casual way of walking and saluting officers, the perpetual dance of his eyeglass, the affectation shewn in the cut of his service dress—the caps always too high, the breeches of too fine a cloth and too pink a shade—they had introduced the idea of a 'tone' which, they were positive, was lacking in the best turned-out officers in the regiment, even the majestic Captain to whom I had been indebted for the privilege of sleeping in bar-racks, who seemed, in comparison, too pompous and almost common.

One of them said that the Captain had bought a new horse. "He can buy as many horses as he likes. I passed Saint-Loup on Sunday morning in the Allée des Acacias; now he's got some style on a horse!" replied his companion, and knew what he was talking about, for these young fellows belonged to a class which, if it does not frequent the same houses and know the same people, yet, thanks to money and leisure, does not differ from the nobility in its experience of all those refinements of life which money can procure. At any rate their refinement had, in the matter of clothes, for instance, something about it more studied, more impeccable than that free and easy negligence which had so delighted my grandmother in Saint-Loup. It gave quite a thrill to these sons of big stockbrokers or bankers, as they sat eating oysters after the theatre, to see at an adjoining table Serjeant Saint-Loup. And what a tale there was to tell in barracks on Monday night, after a week-end leave, by one of them who was in Robert's squadron, and to whom he had said how d'ye do 'most civilly,' while an-other, who was not in the same squadron, was quite positive that, in spite of this, Saint-Loup had recognised him, for two or three times he had put up his eyeglass and stared in the speaker's direction.

"Yes, my brother saw him at the Paix," said another, who had been spending the day with his mistress; "my brother says his dress coat was cut too loose and didn't fit him."

"What was the waistcoat like?"

"He wasn't wearing a white waistcoat; it was purple, with sort of palms on it; stunning!"

To the 'old soldiers' (sons of the soil who had never heard of the Jockey Club and simply put Saint-Loup in the category of ultra-rich non-com-missioned officers, in which they included all those who, whether bankrupt or not, lived in a certain style, whose income or debts ran into several figures, and who were generous towards their men), the gait, the eye-glass, the breeches, the caps of Saint-Loup, even if they saw in them noth-ing particularly aristocratic, furnished nevertheless just as much interest and meaning. They recognised in these peculiarities the character, the style which they had assigned once and for all time to this most popular of the 'stripes' in the regiment, manners like no one's else, scornful indifference to what his superior officers might think, which seemed to them the natural corollary of his goodness to his subordinates. The morning cup of coffee in the canteen, the afternoon 'lay-down' in the barrack-room seemed pleasanter, somehow, when some old soldier fed the hungering, lazy section with some savoury titbit as to a cap in which Saint-Loup had appeared on parade.

"It was the height of my pack."

"Come off it, old chap, you don't expect us to believe that; it couldn't have been the height of your pack," interrupted a young college graduate who hoped by using these slang terms not to appear a 'learned beggar,' and by venturing on this contradiction to obtain confirmation of a fact the thought of which enchanted him.

"Oh, so it wasn't the height of my pack, wasn't it? You measured it, I suppose! I tell you this much, the C. O. glared at it as if he'd have liked to put him in clink. But you needn't think the great Saint-Loup felt squashed; no, he went and he came, and down with his head and up with his head, and that blinking glass screwed in his eye all the time. We'll see what the 'Capstan' has to say when he hears. Oh, very likely he'll say nothing, but you may be sure he won't be pleased. But there's nothing so wonderful about that cap. I hear he's got thirty of 'em and more at home, at his house in town."

"Where did you hear that, old man? From our blasted corporal-dog?" asked the young graduate, pedantically displaying the new forms of speech which he had only recently acquired and with which he took a pride in garnishing his conversation.

"Where did I hear it? From his batman; what d'you think?"

"Ah! Now you're talking. That's a chap who knows when he's well off!"

"I should say so! He's got more in his pocket than I have, certain sure! And besides he gives him all his own things, and everything. He wasn't getting his grub properly, he says. Along comes de Saint-Loup, and gives cooky hell: 'I want him to be properly fed, d'you hear,' he says, 'and I don't care what it costs.'"

The old soldier made up for the triviality of the words quoted by the emphasis of his tone, in a feeble imitation of the speaker which had an immense success.

On leaving the barracks I would take a stroll, and then, to fill up the time before I went, as I did every evening, to dine with Saint-Loup at the hotel in which he and his friends had established their mess, I made for my own, as soon as the sun had set, so as to have a couple of hours in which to rest and read. In the square, the evening light bedecked the pepper-pot turrets of the castle with little pink clouds which matched the colour of the bricks, and completed the harmony by softening the tone of the latter where it bathed them. So strong a current of vitality coursed through my nerves that no amount of movement on my part could exhaust it; each step I took, after touching a stone of the pavement, rebounded off it. I seemed to have growing on my heels the wings of Mercury. One of the fountains was filled with a ruddy glow, while in the other the moonlight had already begun to turn the water opalescent. Between them were children at play, uttering shrill cries, wheeling in circles, obeying some necessity of the hour, like swifts or bats. Next door to the hotel, the old National Courts and the Louis XVI orangery, in which were installed now the savings-bank and the Army Corps headquarters, were lighted from within by the palely gilded globes of their gas-jets which, seen in the still clear daylight outside, suited those vast, tall, eighteenth-century windows from which the last rays of the setting sun had not yet departed, as would have suited a complexion heightened with rouge a head-dress of yellow tortoise-shell, and persuaded me to seek out my fireside and the lamp which, alone in the shadowy front of my hotel, was striving to resist the gathering darkness, and for the sake of which I went indoors before it was quite dark, for pleasure, as to an appetising meal. I kept, when I was in my room, the same fulness of sensation that I had felt outside. It gave such an apparent convexity of surface to things which as a rule seem flat and empty, to the yellow flame of the fire, the coarse blue paper on the ceiling, on which the setting sun had scribbled corkscrews and whirligigs, like a schoolboy with a piece of red chalk, the curiously patterned cloth on the round table, on which a ream of essay paper and an inkpot lay in readiness for me, with one of Bergotte's novels, that ever since then these things have continued to seem to me to be enriched with a whole form of existence which I feel that I should be able to extract from them if it were granted me to set eyes on them again. I thought with joy of the barracks that I had just left and of their weather-cock turning with every wind that blew. Like a diver breathing through a pipe which rises above the surface of the water, I felt that I was in a sense maintaining contact with a healthy, open-air life when I kept as a baiting-place those barracks, that towering observatory, dominating a country-side furrowed with canals of green enamel, into whose various buildings I esteemed as a priceless privilege, which I hoped would last, my freedom to go whenever I chose, always certain of a welcome.

At seven o'clock I dressed myself and went out again to dine with Saint-Loup at the hotel where he took his meals. I liked to go there on foot. It was by now pitch dark, and after the third day of my visit there began to blow, as soon as night had fallen, an icy wind which seemed a harbinger of snow. As I walked, I ought not, strictly speaking, to have ceased for a moment to think of Mme. de Guermantes; it was only in the attempt to draw nearer to her that I had come to visit Robert's garrison. But a memory, a grief, are fleeting things. There are days when they remove so far that we are barely conscious of them, we think that they have gone for ever. Then we pay attention to other things. And the streets of this town had not yet become for me what streets are in the place where one is accustomed to live, simply means of communication between one part and another. The life led by the inhabitants of this unknown world must, it seemed to me, be a marvellous thing, and often the lighted windows of some dwelling-house kept me standing for a long while motionless in the darkness by laying before my eyes the actual and mysterious scenes of

an existence into which I might not penetrate. Here the fire-spirit displayed to me in purple colouring the booth of a chestnut seller in which
a couple of serjeants, their belts slung over the backs of chairs, were playing cards, never dreaming that a magician's wand was making them emerge
from the night, like a transparency on the stage, and presenting them in
their true lineaments at that very moment to the eyes of an arrested passer-
by whom they could not see. In a little curiosity shop a candle, burned almost to its socket, projecting its warm glow over an engraving reprinted it
in sanguine, while, battling against the darkness, the light of the big lamp
tanned a scrap of leather, inlaid a dagger with fiery spangles, on pictures
which were only bad copies spread a priceless film of gold like the patina
of time or the varnish used by a master, made in fact of the whole hovel, in
which there was nothing but pinchbeck rubbish, a marvellous composition
by Rembrandt. Sometimes I lifted my gaze to some huge old dwelling-
house on which the shutters had not been closed and in which amphibious
men and women floated slowly to and fro in the rich liquid that after
nightfall rose incessantly from the wells of the lamps to fill the rooms to
the very brink of the outer walls of stone and glass, the movement of their
bodies sending through it long unctuous golden ripples. I proceeded on my
way, and often, in the dark alley that ran past the cathedral, as long ago
on the road to Méséglise, the force of my desire caught and held me; it
seemed that a woman must be on the point of appearing, to satisfy it; if,
in the darkness, I felt suddenly brush past me a skirt, the violence of the
pleasure which I then felt made it impossible for me to believe that the
contact was accidental and I attempted to seize in my arms a terrified
stranger. This gothic alley meant for me something so real that if I had
been successful in raising and enjoying a woman there, it would have been
impossible for me not to believe that it was the ancient charm of the place
that was bringing us together, and even though she were no more than a
common street-walker, stationed there every evening, still the wintry
night, the strange place, the darkness, the mediaeval atmosphere would
have lent her their mysterious glamour. I thought of what might be in
store for me; to try to forget Mme. de Guermantes seemed to me a dreadful
thing, but reasonable, and for the first time possible, easy perhaps even.
In the absolute quiet of this neighbourhood I could hear ahead of me
shouted words and laughter which must come from tipsy revellers staggering home. I waited to see them, I stood peering in the direction from
which I had heard the sound. But I was obliged to wait for some time,
for the surrounding silence was so intense that it allowed to travel with
the utmost clearness and strength sounds that were still a long way off.
Finally the revellers did appear; not, as I had supposed, in front of me,
but ever so far behind. Whether the intersection of sidestreets, the inter-
position of buildings had, by reverberation, brought about this acoustic
error, or because it is very difficult to locate a sound when the place from
which it comes is not known, I had been as far wrong over direction as
over distance.

  The wind grew stronger. It was thick and bristling with coming snow. I
returned to the main street and jumped on board the little tramway-car

on which, from its platform, an officer, without apparently seeing them, was acknowledging the salutes of the loutish soldiers who trudged past along the pavement, their faces daubed crimson by the cold, reminding me, in this little town which the sudden leap from autumn into early winter seemed to have transported farther north, of the rubicund faces which Breughel gives to his merry, junketing, frostbound peasants.

And sure enough at the hotel where I was to meet Saint-Loup and his friends and to which the fair now beginning had attracted a number of people from near and far, I found, as I hurried across the courtyard with its glimpses of glowing kitchens in which chickens were turning on spits, pigs were roasting, lobsters being flung, alive, into what the landlord called the 'everlasting fire,' an influx (worthy of some *Numbering of the People Before Bethlehem* such as the old Flemish masters used to paint) of new arrivals who assembled there in groups, asking the landlord or one of his staff (who, if he did not like the look of them, would recommend lodgings elsewhere in the town) whether they could have dinner and beds, while a scullion hurried past holding a struggling fowl by the neck. And similarly, in the big dining-room which I crossed the first day before coming to the smaller room in which my friend was waiting for me, it was of some feast in the Gospels portrayed with a mediaeval simplicity and an exaggeration typically Flemish that one was reminded by the quantity of fish, pullets, grouse, woodcock, pigeons, brought in dressed and garnished and piping hot by breathless waiters who slid over the polished floor to gain speed and set them down on the huge carving table where they were at once cut up but where—for most of the people had nearly finished dinner when I arrived—they accumulated untouched, as though their profusion and the haste of those who brought them in were due not so much to the requirements of the diners as to respect for the sacred text, scrupulously followed in the letter but quaintly illustrated by real details borrowed from local custom, and to an aesthetic and religious scruple for making evident to the eye the solemnity of the feast by the profusion of the victuals and the assiduity of the servers. One of these stood lost in thought at the far end of the room by a sideboard; and to find out from him, who alone appeared calm enough to be capable of answering me, in which room our table had been laid, making my way forward among the chafing-dishes that had been lighted here and there to keep the late comers' plates from growing cold (which did not, however, prevent the dessert, in the centre of the room, from being piled on the outstretched hands of a huge mannikin, sometimes supported on the wings of a duck, apparently of crystal, but really of ice, carved afresh every day with a hot iron by a sculptor-cook, quite in the Flemish manner), I went straight—at the risk of being knocked down by his colleagues—towards this servitor, in whom I felt that I recognised a character who is traditionally present in all these sacred subjects, for he reproduced with scrupulous accuracy the blunt features, fatuous and ill-drawn, the musing expression, already half aware of the miracle of a divine presence which the others have not yet begun to suspect. I should add that, in view probably of the coming fair, this presentation was strengthened by a celestial contingent, recruited in mass, of cherubim and seraphim. A young angel musician, whose fair hair enclosed a fourteen-year-old face, was not, it was true, playing on any instrument, but stood musing before a gong or a pile of plates, while other less infantile angels flew swiftly across the boundless expanse of the room, beating the air with the ceaseless fluttering of the napkins which fell along the lines of their bodies like the wings in 'primi- tive' paintings, with pointed ends. Fleeing those ill-defined regions, screened by a hedge of palms through which the angelic servitors looked, from a distance, as though they had floated down out of the empyrean, I explored my way to the smaller room in which Saint-Loup's table was laid. I found there several of his friends who dined with him regularly, nobles except for one or two commoners in whom the young nobles had, in their school days, detected likely friends, and with whom they readily associated, proving thereby that they were not on principle hostile to the middle class, even though it were Republican, provided it had clean hands and went to mass. On the first of these evenings, before we sat down to dinner, I drew Saint- Loup into a corner and, in front of all the rest but so that they should not hear me, said to him:

"Robert, this is hardly the time or the place for what I am going to say, but I shan't be a second. I keep on forgetting to ask you when I'm in the barracks; isn't that Mme. de Guermantes's photograph that you have on your table?"

"Why, yes; my good aunt."

"Of course she is; what a fool I am; you told me before that she was; I'd forgotten all about her being your aunt. I say, your friends will be getting impatient, we must be quick, they're looking at us; another time will do; it isn't at all important."

"That's all right; go on as long as you like. They can wait."

"No, no; I do want to be polite to them; they're so nice; besides, it doesn't really matter in the least, I assure you."

"Do you know that worthy Oriane, then?"

This 'worthy Oriane,' as he might have said, 'that good Oriane,' did not imply that Saint-Loup regarded Mme. de Guermantes as especially good. In this instance the words 'good,' 'excellent,' 'worthy' are mere reinforcements of the demonstrative 'that,' indicating a person who is known to both parties and of whom the speaker does not quite know what to say to someone outside the intimate circle. The word 'good' does duty as a stopgap and keeps the conversation going for a moment until the speaker has hit upon "Do you see much of her?" or "I haven't set eyes on her for months," or "I shall be seeing her on Tuesday," or "She must be getting on, now, you know."

"I can't tell you how funny it is that it should be her photograph, be- cause we're living in her house now, in Paris, and I've been hearing the most astounding things" (I should have been hard put to it to say what) "about her, which have made me immensely interested in her, only from a literary point of view, don't you know, from a—how shall I put it—from a Balzacian point of view; but you're so clever you can see what I mean;

I don't need to explain things to you; but we must hurry up; what on earth will your friends think of my manners?"

"They will think absolutely nothing; I have told them that you are sublime, and they are a great deal more alarmed than you are."

"You are too kind. But listen, what I want to say is this: I suppose Mme. de Guermantes hasn't any idea that I know you, has she?"

"I can't say; I haven't seen her since the summer, because I haven't had any leave since she's been in town."

"What I was going to say is this: I've been told that she looks on me as an absolute idiot."

"That I do not believe; Oriane is not exactly an eagle, but all the same she's by no means stupid."

"You know that, as a rule, I don't care about your advertising the good opinion you're kind enough to hold of me; I'm not conceited. That's why I'm sorry you should have said flattering things about me to your friends here (we will go back to them in two seconds). But Mme. de Guermantes is different; if you could let her know—if you would even exaggerate a trifle—what you think of me, you would give me great pleasure."

"Why, of course I will, if that's all you want me to do; it's not very difficult; but what difference can it possibly make to you what she thinks of you? I suppose you think her no end of a joke, really; anyhow, if that's all you want we can discuss it in front of the others or when we are by ourselves; I'm afraid of your tiring yourself if you stand talking, and it's so inconvenient too, when we have heaps of opportunities of being alone together."

It was precisely this inconvenience that had given me courage to approach Robert; the presence of the others was for me a pretext that justified my giving my remarks a curt and incoherent form, under cover of which I could more easily dissemble the falsehood of my saying to my friend that I had forgotten his connexion with the Duchess, and also did not give him time to frame—with regard to my reasons for wishing that Mme. de Guermantes should know that I was his friend, was clever, and so forth—questions which would have been all the more disturbing in that I should not have been able to answer them.

"Robert, I'm surprised that a man of your intelligence should fail to understand that one doesn't discuss the things that will give one's friends pleasure; one does them. Now I, if you were to ask me no matter what, and indeed I only wish you would ask me to do something for you, I can assure you I shouldn't want any explanations. I may ask you for more than I really want; I have no desire to know Mme. de Guermantes, but just to test you I ought to have said that I was anxious to dine with Mme. de Guermantes; I am sure you would never have done it."

"Not only should I have done it, I will do it."

"When?"

"Next time I'm in Paris, three weeks from now, I expect."

"We shall see; I dare say she won't want to see me, though. I can't tell you how grateful I am."

"Not at all; it's nothing."

"Don't say that; it's everything in the world, because now I can see what sort of friend you are; whether what I ask you to do is important or not, disagreeable or not, whether I am really keen about it or ask you only as a test, it makes no difference; you say you will do it, and there you shew the fineness of your mind and heart. A stupid friend would have started a discussion."

Which was exactly what he had just been doing; but perhaps I wanted to flatter his self-esteem; perhaps also I was sincere, the sole touchstone of merit seeming to me to be the extent to which a friend could be useful in respect of the one thing that seemed to me to have any importance, namely my love. Then I went on, perhaps from cunning, possibly from a genuine increase of affection inspired by gratitude, expectancy, and the copy of Mme. de Guermantes's very features which nature had made in producing her nephew Robert: "But, I say, we mustn't keep them waiting any longer, and I've mentioned only one of the two things I wanted to ask you, the less important; the other is more important to me, but I'm afraid you will never consent. Would it bore you if we were to call each other *tu*?"

"Bore me? My dear fellow! Joy! Tears of joy! Undreamed-of happiness!"

"Thank you—*tu* I mean; you begin first—ever so much. It is such a pleasure to me that you needn't do anything about Mme. de Guermantes if you'd rather not, this is quite enough for me."

"I can do both."

"I say, Robert! Listen to me a minute," I said to him later while we were at dinner. "Oh, it's really too absurd the way our conversation is always being interrupted, I can't think why—you remember the lady I was speaking to you about just now."

"Yes."

"You're quite sure you know who' I mean?"

"Why, what do you take me for, a village idiot?"

"You wouldn't care to give me her photograph, I suppose?"

I had meant to ask him only for the loan of it. But when the time came to speak I felt shy, I decided that the request was indiscreet, and in order to hide my confusion I put the question more bluntly, and increased my demand, as if it had been quite natural.

"No; I should have to ask her permission first," was his answer.

He blushed as he spoke. I could see that he had a reservation in his mind, that he credited me also with one, that he would give only a partial service to my love, under the restraint of certain moral principles, and for this I hated him.

At the same time I was touched to see how differently Saint-Loup behaved towards me now that I was no longer alone with him, and that his friends formed an audience. His increased affability would have left me cold had I thought that it was deliberately assumed; but I could feel that it was spontaneous and consisted only of all that he had to say about me in my absence and refrained as a rule from saying when we were together by ourselves. In our private conversations I might certainly suspect the pleasure that he found in talking to me, but that pleasure he almost always left unexpressed. Now, at the same remarks from me which, as a rule, he enjoyed without shewing it, he watched from the corner of his eye to see whether they produced on his friends the effect on which he had counted, an effect corresponding to what he had promised them before-hand. The mother of a girl in her first season could be no more unrelaxing in her attention to her daughter's responses and to the attitude of the public. If I had made some remark at which, alone in my company, he would merely have smiled, he was afraid that the others might not have seen the point, and put in a "What's that?" to make me repeat what I had said, to attract attention, and turning at once to his friends and making himself automatically, by facing them with a hearty laugh, the fugleman of their laughter, presented me for the first time with the opinion that he actually held of me and must often have expressed to them. So that I caught sight of myself suddenly from without, like a person who reads his name in a newspaper or sees himself in a mirror.

It occurred to me, one of these evenings, to tell a mildly amusing story about Mme. Blandais, but I stopped at once, remembering that Saint-Loup knew it already, and that when I had tried to tell him it on the day following my arrival he had interrupted me with: "You told me that before, at Balbec." I was surprised, therefore, to find him begging me to go on and assuring me that he did not know the story, and that it would amuse him immensely. "You've forgotten it for the moment," I said to him, "but you'll remember as I go on." "No, really; I swear you're mistaken. You've never told me. Do go on." And throughout the story he fixed a feverish and enraptured gaze alternately on myself and on his friends. I realised only after I had finished, amid general laughter, that it had struck him that this story would give his friends a good idea of my wit, and that it was for this reason that he had pretended not to know it. Such is the stuff of friendship.

On the third evening, one of his friends, to whom I had not had an opportunity before of speaking, conversed with me at great length; and I overheard him telling Saint-Loup how much he had been enjoying him-self. And indeed we sat talking together almost all evening, leaving our glasses of sauterne untouched on the table before us, isolated, sheltered from the others by the sumptuous curtains of one of those intuitive sym-pathies between man and man which, when they are not based upon any physical attraction, are the only kind that is altogether mysterious. Of such an enigmatic nature had seemed to me, at Balbec, that feeling which Saint-Loup had for me, which was not to be confused with the interest of our conversations, a feeling free from any material association, invisible, intangible, and yet a thing of the presence of which in himself, like a sort of inflammatory gas, he had been so far conscious as to refer to it with a smile. And yet there was perhaps something more surprising still in this sympathy born here in a single evening, like a flower that had budded and opened in a few minutes in the warmth of this little room. I could not help asking Robert when he spoke to me about Balbec whether it were really settled that he was to marry Mlle. d'Ambresac. He assured me that not only was it not settled, but there had never been any thought of such a match, he had never seen her, he did not know who she was. If at that moment I had happened to see any of the social gossipers who had told me of this coming event, they would promptly have announced the betrothal of Mlle. d'Ambresac to some one who was not Saint-Loup and that of Saint-Loup to some one who was not Mlle. d'Ambresac. I should have surprised them greatly had I reminded them of their incompatible and still so recent predictions. In order that this little game may continue, and multiply false reports by attaching the greatest possible number to every name in turn, nature has furnished those who play it with a memory as short as their credulity is long.

Saint-Loup had spoken to me of another of his friends who was present also, one with whom he was on particularly good terms just then, since they were the only two advocates in their mess of the retrial of Dreyfus.

Just as a brother of this friend of Saint-Loup, who had been trained at the Schola Cantorum, thought about every new musical work not at all what his father, his mother, his cousins, his club friends thought, but exactly what the other students thought at the Schola, so this non-commissioned nobleman (of whom Bloch formed an extraordinary opinion when I told him about him, because, touched to hear that he belonged to the same party as himself, he nevertheless imagined him on account of his aristocratic birth and religious and military upbringing to be as different as possible, endowed with the same romantic attraction as a native of a distant country) had a 'mentality,' as people were now beginning to say, analogous to that of the whole body of Dreyfusards in general and of Bloch in particular, on which the traditions of his family and the interests of his career could retain no hold whatever. Similarly one of Saint-Loup's cousins had married a young Eastern princess who was said to write poetry quite as fine as Victor Hugo's or Alfred de Vigny's, and in spite of this was supposed to have a different type of mind from what one would naturally expect, the mind of an Eastern princess immured in an Arabian Nights palace. For the writers who had the privilege of meeting her was reserved the disappointment or rather the joy of listening to conversation which gave the impression not of Scheherazade but of a person of genius of the type of Alfred de Vigny or Victor Hugo.

"That fellow? Oh, he's not like Saint-Loup, he's a regular devil," my new friend informed me; "he's not even straight about it. At first, he used to say: 'Just wait a little, there's a man I know well, a clever, kindhearted fellow, General de Boisdeffre; you need have no hesitation in accepting his decision.' But as soon as he heard that Boisdeffre had pronounced Dreyfus guilty, Boisdeffre ceased to count: clericalism, staff prejudices, prevented his forming a candid opinion, although there is no one in the world (or was, rather, before this Dreyfus business) half so clerical as our friend. Next he told us that now we were sure to get the truth, the case had been put in the hands of Saussier, and he, a soldier of the Republic (our friend coming of an ultra-monarchist family, if you please), was a man of bronze, a stern unyielding conscience. But when Saussier pronounced Esterhazy innocent, he found fresh reasons to account for the decision, reasons damaging not to Dreyfus but to General Saussier. It was the militarist spirit that blinded Saussier (and I must explain to you that our friend is just as much militarist as clerical, or at least he was; I don't know what to think of him now). His family are all broken-hearted at seeing him possessed by such ideas."

"Don't you think," I suggested, turning half towards Saint-Loup so as not to appear to be cutting myself off from him, as well as towards his friend, and so that we might all three join in the conversation, "that the influence we ascribe to environment is particularly true of intellectual environment. One is the man of one's idea. There are far fewer ideas than men, therefore all men with similar ideas are alike. As there is nothing material in an idea, so the people who are only materially neighbours of the man with an idea can do nothing to alter it."

At this point I was interrupted by Saint-Loup, because another of the young men had leaned across to him with a smile and, pointing to me, exclaimed: "Duroc! Duroc all over!" I had no idea what this might mean, but I felt the expression on the shy young face to be more than friendly. While I was speaking, the approbation of the party seemed to Saint-Loup superfluous; he insisted on silence. And just as a conductor stops his orchestra with a rap from his baton because some one in the audience has made a noise, so he rebuked the author of this disturbance: "Gibergue, you must keep your mouth shut when people are speaking. You can tell us about it afterwards." And to me: "Please go on."

I gave a sigh of relief, for I had been afraid that he was going to make me begin all over again.

"And as an idea," I went on, "is a thing that cannot participate in human interests and would be incapable of deriving any benefit from them, the men who are governed by an idea are not influenced by material considerations."

When I had finished, "That's one in the eye for you, my boys," exclaimed Saint-Loup, who had been following me with his gaze with the same anxious solicitude as if I had been walking upon a tight-rope. "What were you going to say, Gibergue?"

"I was just saying that your friend reminded me of Major Duroc. I seemed to hear him speaking."

"Why, I've often thought so myself," replied Saint-Loup; "they have several points in common, but you'll find there are a thousand things in this fellow that Duroc hasn't got."

Saint-Loup was not satisfied with this comparison. In an ecstasy of joy, into which there no doubt entered the joy that he felt in making me shine before his friends, with extreme volubility, stroking me as though he were rubbing down a horse that had just come first past the post, he reiterated: "You're the cleverest man I know, do you hear?" He corrected himself, and added: "You and Elstir.—You don't mind my bracketing him with you, I hope. You understand—punctiliousness. It's like this: I say it to you as one might have said to Balzac: 'You are the greatest novelist of the century—you and Stendhal.' Excessive punctiliousness, don't you know, and at heart an immense admiration. No? You don't admit Stendhal?" he went on, with an ingenuous confidence in my judgment which found expression in a charming, smiling, almost childish glance of interrogation from his green eyes. "Oh, good! I see you're on my side; Bloch can't stand Stendhal. I think it's idiotic of him. The *Chartreuse* is after all an immense work, don't you think? I am so glad you agree with me. What is it you l,ke best in the *Chartreuse,* answer me?" he appealed to me with a boyish impetuosity. And the menace of his physical strength made the question almost terrifying. "Mosca? Fabrice?" I answered timidly that Mosca reminded me a little of M. de Norpois. Whereupon peals of laughter from the young Siegfried Saint-Loup. And while I was going on to explain: "But Mosca is far more intelligent, not so pedantic," I heard Robert cry: "Bravo!" actually clapping his hands, and, helpless with laughter, gasp: "Oh, perfect! Admirable! You really are astounding."

I took a particular pleasure in talking to this young man, as for that matter to all Robert's friends and to Robert himself, about their barracks, the officers of the garrison, and the army in general. Thanks to the immensely enlarged scale on which we see the things, however petty they may be, in the midst of which we eat, and talk, and lead our real life; thanks to that formidable enlargement which they undergo, and the effect of which is that the rest of the world, not being present, cannot compete with them, and assumes in comparison the unsubstantiality of a dream, I had begun to take an interest in the various personalities of the barracks, in the officers whom I saw in the square when I went to visit Saint-Loup, or, if I was awake then, when the regiment passed beneath my windows. I should have liked to know more about the major whom Saint-Loup so greatly admired, and about the course of military history which would have appealed to me "even from an aesthetic point of view." I knew that with Robert the spoken word was, only too often, a trifle hollow, but at other times implied the assimilation of valuable ideas which he was fully capable of grasping. Unfortunately, from the military point of view Robert was exclusively preoccupied at this time with the case of Dreyfus. He spoke little about it, since he alone of the party at table was a Dreyfusard; the others were violently opposed to the idea of a fresh trial, except my other neighbour, my new friend, and his opinions appeared to be somewhat vague. A firm admirer of the colonel, who was regarded as an exceptionally competent officer and had denounced the current agitation against the Army in several of his regimental orders, which won him the reputation of being an anti-Dreyfusard, my neighbour had heard that his commanding officer had let fall certain remarks which had led to the supposition that he had his doubts as to the guilt of Dreyfus and retained his admiration for Picquart. In the latter respect, at any rate, the rumour of Dreyfusism as applied to the colonel was as ill-founded as are all the rumours, springing from none knows where, which float around any great scandal. For, shortly afterwards, this colonel having been detailed to interrogate the former Chief of the Intelligence Branch, had treated him with a brutality and contempt the like of which had never been known before. However this might be (and naturally he had not taken the liberty of going direct to the colonel for his information), my neighbour had paid

Saint-Loup the compliment of telling him—in the tone in which a Catholic lady might tell a Jewish lady that her parish priest denounced the pogroms in Russia and might openly admire the generosity of certain Israelites— that their colonel was not, with regard to Dreyfusism—to a certain kind of Dreyfusism, at least—the fanatical, narrow opponent that he had been made out to be.

"I am not surprised," was Saint-Loup's comment; "for he's a sensible man. But in spite of that he is blinded by the prejudices of his caste, and above all by his clericalism. Now," he turned to me, "Major Duroc, the lecturer on military history I was telling you about; there's a man who is whole-heartedly in support of our views, or so I'm told. And I should have been surprised to hear that he wasn't, for he's not only a brilliantly clever man, but a Radical-Socialist and a freemason."

Partly out of courtesy to his friends, whom these expressions of Saint-Loup's faith in Dreyfus made uncomfortable, and also because the subject was of more interest to myself, I asked my neighbour if it were true that this major gave a demonstration of military history which had a genuine aesthetic beauty. "It is absolutely true."

"But what do you mean by that?"

"Well, all that you read, let us say, in the narrative of a military historian, the smallest facts, the most trivial happenings, are only the outward signs of an idea which has to be analysed, and which often brings to light other ideas, like a palimpsest. So that you have a field for study as intellectual as any science you care to name, or any art, and one that is satisfying to the mind."

"Give me an example or two, if you don't mind."

"It is not very easy to explain," Saint-Loup broke in. "You read, let us say, that this or that Corps has tried . . . but before we go any further, the serial number of the Corps, its order of battle are not without their significance. If it is not the first time that the operation has been attempted, and if for the same operation we find a different Corps being brought up, it is perhaps a sign that the previous Corps have been wiped out or have suffered heavy casualties in the said operation; that they are no longer in a fit state to carry it through successfully. Next, we must ask ourselves what was this Corps which is now out of action; if it was composed of shock troops, held in reserve for big attacks, a fresh Corps of inferior quality will have little chance of succeeding where the first has failed. Furthermore, if we are not at the start of a campaign, this fresh Corps may itself be a composite formation of odds and ends withdrawn from other Corps, which throws a light on the strength of the forces the belligerent still has at his disposal and the proximity of the moment when his forces shall be definitely inferior to the enemy's, which gives to the operation on which this Corps is about to engage a different meaning, because, if it is no longer in a condition to make good its losses, its successes even will only help mathematically to bring it nearer to its ultimate destruction. And then, the serial number of the Corps that it has facing it is of no less significance. If, for instance, it is a much weaker unit, which has already accounted for several important units of the attacking force, the whole nature of the operation is changed, since, even if it should end in the loss of the position which the defending force has been holding, simply to have held it for any length of time may be a great success if a very small defending force has been sufficient to disable highly important forces on the other side. You can understand that if, in the analysis of the Corps engaged on both sides, there are all these points of importance, the study of the position itself, of the roads, of the railways which it commands, of the lines of communication which it protecʿs, is of the very highest. One must study what I may call the whole geographical context," he added with a laugh. And indeed he was so delighted with this expression that, every time he employed it, even months afterwards, it was always accompanied by the same laugh. "While the operation is being prepared by one of the belligerents, if you read that one of his patrols has been wiped out in the neighbourhood of the position by the other belligerent, one of the conclusions which you are entitled to draw is that one side was attempting to reconnoitre the defensive works with which the other intended to resist his attack. An exceptional burst of activity at a given point may indicate the desire to capture that point, but equally well the desire to hold the enemy in check there, not to retaliate at the point at which he has attacked you; or it may indeed be only a feint, intended to cover by an increased activity the relief of troops in that sector. (Which was a classic feint in Napoleon's wars.) On the other hand, to appreciate the significance of any movement, its probable object, and, as a corollary, the other movements by which it will be accompanied or followed, it is not immaterial to consult, not so much the announcements issued by the Higher Command, which may be intended to deceive the enemy, to mask a possible check, as the manual of field operations in use in the country in question. We are always entitled to assume that the manœuvre which an army has attempted to carry out is that prescribed by the rules that are applicable to the circumstances. If, for instance, the rule lays down that a frontal attack should be accompanied by a flank attack; if, after the flank attack has failed, the Higher Command makes out that it had no connexion with the main attack and was merely a diversion, there is a strong likelihood that the truth will be found by consulting the rules and not the reports issued from Headquarters. And there are not only the regulations governing each army to be considered, but their traditions, their habits, their doctrines; the study of diplomatic activities, with their perpetual action or reaction upon military activities, must not be neglected either. Incidents apparently insignificant, which at the time are not understood, will explain to you how the enemy, counting upon a support which these incidents shew to have been withheld, was able to carry out only a part of his strategic plan. So that, if you can read between the lines of military history, what is a confused jumble for the ordinary reader becomes a chain of reasoning as straightforward as a picture is for the picture-lover who can see what the person portrayed is wearing and has in his hands, while the visitor hurrying through the gallery is bewildered by a blur of colour which gives him a headache. But just as with certain pictures, in which it is not enough to observe that the figure is holding a chalice, but one must

know why the painter chose to place a chalice in his hands, what it is
intended to symbolise, so these military operations, apart from their immediate object, are quite regularly traced, in the mind of the general responsible for the campaign, from the plans of earlier battles, which we may
call the past experience, the literature, the learning, the etymology, the
aristocracy (whichever you like) of the battles of to-day. Observe that I
am not speaking for the moment of the local, the (what shall I call it?)
spatial identity of battles. That exists also. A battle-field has never been,
and never will be throughout the centuries, simply the ground upon which
a particular battle has been fought. If it has been a battle-field, that was
because it combined certain conditions of geographical position, of geological formation, drawbacks even, of a kind that would obstruct the enemy
(a river, for instance, cutting his force in two), which made it a good field
of battle. And so what it has been it will continue to be. A painter doesn't
make a studio out of any old room; so you don't make a battle-field out of
any old piece of ground. There are places set apart for the purpose. But,
once again, this is not what I was telling you about; it was the type of
battle which one follows, in a sort of strategic tracing, a tactical imitation,
if you like. Battles like Ulm, Lodi, Leipzig, Cannae. I can't say whether
there is ever going to be another war, or what nations are going to fight in
it, but, if a war does come, you may be sure that it will include (and deliberately, on the commander's part) a Cannae, an Austerlitz, a Rosbach, a
Waterloo. Some of our people say quite openly that Marshal von Schieffer
and General Falkenhausen have prepared a Battle of Cannae against
France, in the Hannibal style, pinning their enemy down along his whole
front, and advancing on both flanks, especially through Belgium, while
Bernhardi prefers the oblique order of Frederick the Great, Lenthen rather
than Cannae. Others expound their views less crudely, but I can tell you
one thing, my boy, that Beauconseil, the squadron commander I introduced
you to the other day, who is an officer with a very great future before him,
has swotted up a little Pratzen attack of his own; he knows it inside out,
he is keeping it up his sleeve, and if he ever has an opportunity to put it
into practice he will make a clean job of it and let us have it on a big scale.
The break through in the centre at Rivoli, too; that's a thing that will crop
up if there's ever another war. It's no more obsolete than the *Iliad*. I must
add that we are practically condemned to make frontal attacks, because
we can't afford to repeat the mistake we made in Seventy; we must assume
the offensive, and nothing else. The only thing that troubles me is that if
I see only the slower, more antiquated minds among us opposing this
splendid doctrine, still, one of the youngest of my masters, who is a genius,
I mean Mangin, would like us to leave room, provisionally of course, for
the defensive. It is not very easy to answer him when he cites the example
of Austerlitz, where the defence was merely a prelude to attack and victory."

The enunciation of these theories by Saint-Loup made me happy. They
gave me to hope that perhaps I was not being led astray, in my life at
Doncières, with regard to these officers whom I used to hear being discussed
while I sat sipping a sauterne which bathed them in its charming golden
glint, by the same magnifying power which had swollen to such enormous

proportions in my eyes while I was at Balbec the King and Queen of the South Sea Island, the little group of the four epicures, the young gambler, Legrandin's brother-in-law, now shrunken so in my view as to appear non-existent. What gave me pleasure to-day would not, perhaps, leave me indifferent to-morrow, as had always happened hitherto; the creature that I still was at this moment was not, perhaps, doomed to immediate destruction, since to the ardent and fugitive passion which I had felt on these few evenings for everything connected with military life, Saint-Loup, by what he had just been saying to me, touching the art of war, added an intellectual foundation, of a permanent character, capable of attaching me to itself so strongly that I might, without any attempt to deceive myself, feel assured that after I had left Doncières I should continue to take an interest in the work of my friends there, and should not be long in coming to pay them another visit. At the same time, so as to make quite sure that this art of war was indeed an art in the true sense of the word:

"You interest me—I beg your pardon, *tu* interest me enormously," I said to Saint-Loup, "but tell me, there is one point that puzzles me. I feel that I could be keenly thrilled by the art of strategy, but if so I must first be sure that it is not so very different from the other arts, that knowing the rules is not everything. You tell me that plans of battles are copied. I do find something aesthetic, just as you said, in seeing beneath a modern battle the plan of an older one, I can't tell you how attractive it sounds. But then, does the genius of the commander count for nothing? Does he really do no more than apply the rules? Or, in point of science, are there great generals as there are great surgeons, who, when the symptoms exhibited by two states of ill-health are identical to the outward eye, nevertheless feel, for some infinitesimal reason, founded perhaps on their experience, but interpreted afresh, that in one case they ought to do one thing, in another case another; that in one case it is better to operate, in another to wait?"

"I should just say so! You will find Napoleon not attacking when all the rules ordered him to attack, but some obscure divination warned him not to. For instance, look at Austerlitz, or in 1806 take his instructions to Lannes. But you will find certain generals slavishly imitating one of Napoleon's movements and arriving at a diametrically opposite result. There are a dozen examples of that in 1870. But even for the interpretation of what the enemy *may* do, what he actually does is only a symptom which may mean any number of different things. Each of them has an equal chance of being the right thing, if one looks only to reasoning and science, just as in certain difficult cases all the medical science in the world will be powerless to decide whether the invisible tumour is malignant or not, whether or not the operation ought to be performed. It is his instinct, his divination—like Mme. de' Thèbes (you follow me?)—which decides, in the great general as in the great doctor. Thus I've been telling you, to take one instance, what might be meant by a reconnaissance on the eve of a battle. But it may mean a dozen other things also, such as to make the enemy think you are going to attack him at one point whereas you intend to attack him at another, to put out a screen which will prevent him from seeing the preparations for your real operation, to force him to bring up fresh troops, to hold them, to immobilise them in a different place from where they are needed, to form an estimate of the forces at his disposal, to feel him, to force him to shew his hand. Sometimes, indeed, the fact that you employ an immense number of troops in an operation is by no means a proof that that is your true objective; for you may be justified in carrying it out, even if it is only a feint, so that your feint may have a better chance of deceiving the enemy. If I had time now to go through the Napoleonic wars from this point of view, I assure you that these simple classic movements which we study here, and which you will come and see us practising in the field, just for the pleasure of a walk, you young rascal —no, I know you're not well, I apologise!—well, in a war, when you feel behind you the vigilance, the judgment, the profound study of the Higher Command, you are as much moved by them as by the simple lamps of a lighthouse, only a material combustion, but an emanation of the spirit, sweeping through space to warn ships of danger. I may have been wrong, perhaps, in speaking to you only of the literature of war. In reality, as the formation of the soil, the direction of wind and light tell us which way a tree will grow, so the conditions in which a campaign is fought, the features of the country through which you march, prescribe, to a certain extent, and limit the number of the plans among which the general has to choose. Which means that along a mountain range, through a system of valleys, over certain plains, it is almost with the inevitability and the tremendous beauty of an avalanche that you can forecast the line of an army on the march."

"Now you deny me that freedom of choice in the commander, that power of divination in the enemy who is trying to discover his plan, which you allowed me a moment ago."

"Not at all. You remember that book of philosophy we read together at Balbec, the richness of the world of possibilities compared with the real world. Very well. It is the same again with the art of strategy. In a given situation there will be four plans that offer themselves, one of which the general has to choose, as a disease may pass through various phases for which the doctor has to watch. And here again the weakness and greatness of the human elements are fresh causes of uncertainty. For of these four plans let us assume that contingent reasons (such as the attainment of minor objects, or time, which may be pressing, or the smallness of his effective strength and shortage of rations) lead the general to prefer the first, which is less perfect, but less costly also to carry out, is more rapid, and has for its terrain a richer country for feeding his troops. He may, after having begun with this plan, which the enemy, uncertain at first, will soon detect, find that success lies beyond his grasp, the difficulties being too great (that is what I call the element of human weakness), abandon it and try the second or third or fourth. But it may equally be that he has tried the first plan (and this is what I call human greatness) merely as a feint to pin down the enemy, so as to surprise him later at a point where he has not been expecting an attack. Thus at Ulm, Mack, who expected the enemy to advance from the west, was surrounded from the north where he thought he was perfectly safe. My example is not a very good one, as a matter of fact. And Ulm is a better type of enveloping battle, which the future will see reproduced, because it is not only a classic example from which generals will seek inspiration, but a form that is to some extent necessary (one of several necessities, which leaves room for choice, for variety) like a type of crystallisation. But it doesn't much matter, really, because these conditions are after all artificial. To go back to our philosophy book; it is like the rules of logic or scientific laws, reality does conform to it more or less, but bear in mind that the great mathematician Poincaré is by no means certain that mathematics are strictly accurate. As to the rules themselves, which I mentioned to you, they are of secondary importance really, and besides they are altered from time to time. We cavalrymen, for instance, have to go by the *Field Service* of 1895, which, you may say, is out of date since it is based on the old and obsolete doctrine which maintains that cavalry warfare has little more than a moral effect, in the panic that the charge creates in the enemy. Whereas the more intelligent of our teachers, all the best brains in the cavalry, and particularly the major I was telling you about, anticipate on the contrary that the decisive victory will be obtained by a real hand-to-hand encounter in which our weapons will be sabre and lance and the side that can hold out longer will win, not simply morally and by creating panic, but materially."

"Saint-Loup is quite right, and it is probable that the next *Field Service* will shew signs of this evolution," put in my other neighbour.

"I am not ungrateful for your support, for your opinions seem to make more impression upon my friend than mine," said Saint-Loup with a smile, whether because the growing attraction between his comrade and myself annoyed him slightly or because he thought it graceful to solemnise it with this official confirmation. "Perhaps I may have underestimated the importance of the rules; I don't know. They do change, that must be admitted. But in the meantime they control the military situation, the plans of campaign and concentration. If they reflect a false conception of strategy they may be the principal cause of defeat. All this is a little too technical for you," he remarked to me. "After all, you may say that what does most to accelerate the evolution of the art of war is wars themselves. In the course of a campaign, if it is at all long, you will see one belligerent profiting by the lessons furnished him by the successes and mistakes, perfecting the methods of the other, who will improve on him in turn. But all that is a thing of the past. With the terrible advance of artillery, the wars of the future, if there are to be any more wars, will be so short that, before we have had time to think of putting our lessons into practice, peace will have been signed."

"Don't be so touchy," I told Saint-Loup, reverting to the first words of this speech. "I was listening to you quite eagerly."

"If you will kindly not fly into a passion, and will allow me to speak," his friend went on, "I shall add to what you have just been saying that if battles copy and coincide with one another it is not merely due to the mind of the commander. It may happen that a mistake on his part (for instance, his failure to appreciate the strength of the enemy) will lead him to call upon his men for extravagant sacrifices, sacrifices which certain units will make with an abnegation so sublime that their part in the battle will be analogous to that played by some other unit in some other battle, and these will be quoted in history as interchangeable examples: to stick to 1870, we have the Prussian Guard at Saint-Privat, and the Turcos at Frœschviller and Wissembourg."

"Ah! Interchangeable; very neat! Excellent! The lad has brains," was Saint-Loup's comment.

I was not unmoved by these last examples, as always when, beneath the particular instance, I was afforded a glimpse of the general law. Still, the genius of the commander, that was what interested me, I was anxious to discover in what it consisted, what steps, in given circumstances, when the commander who lacked genius could not withstand the enemy, the inspired leader would take to re-establish his jeopardised position, which, according to Saint-Loup, was quite possible and had been done by Napoleon more than once. And to understand what military worth meant I asked for comparisons between the various generals whom I knew by name, which of them had most markedly the character of a leader, the gifts of a tactician; at the risk of boring my new friends, who however shewed no signs of boredom, but continued to answer me with an inexhaustible good nature.

I felt myself isolated, not only from the great, freezing night which extended far around us and in which we heard from time to time the whistle of a train which only rendered more keen the pleasure of being where we were, or the chime of an hour which, happily, was still a long way short of that at which these young men would have to buckle on their sabres and go, but also from all my external obsessions, almost from the memory of Mme. de Guermantes, by the hospitality of Saint-Loup, to which that of his friends, reinforcing it, gave, so to speak, a greater solidity; by the warmth also of this little dining-room, by the savour of the well-chosen dishes that were set before us. They gave as much pleasure to my imagination as to my appetite; sometimes the little piece of still life from which they had been taken, the rugged holy water stoup of the oyster in which lingered a few drops of brackish water, or the knotted stem, the yellow leaves of a bunch of grapes still enveloped them, inedible, poetic and remote as a landscape, and producing, at different points in the course of the meal, the impressions of rest in the shade of a vine and of an excursion out to sea; on other evenings it was the cook alone who threw into relief these original properties of our food, which he presented in its natural setting, like a work of art; and a fish cooked in wine was brought in on a long earthenware dish, on which, as it stood out in relief on a bed of bluish herbs, unbreakable now but still contorted from having been dropped alive into boiling water, surrounded by a circle of satellite creatures in their shells, crabs, shrimps and mussels, it had the appearance of being part of a ceramic design by Bernard Palissy.

"I am jealous, furious," Saint-Loup attacked me, half smiling, half in earnest, alluding to the interminable conversations aside which I had been having with his friend. "Is it because you find him more intelligent than me; do you like him better than me? Well, I suppose he's everything now, and no one else is to have a look in!" Men who are enormously in love with a woman, who live in the society of woman-lovers, allow themselves pleasantries on which others, who would see less innocence in them, would never venture.

When the conversation became general, they avoided any reference to Dreyfus for fear of offending Saint-Loup. The following week, however, two of his friends were remarking what a curious thing it was that, living in so military an atmosphere, he was so keen a Dreyfusard, almost an anti-militarist. "The reason is," I suggested, not wishing to enter into details, "that the influence of environment is not so important as people think . . ." I intended of course to stop at this point, and not to reiterate the observations which I had made to Saint-Loup a few days earlier. Since, however, I had repeated these words almost textually, I proceeded to excuse myself by adding: "As, in fact, I was saying the other day . . ." But I had reckoned without the reverse side of Robert's polite admiration of myself and certain other persons. That admiration reached its fulfilment in so entire an assimilation of their ideas that, in the course of a day or two, he would have completely forgotten that those ideas were not his own. And so, in the matter of my modest theory, Saint-Loup, for all the world as though it had always dwelt in his own brain, and as though I were merely poaching on his preserves, felt it incumbent upon him to greet my discovery with warm approval.

"Why, yes; environment is of no importance."

And with as much vehemence as if he were afraid of my interrupting, or failing to understand him:

"The real influence is that of one's intellectual environment! One is the man of one's idea!"

He stopped for a moment, with the satisfied smile of one who has digested his dinner, dropped his eyeglass and, fixing me with a gimlet-like stare:

"All men with similar ideas are alike," he informed me, with a challenging air. Probably he had completely forgotten that I myself had said to him, only a few days earlier, what on the other hand he remembered so well.

I did not arrive at Saint-Loup's restaurant every evening in the same state of mind. If a memory, a sorrow that weigh on us are able to leave us so effectively that we are no longer aware of them, they can also return and sometimes remain with us for a long time. There were evenings when, as I passed through the town on my way to the restaurant, I felt so keen a longing for Mme. de Guermantes that I could scarcely breathe; you might have said that part of my breast had been cut open by a skilled anatomist, taken out, and replaced by an equal part of immaterial suffering, by an equivalent load of longing and love. And however neatly the wound may have been stitched together, there is not much comfort in life when regret for the loss of another person is substituted for one's entrails, it seems to be occupying more room than they, one feels it perpetually, and besides, what a contradiction in terms to be obliged to *think* a part of one's body. Only it seems that we are worth more, somehow. At the whisper of a breeze we sigh, from oppression, but from weariness also. I would look up at the sky. If it were clear, I would say to myself: "Perhaps she is in the country; she is looking at the same stars; and, for all I know, when I arrive at the restaurant Robert may say to me: 'Good news! I have just heard from my aunt; she wants to meet you; she is coming down here.' " It was not in the firmament alone that I enshrined the thought of Mme. de Guermantes. A passing breath of air, more fragrant than the rest, seemed to bring me a message from her, as, long ago, from Gilberte in the cornfields of Méséglise. We do not change; we introduce into the feeling with which we regard a person many slumbering elements which that feeling revives but which are foreign to it. Besides, with these feelings for particular people, there is always something in us that is trying to bring them nearer to the truth, that is to say, to absorb them in a more general feeling, common to the whole of humanity, with which people and the suffering that they cause us are merely a means to enable us to communicate. What brought a certain pleasure into my grief was that I knew it to be a tiny fragment of the universal love. Simply because I thought that I recognised sorrows which I had felt on Gilberte's account, or else when in the evenings at Combray Mamma would not stay in any room, and also the memory of certain pages of Bergotte, in the agony I now felt, to which Mme. de Guermantes, her coldness, her absence, were not clearly linked, as cause is to effect in the mind of a philosopher, I did not conclude that Mme. de Guermantes was not the cause of that agony. Is there not such a thing as a diffused bodily pain, extending, radiating out into other parts, which, however, it leaves, to vanish altogether, if the practitioner lays his finger on the precise spot from which it springs? And yet, until that moment, its extension gave it for us so vague, so fatal a semblance that, powerless to explain or even to locate it, we imagined that there was no possibility of its being healed. As I made my way to the restaurant I said to myself: "A fortnight already since I last saw Mme. de Guermantes." A fortnight which did not appear so enormous an interval save to me, who, when Mme. de Guermantes was concerned, reckoned time by minutes. For me it was no longer the stars and the breeze merely, but the arithmetical divisions of time that assumed a dolorous and poetic aspect. Each day now was like the loose crest of a crumbling mountain, down one side of which I felt that I could descend into oblivion, but down the other was borne by the necessity of seeing the Duchess again. And I was continually inclining one way or the other, having no stable equilibrium. One day I said to myself: "Perhaps there will be a letter to-night;" and on entering the dining-room I found courage to ask Saint-Loup:

"You don't happen to have had any news from Paris?"

"Yes," he replied gloomily; "bad news."

I breathed a sigh of relief when I realised that it was only he who was unhappy, and that the news came from his mistress. But I soon saw that one of its consequences would be to prevent Robert, for ever so long, from taking me to see his aunt.

I learned that a quarrel had broken out between him and his mistress, through the post presumably, unless she had come down to pay him a flying visit between trains. And the quarrels, even when relatively slight, which they had previously had, had always seemed as though they must prove insoluble. For she was a girl of violent temper, who would stamp her foot and burst into tears for reasons as incomprehensible as those that make children shut themselves into dark cupboards, not come out for dinner, refuse to give any explanation, and only redouble their sobs when, our patience exhausted, we visit them with a whipping. To say that Saint-Loup suffered terribly from this estrangement would be an understatement of the truth, which would give the reader a false impression of his grief. When he found himself alone, the only picture in his mind being that of his mistress parting from him with the respect which she had felt for him at the sight of his energy, the anxieties which he had had at first gave way before the irreparable, and the cessation of an anxiety is so pleasant a thing that the rupture, once it was certain, assumed for him something of the same kind of charm as a reconciliation. What he began to suffer from, a little later, was a secondary and accidental grief, the tide of which flowed incessantly from his own heart, at the idea that perhaps she would be glad to make it up, that it was not inconceivable that she was waiting for a word from him, that in the mean time, to be avenged on him, she would perhaps on a certain evening, in a certain place, do a certain thing, and that he had only to telegraph to her that he was coming for it not to happen, that others perhaps were taking advantage of the time which he was letting slip, and that in a few days it would be too late to recapture her, for she would be already bespoke. Among all these possibilities he was certain of nothing; his mistress preserved a silence which wrought him up to such a frenzy of grief that he began to ask himself whether she might not be in hiding at Doncières, or have sailed for the Indies.

It has been said that silence is a force; in another and widely different sense it is a tremendous force in the hands of those who are loved. It increases the anxiety of the lover who has to wait. Nothing so tempts us to approach another person as what is keeping us apart; and what barrier is there so insurmountable as silence? It has been said also that silence is a torture, capable of goading to madness him who is condemned to it in a prison cell. But what a torture—keener than that of having to keep silence —to have to endure the silence of the person one loves! Robert asked himself: "What can she be doing, never to send me a single word, like this? She hates me, perhaps, and will always go on hating me." And he reproached himself. Thus her silence did indeed drive him mad with jealousy and remorse. Besides, more cruel than the silence of prisons, that kind of silence is in itself a prison. An immaterial enclosure, I admit, but impenetrable, this interposed slice of empty atmosphere through which, despite its emptiness, the visual rays of the abandoned lover cannot pass. Is there a more terrible illumination than that of silence which shews us not one absent love but a thousand, and shews us each of them in the act of indulging in some fresh betrayal? Sometimes, in an abrupt relaxation of his strain, Robert would imagine that this period of silence was just coming to an end, that the long expected letter was on its way. He saw it, it arrived, he started at every sound, his thirst was already quenched, he murmured: "The letter! The letter!" After this glimpse of a phantom oasis of affection, he found himself once more toiling across the real desert of a silence without end.

He suffered in anticipation, without a single omission, all the griefs and pains of a rupture which at other moments he fancied he might somehow contrive to avoid, like people who put all their affairs in order with a view to a migration abroad which they never make, whose minds, no longer certain where they will find themselves living next 'day, flutter helplessly for the time being, detached from them, like a heart that is taken out of a dying man and continues to beat, though disjoined from the rest of his body. Anyhow, this hope that his mistress would return gave him courage to persevere in the rupture, as the belief that one will return alive from the battle helps one to face death. And inasmuch as habit is, of all the plants of human growth, the one that has least need of nutritious soil in order to live, and is the first to appear upon what is apparently the most barren rock, perhaps had he begun by effecting their rupture as a feint he would in the end have grown genuinely accustomed to it. But his uncertainty kept him in a state of emotion which, linked with the memory of the woman herself, was akin to love. He forced himself, nevertheless, not to write to her, thinking perhaps that it was a less cruel torment to live without his mistress than with her in certain conditions, or else that, after the way in which they had parted, it was necessary to wait for excuses from her, if she was to keep what he believed her to feel for him in the way, if not of love, at any rate of esteem and regard. He contented himself with going to the telephone, which had recently been installed at Doncières, and asking for news from, or giving instructions to a lady's maid whom he had procured and placed with his friend. These communications were, as it turned out, complicated and took up much of his time, since, influenced by what her literary friends preached to her about the ugliness of the capital, but principally for the sake of her animals, her dogs, her monkey, her canaries and her parrokeet, whose incessant din her Paris landlord had declined to tolerate for another moment, Robert's mistress had now taken a little house in the neighbourhood of Versailles. Meanwhile he, down at Doncières, no longer slept a wink all night. Once, in my room, overcome by exhaustion, he dozed off for a little. But suddenly he began to talk, tried to get up and run, to stop something from happening, said: "I hear her; you shan't . . . you shan't. . . ." He awoke. He had been dreaming, he explained to me, that he was in the country with the serjeant-major. His host had tried to keep him away from a certain part of the house. Saint-Loup had discovered that the serjeant-major had staying with him a subaltern, extremely rich and extremely vicious, whom he knew to have a violent passion for his mistress. And suddenly in his dream he had distinctly heard the spasmodic, regular cries which his mistress was in the habit of uttering at the moment of gratification. He had tried to force the serjeant-major to take him to the room in which she was. And the other had held him back, to keep him from going there, with an air of annoyance at such a want of discretion in a guest which, Robert said, he would never be able to forget.

"It was an idiotic dream," he concluded, still quite breathless.

All the same I could see that, during the hour that followed, he was more than once on the point of telephoning to his mistress to beg for a reconciliation. My father had now had the telephone for some time at home, but I doubt whether that would have been of much use to Saint-Loup. Besides, it hardly seemed to me quite proper to make my parents, or even a mechanical instrument installed in their house, play pander between Saint-Loup and his mistress, ladylike and high-minded as the latter might be. His bad dream began to fade from his memory. With a fixed and absent stare, he came to see me on each of those cruel days which traced in my mind as they followed one after the other the splendid sweep of a staircase forged in hard metal on which Robert stood asking himself what decision his friend was going to take.

At length she wrote to ask whether he would consent to forgive her. As soon as he realised that a definite rupture had been avoided he saw all the disadvantages of a reconciliation. Besides, he had already begun to suffer less acutely, and had almost accepted a grief the sharp tooth of which he would have, in a few months perhaps, to feel again if their intimacy were to be resumed. He did not hesitate for long. And perhaps he hesitated only because he was now certain of being able to recapture his mistress, of being able to do it and therefore of doing it. Only she asked him, so that she might have time to recover her equanimity, not to come to Paris at the New Year. Now he had not the heart to go to Paris without seeing her. On the other hand, she had declared her willingness to go abroad with him, but for that he would need to make a formal application for leave, which Captain de Borodino was unwilling to grant.

"I'm sorry about it, because of your meeting with my aunt, which will have to be put off. I dare say I shall be in Paris at Easter."

"We shan't be able to call on Mme. de Guermantes then, because I shall have gone to Balbec. But, really, it doesn't matter in the least, I assure you."

"To Balbec? But you didn't go there till August."

"I know; but next year they're making me go there earlier, for my health."

All that he feared was that I might form a bad impression of his mistress, after what he had told me. "She is violent simply because she is too frank, too thorough in her feelings. But she is a sublime creature. You can't imagine what exquisite poetry there is in her. She goes every year to spend all Souls' Day at Bruges. 'Nice' of her, don't you think? If you ever do meet her you'll see what I mean; she has a greatness. . . ." And, as he was infected with certain of the mannerisms used in the literary circles in which the lady moved: "There is something sidereal about her, in fact something bardic; you know what I mean, the poet merging into the priest."

I was searching all through dinner for a pretext which would enable Saint-Loup to ask his aunt to see me without my having to wait until he came to Paris. Now such a pretext was furnished by the desire that I had to see some more pictures by Elstir, the famous painter whom Saint-Loup and I had met at Balbec. A pretext behind which there was, moreover, an element of truth, for if, on my visits to Elstir, what I had asked of his painting had been that it should lead me to the comprehension and love of things better than itself, a real thaw, an authentic square in a country town, live women on a beach (all the more would I have commissioned from it the portraits of the realities which I had not been able to fathom, such as a lane of hawthorn-blossoms, not so much that it might perpetuate their beauty for me as that it might reveal that beauty to me), now, on the other hand, it was the originality, the seductive attraction of those paintings that aroused my desire, and what I wanted above anything else was to look at other pictures by Elstir.

It seemed to me, also, that the least of his pictures were something quite different from the masterpieces even of greater painters than himself. His work was like a realm apart, whose frontiers were not to be passed, matchless in substance. Eagerly collecting the infrequent periodicals in which articles on him and his work had appeared, I had learned that it was only recently that he had begun to paint landscapes and still life, and that he had started with mythological subjects (I had seen photographs of two of these in his studio), and had then been for long under the influence of Japanese art.

Several of the works most characteristic of his various manners were scattered about the provinces. A certain house at les Andelys, in which there was one of his finest landscapes, seemed to me as precious, gave me as keen a desire to go there and see it as did a village in the Chartres district, among whose millstone walls was enshrined a glorious painted window; and towards the possessor of this treasure, towards the man who, inside his ugly house, on the main street, closeted like an astrologer, sat questioning one of those mirrors of the world which Elstir's pictures were, and who had perhaps bought it for many thousands of francs, I felt myself borne by that instinctive sympathy which joins the very hearts, the inmost natures of those who think alike upon a vital subject. Now three important works by my favourite painter were described in one of these articles as belonging to Mme. de Guermantes. So that it was, after all, quite sincerely that, on the evening on which Saint-Loup told me of his lady's projected visit to Bruges, I was able, during dinner, in front of his friends, to let fall, as though on the spur of the moment:

"Listen, if you don't mind. Just one last word on the subject of the lady we were speaking about. You remember Elstir, the painter I met at Balbec?"

"Why, of course I do."

"You remember how much I admired his work?"

"I do, quite well; and the letter we sent him."

"Very well, one of the reasons—not one of the chief reasons, a subordinate reason—why I should like to meet the said lady—you do know who' I mean, don't you?"

"Of course I do. How involved you're getting."

"Is that she has in her house one very fine picture, at least, by Elstir."

"I say, I never knew that."

"Elstir will probably be at Balbec at Easter; you know he stays down there now all the year round, practically. I should very much like to have seen this picture before I leave Paris. I don't know whether you're on sufficiently intimate terms with your aunt: but couldn't you manage, somehow, to give her so good an impression of me that she won't refuse, and then ask her if she'll let me come and see the picture without you, since you won't be there?"

"That's all right. I'll answer for her; I'll make a special point of it."

"Oh, Robert, you are an angel; I do love you."

"It's very nice of you to love me, but it would be equally nice if you were to call me *tu*, as you promised, and as you began to do."

"I hope it's not your departure that you two are plotting together," one of Robert's friends said to me. "You know, if Saint-Loup does go on leave, it needn't make any difference, we shall still be here. It will be less amusing for you, perhaps, but we'll do all we can to make you forget his absence." As a matter of fact, just as we had decided that Robert's mistress would have to go to Bruges by herself, the news came that Captain de Borodino, obdurate hitherto in his refusal, had given authority for Serjeant Saint-Loup to proceed on long leave to Bruges. What had happened was this. The Prince, extremely proud of his luxuriant head of hair, was an assiduous customer of the principal hairdresser in the town, who had started life as a boy under Napoleon III's barber. Captain de Borodino was on the best of terms with the hairdresser, being, in spite of his air of majesty, quite simple in his dealings with his inferiors. But the hairdresser, through whose books the Prince's account had been running without payment for at least five years, swollen no less by bottles of Portugal and Eau des Souverains, irons, razors, and strops, than by the ordinary charges for shampooing, haircutting and the like, had a greater respect for Saint-Loup, who always paid on the nail and kept several carriages and saddle-horses. Having learned of Saint-Loup's vexation at not being able to go with his mistress, he had spoken strongly about it to the Prince at a moment when he was trussed up in a white surplice with his head held firmly over the back of the chair and his throat menaced by a razor. This narrative of a young man's gallant adventures won from the princely captain a smile of Bonapartish indulgence. It is hardly probable that he thought of his unpaid bill, but the barber's recommendation tended to put him in as good a humour as one from a duke would have put him in a bad. While his chin was still smothered in soap, the leave was promised, and the warrant was signed that evening. As for the hairdresser, who was in the habit of boasting all day long of his own exploits, and in order to do so claimed for himself, shewing an astonishing faculty for lying, distinctions that were pure fabrications, having for once rendered this signal service to Saint-Loup, not only did he refrain from publishing it broadcast, but, as if vanity were obliged to lie, and when there was no scope for lying gave place to modesty, he never mentioned the matter to Robert again.

All his friends assured me that, as long as I stayed at Doncières, or if I should come there again at any time, even although Robert were away, their horses, their quarters, their time would be at my disposal, and I felt that it was with the greatest cordiality that these young men put their comfort and youth and strength at the service of my weakness.

"Why on earth," they went on, after insisting that I should stay, "don't you come down here every year; you see how our quiet life appeals to you! Besides you're so keen about everything that goes on in the regiment; quite the old soldier."

For I continued my eager demands that they would classify the different officers whose names I knew according to the degree of admiration which they seemed to deserve, just as, in my schooldays, I used to make the other boys classify the actors of the Théâtre-Français. If, in the place of one of the generals whom I had always heard mentioned at the head of the list, such as Galliffet or Négrier, one of Saint-Loup's friends, with a contemptuous: "But Négrier is one of the feeblest of our general officers," put the new, intact, appetising name of Pau or Geslin de Bourgogne, I felt the same joyful surprise as long ago when the outworn name of Thiron or Febvre was sent flying by the sudden explosion of the unfamiliar name of Amaury. "Better even than Négrier? But in what respect; give me an example?" I should have liked there to exist profound differences even among the junior officers of the regiment, and I hoped in the reason for these differences to seize the essential quality of what constituted military superiority. The one whom I should have been most interested to hear discussed, because he was the one whom I had most often seen, was the Prince de Borodino. But neither Saint-Loup nor his friends, if they did justice to the fine officer who kept his squadron up to the supreme pitch of efficiency, liked the man. Without speaking of him, naturally, in the same tone as of certain other officers, rankers and freemasons, who did not associate much with the rest and had, in comparison, an uncouth, barrack-room manner, they seemed not to include M. de Borodino among the officers of noble birth, from whom, it must be admitted, he differed considerably in his attitude even towards Saint-Loup. The others, taking advantage of the fact that Robert was only an N.C.O., and that therefore his influential relatives might be grateful were he invited to the houses of superior officers on whom ordinarily they would have looked down, lost no opportunity of having him to dine when any bigwig was expected who might be of use to a young cavalry serjeant. Captain de Borodino alone confined himself to his official relations (which, for that matter, were always excellent) with Robert. The fact was that the Prince, whose grandfather had been made a Marshal and a Prince-Duke by the Emperor, with whose family he had subsequently allied himself by marriage, while his father had married a cousin of Napoleon III and had twice been a Minister after the Coup d'Etat, felt that in spite of all this he did not count for much with Saint-Loup and the Guermantes connexion, who in turn, since he did not look at things from the same point of view as they, counted for very little with him. He suspected that, for Saint-Loup, he himself was— he, a kinsman of the Hohenzollern—not a true noble but the grandson of a farmer, but at the same time he regarded Saint-Loup as the son of a man whose Countship had been confirmed by the Emperor—one of what were known in the Faubourg Saint-Germain as 'touched-up' Counts—and who had besought him first for a Prefecture, then for some other post a long way down the list of subordinates to His Highness the Prince de Borodino,

Minister of State, who was styled on his letters 'Monseigneur' and was a nephew of the Sovereign.

Something more than a nephew, possibly. The first Princesse de Borodino was reputed to have bestowed her favours on Napoleon I, whom she followed to the Isle of Elba, and the second hers on Napoleon III. And if, in the Captain's placid countenance, one caught a trace of Napoleon I— if not in his natural features, at least in the studied majesty of the mask— the officer had, particularly in his melancholy and kindly gaze, in his drooping moustache, something that reminded one also of Napoleon III; and this in so striking a fashion that, having asked leave, after Sedan, to join the Emperor in captivity, and having been sent away by Bismarck, before whom he had been brought, the latter, happening to look up at the young man who was preparing to leave the room, was at once impressed by the likeness and, reconsidering his decision, recalled him and gave him the authorisation which he, in common with every one else, had just been refused.

If the Prince de Borodino was not prepared to make overtures to Saint-Loup nor to the other representatives of Faubourg Saint-Germain society that there were in the regiment (while he frequently invited two subalterns of plebeian origin who were pleasant companions) it was because, looking down upon them all from the height of his Imperial grandeur, he drew between these two classes of inferiors the distinction that one set consisted of inferiors who knew themselves to be such and with whom he was delighted to spend his time, being beneath his outward majesty of a simple, jovial humour, and the other of inferiors who thought themselves his superiors, a claim which he could not allow. And so, while all the other officers of the regiment made much of Saint-Loup, the Prince de Borodino, to whose care the young man had been recommended by Marshal X——, confined himself to being obliging with regard to the military duties which Saint-Loup always performed in the most exemplary fashion, but never had him to his house except on one special occasion when he found himself practically compelled to invite him, and when, as this occurred during my stay at Doncières, he asked him to bring me to dinner also. I had no difficulty that evening, as I watched Saint-Loup sitting at his Captain's table, in distinguishing, in their respective manners and refinements, the difference that existed between the two aristocracies: the old nobility and that of the Empire. The offspring of a caste the faults of which, even if he repudiated them with all the force of his intellect, had been absorbed into his blood, a caste which, having ceased to exert any real authority for at least a century, saw nothing more now in the protective affability which formed part of its regular course of education, than an exercise, like horsemanship or fencing, cultivated without any serious purpose, as a sport; on meeting representatives of that middle class on which the old nobility so far looked down as to believe that they were flattered by its intimacy and would be honoured by the informality of its tone, Saint-Loup would take the hand of no matter who might be introduced to him, though he had failed perhaps to catch the stranger's name, in a friendly grip, and as he talked to him (crossing and uncrossing his legs all the time, flinging himself back in his chair in an attitude of absolute unconstraint, one foot in the palm of his hand) call him 'my dear fellow.' Belonging on the other hand to a nobility whose titles still preserved their original meaning, provided that their holders still possessed the splendid emoluments given in reward for glorious services and bringing to mind the record of high offices in which one is in command of numberless men and must know how to deal with men, the Prince de Borodino—not perhaps very distinctly or with any clear personal sense of superiority, but at any rate in his body, which revealed it by its attitudes and behaviour generally—regarded his own rank as a prerogative that was still effective; those same commoners whom Saint-Loup would have slapped on the shoulder and taken by the arm he addressed with a majestic affability, in which a reserve instinct with grandeur tempered the smiling good-fellowship that came naturally to him, in a tone marked at once by a genuine kindliness and a stiffness deliberately assumed. This was due, no doubt, to his being not so far removed from the great Embassies, and the Court itself, at which his father had held the highest posts, whereas the manners of Saint-Loup, the elbow on the table, the foot in the hand, would not have been well received there; but principally it was due to the fact that he looked down less upon the middle classes because they were the inexhaustible source from which the first Emperor had chosen his marshals and his nobles and in which the second had found a Rouher and a Fould.

Son, doubtless, or grandson of an Emperor, who had nothing more important to do than to command a squadron, the preoccupations of his putative father and grandfather could not, for want of an object on which to fasten themselves, survive in any real sense in the mind of M. de Borodino. But as the spirit of an artist continues to model, for many years after he is dead, the statue which he carved, so they had taken shape in him, were materialised, incarnate in him, it was they that his face reflected. It was with, in his voice, the vivacity of the first Emperor that he worded a reprimand to a corporal, with the dreamy melancholy of the second that he puffed out the smoke of a cigarette. When he passed in plain clothes through the streets of Doncières, a certain sparkle in his eyes escaping from under the brim of the bowler hat sent radiating round this captain of cavalry a regal incognito; people trembled when he strode into the serjeant-major's office, followed by the adjutant and the quartermaster, as though by Berthier and Masséna. When he chose the cloth for his squadron's breeches, he fastened on the master-tailor a gaze capable of baffling Talleyrand and deceiving Alexander; and at times, in the middle of an inspection, he would stop, let his handsome blue eyes cloud with dreams, twist his moustache, with the air of one building up a new Prussia and a new Italy. But a moment later, reverting from Napoleon III to Napoleon I, he would point out that the equipment was not properly polished, and would insist on tasting the men's rations. And at home, in his private life, it was for the wives of middle class officers (provided that their husbands were not freemasons) that he would bring out not only a dinner service of royal blue Sèvres, fit for an Ambassador (which had been given to his father by Napoleon, and appeared even more priceless in the commonplace house on a provincial street in which he was living, like those rare porcelains which tourists admire with a special delight in the rustic china-cupboard of some old manor that has been converted into a comfortable and prosperous farmhouse), but other gifts of the Emperor also: those noble and charming manners, which too would have won admiration in some diplomatic post abroad, if, for some men, it did not mean a lifelong condemnation to the most unjust form of ostracism, merely to be well born; his easy gestures, his kindness, his grace, and, embedding beneath an enamel that was of royal blue, also glorious images, the mysterious, illuminated, living reliquary of his gaze. And, in treating of the social relations with the middle classes which the Prince had at Doncières, it may be as well to add these few words. The lieutenant-colonel played the piano beautifully; the senior medical officer's wife sang like a Conservatoire medallist. This latter couple, as well as the lieutenant-colonel and his wife, used to dine every week with M. de Borodino. They were flattered, unquestionably, knowing that when the Prince went to Paris on leave he dined with Mme. de Pourtalès, and the Murats, and people like that. "But," they said to themselves, "he's just a captain, after all; he's only too glad to get us to come. Still, he's a real friend, you know." But when M. de Borodino, who had long been pulling every possible wire to secure an appointment for himself nearer Paris, was posted to Beauvais, he packed up and went, and forgot as completely the two musical couples as he forgot the Doncières theatre and the little restaurant to which he used often to send out for his luncheon, and, to their great indignation, neither the lieutenant-colonel nor the senior medical officer, who had so often sat at his table, ever had so much as a single word from him for the rest of their lives.

One morning, Saint-Loup confessed to me that he had written to my grandmother to give her news of me, with the suggestion that, since there was telephonic connexion between Paris and Doncières, she might make use of it to speak to me. In short, that very day she was to give me a call, and he advised me to be at the post office at about a quarter to four. The telephone was not yet at that date as commonly in use as it is to-day. And yet habit requires so short a time to divest of their mystery the sacred forces with which we are in contact, that, not having had my call at once, the only thought in my mind was that it was very slow, and badly managed, and I almost decided to lodge a complaint. Like all of us nowadays I found not rapid enough for my liking in its abrupt changes the admirable sorcery for which a few moments are enough to bring before us, invisible but present, the person to whom we have been wishing to speak, and who, while still sitting at his table, in the town in which he lives (in my grandmother's case, Paris), under another sky than ours, in weather that is not necessarily the same, in the midst of circumstances and worries of which we know nothing, but of which he is going to inform us, finds himself suddenly transported hundreds of miles (he and all the surroundings in which he remains immured) within reach of our ear, at the precise moment which our fancy has ordained. And we are like the person in the fairy-tale to whom a sorceress, on his uttering the wish, makes appear with supernatural clearness his grandmother or his betrothed in the act of turning over a book, of shedding tears, of gathering flowers, quite close to the spectator and yet ever so remote, in the place in which she actually is at the moment. We need only, so that the miracle may be accomplished, apply our lips to the magic orifice and invoke—occasionally for rather longer than seems to us necessary, I admit—the Vigilant Virgins to whose voices we listen every day without ever coming to know their faces, and who are our Guardian Angels in the dizzy realm of darkness whose portals they so jealously keep; the All Powerful by whose intervention the absent rise up at our side, without our being permitted to set eyes on them; the Danaids of the Unseen who without ceasing empty, fill, transmit the urns of sound; the ironic Furies who, just as we were murmuring a confidence to a friend, in the hope that no one was listening, cry brutally: "I hear you!"; the ever infuriated servants of the Mystery, the umbrageous priestesses of the Invisible, the Young Ladies of the Telephone.

And, the moment our call has sounded, in the night filled with phantoms to which our ears alone are unsealed, a tiny sound, an abstract sound— the sound of distance overcome—and the voice of the dear one speaks to us.

It is she, it is her voice that is speaking, that is there. But how remote it is! How often have I been unable to listen without anguish, as though, confronted by the impossibility of seeing, except after long hours of journeying, her whose voice has been so close to my ear, I felt more clearly the sham and illusion of meetings apparently most pleasant, and at what a distance we may be from the people we love at the moment when it seems that we have only to stretch out our hand to seize and hold them. A real presence indeed that voice so near—in actual separation. But a premonition also of an eternal separation! Over and again, as I listened in this way, without seeing her who spoke to me from so far away, it has seemed to me that the voice was crying to me from depths out of which one does not rise again, and I have known the anxiety that was one day to wring my heart when a voice should thus return (alone, and attached no longer to a body which I was never more to see), to murmur, in my ear, words I would fain have kissed as they issued from lips for ever turned to dust.

This afternoon, alas, at Doncières, the miracle did not occur. When I reached the post office, my grandmother's call had already been received; I stepped into the box; the line was engaged; some one was talking who probably did not realise that there was nobody to answer him, for when I raised the receiver to my ear, the lifeless block began squeaking like Punchinello; I silenced it, as one silences a puppet, by putting it back on its hook, but, like Punchinello, as soon as I took it again in my hand, it resumed its gabbling. At length, giving it up as hopeless, by hanging up the receiver once and for all, I stifled the convulsions of this vociferous stump which kept up its chatter until the last moment, and went in search of the operator, who told me to wait a little; then I spoke, and, after a few seconds of silence, suddenly I heard that voice which I supposed myself, mistakenly, to know so well; for always until then, every time that my grandmother had talked to me, I had been accustomed to follow what she was saying on the open score of her face, in which the eyes figured so largely; but her voice itself I was hearing this afternoon for the first time. And because that voice appeared to me to have altered in its proportions from the moment that it was a whole, and reached me in this way alone and without the accompaniment of her face and features, I discovered for the first time how sweet that voice was; perhaps, too, it had never been so sweet, for my grandmother, knowing me to be alone and unhappy, felt that she might let herself go in the outpouring of an affection which, on her principle of education, she usually restrained and kept hidden. It was sweet, but also how sad it was, first of all on account of its very sweetness, a sweetness drained almost—more than any but a few human voices can ever have been—of every element of resistance to others, of all selfishness; fragile by reason of its delicacy it seemed at every moment ready to break, to expire in a pure flow of tears; then, too, having it alone beside me, seen, without the mask of her face, I noticed for the first time the sorrows that had scarred it in the course of a lifetime.

Was it, however, solely the voice that, because it was alone, gave me this new impression which tore my heart? Not at all; it was rather that this isolation of the voice was like a symbol, a presentation, a direct consequence of another isolation, that of my grandmother, separated, for the first time in my life, from myself. The orders or prohibitions which she addressed to me at every moment in the ordinary course of my life, the tedium of obedience or the fire of rebellion which neutralised the affection that I felt for her were at this moment eliminated, and indeed might be eliminated for ever (since my grandmother no longer insisted on having me with her under her control, was in the act of expressing her hope that I would stay at Doncières altogether, or would at any rate extend my visit for as long as possible, seeing that both my health and my work seemed likely to benefit by the change); also, what I held compressed in this little bell that was ringing in my ear was, freed from the conflicting pressures which had, every day hitherto, given it a counterpoise, and from this moment irresistible, carrying me altogether away, our mutual affection. My grandmother, by telling me to stay, filled me with an anxious, an insensate longing to return. This freedom of action which for the future she allowed me and to which I had never dreamed that she would consent, appeared to me suddenly as sad as might be my freedom of action after her death (when I should still love her and she would for ever have abandoned me). "Granny!" I cried to her, "Granny!" and would fain have kissed her, but I had beside me only that voice, a phantom, as impalpable as that which would come perhaps to revisit me when my grandmother was dead. "Speak to me!" but then it happened that, left more solitary still, I ceased to catch the sound of her voice. My grandmother could no longer hear me; she was no longer in communication with me; we had ceased to stand face to face, to be audible to one another; I continued to call her, sounding the empty night, in which I felt that her appeals also must be straying. I was shaken by the same anguish which, in the distant past, I had felt once before, one day when, a little child, in a crowd, I had lost her, an anguish due less to my not finding her than to the thought that she must be searching for me, must be saying to herself that I was searching for her; an anguish comparable to that which I was to feel on the day when we speak to those who can no longer reply and whom we would so love to have hear all the things that we have not told them, and our assurance that we are not unhappy. It seemed as though it were already a beloved ghost that I had allowed to lose herself in the ghostly world, and, standing alone before the instrument, I went on vainly repeating: "Granny! Granny!" as Orpheus, left alone, repeats the name of his dead wife. I decided to leave the post office, to go and find Robert at his restaurant, in order to tell him that, as I was half expecting a telegram which would oblige me to return to Paris, I wished at all costs to find out at what times the trains left. And yet, before reaching this decision, I felt I must make one attempt more to invoke the Daughters of the Night, the Messengers of the Word, the Deities without form or feature; but the capricious Guardians had not deigned once again to unclose the miraculous portals, or more probably, had not been able; in vain might they untiringly appeal, as was their custom, to the venerable inventor of printing and the young prince, collector of impressionist paintings and driver of motor-cars (who was Captain de Borodino's nephew); Gutenberg and Wagram left their supplications unanswered, and I came away, feeling that the Invisible would continue to turn a deaf ear.

When I came among Robert and his friends, I withheld the confession that my heart was no longer with them, that my departure was now irrevocably fixed. Saint-Loup appeared to believe me, but I learned afterwards that he had from the first moment realised that my uncertainty was feigned and that he would not see me again next day. And while, letting their plates grow cold, his friends joined him in searching through the time-table for a train which would take me to Paris, and while we heard in the cold, starry night the whistling of the engines on the line, I certainly felt no longer the same peace of mind which on all these last evenings I had derived from the friendship of the former and the latter's distant passage. And yet they did not fail me this evening, performing the same office in a different way. My departure overpowered me less when I was no longer obliged to think of it by myself, when I felt that there was concentrated on what was to be done the more normal, more wholesome activity of my strenuous friends, Robert's brothers in arms, and of those other strong creatures, the trains, whose going and coming, night and morning, between Doncières and Paris, broke up in retrospect what had been too compact and insupportable in my long isolation from my grandmother into daily possibilities of return.

"I don't doubt the truth of what you're saying, or that you aren't thinking of leaving us just yet," said Saint-Loup, smiling; "but pretend you are going, and come and say good-bye to me to-morrow morning; early, otherwise there's a risk of my not seeing you; I'm going out to luncheon, I've got leave from the Captain; I shall have to be back in barracks by two, as we are to be on the march all afternoon. I suppose the man to whose house I'm going, a couple of miles out, will manage to get me back in time."

Scarcely had he uttered these words when a messenger came for me from my hotel; the telephone operator had sent to find me. I ran to the post office, for it was nearly closing time. The word 'trunks' recurred incessantly in the answers given me by the officials. I was in a fever of anxiety, for it was my grandmother who had asked for me. The office was closing for the night. Finally I got my connexion. "Is that you, Granny?" A woman's voice, with a strong English accent, answered: "Yes, but I don't know your voice." Neither did I recognise the voice that was speaking to me; besides, my grandmother called me *tu*, and not *vous*. And then all was explained. The young man for whom his grandmother had called on the telephone had a name almost identical with my own, and was staying in an annex of my hotel. This call coming on the very day on which I had been telephoning to my grandmother, I had never for a moment doubted that it was she who was asking for me. Whereas it was by pure coincidence that the post office and the hotel had combined to make a twofold error.

The following morning I rose late, and failed to catch Saint-Loup, who had already started for the country house where he was invited to luncheon. About half past one, I had decided to go in any case to the barracks, so as to be there before he arrived, when, as I was crossing one of the avenues on the way there, I noticed, coming behind me in the same direction as myself, a tilbury which, as it overtook me, obliged me to jump out of its way; an N.C.O. was driving it, wearing an eyeglass; it was Saint-Loup. By his side was the friend whose guest he had been at luncheon, and whom I had met once before at the hotel where we dined. I did not dare shout to Robert since he was not alone, but, in the hope that he would stop and pick me up, I attracted his attention by a sweeping wave of my hat, which might be regarded as due to the presence of a stranger. I knew that Robert was short-sighted; still, I should have supposed that, provided he saw me at all, he could not fail to recognise me; he did indeed see my salute, and returned it, but without stopping; driving on at full speed, without a smile, without moving a muscle of his face, he confined himself to keeping his hand raised for a minute to the peak of his cap, as though he were acknowledging the salute of a trooper whom he did not know personally. I ran to the barracks, but it was a long way; when I arrived, the regiment was parading on the square, on which I was not allowed to stand, and I was heart-broken at not having been able to say good-bye to Saint-Loup; I went up to his room, but he had gone; I was reduced to questioning a group of sick details, recruits who had been excused route-marches, the young graduate, one of the 'old soldiers,' who were watching the regiment parade.

"You haven't seen Serjeant Saint-Loup, have you, by any chance?" I asked.

"He's gone on parade, sir," said the old soldier.

"I never saw him," said the graduate.

"You never saw him," exclaimed the old soldier, losing all interest in me, "you never saw our famous Saint-Loup, the figure he's cutting with his new breeches! When the Capstan sees that, officer's cloth, my word!"

"Oh, you're a wonder, you are; officer's cloth," replied the young graduate, who, reported 'sick in quarters,' was excused marching and tried, not without some misgivings, to be on easy terms with the veterans. "This officer's cloth you speak of is cloth like that, is it?"

"Sir?" asked the old soldier angrily.

He was indignant that the young graduate should throw doubt on the breeches' being made of officer's cloth, but, being a Breton, coming from a village that went by the name of Penguern-Stereden, having learned French with as much difficulty as if it had been English or German, whenever he felt himself overcome by emotion he would go on saying 'Sir?' to give himself time to find words, then, after this preparation, let loose his eloquence, confining himself to the repetition of certain words which he knew better than others, but without haste, taking every precaution to gloss over his unfamiliarity with the pronunciation.

"Ah! It is cloth like that," he broke out, with a fury the intensity of which increased as the speed of his utterance diminished. "Ah! It is cloth like that; when I tell you that it is, officer's cloth, when-I-tell-you-a-thing, if-I-tell-you-a-thing, it's because I know, I should think."

"Very well, then;" replied the young graduate, overcome by the force of this argument. "Keep your hair on, old boy."

"There, look, there's the Capstan coming along. No, but just look at Saint-Loup; the way he throws his leg out; and his head. Would you call that a non-com? And his eyeglass; oh, he's hot stuff, he is."

I asked these troopers, who did not seem at all embarrassed by my presence, whether I too might look out of the window. They neither objected to my doing so nor moved to make room for me. I saw Captain de Borodino go majestically by, putting his horse into a trot, and apparently under the illusion that he was taking part in the Battle of Austerlitz. A few loiterers had stopped by the gate to see the regiment file out. Erect on his charger, his face inclined to plumpness, his cheeks of an Imperial fulness, his eye lucid, the Prince must have been the victim of some hallucination, as I was myself whenever, after the tramway-car had passed, the silence that followed its rumble seemed to me to throb and echo with a vaguely musical palpitation. I was wretched at not having said good-bye to Saint-Loup, but I went nevertheless, for my one anxiety was to return to my grandmother; always until then, in this little country town, when I thought of what my grandmother must be doing by herself, I had pictured her as she was when with me, suppressing my own personality but without taking into account the effects of such a suppression; now, I had to free myself, at the first possible moment, in her arms, from the phantom, hitherto unsuspected and suddenly called into being by her voice, of a grandmother really separated from me, resigned, having, what I had never yet thought of her as having, a definite age, who had just received a letter from me in an empty house, as I had once before imagined Mamma in a house by herself, when I had left her to go to Balbec.

Alas, this phantom was just what I did see when, entering the drawing-room before my grandmother had been told of my return, I found her there, reading. I was in the room, or rather I was not yet in the room since she was not aware of my presence, and, like a woman whom one surprises at a piece of work which she will lay aside if anyone comes in, she had abandoned herself to a train of thoughts which she had never allowed to be visible by me. Of myself—thanks to that privilege which does not last but which one enjoys during the brief moment of return, the faculty of being a spectator, so to speak, of one's own absence,—there was present only the witness, the observer, with a hat and travelling coat, the stranger who does not belong to the house, the photographer who has called to take a photograph of places which one will never see again. The process that mechanically occurred in my eyes when I caught sight of my grandmother was indeed a photograph. We never see the people who are dear to us save in the animated system, the perpetual motion of our incessant love for them, which before allowing the images that their faces present to reach us catches them in its vortex, flings them back upon the idea that we have always had of them, makes them adhere to it, coincide with it. How, since into the forehead, the cheeks of my grandmother I had been accustomed to read all the most delicate, the most permanent qualities of her mind; how, since every casual glance is an act of necromancy, each face that we love a mirror of the past, how could I have failed to overlook what in her had become dulled and changed, seeing that in the most trivial spectacles of our daily life, our eye, charged with thought, neglects, as would a classical tragedy, every image that does not assist the action of the play and retains only those that may help to make its purpose intelligible. But if, in place of our eye, it should be a purely material object, a photographic plate, that has watched the action, then what we shall see, in the courtyard of the Institute, for example, will be, instead of the dignified emergence of an Academician who is going to hail a cab, his staggering gait, his precautions to avoid tumbling upon his back, the parabola of his fall, as though he were drunk, or the ground frozen over. So is it when some casual sport of chance prevents our intelligent and pious affection from coming forward in time to hide from our eyes what they ought never to behold, when it is forestalled by our eyes, and they, arising first in the field and having it to themselves, set to work mechanically, like films, and shew us, in place of the loved friend who has long ago ceased to exist but whose death our affection has always hitherto kept concealed from us, the new person whom a hundred times daily that affection has clothed with a dear and cheating likeness. And, as a sick man who for long has not looked at his own reflexion, and has kept his memory of the face that he never sees refreshed from the ideal image of himself that he carries in his mind, recoils on catching sight in the glass, in the midst of an arid waste of cheek, of the sloping red structure of a nose as huge as one of the pyramids of Egypt, I, for whom my grandmother was still myself, I who had never seen her save in my own soul, always at the same place in the past, through the transparent sheets of contiguous, overlapping memories, suddenly in our drawing-room which formed part of a new world, that of time, that in which dwell the strangers of whom we say "He's begun to age a good deal," for the first time and for a moment only, since she vanished at once, I saw, sitting on the sofa, beneath the lamp, red-faced, heavy and common, sick, lost in thought, following the lines of a book with eyes that seemed hardly sane, a dejected old woman whom I did not know.

My request to be allowed to inspect the Elstirs in Mme. de Guermantes's collection had been met by Saint-Loup with: "I will answer for her." And indeed, as ill luck would have it, it was he and he alone who did answer. We answer readily enough for other people when, setting our mental stage with the little puppets that represent them, we manipulate these to suit our fancy. No doubt even then we take into account the difficulties due to another person's nature being different from our own, and we do not fail to have recourse to some plan of action likely to influence that nature, an appeal to his material interest, persuasion, the rousing of emotion, which will neutralise contrary tendencies on his part. But these differences from our own nature, it is still our own nature that is imagining them, these difficulties, it is we that are raising them; these compelling motives, it is we that are applying them. And so with the actions which before our mind's eye we have made the other person rehearse, and which make him act as we choose; when we wish to see him perform them in real life, the case is altered, we come up against unseen resistances which may prove insuperable. One of the strongest is doubtless that which may be developed in a woman who is not in love with him by the disgust inspired in her, a fetid, insurmountable loathing, by the man who is in love with her; during the long weeks in which Saint-Loup still did not come to Paris, his aunt, to whom I had no doubt of his having written begging her to do so, never once asked me to call at her house to see the Elstirs.

I perceived signs of coldness on the part of another occupant of the building. This was Jupien. Did he consider that I ought to have gone in and said how d'ye do to him, on my return from Doncières, before even going upstairs to our own flat? My mother said no, that there was nothing unusual about it. Françoise had told her that he was like that, subject to sudden fits of ill humour, without any cause. These invariably passed off after a little time.

Meanwhile the winter was drawing to an end. One morning, after several weeks of showers and storms, I heard in my chimney—instead of the wind, formless, elastic, sombre, which convulsed me with a longing to go to the sea—the cooing of the pigeons that were nesting in the wall outside; shimmering, unexpected, like a first hyacinth, gently tearing open its fostering heart that there might shoot forth, purple and satin-soft, its flower of sound, letting in like an opened window into my bedroom still shuttered and dark the heat, the dazzling brightness, the fatigue of a first fine day. That morning, I was surprised to find myself humming a music-hall tune which had never entered my head since the year in which I had been going to Florence and Venice. So profoundly does the atmosphere, as good days and bad recur, act on our organism and draw from dim shelves where we had forgotten them, the melodies written there which our memory could not decipher. Presently a more conscious dreamer accompanied this musician to whom I was listening inside myself, without having recognised at first what he was playing.

I quite realised that it was not for any reason peculiar to Balbec that on my arrival there I had failed to find in its church the charm which it had had for me before I knew it; that at Florence or Parma or Venice my imagination could no more take the place of my eyes when I looked at the sights there. I realised this. Similarly, one New Year's afternoon, as night fell, standing before a column of playbills, I had discovered the illusion that lies in our thinking that certain solemn holidays differ essentially from the other days in the calendar. And yet I could not prevent my memory of the time during which I had looked forward to spending Easter in Florence from continuing to make that festival the atmosphere, so to speak, of the City of Flowers, to give at once to Easter Day something Florentine and to Florence something Paschal. Easter was still a long way off; but in the range of days that stretched out before me the days of Holy Week stood out more clearly at the end of those that merely came between. Touched by a far-flung ray, like certain houses in a village which one sees from a distance when the rest are in shadow, they had caught and kept all the sun.

The weather had now become milder. And my parents themselves, by urging me to take more exercise, gave me an excuse for resuming my morning walks. I had meant to give them up, since they meant my meeting Mme. de Guermantes. But it was for this very reason that I kept thinking all the time of those walks, which led to my finding, every moment, a fresh reason for taking them, a reason that had no connexion with Mme. de Guermantes and no difficulty in convincing me that, had she never existed, I should still have taken a walk, without fail, at that hour every morning.

Alas, if to me meeting any person other than herself would not have mattered, I felt that to her meeting anyone in the world except myself would have been endurable. It happened that, in the course of her morning walks, she received the salutations of plenty of fools whom she regarded as such. But the appearance of these in her path seemed to her, if not to hold out any promise of pleasure, to be at any rate the result of mere accident. And she stopped them at times, for there are moments in which one wants to escape from oneself, to accept the hospitality offered by the soul of another person, provided always that the other, however modest and plain it may be, is a different soul, whereas in my heart she was exasperated to feel that what she would have found was herself. And so, even when I had, for taking the same way as she, another reason than my desire to see her, I trembled like a guilty man as she came past; and sometimes, so as to neutralise anything extravagant that there might seem to have been in my overtures, I would barely acknowledge her bow, or would fasten my eyes on her face without raising my hat, and succeed only in making her angrier than ever, and begin to regard me as insolent and ill-bred besides.

She was now wearing lighter, or at any rate brighter, clothes, and would come strolling down the street in which already, as though it were spring, in front of the narrow shops that were squeezed in between the huge fronts of the old aristocratic mansions, over the booths of the butter-woman and the fruit-woman and the vegetable-woman, awnings were spread to protect them from the sun. I said to myself that the woman whom I could see far off, walking, opening her sunshade, crossing the street, was, in the opinion of those best qualified to judge, the greatest living exponent of the art of performing those movements and of making out of them something exquisitely lovely. Meanwhile she was advancing towards me, unconscious of this widespread reputation, her narrow, stubborn body, which had absorbed none of it, was bent stiffly forward under a scarf of violet silk; her clear, sullen eyes looked absently in front of her, and had perhaps caught sight of me; she was biting her lip; I saw her straighten her muff, give alms to a beggar, buy a bunch of violets from a flower-seller, with the same curiosity that I should have felt in watching the strokes of a great painter's brush. And when, as she reached me, she gave me a bow that was accompanied sometimes by a faint smile, it was as though she had sketched in colour for me, adding a personal inscription to myself, a drawing that was a masterpiece of art. Each of her gowns seemed to me her natural, necessary surroundings, like the projection around her of a particular aspect of her soul. On one of these Lenten mornings, when she was on her way out to luncheon, I met her wearing a gown of bright red velvet, cut slightly open at the throat. The face of Mme. de Guermantes appeared to be dreaming, beneath its pile of fair hair. I was less sad than usual because the melancholy of her expression, the sort of claustration which the startling hue of her gown set between her and the rest of the world, made her seem somehow lonely and unhappy, and this comforted me. The gown struck me as being the materialisation round about her of the scarlet rays of a heart which I did not recognise as hers and might have been able, perhaps, to console; sheltered in the mystical light of the garment with its gently flowing folds, she made me think of some Saint of the early ages of Christianity. After which I felt ashamed of afflicting with the sight of myself this holy martyr. "But, after all, the streets are public."

The streets are public, I reminded myself, giving a different meaning to the words, and marvelling that indeed in the crowded thoroughfare often soaked with rain, which made it beautiful and precious as a street sometimes is in the old towns of Italy, the Duchesse de Guermantes mingled with the public life of the world moments of her own secret life, shewing herself thus to all and sundry, jostled by every passer-by, with the splendid gratuitousness of the greatest works of art. As I had been out in the morning, after staying awake all night, in the afternoon my parents would tell me to lie down for a little and try to sleep. There is no need, when one is trying to find sleep, to give much thought to the quest, but habit is very useful, and even freedom from thought. But in these afternoon hours both were lacking. Before going to sleep, I devoted so much time to thinking that I should not be able to sleep, that even after I was asleep a little of my thought remained. It was no more than a glimmer in the almost total darkness, but it was bright enough to cast a reflexion in my sleep, first of the idea that I could not sleep, and then, a reflexion of this reflexion, that it was in my sleep that I had had the idea that I was not asleep, then, by a further refraction, my awakening . . . to a fresh doze in which I was trying to tell some friends who had come into my room that, a moment earlier, when I was asleep, I had imagined that I was not asleep. These shades were barely distinguishable; it would have required a keen—and quite useless—delicacy of perception to seize them all. Similarly, in later years, at Venice, long after the sun had set, when it seemed to be quite dark, I have seen, thanks to the echo, itself imperceptible, of a last note of light, held indefinitely on the surface of the canals, as though some optical pedal were being pressed, the reflexion of the palaces unfurled, as though for all time, in a darker velvet, on the crepuscular greyness of the water. One of my dreams was the synthesis of what my imagination had often sought to depict, in my waking hours, of a certain seagirt place and its mediaeval past. In my sleep I saw a gothic fortress rising from a sea whose waves were stilled as in a painted window. An arm of the sea cut the town in two; the green water stretched to my feet; it bathed on the opposite shore the foundations of an oriental church, and beyond it houses which existed already in the fourteenth century, so that to go across to them would have been to ascend the stream of time. This dream in which nature had learned from art, in which the sea had turned gothic, this dream in which I longed to attain, in which I believed that I was attaining to the impossible, it seemed to me that I had often dreamed it before. But as it is the property of what we imagine in our sleep to multiply itself in the past, and to appear, even when novel, familiar, I supposed that I was mistaken. I noticed, however, that I did frequently have this dream.

The limitations, too, that are common to all sleep were reflected in mine, but in a symbolical manner; I could not in the darkness make out the faces of the friends who were in the room, for we sleep with our eyes shut. I, who could carry on endless arguments with myself while I dreamed, as soon as I tried to speak to these friends felt the words stick in my throat, for we do not speak distinctly in our sleep; I wanted to go to them, and I could not move my limbs, for we do not walk when we are asleep either; and suddenly I was ashamed to be seen by them, for we sleep without our clothes. So, my eyes blinded, my lips sealed, my limbs fettered, my body naked, the figure of sleep which my sleep itself projected had the appearance of those great allegorical figures (in one of which Giotto has portrayed Envy with a serpent in her mouth) of which Swann had given me photographs.

Saint-Loup came to Paris for a few hours only. He came with assurances that he had had no opportunity of mentioning me to his aunt. "She's not being at all nice just now, Oriane isn't," he explained, with innocent self-betrayal. "She's not my old Oriane any longer, they've gone and changed her. I assure you, it's not worth while bothering your head about her. You pay her far too great a compliment. You wouldn't care to meet my cousin Poictiers?" he went on, without stopping to reflect that this could not possibly give me any pleasure. "Quite an intelligent young woman, she is; you'd like her. She's married to my cousin, the Duc de Poictiers, who is a good fellow, but a bit slow for her. I've told her about you. She said I was to bring you to see her. She's much better looking than Oriane, and younger, too. Really a nice person, don't you know, really a good sort." These were expressions recently—and all the more ardently—taken up by Robert, which meant that the person in question had a delicate nature. "I don't go so far as to say she's a Dreyfusard, you must remember the sort of people she lives among; still, she did say to me: 'If he is innocent, how ghastly for him to be shut up on the Devil's Isle.' You see what I mean, don't you? And then she's the sort of woman who does a tremendous lot for her old governesses; she's given orders that they're never to be sent in by the servants' stair, when they come to the house. She's a very good sort, I assure you. The real reason why Oriane doesn't like her is that she feels she's the cleverer of the two."

Although completely absorbed in the pity which she felt for one of the Guermantes footmen—who had no chance of going to see his girl, even when the Duchess was out, for it would immediately have been reported to her from the lodge,—Françoise was heartbroken at not having been in the house at the moment of Saint-Loup's visit, but this was because now she herself paid visits also. She never failed to go out on the days when I most wanted her. It was always to see her brother, her niece and, more particularly, her own daughter, who had recently come to live in Paris. The intimate nature of these visits itself increased the irritation that I felt at being deprived of her services, for I had a foreboding that she would speak of them as being among those duties from which there was no dispensation, according to the laws laid down at Saint-André-des-Champs. And so I never listened to her excuses without an ill humour which was highly unjust to her, and was brought to a climax by the way Françoise had of saying not: "I have been to see my brother," or "I have been to see my niece," but "I have been to see the brother," "I just looked in as I passed to bid good day to the niece" (or "to my niece the butcheress"). As for her daughter, Françoise would have been glad to see her return to Combray. But this recent Parisian, making use, like a woman of fashion, of abbreviations, though hers were of a vulgar kind, protested that the week she was going shortly to spend at Combray would seem quite long enough without so much as a sight of "the *Intran*." She was still less willing to go to Françoise's sister, who lived in a mountainous country, for "mountains," said the daughter, giving to the adjective a new and terrible meaning, "aren't really interesting." She could not make up her mind to go back to Méséglise, where "the people are so stupid," where in the market the gossips at their stalls would call cousins with her, and say "Why, it's never poor Bazireau's daughter?" She would sooner die than go back and bury herself down there, now that she had "tasted the life of Paris," and Françoise, traditionalist as she was, smiled complacently nevertheless at the spirit of innovation that was incarnate in this new Parisian when she said: "Very well, mother, if you don't get your day out, you have only to send me a pneu."

The weather had turned chilly again. "Go out? What for? To catch your death?" said Françoise, who preferred to remain in the house during the week which her daughter and brother and the butcher-niece had gone to spend at Combray. Being, moreover, the last surviving adherent of the sect in whom persisted obscurely the doctrine of my aunt Léonie—a natural philosopher—Françoise would add, speaking of this unseasonable weather: "It is the remnant of the wrath of God!" But I responded to her complaints only in a languid smile; all the more indifferent to these predictions, in that whatever befell it would be fine for me; already I could see the morning sun shine on the slope of Fiesole, I warmed myself in its rays; their strength obliged me to half open, half shut my eyelids, smiling the while, and my eyelids, like alabaster lamps, were filled with a rosy glow.

It was not only the bells that came from Italy, Italy had come with them. My faithful hands would not lack flowers to honour the anniversary of the pilgrimage which I ought to have made long ago, for since, here in Paris, the weather had turned cold again as in another year at the time of our preparations for departure at the end of Lent, in the liquid, freezing air which bathed the chestnuts and planes on the boulevards, the tree in the courtyard of our house, there were already opening their petals, as in a bowl of pure water, the narcissi, the jonquils, the anemones of the Ponte Vecchio.

My father had informed us that he now knew, from his friend A. J., where M. de Norpois was going when he met him about the place.

"It's to see Mme. de Villeparisis, they are great friends; I never knew anything about it. It seems she's a delightful person, a most superior woman. You ought to go and call on her," he told me. "Another thing that surprised me very much. He spoke to me of M. de Guermantes as quite a distinguished man; I had always taken him for a boor. It seems, he knows an enormous amount, and has perfect taste, only he's very proud of his name and his connexions. But for that matter, according to Norpois, he has a tremendous position, not only here but all over Europe. It appears, the Austrian Emperor and the Tsar treat him just like one of themselves. Old Norpois told me that Mme. de Villeparisis had taken quite a fancy to you, and that you would meet all sorts of interesting people in her house. He paid a great tribute to you; you will see him if you go there, and he may have some good advice for you even if you are going to be a writer. For you're not likely to do anything else; I can see that. It might turn out quite a good career; it's not what I should have chosen for you, myself; but you'll be a man in no time now, we shan't always be here to look after you, and we mustn't prevent you from following your vocation."

If only I had been able to start writing! But whatever the conditions in which I approached the task (as, too, alas, the undertakings not to touch alcohol, to go to bed early, to sleep, to keep fit), whether it were with enthusiasm, with method, with pleasure, in depriving myself of a walk, or postponing my walk and keeping it in reserve as a reward of industry, taking advantage of an hour of good health, utilising the inactivity forced on me by a day of illness, what always emerged in the end from all my effort was a virgin page, undefiled by any writing, ineluctable as that forced card which in certain tricks one invariably is made to draw, however carefully one may first have shuffled the pack. I was merely the instrument of habits of not working, of not going to bed, of not sleeping, which must find expression somehow, cost what it might; if I offered them no resistance, if I contented myself with the pretext they seized from the first opportunity that the day afforded them of acting as they chose, I escaped without serious injury, I slept for a few hours after all, towards morning, I read a little, I did not over-exert myself; but if I attempted to thwart them, if I pretended to go to bed early, to drink only water, to work, they grew restive, they adopted strong measures, they made me really ill, I was obliged to double my dose of alcohol, did not lie down in bed for two days and nights on end, could not even read, and I vowed that another time I would be more reasonable, that is to say less wise, like the victim of an assault who allows himself to be robbed for fear, should he offer resistance, of being murdered.

My father, in the meantime, had met M. de Guermantes once or twice, and, now that M. de Norpois had told him that the Duke was a remarkable man, had begun to pay more attention to what he said. As it happened, they met in the courtyard and discussed Mme. de Villeparisis. "He tells me, she's his aunt; 'Viparisi,' he pronounces it. He tells me, too, she's an extraordinarily able woman. In fact he said she kept a School of Wit," my father announced to us, impressed by the vagueness of this expression, which he had indeed come across now and then in volumes of memoirs, but without attaching to it any definite meaning. My mother, so great was her respect for him, when she saw that he did not dismiss as of no importance the fact that Mme. de Villeparisis kept a School of Wit, decided that this must be of some consequence. Albeit from my grandmother she had known all the time the exact amount of the Marquise's intellectual worth, it was immediately enhanced in her eyes. My grandmother, who was not very well just then, was not in favour at first of the suggested visit, and afterwards lost interest in the matter. Since we had moved into our new flat, Mme. de Villeparisis had several times asked my grandmother to call upon her. And invariably my grandmother had replied that she was not going out just at present, in one of those letters which, by a new habit of hers which we did not understand, she no longer sealed herself, but employed Françoise to lick the envelopes for her. As for myself, without any very clear picture in my mind of this School of Wit, I should not have been greatly surprised to find the old lady from Balbec installed behind a desk, as, for that matter, I eventually did.

My father would have been glad to know, into the bargain, whether the Ambassador's support would be worth many votes to him at the Institute, for which he had thoughts of standing as an independent candidate. To tell the truth, while he did not venture to doubt that he would have M. de Norpois's support, he was by no means certain of it. He had thought it merely malicious gossip when they assured him at the Ministry that M. de Norpois, wishing to be himself the only representative there of the Institute, would put every possible obstacle in the way of my father's candidature, which besides would be particularly awkward for him at that moment, since he was supporting another candidate already. And yet, when M. Leroy-Beaulieu had first advised him to stand, and had reckoned up his chances, my father had been struck by the fact that, among the colleagues upon whom he could count for support, the eminent economist had not mentioned M. de Norpois. He dared not ask the Ambassador point-blank, but hoped that I should return from my call on Mme. de Villeparisis with his election as good as secured. This call was now imminent. That M. de Norpois would carry on propaganda calculated to assure my father the votes of at least two thirds of the Academy seemed to him all the more probable since the Ambassador's willingness to oblige was proverbial, those who liked him least admitting that no one else took such pleasure in being of service. And besides, at the Ministry, his protective influence was extended over my father far more markedly than over any other official.

My father had also another encounter about this time, but one at which his extreme surprise ended in equal indignation. In the street one day he ran into Mme. Sazerat, whose life in Paris her comparative poverty restricted to occasional visits to a friend. There was no one who bored my father quite so intensely as did Mme. Sazerat, so much so that Mamma was obliged, once a year, to intercede with him in sweet and suppliant tones: "My dear, I really must invite Mme. Sazerat to the house, just once; she won't stay long;" and even: "Listen, dear, I am going to ask you to make a great sacrifice; do go and call upon Mme. Sazerat. You know I hate bothering you, but it would be so nice of you." He would laugh, raise various objections, and go to pay the call. And so, for all that Mme. Sazerat did not appeal to him, on catching sight of her in the street my father went towards her, hat in hand; but to his profound astonishment Mme. Sazerat confined her greeting to the frigid bow enforced by politeness towards a person who is guilty of some disgraceful action or has been condemned to live, for the future, in another hemisphere. My father had come home speechless with rage. Next day my mother met Mme. Sazerat in some one's house. She did not offer my mother her hand, but only smiled at her with a vague and melancholy air as one smiles at a person with whom one used to play as a child, but with whom one has since severed all one's relations because she has led an abandoned life, has married a convict or (what is worse still) a co-respondent. Now, from all time my parents had accorded to Mme. Sazerat, and inspired in her, the most profound respect. But (and of this my mother was ignorant) Mme. Sazerat, alone of her kind at Combray, was a Dreyfusard. My father, a friend of M. Méline, was convinced that Dreyfus was guilty. He had flatly refused to listen to some of his colleagues who had asked him to sign a petition demanding a fresh trial. He never spoke to me for a week, after learning that I had chosen to take a different line. His opinions were well known. He came near to being looked upon as a Nationalist. As for my grandmother, in whom alone of the family a generous doubt was likely to be kindled, whenever anyone spoke to her of the possible innocence of Dreyfus, she gave a shake of her head, the meaning of which we did not at the time understand, but which was like the gesture of a person who has been interrupted while thinking of more serious things. My mother, torn between her love for my father and her hope that I might turn out to have brains, preserved an impartiality which she expressed by silence. Finally my grandfather, who adored the Army (albeit his duties with the National Guard had been the bugbear of his riper years), could never, at Combray, see a regiment go by the garden railings without baring his head as the colonel and the colours passed. All this was quite enough to make Mme. Sazerat, who knew every incident of the disinterested and honourable careers of my father and grandfather, regard them as pillars of Injustice. We pardon the crimes of individuals, but not their participation in a collective crime. As soon as she knew my father to be an anti-Dreyfusard she set between him and herself continents and centuries. Which explains why, across such an interval of time and space, her bow had been imperceptible to my father, and why it had not occurred to her to hold out her hand, or to say a few words which would never have carried across the worlds that lay between.

Saint-Loup, who was coming anyhow to Paris, had promised to take me to Mme. de Villeparisis's, where I hoped, though I had not said so to him, that we might meet Mme. de Guermantes. He invited me to luncheon in a restaurant with his mistress, whom we were afterwards to accompany to a rehearsal. We were to go out in the morning and call for her at her home on the outskirts of Paris.

I had asked Saint-Loup that the restaurant to which we went for luncheon (in the lives of young noblemen with money to spend the restaurant plays as important a part as do bales of merchandise in Arabian stories), might, if possible, be that to which Aimé had told me that he would be going as head waiter until the Balbec season started. It was a great attraction to me who dreamed of so many expeditions and made so few to see again some one who formed part not merely of my memories of Balbec but of Balbec itself, who went there year after year, who when ill health or my studies compelled me to stay in Paris would be watching, just the same, through the long July afternoons while he waited for the guests to come in to dinner, the sun creep down the sky and set in the sea, through the glass panels of the great dining-room, behind which, at the hour when the light died, the motionless wings of vessels, smoky blue in the distance, looked like exotic and nocturnal moths in a show-case. Himself magnetised by his contact with the strong lodestone of Balbec, this head waiter became in turn a magnet attracting me. I hoped by talking to him to get at once into communication with Balbec, to have realised here in Paris something of the delights of travel.

I left the house early, with Françoise complaining bitterly because the footman who was engaged to be married had once again been prevented, the evening before, from going to see his girl. Françoise had found him in tears; he had been itching to go and strike the porter, but had restrained himself, for he valued his place.

Before reaching Saint-Loup's, where he was to be waiting for me at the door, I ran into Legrandin, of whom we had lost sight since our Combray days, and who, though now grown quite grey, had preserved his air of youthful candour. Seeing me, he stopped:

"Ah! So it's you," he exclaimed, "a man of fashion, and in a frock coat too! That is a livery in which my independent spirit would be ill at ease. It is true that you are a man of the world, I suppose, and go out paying calls! To go and dream, as I do, before some half ruined tomb, my flowing tie and jacket are not out of place. You know how I admire the charming quality of your soul; that is why I tell you how deeply I regret that you should go forth and deny it among the Gentiles. By being capable of remaining for a moment in the nauseating atmosphere—which I am unable to breathe—of a drawing-room, you pronounce on your own future the condemnation, the damnation of the Prophet. I can see it all, you frequent the 'light hearts,' the houses of the great, that is the vice of our middle class to-day. Ah! Those aristocrats! The Terror was greatly to blame for

not cutting the heads off every one of them. They are all sinister de-
bauchees, when they are not simply dreary idiots. Still, my poor boy, if
that sort of thing amuses you! While you are on your way to your tea-
party your old friend will be more fortunate than you, for alone in an out-
lying suburb he will be watching the pink moon rise in a violet sky. The
truth is that I scarcely belong to this Earth upon which I feel myself such
an exile; it takes all the force of the law of gravity to hold me here, to keep
me from escaping into another sphere. I belong to a different planet. Good-
bye; do not take amiss the old-time frankness of the peasant of the Vivonne,
who has also remained a peasant of the Danube. To prove to you that I
am your sincere well-wisher, I am going to send you my last novel. But you
will not care for it; it is not deliquescent enough, not *fin de siècle* enough
for you; it is too frank, too honest; what you want is Bergotte, you have
confessed it, high game for the jaded palates of pleasure-seeking epicures.
I suppose I am looked upon, in your set, as an old campaigner; I do wrong
to put my heart into what I write, that is no longer done; besides, the life
of the people is not distinguished enough to interest your little snobbicules.
Go, get you gone, try to recall at times the words of Christ: 'Do this and
ye shall live.' Farewell, Friend."

It was not with any particular resentment against Legrandin that I
parted from him. Certain memories are like friends in common, they can
bring about reconciliations; set down amid fields starred with buttercups,
upon which were piled the ruins of feudal greatness, the little wooden
bridge still joined us, Legrandin and me, as it joined the two banks of the
Vivonne.

After coming out of a Paris in which, although spring had begun, the
trees on the boulevards had hardly put on their first leaves, it was a marvel
to Saint-Loup and myself, when the circle train had set us down at the
suburban village in which his mistress was living, to see every cottage
garden gay with huge festal altars of fruit trees in blossom. It was like one
of those peculiar, poetical, ephemeral, local festivals which people travel
long distances to attend on certain fixed occasions, only this one was held
by Nature. The bloom of the cherry tree is stuck so close to its branches,
like a white sheath, that from a distance, among the other trees that
shewed as yet scarcely a flower or leaf, one might have taken it, on this day
of sunshine that was still so cold, for snow, melted everywhere else, which
still clung to the bushes. But the tall pear trees enveloped each house, each
modest courtyard in a whiteness more vast, more uniform, more dazzling,
as if all the dwellings, all the enclosed spaces in the village were on their
way to make, on one solemn date, their first communion.

It had been a country village, and had kept its old mayor's office
sunburned and brown, in front of which, in the place of maypoles
and streamers, three tall pear trees were, as though for some civic
and local festival, gallantly beflagged with white satin. These villages
in the environs of Paris still have at their gates parks of the seventeenth
and eighteenth centuries which were the 'follies' of the stewards and
favourites of the great. A fruit-grower had utilised one of these which was
sunk below the road for his trees, or had simply, perhaps, preserved the

plan of an immense orchard of former days. Laid out in quincunxes, these pear trees, less crowded and not so far on as those that I had seen, formed great quadrilaterals—separated by low walls—of snowy blossom, on each side of which the light fell differently, so that all these airy roofless chambers seemed to belong to a Palace of the Sun, such as one might unearth in Crete or somewhere; and made one think also of the different ponds of a reservoir, or of those parts of the sea which man, for some fishery, or to plant oyster-beds, has subdivided, when one saw, varying with the orientation of the boughs, the light fall and play upon their trained arms as upon water warm with spring, and coax into unfolding here and there, gleaming amid the open, azure-panelled trellis of the branches, the foaming whiteness of a creamy, sunlit flower.

Never had Robert spoken to me so tenderly of his friend as he did during this walk. She alone had taken root in his heart; his future career in the Army, his position in society, his family, he was not, of course, indifferent altogether to these, but they were of no account compared with the veriest trifle that concerned his mistress. That alone had any importance in his eyes, infinitely more importance than the Guermantes and all the kings of the earth put together. I do not know whether he had formulated the doctrine that she was of a superior quality to anyone else, but I do know that he considered, took trouble only about what affected her. Through her and for her he was capable of suffering, of being happy, perhaps of doing murder. There was really nothing that interested, that could excite him except what his mistress wished, was going to do, what was going on, discernible at most in fleeting changes of expression, in the narrow expanse of her face and behind her privileged brow. So nice-minded in all else, he looked forward to the prospect of a brilliant marriage, solely in order to be able to continue to maintain her, to keep her always. If one had asked oneself what was the value that he set on her, I doubt whether one could ever have imagined a figure high enough. If he did not marry her, it was because a practical instinct warned him that as soon as she had nothing more to expect from him she would leave him, or would at least live as she chose, and that he must retain his hold on her by keeping her in suspense from day to day. For he admitted the possibility that she did not love him. No doubt the general affection called love must have forced him—as it forces all men—to believe at times that she did. But in his heart of hearts he felt that this love which she felt for him did not exhaust the possibility of her remaining with him only on account of his money, and that on the day when she had nothing more to expect from him she would make haste (the dupe of her friends and their literary theories, and loving him all the time, really—he thought) to leave him. "If she is nice to me to-day," he confided to me, "I am going to give her something that she'll like. It's a necklace she saw at Boucheron's. It's rather too much for me just at present—thirty thousand francs. But, poor puss, she gets so little pleasure out of life. She will be jolly pleased with it, I know. She mentioned it to me and told me she knew somebody who would perhaps give it to her. I don't believe that is true, really, but I wasn't taking any risks, so I've arranged with Boucheron, who is our family jeweller, to keep it for me. I am glad

to think that you're going to meet her; she's nothing so very wonderful to
look at, you know," (I could see that he thought just the opposite and had
said this only so as to make me, when I did see her, admire her all the more)
"what she has got is a marvellous judgment; she'll perhaps be afraid to talk
much before you, but, by Jove! the things she'll say to me about you
afterwards, you know she says things one can go on thinking about for
hours; there's really something about her that's quite Pythian."

On our way to her house we passed by a row of little gardens, and I was
obliged to stop, for they were all aflower with pear and cherry blossoms;
as empty, no doubt, and lifeless only yesterday as a house that no tenant
has taken, they were suddenly peopled and adorned by these newcomers,
arrived during the night, whose lovely white garments we could see through
the railings along the garden paths.

"Listen; I can see you'd rather stop and look at that stuff, and grow
poetical about it," said Robert, "so just wait for me here, will you; my
friend's house is quite close, I will go and fetch her."

While I waited I strolled up and down the road, past these modest gardens. If I raised my head I could see, now and then, girls sitting in the
windows, but outside, in the open air, and at the height of a half-landing,
here and there, light and pliant, in their fresh pink gowns, hanging among
the leaves, young lilac-clusters were letting themselves be swung by the
breeze without heeding the passer-by who was turning his eyes towards
their green mansions. I recognised in them the platoons in violet uniform
posted at the entrance to M. Swann's park, past the little white fence, in
the warm afternoons of spring, like an enchanting rustic tapestry. I took
a path which led me into a meadow. A cold wind blew keenly along it, as at
Combray, but from the midst of the rich, moist, country soil, which might
have been on the bank of the Vivonne, there had nevertheless arisen, punc-
tual at the trysting place like all its band of brothers, a great white pear
tree which waved smilingly in the sun's face, like a curtain of light materialised and made palpable, its flowers shaken by the breeze but polished
and frosted with silver by the sun's rays.

Suddenly Saint-Loup appeared, accompanied by his mistress, and then,
in this woman who was for him all the love, every possible delight in life,
whose personality, mysteriously enshrined in a body as in a Tabernacle,
was the object that still occupied incessantly the toiling imagination of my
friend, whom he felt that he would never really know, as to whom he was
perpetually asking himself what could be her secret self, behind the veil
of eyes and flesh, in this woman I recognised at once 'Rachel when from
the Lord,' her who, but a few years since—women change their position
so rapidly in that world, when they do change—used to say to the pro-
curess: "To-morrow evening, then, if you want me for anyone, you will
send round, won't you?"

And when they had 'come round' for her, and she found herself alone
in the room with the 'anyone,' she had known so well what was required
of her that after locking the door, as a prudent woman's precaution or a
ritual gesture, she would begin to take off all her things, as one does before
the doctor who is going to sound one's chest, never stopping in the process

unless the 'some one,' not caring for nudity, told her that she might keep on her shift, as specialists do sometimes who, having an extremely fine ear and being afraid of their patient's catching a chill, are satisfied with listening to his breathing and the beating of his heart through his shirt. On this woman whose whole life, all her thoughts, all her past, all the men who at one time or another had had her were to me so utterly unimportant that if she had begun to tell me about them I should have listened to her only out of politeness, and should barely have heard what she said, I felt that the anxiety, the torment, the love of Saint-Loup had been concentrated in such a way as to make—out of what was for me a mechanical toy, nothing more—the cause of endless suffering, the very object and reward of existence. Seeing these two elements separately (because I had known 'Rachel when from the Lord' in a house of ill fame), I realised that many women for the sake of whom men live, suffer, take their lives, may be in themselves or for other people what Rachel was for me. The idea that any one could be tormented by curiosity with regard to her life stupefied me. I could have told Robert of any number of her unchastities, which seemed to me the most uninteresting things in the world. And how they would have pained him! And what had he not given to learn them, without avail!

I realised also then all that the human imagination can put behind a little scrap of face, such as this girl's face was, if it is the imagination that was the first to know it; and conversely into what wretched elements, crudely material and utterly without value, might be decomposed what had been the inspiration of countless dreams if, on the contrary, it should be so to speak controverted by the slightest actual acquaintance. I saw that what had appeared to me to be not worth twenty francs when it had been offered to me for twenty francs in the house of ill fame, where it was then for me simply a woman desirous of earning twenty francs, might be worth more than a million, more than one's family, more than all the most coveted positions in life if one had begun by imagining her to embody a strange creature, interesting to know, difficult to seize and to hold. No doubt it was the same thin and narrow face that we saw, Robert and I. But we had arrived at it by two opposite ways, between which there was no communication, and we should never both see it from the same side. That face, with its stares, its smiles, the movements of its lips, I had known from outside as being simply that of a woman of the sort who for twenty francs would do anything that I asked. And so her stares, her smiles, the movements of her lips had seemed to me significant merely of the general actions of a class without any distinctive quality. And beneath them I should not have had the curiosity to look for a person. But what to me had in a sense been offered at the start, that consenting face, had been for Robert an ultimate goal towards which he had made his way through endless hopes and doubts, suspicions, dreams. He gave more than a million francs in order to have for himself, in order that there might not be offered to others what had been offered to me, as to all and sundry, for a score. That he too should not have enjoyed it at the lower price may have been due to the chance of a moment, the instant in which she who seemed ready to yield herself makes off, having perhaps an assignation elsewhere, some reason which makes her more difficult of access that day. Should the man be a sentimentalist, then, even if she has not observed it, but infinitely more if she has, the direst game begins. Unable to swallow his disappointment, to make himself forget about the woman, he starts afresh in pursuit, she flies him, until a mere smile for which he no longer ventured to hope is bought at a thousand times what should have been the price of the last, the most intimate favours. It happens even at times in such a case, when one has been led by a mixture of simplicity in one's judgment and cowardice in the face of suffering to commit the crowning folly of making an inaccessible idol of a girl, that these last favours, or even the first kiss one is fated never to obtain, one no longer even ventures to ask for them for fear of destroying one's chances of Platonic love. And it is then a bitter anguish to leave the world without having ever known what were the embraces of the woman one has most passionately loved. As for Rachel's favours, however, Saint-Loup had by mere accident succeeded in winning them all. Certainly if he had now learned that they had been offered to all the world for a louis, he would have suffered, of course, acutely, but would still have given a million francs for the right to keep them, for nothing that he might have learned could have made him emerge—since that is beyond human control and can be brought to pass only in spite of it by the action of some great natural law—from the path he was treading, from which that face could appear to him only through the web of the dreams that he had already spun. The immobility of that thin face, like that of a sheet of paper subjected to the colossal pressure of two atmospheres, seemed to me to be being maintained by two infinities which abutted on her without meeting, for she held them apart. And indeed, when Robert and I were both looking at her we did not both see her from the same side of the mystery.

It was not 'Rachel when from the Lord'—who seemed to me a small matter—it was the power of the human imagination, the illusion on which were based the pains of love; these I felt to be vast. Robert noticed that I appeared moved. I turned my eyes to the pear and cherry trees of the garden opposite, so that he might think that it was their beauty that had touched me. And it did touch me in somewhat the same way; it also brought close to me things of the kind which we not only see with our eyes but feel also in our hearts. These trees that I had seen in the garden, likening them in my mind to strange deities, had not my mistake been like the Magdalene's when, in another garden, she saw a human form and 'thought it was the gardener.' Treasurers of our memories of the age of gold, keepers of the promise that reality is not what we suppose, that the splendour of poetry, the wonderful radiance of innocence may shine in it and may be the recompense which we strive to earn, these great white creatures, bowed in a marvellous fashion above the shade propitious for rest, for angling or for reading, were they not rather angels? I exchanged a few words with Saint-Loup's mistress. We cut across the village. Its houses were sordid. But by each of the most wretched, of those that looked as though they had been scorched and branded by a rain of brimstone, a mysterious traveller, halting for a day in the accursed city, a resplendent angel stood erect, extending broadly over it the dazzling protection of the wings of flowering innocence: it was a pear tree. Saint-Loup drew me a little way in front to explain.

"I should have liked it if you and I could have been alone together, in fact I would much rather have had luncheon just with you, and stayed with you until it was time to go to my aunt's. But this poor girl of mine here, it is such a pleasure to her, and she is so decent to me, don't you know, I hadn't the heart to refuse her. You'll like her, however, she's literary, you know, a most sensitive nature, and besides it's such a pleasure to be with her in a restaurant, she is so charming, so simple, always delighted with every-thing."

I fancy nevertheless that, on this same morning, and then probably for the first and last time, Robert did detach himself for a moment from the woman whom out of successive layers of affection he had gradually created, and beheld suddenly at some distance from himself another Rachel, out-wardly the double of his but entirely different, who was nothing more or less than a little light of love. We had left the blossoming orchard and were making for the train which was to take us to Paris when, at the station, Rachel, who was walking by herself, was recognised and accosted by a pair of common little 'tarts' like herself, who first of all, thinking that she was alone, called out: "Hello, Rachel, you come with us; Lucienne and Germaine are in the train, and there's room for one more. Come on. We're all going to the rink," and were just going to introduce to her two counter-jumpers, their lovers, who were escorting them, when, noticing that she seemed a little uneasy, they looked up and beyond her, caught sight of us, and with apologies bade her a good-bye to which she responded in a some-what embarrassed, but still friendly tone. They were two poor little 'tarts' with collars of sham otter skin, looking more or less as Rachel must have looked when Saint-Loup first met her. He did not know them, or their names even, and seeing that they appeared to be extremely intimate with his mistress he could not help wondering whether she too might not once have had, had not still perhaps her place in a life of which he had never dreamed, utterly different from the life she led with him, a life in which one had women for a louis apiece, whereas he was giving more than a hundred thousand francs a year to Rachel. He caught only a fleeting glimpse of that life, but saw also in the thick of it a Rachel other than her whom he knew, a Rachel like the two little 'tarts' in the train, a twenty-franc Rachel. In short, Rachel had for the moment duplicated herself in his eyes, he had seen, at some distance from his own Rachel, the little 'tart' Rachel, the real Rachel, assuming that Rachel the 'tart' was more real than the other. It may then have occurred to Robert that from the hell in which he was living, with the prospect of a rich marriage, of the sale of his name, to enable him to go on giving Rachel a hundred thousand francs every year, he might easily perhaps have escaped, and have enjoyed the favours of his mistress, as the two counter-jumpers enjoyed those of their girls, for next to nothing. But how was it to be done? She had done nothing to forfeit his regard. Less generously rewarded she would be less kind to him, would stop saying and writing the things that so deeply moved him, things which he would quote, with a touch of ostentation, to his friends, taking care to point out how nice it was of her to say them, but omitting to mention that he was maintaining her in the most lavish fashion, or even that he ever gave her anything at all, that these inscriptions on photographs, or greetings at the end of telegrams were but the conversion into the most exiguous, the most precious of currencies of a hundred thousand francs. If he took care not to admit that these rare kindnesses on Rachel's part were handsomely paid for by himself, it would be wrong to say—and yet, by a crude piece of reasoning, we do say it, absurdly, of every lover who pays in cash for his pleasure, and of a great many husbands—that this was from self-esteem or vanity. Saint-Loup had enough sense to perceive that all the pleasures which appeal to vanity he could have found easily and without cost to himself in society, on the strength of his historic name and handsome face, and that his connexion with Rachel had rather, if anything, tended to ostracise him, led to his being less sought after. No; this self-esteem which seeks to appear to be receiving gratuitously the outward signs of the affection of her whom one loves is simply a consequence of love, the need to figure in one's own eyes and in other people's as loved in return by the person whom one loves so well. Rachel rejoined us, leaving the two 'tarts' to get into their compartment; but, no less than their sham otter skins and the self-conscious appearance of their young men, the names Lucienne and Germaine kept the new Rachel alive for a moment longer. For a moment Robert imagined a Place Pigalle existence with unknown associates, sordid love affairs, afternoons spent in simple amusements, excursions or pleasure-parties, in that Paris in which the sunny brightness of the streets from the Boulevard de Clichy onwards did not seem the same as the solar radiance in which he himself strolled with his mistress, but must be something different, for love, and suffering which is one with love, have, like intoxication, the power to alter for us inanimate things. It was almost an unknown Paris in the heart of Paris itself that he suspected, his connexion appeared to him like the exploration of a strange form of life, for if when with him Rachel was somewhat similar to himself, it was nevertheless a part of her real life that she lived with him, indeed the most precious part, in view of his reckless expenditure on her, the part that made her so greatly envied by her friends and would enable her one day to retire to the country or to establish herself in the leading theatres, when she had made her pile. Robert longed to ask her who Lucienne and Germaine were, what they would have said to her if she had joined them in their compartment, how they would all have spent a day which would have perhaps ended, as a supreme diversion, after the pleasures of the rink, at the Olympia Tavern, if Robert and I had not been there. For a moment the purlieus of the Olympia, which until then had seemed to him merely deadly dull, aroused curiosity in him and pain, and the sunshine of this spring day beating upon the Rue Caumartin where, possibly, if she had not known Robert, Rachel might have gone in the course of the evening and have earned a louis, filled him with a vague longing. But what use was it to ply Rachel with questions when he already knew that her answer would be merely silence, or a lie, or something extremely painful for him to hear, which would yet explain nothing. The porters were shutting the doors; we jumped into a first-class carriage; Rachel's magnificent pearls reminded Robert that she was a woman of great price, he caressed her, restored her to her place in his heart where he could contemplate her, internalised, as he had always done hitherto—save during this brief instant in which he had seen her in the Place Pigalle of an impressionist painter—and the train began to move.

It was, by the way, quite true that she was 'literary.' She never stopped talking to me about books, new art and Tolstoyism except to rebuke Saint-Loup for drinking so much wine:

"Ah! If you could live with me for a year, we'd see a fine change. I should keep you on water and you'd be ever so much better."

"Right you are. Let's begin now."

"But you know quite well I have to work all day!" For she took her art very seriously. "Besides, what would your people say?"

And she began to abuse his family to me in terms which for that matter seemed to me highly reasonable, and with which Saint-Loup, while disobeying her orders in the matter of champagne, entirely concurred. I, who was so much afraid of the effect of wine on him, and felt the good influence of his mistress, was quite prepared to advise him to let his family go hang. Tears sprang to the young woman's eyes; I had been rash enough to refer to Dreyfus.

"The poor martyr!" she almost sobbed; "it will be the death of him in that dreadful place."

"Don't upset yourself, Zézette, he will come back, he will be acquitted all right, they will admit they've made a mistake."

"But long before then he'll be dead! Oh, well at any rate his children will bear a stainless name. But just think of the agony he must be going through; that's what makes my heart bleed. And would you believe that Robert's mother, a pious woman, says that he ought to be left on the Devil's Isle, even if he is innocent; isn't it appalling?"

"Yes, it's absolutely true, she does say that," Robert assured me. "She's my mother, I've no fault to find with her, but it's quite clear she hasn't got a sensitive nature, like Zézette."

As a matter of fact these luncheons which were said to be 'such a pleasure' always ended in trouble. For as soon as Saint-Loup found himself in a public place with his mistress, he would imagine that she was looking at every other man in the room, and his brow would darken; she would remark his ill-humour, which she may have thought it amusing to encourage, or, as was more probable, by a foolish piece of conceit preferred, feeling wounded by his tone, not to appear to be seeking to disarm; and would make a show of being unable to take her eyes off some man or other, not that this was always a mere pretence. In fact, the gentleman who, in theatre or café, happened to sit next to them, or, to go no farther, the driver of the cab they had engaged need only have something attractive about him, no matter what, and Robert, his perception quickened by jealousy, would have noticed it before his mistress; he would see in him immediately one of those foul creatures whom he had denounced to me at

Balbec, who corrupted and dishonoured women for their own amusement, would beg his mistress to take her eyes off the man, thereby drawing her attention to him. And sometimes she found that Robert had shewn such good judgment in his suspicion that after a little she even left off teasing him in order that he might calm down and consent to go off by himself on some errand which would give her time to begin conversation with the stranger, often to make an assignation, sometimes even to bring matters quickly to a head. I could see as soon as we entered the restaurant that Robert was looking troubled. The fact of the matter was that he had at once remarked, what had escaped our notice at Balbec, namely that, standing among his coarser colleagues, Aimé, with a modest brilliance, emitted, quite unconsciously of course, that air of romance which emanates until a certain period in life from fine hair and a Grecian nose, features thanks to which he was distinguishable among the crowd of waiters. The others, almost all of them well on in years, presented a series of types, extraordinarily ugly and criminal, of hypocritical priests, sanctimonious confessors, more numerously of comic actors of the old school, whose sugar-loaf foreheads are scarcely to be seen nowadays outside the collections of portraits that hang in the humbly historic green-rooms of little, out of date theatres, where they are represented in the parts of servants or high priests, though this restaurant seemed, thanks to a selective method of recruiting and perhaps to some system of hereditary nomination, to have preserved their solemn type in a sort of College of Augurs. As ill luck would have it, Aimé having recognised us, it was he who came to take our order, while the procession of operatic high priests swept past us to other tables. Aimé inquired after my grandmother's health; I asked for news of his wife and children. He gave it with emotion, being a family man. He had an intelligent, vigorous, but respectful air. Robert's mistress began to gaze at him with a strange attentiveness. But Aimé's sunken eyes, in which a slight short-sightedness gave one the impression of veiled depths, shewed no sign of consciousness in his still face. In the provincial hotel in which he had served for many years before coming to Balbec, the charming sketch, now a trifle discoloured and faded, which was his face, and which, for all those years, like some engraved portrait of Prince Eugène, had been visible always at the same place, at the far end of a dining-room that was almost always empty, could not have attracted any very curious gaze. He had thus for long remained, doubtless for want of sympathetic admirers, in ignorance of the artistic value of his face, and but little inclined for that matter to draw attention to it, for he was temperamentally cold. At the most, some passing Parisian, stopping for some reason in the town, had raised her eyes to his, had asked him perhaps to bring something to her in her room before she left for the station, and in the pellucid, monotonous, deep void of this existence of a faithful husband and servant in a country town had hidden the secret of a caprice without sequel which no one would ever bring to light. And yet Aimé must have been conscious of the insistent emphasis with which the eyes of the young actress were fastened upon him now. Anyhow, it did not escape Robert beneath whose skin I saw gathering a flush, not vivid like that which burned his cheeks when he felt any sudden emotion, but faint, diffused.

"Anything specially interesting about that waiter, Zézette?" he inquired, after sharply dismissing Aimé. "One would think you were studying the part."

"There you are, beginning again; I knew it was coming."

"Beginning what again, my dear girl? I may have been mistaken; I haven't said anything, I'm sure. But I have at least the right to warn you against the fellow, seeing that I knew him at Balbec (otherwise I shouldn't give a damn), and a bigger scoundrel doesn't walk the face of the earth."

She seemed anxious to pacify Robert and began to engage me in a literary conversation in which he joined. I found that it did not bore me to talk to her, for she had a thorough knowledge of the books that I most admired, and her opinion of them agreed more or less with my own; but as I had heard Mme. de Villeparisis declare that she had no talent, I attached but little importance to this evidence of culture. She discoursed wittily on all manner of topics, and would have been genuinely entertaining had she not affected to an irritating extent the jargon of the sets and studios. She applied this, moreover, to everything under the sun; for instance, having acquired the habit of saying of a picture, if it were impressionist, or an opera, if Wagnerian, "Ah! That is *good*!" one day when a young man had kissed her on the ear, and, touched by her pretence of being thrilled, had affected modesty, she said: "Yes, as a sensation I call it distinctly *good*." But what more surprised me was that the expressions peculiar to Robert (which, moreover, had come to him, perhaps, from literary men whom she knew) were used by her to him and by him to her as though they had been a necessary form of speech, and without any conception of the pointlessness of an originality that is universal.

In eating, she managed her hands so clumsily that one assumed that she must appear extremely awkward upon the stage. She recovered her dexterity only when making love, with that touching prescience latent in women who love the male body so intensely that they immediately guess what will give most pleasure to that body, which is yet so different from their own.

I ceased to take part in the conversation when it turned upon the theatre, for on that topic Rachel was too malicious for my liking. She did, it was true, take up in a tone of commiseration—against Saint-Loup, which proved that he was accustomed to hearing Rachel attack her—the defence of Berma, saying: "Oh, no, she's a wonderful person, really. Of course, the things she does no longer appeal to us, they don't correspond quite to what we are looking for, but one must think of her at the period to which she belongs; we owe her a great deal. She has done good work, you know. And besides she's such a fine woman, she has such a good heart; naturally she doesn't care about the things that interest us, but she has had in her time, with a rather impressive face, a charming quality of mind." (Our fingers, by the way, do not play the same accompaniment to all our aesthetic judgments. If it is a picture that is under discussion, to shew that it is a fine work with plenty of paint, it is enough to stick out one's thumb. But the 'charming quality of mind' is more exacting. It requires two fingers, or rather two fingernails, as though one were trying to flick off a particle of dust.) But, with this single exception, Saint-Loup's mistress referred to the best-known actresses in a tone of ironical superiority which annoyed me because I believed—quite mistakenly, as it happened—that it was she who was inferior to them. She was clearly aware that I must regard her as an indifferent actress, and on the other hand have a great regard for those she despised. But she shewed no resentment, because there is in all great talent while it is still, as hers was then, unrecognised, however sure it may be of itself, a vein of humility, and because we make the consideration that we expect from others proportionate not to our latent powers but to the position to which we have attained. (I was, an hour or so later, at the theatre, to see Saint-Loup's mistress shew great deference towards those very artists against whom she was now bringing so harsh a judgment to bear.) And so, in however little doubt my silence may have left her, she insisted nevertheless on our dining together that evening, assuring me that never had anyone's conversation delighted her so much as mine. If we were not yet in the theatre, to which we were to go after luncheon, we had the sense of being in a green-room hung with portraits of old members of the company, so markedly were the waiters' faces those which, one thought, had perished with a whole generation of obscure actors of the Palais-Royal; they had a look, also, of Academicians; stopping before a side table one of them was examining a dish of pears with the expression of detached curiosity that M. de Jussieu might have worn. Others, on either side of him, were casting about the room that gaze instinct with curiosity and coldness which Members of the Institute, who have arrived early, throw at the public, while they exchange a few murmured words which one fails to catch. They were faces well known to all the regular guests. One of them, however, was being pointed out, a newcomer with distended nostrils and a smug upper lip, who looked like a cleric; he was entering upon his duties there for the first time, and everyone gazed with interest at this newly elected candidate. But presently, perhaps to drive Robert away so that she might be alone with Aimé, Rachel began to make eyes at a young student, who was feeding with another man at a neighbouring table.

"Zézette, let me beg you not to look at that young man like that," said Saint-Loup, on whose face the hesitating flush of a moment ago had been gathered now into a scarlet tide which dilated and darkened his swollen features, "if you must make a scene here, I shall simply finish eating by myself and join you at the theatre afterwards."

At this point a messenger came up to tell Aimé that he was wanted to speak to a gentleman in a carriage outside. Saint-Loup, ever uneasy, and afraid now that it might be some message of an amorous nature that was to be conveyed to his mistress, looked out of the window and saw there, sitting up in his brougham, his hands tightly buttoned in white gloves with black seams, a flower in his buttonhole, M. de Charlus.

"There; you see!" he said to me in a low voice, "my family hunt me down even here. Will you, please—I can't very well do it myself, but you can, as you know the head waiter so well and he's certain to give us away—

ask him not to go to the carriage. He can always send some other waiter who doesn't know me. I know my uncle; if they tell him that I'm not known here, he'll never come inside to look for me, he loathes this sort of place. Really, it's pretty disgusting that an old petticoat-chaser like him, who is still at it, too, should be perpetually lecturing me and coming to spy on me!"

Aimé on receiving my instructions sent one of his underlings to explain that he was busy and could not come out at the moment, and (should the gentleman ask for the Marquis de Saint-Loup) that they did not know any such person. But Saint-Loup's mistress, who had failed to catch our whispered conversation and thought that it was still about the young man at whom Robert had been finding fault with her for making eyes, broke out in a torrent of rage.

"Oh, indeed! So it's the young man over there, now, is it? Thank you for telling me; it's a real pleasure to have this sort of thing with one's meals! Don't listen to him, please; he's rather cross to-day, and, you know," she went on, turning to me, "he just says it because he thinks it smart, that it's the gentlemanly thing to appear jealous always."

And she began with feet and fingers to shew signs of nervous irritation.

"But, Zézette, it is I who find it unpleasant. You are making us all ridiculous before that gentleman, who will begin to imagine you're making overtures to him, and an impossible bounder he looks, too."

"Oh, no, I think he's charming; for one thing, he's got the most adorable eyes, and a way of looking at women—you can feel he must love them."

"You can at least keep quiet until I've left the room, if you have lost your senses," cried Robert. "Waiter, my things."

I did not know whether I was expected to follow him.

"No, I want to be alone," he told me in the same tone in which he had just been addressing his mistress, and as if he were quite furious with me. His anger was like a single musical phrase to which in an opera several lines are sung which are entirely different from one another, if one studies the words, in meaning and character, but which the music assimilates by a common sentiment. When Robert had gone, his mistress called Aimé and asked him various questions. She then wanted to know what I thought of him.

"An amusing expression, hasn't he? Do you know what I should like; it would be to know what he really thinks about things, to have him wait on me often, to take him travelling. But that would be all. If we were expected to love all the people who attract us, life would be pretty ghastly, wouldn't it? It's silly of Robert to get ideas like that. All that sort of thing, it's only just what comes into my head, that's all; Robert has nothing to worry about." She was still gazing at Aimé. "Do look, what dark eyes he has. I should love to know what there is behind them."

Presently came a message that Robert was waiting for her in a private room, to which he had gone to finish his luncheon, by another door, without having to pass through the restaurant again. I thus found myself alone, until I too was summoned by Robert. I found his mistress stretched out on a sofa laughing under the kisses and caresses that he was showering on her. They were drinking champagne. "Hallo, you!" she cried to him, having recently picked up this formula which seemed to her the last word in playfulness and wit. I had fed badly, I was extremely uncomfortable, and albeit Legrandin's words had had no effect on me I was sorry to think that I was beginning in a back room of a restaurant and should be finishing in the wings of a theatre this first afternoon of spring. Looking first at the time to see that she was not making herself late, she offered me a glass of champagne, handed me one of her Turkish cigarettes and unpinned a rose for me from her bodice. Whereupon I said to myself: "I have nothing much to regret, after all; these hours spent in this young woman's company are not wasted, since I have had from her, charming gifts which could not be bought too dear, a rose, a scented cigarette and a glass of champagne." I told myself this because I felt that it endowed with an aesthetic character and thereby justified, saved these hours of boredom. I ought perhaps to have reflected that the very need which I felt of a reason that would console me for my boredom was sufficient to prove that I was experiencing no aesthetic sensation. As for Robert and his mistress, they appeared to have no recollection of the quarrel which had been raging between them a few minutes earlier, or of my having been a witness to it. They made no allusion to it, sought no excuse for it any more than for the contrast with it which their present conduct formed. By dint of drinking champagne with them, I began to feel a little of the intoxication that used to come over me at Rivebelle, though probably not quite the same. Not only every kind of intoxication, from that which the sun or travelling gives us to that which we get from exhaustion or wine, but every degree of intoxication—and each must have a different figure, like the numbers of fathoms on a chart—lays bare in us exactly at the depth to which it reaches a different kind of man. The room which Saint-Loup had taken was small, but the mirror which was its sole ornament was of such a kind that it seemed to reflect thirty others in an endless vista; and the electric bulb placed at the top of the frame must at night, when the light was on, followed by the procession of thirty flashes similar to its own, give to the drinker, even when alone, the idea that the surrounding space was multiplying itself simultaneously with his sensations heightened by intoxication, and that, shut up by himself in this little cell, he was reigning nevertheless over something far more extensive in its indefinite luminous curve than a passage in the Jardin de Paris. Being then myself at this moment the said drinker, suddenly, looking for him in the glass, I caught sight of him, hideous, a stranger, who was staring at me. The joy of intoxication was stronger than my disgust; from gaiety or bravado I smiled at him, and simultaneously he smiled back at me. And I felt myself so much under the ephemeral and potent sway of the minute in which our sensations are so strong, that I am not sure whether my sole regret was not at the thought that this hideous self of whom I had just caught sight in the glass was perhaps there for the last time on earth, and that I should never meet the stranger again in the whole course of my life.

Robert was annoyed only because I was not being more brilliant before his mistress.

"What about that fellow you met this morning, who combines snobbery with astronomy; tell her about him, I've forgotten the story," and he watched her furtively.

"But, my dear boy, there's nothing more than what you've just said."

"What a bore you are. Then tell her about Françoise in the Champs-Elysées. She'll enjoy that."

"Oh, do! Bobby is always talking about Françoise." And taking Saint-Loup by the chin, she repeated, for want of anything more original, drawing the said chin nearer to the light: "Hallo, you!"

Since actors had ceased to be for me exclusively the depositaries, in their diction and playing, of an artistic truth, they had begun to interest me in themselves; I amused myself, pretending that what I saw before me were the characters in some old humorous novel, by watching, struck by the fresh face of the young man who had just come into the stalls, the heroine listen distractedly to the declaration of love which the juvenile lead in the piece was addressing to her, while he, through the fiery torrent of his impassioned speech, still kept a burning gaze fixed on an old lady seated in a stage box, whose magnificent pearls had caught his eye; and thus, thanks especially to the information that Saint-Loup gave me as to the private lives of the players, I saw another drama, mute but expressive, enacted beneath the words of the spoken drama which in itself, although of no merit, interested me also; for I could feel in it that there were budding and opening for an hour in the glare of the footlights, created out of the agglutination on the face of an actor of another face of grease paint and pasteboard, on his own human soul the words of a part.

These ephemeral vivid personalities which the characters are in a play that is entertaining also, whom one loves, admires, pities, whom one would like to see again after one has left the theatre, but who by that time are already disintegrated into a comedian who is no longer in the position which he occupied in the play, a text which no longer shews one the comedian's face, a coloured powder which a handkerchief wipes off, who have returned in short to elements that contain nothing of them, since their dissolution, effected so soon after the end of the show, make us—like the dissolution of a dear friend—begin to doubt the reality of our ego and meditate on the mystery of death.

One number in the programme I found extremely trying. A young woman whom Rachel and some of her friends disliked was, with a set of old songs, to make a first appearance on which she had based all her hopes for the future of herself and her family. This young woman was blessed with unduly, almost grotesquely prominent hips and a pretty but too slight voice, weakened still farther by her excitement and in marked contrast to her muscular development. Rachel had posted among the audience a certain number of friends, male and female, whose business it was by their sarcastic comments to put the novice, who was known to be timid, out of countenance, to make her lose her head so that her turn should prove a complete failure, after which the manager would refuse to give her a contract. At the first notes uttered by the wretched woman, several of the male audience, recruited for that purpose, began pointing to her back-

ward profile with jocular comments, several of the women, also in the plot,
laughed out loud, each flute-like note from the stage increased the deliberate hilarity, which grew to a public scandal. The unhappy woman, sweat-
ing with anguish through her grease-paint, tried for a little longer to hold
out, then stopped and looked round the audience with an appealing gaze
of misery and anger which succeeded only in increasing the uproar. The
instinct to imitate others, the desire to shew their own wit and daring added
to the party several pretty actresses who had not been forewarned but now
threw at the others glances charged with malicious connivance, and sat convulsed with laughter which rang out in such violent peals that at the end
of the second song, although there were still five more on the programme,
the stage manager rang down the curtain. I tried to make myself pay no
more heed to the incident than I had paid to my grandmother's sufferings
when my great-aunt, to tease her, used to give my grandfather brandy,
the idea of deliberate wickedness being too painful for me to bear. And
yet, just as our pity for misfortune is perhaps not very exact since in our
imagination we recreate a whole world of grief by which the unfortunate
who has to struggle against it has no time to think of being moved to self-
pity, so wickedness has probably not in the mind of the wicked man that
pure and voluptuous cruelty which it so pains us to imagine. Hatred inspires him, anger gives him an ardour, an activity in which there is no
great joy; he must be a sadist to extract any pleasure from it; ordinarily,
the wicked man supposes himself to be punishing the wickedness of his
victim; Rachel imagined certainly that the actress whom she was making
suffer was far from being of interest to any one, and that anyhow, in having her hissed off the stage, she was herself avenging an outrage on good
taste and teaching an unworthy comrade a lesson. Nevertheless, I preferred not to speak of this incident since I had had neither the courage nor
the power to prevent it, and it would have been too painful for me, by
saying any good of their victim, to approximate to a gratification of the
lust for cruelty the sentiments which animated the tormentors who had
strangled this career in its infancy.

But the opening scene of this afternoon's performance interested me in
quite another way. It made me realise in part the nature of the illusion of
which Saint-Loup was a victim with regard to Rachel, and which had set
a gulf between the images that he and I respectively had in mind of his
mistress, when we beheld her that morning among the blossoming pear
trees. Rachel was playing a part which involved barely more than her
walking on in the little play. But seen thus, she was another woman. She
had one of those faces to which distance—and not necessarily that between stalls and stage, the world being in this respect only a larger theatre
—gives form and outline and which, seen close at hand, dissolve back into
dust. Standing beside her one saw only a nebula, a milky way of freckles,
of tiny spots, nothing more. At a proper distance, all this ceased to be
visible and, from cheeks that withdrew, were reabsorbed into her face, rose
like a crescent moon a nose so fine, so pure that one would have liked to be
the object of Rachel's attention, to see her again as often as one chose, to
keep her close to one, provided that one had not already seen her differ-

ently and at close range. This was not my case but it had been Saint-Loup's when he first saw her on the stage. Then he had asked himself how he might approach her, how come to know her, there had opened in him a whole fairy realm—that in which she lived—from which emanated an exquisite radiance but into which he might not penetrate. He had left the theatre telling himself that it would be madness to write to her, that she would not answer his letter, quite prepared to give his fortune and his name for the creature who was living in him in a world so vastly superior to those too familiar realities, a world made beautiful by desire and dreams of happiness, when at the back of the theatre, a little old building which had itself the air of being a piece of scenery, from the stage door he saw debouch the gay and daintily hatted band of actresses who had just been playing. Young men who knew them were waiting for them outside. The number of pawns on the human chessboard being less than the number of combinations that they are capable of forming, in a theatre from which are absent all the people we know and might have expected to find, there turns up one whom we never imagined that we should see again and who appears so opportunely that the coincidence seems to us providential, although no doubt some other coincidence would have occurred in its stead had we been not in that place but in some other, where other desires would have been aroused and we should have met some other old acquaintance to help us to satisfy them. The golden portals of the world of dreams had closed again upon Rachel before Saint-Loup saw her emerge from the theatre, so that the freckles and spots were of little importance. They vexed him nevertheless, especially as, being no longer alone, he had not now the same opportunity to dream as in the theatre. But she, for all that he could no longer see her, continued to dictate his actions, like those stars which govern us by their attraction even during the hours in which they are not visible to our eyes. And so his desire for the actress with the fine features which had no place now even in Robert's memory had the result that, dashing towards the old friend whom chance had brought to the spot, he insisted upon an introduction to the person with no features and with freckles, since she was the same person, telling himself that later on he would take care to find out which of the two this same person really was. She was in a hurry, she did not on this occasion say a single word to Saint-Loup, and it was only some days later that he finally contrived, by inducing her to leave her companions, to escort her home. He loved her already. The need for dreams, the desire to be made happy by her of whom one has dreamed, bring it about that not much time is required before one entrusts all one's chances of happiness to her who a few days since was but a fortuitous apparition, unknown, unmeaning, upon the boards of the theatre.

When, the curtain having fallen, we moved on to the stage, alarmed at finding myself there for the first time, I felt the need to begin a spirited conversation with Saint-Loup. In this way my attitude, as I did not know what one ought to adopt in a setting that was strange to me, would be entirely dominated by our talk, and people would think that I was so absorbed in it, so unobservant of my surroundings, that it was quite natural that I should not shew the facial expressions proper to a place in which, to judge by what I appeared to be saying, I was barely conscious of standing; and seizing, to make a beginning, upon the first topic that came to my mind:

"You know," I said, "I did come to say good-bye to you the day I left Doncières; I've not had an opportunity to mention it. I waved to you in the street."

"Don't speak about it," he replied, "I was so sorry. I passed you just outside the barracks, but I couldn't stop because I was late already. I assure you, I felt quite wretched about it."

So he had recognised me! I saw again in my mind the wholly impersonal salute which he had given me, raising his hand to his cap, without a glance to indicate that he knew me, without a gesture to shew that he was sorry he could not stop. Evidently this fiction, which he had adopted at that moment, of not knowing me must have simplified matters for him greatly. But I was amazed to find that he had been able to compose himself to it so swiftly and without any instinctive movement to betray his original impression. I had already observed at Balbec that, side by side with that childlike sincerity of his face, the skin of which by its transparence rendered visible the sudden tide of certain emotions, his body had been admirably trained to perform a certain number of well-bred dissimulations, and that, like a consummate actor, he could, in his regimental and in his social life, play alternately quite different parts. In one of his parts he loved me tenderly, he acted towards me almost as if he had been my brother; my brother he had been, he was now again, but for a moment that day he had been another person who did not know me and who, holding the reins, his glass screwed to his eye, without a look or a smile had lifted his disengaged hand to the peak of his cap to give me correctly the military salute.

The stage scenery, still in its place, among which I was passing, seen thus at close range and without the advantage of any of those effects of lighting and distance on which the eminent artist whose brush had painted it had calculated, was a depressing sight, and Rachel, when I came near her, was subjected to a no less destructive force. The curves of her charming nose had stood out in perspective, between stalls and stage, like the relief of the scenery. It was no longer herself, I recognised her only thanks to her eyes, in which her identity had taken refuge. The form, the radiance of this young star, so brilliant a moment ago, had vanished. On the other hand—as though we came close to the moon and it ceased to present the appearance of a disk of rosy gold—on this face, so smooth a surface until now, I could distinguish only protuberances, discolourations, cavities. Despite the incoherence into which were resolved at close range not only the feminine features but the painted canvas, I was glad to be there to wander among the scenery, all that setting which at one time my love of nature had prompted me to dismiss as tedious and artificial until the description of it by Goethe in *Wilhelm Meister* had given it a sort of beauty in my eyes; and I had already observed with delight, in the thick of a crowd of journalists or men of fashion, friends of the actresses, who were greeting one another, talking, smoking, as though in a public thoroughfare, a young man in a black velvet

cap and hortensia-coloured skirt, his cheeks chalked in red like a page from
a Watteau album, who with his smiling lips, his eyes raised to the ceiling, as
he sprang lightly into the air, seemed so entirely of another species than
the rational folk in everyday clothes, in the midst of whom he was pursuing like a madman the course of his ecstatic dream, so alien to the preoccupations of their life, so anterior to the habits of their civilisation, so
enfranchised from all the laws of nature, that it was as restful and as fresh
a spectacle as watching a butterfly straying along a crowded street to
follow with one's eyes, between the strips of canvas, the natural arabesques
traced by his winged capricious painted oscillations. But at that moment
Saint-Loup conceived the idea that his mistress was paying undue attention
to this dancer, who was engaged now in practising for the last time the
figure of fun with which he was going to take the stage, and his face
darkened.

"You might look the other way," he warned her gloomily. "You know
that none of those dancer-fellows is worth the rope they can at least fall
off and break their necks, and they're the sort of people who go about
afterwards boasting that you've taken notice of them. Besides, you know
very well you've been told to go to your dressing-room and change. You'll
be missing your call again."

A group of men—journalists—noticing the look of fury on Saint-Loup's
face, came nearer, amused, to listen to what we were saying. And as the
stage-hands had just set up some scenery on our other side we were forced
into close contact with them.

"Oh, but I know him; he's a friend of mine," cried Saint-Loup's mistress,
her eyes still fixed on the dancer. "Look how well made he is, do watch those
little hands of his dancing away by themselves like his whole body!"

The dancer turned his head towards her, and his human person appeared beneath the sylph that he was endeavouring to be, the clear grey
jelly of his eyes trembled and sparkled between eyelids stiff with paint, and
a smile extended the corners of his mouth into cheeks plastered with rouge;
then, to amuse the girl, like a singer who hums to oblige us the air of the
song in which we have told her that we admired her singing, he began to
repeat the movement of his hands, counterfeiting himself with the fineness
of a parodist and the good humour of a child.

"Oh, that's too lovely, the way he copies himself," she cried, clapping
her hands.

"I implore you, my dearest girl," Saint-Loup broke in, in a tone of utter
misery, "do not make a scene here, I can't stand it; I swear, if you say
another word I won't go with you to your room, I shall walk straight out;
come, don't be so naughty. . . . You oughtn't to stand about in the cigar
smoke like that, it'll make you ill," he went on, to me, with the solicitude
he had shewn for me in our Balbec days.

"Oh! What a good thing it would be if you did go."

"I warn you, if I do I shan't come back."

"That's more than I should venture to hope."

"Listen; you know, I promised you the necklace if you behaved nicely
to me, but the moment you treat me like this. . . ."

"Ah! Well, that doesn't surprise me in the least. You gave me your promise; I ought to have known you'd never keep it. You want the whole world to know you're made of money, but I'm not a money-grubber like you. You can keep your blasted necklace; I know some one else who'll give it to me."

"No one else can possibly give it to you; I've told Boucheron he's to keep it for me, and I have his promise not to let anyone else have it."

"There you are, trying to blackmail me, you've arranged everything, I see. That's what they mean by Marsantes, *Mater Semita*, it smells of the race," retorted Rachel quoting an etymology which was founded on a wild misinterpretation, for *Semita* means 'path' and not 'Semite,' but one which the Nationalists applied to Saint-Loup on account of the Dreyfusard views for which, so far as that went, he was indebted to the actress. She was less entitled than anyone to apply the word 'Jew' to Mme. de Marsantes, in whom the ethnologists of society could succeed in finding no trace of Judaism apart from her connexion with the Lévy-Mirepoix family. "But this isn't the last of it, I can tell you. An agreement like that isn't binding. You have acted treacherously towards me. Boucheron shall be told of it and he'll be paid twice as much for his necklace. You'll hear from me before long; don't you worry."

Robert was in the right a hundred times over. But circumstances are always so entangled that the man who is in the right a hundred times may have been once in the wrong. And I could not help recalling that unpleasant and yet quite innocent expression which he had used at Balbec: "In that way I keep a hold over her."

"You don't understand what I mean about the necklace. I made no formal promise: once you start doing everything you possibly can to make me leave you, it's only natural, surely, that I shouldn't give it to you; I fail to understand what treachery you can see in that, or what my ulterior motive is supposed to be. You can't seriously maintain that I brag about my money, I'm always telling you that I'm only a poor devil without a cent to my name. It's foolish of you take it in that way, my dear. What possible interest can I have in hurting you? You know very well that my one interest in life is yourself."

"Oh, yes, yes, please go on," she retorted ironically, with the sweeping gesture of a barber wielding his razor. And turning to watch the dancer: "Isn't he too wonderful with his hands. A woman like me couldn't do the things he's doing now." She went closer to him and, pointing to Robert's furious face: "Look, he's hurt," she murmured, in the momentary elation of a sadic impulse to cruelty totally out of keeping with the genuine feelings of affection for Saint-Loup.

"Listen, for the last time, I swear to you it doesn't matter what you do—in a week you'll be giving anything to get me back—I shan't come; it's a clean cut, do you hear, it's irrevocable; you will be sorry one day, when it's too late."

Perhaps he was sincere in saying this, and the torture of leaving his mistress may have seemed to him less cruel than that of remaining with her in certain circumstances.

"But, my dear boy," he went on, to me, "you oughtn't to stand about here, I tell you, it will make you cough."

I pointed to the scenery which barred my way. He touched his hat and said to one of the journalists:

"Would you mind, sir, throwing away your cigar; the smoke is bad for my friend."

His mistress had not waited for him to accompany her; on her way to her dressing-room she turned round and:

"Do they do those tricks with women too, those nice little hands?" she flung to the dancer from the back of the stage, in an artificially melodious tone of girlish innocence. "You look just like one yourself, I'm sure I could have a wonderful time with you and a girl I know."

"There's no rule against smoking that I know of; if people aren't well, they have only to stay at home," said the journalist.

The dancer smiled mysteriously back at the actress.

"Oh! Do stop! You'll make me quite mad," she cried to him. "Then there will be trouble."

"In any case, sir, you are not very civil," observed Saint-Loup to the journalist, still with a courteous suavity, in the deliberate manner of a man judging retrospectively the rights and wrongs of an incident that is already closed.

At that moment I saw Saint-Loup raise his arm vertically above his head as if he had been making a signal to some one whom I could not see, or like the conductor of an orchestra, and indeed—without any greater transition than when, at a simple wave of the baton, in a symphony or a ballet, violent rhythms succeed a graceful andante—after the courteous words that he had just uttered he brought down his hand with a resounding smack upon the journalist's cheek.

Now that to the measured conversations of the diplomats, to the smiling arts of peace had succeeded the furious onthrust of war, since blows lead to blows, I should not have been surprised to see the combatants swimming in one another's blood. But what I could not understand (like people who feel that it is not according to the rules when a war breaks out between two countries after some question merely of the rectification of a frontier, or when a sick man dies after nothing more serious than a swelling of the liver) was how Saint-Loup had contrived to follow up those words, which implied a distinct shade of friendliness, with an action which in no way arose out of them, which they had not, so to speak, announced, that action of an arm raised in defiance not only of the rights of man but of the law of cause and effect, that action created *ex nihilo*. Fortunately the journalist who, staggering back from the violence of the blow, had turned pale and hesitated for a moment, did not retaliate. As for his friends, one of them had promptly turned away his head and was looking fixedly into the wings for some one who evidently was not there; the second pretended that a speck of dust had got into his eye, and began rubbing and squeezing his eyelid with every sign of being in pain; while the third had rushed off, exclaiming: "Good heavens, I believe the curtain's going up; we shan't get into our seats."

I wanted to speak to Saint-Loup, but he was so full of his indignation with the dancer that it adhered exactly to the surface of his eyeballs; like a subcutaneous structure it distended his cheeks with the result that, his internal agitation expressing itself externally in an entire immobility, he had not even the power of relaxation, the 'play' necessary to take in a word from me and to answer it. The journalist's friends, seeing that the incident was at an end, gathered round him again, still trembling. But, ashamed of having deserted him, they were absolutely determined that he should be made to suppose that they had noticed nothing. And so they dilated, one upon the speck of dust in his eye, one upon his false alarm when he had thought that the curtain was going up, the third upon the astonishing resemblance between a man who had just gone by and the speaker's brother. Indeed they seemed quite to resent their friend's not having shared their several emotions.

"What, didn't it strike you? You must be going blind."

"What I say is that you're a pack of curs," growled the journalist whom Saint-Loup had punished.

Forgetting the poses they had adopted, to be consistent with which they ought—but they did not think of it—to have pretended not to understand what he meant, they fell back on certain expressions traditional in the circumstances: "What's all the excitement? Keep your hair on, old chap. Don't take the bit in your teeth."

I had realised that morning beneath the pear blossom how illusory were the grounds upon which Robert's love for 'Rachel when from the Lord' was based; I was bound now to admit how very real were the sufferings to which that love gave rise. Gradually the feeling that had obsessed him for the last hour, without a break, began to diminish, receded into him, an unoccupied pliable zone appeared in his eyes. I had stopped for a moment at a corner of the Avenue Gabriel from which I had often in the past seen Gilberte appear. I tried for a few seconds to recall those distant impressions, and was hurrying at a 'gymnastic' pace to overtake Saint-Loup when I saw that a gentleman, somewhat shabbily attired, appeared to be talking to him confidentially. I concluded that this was a personal friend of Robert; at the same time they seemed to be drawing even closer to one another; suddenly, as a meteor flashes through the sky, I saw a number of ovoid bodies assume with a giddy swiftness all the positions necessary for them to form, before Saint-Loup's face and body, a flickering constellation. Flung out like stones from a catapult, they seemed to me to be at the very least seven in number. They were merely, however, Saint-Loup's pair of fists, multiplied by the speed with which they were changing their places in this—to all appearance ideal and decorative—arrangement. But this elaborate display was nothing more than a pummelling which Saint-Loup was administering, the true character of which, aggressive rather than aesthetic, was first revealed to me by the aspect of the shabbily dressed gentleman who appeared to be losing at once his self-possession, his lower jaw and a quantity of blood. He gave fictitious explanations to the people who came up to question him, turned his head and, seeing that Saint-Loup had made off and was hastening to rejoin me, stood gazing after him with an offended, crushed, but by no means furious expression on his face. Saint-Loup, on the other hand, was furious, although he himself had received no blow, and his eyes were still blazing with anger when he reached me. The incident was in no way connected (as I had supposed) with the assault in the theatre. It was an impassioned loiterer who, seeing the fine looking young soldier that Saint-Loup was, had made overtures to him. My friend could not get over the audacity of this 'clique' who no longer even waited for the shades of night to cover their operations, and spoke of the suggestion that had been made to him with the same indignation as the newspapers use in reporting an armed assault and robbery, in broad daylight, in the centre of Paris. And yet the recipient of his blow was excusable in one respect, for the trend of the downward slope brings desire so rapidly to the point of enjoyment that beauty by itself appears to imply consent. Now, that Saint-Loup was beautiful was beyond dispute. Castigation such as he had just administered has this value, for men of the type that had accosted him, that it makes them think seriously of their conduct, though never for long enough to enable them to amend their ways and thus escape correction at the hands of the law. And so, although Saint-Loup's arm had shot out instinctively, without any preliminary thought, all such punishments, even when they reinforce the law, are powerless to bring about any uniformity in morals.

These incidents, particularly the one that was weighing most on his mind, seemed to have prompted in Robert a desire to be left alone for a while. After a moment's silence he asked me to leave him, and to go by myself to call on Mme. de Villeparisis. He would join me there, but preferred that we should not enter the room together, so that he might appear to have only just arrived in Paris, instead of having spent half the day already with me.

As I had supposed before making the acquaintance of Mme. de Villeparisis at Balbec, there was a vast difference between the world in which she lived and that of Mme. de Guermantes. Mme. de Villeparisis was one of those women who, born of a famous house, entering by marriage into another no less famous, do not for all that enjoy any great position in the social world, and, apart from a few duchesses who are their nieces or sisters-in-law, perhaps even a crowned head or two, old family friends, see their drawing-rooms filled only by third-rate people, drawn from the middle classes or from a nobility either provincial or tainted in some way, whose presence there has long since driven away all such smart and snobbish folk as are not obliged to come to the house by ties of blood or the claims of a friendship too old to be ignored. Certainly I had no difficulty after the first few minutes in understanding how Mme. de Villeparisis, at Balbec, had come to be so well informed, better than ourselves even, as to the smallest details of the tour through Spain which my father was then making with M. de Norpois. Even this, however, did not make it possible to rest content with the theory that the intimacy—of more than twenty years' standing—between Mme. de Villeparisis and the Ambassador could have been responsible for the lady's loss of caste in a world where the smartest women boasted the attachment of lovers far less respectable than he, not to mention that it was probably years since he had been anything more to the Marquise than just an old friend. Had Mme. de Villeparisis then had other adventures in days gone by? Being then of a more passionate temperament than now, in a calm and religious old age which nevertheless owed some of its mellow colouring to those ardent, vanished years, had she somehow failed, in the country neighbourhood where she had lived for so long, to avoid certain scandals unknown to the younger generation who simply took note of their effect in the unequal and defective composition of a visiting list bound, otherwise, to have been among the purest of any taint of mediocrity? That 'sharp tongue' which her nephew ascribed to her, had it in those far-off days made her enemies? Had it driven her into taking advantage of certain successes with men so as to avenge herself upon women? All this was possible; nor could the exquisitely sensitive way in which—giving so delicate a shade not merely to her words but to her intonation—Mme. de Villeparisis spoke of modesty or generosity be held to invalidate this supposition; for the people who not only speak with approval of certain virtues but actually feel their charm and shew a marvellous comprehension of them (people in fact who will, when they come to write their memoirs, present a worthy picture of those virtues) are often sprung from but not actually part of the silent, simple, artless generation which practised them. That generation is reflected in them but is not continued. Instead of the character which it possessed we find a sensibility, an intelligence which are not conducive to action. And whether or not there had been in the life of Mme. de Villeparisis any of those scandals, which (if there had) the lustre of her name would have blotted out, it was this intellect, resembling rather that of a writer of the second order than that of a woman of position, that was undoubtedly the cause of her social degradation.

It is true that they were not specially elevating, the qualities, such as balance and restraint, which Mme. de Villeparisis chiefly extolled; but to speak of restraint in a manner that shall be entirely adequate, the word 'restraint' is not enough, we require some of the qualities of authorship which presuppose a quite unrestrained exaltation; I had remarked at Balbec that the genius of certain great artists was completely unintelligible to Mme. de Villeparisis; and that all she could do was to make delicate fun of them and to express her incomprehension in a graceful and witty form. But this wit and grace, at the point to which she carried them, became themselves—on another plane, and even although they were employed to belittle the noblest masterpieces—true artistic qualities. Now the effect of such qualities on any social position is a morbid activity of the kind which doctors call elective, and so disintegrating that the most firmly established pillars of society are hard put to it to hold out for any length of time. What artists call intellect seems pure presumption to the fashionable world which, unable to place itself at the sole point of view from which they, the artists, look at and judge things, incapable of understanding the particular attraction to which they yield when they choose an expression or start a friendship, feel in their company an exhaustion, an irritation, from which antipathy very shortly springs. And yet in her conversation, and the same may be said of the *Memoirs* which she afterwards published, Mme. de Villeparisis shewed nothing but a sort of grace that was eminently social. Having passed by great works without mastering, sometimes without even noticing them, she had preserved from the period in which she had lived and which, moreover, she described with great aptness and charm, little more than the most frivolous of the gifts that they had had to offer her. But a narrative of this sort, even when it treats exclusively of subjects that are not intellectual, is still a work of the intellect, and to give in a book or in conversation, which is almost the same thing, a deliberate impression of frivolity, a serious touch is required which a purely frivolous person would be incapable of supplying. In a certain book of reminiscences written by a woman and regarded as a masterpiece, the phrase that people quote as a model of airy grace has always made me suspect that, in order to arrive at such a pitch of lightness, the author must originally have had a rather stodgy education, a boring culture, and that as a girl she probably appeared to her friends an insufferable prig. And between certain literary qualities and social failure the connexion is so inevitable that when we open Mme. de Villeparisis's *Memoirs* to-day, on any page a fitting epithet, a sequence of metaphors will suffice to enable the reader to reconstruct the deep but icy bow which must have been bestowed on the old Marquise on the staircases of the Embassies by a snob like Mme. Leroi, who perhaps may have left a card on her when she went to call on the Guermantes, but never set foot in her house for fear of losing caste among all the doctors' or solicitors' wives whom she would find there. A bluestocking Mme. de Villeparisis had perhaps been in her earliest youth, and, intoxicated with the ferment of her own knowledge, had perhaps failed to realise the importance of not applying to people in society, less intelligent and less educated than herself, those cutting strokes which the injured party never forgets.

Moreover, talent is not a separate appendage which one artificially attaches to those qualities which make for social success, in order to create from the whole what people in society call a 'complete woman.' It is the living product of a certain moral complexion, from which as a rule many moral qualities are lacking and in which there predominates a sensibility of which other manifestations such as we do not notice in a book may make themselves quite distinctly felt in the course of a life, certain curiosities for instance, certain whims, the desire to go to this place or that for one's own amusement and not with a view to the extension, the maintenance or even the mere exercise of one's social relations. I had seen at Balbec Mme. de Villeparisis hemmed in by a bodyguard of her own servants without even a glance, as she passed, at the people sitting in the hall of the hotel. But I had had a presentiment that this abstention was due not to indifference, and it seemed that she had not always confined herself to it. She would get a sudden craze to know some one or other because she had seen him and thought him good-looking, or merely because she had been told that he was amusing, or because he had struck her as different from the people she knew, who at this period, when she had not yet begun to appreciate them because she imagined that they would never fail her, belonged, all of them, to the purest cream of the Faubourg Saint-Germain. To the bohemian, the humble middle-class gentleman whom she had marked out with her favour she was obliged to address invitations the importance of which he was unable to appreciate, with an insistence which began gradually to depreciate her in the eyes of the snobs who were in the habit of estimating the smartness of a house by the people whom its mistress excluded rather than by those whom she entertained. Certainly, if at a given moment in her youth Mme. de Villeparisis, surfeited with the satisfaction of belonging to the fine flower of the aristocracy, had found a sort of amusement in scandalising the people among whom she lived, and in deliberately impairing her own position in society, she had begun to attach its full importance to that position once it was definitely lost. She had wished to shew the Duchesses that she was better than they, by saying and doing all the things that they dared not say or do. But now that they all, save such as were closely related to her, had ceased to call, she felt herself diminished, and sought once more to reign, but with another sceptre than that of wit. She would have liked to attract to her house all those women whom she had taken such pains to drive away. How many women's lives, lives of which little enough is known (for we all live in different worlds according to our ages, and the discretion of their elders prevents the young from forming any clear idea of the past and so completing the cycle), have been divided in this way into contrasted periods, the last being entirely devoted to the reconquest of what in the second has been so light-heartedly flung on the wind. Flung on the wind in what way? The young people are all the less capable of imagining it, since they see before them an elderly and respectable Marquise de Villeparisis and have no idea that the grave diarist of the present day, so dignified beneath her pile of snowy hair, can ever have been a gay midnight-reveller who was perhaps the delight in those days, devoured the fortunes perhaps of men now sleeping in their graves; that she should also have set to work, with a persevering and natural industry, to destroy the position which she owed to her high birth does not in the least imply that even at that remote period Mme. de Villeparisis did not attach great importance to her position. In the same way the web of isolation, of inactivity in which a neurasthenic lives may be woven by him from morning to night without therefore seeming endurable, and while he is hastening to add another mesh to the net which holds him captive, it is possible that he is dreaming only of dancing, sport and travel. We are at work every moment upon giving its form to our life, but we do so by copying unintentionally, like the example in a book, the features of the person that we are and not of him who we should like to be. The disdainful bow of Mme. Leroi might to some extent be expressive of the true nature of Mme. de Villeparisis; it in no way corresponded to her ambition.

No doubt at the same moment at which Mme. Leroi was—to use an expression beloved of Mme. Swann—'cutting' the Marquise, the latter could seek consolation in remembering how Queen Marie-Amélie had once said to her: "You are just like a daughter to me." But such marks of royal friendship, secret and unknown to the world, existed for the Marquise alone, dusty as the diploma of an old Conservatoire medalist. The only true social advantages are those that create life, that can disappear without the person who has benefited by them needing to try to keep them or to make them public, because on the same day a hundred others will take their place. And for all that she could remember the Queen's using those words to her, she would nevertheless have bartered them gladly for the permanent faculty of being asked everywhere which Mme. Leroi possessed, as in a restaurant a great but unknown artist whose genius is written neither in the lines of his bashful face nor in the antiquated cut of his threadbare coat, would willingly be even the young stock-jobber, of the lowest grade of society, who is sitting with a couple of actresses at a neighbouring table to which in an obsequious and incessant chain come hurrying manager, head waiter, pages and even the scullions who file out of the kitchen to salute him, as in the fairy-tales, while the wine-waiter advances, dust-covered like his bottles, limping and dazed, as if on his way up from the cellar he had twisted his foot before emerging into the light of day.

It must be remarked, however, that in Mme. de Villeparisis's drawing-room the absence of Mme. Leroi, if it distressed the lady of the house, passed unperceived by the majority of her guests. They were entirely ignorant of the peculiar position which Mme. Leroi occupied, a position known only to the fashionable world, and never doubted that Mme. de Villeparisis's receptions were, as the readers of her *Memoirs* to-day are convinced that they must have been, the most brilliant in Paris.

On the occasion of this first call which, after leaving Saint-Loup, I went to pay on Mme. Villeparisis, following the advice given by M. de Norpois to my father, I found her in her drawing-room hung with yellow silk, against which the sofas and the admirable armchairs upholstered in Beauvais tapestry stood out with the almost purple redness of ripe raspberries. Side by side with the Guermantes and Villeparisis portraits one saw those— gifts from the sitters themselves—of Queen Marie-Amélie, the Queen of the Belgians, the Prince de Joinville and the Empress of Austria. Mme. de Villeparisis herself, capped with an old-fashioned bonnet of black lace (which she preserved with the same instinctive sense of local or historical colour as a Breton inn-keeper who, however Parisian his customers may have become, feels it more in keeping to make his maids dress in coifs and wide sleeves), was seated at a little desk on which in front of her, as well as her brushes, her palette and an unfinished flower-piece in water-colours, were arranged in glasses, in saucers, in cups, moss-roses, zinnias, maidenhair ferns, which on account of the sudden influx of callers she had just left off painting, and which had the effect of being piled on a florist's counter in some eighteenth-century mezzotint. In this drawing-room, which had been slightly heated on purpose because the Marquise had caught cold on the journey from her house in the country, there were already when I arrived a librarian with whom Mme. de Villeparisis had spent the morning in selecting the autograph letters to herself from various historical personages which were to figure in facsimile as documentary evidence in the *Memoirs* which she was preparing for the press, and a historian, solemn and tongue-tied, who hearing that she had inherited and still possessed a portrait of the Duchesse de Montmorency, had come to ask her permission to reproduce it as a plate in his work on the Fronde; a party strengthened presently by the addition of my old friend Bloch, now a rising dramatist, upon whom she counted to secure the gratuitous services of actors and actresses at her next series of afternoon parties. It was true that the social kaleidoscope was in the act of turning and that the Dreyfus case was shortly to hurl the Jews down to the lowest rung of the social ladder. But, for one thing, the anti-Dreyfus cyclone might rage as it would, it is not in the first hour of a storm that the waves are highest. In the second place, Mme. de Villeparisis, leaving a whole section of her family to fulminate against the Jews, had hitherto kept herself entirely aloof from the Case and never gave it a thought. Lastly, a young man like Bloch, whom no one knew, might pass unperceived, whereas leading Jews, representatives of their party, were already threatened. He had his chin pointed now by a goat-beard, wore double glasses and a long frock coat, and carried a glove like a roll of papyrus in his hand. The Rumanians, the Egyptians, the Turks may hate the Jews. But in a French drawing-room the differences between those peoples are not so apparent, and an Israelite making his entry as though he were emerging from the heart of the desert, his body crouching like a hyæna's, his neck thrust obliquely forward, spreading himself in profound 'salaams,' completely satisfies a certain taste for the oriental. Only it is essential that the Jew should not be actually 'in' society, otherwise he will readily assume the aspect of a lord and his manners become so Gallicised that on his face a rebellious nose, growing like a nasturtium in any but the right direction, will make one think rather of Mascarille's nose than of Solomon's. But Bloch, not having been rendered supple by the gymnastics of the Faubourg, nor ennobled by a crossing with England or Spain, remained for a lover of the exotic as strange and savoury a spectacle, in spite of his European costume, as one of Decamps's Jews. Marvellous racial power which from the dawn of time thrusts to the surface, even in modern Paris, on the stage of our theatres, behind the pigeonholes of our public offices, at a funeral, in the street, a solid phalanx, setting their mark upon our modern ways of hairdressing, absorbing, making us forget, disciplining the frock coat which on them remains not at all unlike the garment in which Assyrian scribes are depicted in ceremonial attire on the frieze of a monument at Susa before the gates of the Palace of Darius. (Later in the afternoon Bloch might have imagined that it was out of anti-semitic malice that M. de Charlus inquired whether his first name was Jewish, whereas it was simply from aesthetic interest and love of local colour.) But, to revert for a moment, when we speak of racial persistence we do not accurately convey the impression we receive from Jews, Greeks, Persians, all those peoples whom it is better to leave with their differences. We know from classical paintings the faces of the ancient Greeks, we have seen Assyrians on the walls of a palace at Susa. And so we feel, on encountering in a Paris drawing-room Orientals belonging to one or another group, that we are in the presence of creatures whom the forces of necromancy must have called to life. We knew hitherto only a superficial image; behold it has gained depth, it extends into three dimensions, it moves. The young Greek lady, daughter of a rich banker and the latest favourite of society, looks exactly like one of those dancers who in the chorus of a ballet at once historical and aesthetic symbolise in flesh and blood the art of Hellas; and yet in the theatre the setting makes these images somehow trite; the spectacle, on the other hand, to which the entry into a drawing-room of a Turkish lady or a Jewish gentleman admits us, by animating their features makes them appear stranger still, as if they really were creatures evoked by the effort of a medium. It is the soul (or rather the pigmy thing to which—up to the present, at any rate—the soul is reduced in this sort of materialisation), it is the soul of which we have caught glimpses hitherto in museums alone, the soul of the ancient Greeks, of the ancient Hebrews, torn from a life at once insignificant and transcendental, which seems to be enacting before our eyes this disconcerting pantomime. In the young Greek lady who is leaving the room what we seek in vain to embrace is the figure admired long ago on the side of a vase. I felt that if I had in the light of Mme. de Villeparisis's drawing-room taken photographs of Bloch, they would have furnished of Israel the same image—so disturbing because it does not appear to emanate from humanity, so deceiving because all the same it is so strangely like humanity—which we find in spirit photographs. There is nothing, to speak more generally, not even the insignificance of the remarks made by the people among whom we spend our lives, that does not give us a sense of the supernatural, in our everyday world where even a man of genius from whom we expect, gathered as though around a turning-table, to learn the secret of the Infinite utters only these words—the same that had just issued from the lips of Bloch: "Take care of my top hat."

"Oh, Ministers, my dear sir," Mme. de Villeparisis was saying, addressing herself specially to my friend, and picking up the thread of a conversation which had been broken by my arrival: "nobody ever wanted to see them. I was only a child at the time, but I can remember so well the King begging my grandfather to invite M. Decazes to a rout at which my father was to dance with the Duchesse de Berry. 'It will give me pleasure, Florimond,' said the King. My grandfather, who was a little deaf, thought he had said M. de Castries, which seemed a perfectly natural thing to ask. When he understood that it was M. Decazes, he was furious at first, but he gave in, and wrote a note the same evening to M. Decazes, begging him to pay my grandfather the compliment and give him the honour of his presence at the ball which he was giving the following week. For we were polite, sir, in those days, and no hostess would have dreamed of simply sending her card and writing on it 'Tea' or 'Dancing' or 'Music.' But if we understood politeness we were not incapable of impertinence either. M. Decazes accepted, but the day before the ball it was given out that my grandfather felt indisposed and had cancelled his invitations. He had obeyed the King, but he had not had M. Decazes at his ball. . . . Yes, sir, I remember M. Molé very well, he was a clever man—he shewed that in his reception of M. de Vigny at the Academy—but he was very pompous, and I can see him now coming downstairs to dinner in his own house with his tall hat in his hand."

"Ah! that is typically suggestive of what must have been a pretty perniciously philistine epoch, for it was no doubt a universal habit to carry one's hat in one's hand in one's own house," observed Bloch, anxious to make the most of so rare an opportunity of learning from an eyewitness details of the aristocratic life of another day, while the librarian, who was a sort of intermittent secretary to the Marquise, gazed at her tenderly as though he were saying to the rest of us: "There, you see what she's like, she knows everything, she has met everybody, you can ask her anything you like, she's quite amazing."

"Oh, dear, no," replied Mme. de Villeparisis, drawing nearer to her as she spoke the glass containing the maidenhair which presently she would begin again to paint, "it was a habit M. Molé had; that was all. I never saw my father carry his hat in the house, except of course when the King came, because the King being at home wherever he is the master of the house is only a visitor then in his own drawing-room."

"Aristotle tells us in the second chapter of . . ." ventured M. Pierre, the historian of the Fronde, but so timidly that no one paid any attention. Having been suffering for some weeks from a nervous insomnia which resisted every attempt at treatment, he had given up going to bed, and, half-dead with exhaustion, went out only whenever his work made it imperative. Incapable of repeating at all often these expeditions which, simple enough for other people, cost him as much effort as if, to make them, he was obliged to come down from the moon, he was surprised to be brought up so frequently against the fact that other people's lives were not organised on a constant and permanent basis so as to furnish the maximum utility to the sudden outbursts of his own. He sometimes found the doors shut of a library which he had reached only after setting himself artificially on his feet and in a frock coat like some automaton in a story by Mr. Wells. Fortunately he had found Mme. de Villeparisis at home and was going to be shewn the portrait.

Meanwhile he was cut short by Bloch. "Indeed," the latter remarked, referring to what Mme. de Villeparisis had said as to the etiquette for royal visits. "Do you know, I never knew that," as though it were strange that he should not have known it always.

"Talking of that sort of visit, you heard the stupid joke my nephew Basin played on me yesterday morning?" Mme. de Villeparisis asked the librarian. "He told my people, instead of announcing him, to say that it was the Queen of Sweden who had called to see me."

"What! He made them tell you just like that! I say, he must have a nerve," exclaimed Bloch with a shout of laughter, while the historian smiled with a stately timidity.

"I was quite surprised, because I had only been back from the country a few days; I had specially arranged, just to be left in peace for a little, that no one was to be told that I was in Paris, and I asked myself how the Queen of Sweden could have heard so soon," went on Mme. de Villeparisis, leaving her guests amazed to find that a visit from the Queen of Sweden was in itself nothing out of the common to their hostess.

Earlier in the day Mme. de Villeparisis might have been collaborating with the librarian in arranging the illustrations to her *Memoirs*; now she was, quite unconsciously, trying their effect on an average public typical of that from which she would eventually have to enlist her readers. Hers might be different in many ways from a really fashionable drawing-room in which you would have been struck by the absence of a number of middle class ladies to whom Mme. de Villeparisis was 'at home,' and would have noticed instead such brilliant leaders of fashion as Mme. Leroi had in course of time managed to secure, but this distinction is not perceptible in her *Memoirs,* from which certain unimportant friendships of the author have disappeared because there is never any occasion to refer to them; while the absence of those who did not come to see her leaves no gap because, in the necessarily restricted space at the author's disposal, only a few persons can appear, and if these persons are royal personages, historic personalities, then the utmost impression of distinction which any volume of memoirs can convey to the public is achieved. In the opinion of Mme. Leroi, Mme. de Villeparisis's parties were third-rate; and Mme. de Villeparisis felt the sting of Mme. Leroi's opinion. But hardly anyone to-day remembers who Mme. Leroi was, her opinions have vanished into thin air, and it is the drawing-room of Mme. de Villeparisis, frequented as it was by the Queen of Sweden, and as it had been by the Duc d'Aumale, the Duc de Broglie, Thiers, Montalembert, Mgr. Dupanloup, which will be looked upon as one of the most brilliant of the nineteenth century by that posterity which has not changed since the days of Homer and Pindar, and for which the enviable things are exalted birth, royal or quasi-royal, and the friendship of kings, the leaders of the people and other eminent men.

Now of all this Mme. de Villeparisis had her share in the people who still came to her house and in the memories—sometimes slightly 'touched up'—by means of which she extended her social activity into the past. And then there was M. de Norpois who, while unable to restore his friend to any substantial position in society, did indeed bring to her house such foreign or French statesmen as might have need of his services and knew that the only effective method of securing them was to pay court to Mme. de Villeparisis. Possibly Mme. Leroi also knew these European celebrities. But, as a well-mannered woman who avoids anything that suggests the bluestocking, she would as little have thought of mentioning the Eastern question to her Prime Ministers as of discussing the nature of love with her novelists and philosophers. "Love?" she had once replied to a pushing lady who had asked her: "What are your views on love?"—"Love? I make it, constantly, but I never talk about it." When she had any of these literary or political lions in her house she contented herself, as did the Duchesse de Guermantes, with setting them down to play poker. They often preferred this to the serious conversations on general ideas in which Mme. de Villeparisis forced them to engage. But these conversations, ridiculous as in the social sense they may have been, have furnished the *Memoirs* of Mme. de Villeparisis with those admirable passages, those dissertations on politics which read so well in volumes of autobiography, as they do in Corneille's tragedies. Furthermore, the parties of the Villeparisis of this world are alone destined to be handed down to posterity, because the

Lerois of this world cannot write, and, if they could, would not have the time. And if the literary bent of the Villeparisis is the cause of the Lerois' disdain, the disdain of the Lerois does, in its turn, a singular service to the literary bent of the Villeparisis by affording the bluestockings that leisure which the career of letters requires. God, Whose Will it is that there should be a few books in the world well written, breathes with that purpose such disdain into the hearts of the Lerois, for He knows that if these should invite the Villeparisis to dinner the latter would at once rise from their writing tables and order their carriages to be round at eight.

Presently there came into the room, with slow and solemn step, an old lady of tall stature who, beneath the raised brim of her straw hat, revealed a monumental pile of snowy hair in the style of Marie-Antoinette. I did not then know that she was one of three women who were still to be seen in Parisian society and who, like Mme. de Villeparisis, while all of the noblest birth, had been reduced, for reasons which were now lost in the night of time and could have been told us only by some old gallant of their period, to entertaining only certain of the dregs of society who were not sought after elsewhere. Each of these ladies had her own 'Duchesse de Guermantes,' the brilliant niece who came regularly to pay her respects, but none of them could have succeeded in attracting to her house the 'Duchesse de Guermantes' of either of the others. Mme. de Villeparisis was on the best of terms with these three ladies, but she did not like them. Perhaps the similarity between their social position and her own gave her an impression of them which was not pleasing. Besides, soured bluestockings as they were, seeking by the number and frequency of the drawing-room comedies which they arranged in their houses to give themselves the illusion of a regular salon, there had grown up among them a rivalry which the decay of her fortune in the course of a somewhat tempestuous existence reduced for each of them, when it was a question of securing the kind assistance of a professional actor or actress, into a sort of struggle for life. Furthermore, the lady with the Marie-Antoinette hair, whenever she set eyes on Mme. de Villeparisis, could not help being reminded of the fact that the Duchesse de Guermantes did not come to her Fridays. Her consolation was that at these same Fridays she could always count on having, blood being thicker than water, the Princesse de Poix, who was her own personal Guermantes, and who never went near Mme. de Villeparisis, albeit Mme. de Poix was an intimate friend of the Duchess.

Nevertheless from the mansion on the Quai Malaquais to the drawing-rooms of the Rue de Tournon, the Rue de la Chaise and the Faubourg Saint-Honoré, a bond as compelling as it was hateful united the three fallen goddesses, as to whom I would fain have learned by searching in some dictionary of social mythology through what gallant adventure, what sacrilegious presumption, they had incurred their punishment. Their common brilliance of origin, the common decay of their present state entered largely, no doubt, into the necessity which compelled them, while hating one another, to frequent one another's society. Besides, each of them found in the others a convenient way of being polite to her own guests. How should these fail to suppose that they had scaled the most inaccessible peak of the Faubourg when they were introduced to a lady with a string of titles whose sister was married to a Duc de Sagan or a Prince de Ligne? Especially as there was infinitely more in the newspapers about these sham salons than about the genuine ones. Indeed these old ladies' 'men about town' nephews—and Saint-Loup the foremost of them—when asked by a friend to introduce him to people, would answer at once "I will take you to see my aunt Villeparisis," (or whichever it was) "you meet interesting people there." They knew very well that this would mean less trouble for themselves than trying to get the said friends invited by the smart nieces or sisters-in-law of these ladies. Certain very old men, and young women who had heard it from those men, told me that if these ladies were no longer received in society it was because of the extraordinary irregularity of their conduct, which, when I objected that irregular conduct was not necessarily a barrier to social success, was represented to me as having gone far beyond anything that we know to-day. The misconduct of these solemn dames who held themselves so erect assumed on the lips of those who hinted at it something that I was incapable of imagining, proportionate to the magnitude of prehistoric days, to the age of the mammoth. In a word, these three Parcae with their white or blue or red locks had spun the fatal threads of an incalculable number of gentlemen. I felt that the people of to-day exaggerated the vices of those fabulous times, like the Greeks who created Icarus, Theseus, Heracles out of men who had been but little different from those who long afterwards deified them. But one does not tabulate the sum of a person's vices until he has almost ceased to be in a fit state to practise them, when from the magnitude of his social punishment, which is then nearing the completion of its term and which alone one can estimate, one measures, one imagines, one exaggerates that of the crime that has been committed. In that gallery of symbolical figures which is 'society,' the really light women, the true Messalinas, invariably present the solemn aspect of a lady of at least seventy, with an air of lofty distinction, who entertains everyone she can but not everyone she would like to have, to whose house women will never consent to go whose own conduct falls in any way short of perfection, to whom the Pope regularly sends his Golden Rose, and who as often as not has written—on the early days of Lamartine—an essay that has been crowned by the French Academy. "How d'ye do, Alix?" Mme. de Villeparisis greeted the Marie-Antoinette lady, which lady cast a searching glance round the assembly to see whether there was not in this drawing-room any item that might be a valuable addition to her own, in which case she would have to discover it for herself, for Mme. de Villeparisis, she was sure, would be spiteful enough to try to keep it from her. Thus Mme. de Villeparisis took good care not to introduce Bloch to the old lady for fear of his being asked to produce the same play that he was arranging for her in the drawing-room of the Quai Malaquais. Besides it was only tit for tat. For, the evening before, the old lady had had Mme. Ristori, who had recited, and had taken care that Mme. de Villeparisis, from whom she had filched the Italian artist, should not hear of this function until it was over. So that she should not read it first in the newspapers and feel annoyed, the old lady had come in person to tell her about it, shewing no sense of guilt. Mme. de Villeparisis, considering that an introduction of myself was not likely to have the same awkward results as that of Bloch, made me known to the Marie-Antoinette of the Quai Malaquais. The latter, who sought, by making the fewest possible movements, to preserve in her old age those lines, as of a Coysevox goddess, which had years ago charmed the young men of fashion and which spurious poets still celebrated in rhymed charades—and had acquired the habit of a lofty and compensating stiffness common to all those whom a personal degradation obliges to be continually making advances—just perceptibly lowered her head with a frigid majesty, and, turning the other way, took no more notice of me than if I had not existed. By this crafty attitude she seemed to be assuring Mme. de Villeparisis: "You see, I'm nowhere near him; please understand that I'm not interested—in any sense of the word, you old cat—in little boys." But when, twenty minutes later, she left the room, taking advantage of the general conversation, she slipped into my ear an invitation to come to her box the following Friday with another of the three, whose high-sounding name—she had been born a Choiseul, moreover—had a prodigious effect on me.

"I understand, sir, that you are thinkin' of writin' somethin' about Mme. la Duchesse de Montmorency," said Mme. de Villeparisis to the historian of the Fronde in that grudging tone which she allowed, quite unconsciously, to spoil the effect of her great and genuine kindness, a tone due to the shrivelling crossness, the sense of grievance that is a physiological accompaniment of age, as well as to the affectation of imitating the almost rustic speech of the old nobility: "I'm goin' to let you see her portrait, the original of the copy they have in the Louvre."

She rose, laying down her brushes beside the flowers, and the little apron which then came into sight at her waist, and which she wore so as not to stain her dress with paints, added still further to the impression of an old peasant given by her bonnet and her big spectacles, and offered a sharp contrast to the luxury of her appointments, the butler who had brought in the tea and cakes, the liveried footman for whom she now rang to light up the portrait of the Duchesse de Montmorency, Abbess of one of the most famous Chapters in the East of France. Everyone had risen. "What is rather amusin'," said our hostess, "is that in these Chapters where our great-aunts were so often made Abbesses, the daughters of the King of France would not have been admitted. They were very close corporations." "Not admit the King's daughters," cried Bloch in amazement, "why ever not?" "Why, because the House of France had not enough quarterin's after that low marriage." Bloch's bewilderment increased. "A low marriage? The House of France? When was that?" "Why, when they married into the Medicis," replied Mme. de Villeparisis in the most natural manner. "It's a fine picture, ain't it, and in a perfect state of preservation," she added.

"My dear," put in the Marie-Antoinette lady, "surely you remember that when I brought Liszt to see you he said that it was this one that was the copy."

"I should bow to any opinion of Liszt on music, but not on painting. Besides, he was quite off his head then, and I don't remember his ever saying anything of the sort. But it wasn't you that brought him here. I had met him any number of times at dinner at Princess Sayn-Wittgenstein's."

Alix's shot had missed fire; she stood silent, erect and motionless. Plastered with layers of powder, her face had the appearance of a face of stone. And, as the profile was noble, she seemed, on a triangular and moss-grown pedestal hidden by her cape, the time-worn stucco goddess of a park.

"Ah, I see another fine portrait," began the historian.

The door opened and the Duchesse de Guermantes entered the room.

"Well, how are you?" Mme. de Villeparisis greeted her without moving her head, taking from her apron-pocket a hand which she held out to the newcomer; and then ceasing at once to take any notice of her niece, in order to return to the historian: "That is the portrait of the Duchesse de La Rochefoucauld. . . ."

A young servant with a bold manner and a charming face (but so finely chiselled, to ensure its perfection, that the nose was a little red and the rest of the skin slightly flushed as though they were still smarting from the recent and sculptural incision) came in bearing a card on a salver.

"It is that gentleman who has been several times to see Mme. la Marquise."

"Did you tell him I was at home?"

"He heard the voices."

"Oh, very well then, shew him in. It's a man who was introduced to me," she explained. "He told me he was very anxious to come to the house. I certainly never said he might. But here he's taken the trouble to call five times now; it doesn't do to hurt people's feelings. Sir," she went on to me, "and you, Sir," to the historian of the Fronde, "let me introduce my niece, the Duchesse de Guermantes."

The historian made a low bow, as I did also, and since he seemed to suppose that some friendly remark ought to follow this salute, his eyes brightened and he was preparing to open his mouth when he was once more frozen by the sight of Mme. de Guermantes who had taken advantage of the independence of her torso to throw it forward with an exaggerated politeness and bring it neatly back to a position of rest without letting face or eyes appear to have noticed that anyone was standing before them; after breathing a gentle sigh she contented herself with manifesting the nullity of the impression that had been made on her by the sight of the historian and myself by performing certain movements of her nostrils with a precision that testified to the absolute inertia of her unoccupied attention.

The importunate visitor entered the room, making straight for Mme. de Villeparisis with an ingenuous, fervent air: it was Legrandin.

"Thank you so very much for letting me come and see you," he began, laying stress on the word 'very.' "It is a pleasure of a quality altogether rare and subtle that you confer on an old solitary; I assure you that its repercussion . . ." He stopped short on catching sight of me.

"I was just shewing this gentleman a fine portrait of the Duchesse de

La Rochefoucauld, the wife of the author of the *Maxims*; it's a family picture."

Mme. de Guermantes meanwhile had greeted Alix, with apologies for not having been able, that year as in every previous year, to go and see her. "I hear all about you from Madeleine," she added.

"She was at luncheon with me to-day," said the Marquise of the Quai Malaquais, with the satisfying reflexion that Mme. de Villeparisis could never say that.

Meanwhile I had been talking to Bloch, and fearing, from what I had been told of his father's change of attitude towards him, that he might be envying my life, I said to him that his must be the happier of the two. My remark was prompted solely by my desire to be friendly. But such friendliness readily convinces those who cherish a high opinion of themselves of their own good fortune, or gives them a desire to convince other people. "Yes, I do lead a delightful existence," Bloch assured me with a beatified smile. "I have three great friends; I do not wish for one more; an adorable mistress; I am infinitely happy. Rare is the mortal to whom Father Zeus accords so much felicity." I fancy that he was anxious principally to extol himself and to make me envious. Perhaps too there was some desire to shew originality in his optimism. It was evident that he did not wish to reply in the commonplace phraseology that everybody uses: "Oh, it was nothing, really," and so forth, when, to my question: "Was it a good show?" put with regard to an afternoon dance at his house to which I had been prevented from going, he replied in a level, careless tone, as if the dance had been given by some one else: "Why, yes, it was quite a good show, couldn't have been better. It was really charming!"

"What you have just told us interests me enormously," said Legrandin to Mme. de Villeparisis, "for I was saying to myself only the other day that you shewed a marked likeness to him in the clear-cut turn of your speech, in a quality which I will venture to describe by two contradictory terms, monumental rapidity and immortal instantaneousness. I should have liked this afternoon to take down all the things you say; but I shall remember them. They are, in a phrase which comes, I think, from Joubert, friends of the memory. You have never read Joubert? Oh! he would have admired you so! I will take the liberty this evening of sending you a set of him, it is a privilege to make you a present of his mind. He had not your strength. But he had a great deal of charm all the same."

I would have gone up to Legrandin at once and spoken to him, but he kept as far away from me as he could, no doubt in the hope that I might not overhear the stream of flattery which, with a remarkable felicity of expression, he kept pouring out, whatever the topic, to Mme. de Villeparisis.

She shrugged her shoulders, smiling, as though he had been trying to make fun of her, and turned to the historian.

"And this is the famous Marie de Rohan, Duchesse de Chevreuse, who was married first of all to M. de Luynes."

"My dear, speaking of Mme. de Luynes reminds me of Yolande; she came to me yesterday evening, and if I had known that you weren't engaged I'd have sent round to ask you to come. Mme. Ristori turned up quite by chance, and recited some poems by Queen Carmen Sylva in the author's presence. It was too beautiful!"

"What treachery!" thought Mme. de Villeparisis. "Of course that was what she was whispering about the other day to Mme. de Beaulaincourt and Mme. de Chaponay. I had no engagement," she replied, "but I should not have come. I heard Ristori in her great days, she's a mere wreck now. Besides I detest Carmen Sylva's poetry. Ristori came here once, the Duchess of Aosta brought her, to recite a canto of the *Inferno,* by Dante. In that sort of thing she's incomparable."

Alix bore the blow without flinching. She remained marble. Her gaze was piercing and blank, her nose proudly arched. But the surface of one cheek was scaling. A faint, strange vegetation, green and pink, was invading her chin. Perhaps another winter would level her with the dust.

"Now, sir, if you are fond of painting, look at the portrait of Mme. de Montmorency," Mme. de Villeparisis said to Legrandin, to stop the flow of compliments which was beginning again.

Seizing her opportunity, while his back was turned, Mme. de Guermantes pointed to him, with an ironical, questioning look at her aunt.

"It's M. Legrandin," murmured Mme. de Villeparisis, "he has a sister called Mme. de Cambremer, not that that conveys any more to you than it does to me."

"What! Oh, but I know her quite well!" exclaimed Mme. de Guermantes, and put her hand over her lips. "That is to say, I don't know her, but for some reason or other Basin, who meets the husband heaven knows where, took it into his head to tell the wretched woman she might call on me. And she did. I can't tell you what it was like. She informed me that she had been to London, and gave me a complete catalogue of all the things in the British Museum. And this very day, the moment I leave your house, I'm going, just as you see me now, to drop a card on the monster. And don't for a moment suppose that it's an easy thing to do. On the pretence that she's dying of some disease she's always at home, it doesn't matter whether you arrive at seven at night or nine in the morning, she's ready for you with a dish of strawberry tarts.

"No, but seriously, you know, she is a monstrosity," Mme. de Guermantes replied to a questioning glance from her aunt. "She's an impossible person, she talks about 'plumitives' and things like that." "What does 'plumitive' mean?" asked Mme. de Villeparisis. "I haven't the slightest idea!" cried the Duchess in mock indignation. "I don't want to know. I don't speak that sort of language." And seeing that her aunt really did not know what a plumitive was, to give herself the satisfaction of shewing that she was a scholar as well as a purist, and to make fun of her aunt, now, after making fun of Mme. de Cambremer: "Why, of course," she said, with a half-laugh which the last traces of her pretended ill humour kept in check, "everybody knows what it means; a plumitive is a writer, a person who holds a pen. But it's a dreadful word. It's enough to make your wisdom teeth drop out. Nothing will ever make me use words like that.

"And so that's the brother, is it? I hadn't realized that yet. But after all it's not inconceivable. She has the same doormat docility and the same mass of information like a circulating library. She's just as much of a flatterer as he is, and just as boring. Yes, I'm beginning to see the family likeness now quite plainly."

"Sit down, we're just going to take a dish of tea," said Mme. de Villeparisis to her niece. "Help yourself; you don't want to look at the pictures of your great-grandmothers, you know them as well as I do."

Presently Mme. de Villeparisis sat down again at her desk and went on with her painting. The rest of the party gathered round her, and I took the opportunity to go up to Legrandin and, seeing no harm myself in his presence in Mme. de Villeparisis's drawing-room and never dreaming how much my words would at once hurt him and make him believe that I had deliberately intended to hurt him, say: "Well, sir, I am almost excused for coming to a tea-party when I find you here too." M. Legrandin concluded from this speech (at least this was the opinion which he expressed of me a few days later) that I was a thoroughly spiteful little wretch who delighted only in doing mischief.

"You might at least have the civility to begin by saying how d'ye do to me," he replied, without offering me his hand and in a coarse and angry voice which I had never suspected him of possessing, a voice which bearing no traceable relation to what he ordinarily said did bear another more immediate and striking relation to something that he was feeling at the moment. What happens is that since we are determined always to keep our feelings to ourselves, we have never given any thought to the manner in which we should express them. And suddenly there is within us a strange and obscene animal making its voice heard, the tones of which may inspire as much terror in the listener who receives the involuntary elliptical irresistible communication of our defect or vice as would the sudden avowal indirectly and uncouthly proffered by a criminal who can no longer refrain from confessing a murder of which one had never imagined him to be guilty. I knew, of course, that idealism, even subjective idealism, did not prevent great philosophers from still having hearty appetites or from presenting themselves with untiring perseverance for election to the Academy. But really Legrandin had no occasion to remind people so often that he belonged to another planet when all his convulsive movements of anger or affability were governed by the desire to occupy a good position on this.

"Naturally, when people pester me twenty times on end to go anywhere," he went on in lower tones, "although I am perfectly free to do what I choose, still I can't behave like an absolute boor."

Mme. de Guermantes had sat down. Her name, accompanied as it was by her title, added to her corporeal dimensions the duchy which projected itself round about her and brought the shadowy, sun-splashed coolness of the woods of Guermantes into this drawing-room, to surround the tuffet on which she was sitting. I felt surprised only that the likeness of those woods was not more discernible on the face of the Duchess, about which there was nothing suggestive of vegetation, and at the most the ruddy discolouration of her cheeks—which ought rather, surely, to have been emblazoned with the name Guermantes—was the effect, but did not furnish a picture of long gallops in the open air. Later on, when she had ceased to interest me, I came to know many of the Duchess's peculiarities, notably (to speak for the moment only of that one of which I already at this time felt the charm though without yet being able to discover what it was) her eyes, in which was held captive as in a picture the blue sky of an afternoon in France, broadly expansive, bathed in light even when no sun shone; and a voice which one would have thought, from its first hoarse sounds, to be almost plebeian, through which there trailed, as over the steps of the church at Combray or the pastry-cook's in the square, the rich and lazy gold of a country sun. But on this first day I discerned nothing, the warmth of my attention volatilised at once the little that I might otherwise have been able to extract from her, in which I should have found some indication of the name Guermantes. In any case, I told myself that it was indeed she who was designated for all the world by the title Duchesse de Guermantes: the inconceivable life which that name signified, this body did indeed contain; it had just introduced that life into a crowd of different creatures, in this room which enclosed it on every side and on which it produced so violent a reaction that I thought I could see, where the extent of that mysterious life ceased, a fringe of effervescence outline its frontiers: round the circumference of the circle traced on the carpet by the balloon of her blue pekin skirt, and in the bright eyes of the Duchess at the point of intersection of the preoccupations, the memories, the incomprehensible, scornful, amused and curious thoughts which filled them from within and the outside images that were reflected on their surface. Perhaps I should have been not quite so deeply stirred had I met her at Mme. de Villeparisis's at an evening party, instead of seeing her thus on one of the Marquise's 'days,' at one of those tea-parties which are for women no more than a brief halt in the course of their afternoon's outing, when, keeping on the hats in which they have been driving through the streets, they waft into the close atmosphere of a drawing-room the quality of the fresh air outside, and give one a better view of Paris in the late afternoon than do the tall, open windows through which one can hear the bowling wheels of their victorias: Mme. de Guermantes wore a boating-hat trimmed with cornflowers, and what they recalled to me was not, among the tilled fields round Combray where I had so often gathered those flowers, on the slope adjoining the Tansonville hedge, the suns of bygone years; it was the scent and dust of twilight as they had been an hour ago, when Mme. de Guermantes drove through them, in the Rue de la Paix. With a smiling, disdainful, vague air, and a grimace on her pursed lips, with the point of her sunshade, as with the extreme tip of an antenna of her mysterious life, she was tracing circles on the carpet; then, with that indifferent attention which begins by eliminating every point of contact with what one is actually studying, her gaze fastened upon each of us in turn; then inspected the sofas and armchairs, but softened this time by that human sympathy which is aroused by the presence, however insignificant, of a thing one knows, a thing that is almost a person; these pieces of furniture were not like us, they belonged vaguely to her world, they were bound up with the life of her aunt; then from the Beauvais furniture her gaze was carried back to the person sitting on it, and resumed then the same air of perspicacity and that same disapproval which the respect that Mme. de Guermantes felt for her aunt would have prevented her from expressing in words, but which she would obviously have felt had she discovered on the chairs, instead of our presence, that of a spot of grease or a layer of dust.

That admirable writer G—— entered the room; he had come to pay a call on Mme. de Villeparisis which he regarded as a tiresome duty. The Duchess, although delighted to see him again, gave him no sign of welcome, but instinctively he made straight for her, the charm that she possessed, her tact, her simplicity making him look upon her as a woman of exceptional intelligence. He was bound, moreover, in common politeness to go and talk to her, for, since he was a pleasant and a distinguished man, Mme. de Guermantes frequently invited him to luncheon even when there were only her husband and herself besides, or in the autumn to Guermantes, making use of this intimacy to have him to dinner occasionally with Royalties who were curious to meet him. For the Duchess liked to entertain certain eminent men, on condition always that they were bachelors, a condition which, even when married, they invariably fulfilled for her, for, as their wives, who were bound to be more or less common, would have been a blot on a drawing-room in which there were never any but the most fashionable beauties in Paris, it was always without them that their husbands were invited; and the Duke, to avoid hurting any possible susceptibility, used to explain to these involuntary widowers that the Duchess never had women in the house, could not endure feminine society, almost as though this had been under doctor's orders, and as he might have said that she could not stay in a room in which there were smells, or eat salt food, or travel with her back to the engine, or wear stays. It was true that these eminent men used to see at the Guermantes' the Princesse de Parme, the Princesse de Sagan (whom Françoise, hearing her constantly mentioned, had taken to calling, in the belief that this feminine ending was required by the laws of accidence, 'the Sagante'), and plenty more, but their presence was accounted for by the explanation that they were relatives, or such very old friends that it was impossible to exclude them. Whether or not they were convinced by the explanations which the Duc de Guermantes had given of the singular malady that made it impossible for the Duchess to associate with other women, the great men duly transmitted them to their wives. Some of these thought that this malady was only an excuse to cloak her jealousy, because the Duchess wished to reign alone over a court of worshippers. Others more simple still thought that perhaps the Duchess had some peculiar habit, a scandalous past it might be, that women did not care to go to her house and that she gave the name of a whim to what was stern necessity. The better among them, hearing their husbands expatiate on the Duchess's marvellous brain, assumed that she must be so far superior to the rest of womankind that she found their society boring since they could not talk intelligently about anything. And it was true that the Duchess was bored by other women, if their princely rank did not render them specially interesting. But the excluded wives were mistaken when they imagined that she chose to entertain men alone in order to be free to discuss with them literature, science and philosophy. For she never referred to these, at least with the great intellectuals. If, by virtue of a family tradition such as makes the daughters of great soldiers preserve, in the midst of their most frivolous distractions, a respect for military matters, she, the granddaughter of women who had been on terms of friendship with Thiers, Mérimée and Augier, felt that a place must always be kept in her drawing-room for men of intellect, she had on the other hand derived from the manner, at once condescending and intimate, in which those famous men had been received at Guermantes the foible of looking on men of talent as family friends whose talent does not dazzle one, to whom one does not speak of their work, and who would not be at all interested if one did. Moreover the type of mind illustrated by Mérimée and Meilhac and Halévy, which was hers also, led her by reaction from the verbal sentimentality of an earlier generation to a style in conversation that rejects everything to do with fine language and the expression of lofty thoughts, so that she made it a sort of element of good breeding when she was with a poet or a musician to talk only of the food that they were eating or the game of cards to which they would afterwards sit down. This abstention had, on a third person not conversant with her ways, a disturbing effect which amounted to mystification. Mme. de Guermantes having asked him whether it would amuse him to come to luncheon to meet this or that famous poet, devoured by curiosity he would arrive at the appointed hour. The Duchess was talking to the poet about the weather. They sat down to luncheon. "Do you like this way of doing eggs?" she asked the poet. On hearing his approval, which she shared, for everything in her own house appeared to her exquisite, including a horrible cider which she imported from Guermantes: "Give Monsieur some more eggs," she would tell the butler, while the anxious fellow-guest sat waiting for what must surely have been the object of the party, since they had arranged to meet, in spite of every sort of difficulty, before the Duchess, the poet and he himself left Paris. But the meal went on, one after another the courses were cleared away, not without having first provided Mme. de Guermantes with opportunities for clever witticisms or apt stories. Meanwhile the poet went on eating, and neither Duke nor Duchess shewed any sign of remembering that he was a poet. And presently the luncheon came to an end and the party broke up, without a word having been said about the poetry which, for all that, everyone admired but to which, by a reserve analogous to that of which Swann had given me a foretaste, no one might refer. This reserve was simply a matter of good form. But for the fellow-guest, if he thought at all about the matter, there was something strangely melancholy about it all, and these meals in the Guermantes household made him think of the hours which timid lovers often spend together in talking trivialities until it is time to part, without—whether from shyness, from audacity or from awkwardness—the great secret which they would have been happier had they confessed ever succeeding in passing from their hearts to their lips. It must, however, be added that this silence with regard to the serious matters which one was always waiting in vain to see approached, if it might pass as characteristic of the Duchess, was by no means constant with her. Mme. de Guermantes had spent her girlhood in a society somewhat different, equally aristocratic but less brilliant and above all less futile than that in which she now lived, and one of wide culture. It had left beneath her present frivolity a sort of bed-rock of greater solidity, invisibly nutritious, to which indeed the Duchess would repair in search (very rarely, though, for she detested pedantry) of some quotation from Victor Hugo or Lamartine which, extremely appropriate, uttered with a look of true feeling from her fine eyes, never failed to surprise and charm her audience. Sometimes, even, without any pretence of authority, pertinently and quite simply, she would give some dramatist and Academician a piece of sage advice, would make him modify a situation or alter an ending.

If, in the drawing-room of Mme. de Villeparisis, just as in the church at Combray, on the day of Mlle. Percepied's wedding, I had difficulty in discovering, in the handsome, too human face of Mme. de Guermantes the unknown element of her name, I at least thought that, when she spoke, her conversation, profound, mysterious, would have a strangeness as of a mediaeval tapestry or a gothic window. But in order that I should not be disappointed by the words which I should hear uttered by a person who called herself Mme. de Guermantes, even if I had not been in love with her, it would not have sufficed that those words were fine, beautiful and profound, they would have had to reflect that amaranthine colour of the closing syllable of her name, that colour which I had on my first sight of her been disappointed not to find in her person and had driven to take refuge in her mind. Of course I had already heard Mme. de Villeparisis, Saint-Loup, people whose intelligence was in no way extraordinary, pronounce without any precaution this name Guermantes, simply as that of a person who was coming to see them or with whom they had promised to dine, without seeming to feel that there were latent in her name the glow of yellowing woods in autumn and a whole mysterious tract of country. But this must have been an affectation on their part, as when the classic poets give us no warning of the profound purpose which they had, all the same, in writing, an affectation which I myself also strove to imitate, saying in the most natural tone: "The Duchesse de Guermantes," as though it were a name that was just like other names. And then everybody assured me that she was a highly intelligent woman, a clever talker, that she was one of a little group of most interesting people: words which became accomplices of my dream. For when they spoke of an intelligent group, of clever talk, it was not at all the sort of intelligence that I knew that I imagined, not even that of the greatest minds, it was not at all with men like Bergotte that I peopled this group. No, by intelligence I understood an ineffable faculty gilded by the sun, impregnated with a sylvan coolness. Indeed, had she made the most intelligent remarks (in the sense in which I understood the word when it was used of a philosopher or critic), Mme. de Guermantes would perhaps have disappointed even more keenly my expectation of so special a faculty than if, in the course of a trivial conversation, she had confined herself to discussing kitchen recipes or the furnishing of a country house, to mentioning the names of neighbours and relatives of her own, which would have given me a picture of her life.

"I thought I should find Basin here, he was meaning to come and see you to-day," said Mme. de Guermantes to her aunt.

"I haven't set eyes on your husband for some days," replied Mme. de Villeparisis in a somewhat nettled tone. "In fact, I haven't seen him— well, I have seen him once, perhaps—since that charming joke he played on me of making my servants announce him as the Queen of Sweden."

Mme. de Guermantes formed a smile by contracting the corners of her mouth as though she were biting her veil.

"We met her at dinner last night at Blanche Leroi's. You wouldn't know her now, she's positively enormous; I'm sure she must have something the matter with her."

"I was just telling these gentlemen that you said she looked like a frog."

Mme. de Guermantes uttered a sort of raucous sound intended to signify that she acknowledged the compliment.

"I don't remember making such a charming comparison, but if she was one before, now she's the frog that has succeeded in swelling to the size of the ox. Or rather, it isn't quite that, because all her swelling is concentrated in front of her waist, she's more like a frog in an interesting condition."

"Ah, that is quite clever," said Mme. de Villeparisis, secretly proud that her guests should be witnessing this display of her niece's wit.

"It is purely *arbitrary*, though," answered Mme. de Guermantes, ironically detaching this selected epithet, as Swann would have done, "for I must admit I never saw a frog in the family way. Anyhow, the frog in question, who, by the way, is not asking for a king, for I never saw her so skittish as she's been since her husband died, is coming to dine with us one day next week. I promised I'd let you know in good time."

Mme. de Villeparisis gave vent to a confused growl, from which emerged: "I know she was dining with the Mecklenburgs the night before last. Hannibal de Bréauté was there. He came and told me about it, and was quite amusing, I must say."

"There was a man there who's a great deal wittier than Babal," said Mme. de Guermantes who, in view of her close friendship with M. de Bréauté-Consalvi, felt that she must advertise their intimacy by the use of this abbreviation. "I mean M. Bergotte."

I had never imagined that Bergotte could be regarded as witty; in fact, I thought of him always as mingling with the intellectual section of humanity, that is to say infinitely remote from that mysterious realm of which I had caught a glimpse through the purple hangings of a theatre box, behind which, making the Duchess smile, M. de Bréauté was holding with her, in the language of the gods, that unimaginable thing, a conversation between people of the Faubourg Saint-Germain. I was stupefied to see the balance upset, and Bergotte rise above M. de Bréauté. But above all I was dismayed to think that I had avoided Bergotte on the evening of *Phèdre*, that I had not gone up and spoken to him, when I heard Mme. de Guermantes say to Mme. de Villeparisis:

"He is the only person I have any wish to know," went on the Duchess, in whom one could always, as at the turn of a mental tide, see the flow of curiosity with regard to well-known intellectuals sweep over the ebb of her aristocratic snobbishness. "It would be such a pleasure."

The presence of Bergotte by my side, which it would have been so easy for me to secure but which I had thought liable to give Mme. de Guermantes a bad impression of myself, would no doubt, on the contrary, have had the result that she would have signalled to me to join her in her box, and would have invited me to bring the eminent writer, one day, to luncheon.

"I gather that he didn't behave very well, he was presented to M. de Cobourg, and never uttered a word to him," said Mme. de Guermantes, dwelling on this odd characteristic as she might have recounted that a Chinaman had blown his nose on a sheet of paper. "He never once said 'Monseigneur' to him," she added, with an air of amusement at this detail, as important to her mind as the refusal of a Protestant, during an audience with the Pope, to go on his knees before his Holiness.

Interested by these idiosyncrasies of Bergotte, she did not, however, appear to consider them reprehensible, and seemed rather to find a certain merit in them, though she would have been put to it to say of what sort. Despite this unusual mode of appreciating Bergotte's originality, it was a fact which I was later on not to regard as wholly negligible that Mme. de Guermantes, greatly to the surprise of many of her friends, did consider Bergotte more witty than M. de Bréauté. Thus it is that such judgments, subversive, isolated, and yet after all just, are delivered in the world of fashion by those rare minds that are superior to the rest. And they sketch then the first rough outlines of the hierarchy of values as the next generation will establish it, instead of abiding eternally by the old standards.

The Comte d'Argencourt, Chargé d'Affaires at the Belgian Legation and a remote connexion of Mme. de Villeparisis, came limping in, followed presently by two young men, the Baron de Guermantes and H. H. the Duc de Châtellerault, whom Mme. de Guermantes greeted with: "How d'ye do, young Châtellerault," in a careless tone and without moving from her tuffet, for she was a great friend of the young Duke's mother, which had given him a deep and lifelong respect for her. Tall, slender, with golden hair and sunny complexions, thoroughly of the Guermantes type, these two young men looked like a condensation of the light of the spring evening which was flooding the spacious room. Following a custom which was the fashion at that time they laid their silk hats on the floor, by their feet. The historian of the Fronde thought that they were embarrassed, like a peasant coming into the mayor's office and not knowing what to do with his hat. Feeling that he ought in charity to come to the rescue of the awkwardness and timidity which he ascribed to them:

"No, no," he said, "don't leave them on the floor, they'll be trodden on."

A glance from the Baron de Guermantes, tilting the plane of his pupils, shot suddenly from them a wave of pure and piercing azure which froze the well-meaning historian.

"What is that person's name?" I was asked by the Baron, who had just been introduced to me by Mme. de Villeparisis.

"M. Pierre," I whispered.

"Pierre what?"

"Pierre: it's his name, he's a historian, a most distinguished man."

"Really? You don't say so."

"No, it's a new fashion with these young men to put their hats on the floor," Mme. de Villeparisis explained. "I'm like you, I can never get used to it. Still, it's better than my nephew Robert, who always leaves his in the hall. I tell him when I see him come in that he looks just like a clock-maker, and I ask him if he's come to wind the clocks."

"You were speaking just now, Madame la Marquise, of M. Molé's hat; we shall soon be able, like Aristotle, to compile a chapter on hats," said the historian of the Fronde, somewhat reassured by Mme. de Villeparisis's intervention, but in so faint a voice that no one but myself overheard him.

"She really is astonishing, the little Duchess," said M. d'Argencourt, pointing to Mme. de Guermantes who was talking to G——. "Whenever there's a famous man in the room you're sure to find him sitting with her. Evidently that must be the lion of the party over there. It can't always be M. de Borelli, of course, or M. Schlumberger or M. d'Avenel. But then it's bound to be M. Pierre Loti or M. Edmond Rostand. Yesterday evening at the Doudeauvilles', where by the way she was looking splendid in her emerald tiara and a pink dress with a long train, she had M. Deschanel on one side and the German Ambassador on the other: she was holding forth to them about China; the general public, at a respectful distance where they couldn't hear what was being said, were wondering whether there wasn't going to be war. Really, you'd have said she was a Queen, holding her circle."

Everyone had gathered round Mme. de Villeparisis to watch her painting.

"Those flowers are a truly celestial pink," said Legrandin, "I should say sky-pink. For there is such a thing as sky-pink just as there is sky-blue. But," he lowered his voice in the hope that he would not be heard by any-one but the Marquise, "I think I shall still give my vote to the silky, living flesh tint of your rendering of them. You leave Pisanello and Van Huysun a long way behind, with their laborious, dead herbals."

An artist, however modest, is always willing to hear himself preferred to his rivals, and tries only to see that justice is done them.

"What makes you think that is that they painted the flowers of their period, which we don't have now, but they did it with great skill."

"Ah! The flowers of their period! That is a most ingenious theory," exclaimed Legrandin.

"I see you're painting some fine cherry blossoms—or are they may-flowers?" began the historian of the Fronde, not without hesitation as to the flower, but with a note of confidence in his voice, for he was beginning to forget the incident of the hats.

"No; they're apple blossom," said the Duchesse de Guermantes, ad-dressing her aunt.

"Ah! I see you're a good countrywoman like me; you can tell one flower from another."

"Why yes, so they are! But I thought the season for apple blossom was over now," said the historian, seeking wildly to cover his mistake.

"Oh dear, no; far from it, it's not out yet; the trees won't be in blossom for another fortnight, not for three weeks perhaps," said the librarian who, since he helped with the management of Mme. de Villeparisis's estates, was better informed upon country matters.

"At least three weeks," put in the Duchess; "even round Paris, where they're very far forward. Down in Normandy, don't you know, at his father's place," she went on, pointing to the young Duc de Châtellerault, "where they have some splendid apple trees close to the seashore, like a Japanese screen, they're never really pink until after the twentieth of May."

"I never see them," said the young Duke, "because they give me hay fever. Such a bore."

"Hay fever? I never heard of that before," said the historian.

"It's the fashionable complaint just now," the librarian informed him.

"That all depends, you won't get it at all, probably, if it's a good year for apples. You know Le Normand's saying: 'When it's a good year for apples . . .'," put in M. d'Argencourt who, not being really French, was always trying to give himself a Parisian air.

"You're quite right," Mme. de Villeparisis told her niece, "these are from the South. It was a florist who sent them round and asked me to accept them as a present. You're surprised, I dare say, Monsieur Valmère," she turned to the librarian, "that a florist should make me a present of apple blossom. Well, I may be an old woman, but I'm not quite on the shelf yet, I have still a few friends," she went on with a smile that might have been taken as a sign of her simple nature but meant rather, I could not help feeling, that she thought it effective to pride herself on the friendship of a mere florist when she moved in such distinguished circles.

Bloch rose and went over to look at the flowers which Mme. de Villeparisis was painting.

"Never mind, Marquise," said the historian, sitting down again, "even though we should have another of those Revolutions which have stained so many pages of our history with blood—and, upon my soul, in these days one can never tell," he added, with a circular and circumspect glance, as though to make sure that there was no 'disaffected' person in the room, though he had not the least suspicion that there actually was, "with a talent like yours and your five languages you would be certain to get on all right." The historian of the Fronde was feeling quite refreshed, for he had forgotten his insomnia. But he suddenly remembered that he had not slept for the last six nights, whereupon a crushing weariness, born of his mind, paralysed his limbs, made him bow his shoulders, and his melancholy face began to droop like an old man's.

Bloch tried to express his admiration in an appropriate gesture, but only succeeded in knocking over with his elbow the glass containing the spray of apple blossom, and all the water was spilled on the carpet.

"Really, you have the fingers of a fairy," went on (to the Marquise) the historian who, having his back turned to me at that moment, had not noticed Bloch's clumsiness.

But Bloch took this for a sneer at himself, and to cover his shame in insolence retorted: "It's not of the slightest importance; I'm not wet."

Mme. de Villeparisis rang the bell and a footman came to wipe the carpet and pick up the fragments of glass. She invited the two young men to her theatricals, and also Mme. de Guermantes, with the injunction:

"Remember to tell Gisèle and Berthe" (the Duchesses d'Auberjon and de Portefin) "to be here a little before two to help me," as she might have told the hired waiters to come early to arrange the tables.

She treated her princely relatives, as she treated M. de Norpois, without any of the little courtesies which she shewed to the historian, Cottard, Bloch and myself, and they seemed to have no interest for her beyond the possibility of serving them up as food for our social curiosity. This was because she knew that she need not put herself out to entertain people for whom she was not a more or less brilliant woman but the touchy old sister—who needed and received tactful handling—of their father or uncle. There would have been no object in her trying to shine before them, she could never have deceived them as to the strength and weakness of her position, for they knew (none so well) her whole history and respected the illustrious race from which she sprang. But, above all, they had ceased to be anything more for her than a dead stock which would not bear fruit again, they would not let her know their new friends, or share their pleasures. She could obtain from them only their occasional presence, or the possibility of speaking of them, at her five o'clock tea-parties as, later on, in her *Memoirs,* of which these parties were only a sort of rehearsal, a preliminary reading aloud of the manuscript before a selected audience. And the society which all these noble kinsmen and kinswomen served to interest, to dazzle, to enthral, the society of the Cottards, of the Blochs, of the dramatists who were in the public eye at the moment, of the historians of the Fronde and such matters; it was in this society that there existed for Mme. de Villeparisis—failing that section of the fashionable world which did not call upon her—the movement, the novelty, all the entertainment of life, it was from people like these that she was able to derive social benefits (which made it well worth her while to let them meet, now and then, though without ever coming to know her, the Duchesse de Guermantes), dinners with remarkable men whose work had interested her, a light opera or a pantomime staged complete by its author in her drawing-room, boxes for interesting shows. Bloch got up to go. He had said aloud that the incident of the broken flower-glass was of no importance, but what he said to himself was different, more different still what he thought: "If people can't train their servants to put flowers where they won't be knocked over and wet their guests and probably cut their hands, it's much better not to go in for such luxuries," he muttered angrily. He was one of those susceptible, highly strung persons who cannot bear to think of themselves as having made a blunder which, though they do not admit even to themselves that they have made it, is enough to spoil their whole day. In a black rage, he was just making up his mind never to go into society again. He had reached the point at which some distraction was imperative. Fortunately in another minute Mme. de Villeparisis was to press him to stay. Either because she was aware of the general feeling among her friends, and had noticed the tide of anti-semitism that was beginning to rise, or simply from carelessness, she had not introduced him to any of the people in the room. He, however, being little used to society, felt bound before leaving the room to take leave of them all, to shew his manners, but without any friendliness; he lowered his head several times, buried his bearded chin in his collar, scrutinised each of the party in turn through his glasses with a cold, dissatisfied glare. But Mme. de Villeparisis stopped him; she had still to discuss with him the little play which was to be performed in her house, and also she did not wish him to leave before he had had the pleasure of meeting M. de Norpois (whose failure to appear puzzled her), although as an inducement to Bloch this introduction was quite superfluous, he having already decided to persuade the two actresses whose names he had mentioned to her to come and sing for nothing in the Marquise's drawing-room, to enhance their own reputations, at one of those parties to which all that was best and noblest in Europe thronged. He had even offered her, in addition, a tragic actress 'with pure eyes, fair as Hera,' who would recite lyrical prose with a sense of plastic beauty. But on hearing this lady's name Mme. de Villeparisis had declined, for it was that of Saint-Loup's mistress.

"I have better news," she murmured in my ear. "I really believe he's quite cooled off now, and that before very long they'll be parted—in spite of an officer who has played an abominable part in the whole business," she added. For Robert's family were beginning to look with a deadly hatred on M. de Borodino, who had given him leave, at the hairdresser's instance, to go to Bruges, and accused him of giving countenance to an infamous intrigue. "It's really too bad of him," said Mme. de Villeparisis with that virtuous accent common to all the Guermantes, even the most depraved. "Too, too bad," she repeated, giving the word a trio of t's. One felt that she had no doubt of the Prince's being present at all their orgies. But, as kindness of heart was the old lady's dominant quality, her expression of frowning severity towards the horrible captain, whose name she articulated with an ironical emphasis: "The Prince de Borodino!"—speaking as a woman for whom the Empire simply did not count, melted into a gentle smile at myself with a mechanical twitch of the eyelid indicating a vague understanding between us.

"I have a great admiration for de Saint-Loup-en-Bray," said Bloch, "dirty dog as he is, because he's so extremely well-bred. I have a great admiration, not for him but for well-bred people, they're so rare," he went on, without thinking, since he was himself so extremely ill-bred, what offence his words were giving. "I will give you an example which I consider most striking of his perfect breeding. I met him once with a young gentleman just as he was about to spring into his wheelèd chariot, after he himself had buckled their splendid harness on a pair of steeds, whose mangers were heaped with oats and barley, who had no need of the flashing whip to urge them on. He introduced us, but I did not catch the gentleman's name; one never does catch people's names when one's introduced to them," he explained with a laugh, this being one of his father's witticisms. "De Saint-Loup-en-Bray was perfectly calm, made no fuss about the young gentleman, seemed absolutely at his ease. Well, I found out, by pure chance, a day or two later, that the young gentleman was the son of Sir Rufus Israels!"

The end of this story sounded less shocking than its preface, for it remained quite incomprehensible to everyone in the room. The fact was that Sir Rufus Israels, who seemed to Bloch and his father an almost royal personage before whom Saint-Loup ought to tremble, was in the eyes of the Guermantes world a foreign upstart, tolerated in society, on whose friendship nobody would ever have dreamed of priding himself, far from it.

"I learned this," Bloch informed us, "from the person who holds Sir Rufus's power of attorney; he is a friend of my father, and quite an extraordinary man. Oh, an absolutely wonderful individual," he assured us with that affirmative energy, that note of enthusiasm which one puts only into those convictions that did not originate with oneself.

"Tell me," Bloch went on, lowering his voice, to myself, "how much do you suppose Saint-Loup has? Not that it matters to me in the least, you quite understand, don't you. I'm interested from the Balzacian point of view. You don't happen to know what it's in, French stocks, foreign stocks, or land or what?"

I could give him no information whatsoever. Suddenly raising his voice, Bloch asked if he might open the windows, and without waiting for an answer, went across the room to do so. Mme. de Villeparisis protested that he must not, that she had a cold. "Of course, if it's bad for you!" Bloch was downcast. "But you can't say it's not hot in here." And breaking into a laugh he put into the gaze with which he swept the room an appeal for support against Mme. de Villeparisis. He received none, from these well-bred people. His blazing eyes, having failed to seduce any of the guests from their allegiance, faded with resignation to their normal gravity of expression; he acknowledged his defeat with: "What's the temperature? Seventy-two, at least, I should say. I'm not surprised. I'm simply dripping. And I have not, like the sage Antenor, son of the river Alpheus, the power to plunge myself in the paternal wave to stanch my sweat before laying my body in a bath of polished marble and anointing my limbs with fragrant oils." And with that need which people feel to outline for the use of others medical theories the application of which would be beneficial to their own health: "Well, if you believe it's good for you! I must say, I think you're quite wrong. It's exactly what gives you your cold."

Bloch was overjoyed at the idea of meeting M. de Norpois. He would like, he told us, to get him to talk about the Dreyfus case. "There's a mentality at work there which I don't altogether understand, and it would be quite sensational to get an interview out of this eminent diplomat," he said in a tone of sarcasm, so as not to appear to be rating himself below the Ambassador.

Mme. de Villeparisis was sorry that he had said this so loud, but minded less when she saw that the librarian, whose strong Nationalist views kept her, so to speak, on leash, was too far off to have overheard. She was more shocked to hear Bloch, led on by that demon of ill-breeding which made him permanently blind to the consequences of what he said, inquiring, with a laugh at the paternal pleasantry: "Haven't I read a learned treatise by him in which he sets forth a string of irrefutable arguments to prove that the Japanese war was bound to end in a Russian victory and a Japanese defeat? He's fairly paralytic now, isn't he? I'm sure he's the old boy I've seen taking aim at his chair before sliding across the room to it, as if he was on wheels."

"Oh, dear, no! Not in the least like that! Just wait a minute," the Marquise went on, "I don't know what he can be doing."

She rang the bell and, when the servant had appeared, as she made no secret, and indeed liked to advertise the fact that her old friend spent the greater part of his time in her house: "Go and tell M. de Norpois to come in," she ordered him, "he is sorting some papers in my library; he said he would be twenty minutes, and I've been waiting now for an hour and three-quarters. He will tell you about the Dreyfus case, anything you want to know," she said gruffly to Bloch. "He doesn't approve much of the way things are going."

For M. de Norpois was not on good terms with the Government of the day, and Mme. de Villeparisis, although he had never taken the liberty of bringing any actual Ministers to her house (she still preserved all the un-approachable dignity of a great lady, and remained outside and above the political relations which he was obliged to cultivate), was kept well informed by him of everything that went on. Then, too, the politicians of the day would never have dared to ask M. de Norpois to introduce them to Mme. de Villeparisis. But several of them had gone down to see him at her house in the country when they needed his advice or help at critical conjectures. One knew the address. One went to the house. One did not see its mistress. But at dinner that evening she would say:

"I hear they've been down here bothering you. I trust things are going better."

"You are not in a hurry?" she now asked Bloch.

"No, not at all. I wanted to go because I am not very well; in fact there is some talk of my taking a cure at Vichy for my biliary ducts," he explained, articulating the last words with a fiendish irony.

"Why, that's where my nephew Châtellerault's got to go, you must fix it up together. Is he still in the room? He's a nice boy, you know," said Mme. de Villeparisis, and may quite well have meant what she said, feeling that two people whom she knew had no reason not to be friends with each other.

"Oh, I dare say he wouldn't care about that—I don't really know him —at least I barely know him. He is sitting over there," stammered Bloch in ecstasy of confusion.

The butler could not have delivered his mistress's message properly, for M. de Norpois, to make believe that he had just come in from the street, and had not yet seen his hostess, had picked up the first hat that he had found in the hall, and came forward to kiss Mme. de Villeparisis's hand with great ceremony, asking after her health with all the interest that people shew after a long separation. He was not aware that the Marquise had already destroyed any semblance of reality in this charade, which she cut short by taking M. de Norpois and Bloch into an adjoining room. Bloch,

who had observed all the courtesy that was being shewn to a person whom
he had not yet discovered to be M. de Norpois, had said to me, trying to
seem at his ease: "Who is that old idiot?" Perhaps, too, all this bowing
and scraping by M. de Norpois had really shocked the better element in
Bloch's nature, the freer and more straightforward manners of a younger
generation, and he was partly sincere in condemning it as absurd. However that might be, it ceased to appear absurd, and indeed delighted him
the moment it was himself, Bloch, to whom the salutations were addressed.

"Monsieur l'Ambassadeur," said Mme. de Villeparisis, "I should like
you to know this gentleman. Monsieur Bloch, Monsieur le Marquis de
Norpois." She made a point, despite her casual usage of M. de Norpois, of
addressing him always as "Monsieur l'Ambassadeur," as a social convention as well as from an exaggerated respect for his Ambassadorial rank, a
respect which the Marquis had inculcated in her, and also with an instinctive application to him of the special manner, less familiar and more
ceremonious, in relation to one particular man which, in the house of a
distinguished woman, in contrast to the liberties that she takes with her
other guests, marks that man out instantly as her lover.

M. de Norpois drowned his azure gaze in his white beard, bent his tall
body deep down as though he were bowing before all the famous and (to
him) imposing connotations of the name Bloch, and murmured: "I am
delighted . . ." whereat his young listener, moved, but feeling that the
illustrious diplomat was going too far, hastened to correct him, saying:
"Not at all! On the contrary, it is I who am delighted." But this ceremony,
which M. de Norpois, in his friendship for Mme. de Villeparisis, repeated
for the benefit of every fresh person that his old friend introduced to him,
did not seem to her adequate to the deserts of Bloch, to whom she said:

"Just ask him anything you want to know; take him into the other room
if it's more convenient; he will be delighted to talk to you. I think you
wished to speak to him about the Dreyfus case," she went on, no more
considering whether this would suit M. de Norpois than she would have
thought of asking leave of the Duchesse de Montmorency's portrait before
having it lighted up for the historian, or of the tea before pouring it into
a cup.

"You must speak loud," she warned Bloch, "he's a little deaf, but he
will tell you anything you want to know; he knew Bismarck very well,
and Cavour. That is so, isn't it;" she raised her voice, "you knew Bismarck
well?"

"Have you got anything on the stocks?" M. de Norpois asked me with
a knowing air as he shook my hand warmly. I took the opportunity to
relieve him politely of the hat which he had felt obliged to bring cere-
monially into the room, for I saw that it was my own which he had inad-
vertently taken. "You shewed me a somewhat laboured little thing in which
you went in for a good deal of hair-splitting. I gave you my opinion quite
frankly; what you had written was literally not worth the trouble of putting it on paper. Are you thinking of letting us have anything else? You
were greatly smitten with Bergotte, if I remember rightly." "You're not
to say anything against Bergotte," put in the Duchess. "I don't dispute

his talent as a painter; no one would, Duchess. He understands all about etching, if not brush-work on a large scale like M. Cherbuliez. But it seems to me that in these days we have a tendency to confuse the arts, and forget that the novelist's business is rather to weave a plot and edify his readers than to fiddle away at producing a frontispiece or tailpiece in drypoint. I shall be seeing your father on Sunday at our good friend A. J.'s," he went on, turning again to myself.

I had hoped for a moment, when I saw him talking to Mme. de Guermantes, that he would perhaps afford me, for getting myself asked to her house, the help he had refused me for getting to Mme. Swann's. "Another of my great favourites," I told him, "is Elstir. It seems the Duchesse de Guermantes has some wonderful examples of his work, particularly that admirable *Bunch of Radishes* which I remember at the Exhibition and should so much like to see again; what a masterpiece that is!" And indeed, if I had been a prominent person and had been asked to state what picture I liked best, I should have named this *Bunch of Radishes*. "A masterpiece?" cried M. de Norpois with a surprised and reproachful air. "It makes no pretence of being even a picture, it is merely a sketch." (He was right.) "If you label a clever little thing of that sort 'masterpiece,' what have you got to say about Hébert's *Virgin* or Dagnan-Bouveret?"

"I heard you refusing to let him bring Robert's woman," said Mme. de Guermantes to her aunt, after Bloch had taken the Ambassador aside. "I don't think you'll miss much, she's a perfect horror, as you know, without a vestige of talent, and besides she's grotesquely ugly."

"Do you mean to say, you know her, Duchess?" asked M. d'Argencourt.

"Yes, didn't you know that she performed in my house before the whole of Paris, not that that's anything for me to be proud of," explained Mme. de Guermantes with a laugh, glad nevertheless, since the actress was under discussion, to let it be known that she herself had had the first fruits of her foolishness. "Hallo, I suppose I ought to be going now," she added, without moving.

She had just seen her husband enter the room, and these words were an allusion to the absurdity of their appearing to be paying a call together, like a newly married couple, rather than to the often strained relations that existed between her and the enormous fellow she had married, who, despite his increasing years, still led the life of a gay bachelor. Ranging over the considerable party that was gathered round the tea-table the genial, cynical gaze—dazzled a little by the brightness of the setting sun—of the little round pupils lodged in the exact centre of his eyes, like the 'bulls' which the excellent marksman that he was could always hit with such perfect aim and precision, the Duke came forward with a bewildered cautious slowness as though, alarmed by so brilliant a gathering, he was afraid of treading on ladies' skirts and interrupting conversations. A permanent smile —suggesting a 'Good King of Yvetot'—slightly pompous, a half-open hand floating like a shark's fin by his side, which he allowed to be vaguely clasped by his old friends and by the strangers who were introduced to him, enabled him, without his having to make a single movement, or to interrupt his genial, lazy, royal progress, to reward the assiduity of them all by simply murmuring: "How do, my boy; how do, my dear friend; charmed, Monsieur Bloch; how do, Argencourt;" and, on coming to myself, who was the most highly favoured, when he had been told my name: "How do, my young neighbour, how's your father? What a splendid fellow he is!" He made no great demonstration except to Mme. de Villeparisis, who gave him good-day with a nod of her head, drawing one hand from a pocket of her little apron.

Being formidably rich in a world where everyone was steadily growing poorer, and having secured the permanent attachment to his person of the idea of this enormous fortune, he displayed all the vanity of the great nobleman reinforced by that of the man of means, the refinement and breeding of the former just managing to control the latter's self-sufficiency. One could understand, moreover, that his success with women, which made his wife so unhappy, was not due merely to his name and fortune, for he was still extremely good looking, and his profile retained the purity, the firmness of outline of a Greek god's.

"Do you mean to tell me she performed in your house?" M. d'Argencourt asked the Duchess.

"Well, don't you see, she came to recite, with a bunch of lilies in her hand, and more lilies on her *dress*." Mme. de Guermantes shared her aunt's affectation of pronouncing certain words in an exceedingly rustic fashion, but never rolled her r's like Mme. de Villeparisis.

Before M. de Norpois, under constraint from his hostess, had taken Bloch into the little recess where they could talk more freely, I went up to the old diplomat for a moment and put in a word about my father's Academic chair. He tried first of all to postpone the conversation to another day. I pointed out that I was going to Balbec. "What? Going again to Balbec? Why, you're a regular globe-trotter." He listened to what I had to say. At the name of Leroy-Beaulieu, he looked at me suspiciously. I conjectured that he had perhaps said something disparaging to M. Leroy-Beaulieu about my father and was afraid of the economist's having repeated it to him. All at once he seemed animated by a positive affection for my father. And after one of those opening hesitations out of which suddenly a word explodes as though in spite of the speaker, whose irresistible conviction prevails over his half-hearted efforts at silence: "No, no," he said to me with emotion, "your father *must not* stand. In his own interest he must not; it is not fair to himself; he owes a certain respect to his own really great merits, which would be compromised by such an adventure. He is too big a man for that. If he should be elected, he will have everything to lose and nothing to gain. He is not an orator, thank heaven. And that is the one thing that counts with my dear colleagues, even if you only talk platitudes. Your father has an important goal in life; he should march straight ahead towards it, and not allow himself to turn aside to beat bushes, even the bushes (more thorny for that matter than flowery) of the grove of Academe. Besides, he would not get many votes. The Academy likes to keep a postulant waiting for some time before taking him to its bosom. For the present, there is nothing to be done. Later on, I don't say. But he must wait until the Society itself comes in quest of him. It makes a practice, not a very fortunate practice, a fetish rather, of the *farà da sè* of our friends across the Alps. Leroy-Beaulieu spoke to me about all this in a way I did not at all like. I pointed out to him, a little sharply perhaps, that a man accustomed as he is to dealing with colonial imports and metals could not be expected to understand the part played by the imponderables, as Bismarck used to say. But, whatever happens, your father must on no account put himself forward as a candidate. *Principis obsta.* His friends would find themselves placed in a delicate position if he suddenly called upon them for their votes. Indeed," he broke forth, with an air of candour, fixing his blue eyes on my face, "I am going to say a thing that you will be surprised to hear coming from me, who am so fond of your father. Well, simply because I am fond of him (we are known as the inseparables— *Arcades ambo*), simply because I know the immense service that he can still render to his country, the reefs from which he can steer her if he remains at the helm; out of affection, out of high regard for him, out of patriotism, I should not vote for him. I fancy, moreover, that I have given him to understand that I should not." (I seemed to discern in his eyes the stern Assyrian profile of Leroy-Beaulieu.) "So that to give him my vote now would be a sort of recantation on my part." M. de Norpois repeatedly dismissed his brother Academicians as old fossils. Other reasons apart, every member of a club or academy likes to ascribe to his fellow members the type of character that is the direct converse of his own, less for the advantage of being able to say: "Ah! If it only rested with me!" than for the satisfaction of making the election which he himself has managed to secure seem more difficult, a greater distinction. "I may tell you," he concluded, "that in the best interests of you all, I should prefer to see your father triumphantly elected in ten or fifteen years' time." Words which I assumed to have been dictated if not by jealousy, at any rate by an utter lack of any willingness to oblige, and which later on I was to recall when the course of events had given them a different meaning.

"You haven't thought of giving the Institute an address on the price of bread during the Fronde, I suppose," the historian of that movement timidly inquired of M. de Norpois. "You could make a considerable success of a subject like that," (which was to say, "you would give me a colossal advertisement,") he added, smiling at the Ambassador pusillanimously, but with a warmth of feeling which made him raise his eyelids and expose a double horizon of eye. I seemed to have seen this look before, and yet I had met the historian for the first time this afternoon. Suddenly I remembered having seen the same expression in the eyes of a Brazilian doctor who claimed to be able to cure choking fits of the kind from which I suffered by some absurd inhalation of the essential oils of plants. When, in the hope that he would pay more attention to my case, I had told him that I knew Professor Cottard, he had replied, as though speaking in Cottard's interest: "Now this treatment of mine, if you were to tell him about it, would give him the material for a most sensational paper for the Academy of Medicine!" He had not ventured to press the matter but had stood gazing at me with the same air of interrogation, timid, anxious, appealing, which it had just puzzled me to see on the face of the historian of the

Fronde. Obviously the two men were not acquainted and had little or nothing in common, but psychological like physical laws have a more or less general application. And the requisite conditions are the same; an identical expression lights the eyes of different human animals, as a single sunrise lights different places, a long way apart, which have no connexion with one another. I did not hear the Ambassador's reply, for the whole party, with a good deal of noise, had again gathered round Mme. de Ville-parisis to watch her at work.

"You know who' we're talking about, Basin?" the Duchess asked her husband.

"I can make a pretty good guess," said the Duke.

"Ah! As an actress she's not, I'm afraid, in what one would call the great tradition."

"You can't imagine," went on Mme. de Guermantes to M. d'Argencourt, "anything more ridiculous."

"In fact, it was drolatic," put in M. de Guermantes, whose odd vocabulary enabled people in society to declare that he was no fool and literary people, at the same time, to regard him as a complete imbecile.

"What I fail to understand," resumed the Duchess, "is how in the world Robert ever came to fall in love with her. Oh, of course I know one mustn't discuss that sort of thing," she added, with the charming pout of a phi-losopher and sentimentalist whose last illusion had long been shattered. "I know that anybody may fall in love with anybody else. And," she went on, for, though she might still laugh at modern literature, it, either by its dissemination through the popular press or else in the course of conversa-tion, had begun to percolate into her mind, "that is the really nice thing about love, because it's what makes it so 'mysterious.' "

"Mysterious! Oh, I must confess, cousin, that's a bit beyond me," said the Comte d'Argencourt.

"Oh dear, yes, it's a very mysterious thing, love," declared the Duchess, with the sweet smile of a good-natured woman of the world, but also with the rooted conviction with which a Wagnerian assures a bored gentleman from the Club that there is something more than just noise in the *Walküre*. "After all, one never does know what makes one person fall in love with another; it may not be at all what we think," she added with a smile, re-pudiating at once by this interpretation the idea she had just suggested. "After all, one never knows anything, does one?" she concluded with an air of weary scepticism. "Besides, one understands, doesn't one; one simply can't explain other people's choices in love."

But having laid down this principle she proceeded at once to abandon it and to criticise Saint-Loup's choice.

"All the same, don't you know, it is amazing to me that a man can find any attraction in a person who's simply silly."

Bloch, hearing Saint-Loup's name mentioned and gathering that he was in Paris, promptly made a remark about him so outrageous that every-body was shocked. He was beginning to nourish hatreds, and one felt that he would stop at nothing to gratify them. Once he had established the principle that he himself was of great moral worth and that the sort of people who frequented La Boulie (an athletic club which he supposed to be highly fashionable) deserved penal servitude, every blow he could get in against them seemed to him praiseworthy. He went so far once as to speak of a lawsuit which he was anxious to bring against one of his La Boulie friends. In the course of the trial he proposed to give certain evidence which would be entirely untrue, though the defendant would be unable to impugn his veracity. In this way Bloch (who, incidentally, never put his plan into action) counted on baffling and infuriating his antagonist. What harm could there be in that, since he whom he sought to injure was a man who thought only of doing the 'right thing,' a La Boulie man, and against people like that any weapon was justified, especially in the hands of a Saint, such as Bloch himself?

"I say, though, what about Swann?" objected M. d'Argencourt, who having at last succeeded in understanding the point of his cousin's speech, was impressed by her accuracy of observation, and was racking his brains for instances of men who had fallen in love with women in whom he himself had seen no attraction.

"Oh, but Swann's case was quite different," the Duchess protested. "It was a great surprise, I admit, because she's just a well-meaning idiot, but she was never silly, and she was at one time good looking."

"Oh, oh!" muttered Mme. de Villeparisis.

"You never thought so? Surely, she had some charming points, very fine eyes, good hair, she used to dress, and does still dress, wonderfully. Nowadays, I quite agree, she's horrible, but she has been a lovely woman in her time. Not that that made me any less sorry when Charles married her, because it was so unnecessary." The Duchess had not intended to say anything out of the common, but as M. d'Argencourt began to laugh she repeated these last words—either because she thought them amusing or because she thought it nice of him to laugh—and looked up at him with a coaxing smile, to add the enchantment of her femininity to that of her wit. She went on: "Yes, really, it wasn't worth the trouble, was it; still, after all, she did have some charm and I can quite understand anybody's falling in love with her, but if you saw Robert's girl, I assure you, you'd simply die of laughter. Oh, I know somebody's going to quote Augier at me: 'What matters the bottle so long as one gets drunk?' Well, Robert may have got drunk, all right, but he certainly hasn't shewn much taste in his choice of a bottle! First of all, would you believe that she actually expected me to fit up a staircase right in the middle of my drawing-room. Oh, a mere nothing—what?—and she announced that she was going to lie flat on her stomach on the steps. And then, if you'd heard the things she recited, I only remember one scene, but I'm sure nobody could imagine anything like it; it was called the *Seven Princesses*."

"*Seven Princesses!* Dear, dear, what a snob she must be!" cried M. d'Argencourt. "But, wait a minute, why, I know the whole play. The author sent a copy to the King, who couldn't understand a word of it and called on me to explain it to him."

"It isn't by any chance, from the Sar Peladan?" asked the historian of the Fronde, meaning to make a subtle and topical allusion, but in so low a tone that his question passed unnoticed.

"So you know the *Seven Princesses,* do you?" replied the Duchess. "I congratulate you! I only know one, but she's quite enough; I have no wish to make the acquaintance of the other six. If they are all like the one I've seen!"

"What a goose!" I thought to myself. Irritated by the coldness of her greeting, I found a sort of bitter satisfaction in this proof of her complete inability to understand Maeterlinck. "To think that's the woman I walk miles every morning to see. Really, I'm too kind. Well, it's my turn now not to want to see her." Thus I reasoned with myself; but my words ran counter to my thoughts; they were purely conversational words such as we say to ourselves at those moments when, too much excited to remain quietly alone, we feel the need, for want of another listener, to talk to ourselves, without meaning what we say, as we talk to a stranger.

"I can't tell you what it was like," the Duchess went on; "you simply couldn't help laughing. Not that anyone tried; rather the other way, I'm sorry to say, for the young person was not at all pleased and Robert has never really forgiven me. Though I can't say I'm sorry, actually, because if it had been a success the lady would perhaps have come again, and I don't quite see Marie-Aynard approving of that."

This was the name given in the family to Robert's mother, Mme. de Marsantes, the widow of Aynard de Saint-Loup, to distinguish her from her cousin, the Princesse de Guermantes-Bavière, also a Marie, to whose Christian name her nephews and cousins and brothers-in-law added, to avoid confusion, either that of her husband or another of her own, making her Marie-Gilbert or Marie-Hedwige.

"To begin with, there was a sort of rehearsal the night before, which was a wonderful affair!" went on Mme. de Guermantes in ironical pursuit of her theme. "Just imagine, she uttered a sentence, no, not so much, not a quarter of a sentence, and then she stopped; she didn't open her mouth— I'm not exaggerating—for a good five minutes."

"Oh, I say," cried M. d'Argencourt.

"With the utmost politeness I took the liberty of hinting to her that this might seem a little unusual. And she said—I give you her actual words— 'One ought always to repeat a thing as though one were just composing it oneself.' When you think of it, that really is monumental."

"But I understood she wasn't at all bad at reciting poetry," said one of the two young men.

"She hasn't the ghost of a notion what poetry is," replied Mme. de Guermantes. "However, I didn't need to listen to her to tell that. It was quite enough to see her come in with her lilies. I knew at once that she couldn't have any talent when I saw those lilies!"

Everybody laughed.

"I hope, my dear aunt, you aren't angry with me, over my little joke the other day about the Queen of Sweden. I've come to ask your forgiveness."

"Oh, no, I'm not at all angry, I even give you leave to eat at my table, if you're hungry.—Come along, M. Valmère, you're the daughter of the house," Mme. de Villeparisis went on to the librarian, repeating a time-honoured pleasantry.

M. de Guermantes sat upright in the armchair in which he had come to anchor, his hat on the carpet by his side, and examined with a satisfied smile the plate of little cakes that was being held out to him.

"Why, certainly, now that I am beginning to feel at home in this distinguished company, I will take a sponge-cake; they look excellent."

"This gentleman makes you an admirable daughter," commented M. d'Argencourt, whom the spirit of imitation prompted to keep Mme. de Villeparisis's little joke in circulation.

The librarian handed the plate of cakes to the historian of the Fronde.

"You perform your functions admirably," said the latter, startled into speech, and hoping also to win the sympathy of the crowd. At the same time he cast a covert glance of connivance at those who had anticipated him.

"Tell me, my dear aunt," M. de Guermantes inquired of Mme. de Villeparisis, "who was that rather good-looking man who was going out just now as I came in? I must know him, because he gave me a sweeping bow, but I couldn't place him at all; you know I never can remember names, it's such a nuisance," he added, in a tone of satisfaction.

"M. Legrandin."

"Oh, but Oriane has a cousin whose mother, if I'm not mistaken, was a Grandin. Yes, I remember quite well, she was a Grandin de l'Epervier."

"No," replied Mme. de Villeparisis, "no relation at all. These are plain Grandins. Grandins of nothing at all. But they'd be only too glad to be Grandins of anything you chose to name. This one has a sister called Mme. de Cambremer."

"Why, Basin, you know quite well who my aunt means," cried the Duchess indignantly. "He's the brother of that great graminivorous creature you had the weird idea of sending to call on me the other day. She stayed a solid hour; I thought I should go mad. But I began by thinking it was she who was mad when I saw a person I didn't know come browsing into the room looking exactly like a cow."

"Listen, Oriane; she asked me what afternoon you were at home; I couldn't very well be rude to her; and besides, you do exaggerate so, she's not in the least like a cow," he added in a plaintive tone, though not without a quick smiling glance at the audience.

He knew that his wife's lively wit needed the stimulus of contradiction, the contradiction of common sense which protests that one cannot (for instance) mistake a woman seriously for a cow; by this process Mme. de Guermantes, enlarging upon her original idea, had been inspired to produce many of her most brilliant sayings. And the Duke in his innocent fashion helped her, without seeming to do so, to bring off her effects like, in a railway carriage, the unacknowledged partner of the three-card player.

"I admit she doesn't look like a cow, she looks like a dozen," exclaimed Mme. de Guermantes. "I assure you, I didn't know what to do when I saw a herd of cattle come marching into my drawing-room in a hat and heard them ask me how I was. I had half a mind to say: 'Please, herd of cattle, you must be making a mistake, you can't possibly know me, because you're a herd of cattle,' but after racking my brains over her I came to the conclusion that your Cambremer woman must be the Infanta Dorothea, who had said she was coming to see me one day, and is rather bovine also, so that I was just on the point of saying: 'Your Royal Highness' and using the third person to a herd of cattle. The cut of her dewlap reminded me rather, too, of the Queen of Sweden. But this massed attack had been prepared for by long range artillery fire, according to all the rules of war. For I don't know how long before, I was bombarded with her cards; I used to find them lying about all over the house, on all the tables and chairs, like prospectuses. I couldn't think what they were supposed to be advertising. You saw nothing in the house but 'Marquis et Marquise de Cambremer' with some address or other which I've forgotten; you may be quite sure nothing will ever take me there."

"But it's a great distinction to look like a Queen," said the historian of the Fronde.

"Gad, sir, Kings and Queens, in these days, don't amount to much," said M. de Guermantes, partly because he liked to be thought broad-minded and modern, and also so as not to seem to attach any importance to his own royal friendships, which he valued highly.

Bloch and M. de Norpois had returned from the other room and came towards us.

"Well, sir," asked Mme. de Villeparisis, "have you been talking to him about the Dreyfus case?"

M. de Norpois raised his eyes to the ceiling, but with a smile, as though calling on heaven to witness the monstrosity of the caprices to which his Dulcinea compelled him to submit. Nevertheless he spoke to Bloch with great affability of the terrible, perhaps fatal period through which France was passing. As this presumably meant that M. de Norpois (to whom Bloch had confessed his belief in the innocence of Dreyfus) was an ardent anti-Dreyfusard, the Ambassador's geniality, his air of tacit admission that his listener was in the right, of never doubting that they were both of the same opinion, of being prepared to join forces with him to overthrow the Government, flattered Bloch's vanity and aroused his curiosity. What were the important points which M. de Norpois never specified but on which he seemed implicitly to affirm that he was in agreement with Bloch; what opinion, then, did he hold of the case, that could bring them together? Bloch was all the more astonished at the mysterious unanimity which seemed to exist between him and M. de Norpois, in that it was not confined to politics, Mme. de Villeparisis having spoken at some length to M. de Norpois of Bloch's literary work.

"You are not of your age," the former Ambassador told him, "and I congratulate you upon that. You are not of this age in which disinterested work no longer exists, in which writers offer the public nothing but obscenities or ineptitudes. Efforts such as yours ought to be encouraged, and would be, if we had a Government."

Bloch was flattered by this picture of himself swimming alone amid a universal shipwreck. But here again he would have been glad of details, would have liked to know what were the ineptitudes to which M. de Norpois referred. Bloch had the feeling that he was working along the same lines as plenty of others; he had never supposed himself to be so exceptional. He returned to the Dreyfus case, but did not succeed in elucidating M. de Norpois's own views. He tried to induce him to speak of the officers whose names were appearing constantly in the newspapers at that time; they aroused more curiosity than the politicians who were involved also, because they were not, like the politicians, well known already, but, wearing a special garb, emerging from the obscurity of a different kind of life and a religiously guarded silence, simply stood up and spoke and disappeared again, like Lohengrin landing from a skiff drawn by a swan. Bloch had been able, thanks to a Nationalist lawyer of his acquaintance, to secure admission to several hearings of the Zola trial. He would arrive there in the morning and stay until the court rose, with a packet of sandwiches and a flask of coffee, as though for the final examination for a degree, and this change of routine stimulating a nervous excitement which the coffee and the emotional interest of the trial worked up to a climax, he would come out so enamoured of everything that had happened in court that, in the evening, as he sat at home, he would long to immerse himself again in that beautiful dream and would hurry out, to a restaurant frequented by both parties, in search of friends with whom he would go over interminably the whole of the day's proceedings, and make up, by a supper ordered in an imperious tone which gave him the illusion of power, for the hunger and exhaustion of a day begun so early and unbroken by any interval for luncheon. The human mind, hovering perpetually between the two planes of experience and imagination, seeks to fathom the ideal life of the people it knows and to know the people whose life it has had to imagine. To Bloch's questions M. de Norpois replied:

"There are two officers involved in the case now being tried of whom I remember hearing some time ago from a man in whose judgment I felt great confidence, and who praised them both highly—I mean M. de Miribel. They are Lieutenant-Colonel Henry and Lieutenant-Colonel Picquart."

"But," exclaimed Bloch, "the divine Athena, daughter of Zeus, has put in the mind of one the opposite of what is in the mind of the other. And they are fighting against one another like two lions. Colonel Picquart had a splendid position in the Army, but his Moira has led him to the side that was not rightly his. The sword of the Nationalists will carve his tender flesh, and he will be cast out as food for the beasts of prey and the birds that wax fat upon the bodies of men."

M. de Norpois made no reply.

"What are those two palavering about over there?" M. de Guermantes asked Mme. de Villeparisis, indicating M. de Norpois and Bloch.

"The Dreyfus case."

"The devil they are. By the way, do you know who is a red-hot supporter of Dreyfus? I give you a thousand guesses. My nephew Robert! I can tell you that, at the Jockey, when they heard of his goings on, there was a fine gathering of the clans, a regular hue and cry. And as he's coming up for election next week . . ."

"Of course," broke in the Duchess, "if they're all like Gilbert, who keeps on saying that all the Jews ought to be sent back to Jerusalem."

"Indeed; then the Prince de Guermantes is quite of my way of thinking," put in M. d'Argencourt.

The Duke made a show of his wife, but did not love her. Extremely self-centred, he hated to be interrupted, besides he was in the habit, at home, of treating her brutally. Convulsed with the twofold rage of a bad husband when his wife speaks to him, and a good talker when he is not listened to, he stopped short and transfixed the Duchess with a glare which made everyone feel uncomfortable.

"What makes you think we want to hear about Gilbert and Jerusalem? It's nothing to do with that. But," he went on in a gentler tone, "you will agree that if one of our family were to be pilled at the Jockey, especially Robert, whose father was chairman for ten years, it would be a pretty serious matter. What can you expect, my dear, it's got 'em on the raw, those fellows; they're all over it. I don't blame them, either; personally, you know that I have no racial prejudice, all that sort of thing seems to me out of date, and I do claim to move with the times; but damn it all, when one goes by the name of 'Marquis de Saint-Loup' one isn't a Dreyfusard; what more can I say?"

M. de Guermantes uttered the words: "When one goes by the name of Marquis de Saint-Loup," with some emphasis. He knew very well that it was a far greater thing to go by that of Duc de Guermantes. But if his self-esteem had a tendency to exaggerate if anything the superiority of the title Duc de Guermantes over all others, it was perhaps not so much the rules of good taste as the laws of imagination that urged him thus to attenuate it. Each of us sees in the brightest colours what he sees at a distance, what he sees in other people. For the general laws which govern perspective in imagination apply just as much to dukes as to ordinary mortals. And not only the laws of imagination, but those of speech. Now, either of two laws of speech may apply here, one being that which makes us express ourselves like others of our mental category and not of our caste. Under this law M. de Guermantes might be, in his choice of expressions, even when he wished to talk about the nobility, indebted to the humblest little tradesman, who would have said: "When one goes by the name of Duc de Guermantes," whereas an educated man, a Swann, a Legrandin would not have said it. A duke may write novels worthy of a grocer, even about life in high society, titles and pedigrees being of no help to him there, and the epithet 'aristocratic' be earned by the writings of a plebeian. Who had been, in this instance, the inferior from whom M. de Guermantes had picked up 'when one goes by the name,' he had probably not the least idea. But another law of speech is that, from time to time, as there appear and then vanish diseases of which nothing more is ever heard, there come into being, no one knows how, spontaneously perhaps or by an accident like that which introduced into France a certain weed from America, the seeds of which, caught in the wool of a travelling rug, fell on a railway embankment, forms of speech which one hears in the same decade on the lips of people who have not in any way combined together to use them. So, just as in a certain year I heard Bloch say, referring to himself, that "the most charming people, the most brilliant, the best known, the most exclusive had discovered that there was only one man in Paris whom they felt to be intelligent, pleasant, whom they could not do without—namely Bloch," and heard the same phrase used by countless other young men who did not know him and varied it only by substituting their own names for his, so I was often to hear this 'when one goes by the name.'

"What can one expect," the Duke went on, "with the influence he's come under; it's easy to understand."

"Still it is rather comic," suggested the Duchess, "when you think of his mother's attitude, how she bores us to tears with her Patrie Française, morning, noon and night."

"Yes, but there's not only his mother to be thought of, you can't humbug us like that. There's a damsel, too, a fly-by-night of the worst type; she has far more influence over him than his mother, and she happens to be a compatriot of Master Dreyfus. She has passed on her state of mind to Robert."

"You may not have heard, Duke, that there is a new word to describe that sort of mind," said the librarian, who was Secretary to the Anti-revisionist Committee. "They say 'mentality.' It means exactly the same thing, but it has this advantage that nobody knows what you're talking about. It is the very latest expression just now, the 'last word' as people say." Meanwhile, having heard Bloch's name, he was watching him question M. de Norpois with misgivings which aroused others as strong though of a different order in the Marquise. Trembling before the librarian, and always acting the anti-Dreyfusard in his presence, she dreaded what he would say were he to find out that she had asked to her house a Jew more or less affiliated to the 'Syndicate.'

"Indeed," said the Duke, " 'mentality,' you say; I must make a note of that; I shall use it some day." This was no figure of speech, the Duke having a little pocketbook filled with such 'references' which he used to consult before dinner-parties. "I like 'mentality.' There are a lot of new words like that which people suddenly start using, but they never last. I read somewhere the other day that some writer was 'talentuous.' You may perhaps know what it means; I don't. And since then I've never come across the word again."

"But 'mentality' is more widely used than 'talentuous,'" the historian of the Fronde made his way into the conversation. "I am on a Committee at the Ministry of Education at which I have heard it used several times, as well as at my Club, the Volney, and indeed at dinner at M. Emile Ollivier's."

"I, who have not the honour to belong to the Ministry of Education," replied the Duke with a feigned humility but with a vanity so intense that his lips could not refrain from curving in a smile, nor his eyes from casting round his audience a glance sparkling with joy, the ironical scorn in which made the poor historian blush, "I who have not the honour to belong to the Ministry of Education," he repeated, relishing the sound of his words, "nor to the Volney Club (my only clubs are the Union and the Jockey

—you aren't in the Jockey, I think, sir?" he asked the historian, who, blushing a still deeper red, scenting an insult and failing to understand it, began to tremble in every limb), "I, who am not even invited to dine with M. Emile Ollivier, I must confess that I had never heard 'mentality.' I'm sure you're in the same boat, Argencourt.

"You know," he went on, "why they can't produce the proofs of Dreyfus's guilt. Apparently it's because the War Minister's wife was his mistress, that's what people are saying."

"Ah! I thought it was the Prime Minister's wife," said M. d'Argencourt.

"I think you're all equally tiresome about this wretched case," said the Duchesse de Guermantes, who, in the social sphere, was always anxious to shew that she did not allow herself to be led by anyone. "It can't make any difference to me, so far as the Jews are concerned, for the simple reason that I don't know any of them, and I intend to remain in that state of blissful ignorance. But on the other hand I do think it perfectly intolerable that just because they're supposed to hold 'sound' views and don't deal with Jewish tradesmen, or have 'Down with the Jews' printed on their sunshades, we should have a swarm of Durands and Dubois and so forth, women we should never have known but for this business, forced down our throats by Marie-Aynard or Victurnienne. I went to see Marie-Aynard a couple of days ago. It used to be so nice there. Nowadays one finds all the people one has spent one's life trying to avoid, on the pretext that they're against Dreyfus, and others of whom you have no idea who they can be."

"No; it was the War Minister's wife; at least, that's the bedside rumour," went on the Duke, who liked to flavour his conversation with certain expressions which he imagined to be of the old school. "Personally, of course, as everyone knows, I take just the opposite view to my cousin Gilbert. I am not feudal like him. I would go about with a Negro if he was a friend of mine, and I shouldn't care two straws what anybody thought; still after all you will agree with me that when one goes by the name of Saint-Loup one doesn't amuse oneself by running clean against the rails of public opinion, which has more sense than Voltaire or even my nephew. Nor does one go in for what I may be allowed to call these acrobatics of conscience a week before one comes up for a club. It is a bit stiff, really! No, it is probably that little wench of his that has put him on his high horse. I expect she told him that he would be classed among the 'intellectuals.' The intellectuals, they're the very cream of those gentry. It's given rise, by the way, to a rather amusing pun, though a very naughty one."

And the Duke murmured, lowering his voice, for his wife's and M. d'Argencourt's benefit, "Mater Semita," which had already made its way into the Jockey Club, for, of all the flying seeds in the world, that to which are attached the most solid wings, enabling it to be disseminated at the greatest distance from its parent branch, is still a joke.

"We might ask this gentleman, who has a *nerudite* air, to explain it to us," he went on, indicating the historian. "But it is better not to repeat it, especially as there's not a vestige of truth in the suggestion. I am not so ambitious as my cousin Mirepoix, who claims that she can trace the descent of her family before Christ to the Tribe of Levi, and I will undertake to prove that there has never been a drop of Jewish blood in our family. Still there is no good in our shutting our eyes to the fact, you may be sure that my dear nephew's highly original views are liable to make a considerable stir at Landerneau. Especially as Fezensac is ill just now, and Duras will be running the election; you know how he likes to make nuisances," concluded the Duke, who had never succeeded in learning the exact meaning of certain phrases, and supposed 'making nuisances' to mean 'making difficulties.'

Bloch tried to pin M. de Norpois down on Colonel Picquart.

"There can be no two opinions;" replied M. de Norpois, "his evidence had to be taken. I am well aware that, by maintaining this attitude, I have drawn screams of protest from more than one of my colleagues, but to my mind the Government were bound to let the Colonel speak. One can't dance lightly out of a blind alley like that, or if one does there's always the risk of falling into a ditch. As for the officer himself, his statement gave one, at the first hearing, a most excellent impression. When one saw him, looking so well in that smart Chasseur uniform, come into court and relate in a perfectly simple and frank tone what he had seen and what he had deduced, and say: 'On my honour as a soldier' " (here M. de Norpois's voice shook with a faint patriotic throb) " 'such is my conviction,' it is impossible to deny that the impression he made was profound."

"There; he is a Dreyfusard, there's not the least doubt of it," thought Bloch.

"But where he entirely forfeited all the sympathy that he had managed to attract was when he was confronted with the registrar, Gribelin. When one heard that old public servant, a man who had only one answer to make," (here M. de Norpois began to accentuate his words with the energy of his sincere convictions) "when one listened to him, when one saw him look his superior officer in the face, not afraid to hold his head up to him, and say to him in a tone that admitted of no response: 'Colonel, sir, you know very well that I have never told a lie, you know that at this moment, as always, I am speaking the truth,' the wind changed; M. Picquart might move heaven and earth at the subsequent hearings; he made a complete fiasco."

"No; evidently he's an anti-Dreyfusard; it's quite obvious," said Bloch to himself. "But if he considers Picquart a traitor and a liar, how can he take his revelations seriously, and quote them as if he found them charming and believed them to be sincere. And if, on the other hand, he sees in him an honest man easing his conscience, how can he suppose him to have been lying when he was confronted with Gribelin?"

"In any case, if this man Dreyfus is innocent," the Duchess broke in, "he hasn't done much to prove it. What idiotic, raving letters he writes from that island. I don't know whether M. Esterhazy is any better, but he does shew some skill in his choice of words, a different tone altogether. That can't be very pleasant for the supporters of M. Dreyfus. What a pity for them there's no way of exchanging innocents." Everybody laughed. "You heard what Oriane said?" the Duc de Guermantes inquired eagerly of Mme. de Villeparisis. "Yes; I think it most amusing." This was not enough

for the Duke. "Well, I don't know, I can't say that I thought it amusing;
or rather it doesn't make the slightest difference to me whether a thing is
amusing or not. I don't care about wit." M. d'Argencourt protested. "It is
probably because I've been a Member of Parliament, where I have listened
to brilliant speeches that meant absolutely nothing. I learned there to value,
more than anything, logic. That's probably why they didn't elect me
again. Amusing things leave me cold." "Basin, don't play the heavy father
like that, my child, you know quite well that no one admires wit more than
you do." "Please let me finish. It is just because I am unmoved by a certain
type of humour, that I am often struck by my wife's wit. For you will find
it based, as a rule, upon sound observation. She reasons like a man; she
states her case like a writer."

Possibly the explanation of M. de Norpois's speaking in this way to
Bloch, as though they had been in agreement, may have lain in the fact
that he himself was so keen an anti-Dreyfusard that, finding the Government not anti-Dreyfusard enough, he was its enemy just as much as the
Dreyfusards. Perhaps because the object to which he devoted himself in
politics was something more profound, situated on another plane, from
which Dreyfusism appeared as an unimportant modality which did not
deserve the attention of a patriot interested in large questions of foreign
policy. Perhaps, rather, because the maxims of his political wisdom being
applicable only to questions of form, of procedure, of expediency, they
were as powerless to solve questions of fact as in philosophy pure logic is
powerless to tackle the problems of existence; or else because that very
wisdom made him see danger in handling such subjects and so, in his
caution, he preferred to speak only of minor incidents. But where Bloch
made a mistake was in thinking that M. de Norpois, even had he been less
cautious by nature and of a less exclusively formal cast of mind, could
(supposing he would) have told him the truth as to the part played by
Henry, Picquart or du Paty de Clam, or as to any of the different aspects
of the case. The truth, indeed, as to all these matters Bloch could not doubt
that M. de Norpois knew. How could he fail to know it seeing that he was
a friend of all the Ministers? Naturally, Bloch thought that the truth in
politics could be approximately reconstructed by the most luminous minds,
but he imagined, like the man in the street, that it resided permanently,
beyond the reach of argument and in a material form, in the secret files
of the President of the Republic and the Prime Minister, who imparted it
to their Cabinet. Now, even when a political truth does take the form of
written documents, it is seldom that these have any more value than a radio-
graphic plate on which the layman imagines that the patient's disease is
inscribed in so many words, when, as a matter of fact, the plate furnishes
simply one piece of material for study, to be combined with a number of
others, which the doctor's reasoning powers will take into consideration as
a whole and upon them found his diagnosis. So, too, the truth in politics,
when one goes to well-informed men and imagines that one is about to
grasp it, eludes one. Indeed, later on (to confine ourselves to the Dreyfus
case), when so startling an event occurred as Henry's confession, followed
by his suicide, this fact was at once interpreted in opposite ways by the

Dreyfusard Ministers, and by Cavaignac and Cuignet who had themselves made the discovery of the forgery and conducted the examination; still more so among the Dreyfusard Ministers themselves, men of the same shade of Dreyfusism, judging not only from the same documents but in the same spirit, the part played by Henry was explained in two entirely different ways, one set seeing in him an accomplice of Esterhazy, the others assigning that part to du Paty de Clam, thus rallying in support of a theory of their opponent Cuignet and in complete opposition to their supporter Reinach. All that Bloch could elicit from M. de Norpois was that if it were true that the Chief of Staff, M. de Boisdeffre, had had a secret communication sent to M. Rochefort, it was evident that a singularly regrettable irregularity had occurred.

"You may be quite sure that the War Minister must (*in petto* at any rate) be consigning his Chief of Staff to the infernal powers. An official disclaimer would not have been (to my mind) a work of supererogation. But the War Minister expresses himself very bluntly on the matter *inter pocula*. There are certain subjects, moreover, about which it is highly imprudent to create an agitation over which one cannot retain control afterwards."

"But those documents are obviously forged," put in Bloch.

M. de Norpois made no reply to this, but announced that he did not approve of the manifestations that were being made by Prince Henri d'Orléans.

"Besides, they can only ruffle the calm of the pretorium, and encourage agitations which, looked at from either point of view, would be deplorable. Certainly we must put a stop to the anti-militarist conspiracy, but we cannot possibly tolerate, either, a brawl encouraged by those elements on the Right who instead of serving the patriotic ideal themselves are hoping to make it serve them. Heaven be praised, France is not a South American Republic, and the need has not yet been felt here for a military pronunciamento."

Bloch could not get him to speak on the question of Dreyfus's guilt, nor would he utter any forecast as to the judgment in the civil trial then proceeding. On the other hand, M. de Norpois seemed only too ready to indicate the consequences of this judgment.

"If it is a conviction," he said, "it will probably be quashed, for it is seldom that, in a case where there has been such a number of witnesses, there is not some flaw in the procedure which counsel can raise on appeal. To return to Prince Henri's outburst, I greatly doubt whether it has met with his father's approval."

"You think Chartres is for Dreyfus?" asked the Duchess with a smile, her eyes rounded, her cheeks bright, her nose buried in her plate, her whole manner deliciously scandalised.

"Not at all; I meant only that there runs through the whole family, on that side, a political sense which we have seen, in the admirable Princesse Clémentine, carried to its highest power, and which her son, Prince Ferdinand, has kept as a priceless inheritance. You would never have found the Prince of Bulgaria clasping Major Esterhazy to his bosom."

"He would have preferred a private soldier," murmured Mme. de Guermantes, who often met the Bulgarian monarch at dinner at the Prince de Joinville's, and had said to him once, when he asked if she was not envious: "Yes, Sir, of your bracelets."

"You aren't going to Mme. de Sagan's ball this evening?" M. de Norpois asked Mme. de Villeparisis, to cut short his conversation with Bloch. My friend had not failed to interest the Ambassador, who told us afterwards, not without a quaint simplicity, thinking no doubt of the traces that survived in Bloch's speech of the neo-Homeric manner which he had on the whole outgrown: "He is rather amusing, with that way of speaking, a trifle old fashioned, a trifle solemn. You expect him to come out with 'The Learned Sisters,' like Lamartine or Jean-Baptiste Rousseau. It has become quite uncommon in the youth of the present day, as it was indeed in the generation before them. We ourselves were inclined to be romantic." But however exceptional his companion may have seemed to him, M. de Norpois decided that the conversation had lasted long enough.

"No, sir, I don't go to balls any more," she replied with a charming grandmotherly smile. "You're going, all of you, I suppose? You're the right age for that sort of thing," she added, embracing in a comprehensive glance M. de Châtellerault, his friend and Bloch. "Still, I was asked," she went on, pretending, just for fun, to be flattered by the distinction. "In fact, they came specially to ask me." ('They' being the Princesse de Sagan.)

"I haven't had a card," said Bloch, thinking that Mme. de Villeparisis would at once offer to procure him one, and that Mme. de Sagan would be glad to see at her ball the friend of a woman whom she had called in person to invite.

The Marquise made no reply, and Bloch did not press the point, for he had another, more serious matter to discuss with her, and, with that in view, had already asked her whether he might call again in a couple of days. Having heard the two young men say that they had both just resigned from the Rue Royale Club, which was letting in every Tom, Dick and Harry, he wished to ask Mme. de Villeparisis to arrange for his election there.

"Aren't they rather bad form, rather stuck-up snobs, these Sagans?" he inquired in a tone of sarcasm.

"Not at all, they're the best we can do for you in that line," M. d'Argencourt, who adopted all the catch-words of Parisian society, assured him.

"Then," said Bloch, still half in irony, "I suppose it's one of the solemnities, the great social fixtures of the season."

Mme. de Villeparisis turned merrily to Mme. de Guermantes.

"Tell us, is it a great social solemnity, Mme. de Sagan's ball?"

"It's no good asking me," answered the Duchess, "I have never yet succeeded in finding out what a social solemnity is. Besides, society isn't my strong point."

"Indeed; I thought it was just the other way," said Bloch, who supposed Mme. de Guermantes to be speaking seriously.

He continued, to the desperation of M. de Norpois, to ply him with questions about the Dreyfus case. The Ambassador declared that, looking at it from outside, he got the impression from du Paty de Clam of a somewhat cloudy brain, which had perhaps not been very happily chosen to conduct that delicate operation, which required so much coolness and discernment, a judicial inquiry.

"I know that the Socialist Party are crying aloud for his head on a charger, as well as for the immediate release of the prisoner from the Devil's Isle. But I think that we are not yet reduced to the necessity of passing the Caudine Forks of MM. Gérault-Richard and Company. So far, the whole case has been an utter mystery, I don't say that on one side just as much as on the other there has not been some pretty dirty work to be hushed up. That certain of your client's more or less disinterested protectors may have the best intentions I will not attempt to deny, but you know that heaven is paved with such things," he added, with a look of great subtlety. "It is essential that the Government should give the impression that they are not in the hands of the factions of the Left, and that they are not going to surrender themselves, bound hand and foot, at the demand of some pretorian guard or other, which, believe me, is not the same thing as the Army. It stands to reason that, should any fresh evidence come to light, a new trial would be ordered. And what follows from that? Obviously, that to demand a new trial is to force an open door. When the day comes, the Government will speak with no uncertain voice or will let fall into abeyance what is their essential prerogative. Cock and bull stories will no longer be enough. We must appoint judges to try Dreyfus. And that will be an easy matter because, although we have acquired the habit, in our sweet France, where we love to belittle ourselves, of thinking or letting it be thought that, in order to hear the words Truth and Justice, it is necessary to cross the Channel, which is very often only a roundabout way of reaching the Spree, there are judges to be found outside Berlin. But once the machinery of Government has been set in motion, will you have ears for the voice of authority? When it bids you perform your duty as a citizen will you have ears for its voice, will you take your stand in the ranks of law and order? When its patriotic appeal sounds, will you have the wisdom not to turn a deaf ear but to answer: 'Present!'?"

M. de Norpois put these questions to Bloch with a vehemence which, while it alarmed my friend, flattered him also; for the Ambassador spoke to him with the air of one addressing a whole party, questioned him as though he had been in the confidence of that party and might be held responsible for the decisions which it would adopt. "Should you fail to disarm," M. de Norpois went on, without waiting for Bloch's collective answer, "should you, before even the ink had dried on the decree ordering the fresh trial of the case, obeying it matters not what insidious word of command, fail, I say, to disarm, and band yourselves, rather, in a sterile opposition which seems to some minds the *ultima ratio* of policy, should you retire to your tents and burn your boats, you would be doing so to your own damnation. Are you the prisoners of those who foment disorder? Have you given them pledges?" Bloch was in doubt how to answer. M. de Norpois gave him no time. "If the negative be true, as I should like to think, and if you have a little of what seems to me to be lamentably lacking in certain of your leaders and your friends, namely political sense, then, on the day when the Criminal Court assembles, if you do not allow yourselves to be dragooned by the fishers in troubled waters, you will have won your battle. I do not guarantee that the whole of the General Staff is going to get away unscathed, but it will be so much to the good if some of them at least can save their faces without setting the heather on fire.

"It stands to reason, moreover, that it is with the Government that it rests to pronounce judgment, and to close the list—already too long—of unpunished crimes, not certainly at the bidding of Socialist agitators, nor yet of any obscure military mouthpiece," he added, looking Bloch boldly in the face, perhaps with the instinct that leads all Conservatives to establish support for themselves in the enemy's camp. "Government action is not to be dictated by the highest bidder, from wherever the bid may come. The Government are not, thank heaven, under the orders of Colonel Driant, nor, at the other end of the scale, under M. Clemenceau's. We must curb the professional agitators and prevent them from raising their heads again. France, the vast majority here in France, desires only to be allowed to work in orderly conditions. As to that, there can be no question whatever. But we must not be afraid to enlighten public opinion; and if a few sheep, of the kind our friend Rabelais knew so well, should dash headlong into the water, it would be as well to point out to them that the water in question was troubled, that it had been troubled deliberately by an agency not within our borders, in order to conceal the dangers lurking in its depths. And the Government ought not to give the impression that they are emerging from their passivity in self-defence when they exercise the right which is essentially their own, I mean that of setting the wheels of justice in motion. The Government will accept all your suggestions. If it is proved that there has been a judicial error, they can be sure of an overwhelming majority which would give them room to act with freedom."

"You, sir," said Bloch, turning to M. d'Argencourt, to whom he had been made known, with the rest of the party, on that gentleman's arrival, "you are a Dreyfusard, of course; they all are, abroad."

"It is a question that concerns only the French themselves, don't you think?" replied M. d'Argencourt with that peculiar form of insolence which consists in ascribing to the other person an opinion which one must, obviously, know that he does not hold since he has just expressed one directly its opposite.

Bloch coloured; M. d'Argencourt smiled, looking round the room, and if this smile, so long as it was directed at the rest of the company, was charged with malice at Bloch's expense, it became tempered with cordiality when finally it came to rest on the face of my friend, so as to deprive him of any excuse for annoyance at the words which he had heard uttered, though those words remained just as cruel. Mme. de Guermantes murmured something to M. d'Argencourt which I could not hear, but which must have referred to Bloch's religion, for there flitted at that moment over the face of the Duchess that expression to which one's fear of being noticed by the person of whom one is speaking gives a certain hesitancy and unreality, while there is blended with it the inquisitive, malicious amusement inspired in one by a group of human beings to which one feels oneself to be fundamentally alien. To retrieve himself, Bloch turned to the Duc de Châtellerault. "You, sir, as a Frenchman, you must be aware that people abroad are all Dreyfusards, although everyone pretends that in France we never know what is going on abroad. Anyhow, I know I can talk freely to you; Saint-Loup told me so." But the young Duke, who felt that every one was turning against Bloch, and was a coward as people often are in society, employing a mordant and precious form of wit which he seemed, by a sort of collateral atavism, to have inherited from M. de Charlus, replied: "You must not ask me, sir, to discuss the Dreyfus case with you; it is a subject which, on principle, I never mention except to Japhetics." Everyone smiled, except Bloch, not that he was not himself in the habit of making scathing references to his Jewish origin, to that side of his ancestry which came from somewhere near Sinai. But instead of one of these epigrams (doubtless because he had not one ready) the operation of the internal machine brought to Bloch's lips something quite different. And we caught only: "But how on earth did you know? Who told you?" as though he had been the son of a convict. Whereas, given his name, which had not exactly a Christian sound, and his face, his surprise argued a certain simplicity of mind.

What M. de Norpois had said not having completely satisfied him, he went up to the librarian and asked him whether Mme. de Villeparisis did not sometimes have in her house M. du Paty de Clam or M. Joseph Reinach. The librarian made no reply; he was a Nationalist, and never ceased preaching to the Marquise that the social revolution might break out at any moment, and that she ought to shew more caution in the choice of her friends. He asked himself whether Bloch might not be a secret emissary of the Syndicate, come to collect information, and went off at once to repeat to Mme. de Villeparisis the questions that Bloch had put to him. She decided that, at the best, he was ill-bred and might be in a position to compromise M. de Norpois. Also, she wished to give satisfaction to the librarian, the only person of whom she went in fear, by whom she was being indoctrinated, though without any marked success (every morning he read her M. Judet's article in the *Petit Journal*). She decided, therefore, to make it plain to Bloch that he need not come to the house again, and had no difficulty in finding, among her social repertory, the scene by which a great lady shows anyone her door, a scene which does not in any way involve the raised finger and blazing eyes that people imagine. As Bloch came up to her to say good-bye, buried in her deep armchair, she seemed only half-awakened from a vague somnolence. Her sunken eyes gleamed with only the feeble though charming light of a pair of pearls. Bloch's farewell, barely pencilling on the Marquise's face a languid smile, drew from her not a word, nor did she offer him her hand. This scene left Bloch in utter bewilderment, but as he was surrounded by a circle of spectators he felt that it could not be prolonged without disadvantage to himself, and, to force the Marquise, the hand which she had made no effort to take he himself thrust out at her. Mme. de Villeparisis was startled. But doubtless, while still bent upon giving an immediate satisfaction to the librarian and the anti-Dreyfusard clan, she wished at the same time to provide for the future, and so contented herself with letting her eyelids droop over her closing eyes.

"I believe she's asleep," said Bloch to the librarian who, feeling that he had the support of the Marquise, assumed an indignant air. "Good-bye, madame," shouted Bloch.

The old lady made the slight movement with her lips of a dying woman who wants to open her mouth but whose eye can no longer recognise people. Then she turned, overflowing with a restored vitality, to M. d'Argencourt, while Bloch left the room, convinced that she must be 'soft' in the head. Full of curiosity and anxious to have more light thrown upon so strange an incident, he came to see her again a few days later. She received him in the most friendly fashion, because she was a good-natured woman, because the librarian was not there, because she had in mind the little play which Bloch was going to produce for her, and finally because she had acted once and for all the little scene of the indignant lady that she had wished to act, a scene that had been universally admired and discussed the same evening in various drawing-rooms, but in a version which had already ceased to bear any resemblance to the truth.

"You were speaking just now of the *Seven Princesses*, Duchess; you know (not that it's anything to be proud of) that the author of that—what shall I call it?—that production is a compatriot of mine," said M. d'Argencourt with a fine scorn blended with satisfaction at knowing more than anyone else in the room about the author of a work which had been under discussion. "Yes, he's a Belgian, by nationality," he went on.

"Indeed! No, we don't accuse you of any responsibility for the *Seven Princesses*. Fortunately for yourself and your compatriots you are not like the author of that absurdity. I know several charming Belgians, yourself, your King, who is inclined to be shy, but full of wit, my Ligne cousins, and heaps of others, but you, I am thankful to say, do not speak the same language as the author of the *Seven Princesses*. Besides, if you want to know, it's not worth talking about, because really there is absolutely nothing in it. You know the sort of people who are always trying to seem obscure, and even plan to make themselves ridiculous to conceal the fact that they have not an idea in their heads. If there was anything behind it all, I may tell you that I'm not in the least afraid of a little daring," she added in a serious tone, "provided that there is some idea in it. I don't know if you've seen Borelli's piece. Some people seem to have been shocked by it, but I must say, even if they stone me through the streets for saying it," she went on, without stopping to think that she ran no very great risk of such a punishment, "I found it immensely interesting. But the *Seven Princesses*! It's all very well, one of them having a fondness for my nephew, I cannot carry family feeling quite . . ."

The Duchess broke off abruptly, for a lady came in who was the Comtesse de Marsantes, Robert's mother. Mme. de Marsantes was regarded in the Faubourg Saint-Germain as a superior being, of a goodness, a resignation that were positively angelic. So I had been told, and had had no particular reason to feel surprised, not knowing at the same time that she was

the sister of the Duc de Guermantes. Later, I have always been taken aback,
whenever I have learned that such women, melancholy, pure, victimised,
venerated like the ideal forms of saints in church windows, had flowered
from the same genealogical stem as brothers brutal, debauched and vile.
Brothers and sisters, when they are closely alike in features as were the
Duc de Guermantes and Mme. de Marsantes, ought (I felt) to have a
single intellect in common, the same heart, as a person would have who
might vary between good and evil moods but in whom one could not, for
all that, expect to find a vast breadth of outlook if he had a narrow mind,
or a sublime abnegation if his heart was hard.

Mme. de Marsantes attended Brunetière's lectures. She fascinated the
Faubourg Saint-Germain and, by her saintly life, edified it as well. But
the morphological link of handsome nose and piercing gaze led one, nevertheless, to classify Mme. de Marsantes in the same intellectual and moral
family as her brother the Duke. I could not believe that the mere fact of
her being a woman, and perhaps those of her having had an unhappy life
and won everyone's sympathy, could make a person be so different from the
rest of her family, as in the old romances, where all the virtues and graces
are combined in the sister of wild and lawless brothers. It seemed to me
that nature, less unconventional than the old poets, must make use almost
exclusively of the elements common to the family, and I was unable to
credit her with enough power of invention to construct, out of materials
analogous to those that composed a fool and clod, a lofty mind without the
least strain of clownishness, a saint unsoiled by any brutality. Mme. de
Marsantes was wearing a gown of white surah embroidered with large
palms, on which stood out flowers of a different material, these being black.
This was because, three weeks earlier, she had lost her cousin, M. de
Montmorency, a bereavement which did not prevent her from paying calls
or even from going to small dinners, but always in mourning. She was a
great lady. Atavism had filled her with the frivolity of generations of life
at court, with all the superficial, rigorous duties that that implies. Mme.
de Marsantes had not had the strength of character to regret for any length
of time the death of her father and mother, but she would not for anything
in the world have appeared in colours in the month following that of a
cousin. She was more than pleasant to me, both because I was Robert's
friend and because I did not move in the same world as he. This pleasant-
ness was accompanied by a pretence of shyness, by that sort of intermittent withdrawal of the voice, the eyes, the mind which a woman draws
back to her like a skirt that has indiscreetly spread, so as not to take up
too much room, to remain stiff and erect even in her suppleness, as a good
upbringing teaches. A good upbringing which must not, however, be taken
too literally, many of these ladies passing very swiftly into a complete dissolution of morals without ever losing the almost childlike correctness of
their manners. Mme. de Marsantes was a trifle irritating in conversation
since, whenever she had occasion to speak of a plebeian, as for instance
Bergotte or Elstir, she would say, isolating the word, giving it its full
value, intoning it on two different notes with a modulation peculiar to the
Guermantes: "I have had the *honour*, the great *hon*-our of meeting Mon-

sieur Bergotte," or "of making the acquaintance of Monsieur Elstir," whether that her hearers might marvel at her humility or from the same tendency that Mme. de Guermantes shewed to revert to the use of obsolete forms, as a protest against the slovenly usages of the present day, in which people never professed themselves sufficiently 'honoured.' Whichever of these was the true reason, one felt that when Mme. de Marsantes said: "I have had the *honour*, the great *hon*-our," she felt she was playing an important part and shewing that she could take in the names of distinguished men as she would have welcomed the men themselves at her home in the country, had they happened to be in the neighbourhood. On the other hand, as her family connexion was numerous, as she was devoted to all her relatives, as, slow in speech and fond of explaining things at length, she was always trying to make clear the exact degree of kinship, she found herself (without any desire to create an effect and without really caring to talk about anyone except touching peasants and sublime gamekeepers) referring incessantly to all the mediatised houses in Europe, a failing which people less brilliantly connected than herself could not forgive, and, if they were at all intellectual, derided as a sign of stupidity.

In the country, Mme. de Marsantes was adored for the good that she did, but principally because the purity of a strain of blood into which for many generations there had flowed only what was greatest in the history of France had taken from her manner everything that the lower orders call 'manners,' and had given her a perfect simplicity. She never shrank from kissing a poor woman who was in trouble, and would tell her to come up to the castle for a cartload of wood. She was, people said, the perfect Christian. She was determined to find an immensely rich wife for Robert. Being a great lady means playing the great lady, that is to say, to a certain extent, playing at simplicity. It is a pastime which costs an extremely high price, all the more because simplicity charms people only on condition that they know that you are not bound to live simply, that is to say that you are very rich. Some one said to me afterwards, when I had told him of my meeting her: "You saw of course that she must have been lovely as a young woman." But true beauty is so individual, so novel always, that one does not recognise it as beauty. I said to myself this afternoon only that she had a tiny nose, very blue eyes, a long neck and a sad expression.

"Listen," said Mme. de Villeparisis to the Duchesse de Guermantes, "I'm expecting a woman at any moment whom you don't wish to know. I thought I'd better warn you, to avoid any unpleasantness. But you needn't be afraid, I shall never have her here again, only I was obliged to let her come to-day. It's Swann's wife."

Mme. Swann, seeing the dimensions that the Dreyfus case had begun to assume, and fearing that her husband's racial origin might be used against herself, had besought him never again to allude to the prisoner's innocence. When he was not present she went farther and used to profess the most ardent Nationalism; in doing which she was only following the example of Mme. Verdurin, in whom a middle-class anti-semitism, latent hitherto, had awakened and grown to a positive fury. Mme. Swann had won by this attitude the privilege of membership in several of the women's leagues that were beginning to be formed in anti-semitic society, and had succeeded in making friends with various members of the aristocracy. It may seem strange that, so far from following their example, the Duchesse de Guermantes, so close a friend of Swann, had on the contrary always resisted his desire, which he had not concealed from her, to introduce to her his wife. But we shall see in due course that this arose from the peculiar nature of the Duchess, who held that she was not 'bound to' do things, and laid down with despotic force what had been decided by her social 'free will,' which was extremely arbitrary.

"Thank you for telling me," said the Duchess. "It would indeed be most unpleasant. But as I know her by sight I shall be able to get away in time."

"I assure you, Oriane, she is really quite nice; an excellent woman," said Mme. de Marsantes.

"I have no doubt she is, but I feel no need to assure myself of it."

"Have you been invited to Lady Israels's?" Mme. de Villeparisis asked the Duchess, to change the conversation.

"Why, thank heaven, I don't know the woman," replied Mme. de Guermantes. "You must ask Marie-Aynard. She knows her. I never could make out why."

"I did indeed know her at one time," said Mme. de Marsantes. "I confess my faults. But I have decided not to know her any more. It seems she's one of the very worst of them, and makes no attempt to conceal it. Besides, we have all been too trusting, too hospitable. I shall never go near anyone of that race again. While we had old friends, country cousins, people of our own flesh and blood on whom we shut our doors, we threw them open to Jews. And now we see what thanks we get from them. But I've no right to speak; I have an adorable son, and, like a young fool, he says and does all the maddest things you can imagine," she went on, having caught some allusion by M. d'Argencourt to Robert. "But, talking of Robert, haven't you seen him?" she asked Mme. de Villeparisis; "being Saturday, I thought he'd be coming to Paris on leave, and in that case he would be sure to pay you a visit."

As a matter of fact Mme. de Marsantes thought that her son would not obtain leave that week; but knowing that, even if he did, he would never dream of coming to see Mme. de Villeparisis, she hoped, by making herself appear to have expected to find him in the room, to procure his forgiveness from her susceptible aunt for all the visits that he had failed to pay her.

"Robert here! But I have never had a single word from him; I don't think I've seen him since Balbec."

"He is so busy; he has so much to do," pleaded Mme. de Marsantes.

A faint smile made Mme. de Guermantes's eyelashes quiver as she studied the circle which, with the point of her sunshade, she was tracing on the carpet. Whenever the Duke had been too openly unfaithful to his wife, Mme. de Marsantes had always taken up the cudgels against her own brother on her sister-in-law's behalf. The latter had a grateful and bitter memory of this protection, and was not herself seriously shocked by Robert's pranks. At this point the door opened again and Robert himself entered the room.

"Well, talk of the Saint!" said Mme. de Guermantes.

Mme. de Marsantes, who had her back to the door, had not seen her son come in. When she did catch sight of him, her motherly bosom was convulsed with joy, as by the beating of a wing, her body half rose from her seat, her face quivered and she fastened on Robert eyes big with astonishment.

"What! You've come! How delightful! What a surprise!"

"Ah! *Talk of the Saint!*—I see," cried the Belgian diplomat, with a shout of laughter.

"Delicious, ain't it?" came tartly from the Duchess, who hated puns, and had ventured on this one only with a pretence of making fun of herself.

"Good afternoon, Robert," she said, "I believe he's forgotten his aunt."

They talked for a moment, probably about myself, for as Saint-Loup was leaving her to join his mother Mme. de Guermantes turned to me:

"Good afternoon; how are you?" was her greeting.

She allowed to rain on me the light of her azure gaze, hesitated for a moment, unfolded and stretched towards me the stem of her arm, leaned forward her body which sprang rapidly backwards like a bush that has been pulled down to the ground and, on being released, returns to its natural position. Thus she acted under the fire of Saint-Loup's eyes, which kept her under observation and were making frantic efforts to obtain some further concession still from his aunt. Fearing that our conversation might fail altogether, he joined in, to stimulate it, and answered for me:

"He's not very well just now, he gets rather tired; I think he would be a great deal better, by the way, if he saw you more often, for I can't help telling you that he admires you immensely."

"Oh, but that's very nice of him," said Mme. de Guermantes in a deliberately casual tone, as if I had brought her her cloak. "I am most flattered."

"Look, I must go and talk to my mother for a minute; take my chair," said Saint-Loup, thus forcing me to sit down next to his aunt.

We were both silent.

"I see you sometimes in the morning," she said, as though she were telling me something that I did not know, and I for my part had never seen her. "It's so good for one, a walk."

"Oriane," began Mme. de Marsantes in a low tone, "you said you were going on to Mme. de Saint-Ferréol's; would you be so very kind as to tell her not to expect me to dinner, I shall stay at home now that I've got Robert. And one other thing, but I hardly like to ask you, if you would leave word as you pass to tell them to send out at once for a box of the cigars Robert likes. 'Corona,' they're called. I've none in the house."

Robert came up to us; he had caught only the name of Mme. de Saint-Ferréol.

"Who in the world is Mme. de Saint-Ferréol?" he inquired, in a surprised but decisive tone, for he affected a studied ignorance of everything to do with society.

"But, my dear boy, you know quite well," said his mother. "She's Vermandois's sister. It was she gave you that nice billiard table you liked so much."

"What, she's Vermandois's sister, I had no idea of that. Really, my family are amazing," he went on, turning so as to include me in the conversation and adopting unconsciously Bloch's intonation just as he borrowed his ideas, "they know the most unheard-of people, people called Saint-Ferréol" (emphasising the final consonant of each word) "and names like that; they go to balls, they drive in victorias, they lead a fabulous existence. It's prodigious."

Mme. de Guermantes made in her throat a slight, short, sharp sound, as of an involuntary laugh which one chokes back, meaning thereby to shew that she paid just as much tribute as the laws of kinship imposed on her to her nephew's wit. A servant came in to say that the Prince von Faffenheim-Munsterburg-Weinigen had sent word to M. de Norpois that he was waiting.

"Bring him in, sir," said Mme. de Villeparisis to the old Ambassador, who started in quest of the German Minister.

"Stop, sir; do you think I ought to shew him the miniature of the Empress Charlotte?"

"Why, I'm sure he'll be delighted," said the Ambassador in a tone of conviction, and as though he were envying the fortunate Minister the favour that was in store for him.

"Oh, I know he's very *sound*," said Mme. de Marsantes, "and that is so rare among foreigners. But I've found out all about him. He is anti-semitism personified."

The Prince's name preserved in the boldness with which its opening syllables were—to borrow an expression from music—attacked, and in the stammering repetition that scanned them, the impulse, the mannered simplicity, the heavy delicacies of the Teutonic race, projected like green boughs over the 'heim' of dark blue enamel which glowed with the mystic light of a Rhenish window behind the pale and finely wrought gildings of the German eighteenth century. This name included, among the several names of which it was composed, that of a little German watering-place to which as a child I had gone with my grandmother, at the foot of a mountain honoured by the feet of Goethe, from the vineyards of which we used to drink, at the Kurhof, their illustrious vintages with elaborate and sonorous names, like the epithets which Homer applies to his heroes. And so, scarcely had I heard the Prince's name spoken than, before I had recalled the watering-place, the name itself seemed to shrink, to grow rich with humanity, to find large enough a little place in my memory to which it clung, familiar, earth to earth, picturesque, savoury, light, with something about it, too, that was authorised, prescribed. And then, M. de Guermantes, in explaining who the Prince was, quoted a number of his titles, and I recognised the name of a village threaded by the river on which, every evening, my cure finished for the day, I used to go in a boat amid the mosquitoes, and that of a forest so far away that the doctor would not allow me to make the excursion to it. And indeed it was comprehensible that the suzerainty of the lord extended to the surrounding places and associated afresh in the enumeration of his titles the names which one could read, close together, upon a map. Thus beneath the visor of the Prince of the Holy Roman Empire and Knight of Franconia it was the face of a dear and smiling land, on which had often lingered for me the light of the six-o'clock sun, that I saw, at any rate before the Prince, Rheingraf and Elector Palatine had entered the room. For I speedily learned that the revenues which he drew from the forest and river, peopled with gnomes and undines, and from the enchanted mountain on which rose the ancient Burg that cherished memories of Luther and Lewis the Germanic, he employed in keeping five Charron motor-cars, a house in Paris and one in London, a box on Mondays at the Opera and another for the 'Tuesdays' at the 'Francais.' He did not seem to me, nor did he seem to regard himself as different from other men of similar fortune and age who had a less poetic origin. He had their culture, their ideals, he was proud of his rank, but purely on account of the advantages it conferred on him, and had now only one ambition in life, to be elected a Corresponding Member of the Academy of Moral and Political Sciences, which was the reason of his coming to see Mme. de Villeparisis. If he, whose wife was a leader of the most exclusive set in Berlin, had begged to be introduced to the Marquise, it was not the result of any desire on his part for her acquaintance. Devoured for years past by this ambition to be elected to the Institute, he had unfortunately never been in a position to reckon above five the number of Academicians who seemed prepared to vote for him. He knew that M. de Norpois could by himself dispose of at least ten others, a number which he was capable, by skilful negotiations, of increasing still further. And so the Prince, who had known him in Russia when they were both there as Ambassadors, had gone to see him and had done everything in his power to win him over. But in vain might he multiply his friendly overtures, procure for the Marquis Russian decorations, quote him in articles on foreign politics; he had had before him an ingrate, a man in whose eyes all these attentions appeared to count as nothing, who had not advanced the prospects of his candidature one inch, had not even promised him his own vote. No doubt M. de Norpois received him with extreme politeness, indeed begged that he would not put himself out and "take the trouble to come so far out of his way," went himself to the Prince's residence, and when the Teutonic Knight had launched his: "I should like immensely to be your colleague," replied in a tone of deep emotion: "Ah! I should be most happy!" And no doubt a simpleton, a Dr. Cottard would have said to himself: "Well, here he is in my house; it was he who insisted on coming, because he regards me as a more important person than himself; he tells me that he would be happy to see me in the Academy; words do have some meaning after all, damn it, probably if he doesn't offer to vote for me it is because it hasn't occurred to him. He lays so much stress on my great influence; presumably he imagines that larks drop into my mouth ready roasted, that I have all the support I want, and that is why he doesn't offer me his; but I have only got to get him with his back to the wall, and just say to him quietly: 'Very well, vote for me, will you?' and he will be obliged to do it."

But Prince von Faffenheim was no simpleton. He was what Dr. Cottard would have called 'a fine diplomat' and he knew that M. de Norpois was no less fine a one than himself, nor a man who would have failed to realise without needing to be told that he could confer a favour on a candidate by voting for him. The Prince, in his Embassies and as Foreign Minister, had conducted, on his country's behalf instead of, as in the present instance, his own, many of those conversations in which one knows beforehand just how far one is prepared to go and at what point one will decline to commit oneself. He was not unaware that, in this diplomatic language, to talk meant to offer. And it was for this reason that he had arranged for M. de Norpois to receive the Cordon of Saint Andrew. But if he had had to report to his Government the conversation which he had subsequently had with M. de Norpois, he would have stated in his dispatch: "I realised that I had gone the wrong way to work." For as soon as he had returned to the subject of the Institute, M. de Norpois had repeated:

"I should like nothing better; nothing could be better, for my colleagues. They ought, I consider, to feel genuinely honoured that you should have thought of them. It is a really interesting candidature, a little outside our ordinary course. As you know, the Academy is very conventional, it takes fright at everything which has at all a novel sound. Personally, I deplore this. How often have I had occasion to say as much to my colleagues! I cannot be sure, God forgive me, that I did not even once let the word 'hidebound' escape me," he added, in an undertone, with a scandalised smile, almost aside, as in a scene on the stage, casting at the Prince a rapid, sidelong glance from his blue eyes, like a veteran actor studying the effect on his audience. "You understand, Prince, that I should not care to allow a personality so eminent as yourself to embark on a venture which was hopeless from the start. So long as my colleagues' ideas linger so far behind the times, I consider that the wiser course will be to abstain. But you may rest assured that if I were ever to discern a mind that was a little more modern, a little more alive, shewing itself in that college, which is tending to become a mausoleum, if I could reckon upon any possible chance of your success, I should be the first to inform you of it."

"The Cordon was a mistake," thought the Prince; "the negotiations have not advanced in the least; that is not what he wanted. I have not yet laid my hand on the right key."

This was a kind of reasoning of which M. de Norpois, formed in the same school as the Prince, would also have been capable. One may mock at the pedantic silliness with which diplomats of the Norpois type go into ecstasies over some piece of official wording which is, for all practical purposes, meaningless. But their childishness has this compensation; diplomats know that, in the loaded scales which assure that European or other equilibrium which we call peace, good feeling, sounding speeches, earnest entreaties weigh very little; and that the heavy weight, the true determinant consists in something else, in the possibility which the adversary does (if he is strong enough) or does not enjoy of satisfying, in exchange for what one oneself wants, a desire. With this order of truths, which an entirely disinterested person, such as my grandmother for instance, would not have understood, M. de Norpois and Prince von Faffenheim had frequently had to deal. Chargé d'Affaires in countries with which we had been within an ace of going to war, M. de Norpois, in his anxiety as to the turn which events were about to take, knew very well that it was not by the word 'Peace,' nor by the word 'War' that it would be revealed to him, but by some other, apparently commonplace word, a word of terror or blessing, which the diplomat, by the aid of his cipher, would immediately read and to which, to safeguard the honour of France, he would respond in another word, quite as commonplace, but one beneath which the Minister of the enemy nation would at once see written: 'War.' Moreover, in accordance with a time-honoured custom, analogous to that which gave to the first meeting between two young people promised to one another in marriage the form of a chance encounter at a performance in the Théâtre du Gymnase, the dialogue in the course of which destiny was to dictate the word 'War' or the word 'Peace' was held, as a rule, not in the ministerial sanctum but on a bench in a Kurgarten where the Minister and M. de Norpois went independently to a thermal spring to drink at its source their little tumblers of some curative water. By a sort of tacit convention they met at the hour appointed for their cure, began by taking together a short stroll which, beneath its innocent appearance, each of the speakers knew to be as tragic as an order for mobilisation. And so, in a private matter like this nomination for election to the Institute, the Prince had employed the same system of induction which had served him in his public career, the same method of reading beneath superimposed symbols.

And certainly it would be wrong to pretend that my grandmother and the few who resembled her would have been alone in their failure to understand this kind of calculation. For one thing, the average human being, practising a profession the lines of which have been laid down for him from the start, comes near, by his want of intuition, to the ignorance which my grandmother owed to her lofty disinterestedness. Often one has to come down to 'kept' persons, male or female, before one finds the hidden spring of actions or words apparently of the most innocent nature in self-interest, in the bare necessity to keep alive. What man does not know that when a woman whom he is going to pay says to him: "Don't let's talk about money," the speech must be regarded as what is called in music 'a silent beat' and that if, later on, she declares: "You are far too much trouble; you are always keeping things from me; I've done with you," he must interpret this as: "Some one else has been offering me more." And yet this is only the language of a lady of easy virtue, not so far removed from the ladies in society. The *apache* furnishes more striking examples. But M. de Norpois and the German Prince, if *apaches* and their ways were unknown to them, had been accustomed to living on the same plane as nations, which are also, despite their greatness, creatures of selfishness and cunning, kept in order only by force, by consideration of their material interests which may drive them to murder, a murder that is often symbolic also, since its mere hesitation or refusal to fight may spell for a nation the word 'Perish.'

But inasmuch as all this is not set forth in Yellow and otherwise coloured Books, the people as a whole are naturally pacific; should they be warlike, it is instinctively, from hatred, from a sense of injury, not for the reasons which have made up the mind of their ruler, on the advice of his Norpois.

The following winter the Prince was seriously ill; he recovered, but his heart was permanently affected.

"The devil!" he said to himself, "I can't afford to lose any time over the Institute. If I wait too long, I may be dead before they elect me. That really would be unpleasant."

He composed, on the foreign politics of the last twenty years, an essay for the *Revue des Deux Mondes,* in which he referred more than once, and in the most flattering terms, to M. de Norpois. The French diplomat called upon him to thank him. He added that he did not know how to express his gratitude. The Prince said to himself, like a man who has been trying to fit various keys into a stubborn lock: "Still not the right one!" and, feeling somewhat out of breath as he shewed M. de Norpois to the door, thought: "Damn it, these fellows will see me in my grave before letting me in. We must hurry up."

That evening, he met M. de Norpois again at the Opera.

"My dear Ambassador," he began to him, "you told me to-day that you did not know what you could do to prove your gratitude; it was a great exaggeration, for you owe me none, but I am going to be so indelicate as to take you at your word."

M. de Norpois had no less high an esteem for the Prince's tact than the Prince had for his. He understood at once that it was not a request that Prince von Faffenheim was about to present to him, but an offer, and with a radiant affability made ready to hear it.

"Well now, you will think me highly indiscreet. There are two people to whom I am greatly attached—in quite different ways, as you will understand in a moment—two people both of whom have recently settled in Paris, where they intend to remain for the future: my wife, and the Grand Duchess John. They are thinking of giving a few dinners, chiefly in honour of the King and Queen of England, and what they would have liked more than anything in the world would have been to be able to offer their guests the company of a person for whom, without knowing her, they both of them feel a great admiration. I confess that I did not know how I was going to gratify their wish when I learned just now, by the most extraordinary accident, that you were a friend of this person. I know that she lives a most retired life, and sees only a very few people—'happy few,' as Stendhal would say—but if you were to give me your backing, with the generosity that you have always shewn me, I am sure that she would allow you to present me to her and to convey to her the wishes of both the Grand Duchess and the Princess. Perhaps she would consent to dine with us, when the Queen of England comes, and then (one never knows) if we don't bore her too much, to spend the Easter holidays with us at Beaulieu, at the Grand Duchess John's. The person I allude to is called the Marquise de Villeparisis. I confess that the hope of becoming one of the frequenters of such a school of wit would console me, would make me contemplate without regret the abandoning of

my attempt at the Institute. For in her house, too, I understand, there is
a regular flow of intellect and brilliant talk."

With an inexpressible sense of pleasure the Prince felt that the lock no
longer resisted, and that at last the key was turning.

"Such an alternative is wholly unnecessary, my dear Prince," replied
M. de Norpois; "nothing is more in harmony with the Institute than the
house you speak of, which is a regular hotbed of Academicians. I shall
convey your request to Mme. la Marquise de Villeparisis: she will undoubtedly be flattered. As for her dining with you, she goes out very little,
and that will perhaps be more difficult to arrange. But I shall present you
to her and you can plead your cause in person. You must on no account
give up the Academy; to-morrow fortnight, as it happens, I shall be having
luncheon, before going on with him to an important meeting, at Leroy-
Beaulieu's, without whom nobody can be elected; I had already allowed
myself in conversation with him to let fall your name, with which, naturally,
he was perfectly familiar. He raised certain objections. But it so happens
that he requires the support of my group at the next election, and I fully
intend to return to the charge; I shall tell him quite openly of the wholly
cordial ties that unite us, I shall not conceal from him that, if you were to
stand, I should ask all my friends to vote for you," (here the Prince breathed
a deep sigh of relief) "and he knows that I have friends. I consider that if
I were to succeed in obtaining his assistance your chances would become
very strong. Come that evening, at six, to Mme. de Villeparisis's; I will
introduce you to her and I can give you an account then of my conversation
with him."

Thus it was that Prince von Faffenheim had been led to call upon Mme.
de Villeparisis. My profound disillusionment occurred when he spoke. It
had never struck me that, if an epoch in history has features both particular
and general which are stronger than those of a nationality, so that in a
biographical dictionary with illustrations, which go so far as to include an
authentic portrait of Minerva, Leibniz with his wig and ruff differs little
from Marivaux or Samuel Bernard, a nationality has particular features
stronger than those of a caste. In the present instance these were rendered
before me not by a discourse in which I had expected, before I saw him,
to hear the rustling of the elves and the dance of the kobolds, but by a
transposition which certified no less plainly that poetic origin: the fact that,
as he bowed, short, red, corpulent, over the hand of Mme. de Villeparisis,
the Rheingraf said to her: "Aow to you too, Matame la Marquise," in the
accent of an Alsatian porter.

"Won't you let me give you a cup of tea or a little of this cake; it is so
good?" Mme. de Guermantes asked me, anxious to have shewn herself as
friendly as possible. "I do the honours in this house just as if it was mine,"
she explained in an ironical tone which gave a slightly guttural sound to
her voice, as though she were trying to stifle a hoarse laugh.

"Sir," said Mme. de Villeparisis to M. de Norpois, "you won't forget
that you have something to say to the Prince about the Academy?"

Mme. de Guermantes lowered her eyes and gave a semicircular turn to
her wrist to look at the time.

"Gracious! I must fly at once if I'm to get to Mme. de Saint-Ferréol's, and I'm dining with Mme. Leroi."

And she rose without bidding me good-bye. She had just caught sight of Mme. Swann, who appeared considerably embarrassed at finding me in the room. She remembered, doubtless, that she had been the first to assure me that she was convinced of Dreyfus's innocence.

"I don't want my mother to introduce me to Mme. Swann," Saint-Loup said to me. "She's an ex-whore. Her husband's a Jew, and she comes here to pose as a Nationalist. Hallo, here's Uncle Palamède."

The arrival of Mme. Swann had a special interest for me, due to an incident which had occurred a few days earlier and which I am obliged to record on account of the consequences which it was to have at a much later date, as the reader will learn in due course. Well, a few days before this visit to Mme. de Villeparisis, I had myself received a visitor whom I little expected, namely Charles Morel, the son (though I had never heard of his existence) of my great-uncle's old servant. This great-uncle (he in whose house I had met the lady in pink) had died the year before. His servant had more than once expressed his intention of coming to see me; I had no idea of the object of his visit, but should have been glad to see him for I had learned from Françoise that he had a genuine veneration for my uncle's memory and made a pilgrimage regularly to the cemetery in which he was buried. But, being obliged, for reasons of health, to retire to his home in the country, where he expected to remain for some time, he delegated the duty to his son. I was surprised to see come into my room a handsome young fellow of eighteen, dressed with expensive rather than good taste, but looking, all the same, like anything in the world except the son of a gentleman's servant. He made a point, moreover, at the start of our conversation, of severing all connexion with the domestic class from which he sprang, by informing me, with a smile of satisfaction, that he had won the first prize at the Conservatoire. The object of his visit to me was as follows: his father, when going through the effects of my uncle Adolphe, had set aside some which, he felt, could not very well be sent to my parents but were at the same time of a nature likely to interest a young man of my age. These were the photographs of the famous actresses, the notorious courtesans whom my uncle had known, the last fading pictures of that gay life of a man about town which he divided by a watertight compartment from his family life. While young Morel was shewing them to me, I noticed that he addressed me as though he were speaking to an equal. He derived from saying 'you' to me as often, and 'sir' as seldom, as possible the pleasure natural in one whose father had never ventured, when addressing my parents, upon anything but the third person. Almost all these photographs bore an inscription such as: "To my best friend." One actress, less grateful and more circumspect than the rest, had written: "To the best of friends," which enabled her (so I was assured) to say afterwards that my uncle was in no sense and had never been her best friend but was merely the friend who had done the most little services for her, the friend she made use of, a good, kind man, in other words an old fool. In vain might young Morel seek to divest himself of his lowly origin, one felt that the shade of my uncle Adolphe, venerable and gigantic in the eyes of the old servant, had never ceased to hover, almost a holy vision, over the childhood and boyhood of the son. While I was turning over the photographs Charles Morel examined my room. And as I was looking for some place in which I might keep them, "How is it," he asked me (in a tone in which the reproach had no need to find expression, so implicit was it in the words themselves), "that I don't see a single photograph of your uncle in your room?" I felt the blood rise to my cheeks and stammered: "Why, I don't believe I have such a thing." "What, you haven't one photograph of your uncle Adolphe, who was so devoted to you! I will send you one of my governor's—he has quantities of them—and I hope you will set it up in the place of honour above that chest of drawers, which came to you from your uncle." It is true that, as I had not even a photograph of my father or mother in my room, there was nothing so very shocking in there not being one of my uncle Adolphe. But it was easy enough to see that for old Morel, who had trained his son in the same way of thinking, my uncle was the important person in the family, my parents only reflecting a diminished light from his. I was in higher favour, because my uncle used constantly to say that I was going to turn out a sort of Racine, or Vaulabelle, and Morel regarded me almost as an adopted son, as a child by election of my uncle. I soon discovered that this young man was extremely 'pushing.' Thus at this first meeting he asked me, being something of a composer as well and capable of setting short poems to music, whether I knew any poet who had a good position in society. I mentioned one. He did not know the work of this poet and had never heard his name, of which he made a note. Well, I found out that shortly afterwards he wrote to the poet telling him that, a fanatical admirer of his work, he, Morel, had composed a musical setting for one of his sonnets and would be grateful if the author would arrange for its performance at the Comtesse So-and-So's. This was going a little too fast, and exposing his hand. The poet, taking offence, made no reply.

For the rest, Charles Morel seemed to have, besides his ambition, a strong leaning towards more concrete realities. He had noticed, as he came through the courtyard, Jupien's niece at work upon a waistcoat, and although he explained to me only that he happened to want a fancy waistcoat at that very moment, I felt that the girl had made a vivid impression on him. He had no hesitation about asking me to come downstairs and introduce him to her, "but not as a connexion of your family, you follow me, I rely on your discretion not to drag in my father, say just a distinguished artist of your acquaintance, you know how important it is to make a good impression on tradespeople." Albeit he had suggested to me that, not knowing him well enough to call him, he quite realised, 'dear friend,' I might address him, before the girl, in some such terms as "not dear master, of course, . . . although . . . well, if you like, dear distinguished artist," once in the shop, I avoided 'qualifying' him, as Saint-Simon would have expressed it, and contented myself with reiterating his 'you.' He picked out from several patterns of velvet one of the brightest red imaginable and so loud that, for all his bad taste, he was never able to wear the waistcoat when it was made. The girl settled down to work again with her two 'apprentices,' but it struck me that the impression had been mutual, and that Charles Morel, whom she regarded as of her own 'station' (only smarter and richer), had proved singularly attractive to her. As I had been greatly surprised to find among the photographs which his father had sent me one of the portrait of Miss Sacripant (otherwise Odette) by Elstir, I said to Charles Morel as I went with him to the outer gate: "I don't suppose you can tell me, but did my uncle know this lady well? I don't see at what stage in his life I can fit her in exactly; and it interests me, because of M. Swann . . ." "Why, if I wasn't forgetting to tell you that my father asked me specially to draw your attention to that lady's picture. As a matter of fact, she was 'lunching' with your uncle the last time you ever saw him. My father was in two minds whether to let you in. It seems you made a great impression on the wench, and she hoped to see more of you. But just at that time there was some trouble in the family, by what my father tells me, and you never set eyes on your uncle again." He broke off with a smile of farewell, across the court-yard, at Jupien's niece. She was watching him and admiring, no doubt, his thin face and regular features, his fair hair and sparkling eyes. I, as I gave him my hand, was thinking of Mme. Swann and saying to myself with amazement, so far apart, so different were they in my memory, that I should have henceforth to identify her with the 'Lady in pink.'

M. de Charlus was not long in taking his place by the side of Mme. Swann. At every social gathering at which he appeared and, contemptuous towards the men, courted by the women, promptly attached himself to the smartest of the latter, whose garments he seemed almost to put on as an ornament to his own, the Baron's frock coat or swallowtails made one think of a portrait by some great painter of a man dressed in black but having by his side, thrown over a chair, the brilliantly coloured cloak which he is about to wear at some costume ball. This partnership, generally with some royal lady, secured for M. de Charlus various privileges which he liked to enjoy. For instance, one result of it was that his hostesses, at theatricals or concerts, allowed the Baron alone to have a front seat, in a row of ladies, while the rest of the men were crowded together at the back of the room. And then besides, completely absorbed, it seemed, in repeating, at the top of his voice, amusing stories to the enraptured lady, M. de Charlus was dispensed from the necessity of going to shake hands with any of the others, was set free, in other words, from all social duties. Behind the scented barrier in which the beauty of his choice enclosed him, he was isolated amid a crowded drawing-room, as, in a crowded theatre or concert-hall, behind the rampart of a box; and when anyone came up to greet him, through, so to speak, the beauty of his companion, it was permissible for him to reply quite curtly and without interrupting his business of conversation with a lady. Certainly Mme. Swann was scarcely of the rank of the people with whom he liked thus to flaunt himself. But he professed admiration for her, friendship for Swann, he knew that she would be flattered by his attentions and was himself flattered at being compromised by the prettiest woman in the room.

Mme. de Villeparisis meanwhile was not too well pleased to receive a visit from M. de Charlus. He, while admitting serious defects in his aunt's character, was genuinely fond of her. But every now and then, carried away by anger, by an imaginary grievance, he would sit down and write to her, without making any attempt to resist his impulse, letters full of the most violent abuse, in which he made the most of trifling incidents which until then he seemed never even to have noticed. Among other examples I may instance the following, which my stay at Balbec brought to my knowledge: Mme. de Villeparisis, fearing that she had not brought enough money with her to Balbec to enable her to prolong her holiday there, and not caring, since she was of a thrifty disposition and shrank from unnecessary expenditure, to have money sent to her from Paris, had borrowed three thousand francs from M. de Charlus. A month later, annoyed, for some trivial reason, with his aunt, he asked her to repay him this sum by telegraph. He received two thousand nine hundred and ninety-odd francs. Meeting his aunt a few days later in Paris, in the course of a friendly conversation, he drew her attention, with the utmost politeness, to the mistake that her banker had made when sending the money. "But there was no mistake," replied Mme. de Villeparisis, "the money order cost six francs seventy-five." "Oh, of course, if it was intentional, it is all right," said M. de Charlus, "I mentioned it only in case you didn't know, because in that case, if the bank had done the same thing with anyone who didn't know you as well as I do, it might have led to unpleasantness." "No, no, there was no mistake." "After all, you were quite right," M. de Charlus concluded easily, stooping to kiss his aunt's hand. And in fact he bore no resentment and was only amused at this little instance of her thrift. But some time afterwards, imagining that, in a family matter, his aunt had been trying to get the better of him and had 'worked up a regular conspiracy' against him, as she took shelter, foolishly enough, behind the lawyers with whom he suspected her of having plotted to undo him, he had written her a letter boiling over with insolence and rage. "I shall not be satisfied with having my revenge," he added as a postscript; "I shall take care to make you a laughing-stock. To-morrow I shall tell everyone the story of the money order and the six francs seventy-five you kept back from me out of the three thousand I lent you; I shall disgrace you publicly." Instead of so doing, he had gone to his aunt the next day to beg her pardon, having already regretted a letter in which he had used some really terrible language. But apart from this, to whom could he have told the story of the money order? Seeking no longer vengeance but a sincere reconciliation, now was the time for him to keep silence. But already he had repeated the story everywhere, while still on the best of terms with his aunt; he had told it without any malice, as a joke, and because he was the soul of indiscretion. He had repeated the story, but without Mme. de Villeparisis's knowledge. With the result that, having learned from his letter that he intended to disgrace her by making public a transaction in which he had told her with his own lips that she had acted rightly, she concluded that he had been deceiving her from the first, and had lied when he pretended to be fond of her. This storm had now died down, but neither of them knew what opinion exactly the other had of her or him. This sort of intermittent quarrel is of course somewhat exceptional. Of a different order were the quarrels of Bloch and his friends. Of a different order again were those of M. de Charlus, as we shall presently see, with people wholly unlike Mme. de Villeparisis. In spite of which we must bear in mind that the opinions which we hold of one another, our relations with friends and kinsfolk, are in no sense permanent, save in appearance, but are as eternally fluid as the sea itself. Whence all the rumours of divorce between couples who have always seemed so perfectly united and will soon afterwards speak of one another with affection, hence all the terrible things said by one friend of another from whom we supposed him to be inseparable and with whom we shall find him once more reconciled before we have had time to recover from our surprise; all the ruptures of alliances, after so short a time, between nations.

"I say, my uncle and Mme. Swann are getting warm over there!" remarked Saint-Loup. "And look at Mamma in the innocence of her heart going across to disturb them. To the pure all things are pure, I suppose!"

I studied M. de Charlus. The tuft of his grey hair, his eye, the brow of which was raised by his monocle to emit a smile, the red flowers in his buttonhole formed, so to speak, the three mobile apices of a convulsive and striking triangle. I had not ventured to bow to him, for he had given me no sign of recognition. And yet, albeit he had not turned his head in my direction, I was convinced that he had seen me; while he repeated some story to Mme. Swann, whose sumptuous, pansy-coloured cloak floated actually over the Baron's knee, his roving eye, like that of a street hawker who is watching all the time for the 'tecs' to appear, had certainly explored every corner of the room and taken note of all the people who were in it. M. de Châtellerault came up to bid him good day without any indication on M. de Charlus's face that he had seen the young Duke until he was actually standing in front of him. In this way, in fairly numerous gatherings such as this, M. de Charlus kept almost continuously on show a smile without any definite direction or particular object, which, pre-existing before the greetings of new arrivals, found itself, when these entered its zone, devoid of any indication of friendliness towards them. Nevertheless, it was obviously my duty to go across and speak to Mme. Swann. But as she was not certain whether I already knew Mme. de Marsantes and M. de Charlus, she was distinctly cold, fearing no doubt that I might ask her to introduce me to them. I then made my way to M. de Charlus, and at once regretted it, for though he could not have helped seeing me he shewed no sign whatsoever. As I stood before him and bowed I found standing out from his body, which it prevented me from approaching by the full length of his outstretched arm, a finger widowed, one would have said, of an episcopal ring, of which he appeared to be offering, for the kiss of the faithful, the consecrated site, and I was made to appear to have penetrated, without leave from the Baron and by an act of trespass for which he would hold me permanently responsible, the anonymous and vacant dispersion of his smile. This coldness was hardly of a kind to encourage Mme. Swann to melt from hers.

"How tired and worried you look," said Mme. de Marsantes to her son who had come up to greet M. de Charlus.

And indeed the expression in Robert's eyes seemed every minute to reach a depth from which it rose at once like a diver who has touched bottom. This bottom which hurt Robert so when he touched it that he left it at once, to return to it a moment later, was the thought that he had quarrelled with his mistress.

"Never mind," his mother went on, stroking his cheek, "never mind; it's good to see my little boy again."

But this show of affection seeming to irritate Robert, Mme. de Marsantes led her son away to the other end of the room where in an alcove hung with yellow silk a group of Beauvais armchairs massed their violet-hued tapestries like purple irises in a field of buttercups. Mme. Swann, finding herself alone and having realised that I was a friend of Saint-Loup, beckoned to me to come and sit beside her. Not having seen her for so long I did not know what to talk to her about. I was keeping an eye on my hat, among the crowd of hats that littered the carpet, and I asked myself with a vague curiosity to whom one of them could belong which was not that of the Duc de Guermantes and yet in the lining of which a capital 'G' was surmounted by a ducal coronet. I knew who everyone in the room was, and could not think of anyone whose hat this could possibly be.

"What a pleasant man M. de Norpois is," I said to Mme. Swann, looking at the Ambassador. "It is true, Robert de Saint-Loup says he's a pest, but . . ."

"He is quite right," she replied.

Seeing from her face that she was thinking of something which she was keeping from me, I plied her with questions. For the satisfaction of appearing to be greatly taken up by some one in this room where she knew hardly anyone, she took me into a corner.

"I am sure this is what M. de Saint-Loup meant," she began, "but you must never tell him I said so, for he would think me indiscreet, and I value his esteem very highly; I am an 'honest Injun,' don't you know. The other day, Charlus was dining at the Princesse de Guermantes's; I don't know how it was, but your name was mentioned. M. de Norpois seems to have told them—it's all too silly for words, don't go and worry yourself to death over it, nobody paid any attention, they all knew only too well the mischievous tongue that said it—that you were a hypocritical little flatterer."

I have recorded a long way back my stupefaction at the discovery that a friend of my father, such as M. de Norpois was, could have expressed himself thus in speaking of me. I was even more astonished to learn that my emotion on that evening long ago when I had asked him about Mme. Swann and Gilberte was known to the Princesse de Guermantes, whom I imagined never to have heard of my existence. Each of our actions, our words, our attitudes is cut off from the 'world,' from the people who have not directly perceived it, by a medium the permeability of which is of infinite variation and remains unknown to ourselves; having learned by experience that some important utterance which we eagerly hoped would be disseminated (such as those so enthusiastic speeches which I used at one time to make to all comers and on every occasion on the subject of Mme. Swann) has found itself, often simply on account of our anxiety, immediately hidden under a bushel, how immeasurably less do we suppose that some tiny word, which we ourselves have forgotten, or else a word never uttered by us but formed on its course by the imperfect refraction of a different word, can be transported without ever halting for any obstacle to infinite distances—in the present instance to the Princesse de Guermantes —and succeed in diverting at our expense the banquet of the gods. What we actually recall of our conduct remains unknown to our nearest neighbour; what we have forgotten that we ever said, or indeed what we never did say, flies to provoke hilarity even in another planet, and the image that other people form of our actions and behaviour is no more like that which we form of them ourselves, than is like an original drawing a spoiled copy in which, at one point, for a black line, we find an empty gap, and for a blank space an unaccountable contour. It may be, all the same, that what has not been transcribed is some non-existent feature which we behold merely in our purblind self-esteem, and that what seems to us added is indeed a part of ourselves, but so essential a part as to have escaped our notice. So that this strange print which seems to us to have so little resemblance to ourselves bears sometimes the same stamp of truth, scarcely flattering, indeed, but profound and useful, as a photograph taken by X-rays. Not that that is any reason why we should recognise ourselves in it. A man who is in the habit of smiling in the glass at his handsome face and stalwart figure, if you shew him their radiograph, will have, face to face with that rosary of bones, labelled as being the image of himself, the same suspicion of error as the visitor to an art gallery who, on coming to the portrait of a girl, reads in his catalogue: "Dromedary resting." Later on, this discrepancy between our portraits, according as it was our own hand that drew them or another, I was to register in the case of others than myself, living placidly in the midst of a collection of photographs which they themselves had taken while round about them grinned frightful faces, invisible to them as a rule, but plunging them in stupor if an accident were to reveal them with the warning: "This is you."

A few years earlier I should have been only too glad to tell Mme. Swann in what connexion I had fawned upon M. de Norpois, since the connexion had been my desire to know her. But I no longer felt this desire, I was no longer in love with Gilberte. On the other hand I had not succeeded in identifying Mme. Swann with the lady in pink of my childhood. Accordingly I spoke of the woman who was on my mind at the moment.

"Did you see the Duchesse de Guermantes just now?" I asked Mme. Swann.

But since the Duchess did not bow to Mme. Swann when they met, the latter chose to appear to regard her as a person of no importance, whose presence in a room one did not even remark.

"I don't know; I didn't *realise* her," she replied sourly, using an expression borrowed from England.

I was anxious nevertheless for information with regard not only to Mme. de Guermantes but to all the people who came in contact with her, and (for all the world like Bloch), with the tactlessness of people who seek in their conversation not to give pleasure to others but to elucidate, from sheer egoism, facts that are interesting to themselves, in my effort to form an exact idea of the life of Mme. de Guermantes I questioned Mme. de Villeparisis about Mme. Leroi.

"Oh, yes, I know who' you mean," she replied with an affectation of contempt, "the daughter of those rich timber people. I've heard that she's begun to go about quite a lot lately, but I must explain to you that I am rather old now to make new acquaintances. I have known such interesting, such delightful people in my time that really I do not believe Mme. Leroi would be any addition to what I already have." Mme. de Marsantes, who was playing lady in waiting to the Marquise, presented me to the Prince, and, while she was still doing so, M. de Norpois also presented me in the most glowing terms. Perhaps he found it convenient to do me a courtesy which could in no way damage his credit since I had just been presented, perhaps it was because he thought that a foreigner, even so distinguished a foreigner, was unfamiliar with French society and might think that he was having introduced to him a young man of fashion, perhaps to exercise one of his prerogatives, that of adding the weight of his personal recommendation as an Ambassador, or in his taste for the archaic to revive in the Prince's honour the old custom, flattering to his rank, that two sponsors were necessary if one wished to be presented.

Mme. de Villeparisis appealed to M. de Norpois, feeling it imperative that I should have his assurance that she had nothing to regret in not knowing Mme. Leroi.

"Am I not right, M. l'Ambassadeur, Mme. Leroi is quite uninteresting, isn't she, quite out of keeping with the people who come here; I was quite right not to make friends with her, wasn't I?"

Whether from independence or because he was tired, M. de Norpois replied merely in a bow full of respect but devoid of meaning.

"Sir," went on Mme. de Villeparisis with a laugh, "there are some absurd people in the world. Would you believe that I had a visit this afternoon from a gentleman who tried to persuade me that he found more pleasure in kissing my hand than a young woman's?"

I guessed at once that this was Legrandin. M. de Norpois smiled with a slight quiver of the eyelid, as though such a remark had been prompted by a concupiscence so natural that one could not find fault with the person who had uttered it, almost as though it were the beginning of a romance which he was prepared to forgive, if not to encourage, with the perverse indulgence of a Voisenon or the younger Crébillon.

"Many young women's hands would be incapable of doing what I see there," said the Prince, pointing to Mme. de Villeparisis's unfinished water-colours. And he asked her whether she had seen the flower paintings by Fantin-Latour which had recently been exhibited.

"They are of the first order, and indicate, as people say nowadays, a fine painter, one of the masters of the palette," declared M. de Norpois; "I consider, all the same, that they stand no comparison with these, in which I find it easier to recognise the colouring of the flower."

Even supposing that the partiality of an old lover, the habit of flattering people, the critical standard admissible in a small circle, had dictated this speech to the ex-Ambassador, it proved upon what an absolute vacuum of true taste the judgment of people in society is based, so arbitrary that the smallest trifle can make it rush to the wildest absurdities, on the way to which it is stopped, held up by no genuinely felt impression.

"I claim no credit for knowing about flowers, I've lived all my life among the fields," replied Mme. de Villeparisis modestly. "But," she added graciously, turning to the Prince, "if I did, when I was quite a girl, form a rather more serious idea of them than children generally do in the country, I owe that to a distinguished fellow-countryman of yours, Herr von Schlegel. I met him at Broglie, when I was staying there once with my aunt Cordelia (Marshal de Castellane's wife, don't you know?). I remember so well M. Lebrun, M. de Salvandy, M. Doudan, getting him to talk about flowers. I was only a little girl, I wasn't able to follow all he said. But he liked playing with me, and when he went back to your country he sent me a beautiful botany book to remind me of a drive we took together in a phaeton to the Val Richer, when I fell asleep on his knee. I have got the book still, and it taught me to observe many things about flowers which I should not have noticed otherwise. When Mme. de Barante published some of Mme. de Broglie's letters, charming and affected like herself, I hoped to find among them some record of those conversations with Herr von Schlegel. But she was a woman who looked for nothing from nature but arguments in support of religion."

Robert called me away to the far end of the room where he and his mother were.

"You have been good to me," I said, "how can I thank you? Can we dine together to-morrow?"

"To-morrow? Yes, if you like, but it will have to be with Bloch. I met him just now on the doorstep; he was rather stiff with me at first because I had quite forgotten to answer his last two letters. (At least, he didn't tell me that that was what had annoyed him, but I guessed it.) But after that he was so friendly to me that I simply can't disappoint him. Between ourselves, on his side at least, I can feel it's a life and death friendship." Nor do I consider that Robert was altogether mistaken. Furious detraction was often, with Bloch, the effect of a keen affection which he had supposed to be unreturned. And as he had little power of imagining the lives of other people, and never dreamed that one might have been ill, or away from home, or otherwise occupied, a week's silence was at once interpreted by him as meaning a deliberate coldness. And so I have never believed that his most violent outbursts as a friend, or in later years as a writer, went very deep. They rose to a paroxysm if one replied to them with an icy dignity, or by a platitude which encouraged him to redouble his onslaught, but yielded often to a warmly sympathetic attitude. "As for being good," went on Saint-Loup, "you say I have been to you, but I haven't been good at all, my aunt tells me that it's you who avoid her, that you never said a word to her. She wondered whether you had anything against her."

Fortunately for myself, if I had been taken in by this speech, our departure, which I believed to be imminent, for Balbec would have prevented my making any attempt to see Mme. Guermantes again, to assure her that I had nothing against her, and so to put her under the necessity of proving

that it was she who had something against me. But I had only to remind myself that she had not even offered to let me see her Elstirs. Besides, this was
not a disappointment; I had never expected her to begin talking to me
about them; I knew that I did not appeal to her, that I need have no hope
of ever making her like me; the most that I had been able to look forward
to was that, thanks to her kindness, I might there and then receive, since
I should not be seeing her again before I left Paris, an entirely pleasing
impression, which I could take with me to Balbec indefinitely prolonged,
intact, instead of a memory broken by anxiety and sorrow.

Mme. de Marsantes kept on interrupting her conversation with Robert
to tell me how often he had spoken to her about me, how fond he was of
me; she treated me with a deference which almost hurt me because I felt
it to be prompted by her fear of being embroiled, on my account, with this
son whom she had not seen all day, with whom she was eager to be alone,
and over whom she must accordingly have supposed that the influence
which she wielded was not equal to and must conciliate mine. Having heard
me, earlier in the afternoon, make some reference to Bloch's uncle, M.
Nissim Bernard, Mme. de Marsantes inquired whether it was he who had
at one time lived at Nice.

"In that case, he knew M. de Marsantes there before our marriage," she
told me. "My husband used often to speak of him as an excellent man, with
such a delicate, generous nature."

"To think that for once in his life he wasn't lying! It's incredible," would
have been Bloch's comment.

All this time I should have liked to explain to Mme. de Marsantes that
Robert felt infinitely more affection for her than for myself, and that had
she shewn any hostility towards me it was not in my nature to attempt to
set him against her, to detach him from her. But now that Mme. de Guermantes had left the room, I had more leisure to observe Robert, and I
noticed then for the first time that, once again, a sort of flood of anger
seemed to be coursing through him, rising to the surface of his stern and
sombre features. I was afraid lest, remembering the scene in the theatre
that afternoon, he might be feeling humiliated in my presence at having
allowed himself to be treated so harshly by his mistress without making
any rejoinder.

Suddenly he broke away from his mother, who had put her arm round
his neck, and, coming towards me, led me behind the little flower-strewn
counter at which Mme. de Villeparisis had resumed her seat, making a
sign to me to follow him into the smaller room. I was hurrying after him
when M. de Charlus, who must have supposed that I was leaving the house,
turned abruptly from Prince von Faffenheim, to whom he had been talking,
and made a rapid circuit which brought him face to face with me. I saw
with alarm that he had taken the hat in the lining of which were a capital
'G' and a ducal coronet. In the doorway into the little room he said, without looking at me:

"As I see that you have taken to going into society, you must do me the
pleasure of coming to see me. But it's a little complicated," he went on
with a distracted, calculating air, as if the pleasure had been one that he

was afraid of not securing again once he had let slip the opportunity of arranging with me the means by which it might be realised. "I am very seldom at home; you will have to write to me. But I should prefer to explain things to you more quietly. I am just going. Will you walk a short way with me? I shall only keep you a moment."

"You'd better take care, sir," I warned him; "you have picked up the wrong hat by mistake."

"Do you want to stop me taking my own hat?" I assumed, a similar mishap having recently occurred to myself, that someone else having taken his hat he had seized upon one at random, so as not to go home bare-headed, and that I had placed him in a difficulty by exposing his stratagem. I told him that I must say a few words to Saint-Loup. "He is still talking to that idiot the Duc de Guermantes," I added. "That really is charming; I shall tell my brother." "Oh! you think that would interest M. de Charlus?" (I imagined that, if he had a brother, that brother must be called Charlus also. Saint-Loup had indeed explained his family tree to me at Balbec, but I had forgotten the details.) "Who has been talking to you about M. de Charlus?" replied the Baron in an arrogant tone. "Go to Robert."

"I hear," he went on, "that you took part this morning in one of those orgies that he has with a woman who is disgracing him. You would do well to use your influence with him to make him realise the pain he is causing his poor mother, and all of us, by dragging our name in the dirt."

I should have liked to reply that at this degrading luncheon the conversation had been entirely about Emerson, Ibsen and Tolstoy, and that the young woman had lectured Robert to make him drink nothing but water. In the hope of bringing some balm to Robert, whose pride had, I felt, been wounded, I sought to find an excuse for his mistress. I did not know that at that moment, in spite of his anger with her, it was on himself that he was heaping reproaches. But it always happens, even in quarrels between a good man and a worthless woman, and when the right is all on one side, that some trifle crops up which enables the woman to appear not to have been in the wrong on one point. And as she ignores all the other points, the moment the man begins to feel the need of her company, or is demoralised by separation from her, his weakness will make his conscience more exacting, he will remember the absurd reproaches that have been flung at him and will ask himself whether they have not some foundation in fact.

"I've come to the conclusion I was wrong about that matter of the necklace," Robert said to me. "Of course, I never meant for a moment to do anything wrong, but, I know very well, other people don't look at things in the same way as oneself. She had a very hard time when she was young. In her eyes, I was bound to appear just the rich man who thinks he can get anything he wants with his money, and with whom a poor person cannot compete, whether in trying to influence Boucheron or in a lawsuit. Of course she has been horribly cruel to me, when I have never thought of anything but her good. But I do see clearly, she believes that I wanted to make her feel that one could keep a hold on her with money, and that's not true. And she's so fond of me; what must she be thinking of me? Poor darling, if you only knew, she has such charming ways, I simply can't tell you, she has often done the most adorable things for me. How wretched she must be feeling now! In any case, whatever happens in the long run, I don't want to let her think me a cad; I shall dash off to Boucheron's and get the necklace. You never know; very likely when she sees me with it, she will admit that she's been in the wrong. Don't you see, it's the idea that she is suffering at this moment that I can't bear. What one suffers oneself one knows; that's nothing. But with her—to say to oneself that she's suffering and not to be able to form any idea of what she feels—I think I shall go mad in a minute —I'd much rather never see her again than let her suffer. She can be happy without me, if she must; that's all I ask. Listen; you know, to me everything that concerns her is enormously important, it becomes something cosmic; I shall run to the jeweller's and then go and ask her to forgive me. But until I get down there what will she be thinking of me? If she could only know that I was on my way! What about your going down there and telling her? For all we know, that might settle the whole business. Perhaps," he went on with a smile, as though he hardly ventured to believe in so idyllic a possibility, "we can all three dine together in the country. But we can't tell yet. I never know how to handle her. Poor child. I shall perhaps only hurt her more than ever. Besides, her decision may be irrevocable."

Robert swept me back to his mother.

"Good-bye," he said to her. "I've got to go now. I don't know when I shall get leave again. Probably not for a month. I shall write as soon as I know myself."

Certainly Robert was not in the least of the type of son who, when he goes out with his mother, feels that an attitude of exasperation towards her ought to balance the smiles and bows which he bestows on strangers. Nothing is more common than this odious form of vengeance on the part of those who appear to believe that rudeness to one's own family is the natural complement to one's ceremonial behaviour. Whatever the wretched mother may say, her son, as though he had been taken to the house against his will and wished to make her pay dearly for his presence, refutes immediately, with an ironical, precise, cruel contradiction, the timidly ventured assertion; the mother at once conforms, though without thereby disarming him, to the opinion of this superior being of whom she will continue to boast to everyone, when he is not present, as having a charming nature, and who all the same spares her none of his keenest thrusts. Saint-Loup was not at all like this; but the anguish which Rachel's absence provoked in him brought it about that, for different reasons, he was no less harsh with his mother than the sons I have been describing are with theirs. And as she listened to him I saw the same throb, like that of a mighty wing, which Mme. de Marsantes had been unable to repress when her son first entered the room, convulse her whole body once again; but this time it was an anxious face, eyes wide with grief that she fastened on him.

"What, Robert, you're going away? Seriously? My little son! The one day I've seen anything of you!"

And then quite softly, in the most natural tone, in a voice from which she strove to banish all sadness so as not to inspire her son with a pity which would perhaps have been painful to him or else useless and might serve only to irritate him, like an argument prompted by plain common sense she added:

"You know, it's not at all nice of you."

But to this simplicity she added so much timidity, to shew him that she was not trespassing on his freedom, so much affection, so that he should not reproach her with spoiling his pleasures, that Saint-Loup could not fail to observe in himself as it were the possibility of a similar wave of affection, that was to say an obstacle to his spending the evening with his lady. And so he grew angry.

"It's unfortunate, but, nice or not, that's how it is."

And he heaped on his mother the reproaches which no doubt he felt that he himself perhaps deserved; thus it is that egoists have always the last word; having laid down at the start that their determination is unshakeable, the more the sentiment in them to which one appeals to make them abandon it is touched, the more fault they find, not with themselves who resist the appeal but with those persons who put them under the necessity of resisting it, with the result that their own firmness may be carried to the utmost degree of cruelty, which only aggravates all the more in their eyes the culpability of the person who is so indelicate as to be hurt, to be in the right, and to cause them thus treacherously the pain of acting against their natural instinct of pity. But of her own accord Mme. de Marsantes ceased to insist, for she felt that she would not be able to keep him.

"I shall leave you here," he said to me, "but you're not to keep him long, Mamma, because he's got to go somewhere else in a minute."

I was fully aware that my company could not afford any pleasure to Mme. de Marsantes, but I preferred, by not going with Robert, not to let her suppose that I was involved in these pleasures which deprived her of him. I should have liked to find some excuse for her son's conduct, less from affection for him than from pity for her. But it was she who spoke first.

"Poor boy," she began, "I am sure I must have hurt him dreadfully. You see, Sir, mothers are such selfish creatures, after all he hasn't many pleasures, he comes so little to Paris. Oh, dear, if he hadn't gone already I should have liked to stop him, not to keep him of course, but just to tell him that I'm not vexed with him, that I think he was quite right. Will you excuse me if I go and look over the staircase?"

I accompanied her there.

"Robert! Robert!" she called. "No; he's gone; we are too late."

At that moment I would as gladly have undertaken a mission to make Robert break with his mistress as, a few hours earlier, to make him go and live with her altogether. In one case Saint-Loup would have regarded me as a false friend, in the other his family would have called me his evil genius. Yet I was the same man, at an interval of a few hours.

We returned to the drawing-room. Seeing that Saint-Loup was not with us, Mme. de Villeparisis exchanged with M. de Norpois that dubious, derisive and not too pitying glance with which people point out to one another an over-jealous wife or an over-loving mother (spectacles which to outsiders are amusing), as much as to say: "There now, there's been trouble."

Robert went to his mistress, taking with him the splendid ornament which, after what had been said on both sides, he ought not to have given her. But it came to the same thing, for she would not look at it, and even after their reconciliation he could never persuade her to accept it. Certain of Robert's friends thought that these proofs of disinterestedness which she furnished were deliberately planned to draw him closer to her. And yet she was not greedy about money, except perhaps to be able to spend it without thought. I have seen her bestow recklessly on people whom she believed to be in need the most insensate charity. "At this moment," Robert's friends would say to him, seeking to balance by their malicious words a disinterested action on Rachel's part, "at this moment she will be in the promenade at the Folies-Bergères. She's an enigma, that girl is, a regular sphinx." After all, how many women who are not disinterested, since they are kept by men, have we not seen, with a delicacy that flowers from their sordid existence, set with their own hands a thousand little limits to the generosity of their lovers?

Robert knew of scarcely any of the infidelities of his mistress, and tortured his mind over what were mere nothings compared with the real life of Rachel, a life which began every day only after he had left her. He knew of scarcely any of these infidelities. One could have told him of them without shaking his confidence in Rachel. For it is a charming law of nature which manifests itself in the heart of the most complex social organisms, that we live in perfect ignorance of those we love. On one side of the mirror the lover says to himself: "She is an angel, she will never yield herself to me, I may as well die—and yet she does care for me; she cares so much that perhaps—but no, it can never possibly happen." And in the exaltation of his desire, in the anguish of waiting, what jewels he flings at the feet of this woman, how he runs to borrow money to save her from inconvenience; meanwhile, on the other side of the screen, through which their conversation will no more carry than that which visitors exchange outside the glass wall of an aquarium, the public are saying: "You don't know her? I congratulate you, she has robbed, in fact ruined I don't know how many men. There isn't a worse girl in Paris. She's a common swindler. And cunning isn't the word!" And perhaps the public are not entirely wrong in their use of the last epithet, for indeed the sceptical man who is not really in love with the woman and whom she merely attracts says to his friends: "No, no, my dear fellow, she is not in the least a prostitute; I don't say she hasn't had an adventure or two in her time, but she's not a woman one pays, she'd be a damned sight too expensive if she was. With her it's fifty thousand francs or nothing." Well, he has spent fifty thousand francs on her, he has had her once, but she (finding, moreover, a willing accomplice in the man himself) has managed to persuade him that he is one of those who have had her for nothing. Such is society, in which every one of us has two aspects, in which the most obvious, the most notorious faults will never be known by a certain other person save embedded in, under the protection of a shell, a smooth cocoon, a delicious curiosity of nature. There were in Paris two thoroughly respectable men to whom Saint-Loup no longer bowed, and could not refer without a tremor in his voice, calling them exploiters of women: this was because they had both been ruined by Rachel.

"I blame myself for one thing only," Mme. de Marsantes murmured in my ear, "and that was my telling him that he wasn't nice to me. He, such an adorable, unique son, there's no one else like him in the world, the only time I see him, to have told him he wasn't nice to me, I would far rather he'd beaten me, because I am sure that whatever pleasure he may be having this evening, and he hasn't many, will be spoiled for him by that unfair word. But, Sir, I mustn't keep you, since you're in a hurry."

Anxiously, Mme. de Marsantes bade me good-bye. These sentiments bore upon Robert; she was sincere. But she ceased to be, to become a great lady once more.

"I have been so *interested,* so *glad* to have this little talk with you. Thank you! Thank you!"

And with a humble air she fastened on me a look of gratitude, of exhilaration, as though my conversation were one of the keenest pleasures that she had experienced in her life. These charming glances went very well with the black flowers on her white skirt; they were those of a great lady who knew her business.

"But I am in no hurry," I replied; "besides, I must wait for M. de Charlus; I am going with him."

Mme. de Villeparisis overheard these last words. They appeared to vex her. Had the matter in question not been one which could not possibly give rise to such a sentiment, it might have struck me that what seemed to be at that moment alarmed in Mme. de Villeparisis was her modesty. But this hypothesis never even entered my mind. I was delighted with Mme. de Guermantes, with Saint-Loup, with Mme. de Marsantes, with M. de Charlus, with Mme. de Villeparisis; I did not stop to reflect, and I spoke light-heartedly and at random.

"You're going from here with my nephew Palamède?" she asked me.

Thinking that it might produce a highly favourable impression on Mme. de Villeparisis if she learned that I was on intimate terms with a nephew whom she esteemed so greatly, "He has asked me to go home with him," I answered blithely. "I am so glad. Besides, we are greater friends than you think, and I've quite made up my mind that we're going to be better friends still."

From being vexed, Mme. de Villeparisis seemed to have grown anxious. "Don't wait for him," she said to me, with a preoccupied air. "He is talking to M. de Faffenheim. He's certain to have forgotten what he said to you. You'd much better go, now, quickly, while his back is turned."

The first emotion shewn by Mme. de Villeparisis would have suggested, but for the circumstances, offended modesty. Her insistence, her opposition might well, if one had studied her face alone, have appeared to be dictated by virtue. I was not, myself, in any hurry to join Robert and his mistress. But Mme. de Villeparisis seemed to make such a point of my going that, thinking perhaps that she had some important business to discuss with her nephew, I bade her good-bye. Next to her M. de Guermantes, superb and

Olympian, was ponderously seated. One would have said that the notion, omnipresent in all his members, of his vast riches gave him a particular high density, as though they had been melted in a crucible into a single human ingot to form this man whose value was so immense. At the moment of my saying good-bye to him he rose politely from his seat, and I could feel the dead weight of thirty millions which his old-fashioned French breeding set in motion, raised, until it stood before me. I seemed to be looking at that statue of Olympian Zeus which Phidias is said to have cast in solid gold. Such was the power that good breeding had over M. de Guermantes, over the body of M. de Guermantes at least, for it had not an equal mastery over the ducal mind. M. de Guermantes laughed at his own jokes, but did not unbend to other people's.

As I went downstairs I heard behind me a voice calling out to me:

"So this is how you wait for me, is it?"

It was M. de Charlus.

"You don't mind if we go a little way on foot?" he asked dryly, when we were in the courtyard. "We can walk until I find a cab that suits me."

"You wished to speak to me about something, Sir?"

"Oh yes, as a matter of fact there were some things I wished to say to you, but I am not so sure now whether I shall. As far as you are concerned, I am sure that they might be the starting-point which would lead you to inestimable benefits. But I can see also that they would bring into my existence, at an age when one begins to value tranquillity, a great loss of time, great inconvenience. I ask myself whether you are worth all the pains that I should have to take with you, and I have not the pleasure of knowing you well enough to be able to say. Perhaps also to you yourself what I could do for you does not appear sufficiently attractive for me to give myself so much trouble, for I repeat quite frankly that for me it can only be trouble."

I protested that, in that case, he must not dream of it. This summary end to the discussion did not seem to be to his liking.

"That sort of politeness means nothing," he rebuked me coldly. "There is nothing so pleasant as to give oneself trouble for a person who is worth one's while. For the best of us, the study of the arts, a taste for old things, collections, gardens are all mere *ersatz, succedanea,* alibis. In the heart of our tub, like Diogenes, we cry out for a man. We cultivate begonias, we trim yews, as a last resort, because yews and begonias submit to treatment. But we should like to give our time to a plant of human growth, if we were sure that he was worth the trouble. That is the whole question: you must know something about yourself. Are you worth my trouble or not?"

"I would not for anything in the world, Sir, be a cause of anxiety to you," I said to him, "but so far as I am concerned you may be sure that everything which comes to me from you will be a very great pleasure to me. I am deeply touched that you should be so kind as to take notice of me in this way and try to help me."

Greatly to my surprise, it was almost with effusion that he thanked me for this speech, slipping his arm through mine with that intermittent fa-

miliarity which had already struck me at Balbec, and was in such contrast
to the coldness of his tone.

"With the want of consideration common at your age," he told me, "you
are liable to say things at times which would open an unbridgeable gulf
between us. What you have said just now, on the other hand, is exactly
the sort of thing that touches me, and makes me want to do a great deal
for you."

As he walked arm in arm with me and uttered these words, which, albeit
tinged with contempt, were so affectionate, M. de Charlus now fastened
his gaze on me with that intense fixity which had struck me the first morning, when I saw him outside the casino at Balbec, and indeed many years
before that, through the pink hawthorns, standing beside Mme. Swann,
whom I supposed then to be his mistress, in the park at Tansonville; now
let it stray around him and examine the cabs which at this time of the day
were passing in considerable numbers on the way to their stables, looking
so determinedly at them that several stopped, the drivers supposing that
he wished to engage them. But M. de Charlus immediately dismissed them.

"They're not what I want," he explained to me, "it's all a question of
the colour of their lamps, and the direction they're going in. I hope, Sir,"
he went on, "that you will not in any way misinterpret the purely disinterested and charitable nature of the proposal which I am going to make
to you."

I was struck by the similarity of his diction to Swann's, closer now than
at Balbec.

"You have enough intelligence, I suppose, not to imagine that it is from
want of society, from any fear of solitude and boredom that I have recourse to you. I do not, as a rule, care to talk about myself, but you may
possibly have heard—it was alluded to in a leading article in *The Times,*
which made a considerable impression—that the Emperor of Austria, who
has always honoured me with his friendship, and is good enough to insist
on keeping up terms of cousinship with me, declared the other day in an
interview which was made public that if the Comte de Chambord had had
by his side a man as thoroughly conversant with the undercurrents of
European politics as myself he would be King of France to-day. I have
often thought, Sir, that there was in me, thanks not to my own humble
talents but to circumstances which you may one day have occasion to
learn, a sort of secret record of incalculable value, of which I have not felt
myself at liberty to make use, personally, but which would be a priceless
acquisition to a young man to whom I would hand over in a few months
what it has taken me more than thirty years to collect, what I am perhaps
alone in possessing. I do not speak of the intellectual enjoyment which
you would find in learning certain secrets which a Michelet of our day
would give years of his life to know, and in the light of which certain events
would assume for him an entirely different aspect. And I do not speak only
of events that have already occurred, but of the chain of circumstances."
(This was a favourite expression with M. de Charlus, and often, when he
used it, he joined his hands as if in prayer, but with his fingers stiffened,
as though to illustrate by their complexity the said circumstances, which

he did not specify, and the chain that linked them.) "I could give you an explanation that no one has dreamed of, not only of the past but of the future." M. de Charlus broke off to question me about Bloch, whom he had heard discussed, though without appearing to be listening, in his aunt's drawing-room. And with that ironical accent he so skilfully detached what he was saying that he seemed to be thinking of something else altogether, and to be speaking mechanically, simply out of politeness. He asked if my friend was young, good looking and so forth. Bloch, if he had heard him, would have been more puzzled even than with M. de Norpois, but for very different reasons, to know whether M. de Charlus was for or against Dreyfus. "It is not a bad idea, if you wish to learn about life," went on M. de Charlus when he had finished questioning me, "to include among your friends an occasional foreigner." I replied that Bloch was French. "Indeed," said M. de Charlus, "I took him to be a Jew." His assertion of this incompatibility made me suppose that M. de Charlus was more anti-Dreyfusard than anyone I had met. He protested, however, against the charge of treason levelled against Dreyfus. But his protest took this form: "I understand the newspapers to say that Dreyfus has committed a crime against his country—so I understand, I pay no attention to the newspapers, I read them as I wash my hands, without finding that it is worth my while to take any interest in what I am doing. In any case, the crime is non-existent, your friend's compatriot would have committed a crime if he had betrayed Judaea, but what has he to do with France?" I pointed out that if there should be a war the Jews would be mobilised just as much as anyone else. "Perhaps so, and I am not sure that it would not be an imprudence. If we bring over Senegalese and Malagasies, I hardly suppose that their hearts will be in the task of defending France, which is only natural. Your Dreyfus might rather be convicted of a breach of the laws of hospitality. But we need not discuss that. Perhaps you could ask your friend to allow me to be present at some great festival in the Temple, at a circumcision, with Jewish chants. He might perhaps take a hall, and give me some biblical entertainment, as the young ladies of Saint-Cyr performed scenes taken from the Psalms by Racine, to amuse Louis XIV. You might even arrange parties to give us a good laugh. For instance a battle between your friend and his father, in which he would smite him as David smote Goliath. That would make quite an amusing farce. He might even, while he was about it, deal some stout blows at his hag (or, as my old nurse would say, his 'haggart') of a mother. That would be an excellent show, and would not be unpleasing to us, eh, my young friend, since we like exotic spectacles, and to thrash that non-European creature would be giving a well-earned punishment to an old camel." As he poured out this terrible, almost insane language, M. de Charlus squeezed my arm until it ached. I reminded myself of all that his family had told me of his wonderful kindness to this old nurse, whose Molièresque vocabulary he had just quoted, and thought to myself that the connexions, hitherto, I felt, little studied, between goodness and wickedness in the same heart, various as they might be, would be an interesting subject for research.

I warned him that, anyhow, Mme. Bloch no longer existed, while as for M. Bloch, I questioned to what extent he would enjoy a sport which might easily result in his being blinded. M. de Charlus seemed annoyed. "That," he said, "is a woman who made a great mistake in dying. As for blinding him, surely the Synagogue is blind, it does not perceive the truth of the Gospel. In any case, think, at this moment, when all these unhappy Jews are trembling before the stupid fury of the Christians, what an honour it would be for him to see a man like myself condescend to be amused by their sports." At this point I caught sight of M. Bloch senior, who was coming towards us, probably on his way to meet his son. He did not see us, but I offered to introduce him to M. de Charlus. I had no conception of the torrent of rage which my words were to let loose. "Introduce him to me! But you must have singularly little idea of social values! People do not get to know me as easily as that. In the present instance, the awkwardness would be twofold, on account of the youth of the introducer and the unworthiness of the person introduced. At the most, if I am ever permitted to enjoy the Asiatic spectacle which I suggested to you, I might address to the horrible creature a few words indicative of generous feeling. But on condition that he allows himself to be thoroughly thrashed by his son, I might go so far as to express my satisfaction." As it happened, M. Bloch paid no attention to us. He was occupied in greeting Mme. Sazerat with a series of sweeping bows, which were very favourably received. I was surprised at this, for in the old days at Combray she had been indignant at my parents for having young Bloch in the house, so anti-semitic was she then. But Dreyfusism, like a strong gust of wind, had, a few days before this, wafted M. Bloch to her feet. My father's friend had found Mme. Sazerat charming and was particularly gratified by the anti-semitism of the lady, which he regarded as a proof of the sincerity of her faith and the soundness of her Dreyfusard opinions, and also as enhancing the value of the call which she had authorised him to pay her. He had not even been offended when she had said to him stolidly: "M. Drumont has the impudence to put the Revisionists in the same bag as the Protestants and the Jews. A delightful promiscuity!" "Bernard," he had said with pride, on reaching home, to M. Nissim Bernard, "you know, she has that prejudice!" But M. Nissim Bernard had said nothing, only raising his eyes to heaven in an angelic gaze. Saddened by the misfortunes of the Jews, remembering his old friendships with Christians, grown mannered and precious with increasing years, for reasons which the reader will learn in due course, he had now the air of a pre-Raphaelite ghost on to which hair had been incongruously grafted, like threads in the heart of an opal. "All this Dreyfus business," went on the Baron, still clasping me by the arm, "has only one drawback. It destroys society (I do not say polite society; society has long ceased to deserve that laudatory epithet) by the influx of Mr. and Mrs. Camels and Camelries and Camelyards, astonishing creatures whom I find even in the houses of my own cousins, because they belong to the Patrie Française, or the Anti-Jewish, or some such league, as if a political opinion entitled one to any social qualification." This frivolity in M. de Charlus brought out his family likeness to the Duchesse de Guermantes. I remarked to him on the resemblance. As he appeared to think that I did not know her, I reminded him of the evening at the Opera when he had seemed to be trying to avoid me. He assured me with such insistence that he had never even seen me there that I should have begun to believe him, if presently a trifling incident had not led me to think that M. de Charlus, in his excessive pride perhaps, did not care to be seen with me.

"Let us return to yourself," he said, "and my plans for you. There exists among certain men, Sir, a freemasonry of which I cannot now say more than that it numbers in its ranks four of the reigning sovereigns of Europe. Now, the courtiers of one of these are trying to cure him of his fancy. That is a very serious matter, and may bring us to war. Yes, Sir, that is a fact. You remember the story of the man who believed that he had the Princess of China shut up in a bottle. It was a form of insanity. He was cured of it. But as soon as he ceased to be mad he became merely stupid. There are maladies which we must not seek to cure because they alone protect us from others that are more serious. A cousin of mine had trouble with his stomach; he could not digest anything. The most learned specialists on the stomach treated him, with no effect. I took him to a certain doctor (another highly interesting man, by the way, of whom I could tell you a great deal). He guessed at once that the trouble was nervousness; he persuaded his patient, ordered him to eat whatever he liked quite boldly and assured him that his digestion would stand it. But my cousin had nephritis also. What the stomach can digest perfectly well the kidneys cease, after a time, to eliminate, and my cousin, instead of living to a good old age with an imaginary disease of the stomach which obliged him to keep to a diet, died at forty with his stomach cured but his kidneys ruined. Given a very considerable advantage over people of your age, for all one knows, you will perhaps become what some eminent man of the past might have been if a good angel had revealed to him, in the midst of a humanity that knew nothing of them, the secrets of steam and electricity. Do not be foolish, do not refuse from discretion. Understand that, if I do you a great service, I expect my reward from you to be no less great. It is many years now since people in society ceased to interest me. I have but one passion left, to seek to redeem the mistakes of my life by conferring the benefit of my knowledge on a soul that is still virgin and capable of being inflamed by virtue. I have had great sorrows, Sir, of which I may tell you perhaps some day; I have lost my wife, who was the loveliest, the noblest, the most perfect creature that one could dream of seeing. I have young relatives who are not—I do not say worthy, but who are not capable of accepting the moral heritage of which I have been speaking. For all I know, you may be he into whose hands it is to pass, he whose life I shall be able to direct and to raise to so lofty a plane. My own would gain in return. Perhaps in teaching you the great secrets of diplomacy I might recover a taste for them myself, and begin at last to do things of real interest in which you would have an equal share. But before I can tell I must see you often, very often, every day."

I was thinking of taking advantage of this unexpected kindness on M. de Charlus's part to ask him whether he could not arrange for me to meet his sister-in-law when, suddenly, I felt my arm violently jerked, as though by an electric shock. It was M. de Charlus who had hurriedly withdrawn his arm from mine. Although as he talked he had allowed his eyes to wander in all directions he had only just caught sight of M. d'Argencourt, who was coming towards us from a side street. On seeing us, M. d'Argencourt appeared worried, cast at me a look of distrust, almost that look intended for a creature of another race than one's own with which Mme. de Guermantes had quizzed Bloch, and tried to avoid us. But one would have said that M. de Charlus was determined to shew him that he was not at all anxious not to be seen by him, for he called to him, simply to tell him something that was of no importance. And fearing perhaps that M. d'Argencourt had not recognised me, M. de Charlus informed him that I was a great friend of Mme. de Villeparisis, of the Duchesse de Guermantes, of Robert de Saint-Loup, and that he himself, Charlus, was an old friend of my grandmother, and glad to be able to shew her grandson a little of the affection that he felt for her. Nevertheless I observed that M. d'Argencourt, albeit I had barely been introduced to him at Mme. de Villeparisis's, and M. de Charlus had now spoken to him at great length about my family, was distinctly colder to me than he had been in the afternoon; and for a long time he shewed the same aloofness whenever we met. He watched me now with a curiosity in which there was no sign of friendliness, and seemed even to have to overcome an instinctive repulsion when, on leaving us, after a moment's hesitation, he held out a hand to me which he at once withdrew.

"I am sorry about that," said M. de Charlus. "That fellow Argencourt, well born but ill bred, more than feeble as a diplomat, an impossible husband, always running after women like a person in a play, is one of those men who are incapable of understanding but perfectly capable of destroying the things in life that are really great. I hope that our friendship will be one of them, if it is ever to be formed, and I hope also that you will honour me by keeping it—as I shall—well clear of the heels of any of those donkeys who, from idleness or clumsiness or deliberate wickedness trample upon what would seem to have been made to endure. Unfortunately, that is the mould in which most of the men one meets have been cast."

"The Duchesse de Guermantes seems to be very clever. We were talking this afternoon about the possibility of war. It appears that she is specially well informed on that subject."

"She is nothing of the sort," replied M. de Charlus tartly. "Women, and most men, for that matter, understand nothing of what I was going to tell you. My sister-in-law is a charming woman who imagines that we are still living in the days of Balzac's novels, when women had an influence on politics. Going to her house could at present have only a bad effect on you, as for that matter going anywhere. That was one of the very things I was just going to tell you when that fool interrupted me. The first sacrifice that you must make for me—I shall claim them from you in proportion to the gifts I bestow on you—is to give up going into society. It distressed me this afternoon to see you at that idiotic tea-party. You may remind me that I was there myself, but for me it was not a social gathering, it was simply a family visit. Later on, when you have established your position, if it amuses you to step down for a little into that sort of thing, it may, perhaps, do no harm. And then, I need not point out how invaluable I can be to you. The 'Open Sesame' to the Guermantes house and any others that it is worth while throwing open the doors of to you, rests with me. I shall be the judge, and intend to remain master of the situation."

I thought I would take advantage of what M. de Charlus had said about my call on Mme. de Villeparisis to try to find out what position exactly she occupied in society, but the question took another form on my lips than I had intended, and I asked him instead what the Villeparisis family was.

"That is absolutely as though you had asked me what the Nobody family was," replied M. de Charlus. "My aunt married, for love, a M. Thirion, who was extremely rich, for that matter, and whose sisters had married surprisingly well; and from that day onwards he called himself Marquis de Villeparisis. It did no harm to anyone, at the most a little to himself, and very little! What his reason was I cannot tell; I suppose he was actually a 'Monsieur de Villeparisis,' a gentleman born at Villeparisis, which as you know is the name of a little place outside Paris. My aunt tried to make out that there was such a Marquisate in the family, she wanted to put things on a proper footing; I can't tell you why. When one takes a name to which one has no right it is better not to copy the regular forms."

Mme. de Villeparisis being merely Mme. Thirion completed the fall which had begun in my estimation of her when I had seen the composite nature of her party. I felt it to be unfair that a woman whose title and name were of quite recent origin should be able thus to impose upon her contemporaries, with the prospect of similarly imposing upon posterity, by virtue of her friendships with royal personages. Now that she had become once again what I had supposed her to be in my childhood, a person who had nothing aristocratic about her, these distinguished kinsfolk who gathered round her seemed to remain alien to her. She did not cease to be charming to us all. I went occasionally to see her and she sent me little presents from time to time. But I had never any impression that she belonged to the Faubourg Saint-Germain, and if I had wanted any information about it she would have been one of the last people to whom I should have applied.

"At present," went on M. de Charlus, "by going into society, you will only damage your position, warp your intellect and character. Also, you must be particularly careful in choosing your friends. Keep mistresses, if your family have no objection, that doesn't concern me, indeed I can only advise it, you young rascal, young rascal who will soon have to start shaving," he rallied me, passing his fingers over my chin. "But the choice of your men friends is more important. Eight out of ten young men are little scoundrels, little wretches capable of doing you an injury which you will never be able to repair. Wait, now, my nephew Saint-Loup is quite a suitable companion for you, at a pinch. As far as your future is concerned, he can be of no possible use to you, but for that I am sufficient. And really, when all's said and done, as a person to go about with, at times when you have had enough of me, he does not seem to present any serious drawback

that I know of. At any rate he is a man, not one of those effeminate creatures one sees so many of nowadays, who look like little renters, and at
any moment may bring their innocent victims to the gallows." I did not
know the meaning of this slang word 'renter'; anyone who had known it
would have been as greatly surprised by his use of it as myself. People in
society always like talking slang, and people against whom certain things
may be hinted like to shew that they are not afraid to mention them. A
proof of innocence in their eyes. But they have lost their sense of proportion, they are no longer capable of realising the point at which a certain
pleasantry will become too technical, too shocking, will be a proof rather
of corruption than of simplicity. "He is not like the rest of them; he has
nice manners; he is really serious."

I could not help smiling at this epithet 'serious,' to which the intonation
that M. de Charlus gave to it seemed to impart the sense of 'virtuous,' of
'steady,' as one says of a little shop-girl that she is 'serious.' At this moment a cab passed, zigzagging along the street; a young cabman, who had
deserted his box, was driving it from inside, where he lay sprawling upon
the cushions, apparently half drunk. M. de Charlus instantly stopped him.
The driver began to argue.

"Which way are you going?"

"Yours." This surprised me, for M. de Charlus had already refused
several cabs with similarly coloured lamps.

"Well, I don't want to get up on the box. D'you mind if I stay down
here?"

"No; but you must put down the hood. Well, think over my proposal,"
said M. de Charlus, preparing to leave me, "I give you a few days to consider my offer; write to me. I repeat, I shall need to see you every day,
and to receive from you guarantees of loyalty, of discretion which, for
that matter, you do appear, I must say, to furnish. But in the course of my
life I have been so often taken in by appearances that I never wish to trust
them again. Damn it, it's the least you can expect that before giving up
a treasure I should know into what hands it is going to pass. Very well,
bear in mind what I'm offering you; you are like Hercules (though, unfortunately for yourself, you do not appear to me to have quite his muscular
development) at the parting of the ways. Try not to have to regret all your
life not having chosen the way that leads to virtue. Hallo!" he turned to
the cabman, "haven't you put the hood down? I'll do it myself. I think,
too, I'd better drive, seeing the state you appear to be in."

He jumped in beside the cabman, took the reins, and the horse trotted off.

As for myself, no sooner had I turned in at our gate than I found the
pendant to the conversation which I had heard exchanged that afternoon
between Bloch and M. de Norpois, but in another form, brief, inverted
and cruel. This was a dispute between our butler, who believed in Dreyfus,
and the Guermantes', who was an anti-Dreyfusard. The truths and counter-
truths which came in conflict above ground, among the intellectuals of the
rival Leagues, the Patrie Française and the Droits de l'Homme, were fast
spreading downwards into the subsoil of popular opinion. M. Reinach was
manipulating, by appeals to sentiment, people whom he had never seen,

while for himself the Dreyfus case simply presented itself to his reason as an incontrovertible theory which he proved in the sequel by the most astonishing victory for rational policy (a victory against France, according to some) that the world has ever seen. In two years he replaced a Billot by a Clemenceau Ministry, revolutionised public opinion from top to bottom, took Picquart from his prison to install him, ungrateful, in the Ministry of War. Perhaps this rationalist manipulator of crowds was himself the puppet of his ancestry. When we find that the systems of philosophy which contain the most truths were dictated to their authors, in the last analysis, by reasons of sentiment, how are we to suppose that in a simple affair of politics like the Dreyfus case reasons of this order may not, unknown to the reasoner, have controlled his reason. Bloch believed himself to have been led by a logical sequence to choose Dreyfusism, yet he knew that his nose, skin and hair had been imposed on him by his race. Doubtless the reason enjoys more freedom; yet it obeys certain laws which it has not prescribed for itself. The case of the Guermantes' butler and our own was peculiar. The waves of the two currents of Dreyfusism and anti-Dreyfusism which now divided France from end to end were, on the whole, silent, but the occasional echoes which they emitted were sincere. When you heard anyone in the middle of a conversation which was being deliberately kept off the Case announce furtively some piece of political news, generally false, but always with a hopefulness of its truth, you could induce from the nature of his predictions where his heart lay. Thus there came into conflict on certain points, on one side a timid apostolate, on the other a righteous indignation. The two butlers whom I heard arguing as I came in furnished an exception to the rule. Ours let it be understood that Dreyfus was guilty, the Guermantes' butler that he was innocent. This was done not to conceal their personal convictions, but from cunning, and in the keenness of their rivalry. Our butler, being uncertain whether the fresh trial would be ordered, wished beforehand, in the event of failure, to deprive the Duke's butler of the joy of seeing a just cause vanquished. The Duke's butler thought that, in the event of a refusal, ours would be more indignant at the detention on the Devil's Isle of an innocent man. The porter looked on. I had the impression that it was not he who was the cause of dissension in the Guermantes household.

I went upstairs, and found my grandmother not so well. For some time past, without knowing exactly what was wrong, she had been complaining of her health. It is in moments of illness that we are compelled to recognise that we live not alone but chained to a creature of a different kingdom, whole worlds apart, who has no knowledge of us and by whom it is impossible to make ourselves understood: our body. Say that we met a brigand by the way; we might yet convince him by an appeal to his personal interest, if not to our own plight. But to ask pity of our body is like discoursing before an octopus, for which our words can have no more meaning than the sound of the tides, and with which we should be appalled to find ourselves condemned to live. My grandmother's attacks passed, often enough, unnoticed by the attention which she kept always diverted to ourselves. When the pain was severe, in the hope of curing it, she would try in vain to understand what the trouble was. If the morbid phenomena of which her body was the theatre remained obscure and beyond the reach of her mind, they were clear and intelligible to certain creatures belonging to the same natural kingdom as themselves, creatures to which the human mind has learned gradually to have recourse in order to understand what the body is saying to it, as when a foreigner accosts us we try to find some one belonging to his country who will act as interpreter. These can talk to our body, and tell us if its anger is serious or will soon be appeased. Cottard, whom we had called in to see my grandmother, and who had infuriated us by asking with a dry smile, the moment we told him that she was ill: "Ill? You're sure it's not what they call a diplomatic illness?" He tried to soothe his patient's restlessness by a milk diet. But incessant bowls of milk soup gave her no relief, because my grandmother sprinkled them liberally with salt (the toxic effects of which were as yet, Widal not having made his dis-coveries, unknown). For, medicine being a compendium of the successive and contradictory mistakes of medical practioners, when we summon the wisest of them to our aid, the chances are that we may be relying on a scientific truth the error of which will be recognised in a few years' time. So that to believe in medicine would be the height of folly, if not to believe in it were not greater folly still, for from this mass of errors there have emerged in the course of time many truths. Cottard had told us to take her temperature. A thermometer was fetched. Throughout almost all its length it was clear of mercury. Scarcely could one make out, crouching at the foot of the tube, in its little cell, the silver salamander. It seemed dead. The glass reed was slipped into my grandmother's mouth. We had no need to leave it there for long; the little sorceress had not been slow in casting her horoscope. We found her motionless, perched half-way up her tower, and declining to move, shewing us with precision the figure that we had asked of her, a figure with which all the most careful examination that my grandmother's mind could have devoted to herself would have been incapable of furnishing her: 101 degrees. For the first time we felt some anxiety. We shook the thermometer well, to erase the ominous line, as though we were able thus to reduce the patient's fever simultaneously with the figure shewn on the scale. Alas, it was only too clear that the little sibyl, unreasoning as she was, had not pronounced judgment arbitrarily, for the next day, scarcely had the thermometer been inserted between my grand-mother's lips when almost at once, as though with a single bound, exulting in her certainty and in her intuition of a fact that to us was imperceptible, the little prophetess had come to a halt at the same point, in an implacable immobility, and pointed once again to that figure 101 with the tip of her gleaming wand. Nothing more did she tell us; in vain might we long, seek, pray, she was deaf to our entreaties; it seemed as though this were her final utterance, a warning and a menace. Then, in an attempt to constrain her to modify her response, we had recourse to another creature of the same kingdom, but more potent, which is not content with questioning the body but can command it, a febrifuge of the same order as the modern aspirin, which had not then come into use. We had not shaken the thermometer down below 99.5, and hoped that it would not have to rise from there. We made my grandmother swallow this drug and then replaced the thermometer in her mouth. Like an implacable warder to whom one presents a permit signed by a higher authority whose protecting influence one has sought, and who, finding it to be in order, replies: "Very well; I have nothing to say; if it's like that you may pass," this time the watcher in the tower did not move. But sullenly she seemed to be saying: "What use will that be to you? Since you are friends with quinine, she may give me the order not to go up, once, ten times, twenty times. And then she will grow tired of telling me, I know her; get along with you. This won't last for ever. And then you'll be a lot better off." Thereupon my grandmother felt the presence within her of a creature which knew the human body better than herself, the presence of a contemporary of the races that have vanished from the earth, the presence of earth's first inhabitant—long anterior to the creation of thinking man—she felt that aeonial ally who was sounding her, a little roughly even, in the head, the heart, the elbow; he found out the weak places, organised everything for the prehistoric combat which began at once to be fought. In a moment a trampled Python, the fever, was vanquished by the potent chemical substance to which my grandmother, across the series of kingdoms, reaching out beyond all animal and vegetable life, would fain have been able to give thanks. And she remained moved by this glimpse which she had caught, through the mists of so many centuries, of a climate anterior to the creation even of plants. Meanwhile the thermometer, like a Weird Sister momentarily vanquished by some more ancient god, held motionless her silver spindle. Alas! other inferior creatures which man has trained to the chase of the mysterious quarry which he cannot pursue within the pathless forest of himself, reported cruelly to us every day a certain quantity of albumen, not large, but constant enough for it also to appear to bear relation to some persistent malady which we could not detect. Bergotte had shocked that scrupulous instinct in me which made me subordinate my intellect when he spoke to me of Dr. du Boulbon as of a physician who would not bore me, who would discover methods of treatment which, however strange they might appear, would adapt themselves to the singularity of my mind. But ideas transform themselves in us, they overcome the resistance with which we at first meet them, and feed upon rich intellectual reserves which we did not know to have been prepared for them. So, as happens whenever anything we have heard said about some one whom we do not know has had the faculty of awakening in us the idea of great talent, of a sort of genius, in my inmost mind I gave Dr. du Boulbon the benefit of that unlimited confidence which he inspires in us who with an eye more penetrating than other men's perceives the truth. I knew indeed that he was more of a specialist in nervous diseases, the man to whom Charcot before his death had predicted that he would reign supreme in neurology and psychiatry. "Ah! I don't know about that. It's quite possible," put in Françoise, who was in the room, and heard Charcot's name, as she heard du Boulbon's, for the first time. But this in no way prevented her from saying "It's possible." Her 'possibles,' her 'perhapses,' her 'I don't knows' were peculiarly irritating at such a moment. One wanted to say to her: "Naturally you don't know, since you haven't the faintest idea of what we are talking about, how can you even say whether it's possible or not; you know nothing about it. Anyhow, you can't say now that you don't know what Charcot said to du Boulbon. You do know because we have just told you, and your 'perhapses' and 'possibles' don't come in, because it's a fact."

In spite of this more special competence in cerebral and nervous matters, as I knew that du Boulbon was a great physician, a superior man, of a profound and inventive intellect, I begged my mother to send for him, and the hope that, by a clear perception of the malady, he might perhaps cure it, carried the day finally over the fear that we had of (if we called in a specialist) alarming my grandmother. What decided my mother was the fact that, encouraged unconsciously by Cottard, my grandmother no longer went out of doors, and scarcely rose from her bed. In vain might she answer us in the words of Mme. de Sévigné's letter on Mme. de la Fayette: "Everyone said she was mad not to wish to go out. I said to these persons, so headstrong in their judgment: 'Mme. de la Fayette is not mad!' and I stuck to that. It has taken her death to prove that she was quite right not to go out." Du Boulbon when he came decided against—if not Mme. de Sévigné, whom we did not quote to him—my grandmother, at any rate. Instead of sounding her chest, fixing on her steadily his wonderful eyes, in which there was perhaps the illusion that he was making a profound scrutiny of his patient, or the desire to give her that illusion, which seemed spontaneous but must be mechanically produced, or else not to let her see that he was thinking of something quite different, or simply to obtain the mastery over her, he began talking about Bergotte.

"I should think so, indeed, he's magnificent, you are quite right to admire him. But which of his books do you prefer? Indeed! Well, perhaps that is the best after all. In any case it is the best composed of his novels. Claire is quite charming in it; of his male characters which appeals to you most?"

I supposed at first that he was making her talk like this about literature because he himself found medicine boring, perhaps also to display his breadth of mind and even, with a more therapeutic aim, to restore confidence to his patient, to shew her that he was not alarmed, to take her mind from the state of her health. But afterwards I realised that, being distinguished particularly as an alienist and by his work on the brain, he had been seeking to ascertain by these questions whether my grandmother's memory was in good order. As though reluctantly he began to inquire about her past life, fixing a stern and sombre eye on her. Then suddenly, as though catching sight of the truth and determined to reach it at all costs, with a preliminary rubbing of his hands, which he seemed to have some difficulty in wiping dry of the final hesitations which he himself might feel and of all the objections which we might have raised, looking down at my grandmother with a lucid eye, boldly and as though he were at last upon solid ground, punctuating his words in a quiet, impressive tone, every inflexion of which bore the mark of intellect, he began. (His voice, for that matter, throughout this visit remained what it naturally was, caressing. And under his bushy brows his ironical eyes were full of kindness.)

"You will be quite well, Madame, on the day—when it comes, and it rests entirely with you whether it comes to-day—on which you realise that there is nothing wrong with you, and resume your ordinary life. You tell me that you have not been taking your food, not going out?"

"But, Sir, I have a temperature."

He laid a finger on her wrist.

"Not just now, at any rate. Besides, what an excuse! Don't you know that we keep out in the open air and overfeed tuberculous patients with temperatures of 102?"

"But I have a little albumen as well."

"You ought not to know anything about that. You have what I have had occasion to call 'mental albumen.' We have all of us had, when we have not been very well, little albuminous phases which our doctor has done his best to make permanent by calling our attention to them. For one disorder that doctors cure with drugs (as I am told that they do occasionally succeed in doing) they produce a dozen others in healthy subjects by inoculating them with that pathogenic agent a thousand times more virulent than all the microbes in the world, the idea that one is ill. A belief of that sort, which has a disturbing effect on any temperament, acts with special force on neurotic people. Tell them that a shut window is open behind their back, they will begin to sneeze; make them believe that you have put magnesia in their soup, they will be seized with colic; that their coffee is stronger than usual, they will not sleep a wink all night. Do you imagine, Madame, that I needed to do any more than look into your eyes, listen to the way in which you express yourself, look, if I may say so, at this lady, your daughter, and at your grandson, who takes so much after you, to learn what was the matter with you?" "Your grandmother might perhaps go and sit, if the Doctor allows it, in some quiet path in the Champs-Elysées, near that laurel shrubbery where you used to play when you were little," said my mother to me, thus indirectly consulting Dr. du Boulbon, her voice for that reason assuming a tone of timid deference which it would not have had if she had been addressing me alone. The Doctor turned to my grandmother and, being apparently as well-read in literature as in science, adjured her as follows: "Go to the Champs-Elysées, Madame, to the laurel shrubbery which your grandson loves. The laurel you will find health-giving. It purifies. After he had exterminated the serpent Python, it was with a bough of laurel in his hand that Apollo made his entry into Delphi. He sought thus to guard himself from the deadly germs of the venomous monster. So you see that the laurel is the most ancient, the most venerable and, I will add—what is of therapeutic as well as of prophylactic value—the most beautiful of antiseptics."

Inasmuch as a great part of what doctors know is taught them by the sick, they are easily led to believe that this knowledge which patients exhibit is common to them all, and they pride themselves on taking the patient of the moment by surprise with some remark picked up at a previous bedside. Thus it was with the superior smile of a Parisian who, in conversation with a peasant, might hope to surprise him by using suddenly a word of the local dialect that Dr. du Boulbon said to my grandmother: "Probably a windy night will make you sleep when the strongest soporifics would have no effect." "On the contrary, Sir, when the wind blows I can never sleep at all." But doctors are touchy people. "Ach!" muttered du Boulbon, knitting his brows, as if some one had trodden on his toe, or as if my grandmother's sleeplessness on stormy nights were a personal insult to himself. He had not, however, an undue opinion of himself, and since, in his character as a 'superior' person, he felt himself bound not to put any faith in medicine, he quickly recovered his philosophic serenity.

My mother, in her passionate longing for reassurance from Bergotte's friend, added in support of his verdict that a first cousin of my grandmother, who suffered from a nervous complaint, had lain for seven years cloistered in her bedroom at Combray, without leaving her bed more than once or twice a week.

"You see, Madame, I didn't know that, and yet I could have told you."

"But, Sir, I am not in the least like her; on the contrary, my doctor complains that he cannot get me to stay in bed," said my grandmother, whether because she was a little annoyed by the doctor's theories, or was anxious to submit to him any objections that might be raised to them, in the hope that he would refute these and that, after he had gone, she would no longer find any doubt lurking in her own mind as to the accuracy of his encouraging diagnosis.

"Why, naturally, Madame, you cannot have all the forms of—if you'll excuse my saying so—mania at once; you have others, but not that particular one. Yesterday I visited a home for neurasthenics. In the garden, I saw a man standing on a seat, motionless as a fakir, his neck bent in a position which must have been highly uncomfortable. On my asking him what he was doing there, he replied, without turning his head, or moving a muscle: 'You see, Doctor, I am extremely rheumatic and catch cold very easily; I have just been taking a lot of exercise, and while I was getting hot, like a fool, my neck was touching my flannels. If I move it away from my flannels now before letting myself cool down, I am certain to get a stiff neck, and possibly bronchitis.' Which he would, in fact, have done. 'You're a fine specimen of neurasthenia, that's what you are,' I told him. And do you know what argument he advanced to prove that I was mistaken? It was this; that while all the other patients in the place had a mania for testing their weight, so much so that the weighing machine had to be padlocked so that they should not spend the whole day on it, he had to be lifted on to it bodily, so little did he care to be weighed. He prided himself on not sharing the mania of the others without thinking that he had also one of his own, and that it was this which saved him from the other. You must not be offended by the comparison, Madame, for the man who dared not turn his neck for fear of catching a chill is the greatest poet of our day. That poor maniac is the most lofty intellect that I know. Submit to being called a neurotic. You belong to that splendid and pitiable family which is the salt of the earth. All the greatest things we know have come to us from neurotics. It is they and they only who have founded religions and created great works of art. Never will the world be conscious of how much it owes to them, nor above all of what they have suffered in order to bestow their gifts on it. We enjoy fine music, beautiful pictures, a thousand exquisite things, but we do not know what they cost those who wrought them in sleeplessness, tears, spasmodic laughter, rashes, asthma, epilepsy, a terror of death which is worse than any of these, and which you perhaps have felt, Madame," he added with a smile at my grandmother, "for confess now, when I came into the room, you were not feeling very confident. You thought that you were ill; dangerously ill, perhaps. Heaven only knows what the disease was of which you thought you had detected the symptoms. And you were not mistaken; they were there. Neurosis has an absolute genius for malingering. There is no illness which it cannot counterfeit perfectly. It will produce life-like imitations of the dilatations of dyspepsia, the sicknesses of pregnancy, the broken rhythm of the cardiac, the feverishness of the consumptive. If it is capable of deceiving the doctor, how should it fail to deceive the patient? No, no; you mustn't think I'm making fun of your sufferings. I should not undertake to heal them unless I understood them thoroughly. And, well, they say there's no good confession unless it's mutual. I have told you that without nervous trouble there can be no great artist. What is more," he added, raising a solemn forefinger, "there can be no great scientist either. I will go further, and say that, unless he himself is subject to nervous trouble, he is not, I won't say a good doctor, but I do say the right doctor to treat nervous troubles. In nervous pathology a doctor who doesn't say too many foolish things is a patient half-cured, just as a critic is a poet who has stopped writing verse and a policeman a burglar who has retired from practice. I, Madame, I do not, like you, fancy myself to be suffering from albuminuria, I have not your nervous fear of food, nor of fresh air, but I can never go to sleep without getting out of bed at least twenty times to see if my door is shut. And in that home where I found the poet yesterday who would not move his neck, I had gone to secure a room, for—this is between ourselves—I spend my holidays there looking after myself when I have increased my own trouble by wearing myself out in the attempt to cure other people."

"But do you want me to take a cure like that, Sir?" came in a frightened voice from my grandmother.

"It is not necessary, Madame. The symptoms which you describe will vanish at my bidding. Besides, you have with you a very efficient person whom I appoint as your doctor from now onwards. That is your trouble itself, the super-activity of your nerves. Even if I knew how to cure you of that, I should take good care not to. All I need do is to control it. I see on your table there one of Bergotte's books. Cured of your neurosis you would no longer care for it. Well, I might feel it my duty to substitute for the joys that it procures for you a nervous stability which would be quite incapable of giving you those joys. But those joys themselves are a strong remedy, the strongest of all perhaps. No; I have nothing to say against your nervous energy. All I ask is that it should listen to me; I leave you in its charge. It must reverse its engines. The force which it is now using to prevent you from getting up, from taking sufficient food, let it employ in making you eat, in making you read, in making you go out, and in distracting you in every possible way. You needn't tell me that you are fatigued. Fatigue is the organic realisation of a preconceived idea. Begin by not thinking it. And if ever you have a slight indisposition, which is a thing that may happen to anyone, it will be just as if you hadn't it, for your nervous energy will have endowed you with what M. de Talleyrand, in an expression full of meaning, called 'imaginary health.' See, it has begun to cure you already, you have been sitting up in bed listening to me without once leaning back on your pillows; your eye is bright, your complexion is good, I have been talking to you for half an hour by the clock and you have never noticed the time. Well, Madame, I shall now bid you good-day."

When, after seeing Dr. du Boulbon to the door, I returned to the room in which my mother was by herself, the oppression that had been weighing on me for the last few weeks lifted, I felt that my mother was going to break out with a cry of joy and would see my joy, I felt that inability to endure the suspense of the coming moment at which a person is going to be overcome with emotion in our presence, which in another category is a little like the thrill of fear that goes through one when one knows that somebody is going to come in and startle one by a door that is still closed; I tried to speak to Mamma but my voice broke, and, bursting into tears, I stayed for a long time, my head on her shoulder, crying, tasting, accepting, relishing my grief, now that I knew that it had departed from my life, as we like to exalt ourselves by forming virtuous plans which circumstances do not permit us to put into execution. Françoise annoyed me by her refusal to share in our joy. She was quite overcome because there had just been a terrible scene between the lovesick footman and the tale-bearing porter. It had required the Duchess herself, in her unfailing benevolence, to intervene, restore an apparent calm to the household and forgive the footman. For she was a good mistress, and that would have been the ideal 'place' if only she didn't listen to 'stories.'

During the last few days people had begun to hear of my grandmother's illness and to inquire for news of her. Saint-Loup had written to me: "I do not wish to take advantage of a time when your dear grandmother is unwell to convey to you what is far more than mere reproaches, on a matter with which she has no concern. But I should not be speaking the truth were I to say to you, even out of politeness, that I shall ever forget the perfidy of your conduct, or that there can ever be any forgiveness for so scoundrelly a betrayal." But some other friends, supposing that my grandmother was not seriously ill (they may not even have known that she was ill at all), had asked me to meet them next day in the Champs-Elysées, to go with them from there to pay a call together, ending up with a dinner in the country, the thought of which appealed to me. I had no longer any reason to forego these two pleasures. When my grandmother had been told that it was now imperative, if she was to obey Dr. du Boulbon's orders, that she should go out as much as possible, she had herself at once suggested the Champs-Elysées. It would be easy for me to escort her there; and, while she sat reading, to arrange with my friends where I should meet them later; and I should still be in time, if I made haste, to take the train with them to Ville d'Avray. When the time came, my grandmother did not want to go out; she felt tired. But my mother, acting on du Boulbon's instructions, had the strength of mind to be firm and to insist on obedience. She was almost in tears at the thought that my grandmother was going to relapse again into her nervous weakness, which she might never be able to shake off. Never again would there be such a fine, warm day for an outing. The sun as it moved through the sky interspersed here and there in the broken solidity of the balcony its unsubstantial muslins, and gave to the freestone ledge a warm epidermis, an indefinite halo of gold. As Françoise had not had time to send a 'tube' to her daughter, she left us immediately after luncheon. She very kindly consented, however, to call first at Jupien's, to get a stitch put in the cloak which my grandmother was going to wear. Returning at that moment from my morning walk I accompanied her into the shop. "Is it your young master who brings you here," Jupien asked Françoise, "is it you who are bringing him to see me, or is it some good wind and fortune that bring you both?" For all his want of education, Jupien respected the laws of grammar as instinctively as M. de Guermantes, in spite of every effort, broke them. With Françoise gone and the cloak mended, it was time for my grandmother to get ready. Having obstinately refused to let Mamma stay in the room with her, she took, left to herself, an endless time over her dressing, and now that I knew her to be quite well, with that strange indifference which we feel towards our relatives so long as they are alive, which makes us put everyone else before them, I felt it to be very selfish of her to take so long, to risk making me late when she knew that I had an appointment with my friends and was dining at Ville d'Avray. In my impatience I finally went downstairs without waiting for her, after I had twice been told that she was just ready. At last she joined me, without apologising to me, as she generally did, for having kept me waiting, flushed and bothered like a person who has come to a place in a hurry and has forgotten half her belongings, just as I was reaching the half-opened glass door which, without warming them with it in the least, let in the liquid, throbbing, tepid air from the street (as though the sluices of a reservoir had been opened) between the frigid walls of the passage.

"Oh, dear, if you're going to meet your friends I ought to have put on another cloak. I look rather poverty-stricken in this one."

I was startled to see her so flushed, and supposed that having begun by making herself late she had had to hurry over her dressing. When we left the cab at the end of the Avenue Gabriel, in the Champs-Elysées, I saw my grandmother, without a word to me, turn aside and make her way to the little old pavilion with its green trellis, at the door of which I had once waited for Françoise. The same park-keeper who had been standing there then was still talking to Françoise's 'Marquise' when, following my grandmother who, doubtless because she was feeling sick, had her hand in front of her mouth, I climbed the steps of that little rustic theatre, erected there among the gardens. At the entrance, as in those circus booths where the clown, dressed for the ring and smothered in flour, stands at the door and takes the money himself for the seats, the 'Marquise,' at the receipt of custom, was still there in her place with her huge, uneven face smeared with a coarse plaster and her little bonnet of red flowers and black lace surmounting her auburn wig. But I do not suppose that she recognised me. The park-keeper, abandoning his watch over the greenery, with the colour of which his uniform had been designed to harmonise, was talking to her, on a chair by her side.

"So you're still here?" he was saying. "You don't think of retiring?"

"And what have I to retire for, Sir? Will you kindly tell me where I shall be better off than here, where I should live more at my ease, and with every comfort? And then there's all the coming and going, plenty of distraction; my little Paris, I call it; my customers keep me in touch with everything that's going on. Just to give you an example, there's one of them who went out not more than five minutes ago; he's a magistrate, in the very highest position there is. Very well, Sir," she cried with ardour, as though prepared to maintain the truth of this assertion by violence, should the agent of civic authority shew any sign of challenging its accuracy, "for the last eight years, do you follow me, every day God has made, regularly on the stroke of three he's been here, always polite, never saying one word louder than another, never making any mess; and he stays half an hour and more to read his papers and do his little jobs. There was one day he didn't come. I never noticed it at the time, but that evening, all of a sudden I said to myself: 'Why, that gentleman never came to-day; perhaps he's dead!' And that gave me a regular turn, you know, because, of course, I get quite fond of people when they behave nicely. And so I was very glad when I saw him come in again next day, and I said to him, I did: 'I hope there was nothing wrong yesterday, Sir?' Then he told me that it was his wife that had died, and he'd been so put out, poor gentleman, what with one thing and another, he hadn't been able to come. He had that really sad look, you know, people have when they've been married five-and-twenty years, and then the parting, but he seemed pleased, all the same, to be back here. You could see that all his little habits had been quite upset. I did what I could to make him feel at home. I said to him: 'Y' mustn't let go of things, Sir. Just come here the same as before, it will be a little distraction for you in your sorrow.' "

The 'Marquise' resumed a gentler tone, for she had observed that the guardian of groves and lawns was listening to her complacently and with no thought of contradiction, keeping harmlessly in its scabbard a sword which looked more like a horticultural implement or some symbol of a garden-god.

"And besides," she went on, "I choose my customers, I don't let everyone into my little parlours, as I call them. And doesn't the place just look like a parlour with all my flowers? Such friendly customers I have; there's always some one or other brings me a spray of nice lilac, or jessamine or roses; my favourite flowers, roses are."

The thought that we were perhaps despised by this lady because we never brought any sprays of lilac or fine roses to her bower made me redden, and in the hope of making a bodily escape—or of being condemned only by default—from an adverse judgment, I moved towards the exit. But it is not always in this world the people who bring us fine roses to whom we are most friendly, for the 'Marquise,' thinking that I was bored, turned to me.

"You wouldn't like me to open a little place for you?"

And, on my declining:

"No? You're sure you won't?" she persisted, smiling. "Well, just as you please. You're welcome to it, but I know quite well, not having to pay for a thing won't make you want to do it if you don't want to."

At this moment a shabbily dressed woman hurried into the place who seemed to be feeling precisely the want in question. But she did not belong to the 'Marquise's' world, for the latter, with the ferocity of a snob, flung at her:

"I've nothing disengaged, Ma'am."

"Will they be long?" asked the poor lady, reddening beneath the yellow flowers in her hat.

"Well, Ma'am, if you'll take my advice, you'll try somewhere else; you see, there are still these two gentlemen waiting, and I've only one closet; the others are out of order."

"Not much money there," she explained when the other had gone. "It's not the sort we want here, either; they're not clean, don't treat the place with respect, it would be your humble here that would have to spend the next hour cleaning up after her ladyship. I'm not sorry to lose her penny."

Finally my grandmother emerged, and feeling that she probably would not seek to atone by a lavish gratuity for the indiscretion that she had shewn by remaining so long inside, I beat a retreat, so as not to have to share in the scorn which the 'Marquise' would no doubt heap on her, and began strolling along a path, but slowly, so that my grandmother should not have to hurry to overtake me; as presently she did. I expected her to begin: "I am afraid I've kept you waiting; I hope you'll still be in time for your friends," but she did not utter a single word, so much so that, feeling a little hurt, I was disinclined to speak first; until looking up at her I noticed that as she walked beside me she kept her face turned the other way. I was afraid that her heart might be troubling her again. I studied her more carefully and was struck by the disjointedness of her gait. Her hat was crooked, her cloak stained; she had the confused and worried look, the flushed, slightly dazed face of a person who has just been knocked down by a carriage or pulled out of a ditch.

"I was afraid you were feeling sick, Grandmamma; are you feeling better now?" I asked her.

Probably she thought that it would be impossible for her, without alarming me, not to make some answer.

"I heard the whole of her conversation with the keeper," she told me. "Could anything have been more typical of the Guermantes, or the Verdurins and their little circle? Heavens, what fine language she put it all in!" And she quoted, with deliberate application, this sentence from her own special Marquise, Mme. de Sévigné: "As I listened to them I thought that they were preparing for me the pleasures of a farewell."

Such was the speech that she made me, a speech into which she had put all her critical delicacy, her love of quotations, her memory of the classics, more thoroughly even than she would naturally have done, and as though to prove that she retained possession of all these faculties. But I guessed rather than heard what she said, so inaudible was the voice in which she muttered her sentences, clenching her teeth more than could be accounted for by the fear of being sick again.

"Come!" I said lightly, so as not to seem to be taking her illness too seriously, "since your heart is bothering you, shall we go home now? I don't want to trundle a grandmother with indigestion about the Champs-Elysées."

"I didn't like to suggest it, because of your friends," she replied. "Poor boy! But if you don't mind, I think it would be wiser."

I was afraid of her noticing the strange way in which she uttered these words.

"Come!" I said to her sharply, "you mustn't tire yourself talking; if your heart is bad, it's silly; wait till we get home."

She smiled at me sorrowfully and gripped my hand. She had realised that there was no need to hide from me what I had at once guessed, that she had had a slight stroke.

PART II

CHAPTER ONE

MY GRANDMOTHER'S ILLNESS
(Continued)

WE MADE our way back along the Avenue Gabriel, through the strolling crowd. I left my grandmother to rest on a seat and went in search of a cab. She, in whose heart I always placed myself when I had to form an opinion of the most unimportant person, she was now closed to me, had become part of the world outside, and, more than from any casual passer-by, I was obliged to keep from her what I thought of her condition, to say no word of my uneasiness. I could not have spoken of it to her in greater confidence than to a stranger. She had suddenly handed back to me the thoughts, the griefs which, from the days of my infancy, I had entrusted for all time to her keeping. She was not yet dead. I was already alone. And even those allusions which she had made to the Guermantes, to Mme. de Sévigné, to our conversations about the little clan, assumed an air of being without point or occasion, fantastic, because they sprang from the nullity of this very being who to-morrow possibly would have ceased to exist, for whom they would no longer have any meaning, from that nullity, incapable of conceiving them, which my grandmother would shortly be.

"Well, Sir, I don't like to say no, but you have not made an appointment, you have no time fixed. Besides, this is not my day for seeing patients. You surely have a doctor of your own. I cannot interfere with his practice, unless he were to call me in for a consultation. It's a question of professional etiquette . . ."

Just as I was signalling to a cabman, I had caught sight of the famous Professor E——, almost a friend of my father and grandfather, acquainted at any rate with them both, who lived in the Avenue Gabriel, and, with a sudden inspiration, had stopped him just as he was entering his house, thinking that he would perhaps be the very person to advise my grandmother. But he was evidently in a hurry and, after calling for his letters, seemed anxious to get rid of me, so that my only chance of speaking to him lay in going up with him in the lift, of which he begged me to allow him to work the switches himself, this being a mania with him.

"But, Sir, I am not asking you to see my grandmother here; you will realise from what I am trying to tell you that she is not in a fit state to come; what I am asking is that you should call at our house in half an hour's time, when I have taken her home."

"Call at your house! Really, Sir, you must not expect me to do that. I am dining with the Minister of Commerce. I have a call to pay first. I must change at once, and to make matters worse I have torn my coat and my other one has no buttonholes for my decorations. I beg you, please, to oblige me by not touching the switches. You don't know how the lift works; one can't be too careful. Getting that buttonhole made means more delay. Well, as I am a friend of your people, if your grandmother comes here at once I will see her. But I warn you that I shall be able to give her exactly a quarter of an hour, nor a moment more."

I had started off at once, without even getting out of the lift which Professor E—— had himself set in motion to take me down again, casting a suspicious glance at me as he did so.

We may, indeed, say that the hour of death is uncertain, but when we say so we represent that hour to ourselves as situated in a vague and remote expanse of time, it never occurs to us that it can have any connexion with the day that has already dawned, or may signify that death—or its first assault and partial possession of us, after which it will never leave hold of us again—may occur this very afternoon, so far from uncertain, this afternoon every hour of which has already been allotted to some occupation. You make a point of taking your drive every day so that in a month's time you will have had the full benefit of the fresh air; you have hesitated over which cloak you will take, which cabman to call, you are in the cab, the whole day lies before you, short because you have to be at home early, as a friend is coming to see you; you hope that it will be as fine again to-morrow; and you have no suspicion that death, which has been making its way towards you along another plane, shrouded in an impenetrable darkness, has chosen precisely this day of all days to make its appearance, in a few minutes' time, more or less, at the moment when the carriage has reached the Champs-Elysées. Perhaps those who are haunted as a rule by the fear of the utter strangeness of death will find something reassuring in this kind of death—in this kind of first contact with death—because death thus assumes a known, familiar guise of everyday life. A good luncheon has preceded it, and the same outing that people take who are in perfect health. A drive home in an open carriage comes on top of its first onslaught; ill as my grandmother was, there were, after all, several people who could testify that at six o'clock, as we came home from the Champs-Elysées, they had bowed to her as she drove past in an open carriage, in perfect weather. Legrandin, making his way towards the Place de la Concorde, raised his hat to us, stopping to look after us with an air of surprise. I, who was not yet detached from life, asked my grandmother if she had acknowledged his greeting, reminding her of his readiness to take offence. My grandmother, thinking me no doubt very frivolous, raised her hand in the air as though to say: "What does it matter? It is not of the least importance."

Yes, one might have said that, a few minutes earlier, when I was looking for a cab, my grandmother was resting on a seat in the Avenue Gabriel, and that a little later she had driven past in an open carriage. But would that have been really true? The seat, for instance, to maintain its position at the side of an avenue—for all that it may be subjected also to certain conditions of equilibrium—has no need of energy. But in order that a living person may be stable, even when supported by a seat or in a carriage, there is required a tension of forces which we do not ordinarily perceive, any more than we perceive (because its action is universal) atmospheric pressure. Possibly if we were to be hollowed out and then left to support the pressure of the air we might feel, in the moment that preceded our extinction, that terrible weight which there was nothing left in us to neutralise. Similarly when the abyss of sickness and death opens within us, and we have no longer any resistance to offer to the tumult with which the world and our own body rush upon us, then to endure even the tension of our own muscles, the shudder that freezes us to the marrow, then even to keep ourselves motionless in what we ordinarily regard as nothing but the simple negative position of a lifeless thing requires, if we wish our head to remain erect and our eyes calm, an expense of vital energy and becomes the object of an exhausting struggle.

And if Legrandin had looked back at us with that astonished air, it was because to him, as to the other people who passed us then, in the cab in which my grandmother was apparently seated she had seemed to be foundering, sliding into the abyss, clinging desperately to the cushions which could barely arrest the downward plunge of her body, her hair in disorder, her eye wild, unable any longer to face the assault of the images which its pupil was not strong enough now to bear. She had appeared to them, although I was still by her side, submerged in that unknown world somewhere in which she had already received the blows, traces of which she still bore when I looked up at her a few minutes earlier in the Champs-Elysées, her hat, her face, her cloak left in disorder by the hand of the invisible angel with whom she had wrestled. I have thought, since, that this moment of her stroke cannot have altogether surprised my grandmother, that indeed she had perhaps foreseen it a long time back, had lived in expectation of it. She had not known, naturally, when this fatal moment would come, had never been certain, any more than those lovers whom a similar doubt leads alternately to found unreasonable hopes and unjustified suspicions on the fidelity of their mistresses. But it is rarely that these grave maladies, like that which now at last had struck her full in the face, do not take up their abode in the sick man for a long time before killing him, during which time they make haste, like a 'sociable' neighbour or tenant, to introduce themselves to him. A terrible acquaintance, not so much from the sufferings that it causes as from the strange novelty of the definite restriction which it imposes upon life. A woman sees herself dying, in these cases not at the actual moment of death but months, sometimes years before, when death has hideously come to dwell in her. The sufferer makes the acquaintance of the stranger whom she hears coming and going in her brain. She does not know him by sight, it is true, but from the sounds which she hears him regularly make she can form an idea of his habits. Is he a criminal? One morning, she can no longer hear him. He has gone. Ah! If it were only for ever! In the evening he has returned. What are his plans? Her specialist, put to the question, like an adored mistress, replies with avowals that one day are believed, another day fail to convince her. Or rather it is not the mistress's part but that of the servants one interrogates that the doctor plays. They are only third parties. The person whom we press for an answer, whom we suspect of being about to play us false, is life itself, and although we feel her to be no longer the same we believe in her still or at least remain undecided until the day on which she finally abandons us.

I helped my grandmother into Professor E——'s lift and a moment later he came to us and took us into his consulting room. But there, busy as he was, his bombastic manner changed, such is the force of habit; for his habit was to be friendly, that is to say lively with his patients. Since he knew that my grandmother was a great reader, and was himself one also, he devoted the first few minutes to quoting various favourite passages of poetry appropriate to the glorious summer weather. He had placed her in an armchair and himself with his back to the light so as to have a good view of her. His examination was minute and thorough, even obliging me at one moment to leave the room. He continued it after my return, then, having finished, went on, although the quarter of an hour was almost at an end, repeating various quotations to my grandmother. He even made a few jokes, which were witty enough, though I should have preferred to hear them on some other occasion, but which completely reassured me by the tone of amusement in which he uttered them. I then remembered that M. Fallières, the President of the Senate, had, many years earlier, had a false seizure, and that to the consternation of his political rivals he had returned a few days later to his duties and had begun, it was said, his preparations for a more or less remote succession to the Presidency of the Republic. My confidence in my grandmother's prompt recovery was all the more complete in that, just as I was recalling the example of M. Fallières, I was distracted from following up the similarity by a shout of laughter, which served as conclusion to one of the Professor's jokes. After which he took out his watch, wrinkled his brows petulantly on seeing that he was five minutes late, and while he bade us good-bye rang for his other coat to be brought to him at once. I waited until my grandmother had left the room, closed the door and asked him to tell me the truth.

"There is not the slightest hope," he informed me. "It is a stroke brought on by uraemia. In itself, uraemia is not necessarily fatal, but this case seems to me desperate. I need not tell you that I hope I am mistaken. Anyhow, you have Cottard, you're in excellent hands. Excuse me," he broke off as a maid came into the room with his coat over her arm. "I told you, I'm dining with the Minister of Commerce, and I have a call to pay first. Ah! Life is not all a bed of roses, as one is apt to think at your age."

And he graciously offered me his hand. I had shut the door behind me, and a footman was shewing us into the hall when we heard a loud shout of rage. The maid had forgotten to cut and hem the buttonhole for the decorations. This would take another ten minutes. The Professor continued to storm while I stood on the landing gazing at a grandmother for whom there was not the slightest hope. Each of us is indeed alone. We started for home.

The sun was sinking, it burnished an interminable wall along which our cab had to pass before reaching the street in which we lived, a wall against which the shadow cast by the setting sun of horse and carriage stood out

in black on a ruddy background, like a funeral car on some Pompeian terra-
cotta. At length we arrived at the house. I made the invalid sit at the foot
of the staircase in the hall, and went up to warn my mother. I told her
that my grandmother had come home feeling slightly unwell, after an
attack of giddiness. As soon as I began to speak, my mother's face was
convulsed by the paroxysm of a despair which was yet already so resigned
that I realised that for many years she had been holding herself quietly in
readiness for an uncalendared but final day. She asked me no question; it
seemed that, just as malevolence likes to exaggerate the sufferings of other
people, so in her devotion she would not admit that her mother was seriously
ill, especially with a disease which might affect the brain. Mamma shuddered, her eyes wept without tears, she ran to give orders for the doctor
to be fetched at once; but when Françoise asked who was ill she could not
reply, her voice stuck in her throat. She came running downstairs with me,
struggling to banish from her face the sob that contracted it. My grandmother was waiting below on the sofa in the hall, but, as soon as she heard
us coming, drew herself together, stood up, and waved her hand cheerfully
at Mamma. I had partially wrapped her head in a white lace shawl, telling
her that it was so that she should not catch cold on the stairs. I had hoped
that my mother would not notice the change in her face, the distortion of her
mouth; my precaution proved unnecessary; my mother went up to my
grandmother, kissed her hand as though it were that of her God, raised her
up, carried her to the lift with infinite precautions in which there was, with
the fear of hurting her by any clumsy movement, the humility of one who
felt herself unworthy to touch the most precious thing, to her, in the world,
but never once did she raise her eyes, nor look at the sufferer's face. Perhaps this was in order that my grandmother might not be saddened by
the thought that the sight of her could alarm her daughter. Perhaps from
fear of a grief so piercing that she dared not face it. Perhaps from reverence,
because she did not feel it permissible to herself, without impiety, to
remark the trace of any mental weakening on those venerated features.
Perhaps to be better able to preserve intact in her memory the image of the
true face of my grandmother, radiant with wisdom and goodness. So they
went up side by side, my grandmother half hidden by her shawl, my mother
turning away her eyes.

Meanwhile there was one person who never took hers from what could
be made out of my grandmother's altered features, at which her daughter
dared not look, a person who fastened on them a gaze wondering, indiscreet and of evil omen: this was Françoise. Not that she was not sincerely
attached to my grandmother (indeed she had been disappointed and
almost scandalised by the coldness shewn by Mamma, whom she would
have liked to see fling herself weeping into her mother's arms), but she
had a certain tendency always to look at the worse side of things, she had
retained from her childhood two peculiarities which would seem to be
mutually exclusive, but which when combined strengthened one another:
the want of restraint common among people of humble origin who make no
attempt to conceal the impression, in other words the painful alarm, aroused
in them by the sight of a physical change which it would be in better taste

to appear not to notice, and the unfeeling coarseness of the peasant who begins by tearing the wings off dragon-flies until she is allowed to wring the necks of chickens, and lacks that modesty which would make her conceal the interest that she feels in the sight of suffering flesh.

When, thanks to the faultless ministrations of Françoise, my grandmother had been put to bed, she discovered that she could speak much more easily, the little rupture or obstruction of a blood-vessel which had produced the uraemia having apparently been quite slight. And at once she was anxious not to fail Mamma in her hour of need, to assist her in the most cruel moments through which she had yet had to pass.

"Well, my child," she began, taking my mother's hand in one of her own, and keeping the other in front of her lips, so as to account for the slight difficulty which she still found in uttering certain words. "So this is all the pity you shew your mother! You look as if you thought that indigestion was quite a pleasant thing!"

Then for the first time my mother's eyes gazed passionately into those of my grandmother, not wishing to see the rest of her face, and she replied, beginning the list of those false promises which we swear but are unable to fulfil:

"Mamma, you will soon be quite well again, your daughter will see to that."

And embodying all her dearest love, all her determination that her mother should recover, in a kiss to which she entrusted them, and which she followed with her mind, with her whole being until it flowered upon her lips, she bent down to lay it humbly, reverently upon the precious brow. My grandmother complained of a sort of alluvial deposit of bedclothes which kept gathering all the time in the same place, over her left leg, and from which she could never manage to free herself. But she did not realise that she was herself the cause of this (so that day after day she accused Françoise unjustly of not 'doing' her bed properly). By a convulsive movement she kept flinging to that side the whole flood of those billowing blankets of fine wool, which gathered there like the sand in a bay which is very soon transformed into a beach (unless the inhabitants construct a breakwater) by the successive deposits of the tide.

My mother and I (whose falsehood was exposed before we spoke by the obnoxious perspicacity of Françoise) would not even admit that my grandmother was seriously ill, as though such an admission might give pleasure to her enemies (not that she had any) and it was more loving to feel that she was not so bad as all that, in short from the same instinctive sentiment which had led me to suppose that Andrée was too sorry for Albertine to be really fond of her. The same individual phenomena are reproduced in the mass, in great crises. In a war, the man who does not love his country says nothing against it, but regards it as lost, commiserates it, sees everything in the darkest colours.

Françoise was of infinite value to us owing to her faculty of doing without sleep, of performing the most arduous tasks. And if, when she had gone to bed after several nights spent in the sick-room, we were obliged to call her a quarter of an hour after she had fallen asleep, she

was so happy to be able to do the most tiring duties as if they had
been the simplest things in the world that, so far from looking cross,
her face would light up with a satisfaction tinged with modesty. Only
when the time came for mass, or for breakfast, then, had my grandmother
been in her death agony, still Françoise would have quietly slipped away
so as not to make herself late. She neither could nor would let her place be
taken by her young footman. It was true that she had brought from Combray an extremely exalted idea of everyone's duty towards ourselves; she
would not have tolerated that any of our servants should 'fail' us. This
doctrine had made her so noble, so imperious, so efficient an instructor
that there had never come to our house any servants, however corrupted,
who had not speedily modified, purified their conception of life so far as
to refuse to touch the usual commissions from tradesmen and to come
rushing—however little they might previously have sought to oblige—to
take from my hands and not let me tire myself by carrying the smallest
package. But at Combray Françoise had contracted also—and had brought
with her to Paris—the habit of not being able to put up with any assistance
in her work. The sight of anyone coming to help her seemed to her like
receiving a deadly insult, and servants had remained for weeks in the house
without receiving from her any response to their morning greeting, had
even gone off on their holidays without her bidding them good-bye or their
guessing her reason, which was simply and solely that they had offered to
do a share of her work on some day when she had not been well. And at
this moment when my grandmother was so ill Françoise's duties seemed
to her peculiarly her own. She would not allow herself, she, the official
incumbent, to be done out of her part in the ritual of these festal days.
And so her young footman, sent packing by her, did not know what to do
with himself, and not content with having copied the butler's example
and supplied himself with note-paper from my desk had begun as well to
borrow volumes of poetry from my bookshelves. He sat reading them for
a good half of the day, out of admiration for the poets who had written
them, but also so as, during the rest of his time, to begem with quotations
the letters which he wrote to his friends in his native village. Naturally he
expected these to dazzle them. But as there was little sequence in his
ideas he had formed the notion that these poems, picked out at random
from my shelves, were matters of common knowledge, to which it was customary to refer. So much so that in writing to these peasants, whose stupefaction he discounted, he interspersed his own reflexions with lines from
Lamartine, just as he might have said "Who laughs last, laughs longest!"
or merely "How are you keeping?"

To ease her pain my grandmother was given morphine. Unfortunately,
if this relieved her in other ways, it increased the quantity of albumen.
The blows which we aimed at the wicked ogre who had taken up his abode
in my grandmother were always wide of the mark, and it was she, her poor
interposed body that had to bear them, without her ever uttering more
than a faint groan by way of complaint. And the pain that we caused her
found no compensation in a benefit which we were unable to give her.
The savage ogre whom we were anxious to exterminate we barely suc-

ceeded in touching, and all we did was to enrage him still further, and possibly hasten the moment at which he would devour his luckless captive. On certain days when the discharge of albumen had been excessive Cottard, after some hesitation, stopped the morphine. In this man, so insignificant, so common, there was, in these brief moments in which he deliberated, in which the relative dangers of one and another course of treatment presented themselves alternately to his mind until he arrived at a decision, the same sort of greatness as in a general who, vulgar in all the rest of his life, is a great strategist, and in an hour of peril, after a moment's reflexion, decides upon what is from the military point of view the wisest course, and gives the order: "Advance eastwards." Medically, however little hope there might be of setting any limit to this attack of uraemia, it did not do to tire the kidneys. But, on the other hand, when my grandmother did not have morphine, her pain became unbearable; she perpetually attempted a certain movement which it was difficult for her to perform without groaning. To a great extent, suffering is a sort of need felt by the organism to make itself familiar with a new state, which makes it uneasy, to adapt its sensibility to that state. We can discern this origin of pain in the case of certain inconveniences which are not such for everyone. Into a room filled with a pungent smoke two men of a coarse fibre will come and attend to their business; a third, more highly strung, will betray an incessant discomfort. His nostrils will continue to sniff anxiously the odour he ought, one would say, to try not to notice but will keep on attempting to attach, by a more exact apprehension of it, to his troubled sense of smell. One consequence of which may well be that his intense preoccupation will prevent him from complaining of a toothache. When my grandmother was in pain the sweat trickled over the pink expanse of her brow, glueing to it her white locks, and if she thought that none of us was in the room she would cry out: "Oh, it's dreadful!" but if she caught sight of my mother, at once she employed all her energy in banishing from her face every sign of pain, or—an alternative stratagem—repeated the same plaints, accompanying them with explanations which gave a different sense, retrospectively, to those which my mother might have overheard.

"Oh! My dear, it's dreadful to have to stay in bed on a beautiful sunny day like this when one wants to be out in the air; I am crying with rage at your orders."

But she could not get rid of the look of anguish in her eyes, the sweat on her brow, the convulsive start, checked at once, of her limbs.

"There is nothing wrong. I'm complaining because I'm not lying very comfortably. I feel my hair is untidy, my heart is bad, I knocked myself against the wall."

And my mother, at the foot of the bed, riveted to that suffering form, as though, by dint of piercing with her gaze that pain-bedewed brow, that body which hid the evil thing within it, she could have succeeded in reaching that evil thing and carrying it away, my mother said:

"No, no, Mamma dear, we won't let you suffer like that, we will find something to take it away, have patience just for a moment; let me give you a kiss, darling—no, you're not to move."

And stooping over the bed, with bended knees, almost kneeling on the ground, as though by an exercise of humility she would have a better chance of making acceptable the impassioned gift of herself, she lowered towards my grandmother her whole life contained in her face as in a ciborium which she extended over her, adorned in relief with dimples and folds so passionate, so sorrowful, so sweet that one knew not whether they had been carved by the chisel of a kiss, a sob or a smile. My grandmother, also, tried to lift up her face to Mamma's. It was so altered that probably, had she been strong enough to go out, she would have been recognised only by the feather in her hat. Her features, like the clay in a sculptor's hands, seemed to be straining, with an effort which distracted her from everything else, to conform to some particular model which we failed to identify. This business of modelling was now almost finished, and if my grandmother's face had shrunk in the process it had at the same time hardened. The veins that ran beneath its surface seemed those not of a piece of marble but of some more rugged stone. Constantly thrust forwards by the difficulty that she found in breathing and as constantly forced back on to her pillow by exhaustion, her face, worn, diminished, terribly expressive, seemed like, in a primitive, almost prehistoric carving, the rude, flushed, purplish, desperate face of some savage guardian of a tomb. But the whole task was not yet accomplished. Next, her resistance must be overcome, and that tomb, the entrance to which she had so painfully guarded, with that tense contraction, entered.

In one of those moments in which, as the saying goes, one does not know what saint to invoke, as my grandmother was coughing and sneezing a good deal, we took the advice of a relative who assured us that if we sent for the specialist X—— he would get rid of all that in a couple of days. People say that sort of thing about their own doctors, and their friends believe them just as Françoise always believed the advertisements in the newspapers. The specialist came with his bag packed with all the colds and coughs of his other patients, like Aeolus's bottle. My grandmother refused point-blank to let herself be examined. And we, out of consideration for the doctor, who had had his trouble for nothing, deferred to the desire that he expressed to inspect each of our noses in turn, albeit there was nothing the matter with any of them. According to him, however, there was; everything, whether headache or colic, heart-disease or diabetes, was a disease of the nose that had been wrongly diagnosed. To each of us he said: "I should like to have another look at that little cornea. Don't put it off too long. I can soon get rid of it for you with a hot needle." We were, of course, thinking of something quite different. And yet we asked ourselves: "Get rid of what?" In a word, every one of our noses was diseased; his mistake lay only in his use of the present tense. For by the following day his examination and provisional treatment had taken effect. Each of us had his or her catarrh. And when in the street he ran into my father doubled up with a cough, he smiled to think that an ignorant layman might suppose the attack to be due to his intervention. He had examined us at a moment when we were already ill.

My grandmother's illness gave occasion to various people to manifest an excess or deficiency of sympathy which surprised us quite as much as the sort of chance which led one or another of them to reveal to us connecting links of circumstances, or of friendship for that matter, which we had never suspected. And the signs of interest shewn by the people who called incessantly at the house to inquire revealed to us the gravity of an illness which, until then, we had not sufficiently detached from the countless painful impressions that we received in my grandmother's room. Summoned by telegram, her sisters declined to leave Combray. They had discovered a musician there who gave them excellent chamber concerts, in listening to which they thought that they could find, better than by the invalid's bedside, food for thought, a melancholy exaltation the form of which was, to say the least of it, unusual. Mme. Sazerat wrote to Mamma, but in the tone of a person whom the sudden breaking off of a betrothal (the cause of the rupture being her Dreyfusism) has parted from one for ever. Bergotte, on the other hand, came every day and spent several hours with me.

He had always made a habit of going regularly for some time to the same house, where, accordingly, he need not stand on ceremony. But formerly it had been in order that he might talk without being interrupted; now it was so that he might sit for as long as he chose in silence, without being expected to talk. For he was very ill, some people said with albuminuria, like my grandmother. According to another version, he had a tumour. He grew steadily weaker; it was with difficulty that he came up our staircase, with greater difficulty still that he went down it. Even though he held on to the banisters he often stumbled, and he would, I believe, have stayed at home had he not been afraid of losing altogether the habit of going out, the capacity to go out, he, the 'man with the little beard' whom I had seen so alert, not very long since. He was now quite blind and even his speech was frequently obstructed.

But at the same time, by a directly opposite process, the body of his work, known only to a few literary people at the period when Mme. Swann used to patronise their timid efforts to disseminate it, now grown in stature and strength before the eyes of all, had acquired an extraordinary power of expansion among the general public. The general rule is, no doubt, that only after his death does a writer become famous. But it was while he still lived, and during his slow progress towards a death that he had not yet reached that this writer was able to watch the progress of his works towards Renown. A dead writer can at least be illustrious without any strain on himself. The effulgence of his name is stopped short by the stone upon his grave. In the deafness of the eternal sleep he is not importuned by Glory. But for Bergotte the antithesis was still incomplete. He existed still sufficiently to suffer from the tumult. He was moving still, though with difficulty, while his books, bounding about him, like daughters whom one loves but whose impetuous youthfulness and noisy pleasures tire one, brought day after day, to his very bedside, a crowd of fresh admirers.

The visits which he now began to pay us came for me several years too late, for I had no longer the same admiration for him as of old. Which is not in any sense incompatible with the growth of his reputation. A man's work seldom becomes completely understood and successful before that of another writer, still obscure, has begun in the minds of certain people more difficult to please to substitute a fresh cult for one that has almost ceased to command observance. In the books of Bergotte which I constantly re-read, his sentences stood out as clearly before my eyes as my own thoughts, the furniture in my room and the carriages in the street. All the details were quite easily seen, not perhaps precisely as one had always seen them, but at any rate as one was accustomed to see them now. But a new writer had recently begun to publish work in which the relations between things were so different from those that connected them for me that I could under-stand hardly anything of what he wrote. He would say, for instance: "The hose-pipes admired the smart upkeep of the roads" (and so far it was simple, I followed him smoothly along those roads) "which started every five minutes from Briand and Claudel." At that point I ceased to understand, because I had expected the name of a place and was given that of a person instead. Only I felt that it was not the sentence that was badly constructed but I myself that lacked the strength and ability necessary to reach the end. I would start afresh striving tooth and nail to climb to the pinnacle from which I would see things in their novel relations. And each time, after I had got about halfway through the sentence, I would fall back again, as later on, when I joined the Army, in my attempts at the exercise known as the 'bridge-ladder.' I felt nevertheless for the new writer the admiration which an awkward boy who never receives any marks for gym-nastics feels when he watches another more nimble. And from then onwards I felt less admiration for Bergotte, whose limpidity began to strike me as insufficient. There was a time at which people recognised things quite easily in pictures when it was Fromentin who had painted them, and could not recognise them at all when it was Renoir.

People of taste and refinement tell us nowadays that Renoir is one of the great painters of the last century. But in so saying they forget the element of Time, and that it took a great deal of time, well into the present century, before Renoir was hailed as a great artist. To succeed thus in gaining recognition, the original painter, the original writer proceeds on the lines adopted by oculists. The course of treatment they give us by their painting or by their prose is not always agreeable to us. When it is at an end the operator says to us: "Now look!" And, lo and behold, the world around us (which was not created once and for all, but is created afresh as often as an original artist is born) appears to us entirely different from the old world, but perfectly clear. Women pass in the street, different from what they used to be, because they are Renoirs, those Renoir types which we persistently refused to see as women. The carriages, too, are Renoirs, and the water, and the sky: we feel tempted to go for a walk in the forest which reminds us of that other which when we first saw it looked like anything in the world except a forest, like for instance a tapestry of innu-merable shades but lacking precisely the shades proper to forests. Such is the new and perishable universe which has just been created. It will last until the next geological catastrophe is precipitated by a new painter or writer of original talent.

This writer who had taken Bergotte's place in my affections wearied me not by the incoherence but by the novelty of associations—perfectly coherent—which my mind was not trained to follow. The fact that it was always at the same point that I felt myself relinquish my grasp pointed to a common character in the efforts that I had always to make. Moreover, when once in a thousand times I did succeed in following the writer to the end of his sentence, what I saw there was always of a humour, a truth, a charm similar to those which I had found long ago in reading Bergotte, only more delightful. I reflected that it was not so many years since a similar reconstruction of the world, like that which I was waiting now for his successor to produce, had been wrought for me by Bergotte himself. Until I was led to ask myself whether there was indeed any truth in the distinction which we are always making between art, which is no more advanced now than in Homer's day, and science with its continuous progress. Perhaps, on the contrary, art was in this respect like science; each new writer seemed to me to have advanced beyond the stage of his immediate predecessor; and how was I to know that in twenty years' time, when I should be able to accompany without strain or effort the newcomer of to-day, another might not appear at whose approach he in turn would be packed off to the limbo to which his own coming would have consigned Bergotte?

I spoke to the latter of the new writer. He gave me a distaste for him not so much when he said that his art was uncouth, easy and vacuous, as when he told me that he had seen him, and had almost mistaken him (so strong was the likeness) for Bloch. From that moment my friend's features outlined themselves on the printed pages, and I no longer felt any obligation to make the effort necessary to understand them. If Bergotte had decried him to me it was less, I fancy, out of jealousy for a success that was yet to come than out of ignorance of his work. He read scarcely anything. The bulk of his thought had long since passed from his brain into his books. He had grown thin, as though they had been extracted from him by surgical operations. His reproductive instinct no longer impelled him to any activity, now that he had given an independent existence to almost all his thoughts. He led the vegetative life of a convalescent, of a woman after childbirth; his fine eyes remained motionless, vaguely dazed, like the eyes of a man who lies on the seashore and in a vague daydream sees only each little breaking wave. However, if it was less interesting to talk to him now than I should once have found it, I felt no compunction for that. He was so far a creature of habit that the simplest habits, like the most elaborate, once he had formed them, became indispensable to him for a certain length of time. I do not know what made him come to our house first of all, but after that every day it was simply because he had been there the day before. He would come to the house as he might have gone to a café, so that no one should talk to him, so that he might—very rarely—talk himself; one might in short have found in his conduct a sign that he was moved to sympathise with us in our anxiety, or that he enjoyed my company, had one sought to draw any conclusion from such an assiduity in calling. It did not fail to impress my mother, sensitive to everything that might be regarded as an act of homage to her invalid. And every day she reminded me: "See that you don't forget to thank him nicely."

We had also—a discreet feminine attention like the refreshments that are brought to us in the studio, between sittings, by a painter's mistress— a courteous supplement to those which her husband paid us professionally, a visit from Mme. Cottard. She came to offer us her 'waiting-woman,' or, if we preferred the services of a man, she would 'scour the country' for one, and, best of all, on our declining, said that she did hope this was not just a 'put-off' on our part, a word which in her world signifies a false pretext for not accepting an invitation. She assured us that the Professor, who never referred to his patients when he was at home, was as sad about it as if it had been she herself who was ill. We shall see in due course that even if this had been true it would have been at once a very small and a considerable admission on the part of the most faithless and the most attentive of husbands.

Offers as helpful and infinitely more touching owing to the form in which they were couched (which was a blend of the highest intelligence, the warmest sympathy, and a rare felicity of expression) were addressed to me by the Hereditary Grand Duke of Luxembourg. I had met him at Balbec where he had come on a visit to one of his aunts, the Princesse de Luxembourg, being himself at that time merely Comte de Nassau. He had married, some months later, the charming daughter of another Luxembourg Princess, extremely rich, because she was the only daughter of a Prince who was the proprietor of an immense flour-mill. Whereupon the Grand Duke of Luxembourg, who had no children of his own and was devoted to his nephew Nassau, had obtained the approval of his Chamber to his declaring the young man his heir. As with all marriages of this nature, the origin of the bride's fortune was the obstacle as it was also the deciding factor. I remembered this Comte de Nassau as one of the most striking young men I had ever met, already devoured, at that time, by a dark and blazing passion for his betrothed. I was deeply touched by the letters which he wrote me, day after day, during my grandmother's illness, and Mamma herself, in her emotion, quoted sadly one of her mother's expressions: "Sévigné would not have put it better."

On the sixth day Mamma, yielding to my grandmother's entreaties, left her for a little and pretended to go and lie down. I should have liked (so that my grandmother might go to sleep) Françoise to sit quite still and not disturb her by moving. In spite of my supplications, she got up and left the room; she was genuinely devoted to my grandmother; with her uncanny insight and her natural pessimism she regarded her as doomed. She would therefore have liked to pay her every possible attention. But word had just come that an electrician was in the house, one of the oldest servants of his firm, the head of which was his brother-in-law, highly esteemed throughout the building, where he had worked for many years, and especially by Jupien. This man had been ordered to come before my grandmother's illness. It seemed to me that he might have been sent away again, or told to wait. But Françoise's code of manners would not permit of this; it would have been a want of courtesy towards this worthy man; my grandmother's condition ceased at once to matter. When, after waiting a quarter of an hour, I lost my patience and went to look for her in the kitchen, I found her talking to him on the landing of the back staircase, the door of which stood open, a device which had the advantage, should any of us come on the scene, of letting it be thought that they were just saying good-bye, but had also the drawback of sending a terrible draught through the house. Françoise tore herself from the workman, not without turning to shout down after him various greetings, forgotten in her haste, to his wife and brother-in-law. A typical Combray scruple, not to be found wanting in politeness, which Françoise extended even to foreign politics. People foolishly imagine that the vast dimensions of social phenomena afford them an excellent opportunity to penetrate farther into the human soul; they ought, on the contrary, to realise that it is by plumbing the depths of a single personality that they might have a chance of understanding those phenomena. A thousand times over Françoise told the gardener at Combray that war was the most senseless of crimes, that life was the only thing that mattered. Yet, when the Russo-Japanese war broke out, she was quite ashamed, when she thought of the Tsar, that we had not gone to war also to help the 'poor Russians,' "since," she reminded us, "we're allianced to them." She felt this abstention to be not quite polite to Nicholas II, who had always "said such nice things about us"; it was a corollary of the same code which would have prevented her from refusing a glass of brandy from Jupien, knowing that it would 'upset' her digestion, and which brought it about that now, with my grandmother lying at death's door, the same meanness of which she considered France guilty in remaining neutral with regard to Japan she would have had to admit in herself, had she not gone in person to make her apologies to this good electrician who had been put to so much trouble.

Luckily for ourselves, we were soon rid of Françoise's daughter, who was obliged to be away for some weeks. To the regular stock of advice which people at Combray gave to the family of an invalid: "You haven't tried taking him away for a little . . . the change of air, you know . . . pick up an appetite . . . etc?" she had added the almost unique idea, which she had specially created in her own imagination, and repeated accordingly whenever we saw her, without fail, as though hoping by dint of reiteration to force it through the thickness of people's heads: "She ought to have taken herself in hand *radically* from the first." She did not recommend any one cure rather than another, provided that it were 'radical.' As for Françoise herself, she noticed that we were not giving my grandmother many medicines. Since, according to her, they only destroyed the stomach, she was quite glad of this, but at the same time even more humiliated. She had, in the South of France, some cousins—relatively well-to-do—whose daughter, after falling ill just as she was growing up, had died at twenty-three; for several years the father and mother had ruined themselves on drugs, on different doctors, on pilgrimages from one watering-place to another, until her decease. Now all this seemed to Françoise, for the parents in question, a kind of luxury, as though they had owned racehorses, or a place in the country. They themselves, in the midst of their affliction, derived a certain gratification from the thought of such lavish expenditure. They had now nothing left, least of all their most precious possession, their child, but they did enjoy telling people how they had done as much for her and more than the richest in the land. The ultra-violet rays to the action of which, several times a day for months on end, the poor girl had been subjected, delighted them more than anything. The father, elated in his grief by the glory of it all, was led to speak of his daughter at times as of an operatic star for whose sake he had ruined himself. Françoise was not unmoved by this wealth of scenic effect; that which framed my grandmother's sickbed seemed to her a trifle meagre, suited rather to an illness on the stage of a small provincial theatre.

There came a time when her uraemic trouble affected my grandmother's eyes. For some days she could not see at all. Her eyes were not at all like those of a blind person, but remained just the same as before. And I gathered that she could see nothing only from the strangeness of a certain smile of welcome which she assumed the moment one opened the door, until one had come up to her and taken her hand, a smile which began too soon and remained stereotyped on her lips, fixed, but always full-faced, and endeavouring to be visible from all points, because she could no longer rely upon her sight to regulate it, to indicate the right moment, the proper direction, to bring it to the point, to make it vary according to the change of position or of facial expression of the person who had come in; because it was left isolated, without the accompanying smile in her eyes which would have distracted a little from it the attention of the visitor, it assumed in its awkwardness an undue importance, giving one the impression of an exaggerated friendliness. Then her sight was completely restored; from her eyes the wandering affliction passed to her ears. For several days my grandmother was deaf. And as she was afraid of being taken by surprise by the sudden entry of some one whom she would not have heard come in, all day long, albeit she was lying with her face to the wall, she kept turning her head sharply towards the door. But the movement of her neck was clumsy, for one cannot adapt oneself in a few days to this transposition of faculties, so as, if not actually to see sounds, to listen with one's eyes. Finally her pain grew less, but the impediment of her speech increased. We were obliged to ask her to repeat almost everything that she said.

And now my grandmother, realising that we could no longer understand her, gave up altogether the attempt to speak and lay perfectly still. When she caught sight of me she gave a sort of convulsive start like a person who suddenly finds himself unable to breathe, but could make no intelligible sound. Then, overcome by her sheer powerlessness, she let her head drop on to the pillows, stretched herself out flat in her bed, her face grave, like a face of marble, her hands motionless on the sheet or occupied in some purely physical action such as that of wiping her fingers with her handkerchief. She made no effort to think. Then came a state of perpetual agitation. She was incessantly trying to get up. But we restrained her so far as we could from doing so, for fear of her discovering how paralysed she was. One day when she had been left alone for a moment I found her standing on the floor in her nightgown trying to open the window.

At Balbec, once, when a widow who had jumped into the sea had been rescued against her will, my grandmother had told me (moved perhaps by one of those presentiments which we discern at times in the mystery—so obscure, for all that—of the organic life around us, in which nevertheless it seems that our own future is foreshadowed) that she could think of nothing so cruel as to tear a poor wretch from the death that she had deliberately sought and restore her to her living martyrdom.

We were just in time to catch my grandmother, she put up an almost violent resistance to my mother, then, overpowered, seated forcibly in an armchair, she ceased to wish for death, to regret being alive, her face resumed its impassivity and she began laboriously to pick off the hairs that had been left on her nightgown by a fur cloak which somebody had thrown over her shoulders.

The look in her eyes changed completely; often uneasy, plaintive, haggard, it was no longer the look we knew, it was the sullen expression of a doddering old woman. . . .

By dint of repeatedly asking her whether she would not like her hair done, Françoise managed to persuade herself that the request had come from my grandmother. She armed herself with brushes, combs, eau de Cologne, a wrapper. "It can't hurt Madame Amédée," she said to herself, "if I just comb her; nobody's ever too ill for a good combing." In other words, one was never too weak for another person to be able, for her own satisfaction, to comb one. But when I came into the room I saw between the cruel hands of Françoise, as blissfully happy as though she were in the act of restoring my grandmother to health, beneath a thin rain of aged tresses which had not the strength to resist the action of the comb, a head which, incapable of maintaining the position into which it had been forced, was rolling to and fro with a ceaseless swirling motion in which sheer debility alternated with spasms of pain. I felt that the moment at which Françoise would have finished her task was approaching, and I dared not hasten it by suggesting to her: "That is enough," for fear of her disobeying me. But I did forcibly intervene when, in order that my grandmother might see whether her hair had been done to her liking, Françoise, with innocent savagery, brought her a glass. I was glad for the moment that I had managed to snatch it from her in time, before my grandmother, whom we had carefully kept without a mirror, could catch even a stray glimpse of a face unlike anything she could have imagined. But, alas, when, a moment later, I leaned over her to kiss that dear forehead which had been so harshly treated, she looked up at me with a puzzled, distrustful, shocked expression: she did not know me.

According to our doctor, this was a symptom that the congestion of her brain was increasing. It must be relieved in some way.

Cottard was in two minds. Françoise hoped at first that they were going to apply 'clarified cups.' She looked for the effects of this treatment in my dictionary, but could find no reference to it. Even if she had said 'scarified' instead of 'clarified' she still would not have found any reference to this adjective, since she did not look any more for it under 'S' than under 'C'; she did indeed say 'clarified' but she wrote (and consequently assumed that the printed word was) 'esclarified.' Cottard, to her disappointment, gave the preference, though without much hope, to leeches. When, a few hours later, I went into my grandmother's room, fastened to her neck, her temples, her ears, the tiny black serpents were writhing among her blood-stained locks, as on the head of Medusa. But in her pale and peaceful, entirely motionless face I saw wide open, luminous and calm, her own beautiful eyes, as in days gone by (perhaps even more charged with the light of intelligence than they had been before her illness, since, as she could not speak and must not move, it was to her eyes alone that she entrusted her thought, that thought which at one time occupies an immense place in us, offering us undreamed-of treasures, at another time seems reduced to nothing, then may be reborn, as though by spontaneous generation, by the withdrawal of a few drops of blood), her eyes, soft and liquid like two pools of oil in which the rekindled fire that was now burning lighted before the face of the invalid a reconquered universe. Her calm was no longer the wisdom of despair, but that of hope. She realised that she was better, wished to be careful, not to move, and made me the present only of a charming smile so that I should know that she was feeling better, as she gently pressed my hand.

I knew the disgust that my grandmother felt at the sight of certain animals, let alone being touched by them. I knew that it was in consideration of a higher utility that she was enduring the leeches. And so it infuriated me to hear Françoise repeating to her with that laugh which people use to a baby, to make it crow: "Oh, look at the little beasties running about on Madame." This was, moreover, treating our patient with a want of respect, as though she were in her second childhood. But my grandmother, whose face had assumed the calm fortitude of a stoic, did not seem even to hear her.

Alas! No sooner had the leeches been taken off than the congestion returned and grew steadily worse. I was surprised to find that at this stage, when my grandmother was so ill, Françoise was constantly disappearing. The fact was that she had ordered herself a mourning dress, and did not wish to keep her dressmaker waiting. In the lives of most women, everything, even the greatest sorrow, resolves itself into a question of 'trying-on.'

A few days later, when I was in bed and sleeping, my mother came to call me in the early hours of the morning. With that tender consideration which, in great crises, people who are crushed by grief shew even for the slightest discomfort of others:

"Forgive me for disturbing your sleep," she said to me.

"I was not asleep," I answered as I awoke.

I said this in good faith. The great modification which the act of awakening effects in us is not so much that of introducing us to the clear life of consciousness, as that of making us lose all memory of that other, rather more diffused light in which our mind has been resting, as in the opaline depths of the sea. The tide of thought, half veiled from our perception, over which we were drifting still a moment ago, kept us in a state of motion perfectly sufficient to enable us to refer to it by the name of wakefulness. But then our actual awakenings produce an interruption of memory. A little later we describe these states as sleep because we no longer remember them. And when shines that bright star which at the moment of waking illuminates behind the sleeper the whole expanse of his sleep, it makes him imagine for a few moments that this was not a sleeping but a waking state; a shooting star, it must be added, which blots out with the fading of its light not only the false existence but the very appearance of our dream, and merely enables him who has awoken to say to himself: "I was asleep."

In a voice so gentle that she seemed to be afraid of hurting me, my mother asked whether it would tire me too much to get out of bed, and, stroking my hands, went on:

"My poor boy, you have only your Papa and Mamma to help you now."

We went into the sickroom. Bent in a semicircle on the bed a creature other than my grandmother, a sort of wild beast which was coated with her hair and couched amid her bedclothes lay panting, groaning, making the blankets heave with its convulsions. The eyelids were closed, and it was because the one nearer me did not shut properly, rather than because it opened at all that it left visible a chink of eye, misty, filmed, reflecting the dimness both of an organic sense of vision and of a hidden, internal pain. All this agitation was not addressed to us, whom she neither saw nor knew. But if this was only a beast that was stirring there, where could my grandmother be? Yes, I could recognise the shape of her nose, which bore no relation now to the rest of her face, but to the corner of which a beauty spot still adhered, and the hand that kept thrusting the blankets aside with a gesture which formerly would have meant that those blankets were pressing upon her, but now meant nothing.

Mamma asked me to go for a little vinegar and water with which to sponge my grandmother's forehead. It was the only thing that refreshed her, thought Mamma, who saw that she was trying to push back her hair. But now one of the servants was signalling to me from the doorway. The news that my grandmother was in the last throes had spread like wildfire through the house. One of those 'extra helps' whom people engage at exceptional times to relieve the strain on their servants (a practice which gives deathbeds an air of being social functions) had just opened the front door to the Duc de Guermantes, who was now waiting in the hall and had asked for me: I could not escape him.

"I have just, my dear Sir, heard your tragic news. I should like, as a mark of sympathy, to shake hands with your father." I made the excuse that I could not very well disturb him at the moment. M. de Guermantes was like a caller who turns up just as one is about to start on a journey. But he felt so intensely the importance of the courtesy he was shewing us that it blinded him to all else, and he insisted upon being taken into the drawing-room. As a general rule, he made a point of going resolutely through the formalities with which he had decided to honour anyone, and took little heed that the trunks were packed or the coffin ready.

"Have you sent for Dieulafoy? No? That was a great mistake. And if you had only asked me, I would have got him to come, he never refuses me anything, although he has refused the Duchesse de Chartres before now. You see, I set myself above a Princess of the Blood. However, in the presence of death we are all equal," he added, not that he meant to suggest that my grandmother was becoming his equal, but probably because he felt that a prolonged discussion of his power over Dieulafoy and his pre-eminence over the Duchesse de Chartres would not be in very good taste.

This advice did not in the least surprise me. I knew that, in the Guermantes set, the name of Dieulafoy was regularly quoted (only with slightly more respect) among those of other tradesmen who were 'quite the best' in their respective lines. And the old Duchesse de Mortemart *née* Guermantes (I never could understand, by the way, why, the moment one speaks of a Duchess, one almost invariably says: "The old Duchess of So-and-so," or, alternatively, in a delicate Watteau tone, if she is still young: "The little Duchess of So-and-so,") would prescribe almost automatically, with a droop of the eyelid, in serious cases: "Dieulafoy, Dieulafoy!" as, if one wanted a place for ices, she would advise: 'Poiré Blanche,' or for small pastry 'Rebattet, Rebattet.' But I was not aware that my father had, as a matter of fact, just sent for Dieulafoy.

At this point my mother, who was waiting impatiently for some cylinders of oxygen which would help my grandmother to breathe more easily, came out herself to the hall where she little expected to find M. de Guermantes. I should have liked to conceal him, had that been possible. But convinced in his own mind that nothing was more essential, could be more gratifying to her or more indispensable to the maintenance of his reputation as a perfect gentleman, he seized me violently by the arm and, although I defended myself as against an assault with repeated protestations of "Sir, Sir, Sir," dragged me across to Mamma, saying: "Will you do me the great honour of presenting me to your mother?" letting go a little as he came to the last word. And it was so plain to him that the honour was hers that he could not help smiling at her even while he was composing a grave face. There was nothing for it but to mention his name, the sound of which at once started him bowing and scraping, and he was just going to begin the complete ritual of salutation. He apparently proposed to enter into conversation, but my mother, overwhelmed by her grief, told me to come at once and did not reply to the speeches of M. de Guermantes who, expecting to be received as a visitor and finding himself instead left alone in the hall, would have been obliged to retire had he not at that moment caught sight of Saint-Loup who had arrived in Paris that morning and had come to us in haste to inquire for news. "I say, this is a piece of luck!" cried the Duke joyfully, catching his nephew by the sleeve, which he nearly tore off, regardless of the presence of my mother who was again crossing the hall. Saint-Loup was not sorry, I fancy, despite his genuine sympathy, at having missed seeing me, considering his attitude towards myself. He left the house, carried off by his uncle who, having had something very important to say to him and having very nearly gone down to Doncières on purpose to say it, was beside himself with joy at being able to save himself so much exertion. "Upon my soul, if anybody had told me I had only to cross the courtyard and I should find you here, I should have thought it a huge joke; as your friend M. Bloch would say, it's a regular farce." And as he disappeared down the stairs with Robert whom he held by the shoulder:

"All the same," he went on, "it's quite clear I must have touched the hangman's rope or something; I do have the most astounding luck." Not that the Duc de Guermantes was ill-bred; far from it. But he was one of those men who are incapable of putting themselves in the place of other people, who resemble in that respect undertakers and the majority of doctors, and who, after composing their faces and saying: "This is a very painful occasion," after, if need be, embracing you and advising you to rest, cease to regard a deathbed or a funeral as anything but a social gathering of a more or less restricted kind at which, with a joviality that has been checked for a moment only, they scan the room in search of the person whom they can tell about their own little affairs, or ask to introduce them to some one else, or offer a 'lift' in their carriage when it is time to go home. The Duc de Guermantes, while congratulating himself on the 'good wind' that had blown him into the arms of his nephew, was still so surprised at the reception—natural as it was—that had been given him by my mother, that he declared later on that she was as disagreeable as my father was civil, that she had 'absent fits' during which she seemed literally not to hear a word you said to her, and that in his opinion she had no self-possession and perhaps even was not quite 'all there.' At the same time he had been quite prepared (according to what I was told) to put this state of mind down, in part at any rate, to the circumstances, and declared that my mother had seemed to him greatly 'affected' by the sad event. But he had still stored up in his limbs all the residue of bows and reverences which he had been prevented from using up, and had so little idea of the real nature of Mamma's sorrow that he asked me, the day before the funeral, if I was not doing anything to distract her.

A half-brother of my grandmother, who was in religion, and whom I had never seen, had telegraphed to Austria, where the head of his Order was, and having as a special privilege obtained leave, arrived that day. Bowed down with grief, he sat by the bedside reading prayers and meditations from a book, without, however, taking his gimlet eyes from the invalid's face. At one point, when my grandmother was unconscious, the sight of this cleric's grief began to upset me, and I looked at him tenderly. He appeared surprised by my pity, and then an odd thing happened. He joined his hands in front of his face, like a man absorbed in painful meditation, but, on the assumption that I would then cease to watch him, left, as I observed, a tiny chink between his fingers. And at the moment when my gaze left his face, I saw his sharp eye, which had been making use of its vantage-point behind his hands to observe whether my sympathy were sincere. He was hidden there as in the darkness of a confessional. He saw that I was still looking and at once shut tight the lattice which he had left ajar. I have met him again since then, but never has any reference been made by either of us to that minute. It was tacitly agreed that I had not noticed that he was spying on me. In the priest as in the alienist, there is always an element of the examining magistrate. Besides, what friend is there, however cherished, in whose and our common past there has not been some such episode which we find it convenient to believe that he must have forgotten?

The doctor gave my grandmother an injection of morphine, and to make her breathing less troublesome ordered cylinders of oxygen. My mother, the doctor, the nursing sister held these in their hands; as soon as one was exhausted another was put in its place. I had left the room for a few minutes. When I returned I found myself face to face with a miracle. Accompanied on a muted instrument by an incessant murmur, my grandmother seemed to be greeting us with a long and blissful chant, which filled the room, rapid and musical. I soon realized that this was scarcely less unconscious, that it was as purely mechanical as the hoarse rattle that I had heard before leaving the room. Perhaps to a slight extent it reflected some improvement brought about by the morphine. Principally it was the result (the air not passing quite in the same way through the bronchial tubes) of a change in the register of her breathing. Released by the twofold action of the oxygen and the morphine, my grandmother's breath no longer laboured, panted, groaned, but, swift and light, shot like a skater along the delicious stream. Perhaps with her breath, unconscious like that of the wind in the hollow stem of a reed, there were blended in this chant some of those more human sighs which, liberated at the approach of death, make us imagine impressions of suffering or happiness in minds which already have ceased to feel, and these sighs came now to add a more melodious accent, but without changing its rhythm, to that long phrase which rose, mounted still higher, then declined, to start forth afresh, from her unburdened bosom in quest of the oxygen. Then, having risen to so high a pitch, having been sustained with so much vigour, the chant, mingled with a murmur of supplication from the midst of her ecstasy, seemed at times to stop altogether like a spring that has ceased to flow.

Françoise, in any great sorrow, felt the need but did not possess the art—as simple as that need was futile—of giving it expression. Regarding my grandmother's case as quite hopeless, it was her own personal impressions that she was impelled to communicate to us. And all that she could do was to repeat: "It makes me feel all queer," in the same tone in which she would say, when she had taken too large a plateful of cabbage broth: "It's like a load on my stomach," sensations both of which were more natural than she seemed to think. Though so feebly expressed, her grief was nevertheless very great, and was aggravated moreover by her annoyance that her daughter, detained at Combray (to which this young Parisian now referred as 'the Cambrousse' and where she felt herself growing '*pétrousse*,' in other words fossilised), would not, presumably, be able to return in time for the funeral ceremony, which was certain, Françoise felt, to be a superb spectacle. Knowing that we were not inclined to be expansive, she made Jupien promise at all costs to keep every evening in the week free. She knew that he would be engaged elsewhere at the hour of the funeral. She was determined at least to 'go over it all' with him on his return.

For several nights now my father, my grandfather and one of our cousins had been sitting up, and never left the house during the day. Their continuous devotion ended by assuming a mask of indifference, and their interminable leisure round the deathbed made them indulge in that small talk which is an inseparable accompaniment of prolonged confinement in a railway carriage. Anyhow this cousin (a nephew of my great-aunt) aroused in me an antipathy as strong as the esteem which he deserved and generally enjoyed. He was always 'sent for' in times of great trouble, and was so assiduous in his attentions to the dying that their mourning families, on the pretext that he was in delicate health, despite his robust appearance, his bass voice and bristling beard, invariably besought him, with the customary euphemisms, not to come to the cemetery. I could tell already that Mamma, who thought of others in the midst of the most crushing grief, would soon be saying to him, in a very different form of words, what he was in the habit of hearing said on all such occasions:

"Promise me that you won't come 'to-morrow.' Please, for 'her sake.' At any rate, you won't go 'all the way.' It's what she would have wished."

But there was nothing for it; he was always the first to arrive 'at the house,' by reason of which he had been given, among another set, the nickname (unknown to us) of 'No flowers by request.' And before attending everything he had always 'attended to everything,' which entitled him to the formula: "We don't know how to thank you."

"What's that?" came in a loud voice from my grandfather, who had grown rather deaf and had failed to catch something which our cousin had just said to my father.

"Nothing," answered the cousin. "I was just saying that I'd heard from Combray this morning. The weather is appalling down there, and here we've got too much sun."

"Yet the barometer is very low," put in my father.

"Where did you say the weather was bad?" asked my grandfather.

"At Combray."

"Ah! I'm not surprised; whenever it's bad here it's fine at Combray, and vice versa. Good gracious! Talking of Combray, has anyone remembered to tell Legrandin?"

"Yes, don't worry about that, it's been done," said my cousin, whose cheeks, bronzed by an irrepressible growth of beard, dimpled faintly with the satisfaction of having 'remembered' it.

At this point my father hurried from the room. I supposed that a sudden change, for better or worse, had occurred. It was simply that Dr. Dieulafoy had just arrived. My father went to receive him in the drawing-room, like the actor who is to come next on the stage. We had sent for him not to cure but to certify, in almost a legal capacity. Dr. Dieulafoy might indeed be a great physician, a marvellous professor; to these several parts, in which he excelled, he added a third, in which he remained for forty years without a rival, a part as original as that of the arguer, the scaramouch or the noble father, which consisted in coming to certify an agony or a death. The mere sound of his name foreshadowed the dignity with which he would sustain the part, and when the servant announced: "M. Dieulafoy," one imagined oneself at a play by Molière. To the dignity of his attitude was added, without being conspicuous, the suppleness of a perfect figure. A face in itself too good-looking was toned down by the convention due to distressing circumstances. In the sable majesty of his frock coat the Professor entered the room, melancholy without affectation, uttered not the least word of condolence, which might have been thought insincere, nor was he guilty of the slightest infringement of the rules of tact. At the foot of a deathbed it was he and not the Duc de Guermantes who was the great gentleman. Having examined my grandmother, but not so as to tire her, and with an excess of reserve which was an act of courtesy to the doctor who was treating the case, he murmured a few words to my father, bowed respectfully to my mother to whom I felt that my father had positively to restrain himself from saying: "Professor Dieulafoy." But already our visitor had turned away, not wishing to seem to be soliciting an introduction, and left the room in the most polished manner conceivable, simply taking with him the sealed envelope that was slipped into his hand. He had not appeared to see it, and we ourselves were left wondering for a moment whether we had really given it to him, such a conjurer's nimbleness had he put into the act of making it vanish without thereby losing anything of the gravity— which was increased rather—of the great consultant in his long frock coat with its silken lapels, and his handsome head full of a noble commiseration. The slowness and vivacity of his movements shewed that, even if he had a hundred other visits to pay and patients waiting, he refused to appear hurried. For he was the embodiment of tact, intelligence and kindness. That eminent man is no longer with us. Other physicians, other professors may have rivalled, may indeed have surpassed him. But the 'capacity' in which his knowledge, his physical endowments, his distinguished manners made him triumph exists no longer for want of any successor capable of taking his place. Mamma had not even noticed M. Dieulafoy, everything that was not my grandmother having no existence for her. I remember (and here I anticipate) that at the cemetery, where we saw her, like a supernatural apparition, go up timidly to the grave and seem to be gazing in the wake of a flying form that was already far away, my father having remarked to her: "Old Norpois came to the house and to the church and on here; he gave up a most important committee meeting to come; you ought really to say a word to him, he'll be so gratified if you do," my mother, when the Ambassador stood before her and bowed, could do no more than gently incline a face that shewed no tears. A couple of days earlier—to anticipate once again before returning to where we were just now by the bed on which my grandmother lay dying—while they were watching by the body, Françoise, who, not disbelieving entirely in ghosts, was terrified by the least sound, had said: "I believe that's her." But in place of fear it was an ineffable sweetness that her words aroused in my mother, who would have been so glad that the dead should return, to have her mother with her sometimes still.

To return now to those last hours, "You heard about the telegram her sisters sent us?" my grandfather asked the cousin.

"Yes, Beethoven, they told me about it, it's worth framing; still, I'm not surprised."

"My poor wife, who was so fond of them, too," said my grandfather, wiping away a tear. "We mustn't blame them. They're stark mad, both of them, as I've always said. What's the matter now; aren't you going on with the oxygen?"

My mother spoke: "Oh, but then Mamma will be having more trouble with her breathing."

The doctor reassured her: "Oh, no! The effect of the oxygen will last a good while yet; we can begin it again presently."

It seemed to me that he would not have said this of a dying woman, that if this good effect were to last it meant that we could still do something to keep her alive. The hiss of the oxygen ceased for a few moments. But the happy plaint of her breathing poured out steadily, light, troubled, unfinished, without end, beginning afresh. Now and then it seemed that all was over, her breath stopped, whether owing to one of those transpositions to another octave that occur in the breathing of a sleeper, or else from a natural interruption, an effect of unconsciousness, the progress of asphyxia, some failure of the heart. The doctor stooped to feel my grandmother's pulse, but already, as if a tributary were pouring its current into the dried river-bed, a fresh chant broke out from the interrupted measure. And the first was resumed in another pitch with the same inexhaustible force. Who knows whether, without indeed my grandmother's being conscious of them, a countless throng of happy and tender memories compressed by suffering were not escaping from her now, like those lighter gases which had long been compressed in the cylinders? One would have said that everything that she had to tell us was pouring out, that it was to us that she was addressing herself with this prolixity, this earnestness, this effusion. At the foot of the bed, convulsed by every gasp of this agony, not weeping but now and then drenched with tears, my mother presented the unreasoning desolation of a leaf which the rain lashes and the wind twirls on its stem. They made me dry my eyes before I went up to kiss my grandmother.

"But I thought she couldn't see anything now?" said my father.

"One can never be sure," replied the doctor.

When my lips touched her face, my grandmother's hands quivered, a long shudder ran through her whole body, reflex perhaps, perhaps because certain affections have their hyperaesthesia which recognises through the veil of unconsciousness what they barely need senses to enable them to love. Suddenly my grandmother half rose, made a violent effort, as though struggling to resist an attempt on her life. Françoise could not endure this sight and burst out sobbing. Remembering what the doctor had just said I tried to make her leave the room. At that moment my grandmother opened her eyes. I thrust myself hurriedly in front of Françoise to hide her tears, while my parents were speaking to the sufferer. The sound of the oxygen had ceased; the doctor moved away from the bedside. My grandmother was dead.

An hour or two later Françoise was able for the last time, and without causing them any pain, to comb those beautiful tresses which had only begun to turn grey and hitherto had seemed not so old as my grandmother herself. But now on the contrary it was they alone that set the crown of age on a face grown young again, from which had vanished the wrinkles, the contractions, the swellings, the strains, the hollows which in the long course of years had been carved on it by suffering. As at the far-off time when her parents had chosen for her a bridegroom, she had the features delicately traced by purity and submission, the cheeks glowing with a chaste expectation, with a vision of happiness, with an innocent gaiety even, which the years had gradually destroyed. Life in withdrawing from her had taken with it the disillusionments of life. A smile seemed to be hovering on my grandmother's lips. On that funeral couch, death, like a sculptor of the middle ages, had laid her in the form of a young maiden.

CHAPTER TWO

A VISIT FROM ALBERTINE

ALBEIT it was simply a Sunday in autumn, I had been born again, life lay intact before me, for that morning, after a succession of mild days, there had been a cold mist which had not cleared until nearly midday. A change in the weather is sufficient to create the world and oneself anew. Formerly, when the wind howled in my chimney, I would listen to the blows which it struck on the iron trap with as keen an emotion as if, like the famous bow-taps with which the C Minor Symphony opens, they had been the irresistible appeal of a mysterious destiny. Every change in the aspect of nature offers us a similar transformation by adapting our desires so as to harmonise with the new form of things. The mist, from the moment of my awakening, had made of me, instead of the centrifugal being which one is on fine days, a self-centred man, longing for the chimney corner and the nuptial couch, a shivering Adam in quest of a sedentary Eve, in this different world.

Between the soft grey tint of a morning landscape and the taste of a cup of chocolate I tried to account for all the originality of the physical, intellectual and moral life which I had taken with me, about a year earlier, to Doncières, and which, blazoned with the oblong form of a bare hillside—always present even when it was invisible—formed in me a series of pleasures entirely distinct from all others, incommunicable to my friends, in the sense that the impressions, richly interwoven with one another, which gave them their orchestral accompaniment were a great deal more characteristic of them, to my subconscious mind, than any facts that I might have related. From this point of view the new world in which the mist of this morning had immersed me was a world already known to me (which only made it more real) and forgotten for some time (which restored all its novelty). And I was able to look at several of the pictures of misty landscapes which my memory had acquired, notably a series of 'Mornings at Doncières,' including my first morning there in barracks and another, in a neighbouring country house, where I had gone with Saint-Loup to spend the night: in which from the windows, whose curtains I had drawn back at daybreak, before getting into bed again, in the first a trooper, in the second (on the thin margin of a pond and a wood all the rest of which was engulfed in the uniform and liquid softness of the mist) a coachman busy polishing a strap had appeared to me like those rare figures, scarcely visible to the eye obliged to adapt itself to the mysterious vagueness of their half-lights, which emerge from an obliterated fresco.

It was from my bed that I was looking this afternoon at these pictorial memories, for I had gone back to bed to wait until the hour came at which, taking advantage of the absence of my parents, who had gone for a few

days to Combray, I proposed to get up and go to a little play which was
being given that evening in Mme. de Villeparisis's drawing-room. Had they
been at home I should perhaps not have ventured to go out; my mother, in
the delicacy of her respect for my grandmother's memory, wished the tokens
of regret that were paid to it to be freely and sincerely given; she would
not have forbidden me this outing, she would have disapproved of it. From
Combray, on the other hand, had I consulted her wishes, she would not have
replied in a melancholy: "Do just as you like; you are old enough now to
know what is right or wrong," but, reproaching herself for having left me
alone in Paris, and measuring my grief by her own, would have wished for
it distractions of a sort which she would have refused to herself, and which
she persuaded herself that my grandmother, solicitous above all things for
my health and the preservation of my nervous balance, would have advised
me to take.

That morning the furnace of the new steam heater had for the first time
been lighted. Its disagreeable sound—an intermittent hiccough—had no
part whatsoever in my memories of Doncières. But its prolonged encounter,
in me this afternoon, with them was to give it so lasting an affinity with
them that whenever, after succeeding more or less in forgetting it, I heard
the central heater hiccough again it reminded me of them.

There was no one else in the house but Françoise. The grey light, falling
like a fine rain on the earth, wove without ceasing a transparent web
through which the Sunday holiday-makers appeared in a silvery sheen. I
had flung to the foot of my bed the *Figaro*, for which I had been sending
out religiously every morning, ever since I had sent in an article which it
had not yet printed; despite the absence of the sun, the intensity of the
daylight was an indication that we were still only half-way through the
afternoon. The tulle window-curtains, vaporous and friable as they would
not have been on a fine day, had that same blend of beauty and fragility
that dragon flies' wings have, and Venetian glass. It depressed me all the
more that I should be spending this Sunday by myself because I had sent
a note that morning to Mlle. de Stermaria. Robert de Saint-Loup, whom
his mother had at length succeeded in parting—after painful and abortive
attempts—from his mistress, and who immediately afterwards had been
sent to Morocco in the hope of his there forgetting one whom he had already
for some little time ceased to love, had sent me a line, which had reached
me the day before, announcing his arrival, presently, in France for a short
spell of leave. As he would only be passing through Paris (where his family
were doubtless afraid of seeing him renew relations with Rachel), he informed me, to shew me that he had been thinking of me, that he had met
at Tangier Mlle. or rather Mme. (for she had divorced her husband three
months after their marriage) de Stermaria. And Robert, remembering what
I had told him at Balbec, had asked her, on my behalf, to arrange a meeting. She would be delighted to dine with me, she had told him, on one of
the evenings which, before her return to Brittany, she would be spending
in Paris. He warned me to lose no time in writing to Mme. de Stermaria,
for she would certainly have arrived before I got his letter. This had come
as no surprise to me, even although I had had no news of him since, at the

time of my grandmother's last illness, he had accused me of perfidy and treachery. It had then been quite easy to see what must have happened. Rachel, who liked to provoke his jealousy—she had other reasons also for wishing me harm—had persuaded her lover that I had made a dastardly attempt to have relations with her in his absence. It is probable that he continued to believe in the truth of this allegation, but he had ceased to be in love with her, which meant that its truth or falsehood had become a matter of complete indifference to him, and our friendship alone remained. When, on meeting him again, I attempted to speak to him about his attack on me his sole answer was a cordial and friendly smile, which gave him the air of begging my pardon; then he turned the conversation to something else. All this was not to say that he did not, a little later, see Rachel occasionally when he was in Paris. The fellow-creatures who have played a leading part in one's life very rarely disappear from it suddenly with any finality. They return to take their old place in it at odd moments (so much so as to lead people to believe in a renewal of old love) before leaving it for ever. Saint-Loup's breach with Rachel had very soon become less painful to him, thanks to the soothing pleasure that was given him by her incessant demands for money. Jealousy, which prolongs the course of love, is not capable of containing many more ingredients than are the other forms of imagination. If one takes with one, when one starts on a journey, three or four images which incidentally one is sure to lose on the way (such as the lilies and anemones heaped on the Ponte Vecchio, or the Persian church shrouded in mist), one's trunk is already pretty full. When one parts from a mistress one would be just as glad, until one has begun to forget her, that she should not become the property of three or four potential protectors whom one has in one's mind's eye, of whom, that is to say, one is jealous: all those whom one does not so picture count for nothing. Now frequent demands for money from a cast-off mistress no more give one a complete idea of her life than charts shewing a high temperature would of her illness. But the latter would at any rate be an indication that she was ill, and the former furnish a presumption, vague enough, it is true, that the forsaken one, or forsaker (whichever she be) cannot have found anything very remarkable in the way of rich protectors. And so each demand is welcomed with the joy which a lull produces in the jealous one's sufferings, while he responds to it at once by dispatching money, for naturally he does not like to think of her being in want of anything, except lovers (one of the three lovers he has in his mind's eye), until time has enabled him to regain his composure and he can learn without the slightest emotion the name of his successor. Sometimes Rachel came in so late at night that she could ask her former lover's permission to lie down beside him until the morning. This was a great comfort to Robert, for it refreshed his memory of how they had, after all, lived in intimacy together merely to see that even if he took the greater part of the bed for himself it did not in the least interfere with her sleep. He realised that she was more comfortable, lying close to his body, than she would have been elsewhere, that she felt herself, by his side—even in an hotel—to be in a bedroom known of old, in which the force of habit prevails and one sleeps better. He felt that his shoulders, his limbs, all of him were for her, even when he was unduly restless, from sleeplessness or from having to get up in the night, things so entirely usual that they could not disturb her, and that the perception of them added still further to her sense of repose.

To revert to where we were, I had been all the more disquieted by Robert's letter in that I could read between the lines what he had not ventured to write more explicitly. "You can most certainly ask her to dine in a private room," he told me. "She is a charming young person, a delightful nature, you will get on splendidly with her, and I am sure you will have a capital evening together." As my parents were returning at the end of the week, on Saturday or Sunday, and as after that I should be forced to dine every evening at home, I had written at once to Mme. de Stermaria, proposing any evening that might suit her, up to Friday. A message was brought back that I should hear from her in writing the same evening, about eight o'clock. The time would have passed quickly enough if I had had, during the afternoon that separated me from her letter, the help of a visit from anyone else. When the hours pass wrapped in conversation one ceases to count, or indeed to notice them, they vanish, and suddenly it is a long way beyond the point at which it escaped you that there reappears the nimble truant time. But if we are alone, our preoccupation, by bringing before us the still distant and incessantly awaited moment with the frequency and uniformity of a ticking pendulum, divides, or rather multiplies the hours by all the minutes which, had we been with friends, we should not have counted. And confronted, by the incessant return of my desire, with the ardent pleasure which I was going to taste—not for some days though, alas!—in Mme. de Stermaria's company, this afternoon, which I should have to spend by myself, seemed to me very empty and very melancholy.

Every now and then I heard the sound of the lift coming up, but it was followed by a second sound, not that for which I was hoping, namely the sound of its coming to a halt at our landing, but another very different sound which the lift made in continuing its progress to the floors above and which, because it so often meant the desertion of my floor when I was expecting a visitor, remained for me at other times, even when I had no wish to see anyone, a sound lugubrious in itself, in which there echoed, as it were, a sentence of solitary confinement. Weary, resigned, busy for several hours still over its immemorial task, the grey day stitched its shimmering needlework of light and shade, and it saddened me to think that I was to be left alone with a thing that knew me no more than would a seamstress who, installed by the window so as to see better while she finished her work, paid no attention to the person present with her in the room. Suddenly, although I had heard no bell, Françoise opened the door to let in Albertine, who came forward smiling, silent, plump, containing in the fulness of her body, made ready so that I might continue living them, come in search of me, the days we had spent together at that Balbec to which I had never since returned. No doubt, whenever we see again a person with whom our relations—however trivial they may have been—are altered, it is like a juxtaposition of two different periods. For this, we do not require that a former mistress should come to call upon us as a friend, all that we need is the visit to Paris of a person whom we had known in the daily round of some particular kind of life, and that this life should have ceased for us, were it no more than a week ago. On each of Albertine's smiling, questioning, blushing features I could read the questions: "And Madame de Villeparisis? And the dancing-master? And the pastry-cook?" When she sat down her back seemed to be saying: "Gracious! There's no cliff here; you don't mind if I sit down beside you, all the same, as I used to do at Balbec?" She was like an enchantress handing me a mirror that reflected time. In this she was like all the people whom we seldom see now but with whom at one time we lived on more intimate terms. With Albertine, however, there was something more than this. Certainly, even at Balbec, in our daily encounters, I had always been surprised when she came in sight, so variable was her appearance from day to day. But now it was difficult to recognise her. Cleared of the pink vapour that used to bathe them, her features had emerged like those of a statue. She had another face, or rather she had a face at last; her body too had grown. There remained scarcely anything now of the shell in which she had been enclosed and on the surface of which, at Balbec, her future outline had been barely visible.

This time, Albertine had returned to Paris earlier than usual. As a rule she came only in the spring, which meant that, already disturbed for some weeks past by the storms that were beating down the first flowers, I did not distinguish, in the elements of the pleasure that I felt, the return of Albertine from that of the fine weather. It was enough that I should be told that she was in Paris and that she had called at the house, for me to see her again like a rose flowering by the sea. I cannot say whether it was the desire for Balbec or for herself that overcame me at such moments; possibly my desire for her was itself a lazy, cowardly, and incomplete method of possessing Balbec, as if to possess a thing materially, to take up one's abode in a town, were equivalent to possessing it spiritually. Besides, even materially, when she was no longer posed by my imagination before a horizon of sea, but sitting still in a room with me, she seemed to me often a very poor specimen of a rose, so poor, indeed, that I would gladly have shut my eyes in order not to observe this or that blemish of its petals, and to imagine instead that I was inhaling the salt air on the beach.

I must say it at this point, albeit I was not then aware of what was to happen only later on. Certainly, it is more reasonable to devote one's life to women than to postage stamps or old snuff-boxes, even to pictures or statues. Only the example of other collectors should be a warning to us to make changes, to have not one woman only but several. Those charming suggestions in which a girl abounds of a sea-beach, of the braided hair of a statue in church, of an old print, of everything that makes one see and admire in her, whenever she appears, a charming composition, those suggestions are not very stable. Live with a woman altogether and you will soon cease to see any of the things that made you love her; though I must add that these two sundered elements can be reunited by jealousy. If, after a long period of life in common, I was to end by seeing nothing more in Albertine than an ordinary woman, an intrigue between her and some person whom she had loved at Balbec would still suffice, perhaps, to rein-corporate in her, to amalgamate the beach and the unrolling of the tide. Only, as these secondary suggestions no longer captivate our eyes, it is to the heart that they are perceptible and fatal. We cannot, under so danger-ous a form, regard the repetition of the miracle as a thing to be desired. But I am anticipating the course of years. And here I need only state my regret that I did not have the sense simply to have kept my collection of women as people keep their collections of old quizzing glasses, never so complete, in their cabinet, that there is not room always for another and rarer still.

Departing from the customary order of her holiday movements, this year she had come straight from Balbec, where furthermore she had not stayed nearly so late as usual. It was a long time since I had seen her, and as I did not know even by name the people with whom she was in the habit of mixing in Paris, I could form no impression of her during the periods in which she abstained from coming to see me. These lasted often for quite a time. Then, one fine day, in would burst Albertine whose rosy apparitions and silent visits left me little if any better informed as to what she might have been doing in an interval which remained plunged in that darkness of her hidden life which my eyes felt little anxiety to pierce.

This time, however, certain signs seemed to indicate that some new experience must have entered into that life. And yet, perhaps, all that one was entitled to conclude from them was that girls change very rapidly at the age which Albertine had now reached. For instance, her intellect was now more in evidence, and on my reminding her of the day when she had insisted with so much ardour on the superiority of her idea of making Sophocles write: "My dear Racine," she was the first to laugh, quite whole-heartedly, at her own stupidity. "Andrée was quite right; it was stupid of me," she admitted. "Sophocles ought to have begun: 'Sir.' " I replied that the 'Sir,' and 'Dear Sir,' of Andrée were no less comic than her own 'My dear Racine,' or Gisèle's 'My dear Friend,' but that after all the really stupid people were the Professors who still went on making Sophocles write letters to Racine. Here, however, Albertine was unable to follow me. She could not see in what the silliness consisted; her intelligence was dawning, but had not fully developed. There were other more attractive novelties in her; I felt, in this same pretty girl who had just sat down by my bed, something that was different; and in those lines which, in one's eyes and other features, express one's general attitude towards life, a change of front, a partial conversion, as though there had now been shattered those resistances against which I had hurled my strength in vain at Balbec, one evening, now remote in time, on which we formed a couple symmetrical with but the converse of our present arrangement, since then it had been she who was lying down and I who sat by her bedside. Wishing and not venturing to make certain whether now she would let herself be kissed, every time that she rose to go I asked her to stay beside me a little longer. This was a concession not very easy to obtain, for albeit she had nothing to do (otherwise she would have rushed from the house) she was a person methodical in her habits and moreover not very gracious towards me, seeming scarcely to be at ease in my company, and yet each time, after looking at her watch, she sat down again at my request until finally she had spent several hours with me without my having asked her for anything; the things I was saying to her followed logically those that I had said during the hours before, and bore no relation to what I was thinking about, what I desired from her, remained indefinitely parallel. There is nothing like desire for preventing the thing one says from bearing any resemblance to what one has in one's mind. Time presses, and yet it seems as though we were seeking to gain time by speaking of subjects absolutely alien to that by which we are obsessed. We then arrange that the sentence which we should like to utter shall be accompanied, or rather preluded, by a gesture, supposing that is to say that we have not to give ourselves the pleasure of an immediate demonstration and to gratify the curiosity we feel as to the reactions which will follow it, without a word said, without even a 'By your leave,' already made this gesture. Certainly I was not in the least in love with Albertine; child of the mists outside, she could merely content the imaginative desire which the change of weather had awakened in me and which was midway between the desires that are satisfied by the arts of the kitchen and of monumental sculpture respectively, for it made me dream simultaneously of mingling with my flesh a substance different and warm, and of attaching at some point to my outstretched body a body divergent, as the body of Eve barely holds by the feet to the side of Adam, to whose body hers is almost perpendicular, in those romanesque bas-reliefs on the church at Balbec which represent in so noble and so reposeful a fashion, still almost like a classical frieze, the Creation of Woman; God in them is everywhere followed, as by two ministers, by two little angels in whom the visitor recognises—like winged, swarming summer creatures which winter has surprised and spared—cupids from Herculaneum, still surviving well into the thirteenth century, and winging their last slow flight, weary but never failing in the grace that might be expected of them, over the whole front of the porch.

As for this pleasure which by accomplishing my desire would have set me free from these meditations and which I should have sought quite as readily from any other pretty woman, had I been asked upon what—in the course of this endless flow of talk throughout which I took care to keep from Albertine the one thing that was in my mind—was based my optimistic hypothesis with regard to her possible complaisances, I should perhaps have answered that this hypothesis was due (while the forgotten outlines of Albertine's voice retraced for me the contour of her personality) to the apparition of certain words which did not form part of her vocabulary, or at least not in the acceptation which she now gave them. Thus she said to me that Elstir was stupid, and, on my protesting:

- "You don't understand," she replied, smiling, "I mean that it was stupid of him to behave like that; of course I know he's quite a distinguished person, really."

Similarly, wishing to say of the Fontainebleau golf club that it was smart, she declared: "They are quite a selection."

Speaking of a duel that I had fought, she said of my seconds: "What very choice seconds," and looking at my face confessed that she would like to see me 'wear a moustache.' She even went so far (and my chances appeared then enormous) as to announce, in a phrase of which I would have sworn that she was ignorant a year earlier, that since she had last seen Gisèle there had passed a certain 'lapse of time.' This was not to say that Albertine had not already possessed, when I was at Balbec, a quite adequate assortment of those expressions which reveal at once that one's people are in easy circumstances, and which, year by year, a mother passes on to her daughter just as she bestows on her, gradually, as the girl grows up, on important occasions, her own jewels. It was evident that Albertine had ceased to be a little girl when one day, to express her thanks for a present which a strange lady had given her, she had said: "I am quite confused." Mme. Bontemps could not help looking across at her husband, whose comment was:

"Gad, she's old for fourteen."

The approach of nubility had been more strongly marked still when Albertine, speaking of another girl whose tone was bad, said: "One can't even tell whether she's pretty, she paints her face a foot thick." Finally, though still a schoolgirl, she already displayed the manner of a grown woman of her upbringing and station when she said, of some one whose face twitched: "I can't look at him, because it makes me want to do the same," or, if some one else were being imitated: "The absurd thing about it is that when you imitate her voice you look exactly like her." All these are drawn from the social treasury. But it did not seem to me possible that Albertine's natural environment could have supplied her with 'distinguished,' used in the sense in which my father would say of a colleague whom he had not actually met, but whose intellectual attainments he had heard praised: "It appears he's quite a distinguished person." 'Selection,' even when used of a golf club, seemed to me as incompatible with the Simonet family as it would be if preceded by the adjective 'Natural,' with a text published centuries before the researches of Darwin. 'Lapse of time' struck me as being of better augury still. Finally there appeared the evidence of certain upheavals, the nature of which was unknown to me, but sufficient to justify me in all my hopes when Albertine announced, with the satisfaction of a person whose opinion is by no means to be despised:

"To my mind, that is the best thing that could possibly happen. I regard it as the best solution, the stylish way out."

This was so novel, so manifestly an alluvial deposit giving one to suspect such capricious wanderings over soil hitherto unknown to her, that on hearing the words 'to my mind' I drew Albertine towards me, and at 'I regard' made her sit on the side of my bed.

No doubt it does happen that women of moderate culture, on marrying well-read men, receive such expressions as part of their paraphernalia. And shortly after the metamorphosis which follows the wedding night, when they begin to pay calls, and talk shyly to the friends of their girlhood, one notices with surprise that they have turned into matrons if, in deciding that some person is intelligent, they sound both l's in the word; but that is precisely the sign of a change of state, and I could see a difference when

I thought of the vocabulary of the Albertine I had known of old—a vocabulary in which the most daring flights were to say of any unusual person: 'He's a type,' or, if you suggested a game of cards to her: 'I've no money to lose,' or again, if any of her friends were to reproach her, in terms which she felt to be undeserved: 'That really is magnificent!' an expression dictated in such cases by a sort of middle-class tradition almost as old as the *Magnificat* itself, and one which a girl slightly out of temper and confident that she is in the right employs, as the saying is, 'quite naturally,' that is to say because she has learned the words from her mother, just as she has learned to say her prayers or to greet a friend. All these expressions Mme. Bontemps had imparted to her at the same time as her hatred of the Jews and her feeling for black, which was always suitable and becoming, indeed without any formal instruction, but as the piping of the parent goldfinches serves as a model for that of the young ones, recently hatched, so that they in turn grow into true goldfinches also. But when all was said, 'selection' appeared to me of alien growth and 'I regard' encouraging. Albertine was no longer the same; which meant that she would not perhaps act, would not react in the same way.

Not only did I no longer feel any love for her, but I had no longer to consider, as I should have had at Balbec, the risk of shattering in her an affection for myself, which no longer existed. There could be no doubt that she had long since become quite indifferent to me. I was well aware that to her I was in no sense a member now of the 'little band' into which I had at one time so anxiously sought and had then been so happy to have secured admission. Besides, as she had no longer even, as in Balbec days, an air of frank good nature, I felt no serious scruples: still I believe that what made me finally decide was another philological discovery. As, continuing to add fresh links to the external chain of talk behind which I hid my intimate desire, I spoke, having Albertine secure now on the corner of my bed, of one of the girls of the little band, one smaller than the rest, whom, nevertheless, I had thought quite pretty, "Yes," answered Albertine, "she reminds me of a little *mousmé*." There had been nothing in the world to shew, when I first knew Albertine, that she had ever heard the word *mousmé*. It was probable that, had things followed their normal course, she would never have learned it, and for my part I should have seen no cause for regret in that, for there is no more horrible word in the language. The mere sound of it makes one's teeth ache as they do when one has put too large a spoonful of ice in one's mouth. But coming from Albertine, as she sat there looking so pretty, not even '*mousmé*' could strike me as unpleasant. On the contrary, I felt it to be a revelation, if not of an outward initiation, at any rate of an inward evolution. Unfortunately it was now time for me to bid her good-bye if I wished her to reach home in time for her dinner, and myself to be out of bed and dressed in time for my own. It was Françoise who was getting it ready; she did not like having to keep it back, and must already have found it an infringement of one of the articles of her code that Albertine, in the absence of my parents, should be paying me so prolonged a visit, and one which was going to make everything late.

But before *'mousmé'* all these arguments fell to the ground and I hastened to say:

"Just fancy; I'm not in the least ticklish; you can go on tickling me for an hour on end and I won't even feel it."

"Really?"

"I assure you."

She understood, doubtless, that this was the awkward expression of a desire on my part, for, like a person who offers to give you an introduction for which you have not ventured to ask him, though what you have said has shewn him that it would be of great service to you.

"Would you like me to try?" she inquired, with womanly meekness.

"Just as you like, but you would be more comfortable if you lay down properly on the bed."

"Like that?"

"No; get right on top."

"You're sure I'm not too heavy?"

As she uttered these words the door opened and Françoise, carrying a lamp, came in. Albertine had just time to fling herself back upon her chair. Perhaps Françoise had chosen this moment to confound us, having been listening at the door or even peeping through the keyhole. But there was no need to suppose anything of the sort; she might have scorned to assure herself, by the use of her eyes, of what her instinct must plainly enough have detected, for by dint of living with me and my parents her fears, her prudence, her alertness, her cunning had ended by giving her that instinctive and almost prophetic knowledge of us all that the mariner has of the sea, the quarry of the hunter, and, of the malady, if not the physician, often at any rate the patient. The amount of knowledge that she managed to acquire would have astounded a stranger, and with as good reason as does the advanced state of certain arts and sciences among the ancients, seeing that there was practically no source of information open to them. (Her sources were no larger. They were a few casual remarks forming barely a twentieth part of our conversation at dinner, caught on the wing by the butler and inaccurately transmitted to the kitchen.) Again, her mistakes were due, like theirs, like the fables in which Plato believed, rather to a false conception of the world and to preconceived ideas than to the insufficiency of the materials at her disposal. Only the other day, has it not been possible for the most important discoveries as to the habits of insects to be made by a scientist who had access to no laboratory and used no instruments of any sort? But if the drawbacks arising from her menial position had not prevented her from acquiring a stock of learning indispensable to the art which was its ultimate goal—and which consisted in putting us to confusion by communicating to us the results of her discoveries—the limitations under which she worked had done more; in this case the impediment, not content with merely not paralysing the flight of her imagination, had greatly strengthened it. Of course Françoise never let slip any artificial device, those for example of diction and attitude. Since (if she never believed what we said to her, hoping that she would believe it) she admitted without any shadow of doubt the truth of anything that any person of her own condition in life might tell her, however absurd, which might at the same time prove shocking to our ideas, just as her way of listening to our assertions bore witness to her incredulity, so the accents in which she reported (the use of indirect speech enabling her to hurl the most deadly insults at us with impunity) the narrative of a cook who had told her how she had threatened her employers, and won from them, by treating them before all the world like dirt, any number of privileges and concessions, shewed that the story was to her as gospel. Françoise went so far as to add: "I'm sure, if I had been the mistress I should have been quite vexed." In vain might we, despite our scant sympathy at first with the lady on the fourth floor, shrug our shoulders, as though at an unlikely fable, at this report of so shocking an example; in making it the teller was able to speak with the crushing, the lacerating force of the most unquestionable, most irritating affirmation.

But above all, just as great writers often attain to a power of concentration from which they would have been dispensed under a system of political liberty or literary anarchy, when they are bound by the tyranny of a monarch or of a school of poetry, by the severity of prosodic laws or of a state religion, so Françoise, not being able to reply to us in an explicit fashion, spoke like Tiresias and would have written like Tacitus. She managed to embody everything that she could not express directly in a sentence for which we could not find fault with her without accusing ourselves, indeed in less than a sentence, in a silence, in the way in which she placed a thing in a room.

Thus when I happened to leave, by accident, on my table, among a pile of other letters, one which it was imperative that she should not see, because, let us say, it referred to her with a dislike which afforded a presumption of the same feeling towards her in the recipient as in the writer, that evening, if I came home with a troubled conscience and went straight to my room, there on top of my letters, neatly arranged in a symmetrical pile, the compromising document caught my eye as it could not possibly have failed to catch the eye of Françoise, placed by her right at the top, almost separated from the rest, in a prominence that was a form of speech, that had an eloquence all its own, and, as I stood in the doorway, made me shudder like a cry. She excelled in the preparation of these scenic effects, intended so to enlighten the spectator, in her absence, that he already knew that she knew everything when in due course she made her appearance. She possessed, for thus making an inanimate object speak, the art, at once inspired and painstaking, of Irving or Frédéric Lemaître. On this occasion, holding over Albertine and myself the lighted lamp whose searching beams missed none of the still visible depressions which the girl's body had hollowed in the counterpane, Françoise made one think of a picture of 'Justice throwing light upon Crime.' Albertine's face did not suffer by this illumination. It revealed on her cheeks the same sunny burnish that had charmed me at Balbec. This face of Albertine, the general effect of which sometimes was, out of doors, a sort of milky pallor, now shewed, according as the lamp shone on them, surfaces so dazzlingly, so uniformly coloured, so firm, so glowing that one might have compared them to the sustained flesh tints of certain flowers. Taken aback meanwhile by the unexpected entry of Françoise, I exclaimed:

"What? The lamp already? I say, the light is strong!"

My object, as may be imagined, was by the second of these ejaculations to account for my confusion, by the first to excuse my lateness in rising. Françoise replied with a cruel ambiguity:

"Do you want me to extinglish it?"

"—guish!" Albertine slipped into my ear, leaving me charmed by the familiar vivacity with which, taking me at once for teacher and for accomplice, she insinuated this psychological affirmation as though asking a grammatical question.

When Françoise had left the room and Albertine was seated once again on my bed:

"Do you know what I'm afraid of?" I asked her. "It is that if we go on like this I may not be able to resist the temptation to kiss you."

"That would be a fine pity."

I did not respond at once to this invitation, which another man might even have found superfluous, for Albertine's way of pronouncing her words was so carnal, so seductive that merely in speaking to you she seemed to be caressing you. A word from her was a favour, and her conversation covered you with kisses. And yet it was highly attractive to me, this invitation. It would have been so, indeed, coming from any pretty girl of Albertine's age; but that Albertine should be now so accessible to me gave me more than pleasure, brought before my eyes a series of images that bore the stamp of beauty. I recalled the original Albertine standing between me and the beach, almost painted upon a background of sea, having for me no more real existence than those figures seen on the stage, when one knows not whether one is looking at the actress herself who is supposed to appear, at an understudy who for the moment is taking her principal's part, or at a mere projection from a lantern. Then the real woman had detached herself from the luminous mass, had come towards me, with the sole result that I had been able to see that she had nothing in real life of that amorous facility which one supposed to be stamped upon her in the magic pictures. I had learned that it was not possible to touch her, to embrace her, that one might only talk to her, that for me she was no more a woman than the jade grapes, an inedible decoration at one time in fashion on dinner tables, are really fruit. And now she was appearing to me in a third plane, real as in the second experience that I had had of her but facile as in the first; facile, and all the more deliciously so in that I had so long imagined that she was not. My surplus knowledge of life (of a life less uniform, less simple than I had at first supposed it to be) inclined me provisionally towards agnosticism. What can one positively affirm, when the thing that one thought probable at first has then shewn itself to be false and in the third instance turns out true? And alas, I was not yet at the end of my discoveries with regard to Albertine. In any case, even if there had not been the romantic attraction of this disclosure of a greater wealth of planes revealed one after another by life (an attraction the opposite of that which Saint-Loup had felt during our dinners at Rivebelle on recognising beneath the mask with which the course of existence had overlaid them, in a calm face, features to which his lips had once been pressed), the knowledge that to kiss Albertine's cheeks was a possible thing was a pleasure perhaps greater even than that of kissing them. What a difference between possessing a woman to whom one applies one's body alone, because she is no more than a piece of flesh, and possessing the girl whom one used to see on the beach with her friends on certain days without even knowing why one saw her on those days and not on others, which made one tremble to think that one might not see her again. Life had obligingly revealed to one in its whole extent the romance of this little girl, had lent one, for the study of her, first one optical instrument, then another, and had added to one's carnal desire an accompaniment which multiplied it an hundredfold and diversified it with those other desires, more spiritual and less easily assuaged, which do not emerge from their torpor, leaving carnal desire to move by itself, when it aims only at the conquest of a piece of flesh, but which to gain possession of a whole tract of memories, whence they have felt the wretchedness of exile, rise in a tempest round about it, enlarge, extend it, are unable to follow it to the accomplishment, the assimilation, impossible in the form in which it is looked for, of an immaterial reality, but wait for this desire halfway and at the moment of recollection, of return furnish it afresh with their escort; to kiss, instead of the cheeks of the first comer, however cool and fresh they might be, but anonymous, with no secret, with no distinction, those of which I had so long been dreaming, would be to know the taste, the savour of a colour on which I had endlessly gazed. One has seen a woman, a mere image in the decorative setting of life, like Albertine, outlined against the sea, and then one has been able to take that image, to detach it, to bring it close to oneself, gradually to discern its solidity, its colours, as though one had placed it behind the glasses of a stereoscope. It is for this reason that the women who are a little difficult, whose resistance one does not at once overcome, of whom one does not indeed know at first whether one ever will overcome it, are alone interesting. For to know them, to approach them, to conquer them is to make fluctuate in form, in dimensions, in relief the human image, is an example of relativity in the appreciation of an image which it is delightful to see afresh when it has resumed the slender proportions of a silhouette in the setting of one's life. The women one meets first of all in a brothel are of no interest because they remain invariable.

In addition, Albertine preserved, inseparably attached to her, all my impressions of a series of seascapes of which I was particularly fond. I felt that it was possible for me, on the girl's two cheeks, to kiss the whole of the beach at Balbec.

"If you really don't mind my kissing you, I would rather put it off for a little and choose a good moment. Only you mustn't forget that you've said I may. I shall want a voucher: 'Valid for one kiss.'"

"Shall I have to sign it?"

"But if I took it now, should I be entitled to another later on?"

"You do make me laugh with your vouchers; I shall issue a new one every now and then."

"Tell me; just one thing more. You know, at Balbec, before I had been introduced to you, you used often to have a hard, calculating look; you can't tell me what you were thinking about when you looked like that?"

"No; I don't remember at all."

"Wait; this may remind you: one day your friend Gisèle put her feet together and jumped over the chair an old gentleman was sitting in. Try to remember what was in your mind at that moment."

"Gisèle was the one we saw least of; she did belong to the band, I suppose, but not properly. I expect I thought that she was very ill-bred and common."

"Oh, is that all?"

I should certainly have liked, before kissing her, to be able to fill her afresh with the mystery which she had had for me on the beach before I knew her, to find latent in her the place in which she had lived earlier still; for that, at any rate, if I knew nothing of it, I could substitute all my memories of our life at Balbec, the sound of the waves rolling up and breaking beneath my window, the shouts of the children. But when I let my eyes glide over the charming pink globe of her cheeks, the gently curving surfaces of which ran up to expire beneath the first foothills of her piled black tresses which ran in undulating mountain chains, thrust out escarped ramparts and moulded the hollows of deep valleys, I could not help saying to myself: "Now at last, after failing at Balbec, I am going to learn the fragrance of the secret rose that blooms in Albertine's cheeks, and, since the cycles through which we are able to make things and people pass in the course of our existence are comparatively few, perhaps I ought now to regard mine as nearing its end when, having made to emerge from its remoteness the flowering face that I had chosen from among all others, I shall have brought it into this new plane in which I shall at last acquire a tactual experience of it with my lips." I told myself this because I believed that there was such a thing as knowledge acquired by the lips; I told myself that I was going to know the taste of this fleshly rose, because I had never stopped to think that man, a creature obviously less rudimentary in structure than the sea-urchin or even the whale, is nevertheless still unprovided with a certain number of essential organs, and notably possesses none that will serve for kissing. The place of this absent organ he supplies with his lips, and thereby arrives perhaps at a slightly more satisfying result than if he were reduced to caressing the beloved with a horny tusk. But a pair of lips, designed to convey to the palate the taste of whatever whets the appetite, must be content, without ever realising their mistake or admitting their disappointment, with roaming over the surface and with coming to a halt at the barrier of the impenetrable but irresistible cheek. Besides, at such moments, at the actual contact between flesh and flesh, the lips, even supposing them to become more expert and better endowed, could taste no better probably the savour which nature prevents their ever actually grasping, for in that desolate zone in which they are unable to find their proper nourishment, they are alone; the sense of sight, then that of smell have long since deserted them. To begin with, as my mouth began gradually to approach the cheeks which my eyes had suggested to it that it should kiss, my eyes, changing their position, saw a different pair of cheeks; the throat, studied at closer range and as though through a magnifying glass shewed in its coarse grain a robustness which modified the character of the face.

Apart from the most recent applications of the art of photography—which set crouching at the foot of a cathedral all the houses which, time and again, when we stood near them, have appeared to us to reach almost to the height of the towers, drill and deploy like a regiment, in file, in open order, in mass, the same famous and familiar structures, bring into actual contact the two columns on the Piazzetta which a moment ago were so far apart, thrust away the adjoining dome of the Salute, and in a pale and toneless background manage to include a whole immense horizon within the span of a bridge, in the embrasure of a window, among the leaves of a tree that stands in the foreground and is portrayed in a more vigorous tone, give successively as setting to the same church the arched walls of all the others—I can think of nothing that can so effectively as a kiss evoke from what we believe to be a thing with one definite aspect, the hundred other things which it may equally well be since each is related to a view of it no less legitimate. In short, just as at Balbec Albertine had often appeared to me different, so now, as if, wildly accelerating the speed of the changes of aspect and changes of colouring which a person presents to us in the course of our various encounters, I had sought to contain them all in the space of a few seconds so as to reproduce experimentally the phenomenon which diversifies the individuality of a fellow creature, and to draw out one from another, like a nest of boxes, all the possibilities that it contains, in this brief passage of my lips towards her cheek it was ten Albertines that I saw; this single girl being like a goddess with several heads, that which I had last seen, if I tried to approach it, gave place to another. At least so long as I had not touched it, that head, I could still see it, a faint perfume reached me from it. But alas—for in this matter of kissing our nostrils and eyes are as ill placed as our lips are shaped—suddenly my eyes ceased to see; next, my nose, crushed by the collision, no longer perceived any fragrance, and, without thereby gaining any clearer idea of the taste of the rose of my desire, I learned, from these unpleasant signs, that at last I was in the act of kissing Albertine's cheek.

Was it because we were enacting—as may be illustrated by the rotation of a solid body—the converse of our scene together at Balbec, because it was I, now, who was lying in bed and she who sat beside me, capable of evading any brutal attack and of dictating her pleasure to me, that she allowed me to take so easily now what she had refused me on the former occasion with so forbidding a frown? (No doubt from that same frown the voluptuous expression which her face assumed now at the approach of my lips differed only by a deviation of its lines immeasurably minute but one in which may be contained all the disparity that there is between the gesture of 'finishing off' a wounded man and that of bringing him relief, between a sublime and a hideous portrait.) Not knowing whether I had to give the credit, and to feel grateful for this change of attitude to some unwitting benefactor who in these last months, in Paris or at Balbec, had been working on my behalf, I supposed that the respective positions in which we were now placed might account for it. It was quite another explanation, however, that Albertine offered me; this, in short: "Oh, well, you see, that time at Balbec I didn't know you properly. For all I knew, you might have meant mischief." This argument left me in perplexity. Albertine was no doubt sincere in advancing it. So difficult is it for a woman to recognise in the movements of her limbs, in the sensations felt by her body in the course of an intimate conversation with a friend, the unknown sin into which she would tremble to think that a stranger was planning her fall.

In any case, whatever the modifications that had occurred at some recent time in her life, which might perhaps have explained why it was that she now readily accorded to my momentary and purely physical desire what at Balbec she had with horror refused to allow to my love, another far more surprising manifested itself in Albertine that same evening as soon as her caresses had procured in me the satisfaction which she could not have failed to notice, which, indeed, I had been afraid might provoke in her the instinctive movement of revulsion and offended modesty which Gilberte had given at a corresponding moment behind the laurel shrubbery in the Champs-Elysées.

The exact opposite happened. Already, when I had first made her lie on my bed and had begun to fondle her, Albertine had assumed an air which I did not remember in her, of docile good will, of an almost childish simplicity. Obliterating every trace of her customary anxieties and interests, the moment preceding pleasure, similar in this respect to the moment after death, had restored to her rejuvenated features what seemed like the innocence of earliest childhood. And no doubt everyone whose special talent is suddenly brought into play becomes modest, devoted, charming; especially if by this talent he knows that he is giving us a great pleasure, he is himself happy in the display of it, anxious to present it to us in as complete a form as possible. But in this new expression on Albertine's face there was more than a mere profession of disinterestedness, conscience, generosity, a sort of conventional and unexpected devotion; and it was farther than to her own childhood, it was to the infancy of the race that she had reverted. Very different from myself who had looked for nothing more than a physical alleviation, which I had finally secured, Albertine seemed to feel that it would indicate a certain coarseness on her part were she to seem to believe that this material pleasure could be unaccompanied by a moral sentiment or was to be regarded as terminating anything. She, who had been in so great a hurry a moment ago, now, presumably because she felt that kisses implied love and that love took precedence of all other duties, said when I reminded her of her dinner:

"Oh, but that doesn't matter in the least; I have plenty of time."

She seemed embarrassed by the idea of getting up and going immediately after what had happened, embarrassed by good manners, just as Françoise when, without feeling thirsty, she had felt herself bound to accept with a seemly gaiety the glass of wine which Jupien offered her, would never have dared to leave him as soon as the last drops were drained, however urgent the call of duty. Albertine—and this was perhaps, with another which the reader will learn in due course, one of the reasons which had made me unconsciously desire her—was one of the incarnations of the little French peasant whose type may be seen in stone at Saint-André-des-Champs. As in Françoise, who presently nevertheless was to become her deadly enemy, I recognised in her a courtesy towards friend and stranger, a sense of decency, of respect for the bedside.

Françoise who, after the death of my aunt, felt obliged to speak only in a plaintive tone, would, in the months that preceded her daughter's marriage, have been quite shocked if, when the young couple walked out together, the girl had not taken her lover's arm. Albertine lying motionless beside me said:

"What nice hair you have; what nice eyes; you are a dear boy."

When, after pointing out to her that it was getting late, I added: "You don't believe me?" she replied, what was perhaps true but could be so only since the minute before and for the next few hours:

"I always believe you."

She spoke to me of myself, my family, my social position. She said: "Oh, I know your parents know some very nice people. You are a friend of Robert Forestier and Suzanne Delage." For the moment these names conveyed absolutely nothing to me. But suddenly I remembered that I had indeed played as a child in the Champs-Elysées with Robert Forestier, whom I had never seen since then. As for Suzanne Delage, she was the great-niece of Mme. Blatin, and I had once been going to a dancing lesson, and had even promised to take a small part in a play that was being acted in her mother's drawing-room. But the fear of being sent into fits of laughter, and of a bleeding nose, had made me decline, so that I had never set eyes on her. I had at the most a vague idea that I had once heard that the Swanns' governess with the feather in her hat had at one time been with the Delages, but perhaps it was only a sister of this governess, or a friend. I protested to Albertine that Robert Forestier and Suzanne Delage occupied a very small place in my life. "That may be; but your mothers are friends, I can place you by that. I often pass Suzanne Delage in the Avenue de Messine, I admire her style." Our mothers were acquainted only in the imagination of Mme. Bontemps, who having heard that I had at one time played with Robert Forestier, to whom, it appeared, I used to recite poetry, had concluded from that that we were bound by family ties. She could never, I gathered, hear my mother's name mentioned without observing: "Oh, yes, she is in the Delage Forestier set," giving my parents a good mark which they had done nothing to deserve.

Apart from this, Albertine's social ideas were fatuous in the extreme. She regarded the Simonnets with a double 'n' as inferior not only to the Simonets with a single 'n' but to everyone in the world. That some one else should bear the same name as yourself without belonging to your family is an excellent reason for despising him. Of course there are exceptions. It may happen that two Simonnets (introduced to one another at one of those gatherings where one feels the need to converse, no matter on what subject, and where moreover one is instinctively well disposed towards strangers, for instance in a funeral procession on its way to the cemetery), finding that they have the same name, will seek with a mutual friendliness though without success to discover a possible connexion. But that is only an exception. Plenty of people are of dubious character, but we either know nothing or care nothing about them. If, however, a similarity of names brings to our door letters addressed to them, or vice versa, we at once feel a mistrust, often justified, as to their moral worth. We are afraid of being confused with them, we forestall the mistake by a grimace of disgust when anyone refers to them in our hearing. When we read our own name, as borne by them, in the newspaper, they seem to have usurped it. The transgressions of other members of the social organism leave us cold. We lay the burden of them more heavily upon our namesakes. The hatred which we bear towards the other Simonnets is all the stronger in that it is not a personal feeling but has been transmitted by heredity. After the second generation we remember only the expression of disgust with which our grandparents used to refer to the other Simonnets, we know nothing of the reason, we should not be surprised to learn that it had begun with a murder. Until, as is not uncommon, the time comes when a male and female Simonnet, who are not related in any way, are joined together in matrimony and so repair the breach.

Not only did Albertine speak to me of Robert Forestier and Suzanne Delage, but spontaneously, with that impulse to confide which the approximation of two human bodies creates, that is to say at first, before it has engendered a special duplicity and reticence in one person towards the other, she told me a story about her own family and one of Andrée's uncles, as to which, at Balbec, she had refused to utter a word; thinking that now she ought not to appear to have any secrets in which I might not share. From this moment, had her dearest friend said anything to her against me, she would have made it her duty to inform me. I insisted upon her going home, and finally she did go, but so ashamed on my account at my discourtesy that she laughed almost as though to apologise for me, as a hostess to whose party you have gone without dressing makes the best of you but is offended nevertheless.

"Are you laughing at me?" I inquired.

"I am not laughing, I am smiling at you," she replied lovingly. "When am I going to see you again?" she went on, as though declining to admit that what had just happened between us, since it is generally the crowning consummation, might not be at least the prelude to a great friendship, a friendship already existing which we should have to discover, to confess, and which alone could account for the surrender we had made of ourselves.

"Since you give me leave, I shall send for you when I can." I dared not let her know that I was subordinating everything else to the chance of seeing Mme. de Stermaria. "It will have to be at short notice, unfortunately," I went on, "I never know beforehand. Would it be possible for me to send round for you in the evenings, when I am free?"

"It will be quite possible in a little while, I am going to have a latch-key of my own. But just at present it can't be done. Anyhow I shall come round to-morrow or next day in the afternoon. You needn't see me if you're busy."

On reaching the door, surprised that I had not anticipated her, she offered me her cheek, feeling that there was no need now for any coarse physical desire to prompt us to kiss one another. The brief relations in which we had just indulged being of the sort to which an absolute intimacy and a heartfelt choice often tend, Albertine had felt it incumbent upon her to improvise and add provisionally to the kisses which we had exchanged on my bed the sentiment of which those kisses would have been the symbol for a knight and his lady such as they might have been conceived in the mind of a gothic minstrel.

When she had left me, this young Picard, who might have been carved on his porch by the image-maker of Saint-André-des-Champs, Françoise brought me a letter which filled me with joy, for it was from Mme. de Stermaria, who accepted my invitation to dinner. From Mme. de Stermaria, that was to say for me not so much from the real Mme. de Stermaria as from her of whom I had been thinking all day before Albertine's arrival. It is the terrible deception of love that it begins by engaging us in play not with a woman of the external world but with a puppet fashioned and kept in our brain, the only form of her moreover that we have always at our disposal, the only one that we shall ever possess, one which the arbitrary power of memory, almost as absolute as that of imagination, may have made as different from the real woman as had been from the real Balbec the Balbec of my dreams; an artificial creation to which by degrees, and to our own hurt, we shall force the real woman into resemblance.

Albertine had made me so late that the play had just finished when I entered Mme. de Villeparisis's drawing-room; and having little desire to be caught in the stream of guests who were pouring out, discussing the great piece of news, the separation, said to be already effected, of the Duc de Guermantes from his wife, I had, until I should have an opportunity of shaking hands with my hostess, taken my seat on an empty sofa in the outer room, when from the other, in which she had no doubt had her chair in the very front row of all, I saw emerging, majestic, ample and tall in a flowing gown of yellow satin upon which stood out in relief huge black poppies, the Duchess herself. The sight of her no longer disturbed me in the least. There had been a day when, laying her hands on my forehead (as was her habit when she was afraid of hurting my feelings) and saying: "You really must stop hanging about trying to meet Mme. de Guermantes. All the neighbours are talking about you. Besides, look how ill your grandmother is, you really have something more serious to think about than waylaying a woman who only laughs at you," in a moment, like a hypnotist who brings one back from the distant country in which one imagined oneself to be, and opens one's eyes for one, or like the doctor who, by recalling one to a sense of duty and reality, cures one of an imaginary disease in which one has been indulging one's fancy, my mother had awakened me from an unduly protracted dream. The rest of the day had been consecrated to a last farewell to this malady which I was renouncing; I had sung, for hours on end and weeping as I sang, the sad words of Schubert's *Adieu*:

> Farewell, strange voices call thee
> Away from me, dear sister of the angels.

And then it had finished. I had given up my morning walks, and with so little difficulty that I thought myself justified in the prophecy (which we shall see was to prove false later on) that I should easily grow accustomed in the course of my life to ceasing to see a woman. And when, shortly afterwards, Françoise had reported to me that Jupien, anxious to enlarge his business, was looking for a shop in the neighbourhood, wishing to find one for him (quite happy, moreover, when strolling along a street which already from my bed I had heard luminously vociferous like a peopled beach, to see behind the raised iron shutters of the dairies the young milk-girls with their white sleeves), I had been able to begin these excursions again. Nor did I feel the slightest constraint; for I was conscious that I was no longer going out with the object of seeing Mme. de Guermantes; much as a married woman who takes endless precautions so long as she has a lover, from the day on which she has broken with him leaves his letters lying about, at the risk of disclosing to her husband an infidelity which ceased to alarm her the moment she ceased to be guilty of it. What troubled me now was the discovery that almost every house sheltered some unhappy person. In one the wife was always in tears because her husband was unfaithful to her. In the next it was the other way about. In another a hardworking mother, beaten black and blue by a drunkard son, was endeavouring to conceal her sufferings from the eyes of the neighbours. Quite half of the human race was in tears. And when I came to know the people who composed it I saw that they were so exasperating that I asked myself whether it might not be the adulterous husband and wife (who were so simply because their lawful happiness had been withheld from them, and shewed themselves charming and faithful to everyone but their respective wife and husband) who were in the right. Presently I ceased to have even the excuse of being useful to Jupien for continuing my morning wanderings. For we learned that the cabinet-maker in our courtyard, whose workrooms were separated from Jupien's shop only by the flimsiest of partitions, was shortly to be 'given notice' by the Duke's agent because his hammering made too much noise. Jupien could have hoped for nothing better; the workrooms had a basement for storing timber, which communicated with our cellars. He could keep his coal in this, he could knock down the partition, and would then have a huge shop all in one room. But even without the amusement of house-hunting on his behalf I had continued to go out every day before luncheon, just as Jupien himself, finding the rent that M. de Guermantes was asking him exorbitant, was allowing the premises to be inspected in the hope that, discouraged by his failure to find a tenant, the Duke would resign himself to accepting a lower offer. Françoise, noticing that, even at an hour when no prospective tenant was likely to call, the porter left the door of the empty shop on the latch, scented a trap laid by him to entice the young woman who was engaged to the Guermantes footman (they would find a lovers' retreat there) and to catch them red-handed.

However that might be, and for all that I had no longer to find Jupien a new shop, I still went out before luncheon. Often, on these excursions, I met M. de Norpois. It would happen that, conversing as he walked with a colleague, he cast at me a glance which after making a thorough scrutiny of my person returned to his companion without his having smiled at me or given me any more sign of recognition than if he had never set eyes on me before. For, with these eminent diplomats, looking at you in a certain way is intended to let you know not that they have seen you but that they have not seen you and that they have some serious question to discuss with the colleague who is accompanying them. A tall woman whom I frequently encountered near the house was less discreet with me. For in spite of the fact that I did not know her, she would turn round to look at me, would wait for me, unavailingly, before shop windows, smile at me as though she were going to kiss me, make gestures indicative of a complete surrender. She resumed an icy coldness towards me if anyone appeared whom she knew. For a long time now in these morning walks, thinking only of what I had to do, were it but the most trivial purchase of a newspaper, I had chosen the shortest way, with no regret were it outside the ordinary course which the Duchess followed in her walks, and if on the other hand it lay along that course, without either compunction or concealment, because it no longer appeared to me the forbidden way on which I should snatch from an ungrateful woman the favour of setting eyes on her against her will. But it had never occurred to me that my recovery, when it restored me to a normal attitude towards Mme. de Guermantes, would have a corresponding effect on her, and so render possible a friendliness, even a friendship in which I no longer felt any interest. Until then, the efforts of the entire world banded together to bring me into touch with her would have been powerless to counteract the evil spell that is cast by an ill-starred love. Fairies more powerful than mankind have decreed that in such cases nothing can avail us until the day on which we have uttered sincerely and from our hearts the formula: "I am no longer in love." I had been vexed with Saint-Loup for not having taken me to see his aunt. But he was no more capable than anyone else of breaking an enchantment. So long as I was in love with Mme. de Guermantes, the marks of politeness that I received from others, their compliments actually distressed me, not only because they did not come from her but because she would never hear of them. And yet even if she had known of them it would not have been of the slightest use to me. Indeed, among the lesser auxiliaries to success in love, an absence, the declining of an invitation to dinner, an unintentional, unconscious harshness are of more service than all the cosmetics and fine clothes in the world. There would be plenty of social success, were people taught upon these lines the art of succeeding.

As she swept through the room in which I was sitting, her mind filled with thoughts of friends whom I did not know and whom she would perhaps be meeting presently at some other party, Mme. de Guermantes caught sight of me on my sofa, genuinely indifferent and seeking only to be polite whereas while I was in love I had tried so desperately, without ever succeeding, to assume an air of indifference; she swerved aside, came towards me and, reproducing the smile she had worn that evening at the Opéra-Comique, which the unpleasant feeling of being cared for by some one for whom she did not care was no longer there to obliterate: "No, don't move; you don't mind if I sit down beside you for a moment?" she asked, gracefully gathering in her immense skirt which otherwise would have covered the entire sofa.

Of less stature than she, who was further expanded by the volume of her gown, I was almost brushed by her exquisite bare arm round which a faint, innumerable down rose in perpetual smoke like a golden mist, and by the fringe of her fair tresses which wafted their fragrance over me. Having barely room to sit down, she could not turn easily to face me, and so, obliged to look straight before her rather than in my direction, assumed the sort of dreamy, sweet expression one sees in a portrait.

"Have you any news of Robert?" she inquired.

At that moment Mme. de Villeparisis entered the room.

"Well, Sir, you arrive at a fine time, when we do see you here for once in a way!" And noticing that I was talking to her niece, concluding, perhaps, that we were more intimate than she had supposed: "But don't let me interrupt your conversation with Oriane," she went on, and (for these good offices as pander are part of the duties of the perfect hostess): "You wouldn't care to dine with her here on Thursday?"

It was the day on which I was to entertain Mme. de Stermaria, so I declined.

"Saturday, then?"

As my mother was returning on Saturday or Sunday, it would never do for me not to stay at home every evening to dine with her; I therefore declined this invitation also.

"Ah, you're not an easy person to get hold of."

"Why do you never come to see me?" inquired Mme. de Guermantes when Mme. de Villeparisis had left us to go and congratulate the performers and present the leading lady with a bunch of roses upon which the hand that offered it conferred all its value, for it had cost no more than twenty francs. (This, incidentally, was as high as she ever went when an artist had performed only once. Those who gave their services at all her afternoons and evenings throughout the season received roses painted by the Marquise.)

"It's such a bore that we never see each other except in other people's houses. Since you won't meet me at dinner at my aunt's, why not come and dine with me?" Various people who had stayed to the last possible moment, upon one pretext or another, but were at length preparing to leave, seeing that the Duchess had sat down to talk to a young man on a seat so narrow as just to contain them both, thought that they must have been misinformed, that it was the Duchess, and not the Duke, who was seeking a separation, and on my account. Whereupon they hastened to spread abroad this intelligence. I had better grounds than anyone to be aware of its falsehood. But I was myself surprised that at one of those difficult periods in which a separation that is not yet completed is beginning to take effect, the Duchess, instead of withdrawing from society should go out of her way to invite a person whom she knew so slightly. The suspicion crossed my mind that it had been the Duke alone who had been opposed to her having me in the house, and that now that he was leaving her she saw no further obstacle to her surrounding herself with the people that she liked.

A minute earlier I should have been stupefied had anyone told me that Mme. de Guermantes was going to ask me to call on her, let alone to dine with her. I might be perfectly aware that the Guermantes drawing-room could not furnish those particular refinements which I had extracted from the name of its occupants, the fact that it had been forbidden ground to me, by obliging me to give it the same kind of existence that we give to the drawing-rooms of which we have read the description in a novel, or seen the image in a dream, made me, even when I was certain that it was just like any other, imagine it as quite different. Between myself and it was the barrier at which reality ends. To dine with the Guermantes was like travelling to a place I had long wished to see, making a desire emerge from my brain and take shape before my eyes, forming acquaintance with a dream. At the most, I might have supposed that it would be one of those dinners to which one's hosts invite one with: "Do come; there'll be *absolutely* nobody but ourselves," pretending to attribute to the pariah the alarm which they themselves feel at the thought of his mixing with their other friends, seeking indeed to convert into an enviable privilege, reserved for their intimates alone, the quarantine of the outsider, hopelessly uncouth, whom they are befriending. I felt on the contrary that Mme. de Guermantes was anxious for me to enjoy the most delightful society that she had to offer me when she went on, projecting as she spoke before my eyes as it were the violet-hued loveliness of a visit to Fabrice's aunt with the miracle of an introduction to Count Mosca:

"On Friday, now, couldn't you? There are just a few people coming; the Princesse de Parme, who is charming, not that I'd ask you to meet anyone who wasn't nice."

Discarded in the intermediate social grades which are engaged in a perpetual upward movement, the family still plays an important part in certain stationary grades, such as the lower middle class and the semi-royal aristocracy, which latter cannot seek to raise itself since above it, from its own special point of view, there exists nothing higher. The friendship shewn me by her 'aunt Villeparisis' and Robert had perhaps made me, for Mme. de Guermantes and her friends, living always upon themselves and in the same little circle, the object of a curious interest of which I had no suspicion.

She had of those two relatives a familiar, everyday, homely knowledge, of a sort, utterly different from what we imagine, in which if we happen to be comprised in it, so far from our actions being at once ejected, like the grain of dust from the eye or the drop of water from the windpipe, they are capable of remaining engraved, and will still be related and discussed years after we ourselves have forgotten them, in the palace in which we are astonished to find them preserved, like a letter in our own handwriting among a priceless collection of autographs.

People who are merely fashionable may set a guard upon doors which are too freely invalided. But the Guermantes door was not that. Hardly ever did a stranger have occasion to pass by it. If, for once in a way, the Duchess had one pointed out to her, she never dreamed of troubling herself about the social increment that he would bring, since this was a thing that she conferred and could not receive. She thought only of his real merits. Both Mme. de Villeparisis and Saint-Loup had testified to mine. Doubtless she might not have believed them if she had not at the same time observed that they could never manage to secure me when they wanted me, and therefore that I attached no importance to worldly things, which seemed to the Duchess a sign that the stranger was to be numbered among what she called 'nice people.'

It was worth seeing, when one spoke to her of women for whom she did not care, how her face changed as soon as one named, in connexion with one of these, let us say, her sister-in-law. "Oh, she is charming!" the Duchess would exclaim in a judicious, confident tone. The only reason that she gave was that this lady had declined to be introduced to the Marquise de Chaussegros and the Princesse de Silistrie. She did not add that the lady had declined also an introduction to herself, the Duchesse de Guermantes. This had, nevertheless, been the case, and ever since the mind of the Duchess had been at work trying to unravel the motives of a woman who was so hard to know, she was dying to be invited to call on her. People in society are so accustomed to be sought after that the person who shuns them seems to them a phoenix and at once monopolises their attention.

Was the true motive in the mind of Mme. de Guermantes for thus inviting me (now that I was no longer in love with her) that I did not run after her relatives, although apparently run after myself by them? I cannot say. In any case, having made up her mind to invite me, she was anxious to do me the honours of the best company at her disposal and to keep away those of her friends whose presence might have dissuaded me from coming again, those whom she knew to be boring. I had not known to what to attribute her change of direction, when I had seen her deviate from her stellar path, come to sit down beside me and had heard her invite me to dinner, the effect of causes unknown for want of a special sense to enlighten us in this respect. We picture to ourselves the people who know us but slightly—such as, in my case, the Duchesse de Guermantes—as thinking of us only at the rare moments at which they set eyes on us. As a matter of fact this ideal oblivion in which we picture them as holding us is a purely arbitrary conception on our part. So that while, in our solitary silence, like that of a cloudless night, we imagine the various queens of society pursuing their course in the heavens at an infinite distance, we cannot help an involuntary start of dismay or pleasure if there falls upon us from that starry height, like a meteorite engraved with our name which we supposed to be unknown on Venus or Cassiopeia, an invitation to dinner or a piece of malicious gossip.

Perhaps now and then when, following the example of the Persian princes who, according to the Book of Esther, made their scribes read out to them the registers in which were enrolled the names of those of their subjects who had shewn zeal in their service, Mme. de Guermantes consulted her list of the well-disposed, she had said to herself, on coming to my name: "A man we must ask to dine some day." But other thoughts had distracted her

> (Beset by surging cares, a Prince's mind
> Towards fresh matters ever is inclined)

until the moment when she had caught sight of me sitting alone like Mordecai at the palace gate; and, the sight of me having refreshed her memory, sought, like Ahasuerus, to lavish her gifts upon me.

I must at the same time add that a surprise of a totally different sort was to follow that which I had felt on hearing Mme. de Guermantes ask me to dine with her. Since I had decided that it would shew greater modesty, on my part, and gratitude also not to conceal this initial surprise, but rather to exaggerate my expression of the delight that it gave me, Mme. de Guermantes, who was getting ready to go on to another, final party, had said to me, almost as a justification and for fear of my not being quite certain who she was, since I appeared so astonished at being invited to dine with her: "You know I'm the aunt of Robert de Saint-Loup, who is such a friend of yours; besides we have met before." In replying that I was aware of this I added that I knew also M. de Charlus, "who had been very good to me at Balbec and in Paris." Mme. de Guermantes appeared dumbfoundered, and her eyes seemed to turn, as though for a verification of this statement, to some page, already filled and turned, of her internal register of events. "What, so you know Palamède, do you?" This name assumed on the lips of Mme. de Guermantes a great charm, due to the instinctive simplicity with which she spoke of a man who was socially so brilliant a figure, but for her was no more than her brother-in-law and the cousin with whom she had grown up. And on the confused greyness which the life of the Duchesse de Guermantes was for me this name, Palamède, shed as it were the radiance of long summer days on which she had played with him as a girl, at Guermantes, in the garden. Moreover, in this long outgrown period in their lives, Oriane de Guermantes and her cousin Palamède had been very different from what they had since become; M. de Charlus in particular, entirely absorbed in the artistic pursuits from which he had so effectively restrained himself in later life that I was stupefied to learn that it was he who had painted the huge fan with black and yellow irises which the Duchess was at this moment unfurling. She could also have shewn me a little sonatina which he had once composed for her. I was completely unaware that the Baron possessed all these talents, of which he never spoke. Let me remark in passing that M. de Charlus did not at all relish being called 'Palamède' by his family. That the form 'Mémé' might not please him one could easily understand. These stupid abbreviations are a sign of the utter inability of the aristocracy to appreciate its own poetic beauty (in Jewry, too, we may see the same defect, since a nephew of Lady Israels, whose name was Moses, was commonly known as 'Momo') concurrently with its anxiety not to appear to attach any importance to what is aristocratic. Now M. de Charlus had, in this connexion, a greater wealth of poetic imagination and a more blatant pride. But the reason for his distaste for 'Mémé' could not be this, since it extended also to the fine name Palamède. The truth was that, considering, knowing himself to come of a princely stock, he would have liked his brother and sister-in-law to refer to him as 'Charlus,' just as Queen Marie-Amélie and Duc d'Orléans might have spoken of their sons and grandsons, brothers and nephews as 'Joinville, Nemours, Chartres, Paris.'

"What a humbug Mémé is!" she exclaimed. "We talked to him about you for hours; he told us that he would be delighted to make your acquaintance, just as if he had never set eyes on you. You must admit he's odd, and—though it's not very nice of me to say such a thing about a brother-in-law I'm devoted to, and really do admire immensely—a trifle mad at times."

I was struck by the application of this last epithet to M. de Charlus, and said to myself that this half-madness might perhaps account for certain things, such as his having appeared so delighted by his own proposal that I should ask Bloch to castigate his mother. I decided that, by reason not only of the things he said but of the way in which he said them, M. de Charlus must be a little mad. The first time that one listens to a barrister or an actor, one is surprised by his tone, so different from the conversational. But, observing that everyone else seems to find this quite natural, one says nothing about it to other people, one says nothing in fact to oneself, one is content with appreciating the degree of talent shewn. At the most, one may think, of an actor at the Théâtre-Français: "Why, instead of letting his raised arm fall naturally, did he make it drop in a series of little jerks broken by pauses for at least ten minutes?" or of a Labori: "Why, whenever he opened his mouth, did he utter those tragic, unexpected sounds to express the simplest things?" But as everybody admits these actions to be necessary and obvious one is not shocked by them. So, upon thinking it over, one said to oneself that M. de Charlus spoke of himself with undue emphasis in a tone which was not in the least that of ordinary speech. It seemed as though one might have at any moment interrupted him with: "But why do you shout so? Why are you so offensive?" only everyone seemed to have tacitly agreed that it was all right. And one took one's place in the circle which applauded his outbursts. But certainly, at certain moments, a stranger might have thought that he was listening to the ravings of a maniac.

"But are you sure you're not thinking of some one else? Do you really mean my brother-in-law Palamède?" went on the Duchess, a trace of impertinence grafted upon her natural simplicity.

I replied that I was absolutely sure, and that M. de Charlus must have failed to catch my name.

"Oh well! I shall leave you now," said Mme. de Guermantes, as though she regretted the parting. "I must look in for a moment at the Princesse de Ligne's. You aren't going on there? No? You don't care for parties? You're very wise, they are too boring for words. If only I hadn't got to go. But she's my cousin; it wouldn't be polite. I am sorry, selfishly, for my own sake, because I could have taken you there, and brought you back afterwards, too. So I shall say good-bye now, and look forward to Friday."

That M. de Charlus should have blushed to be seen with me by M. d'Argencourt was all very well. But that to his own sister-in-law, who had so high an opinion of him besides, he should deny all knowledge of me, knowledge which was perfectly natural seeing that I was a friend of both his aunt and his nephew, was a thing that I could not understand.

I shall end my account of this incident with the remark that from one point of view there was in Mme. de Guermantes a true greatness which consisted in her entirely obliterating from her memory what other people would have only partially forgotten. Had she never seen me waylaying her, following her, tracking her down as she took her morning walks, had she never responded to my daily salute with an angry impatience, had she never refused Saint-Loup when he begged her to invite me to her house, she could not have greeted me now in a nobler or more gracious manner. Not only did she waste no time in retrospective explanations, in hints, allusions or ambiguous smiles, not only was there in her present affability, without any harking back to the past, without any reticence, something as proudly rectilinear as her majestic stature, but the resentment which she might have felt against anyone in the past was so entirely reduced to ashes, the ashes were themselves cast so utterly from her memory, or at least from her manner, that on studying her face whenever she had occasion to treat with the most exquisite simplification what in so many other people would have been a pretext for reviving stale antipathies and recriminations one had the impression of an intense purity of mind.

But if I was surprised by the modification that had occurred in her opinion of me, how much more did it surprise me to find a similar but ever so much greater change in my feeling for her. Had there not been a time during which I could regain life and strength only if—always building new castles in the air!—I had found some one who would obtain for me an invitation to her house and, after this initial boon, would procure many others for my increasingly exacting heart? It was the impossibility of finding any avenue there that had made me leave Paris for Doncières to visit Robert de Saint-Loup. And now it was indeed by the consequence of a letter from him that I was agitated, but on account this time of Mme. de Stermaria, not of Mme. de Guermantes.

Let me add further, to conclude my account of this party, that there occurred at it an incident, contradicted a few days later, which continued to puzzle me, interrupted for some time my friendship with Bloch, and constitutes in itself one of those curious paradoxes the explanation of which will be found in the next part of this work. At this party at Mme. de Villeparisis's, Bloch kept on boasting to me about the friendly attentions shewn him by M. de Charlus, who, when he passed him in the street, looked him straight in the face as though he recognised him, was anxious to know him personally, knew quite well who he was. I smiled at first, Bloch having expressed so vehemently at Balbec his contempt for the said M. de Charlus. And I supposed merely that Bloch, like his father in the case of Bergotte, knew the Baron 'without actually knowing him,' and that what he took for a friendly glance was due to absent-mindedness. But finally Bloch became so precise and appeared so confident that on two or three occasions M. de Charlus had wished to address him that, remembering that I had spoken of my friend to the Baron, who had, as we walked away together from this very house, as it happened, asked me various questions about him, I came to the conclusion that Bloch was not lying, that M. de Charlus had heard his name, realised that he was my friend, and so forth. And so, a little later, at the theatre one evening, I asked M. de Charlus if I might introduce Bloch to him, and, on his assenting, went in search of my friend. But as soon as M. de Charlus caught sight of him an expression of astonishment, instantly repressed, appeared on his face, where it gave way to a blazing fury. Not only did he not offer Bloch his hand but whenever Bloch spoke to him he replied in the most insolent manner, in an angry and wounding tone. So that Bloch, who, according to his version, had received nothing until then from the Baron but smiles, assumed that I had not indeed commended but disparaged him in the short speech in which, knowing M. de Charlus's liking for formal procedure, I had told him about my friend before bringing him up to be introduced. Bloch left us, his spirit broken, like a man who has been trying to mount a horse which is always ready to take the bit in its teeth, or to swim against waves which continually dash him back on the shingle, and did not speak to me again for six months.

The days that preceded my dinner with Mme. de Stermaria were for me by no means delightful, in fact it was all I could do to live through them. For as a general rule, the shorter the interval is that separates us from our planned objective, the longer it seems to us, because we apply to it a more minute scale of measurement, or simply because it occurs to us to measure it at all. The Papacy, we are told, reckons by centuries, and indeed may not think perhaps of reckoning time at all, since its goal is in eternity. Mine was no more than three days off; I counted by seconds, I gave myself up to those imaginings which are the first movements of caresses, of caresses which it maddens us not to be able to make the woman herself reciprocate and complete—those identical caresses, to the exclusion of all others. And, as a matter of fact, it is true that, generally speaking, the difficulty of attaining to the object of a desire enhances that desire (the difficulty, not the impossibility, for that suppresses it altogether), yet in the case of a desire that is wholly physical the certainty that it will be realised, at a fixed and not distant point in time, is scarcely less exciting than uncertainty; almost as much as an anxious doubt, the absence of doubt makes intolerable the period of waiting for the pleasure that is bound to come, because it makes of that suspense an innumerably rehearsed accomplishment and by the frequency of our proleptic representations divides time into sections as minute as could be carved by agony. What I required was to possess Mme. de Stermaria, for during the last few days, with an incessant activity, my desires had been preparing this pleasure, in my imagination, and this pleasure alone, for any other kind (pleasure, that is, taken with another woman) would not have been ready, pleasure being but the realisation of a previous wish, and of one which is not always the same, but changes according to the endless combinations of one's fancies, the accidents of one's memory, the state of one's temperament, the variability of one's desires, the most recently granted of which lie dormant until the disappointment of their satisfaction has been to some extent forgotten; I should not have been prepared, I had already turned from the main road of general desires and had ventured along the bridle-path of a particular desire; I should have had—in order to wish for a different assignation—to retrace my steps too far before rejoining the main road and taking another path. To take possession of Mme. de Stermaria on the island in the Bois de Boulogne where I had asked her to dine with me, this was the pleasure that I imagined to myself afresh every moment. It would have automatically perished if I had dined on that island without Mme. de Stermaria; but perhaps as greatly diminished had I dined, even with her, somewhere else. Besides, the attitudes in which one pictures a pleasure to oneself exist previously to the woman, to the type of woman required to give one that pleasure. They dictate the pleasure, and the place as well, and on that account bring to the fore alternatively, in our capricious fancy, this or that woman, this or that scene, this or that room, which in other weeks we should have dismissed with contempt. Child of the attitude that produced her, one woman will not appeal to us without the large bed in which we find peace by her side, while others, to be caressed with a more secret intention, require leaves blown by the wind, water rippling in the night, are as frail and fleeting as they.

No doubt in the past, long before I received Saint-Loup's letter and when there was as yet no question of Mme. de Stermaria, the island in the Bois had seemed to me to be specially designed for pleasure, because I had found myself going there to taste the bitterness of having no pleasure to enjoy in its shelter. It is to the shores of the lake from which one goes to that island, and along which, in the last weeks of summer, those ladies of Paris who have not yet left for the country take the air, that, not knowing where to look for her, or if indeed she has not already left Paris, one wanders in the hope of seeing the girl go by with whom one fell in love at the last ball of the season, whom one will not have a chance of meeting again in any drawing-room until the following spring. Feeling it to be at least the eve, if not the morrow, of the beloved's departure, one follows along the brink of the shivering water those attractive paths by which already a first red leaf is blooming like a last rose, one scans that horizon where, by a device the opposite of that employed in those panoramas beneath whose domed roofs the wax figures in the foreground impart to the painted canvas beyond them the illusory appearance of depth and mass, our eyes, passing without any transition from the cultivated park to the natural heights of Meudon and the Mont Valérien, do not know where to set the boundary, and make the natural country trespass upon the handiwork of the gardener, of which they project far beyond its own limits the artificial charm; like those rare birds reared in the open in a botanical garden which every day in the liberty of their winged excursions sally forth to strike, among the surrounding woods, an exotic note. Between the last festivity of summer and one's winter exile, one ranges anxiously that ro-

mantic world of chance encounters and lover's melancholy, and one would
be no more surprised to learn that it was situated outside the mapped
universe than if, at Versailles, looking down from the terrace, an observatory round which the clouds are massed against a blue sky in the manner
of Van der Meulen, after having thus risen above the bounds of nature, one
were informed that, there where nature begins again at the end of the great
canal, the villages which one just could not make out, on a horizon as
dazzling as the sea, were called Fleurus or Nimègue.

And then, the last carriage having rolled by, when one feels with a throb
of pain that she will not come now, one goes to dine on the island; above
the shivering poplars which suggest endless mysteries of evening though
without response, a pink cloud paints a last touch of life in the tranquil
sky. A few drops of rain fall without noise on the water, ancient but still
in its divine infancy coloured always by the weather and continually forgetting the reflexions of clouds and flowers. And after the geraniums have
vainly striven, by intensifying the brilliance of their scarlet, to resist the
gathering darkness, a mist rises to envelop the now slumbering island; one
walks in the moist dimness along the water's edge, where at the most the
silent passage of a swan startles one like, in a bed, at night, the eyes, for
a moment wide open, and the swift smile of a child whom one did not suppose to be awake. Then one would like to have with one a loving companion, all the more as one feels oneself to be alone and can imagine oneself
to be far away from the world.

But to this island, where even in summer there was often a mist, how
much more gladly would I have brought Mme. de Stermaria now that the
cold season, the back end of autumn had come. If the weather that had prevailed since Sunday had not by itself rendered grey and maritime the
scenes in which my imagination was living—as other seasons made them
balmy, luminous, Italian—the hope of, in a few days' time, making Mme.
de Stermaria mine would have been quite enough to raise, twenty times in
an hour, a curtain of mist in my monotonously lovesick imagination. In
any event the mist, which since yesterday had risen even in Paris, not
only made me think incessantly of the native place of the young woman
whom I had invited to dine with me, but, since it was probable that, far
more thickly than in the streets of the town, it must after sunset be invading the Bois, especially the shores of the lake, I thought that it would make
the Swans' Island, for me, something like that Breton island the marine
and misty atmosphere of which had always enwrapped in my mind like
a garment the pale outline of Mme. de Stermaria. Of course when we are
young, at the age I had reached at the period of my walks along the
Méséglise way, our desires, our faith bestow on a woman's clothing an
individual personality, an ultimate quintessence. We pursue reality. But
by dint of allowing it to escape we end by noticing that, after all those
vain endeavours which have led to nothing, something solid subsists, which
is what we have been seeking. We begin to separate, to recognise what we
love, we try to procure it for ourselves, be it only by a stratagem. Then, in
the absence of our vanished faith, costume fills the gap, by means of a
deliberate illusion. I knew quite well that within half an hour of home I

should not find myself in Brittany. But in walking arm in arm with Mme. de Stermaria in the dusk of the island, by the water's edge, I should be acting like other men who, unable to penetrate the walls of a convent, do at least, before enjoying a woman, clothe her in the habit of a nun.

I could even look forward to hearing, as I sat with the lady, the lapping of waves, for, on the day before our dinner, a storm broke over Paris. I was beginning to shave myself before going to the island to engage the room (albeit at this time of year the island was empty and the restaurant deserted) and order the food for our dinner next day when Françoise came in to tell me that Albertine had called. I made her come in at once, indifferent to her finding me disfigured by a bristling chin, her for whom at Balbec I had never felt smart enough and who had cost me then as much agitation and distress as Mme. de Stermaria was costing me now. The latter, I was determined, must go away with the best possible impression from our evening together. Accordingly I asked Albertine to come with me there and then to the island to order the food. She to whom one gives everything is so quickly replaced by another that one is surprised to find oneself giving all that one has, afresh, at every moment, without any hope of future reward. At my suggestion the smiling rosy face beneath Albertine's flat cap, which came down very low, to her eyebrows, seemed to hesitate. She had probably other plans; if so she sacrificed them willingly, to my great satisfaction, for I attached the utmost importance to my having with me a young housewife who would know a great deal more than myself about ordering dinner.

It is quite true that she had represented something utterly different for me at Balbec. But our intimacy, even when we do not consider it close enough at the time, with a woman with whom we are in love creates between her and us, in spite of the shortcomings that pain us while our love lasts, social ties which outlast our love and even the memory of our love. Then, in her who is nothing more for us than a means of approach, an avenue towards others, we are just as astonished and amused to learn from our memory what her name meant originally to that other creature which we then were as if, after giving a cabman an address in the Boulevard des Capucines or the Rue du Bac, thinking only of the person whom we are going to see there, we remind ourself that the names were once those of, respectively, the Capuchin nuns whose convent stood on the site and the ferry across the Seine.

At the same time, my Balbec desires had so generously ripened Albertine's body, had gathered and stored in it savours so fresh and sweet that, as we drove through the Bois, while the wind like a careful gardener shook the trees, brought down the fruit, swept up the fallen leaves, I said to myself that had there been any risk of Saint-Loup's being mistaken, or of my having misunderstood his letter, so that my dinner with Mme. de Stermaria might lead to no satisfactory result, I should have made an appointment for the same evening, later on, with Albertine, so as to forget, for a purely voluptuous hour, as I held in my arms a body of which my curiosity had long since computed, weighed up all the possible charms in which now it abounded, the emotions and perhaps the regrets of this first phase of love for Mme. de Stermaria. And certainly if I could have supposed that Mme. de Stermaria would not grant me any of her favours at our first meeting, I should have formed a slightly depressing picture of my evening with her. I knew too well from experience how the two stages which occur in us in the first phase of our love for a woman whom we have desired without knowing her, loving in her rather the particular kind of existence in which she is steeped than her still unfamiliar self—how distorted is the reflexion of those two stages in the world of facts, that is to say not in ourselves any longer but in our meetings with her. We have, without ever having talked to her, hesitated, tempted as we were by the poetic charm which she represented for us. Shall it be this woman or another? And lo, our dreams become fixed round about her, cease to have any separate existence from her. The first meeting with her which will shortly follow should reflect this dawning love. Nothing of the sort. As if it were necessary that our material life should have its first period also, in love with her already, we talk to her in the most trivial fashion: "I asked you to dine on this island because I thought the surroundings would amuse you. I've nothing particular to say to you, don't you know. But it's rather damp, I'm afraid, and you may find it cold—" "Oh, no, not at all!" "You just say that out of politeness. Very well, Madame, I shall allow you to battle against the cold for another quarter of an hour, as I don't want to bother you, but in fifteen minutes I shall carry you off by force. I don't want to have you catching a chill." And without another word said we take her home, remembering nothing about her, at the most a certain look in her eyes, but thinking only of seeing her again. Well, at our second meeting (when we do not find even that look, our sole memory of her, but nevertheless have been thinking only of seeing her again), the first stage is passed. Nothing has happened in the interval. And yet, instead of talking about the comfort or want of comfort of the restaurant, we say, without our words appearing to surprise the new person, who seems to us positively plain but to whom we should like to think that people were talking about us at every moment in her life: "We are going to have our work cut out to overcome all the obstacles in our way. Do you think we shall be successful? Do you suppose that we can triumph over our enemies—live happily ever afterwards, and all that sort of thing?" But these conversational openings, trivial to begin with, then hinting at love, would not be required; I could trust Saint-Loup's letter for that. Mme. de Stermaria would yield herself to me from the first, I should have no need therefore to engage Albertine to come to me, as a makeshift, later in the evening. It would be superfluous; Robert never exaggerated, and his letter was explicit.

Albertine spoke hardly at all, conscious that my thoughts were elsewhere. We went a little way on foot into the greenish, almost submarine grotto of a dense mass of trees, on the domed tops of which we heard the wind sweep and the rain pelt. I trod underfoot dead leaves which, like shells, were trampled into the soil, and poked with my stick at fallen chestnuts prickly as sea-urchins.

On the boughs the last clinging leaves, shaken by the wind, followed it only as far as their stems would allow, but sometimes these broke, and they fell to the ground, along which they coursed to overtake it. I thought with joy how much more remote still, if this weather lasted, the island would be on the morrow—and in any case quite deserted. We returned to our carriage and, as the storm had passed off, Albertine asked me to take her on to Saint-Cloud. As on the ground the drifting leaves so up above the clouds were chasing the wind. And a stream of migrant evenings, of which a sort of conic section cut through the sky made visible the successive layers, pink, blue and green, were gathered in readiness for departure to warmer climes. To obtain a closer view of a marble goddess who had been carved in the act of leaping from her pedestal and, alone in a great wood which seemed to be consecrated to her, filled it with the mythological terror, half animal, half divine, of her frenzied bounding, Albertine climbed a grassy slope while I waited for her in the road. She herself, seen thus from below, no longer coarse and plump as, a few days earlier, on my bed when the grain of her throat became apparent in the lens of my eye as it approached her person, but chiselled and delicate, seemed a little statue on which our happy hours together at Balbec had left their patina. When I found myself alone again at home, and remembered that I had taken a drive that afternoon with Albertine, that I was to dine in two days' time with Mme. de Guermantes and that I had to answer a letter from Gilberte, three women each of whom I had once loved, I said to myself that our social existence is, like an artist's studio, filled with abandoned sketches in which we have fancied for a moment that we could set down in permanent form our need of a great love, but it did not occur to me that sometimes, if the sketch be not too old, it may happen that we return to it and make of it a work wholly different, and possibly more important than what we had originally planned.

The next day was cold and fine; winter was in the air—indeed the season was so far advanced that it had seemed miraculous that we should find in the already pillaged Bois a few domes of gilded green. When I awoke I saw, as from the window of the barracks at Doncières, a uniform, dead white mist which hung gaily in the sunlight, consistent and sweet as a web of spun sugar. Then the sun withdrew, and the mist thickened still further in the afternoon. Night fell early, I made ready for dinner, but it was still too soon to start; I decided to send a carriage for Mme. de Stermaria. I did not like to go for her in it myself, not wishing to force my company on her, but I gave the driver a note for her in which I asked whether she would mind my coming to call for her. While I waited for her answer I lay down on my bed, shut my eyes for a moment, then opened them again. Over the top of the curtains there was nothing now but a thin strip of daylight which grew steadily fainter. I recognised that wasted hour, the large ante-room of pleasure, the dark, delicious emptiness of which I had learned at Balbec to know and to enjoy when, alone in my room as I was now, while all the rest were at dinner, I saw without regret the daylight fade from above my curtains, knowing that, presently, after a night of arctic brevity, it was to be resuscitated in a more dazzling brightness in the lighted rooms of Rivebelle. I sprang from my bed, tied my black necktie, passed a brush over my hair, final gestures of a belated tidying carried out at Balbec with my mind not on myself but on the women whom I should see at Rivebelle, while I smiled at them in anticipation in the mirror that stood across a corner of my room, gestures which, on that account, had continued to herald a form of entertainment in which music and lights would be mingled. Like magic signs they summoned, nay rather presented this entertainment already; thanks to them I had, of its intoxicating frivolous charm, as complete an enjoyment as I had had at Combray, in the month of July, when I heard the hammer-blows ring on the packing cases and enjoyed, in the coolness of my darkened room, a sense of warmth and sunshine.

Also, it was no longer exactly Mme. de Stermaria that I should have wished most to see. Forced now to spend my evening with her, I should have preferred, as it was almost the last before the return of my parents, that it should remain free and myself try instead to find some of the women from Rivebelle. I gave my hands one more final wash and, my sense of pleasure keeping me on the move, dried them as I walked through the shuttered dining-room. It appeared to have a door open on to the lighted hall, but what I had taken for the bright chink of the door, which as a matter of fact was closed, was only the gleaming reflexion of my towel in a mirror that had been laid against the wall in readiness to be fixed in its place before Mamma's return. I thought of all the other illusions of the sort which I had discovered in different parts of the house, and which were not optical only, for when we first came there I had supposed that our next-door neighbour kept a dog on account of the continuous, almost human yapping which came from a certain pipe in the kitchen whenever the tap was turned on. And the door on to the outer landing never closed by itself, very gently, caught by a draught on the staircase, without rendering those broken, voluptuous, whimpering passages which sound over the chant of the pilgrims towards the end of Overture to *Tannhäuser*. I had, moreover, just as I had put my towel back on its rail, an opportunity of hearing a fresh rendering of this brilliant symphonic fragment, for at a peal of the bell I hurried out to open the door to the driver who had come with Mme. de Stermaria's answer. I thought that his message would be: "The lady is downstairs," or "The lady is waiting." But he had a letter in his hand. I hesitated for a moment before looking to see what Mme. de Stermaria had written, who, while she held the pen in her hand, might have been anything but was now, detached from herself, an engine of fate, pursuing a course alone, which she was utterly powerless to alter. I asked the driver to wait downstairs for a moment, although he was cursing the fog. As soon as he had gone I opened the envelope. On her card, inscribed *Vicomtesse Alix de Stermaria*, my guest had written: "Am so sorry—am unfortunately prevented from dining with you this evening on the island in the Bois. Had been so looking forward to it. Will write you a proper letter from Stermaria. Very sorry. Kindest regards." I stood motionless, stunned by the shock that I had received. At my feet lay the card and envelope, fallen like the spent cartridge from a gun when the shot has been fired. I picked them up, tried to analyse her message. "She says that she cannot dine with me on the island in the Bois. One might gather from that that she would dine with me somewhere else. I shall not be so indiscreet as to go and fetch her, but, after all, that is quite a reasonable interpretation." And from that island in the Bois, as for the last few days my thoughts had been installed there beforehand with Mme. de Stermaria, I could not succeed in bringing them back to where I was. My desire responded automatically to the gravitational force which had been pulling it now for so many hours on end, and in spite of this message, too recent to counteract that force, I went on instinctively getting ready to start, just as a student, although ploughed by the examiners, tries to answer one question more. At last I decided to tell Françoise to go down and pay the driver. I went along the passage without finding her, I passed through the dining-room, where suddenly my feet ceased to sound on the bare boards as they had been doing and were hushed to a silence which, even before I had realised the explanation of it, gave me a feeling of suffocation and confinement. It was the carpets which, in view of my parents' return, the servants had begun to put down again, those carpets which look so well on bright mornings when amid their disorder the sun stays and waits for you like a friend come to take you out to luncheon in the country, and casts over them the dappled light and shade of the forest, but which now on the contrary were the first installation of the wintry prison from which, obliged as I should be to live, to take my meals at home, I should no longer be free now to escape when I chose.

"Take care you don't slip, Sir; they're not tacked yet," Françoise called to me. "I ought to have lighted up. Oh, dear, it's the end of 'Sectember' already, the fine days are over." In no time, winter; at the corner of a window, as in a Gallé glass, a vein of crusted snow; and even in the Champs-Elysées, instead of the girls one waits to see, nothing but solitary sparrows.

What added to my distress at not seeing Mme. de Stermaria was that her answer led me to suppose that whereas, hour by hour, since Sunday, I had been living for this dinner alone, she had presumably never given it a second thought. Later on I learned of an absurd love match that she had suddenly made with a young man whom she must already have been seeing at this time, and who had presumably made her forget my invitation. For if she had remembered it she would surely never have waited for the carriage which I was not, for that matter, supposed to be sending for her, to inform me that she was otherwise engaged. My dreams of a young feudal maiden on a misty island had cleared the way to a still non-existent love. Now my disappointment, my rage, my desperate desire to recapture her who had just refused me were able, by bringing my sensibility into play, to make definite the possible love which until then my imagination alone had—and that more loosely—offered me.

How many are there in our memories, how many more have we forgotten, of these faces of girls and young women, all different, to which we have added a certain charm and a frenzied desire to see them again only because at the last moment they eluded us? In the case of Mme. de Stermaria there was a good deal more than this, and it was enough now to make me love her for me to see her again so that I might refresh those impressions, so vivid but all too brief, which my memory would not, without such refreshment, have the strength to keep alive when we were apart.

Circumstances decided against me; I did not see her again. It was not she that I loved, but it might well have been. And one of the things that made most cruel, perhaps, the great love which was presently to come to me was that when I thought of this evening I used to say to myself that my love might, given a slight modification of very ordinary circumstances, have been directed elsewhere, to Mme. de Stermaria; its application to her who inspired it in me so soon afterwards was not therefore—as I so longed, so needed to believe—absolutely necessary and predestined.

Françoise had left me by myself in the dining-room with the remark that it was foolish of me to stay there before she had lighted the fire. She went to get me some dinner, for even before the return of my parents, from this very evening, my seclusion was to begin. I caught sight of a huge bundle of carpets, still rolled up, and leaning against one end of the sideboard, and burying my head in it, swallowing its dust with my own tears, as the Jews used to cover their heads with ashes in times of mourning, I began to sob. I shuddered not only because the room was cold, but because a distinct lowering of temperature (against the danger and—I should add, perhaps—the by no means disagreeable sensation of which we make no attempt to react) is brought about by a certain kind of tears which fall from our eyes, drop by drop, like a fine, penetrating, icy rain, and seem as though never would they cease to flow. Suddenly I heard a voice:

"May I come in? Françoise told me you would be in the dining-room. I looked in to see whether you would care to come out and dine somewhere, if it isn't bad for your throat—there's a fog outside you could cut with a knife."

It was—arrived in Paris that morning, when I imagined him to be still in Morocco or on the sea—Robert de Saint-Loup.

I have already said (as a matter of fact, it was Robert himself who, at Balbec, had helped me, quite without meaning it, to arrive at this conclusion) what I think about friendship: to wit that it is so small a thing that I find it hard to understand how men with some claim to genius—Nietzsche, for instance—can have been such simpletons as to ascribe to it a certain intellectual value, and consequently to deny themselves friendships in which intellectual esteem would have no part. Yes, it has always been a surprise to me to find a man who carried sincerity towards himself to so high a pitch as to cut himself off, by a scruple of conscience, from Wagner's music, imagining that the truth could ever be attained by the mode of expression, naturally vague and inadequate, which our actions in general and acts of friendship in particular furnish, or that there could be any kind of significance in the fact of one's leaving one's work to go and see a friend and shed tears with him on hearing the false report that the Louvre was burned. I had got so far, at Balbec, as to find that the pleasure of playing with a troop of girls is less destructive of the spiritual life, to which at least it remains alien, than friendship, the whole effort of which is directed towards making us sacrifice the one real and (save by the channel of art) incommunicable part of ourself to a superficial self which finds—not, like the other, any joy in itself, but rather a vague, sentimental attraction in the feeling that it is being supported by external props, hospitably entertained by a strange personality, through which, happy in the protection that is afforded it there, it makes its own comfort radiate in warm approval, and marvels at qualities which it would denounce as faults and seek to correct in itself. Moreover the scorners of friendship can, without illusion and not without remorse, be the finest friends in the world, just as an artist carrying in his brain a masterpiece and feeling that his duty is rather to live and carry on his work, nevertheless, so as not to be thought or to run the risk of actually being selfish, gives his life for a vain cause, and gives it all the more gallantly in that the reasons for which he would have preferred not to give it were disinterested. But whatever might be my opinion of friendship, to mention only the pleasure that it procured me, of a quality so mediocre as to be like something halfway between physical exhaustion and mental boredom, there is no brew so deadly that it cannot at certain moments become precious and invigorating by giving us just the stimulus that was necessary, the warmth that we cannot generate in ourselves.

The thought of course never entered my mind now of asking Saint-Loup to take me (as, an hour earlier, I had been longing to go) to see some of the Rivebelle women; the scar left by my disappointment with Mme. de Stermaria was too recent still to be so easily healed, but at the moment when I had ceased to feel in my heart any reason for happiness Saint-Loup's bursting in upon me was like a sudden apparition of kindness, mirth, life, which were external to me, no doubt, but offered themselves to me, asked only to be made mine. He did not himself understand my shout of gratitude, my tears of affection. And yet is there anything more unaccountably affecting than one of those friends, be he diplomat, explorer, airman or soldier like Saint-Loup, who, having to start next day for the country, from where they will go on heaven knows where, seem to form for themselves, in the evening which they devote to us, an impression which we are astonished both to find, so rare and fleeting is it, can be so pleasant to them, and, since it does so delight them, not to see them prolong farther or repeat more often. A meal with us, an event so natural in itself, affords these travellers the same strange and exquisite pleasure as our boulevards give to an Asiatic. We set off together to dine, and as I went downstairs I thought of Doncières where every evening I used to meet Robert at his restaurant, and the little dining-rooms there that I had forgotten. I remembered one of these to which I had never given a thought, and which was not in the hotel where Saint-Loup dined but in another, far humbler, a cross between an inn and a boarding-house, where the waiting was done by the landlady and one of her servants. I had been forced to take shelter there once from a snowstorm. Besides, Robert was not to be dining at the hotel that evening and I had not cared to go any farther. My food was brought to me, upstairs, in a little room with bare wooden walls. The lamp went out during dinner and the servant lighted a couple of candles. I, pretending that I could not see very well as I held out my plate, while she helped me to potatoes, took her bare fore-arm in my hand, as though to guide her. Seeing that she did not withdraw it, I began to fondle it, then, without saying a word, pulled her bodily to me, blew out the candles and told her to feel in my pocket for some money. For the next few days physical pleasure seemed to me to require, to be properly enjoyed, not only this servant but the timbered dining-room, so remote and lonely. And yet it was to the other, in which Saint-Loup and his friends dined, that I returned every evening, from force of habit and in friendship for them, until I left Doncières. But even of this hotel, where he took his meals with his friends, I had long ceased to think; we make little use of our experience, we leave unconsumed in the summer dusk or precocious nights of winter the hours in which it had seemed to us that there might nevertheless be contained some element of tranquillity or pleasure. But those hours are not altogether wasted. When, in their turn, come and sing to us fresh moments of pleasure, which by themselves would pass by equally bare in outline, the others recur, bringing with them the groundwork, the solid consistency of a rich orchestration. They are in this way prolonged into one of those types of happiness which we recapture only now and again but which continue to exist; in the present instance the type was that of forsaking everything else to dine in comfortable surroundings, which by the help of memory embody in a scene from nature suggestions of the rewards of travel, with a friend who is going to stir our dormant life with all his energy, his affection, to communicate to us an emotional pleasure, very different from anything that we could derive from our own efforts or from social distractions; we are going to exist solely for him, to utter vows of friendship which, born within the confines of the hour, remaining imprisoned in it, will perhaps not be kept on the morrow but which I need have no scruple in taking before Saint-Loup since, with a courage into which there entered a great deal of common sense and the presentiment that friendship cannot explore its own depths, on the morrow he would be gone.

If as I came downstairs I lived over again the evenings at Doncières, when we reached the street, in a moment the darkness, now almost total, in which the fog seemed to have put out the lamps, which one could make out, glimmering very faintly, only when close at hand, took me back to I could not say what arrival, by night, at Combray, when the streets there were still lighted only at long intervals and one felt one's way through a darkness moist, warm, consecrated, like that of a Christmas manger, just visibly starred here and there by a wick that burned no brighter than a candle. Between that year—to which I could ascribe no precise date—of my Combray life and the evenings at Rivebelle which had, an hour earlier, been reflected above my drawn curtains, what a world of differences! I felt on perceiving them an enthusiasm which might have borne fruit had I been left alone and would then have saved me the unnecessary round of many wasted years through which I was yet to pass before there was revealed to me that invisible vocation of which these volumes are the history. Had the revelation come to me this evening, the carriage in which I sat would have deserved to rank as more memorable with me than Dr. Percepied's, on the box seat of which I had composed that little sketch—on which, as it happened, I had recently laid my hands, altered it and sent it in vain to the *Figaro*—of the spires of Martinville. Is it because we live

over our past years not in their continuous sequence, day by day, but in
a memory that fastens upon the coolness or sun-parched heat of some
morning or afternoon, receives the shadow of some solitary place, is enclosed, immovable, arrested, lost, remote from all others, because, therefore, the changes gradually wrought not only in the world outside but in
our dreams and our evolving character (changes which have impercepti-
bly carried us through life from one to another, wholly different time), are
of necessity eliminated, that, if we revive another memory taken from a
different year, we find between the two, thanks to lacunae, to vast stretches
of oblivion, as it were the gulf of a difference in altitude or the incompatibility of two divers qualities, that of the air we breathe and the colour of the
scene before our eyes? But between one and another of the memories that
had now come to me in turn of Combray, of Doncières and of Rivebelle,
I was conscious at the moment of more than a distance in time, of the distance that there would be between two separate universes the material
elements in which were not the same. If I had sought to reproduce the element in which appeared carven my most trivial memories of Rivebelle, I
should have had to streak with rosy veins, to render at once translucent,
compact, refreshing, resonant a substance hitherto analogous to the coarse
dark sandstone walls of Combray. But Robert having finished giving his
instructions to the driver joined me now in the carriage. The ideas that had
appeared before me took flight. Ideas are goddesses who deign at times to
make themselves visible to a solitary mortal, at a turning in the road, even
in his bedroom while he sleeps, when they, standing framed in the doorway, bring him the annunciation of their tidings. But as soon as a companion joins him they vanish, in the society of his fellows no man has ever
beheld them. And I found myself cast back upon friendship. When he first
appeared Robert had indeed warned me that there was a good deal of fog
outside, but while we were indoors, talking, it had grown steadily thicker.
It was no longer merely the light mist which I had looked forward to seeing
rise from the island and envelop Mme. de Stermaria and myself. A few feet
away from us the street lamps were blotted out and then it was night, as
dark as in the open fields, in a forest, or rather on a mild Breton island
whither I would fain have gone; I lost myself, as on the stark coast of some
Northern sea where one risks one's life twenty times over before coming to
the solitary inn; ceasing to be a mirage for which one seeks, the fog became
one of those dangers against which one has to fight, so that we had, in finding our way and reaching a safe haven, the difficulties, the anxiety and
finally the joy which safety, so little perceived by him who is not threatened with the loss of it, gives to the perplexed and benighted traveller. One
thing only came near to destroying my pleasure during our adventurous
ride, owing to the angry astonishment into which it flung me for a moment.
"You know, I told Bloch," Saint-Loup suddenly informed me, "that you
didn't really think all that of him, that you found him rather vulgar at
times. I'm like that, you see, I want people to know where they stand,"
he wound up with a satisfied air and in a tone which brooked no reply. I
was astounded. Not only had I the most absolute confidence in Saint-
Loup, in the loyalty of his friendship, and he had betrayed it by what he

had said to Bloch, but it seemed to me that he of all men ought to have been restrained from doing so, by his defects as well as by his good qualities, by that astonishing veneer of breeding which was capable of carrying politeness to what was positively a want of frankness. His triumphant air, was it what we assume to cloak a certain embarrassment in admitting a thing which we know that we ought not to have done, or did it mean complete unconsciousness; stupidity making a virtue out of a defect which I had not associated with him; a passing fit of ill humour towards me, prompting him to make an end of our friendship, or the notation in words of a passing fit of ill humour in the company of Bloch to whom he had felt that he must say something disagreeable, even although I should be compromised by it? However that might be, his face was seared, while he uttered this vulgar speech, by a frightful sinuosity which I saw on it once or twice only in all the time I knew him, and which, beginning by running more or less down the middle of his face, when it came to his lips twisted them, gave them a hideous expression of baseness, almost of bestiality, quite transitory and no doubt inherited. There must have been at such moments, which recurred probably not more than once every other year, a partial eclipse of his true self by the passage across it of the personality of some ancestor whose shadow fell on him. Fully as much as his satisfied air, the words: "I want people to know where they stand," encouraged the same doubt and should have incurred a similar condemnation. I felt inclined to say to him that if one wants people to know where they stand one ought to confine these outbursts of frankness to one's own affairs and not to acquire a too easy merit at the expense of others. But by this time the carriage had stopped outside the restaurant, the huge front of which, glazed and streaming with light, alone succeeded in piercing the darkness. The fog itself, beside the comfortable brightness of the lighted interior, seemed to be waiting outside on the pavement to shew one the way in with the joy of servants whose faces reflect the hospitable instincts of their master; shot with the most delicate shades of light, it pointed the way like the pillar of fire which guided the Children of Israel. Many of whom, as it happened, were to be found inside. For this was the place to which Bloch and his friends had long been in the habit, maddened by a hunger as famishing as the Ritual Fast, which at least occurs only once a year, for coffee and the satisfaction of political curiosity, of repairing in the evenings. Every mental excitement creating a value that overrides others, a quality superior to the rest of one's habits, there is no taste at all keenly developed that does not thus gather round it a society which it unites and in which the esteem of his fellows is what each of its members seeks before anything else from life. Here, in their café, be it in a little provincial town, you will find impassioned music-lovers; the greater part of their time, all their spare cash is spent in chamber-concerts, in meetings for musical discussion, in cafés where one finds oneself among musical people and rubs shoulders with the members of the orchestra. Others, keen upon flying, seek to stand well with the old waiter in the glazed bar perched on top of the aerodrome; sheltered from the wind as in the glass cage of a lighthouse, they can follow in the company of an airman who is not going up that day the evolutions of a pilot practising loops, while another, invisible a moment ago, comes suddenly swooping down to land with the great winged roar of an Arabian roc. The little group which met to try to perpetuate, to explore the fugitive emotions aroused by the Zola trial attached a similar importance to this particular café. But they were not viewed with favour by the young nobles who composed the rest of its patrons and had taken possession of a second room, separated from the other only by a flimsy parapet topped with a row of plants. These looked upon Dreyfus and his supporters as traitors, albeit twenty-five years later, ideas having had time to classify themselves and Dreyfusism to acquire, in the light of history, a certain distinction, the sons, dance-mad Bolshevists, of these same young nobles were to declare to the 'intellectuals' who questioned them that undoubtedly, had they been alive at the time, they would have stood up for Dreyfus, without having any clearer idea of what the great Case had been about than Comtesse Edmond de Pourtalès or the Marquise de Galliffet, other luminaries already extinct at the date of their birth. For on the night of the fog the noblemen of the café, who were in due course to become the fathers of these young intellectuals, Dreyfusards in retrospect, were still bachelors. Naturally the idea of a rich marriage was present in the minds of all their families, but none of them had yet brought such a marriage off. While still potential, the only effect of this rich marriage, the simultaneous ambition of several of them (there were indeed several heiresses in view, but after all the number of big dowries was considerably below that of the aspirants to them), was to create among these young men a certain amount of rivalry.

As ill luck would have it, Saint-Loup remaining outside for a minute to explain to the driver that he was to call for us again after dinner, I had to make my way in by myself. In the first place, once I had involved myself in the spinning door, to which I was not accustomed, I began to fear that I should never succeed in escaping from it. (Let me note here for the benefit of lovers of verbal accuracy that the contrivance in question, despite its peaceful appearance, is known as a 'revolver,' from the English 'revolving door.') This evening the proprietor, not venturing either to brave the elements outside or to desert his customers, remained standing near the entrance so as to have the pleasure of listening to the joyful complaints of the new arrivals, all aglow with the satisfaction of people who have had difficulty in reaching a place and have been afraid of losing their way. The smiling cordiality of his welcome was, however, dissipated by the sight of a stranger incapable of disengaging himself from the rotating sheets of glass. This flagrant sign of social ignorance made him knit his brows like an examiner who has a good mind not to utter the formula: *Dignus est intrare.* As a crowning error I went to look for a seat in the room set apart for the nobility, from which he at once expelled me, indicating to me, with a rudeness to which all the waiters at once conformed, a place in the other room. This was all the less to my liking because the seat was in the middle of a crowded row and I had opposite me the door reserved for the Hebrews which, as it did not revolve, opening and shutting at every moment kept me in a horrible draught. But the proprietor declined to move me, saying: "No, Sir, I cannot have the whole place upset for you." Presently, however, he forgot this belated and troublesome guest, captivated as he was by the arrival of each newcomer who, before calling for his beer, his wing of cold chicken or his hot grog (it was by now long past dinner-time), must first, as in the old romances, pay his scot by relating his adventure at the moment of his entry into this asylum of warmth and security where the contrast with the perils just escaped made that gaiety and sense of comradeship prevail which create a cheerful harmony round the campfire.

One reported that his carriage, thinking it had got to the Pont de la Concorde, had circled three times round the Invalides, another that his, in trying to make its way down the Avenue des Champs-Elysées, had driven into a clump of trees at the Rond Point, from which it had taken him three quarters of an hour to get clear. Then followed lamentations upon the fog, the cold, the deathly stillness of the streets, uttered and received with the same exceptionally jovial air, which was accounted for by the pleasant atmosphere of the room which, except where I sat, was warm, the dazzling light which set blinking eyes already accustomed to not seeing, and the buzz of talk which restored their activity to deafened ears.

It was all the newcomers could do to keep silence. The singularity of the mishaps which each of them thought unique burned their tongues, and their eyes roved in search of some one to engage in conversation. The proprietor himself lost all sense of social distinction. "M. le Prince de Foix lost his way three times coming from the Porte Saint-Martin," he was not afraid to say with a laugh, actually pointing out, as though introducing one to the other, the illustrious nobleman to an Israelite barrister, who, on any evening but this, would have been divided from him by a barrier far harder to surmount than the ledge of greenery. "Three times—fancy that!" said the barrister, touching his hat. This note of personal interest was not at all to the Prince's liking. He formed one of an aristocratic group for whom the practice of impertinence, even at the expense of their fellow-nobles when these were not of the very highest rank, seemed the sole possible occupation. Not to acknowledge a bow, and, if the polite stranger repeated the offence, to titter with sneering contempt or fling back one's head with a look of fury, to pretend not to know some elderly man who might have done them a service, to reserve their handclasp for dukes and the really intimate friends of dukes whom the latter introduced to them, such was the attitude of these young men, and especially of the Prince de Foix. Such an attitude was encouraged by the ill-balanced mentality of early manhood (a period in which, even in the middle class, one appears ungrateful and behaves like a cad because, having forgotten for months to write to a benefactor after he has lost his wife, one then ceases to nod to him in the street so as to simplify matters), but it was inspired above all by an over-acute caste snobbishness. It is true that, after the fashion of certain nervous affections the symptoms of which grow less pronounced in later life, this snobbishness was on the whole to cease to express itself in so offensive a form in these men who had been so intolerable when young. Once youth is outgrown, it is seldom that anyone remains hidebound by insolence. He had supposed it to be the only thing in the world; suddenly he discovers, for all the Prince that he is, that there also are such things as music, literature, even standing for parliament. The scale of human values is correspondingly altered and he joins in conversation with people whom at one time he would have slain with a glare of lightning. Which is fortunate for those of the latter who have had the patience to wait, and whose character is sufficiently formed—if one may so put it—for them to feel pleasure in receiving in their forties the civility and welcome that had been coldly withheld from them at twenty.

As I have mentioned the Prince de Foix, it may not be inconsequent here to add that he belonged to a set of a dozen or fifteen young men and to an inner group of four. The dozen or fifteen shared this characteristic (which the Prince lacked, I fancy) that each of them faced the world in a dual aspect. Up to their own eyes in debt, they were of no account in those of their tradesmen, notwithstanding the pleasure these took in addressing them as 'Monsieur le Comte,' 'Monsieur le Marquis,' 'Monsieur le Duc.' They hoped to retrieve their fortunes by means of the famous rich marriage ('money-bags' as the expression still was) and, as the fat dowries which they coveted numbered at the most four or five, several of them would be silently training their batteries on the same damsel. And the secret would be so well kept that when one of them, on arriving at the café, announced: "My dear fellows, I am too fond of you all not to tell you of my engagement to Mlle. d'Ambresac," there was a general outburst, more than one of the others imagining that the marriage was as good as settled already between Mlle. d'Ambresac and himself, and not having enough self-control to stifle a spontaneous cry of stupefaction and rage. "So you like the idea of marriage, do you Bibi?" the Prince de Châtellerault could not help exclaiming, letting his fork drop in his surprise and despair, for he had been fully expecting the engagement of this identical Mlle. d'Ambresac to be announced, but with himself, Châtellerault, as her bridegroom. And heaven only knew all that his father had cunningly hinted to the Ambresacs against Bibi's mother. "So you think it'll be fun, being married, do you?" he was impelled to repeat his question to Bibi, who, better prepared to meet it, for he had had plenty of time to decide on the right attitude to adopt since the engagement had reached the semi-official stage, replied with a smile: "What pleases me is not the idea of marriage, which never appealed much to me, but marrying Daisy d'Ambresac, whom I think charming." In the time taken up by this response M. de Châtellerault had recovered his composure, but he was thinking that he must at the earliest possible moment execute a change of front in the direction of Mlle. de la Canourque or Miss Foster, numbers two and three on the list of heiresses, pacify somehow the creditors who were expecting the Ambresac marriage and finally explain to the people to whom he too had declared that Mlle. d'Ambresac was charming that this marriage was all very well for Bibi, but that he himself would have had all his family down on him like a ton of bricks if he had married her. Mme. Soléon (he decided to say) had actually announced that she would not have them in her house.

But if in the eyes of tradesmen, proprietors of restaurants and the like they seemed of little account, conversely, being creatures of dual personality, the moment they appeared in society they ceased to be judged by the decay of their fortunes and the sordid occupations by which they sought to repair them. They became once more M. le Prince this, M. le Duc that, and were reckoned only in terms of their quarterings. A duke who was practically a multi-millionaire and seemed to combine in his own person every possible distinction gave precedence to them because, the heads of their various houses, they were by descent sovereign princes of minute territories in which they were entitled to coin money and so forth. Often in this café one of them lowered his eyes when another came in so as not to oblige the newcomer to greet him. This was because in his imaginative pursuit of riches he had invited a banker to dine. Every time that a man about town enters into relations, on this footing, with a banker, the latter leaves him the poorer by a hundred thousand francs, which does not prevent the man about town from at once repeating the process with another. We continue to burn candles in churches and to consult doctors.

But the Prince de Foix, who was rich already, belonged not only to this fashionable set of fifteen or so young men, but to a more exclusive and inseparable group of four which included Saint-Loup. These were never asked anywhere separately, they were known as the four *gigolos*, they were always to be seen riding together, in country houses their hostesses gave them communicating bedrooms, with the result that, especially as they were all four extremely good looking, rumours were current as to the extent of their intimacy. I was in a position to give these the lie direct so far as Saint-Loup was concerned. But the curious thing is that if, later on, one was to learn that these rumours were true of all four, each of the quartet had been entirely in the dark as to the other three. And yet each of them had done his utmost to find out about the others, to gratify a desire or (more probably) a resentment, to prevent a marriage or to secure a hold over the friend whose secret he discovered. A fifth (for in these groups of four there are never four only) had joined this Platonic party who was more so than any of the others. But religious scruples restrained him until long after the group had broken up, and he himself was a married man, the father of a family, fervently praying at Lourdes that the next baby might be a boy or a girl, and spending the intervals of procreation in the pursuit of soldiers.

Despite the Prince's code of manners, the fact that the barrister's comment, though uttered in his hearing, had not been directly addressed to him made him less angry than he would otherwise have been. Besides, this evening was somewhat exceptional. Finally, the barrister had no more prospect of coming to know the Prince de Foix than the cabman who had driven that noble lord to the restaurant. The Prince felt, accordingly, that he might allow himself to reply, in an arrogant tone, as though speaking to some one 'off stage,' to this stranger who, thanks to the fog, was in the position of a travelling companion whom one meets at some seaside place at the ends of the earth, scoured by all the winds of heaven or shrouded in mist: "Losing your way's nothing; the trouble is, you can't find it again." The wisdom of this aphorism impressed the proprietor, for he had already heard it several times in the course of the evening.

He was, in fact, in the habit of always comparing what he heard or read with an already familiar canon, and felt his admiration aroused if he could detect no difference. This state of mind is by no means to be ignored, for, applied to political conversations, to the reading of newspapers, it forms public opinion and thereby makes possible the greatest events in history. An aggregation of German landlords, simply by being impressed by a customer or a newspaper when he or it said that France, England and Russia were 'out to crush' Germany, made war, at the time of Agadir, possible, even if no war occurred. Historians, if they have not been wrong to abandon the practice of attributing the actions of peoples to the will of kings, ought to substitute for the latter the psychology of the person of no importance.

In politics the proprietor of this particular café had for some time now concentrated his pupil-teacher's mind on certain particular details of the Dreyfus case. If he did not find the terms that were familiar to him in the conversation of a customer or the columns of a newspaper he would pronounce the article boring or the speaker insincere. The Prince de Foix, however, impressed him so forcibly that he barely gave him time to finish what he was saying. "That's right, Prince, that's right," (which meant neither more nor less than 'repeated without a mistake') "that's exactly how it is!" he exclaimed, expanding, like people in the Arabian Nights 'to the limit of repletion.' But the Prince had by this time vanished into the smaller room. Then, as life resumes its normal course after even the most sensational happenings, those who had emerged from the sea of fog began to order whatever they wanted to eat or drink; among them a party of young men from the Jockey Club who, in view of the abnormality of the situation, had no hesitation in taking their places at a couple of tables in the big room, and were thus quite close to me. So the cataclysm had established even between the smaller room and the bigger, among all these people stimulated by the comfort of the restaurant after their long wanderings across the ocean of fog, a familiarity from which I alone was excluded, not unlike the spirit that must have prevailed in Noah's ark. Suddenly I saw the landlord's body whipped into a series of bows, the head waiters hurrying to support him in a full muster which drew every eye towards the door. "Quick, send Cyprien here, lay a table for M. le Marquis de Saint-Loup," cried the proprietor, for whom Robert was not merely a great nobleman possessing a real importance even in the eyes of the Prince de Foix, but a client who drove through life four-in-hand, so to speak, and spent a great deal of money in this restaurant. The customers in the big room looked on with interest, those in the small room shouted simultaneous greetings to their friend as he finished wiping his shoes. But just as he was about to make his way into the small room he caught sight of me in the big one. "Good God," he exclaimed, "what on earth are you doing there? And with the door wide open too?" he went on, with an angry glance at the proprietor, who ran to shut it, throwing the blame on his staff: "I'm always telling them to keep it shut."

I had been obliged to shift my own table and to disturb others which stood in the way in order to reach him. "Why did you move? Would you sooner dine here than in the little room? Why, my poor fellow, you're freezing. You will oblige me by keeping that door locked;" he turned to the proprietor. "This very instant, M. le Marquis; the gentlemen will have to go out of this room through the other, that is all." And the better to

shew his zeal he detailed for this operation a head waiter and several satel-
lites, vociferating the most terrible threats of punishment were it not
properly carried out. He began to shew me exaggerated marks of respect,
so as to make me forget that these had begun not upon my arrival but only
after that of Saint-Loup, while, lest I should think them to have been
prompted by the friendliness shewn me by his rich and noble client, he
gave me now and again a surreptitious little smile which seemed to indicate
a regard that was wholly personal.

Something said by one of the diners behind me made me turn my head
for a moment. I had caught, instead of the words: "Wing of chicken, excellent; and a glass of champagne, only not too dry," the unexpected: "I
should prefer glycerine. Yes, hot, excellent." I wanted to see who the ascetic
was that was inflicting upon himself such a diet. I turned quickly back to
Saint-Loup so as not to be recognised by the man of strange appetite. It
was simply a doctor, whom I happened to know, and of whom another
customer, taking advantage of the fog to buttonhole him here in the café,
was asking his professional advice. Like stockbrokers, doctors employ the
first person singular.

Meanwhile I was studying Saint-Loup, and my thoughts took a line of
their own. They were in this café, I had myself known at other times,
plenty of foreigners, intellectuals, budding geniuses of all sorts, resigned to
the laughter excited by their pretentious capes, their 1830 neckties and still
more by the clumsiness of their movements, going so far as to provoke that
laughter in order to shew that they paid no heed to it, who yet were men
of real intellectual and moral worth, of an extreme sensibility. They repelled—the Jews among them principally, the unassimilated Jews, that is
to say, for with the other kind we are not concerned—those who could not
endure any oddity or eccentricity of appearance (as Bloch repelled Albertine). Generally speaking, one realised afterwards that if they had
against them hair worn too long, noses and eyes that were too big, stilted
theatrical gestures, it was puerile to judge them by these only, they had
plenty of intelligence and spirit and were men to whom, in the long run,
one could become closely attached. Among the Jews especially there were
few whose parents and kinsfolk had not a warmth of heart, a breadth of
mind in comparison with which Saint-Loup's mother and the Duc de Guermantes cut the poorest of figures by their sereness, their skin-deep religiosity
which denounced only the most open scandals, their apology for a Christianity which led invariably (by the unexpected channel of a purely calculating mind) to an enormously wealthy marriage. But in Saint-Loup,
when all was said, however the faults of his relatives might be combined
in a fresh creation of character, there reigned the most charming openness
of mind and heart. And whenever (it must be frankly admitted, to the
undying glory of France) these qualities are found in a man who is purely
French, be he noble or plebeian, they flower—flourish would be too strong
a word, for a sense of proportion persists and also a certain restraint—with
a grace which the foreign visitor, however estimable he may be, does not
present to us. Of these intellectual and moral qualities others undoubtedly
have their share, and if we have first to overcome what repels us and what

makes us smile they remain no less precious. But it is all the same a pleasant thing, and one which is perhaps exclusively French that what is fine from the standpoint of equity, what is of value to the heart and mind should be first of all attractive to the eyes, charmingly coloured, consummately chiselled, should express outwardly as well in substance as in form an inward perfection. I studied Saint-Loup's features and said to myself that it is a thing to be glad of when there is no lack of bodily grace to prepare one for the graces within, and when the winged nostrils are spread as delicately and with as perfect a design as the wings of the little butterflies that hover over the field-flowers round Combray; and that the true *opus francigenum,* the secret of which was not lost in the thirteenth century, the beauty of which would not be lost with the destruction of our churches, consists not so much in the stone angels of Saint-André-des-Champs as in the young sons of France, noble, citizen or peasant, whose faces are carved with that delicacy and boldness which have remained as traditional there as on the famous porch, but are creative still as well.

After leaving us for a moment in order to supervise personally the barring of the door and the ordering of our dinner (he laid great stress on our choosing 'butcher's meat,' the fowls being presumably nothing to boast of) the proprietor came back to inform us that M. le Prince de Foix would esteem it a favour if M. le Marquis would allow him to dine at a table next to ours. "But they are all taken," objected Robert, casting an eye over the tables which blocked the way to mine. "That doesn't matter in the least, if M. le Marquis would like it, I can easily ask these people to move to another table. It is always a pleasure to do anything for M. le Marquis!" "But you must decide," said Saint-Loup to me. "Foix is a good fellow, he may bore you or he may not; anyhow he's not such a fool as most of them." I told Robert that of course I should like to meet his friend but that now that I was for once in a way dining with him and was so entirely happy, I should be just as well pleased to have him all to myself. "He's got a very fine cloak, the Prince has," the proprietor broke in upon our deliberation. "Yes, I know," said Saint-Loup. I wanted to tell Robert that M. de Charlus had disclaimed all knowledge of me to his sister-in-law, and to ask him what could be the reason of this, but was prevented by the arrival of M. de Foix. Come to see whether his request had been favourably received, we caught sight of him standing beside our table. Robert introduced us, but did not hide from his friend that as we had things to talk about he would prefer not to be disturbed. The Prince withdrew, adding to the farewell bow which he made me a smile which, pointed at Saint-Loup, seemed to transfer to him the responsibility for the shortness of a meeting which the Prince himself would have liked to see prolonged. As he turned to go, Robert, struck, it appeared, by a sudden idea, dashed off after his friend, with a "Stay where you are and get on with your dinner, I shall be back in a moment," to me; and vanished into the smaller room. I was pained to hear the smart young men sitting near me, whom I did not know, repeat the most absurd and malicious stories about the young Hereditary Grand Duke of Luxembourg (formerly Comte de Nassau) whom I had met at Balbec and who had shewn me such delicate marks of sympathy at the time of my grandmother's illness. According to one of these young men, he had said to the Duchesse de Guermantes: "I expect everyone to get up when my wife passes," to which the Duchess had retorted (with as little truth, had she said any such thing, as humour, the grandmother of the young Princess having always been the very pink of propriety): "Get up when your wife passes, do they? Well, that's a change from her grand-mother's day. She expected the gentlemen to lie down." Then some one alleged that, having gone down to see his aunt the Princesse de Luxem-bourg at Balbec, and put up at the Grand Hotel, he had complained to the manager there (my friend) that the royal standard of Luxembourg was not flown in front of the hotel, over the sea. And that this flag being less familiar and less generally in use than the British or Italian, it had taken him several days to procure one, greatly to the young Grand Duke's annoyance. I did not believe a word of this story, but made up my mind, as soon as I went to Balbec, to inquire of the manager, so as to make certain that it was a pure invention. While waiting for Saint-Loup to return I asked the proprietor to get me some bread. "Certainly, Monsieur le Baron!" "I am not a Baron," I told him. "Oh, beg pardon, Monsieur le Comte!" I had no time to lodge a second protest which would certainly have pro-moted me to the rank of marquis; faithful to his promise of an immediate return, Saint-Loup reappeared in the doorway carrying over his arm the thick vicuna cloak of the Prince de Foix, from whom I guessed that he had borrowed it in order to keep me warm. He signed to me not to get up, and came towards me, but either my table would have to be moved again or I must change my seat if he was to get to his. Entering the big room he sprang lightly on to one of the red plush benches which ran round its walls and on which, apart from myself, there were sitting only three or four of the young men from the Jockey Club, friends of his own, who had not managed to find places in the other room. Between the tables and the wall electric wires were stretched at a certain height; without the least hesitation Saint-Loup jumped nimbly over them like a horse in a steeplechase; em-barrassed that it should be done wholly for my benefit and to save me the trouble of a slight movement, I was at the same time amazed at the precision with which my friend performed this exercise in levitation; and in this I was not alone; for, albeit they would probably have had but little admiration for a similar display on the part of a more humbly born and less generous client, the proprietor and his staff stood fascinated, like race-goers in the enclosure; one underling, apparently rooted to the ground, stood there gaping with a dish in his hand for which a party close beside him were waiting; and when Saint-Loup, having to get past his friends, climbed on the narrow ledge behind them and ran along it, balancing him-self with his arms, discreet applause broke from the body of the room. On coming to where I was sitting he stopped short in his advance with the precision of a tributary chieftain before the throne of a sovereign, and, stooping down, handed to me with an air of courtesy and submission the vicuna cloak which, a moment later, having taken his place beside me, without my having to make a single movement he arranged as a light but warm shawl about my shoulders.

"By the way, while I think of it, my uncle Charlus has something to say to you. I promised I'd send you round to him to-morrow evening."

"I was just going to speak to you about him. But to-morrow evening I am dining with your aunt Guermantes."

"Yes there's a regular beanfeast to-morrow at Oriane's. I'm not asked. But my uncle Palamède doesn't want you to go there. You can't get out of it, I suppose? Well, anyhow, go on to my uncle's afterwards. I'm sure he really does want to see you. Look here, you can easily manage to get there by eleven. Eleven o'clock; don't forget; I'll let him know. He's very touchy. If you don't turn up he'll never forgive you. And Oriane's parties are always over quite early. If you are only going to dine there you can quite easily be at my uncle's by eleven. I ought really to go and see Oriane, about getting shifted from Morocco; I want an exchange. She is so nice about all that sort of thing, and she can get anything she likes out of General de Saint-Joseph, who runs that branch. But don't say anything about it to her. I've mentioned it to the Princesse de Parme, everything will be all right. Interesting place, Morocco. I could tell you all sorts of things. Very fine lot of men out there. One feels they're on one's own level, mentally."

"You don't think the Germans are going to go to war about it?"

"No; they're annoyed with us, as after all they have every right to be. But the Emperor is out for peace. They are always making us think they want war, to force us to give in. Pure bluff, you know, like poker. The Prince of Monaco, one of Wilhelm's agents, comes and tells us in confidence that Germany will attack us. Then we give way. But if we didn't give way, there wouldn't be war in any shape or form. You have only to think what a comic spectacle a war would be in these days. It'd be a bigger catastrophe than the Flood and the *Götterdämmerung* rolled in one. Only it wouldn't last so long."

He spoke to me of friendship, affection, regret, albeit like all visitors of his sort he was going off the next morning for some months, which he was to spend in the country, and would only be staying a couple of nights in Paris on his way back to Morocco (or elsewhere); but the words which he thus let fall into the heated furnace which my heart was this evening kindled a pleasant glow there. Our infrequent meetings, this one in particular, have since formed a distinct episode in my memories. For him, as for me, this was the evening of friendship. And yet the friendship that I felt for him at this moment was scarcely, I feared (and felt therefore some remorse at the thought), what he would have liked to inspire. Filled still with the pleasure that I had had in seeing him come bounding towards me and gracefully pause on arriving at his goal, I felt that this pleasure lay in my recognising that each of the series of movements which he had developed against the wall, along the bench, had its meaning, its cause in Saint-Loup's own personal nature, possibly, but even more in that which by birth and upbringing he had inherited from his race.

A certainty of taste in the region not of beauty but manners, which when he was faced by a novel combination of circumstances enabled the man of breeding to grasp at once—like a musician who has been asked to play a piece he has never seen—the feeling, the motions that were required, and to apply the appropriate mechanism and technique; which then allowed this taste to display itself without the constraint of any other consideration, by which the average young man of the middle class would have been paralysed, from fear as well of making himself ridiculous in the eyes of strangers by his disregard of convention as of appearing too deferential in the eyes of his friends; the place of this constraint being taken in Robert by a lofty disdain which certainly he had never felt in his heart but which he had received by inheritance in his body, and which had moulded the attitudes of his ancestors to a familiarity with their inferiors which, they imagined, could only flatter and enchant those to whom it was displayed; lastly, a noble liberality which, taking no account of his boundless natural advantages (lavish expenditure in this restaurant had succeeded in making him, here as elsewhere, the most fashionable customer and the general favourite, a position which was underlined by the deference shewn him throughout the place not only by the waiters but by all its most exclusive young patrons), led him to trample them underfoot, just as he had, actually and symbolically, trodden upon those benches decked with purple, like a triumphal way which pleased my friend only because it enabled him more gracefully and swiftly to arrive at my side; such were the qualities, essential to aristocracy, which through the husk of this body, not opaque and vague as mine would have been, but significant and limpid, transmitted as through a work of art the industrious, energetic force which had created it and rendered the movements of this lightfoot course which Robert had pursued along the wall intelligible and charming as those of a row of knights upon a marble frieze. "Alas!" Robert might have thought, "was it worth while to have grown up despising birth, honouring only justice and intellect, choosing outside the ranks of the friends provided for me companions who were awkward and ill-dressed, provided they had the gift of eloquence, only for the sole personality apparent in me, which is to remain a treasured memory, to be not that which my will, with the most praiseworthy effort, has fashioned in my likeness, but one which is not of my making, which is not even myself, which I have always disliked and striven to overcome; was it worth while to love my chosen friend as I have loved him, for the greatest pleasure that he can find in me to be that of discovering something far more general than myself, a pleasure which is not in the least (as he says, though he cannot seriously believe it) one of the pleasures of friendship, but an intellectual and detached, a sort of artistic pleasure?" This is what I am now afraid that Saint-Loup may at times have thought. If so, he was mistaken. If he had not (as he steadfastly had) cherished something more lofty than the suppleness innate in his body, if he had not kept aloof for so long from the pride that goes with noble birth, there would have been something more studied, a certain heaviness in his very agility, a self-important vulgarity in his manners. As with Mme. de Villeparisis a strong vein of seriousness had been necessary for her to give in her conversation and in her Memoirs a sense of the frivolous, which is intellectual, so, in order that Saint-Loup's body might be indwelt by so much nobility, the latter had first to desert a mind that was aiming at higher things, and, reabsorbed into his body, to be fixed there in unconscious, noble lines. In this way his distinction of mind was not absent from a bodily distinction which otherwise would not have been complete. An artist has no need to express his mind directly in his work for it to express the quality of that mind; it has indeed been said that the highest praise of God consists in the denial of Him by the atheist, who finds creation so perfect that it can dispense with a creator. And I was quite well aware that it was not merely a work of art that I was admiring in this young man unfolding along the wall the frieze of his flying course; the young Prince (a descendant of Catherine de Foix, Queen of Navarre and grand-daughter of Charles VII) whom he had just left for my sake, the endowments, by birth and fortune, which he was laying at my feet, the proud and shapely ancestors who survived in the assurance, the agility, the courtesy with which he now arranged about my shivering body the warm woollen cloak, were not all these like friends of longer standing in his life, by whom I might have expected that we should be permanently kept apart, and whom, on the contrary, he was sacrificing to me by a choice which one can make only in the loftiest places of the mind, with that sovereign liberty of which Robert's movements were the presentment and in which is realised perfect friendship?

How much familiar intercourse with a Guermantes—in place of the distinction that it had in Robert, because there the inherited scorn of humanity was but the outer garment, become an unconscious charm, of a real moral humility—could disclose of vulgar arrogance I had had an opportunity of seeing, not in M. de Charlus, in whom certain characteristic faults, for which I had been unable, so far, to account, were overlaid upon his aristocratic habits, but in the Duc de Guermantes. And yet he too, in the general impression of commonness which had so strongly repelled my grandmother when she had met him once, years earlier, at Mme. de Villeparisis's, included glimpses of historic grandeur of which I became conscious when I went to dine in his house, on the evening following that which I had spent with Saint-Loup.

They had not been apparent to me either in himself or in the Duchess when I had met them first in their aunt's drawing-room, any more than I had discerned, on first seeing her, the differences that set Berma apart from her fellow-players, all the more that in her the individuality was infinitely more striking than in any social celebrity, such distinctions becoming more marked in proportion as the objects are more real, more conceivable by the intellect. And yet, however slight the shades of social distinction may be (and so slight are they that when an accurate portrayer like Sainte-Beuve tries to indicate the shades of difference between the salons of Mme. Geoffrin, Mme. Récamier and Mme. de Boigne, they appear so much alike that the cardinal tru+h which, unknown to the author, emerges from his investigations is the vacuity of that form of life), with them, and for the same reason as with Berma, when the Guermantes had ceased to impress me and the tiny drop of their originality was no longer vaporised by my imagination, I was able to distil and analyse it, imponderable as it was.

The Duchess having made no reference to her husband when she talked to me at her aunt's party, I wondered whether, in view of the rumours of a divorce that were current, he would be present at the dinner. But my doubts were speedily set at rest, for through the crowd of footmen who stood about in the hall and who (since they must until then have regarded me much as they regarded the children of the evicted cabinet-maker, that is to say with more fellow-feeling perhaps than their master but as a person incapable of being admitted to his house) must have been asking themselves to what this social revolution could be due, I saw slip towards me M. de Guermantes himself, who had been watching for my arrival so as to receive me upon his threshold and take off my greatcoat with his own hands.

"Mme. de Guermantes will be as pleased as punch," he greeted me in a glibly persuasive tone. "Let me help you off with your duds." (He felt it to be at once companionable and comic to employ the speech of the people.) "My wife was just the least bit afraid you might fail us, although you had fixed a date. We've been saying to each other all day long: 'Depend upon it, he'll never turn up.' I am bound to say, Mme. de Guermantes was a better prophet than I was. You are not an easy man to get hold of, and I was quite sure you were going to play us false." And the Duke was so bad a husband, so brutal even (people said), that one felt grateful to him, as one feels grateful to wicked people for their occasional kindness of heart, for those words 'Mme. de Guermantes' with which he appeared to be spreading out over the Duchess a protecting wing, that she might be but one flesh with him. Meanwhile, taking me familiarly by the hand, he began to lead the way, to introduce me into his household. Just as some casual phrase may delight us coming from the lips of a peasant if it points to the survival of a local tradition, shews the trace of some historic event unknown, it may be, to him who thus alludes to it; so this politeness on the part of M. de Guermantes, which, moreover, he was to continue to shew me throughout the evening, charmed me as a survival of habits of many centuries' growth, habits of the seventeenth century in particular. The people of bygone ages seem to us infinitely remote. We do not feel justified in ascribing to them any underlying intention apart from those to which they give formal expression; we are amazed when we come upon a sentiment more or less akin to what we are feeling to-day in a Homeric hero, or upon a skilful tactical feint in Hannibal, during the battle of Cannae, where he let his flank be driven back in order to take the enemy by surprise and surround him; it would seem that we imagined the epic poet and the Punic general as being as remote from ourselves as an animal seen in a zoological garden. Even in certain personages of the court of Louis XIV, when we find signs of courtesy in the letters written by them to some man of inferior rank who could be of no service to them whatever, they leave us bewildered because they reveal to us suddenly, as existing among these great gentlemen, a whole world of beliefs to which they never give any direct expression but which govern their conduct, and especially the belief that they are bound in politeness to feign certain sentiments and to carry out with the most scrupulous care certain obligations of friendship.

This imagined remoteness of the past is perhaps one of the things that enable us to understand how even great writers have found an inspired beauty in the works of mediocre mystifiers, such as Macpherson's *Ossian*.

We so little expected to learn that bards long dead could have modern ideas that we marvel if in what we believe to be an ancient Gaelic ode we come upon one which we should have thought, at the most, ingenious in a contemporary. A translator of talent has simply to add to an ancient writer whom he presents to us more or less faithfully reproduced fragments which, signed with a contemporary name and published separately, would seem entertaining only; at once he imparts a moving grandeur to his poet, who is thus made to play upon the keyboards of several ages at once. This translator was capable only of a mediocre book, if that book had been published as his original work. Given out as a translation, it seems that of a masterpiece. The past not merely is not fugitive, it remains present. It is not within a few months only after the outbreak of a war that laws passed without haste can effectively influence its course, it is not within fifteen years only after a crime which has remained obscure that a magistrate can still find the vital evidence which will throw a light on it; after hundreds and thousands of years the scholar who has been studying in a distant land the place-names, the customs of the inhabitants, may still extract from them some legend long anterior to the Christian era, already unintelligible, if not actually forgotten, at the time of Herodotus, which in the name given to a rock, in a religious rite, dwells surrounded by the present, like an emanation of greater density, immemorial and stable. There was similarly an emanation, though far less ancient, of the life of the court, if not in the manners of M. de Guermantes, which were often vulgar, at least in the mind that controlled them. I was to breathe this again, like the odour of antiquity, when I joined him a little later in the drawing-room. For I did not go there at once.

As we left the outer hall, I had mentioned to M. de Guermantes that I was extremely anxious to see his Elstirs. "I am at your service. Is M. Elstir a friend of yours, then? If so, it is most vexing, for I know him slightly; he is a pleasant fellow, what our fathers used to call an 'honest fellow'; I might have asked him to honour us with his company, and to dine to-night. I am sure he would have been highly flattered at being invited to spend the evening in your society." Very little suggestive of the old order when he tried thus to assume its manner, the Duke relapsed unconsciously into it. After inquiring whether I wished him to shew me the pictures, he conducted me to them, gracefully standing aside for me at each door, apologising when, to shew me the way, he was obliged to precede me, a little scene which (since the days when Saint-Simon relates that an ancestor of the Guermantes did him the honours of his town house with the same punctilious exactitude in the performance of the frivolous duties of a gentleman) must, before coming gradually down to us, have been enacted by many other Guermantes for numberless other visitors. And as I had said to the Duke that I would like very much to be left alone for a few minutes with the pictures, he discreetly withdrew, telling me that I should find him in the drawing-room when I was ready.

Only, once I was face to face with the Elstirs, I completely forgot about dinner and the time; here again as at Balbec I had before me fragments of that strangely coloured world which was no more than the projection,

the way of seeing things peculiar to that great painter, which his speech
in no way expressed. The parts of the walls that were covered by paintings
from his brush, all homogeneous with one another, were like the luminous
images of a magic lantern, which would have been in this instance the brain
of the artist, and the strangeness of which one could never have suspected
so long as one had known only the man, which was like seeing the iron
lantern boxing its lamp before any coloured slide had been slid into its
groove. Among these pictures several of the kind that seemed most absurd
to ordinary people interested me more than the rest because they recreated
those optical illusions which prove to us that we should never succeed in
identifying objects if we did not make some process of reasoning intervene.
How often, when driving in the dark, do we not come upon a long, lighted
street which begins a few feet away from us, when what we have actually
before our eyes is nothing but a rectangular patch of wall with a bright
light falling on it, which has given us the mirage of depth. In view of which
is it not logical, not by any artifice of symbolism but by a sincere return
to the very root of the impression, to represent one thing by that other for
which, in the flash of a first illusion, we mistook it? Surfaces and volumes
are in reality independent of the names of objects which our memory imposes on them after we have recognised them. Elstir attempted to wrest
from what he had just felt what he already knew, his effort had often been
to break up that aggregate of impressions which we call vision.

The people who detested these 'horrors' were astonished to find that
Elstir admired Chardin, Perroneau, any number of painters whom they,
the ordinary men and women of society, liked. They did not take into
account that Elstir had had to make, for his own part, in striving to reproduce reality (with the particular index of his taste for certain lines of approach), the same effort as a Chardin or a Perroneau and that consequently,
when he ceased to work for himself, he admired in them attempts of the
same order, fragments anticipatory so to speak of works of his own. Nor
did these society people include in their conception of Elstir's work that
temporal perspective which enabled them to like, or at least to look without
discomfort at Chardin's painting. And yet the older among them might
have reminded themselves that in the course of their lives they had seen
gradually, as the years bore them away from it, the unbridgeable gulf between what they considered a masterpiece by Ingres and what, they had
supposed, must remain for ever a 'horror' (Manet's *Olympia*, for example)
shrink until the two canvases seemed like twins. But we learn nothing from
any lesson because we have not the wisdom to work backwards from the
particular to the general, and imagine ourselves always to be going through
an experience which is without precedents in the past.

I was moved by the discovery in two of the pictures (more realistic,
these, and in an earlier manner) of the same person, in one in evening dress
in his own drawing-room, in the other wearing a frock coat and tall hat
at some popular regatta where he had evidently no business to be, which
proved that for Elstir he was not only a regular sitter but a friend, perhaps
a patron whom it pleased him (just as Carpaccio used to introduce prominent figures, and in speaking likenesses, from contemporary life in Venice)

to introduce into his pictures, just as Beethoven, too, found pleasure in inscribing at the top of a favourite work the beloved name of the Archduke Rudolph. There was something enchanting about this waterside carnival. The river, the women's dresses, the sails of the boats, the innumerable reflexions of one thing and another came crowding into this little square panel of beauty which Elstir had cut out of a marvellous afternoon. What delighted one in the dress of a woman who had stopped for a moment in the dance because it was hot and she was out of breath was irresistible also in the same way in the canvas of a motionless sail, in the water of the little harbour, in the wooden bridge, in the leaves of the trees and in the sky. As in one of the pictures that I had seen at Balbec, the hospital, as beautiful beneath its sky of lapis lazuli as the cathedral itself, seemed (more bold than Elstir the theorician, then Elstir the man of taste, the lover of things mediaeval) to be intoning: "There is no such thing as gothic, there is no such thing as a masterpiece; this tasteless hospital is just as good as the glorious porch," so I now heard: "The slightly vulgar lady at whom a man of discernment would refrain from glancing as he passed her by, would except from the poetical composition which nature has set before him— her dress is receiving the same light as the sail of that boat, and there are no degrees of value and beauty; the commonplace dress and the sail, beautiful in itself, are two mirrors reflecting the same gleam; the value is all in the painter's eye." This eye had had the skill to arrest for all time the motion of the hours at this luminous instant, when the lady had felt hot and had stopped dancing, when the tree was fringed with a belt of shadow, when the sails seemed to be slipping over a golden glaze. But just because the depicted moment pressed on one with so much force, this so permanent canvas gave one the most fleeting impression, one felt that the lady would presently move out of it, the boats drift away, the night draw on, that pleasure comes to an end, that life passes and that the moments illuminated by the convergence, at once, of so many lights do not recur. I recognized yet another aspect, quite different it is true, of what the moment means in a series of water-colours of mythological subjects, dating from Elstir's first period, which also adorned this room. Society people who held 'advanced' views on art went 'as far as' this earliest manner, but no further. These were certainly not the best work that he had done, but already the sincerity with which the subject had been thought out melted its natural coldness. Thus the Muses, for instance, were represented as it might be creatures belonging to a species now fossilised, but creatures which it would not have been surprising in mythological times to see pass in the evening, in twos or threes, along some mountain path. Here and there a poet, of a race that had also a peculiar interest for the zoologist (characterised by a certain sexlessness) strolled with a Muse, as one sees in nature creatures of different but of kindred species consort together. In one of these water-colours one saw a poet wearied by long wanderings on the mountains, whom a Centaur, meeting him and moved to pity by his weakness, had taken on his back and was carrying home. In more than one other, the vast landscape (in which the mythical scene, the fabulous heroes, occupied a minute place and were almost lost) was rendered, from the mountain tops to the sea, with an exactitude which told one more than the hour, told one to the very minute what time of day it was, thanks to the precise angle of the setting sun, to the fleeting fidelity of the shadows. In this way the artist managed to give, by making it instantaneous, a sort of historical reality, as of a thing actually lived, to the symbol of his fable, painted it and set it at a definite point in the past.

While I was examining Elstir's paintings the bell, rung by arriving guests, had been pealing uninterruptedly, and had lulled me into a pleasing unconsciousness. But the silence which followed its clangour and had already lasted for some time succeeded—less rapidly, it is true—in awakening me from my dream, as the silence that follows Lindor's music arouses Bartolo from his sleep. I was afraid that I had been forgotten, that they had sat down to dinner, and hurried to the drawing-room. At the door of the Elstir gallery I found a servant waiting for me, white-haired, though whether with age or powder I cannot say, with the air of a Spanish Minister, but treating me with the same respect that he would have shewn to a King. I felt from his manner that he must have been waiting for at least an hour, and I thought with alarm of the delay I had caused in the service of dinner, especially as I had promised to be at M. de Charlus's by eleven.

The Spanish Minister (though I also met on the way the footman persecuted by the porter, who, radiant with delight when I inquired after his girl, told me that the very next day they were both to be off duty, so that he would be able to spend the whole day with her, and extolled the generosity of Madame la Duchesse) conducted me to the drawing-room, where I was afraid of finding M. de Guermantes in an ill humour. He welcomed me, on the contrary, with a joy that was evidently to a certain extent artificial and dictated by politeness, but was also sincere, prompted both by his stomach which so long a delay had begun to famish, and his consciousness of a similar impatience in all his other guests, who completely filled the room. Indeed I heard afterwards that I had kept them waiting for nearly three-quarters of an hour. The Duc de Guermantes probably thought that to prolong the general torment for two minutes more would not intensify it and that, politeness having driven him to postpone for so long the moment of moving into the dining-room, this politeness would be more complete if, by not having dinner announced immediately, he could succeed in persuading me that I was not late, and that they had not been waiting for me. And so he asked me, as if we had still an hour before dinner and some of the party had not yet arrived, what I thought of his Elstirs. But at the same time, and without letting the cravings of his stomach become apparent, so as not to lose another moment, he, in concert with the Duchess, proceeded to the ceremony of introduction. Then only I perceived that there had occurred round about me, me who until this evening, save for my novitiate in Mme. Swann's drawing-room, had been accustomed, in my mother's homes, at Combray and in Paris, to the manners, either protecting or defensive, of the grim ladies of our middle-world, who treated me as a child, a change of surroundings comparable to that which introduces Parsifal suddenly into the midst of the Flower-Maidens. Those who surrounded me now, their bosoms entirely bare (the naked flesh appeared on either side of a sinuous spray of mimosa or behind the broad petals of a rose) could not murmur a word of greeting without at the same time bathing me in long, caressing glances, as though shyness alone restrained them from kissing me. Many of them were nevertheless highly respectable from the moral standpoint; many, not all, for the most virtuous had not for those of a lighter vein the same repulsion that my mother would have felt. The caprices of one's conduct, denied by saintlier friends, in the face of the evidence, seemed in the Guermantes world to matter far less than the relations which one had been able to maintain. One pretended not to know that the body of one's hostess was at the disposal of all comers, provided that her visiting list showed no gaps. As the Duke put himself out not at all for his other guests (of whom he had long known everything that there was to know, and they of him) but quite markedly for me, whose kind of superiority, being outside his experience, inspired in him something akin to the respect which the great nobleman of the court of Louis XIV used to feel for his plebeian Ministers, he evidently considered that the fact of my not knowing his other guests mattered not at all—to me at least, though it might to them—and while I was anxious, on his account, as to the impression that I was going to make on them he was thinking only of how his friends would impress me.

At the very outset I found myself completely bewildered. No sooner had I entered the drawing-room than M. de Guermantes, without even allowing me time to shake hands with the Duchess, had led me, as though I were a delightful surprise to the person in question to whom he seemed to be saying: "Here's your friend! You see, I'm bringing him to you by the scruff of his neck," towards a lady of smallish stature. Whereupon, long before, thrust forward by the Duke, I had reached her chair, the lady had begun to flash at me continuously from her large, soft, dark eyes the thousand smiles of understanding which we address to an old friend who perhaps has not recognised us. As this was precisely my case and I could not succeed in calling to mind who she was I averted my eyes from her as I approached so as not to have to respond until our introduction should have released me from my predicament. Meanwhile the lady continued to maintain in unstable equilibrium the smile intended for myself. She looked as though she were anxious to be relieved of it and to hear me say: "Oh, but this is a pleasure! Mamma will be pleased when I tell her I've met you!" I was as impatient to learn her name as she was to see that I did finally greet her, fully aware of what I was doing, so that the smile which she was holding on indefinitely, like the note of a tuning-fork, might at length be let go. But M. de Guermantes managed things so badly (to my mind, at least) that I seemed to have heard only my own name uttered and was given no clue to the identity of my unknown friend, to whom it never occurred to tell me herself what her name was, so obvious did the grounds of our intimacy, which baffled me completely, seem to her. Indeed, as soon as I had come within reach, she did not offer me her hand, but took mine in a familiar clasp, and spoke to me exactly as though I had been equally conscious with herself of the pleasant memories to which her mind reverted. She told me how sorry Albert (who, I gathered, was her son) would be to have missed seeing me. I tried to remember who, among the people I had known as boys, was called Albert, and could think only of Bloch, but this could not be Bloch's mother that I saw before me since she had been dead for some time. In vain I struggled to identify the past experience common to herself and me to which her thoughts had been carried back. But I could no more distinguish it through the translucent jet of her large, soft pupils which allowed only her smile to pierce their surface than one can distinguish a landscape that lies on the other side of a smoked glass, even when the sun is blazing on it. She asked me whether my father was not working too hard, if I would not come to the theatre some evening with Albert, if I was stronger now, and as my replies, stumbling through the mental darkness in which I was plunged, became distinct only to explain that I was not feeling well that evening, she pushed forward a chair for me herself, going to all sorts of trouble which I was not accustomed to see taken by my parents' friends. At length the clue to the riddle was furnished me by the Duke: "She thinks you're charming," he murmured in my ear, which felt somehow that it had heard these words before. They were what Mme. de Villeparisis had said to my grandmother and myself after we had made the acquaintance of the Princesse de Luxembourg. Everything became clear; the lady I now saw had nothing in common with Mme. de Luxembourg, but from the language of him who thus served me with her I could discern the nature of the animal. It was a Royalty. She had never before heard of either my family or myself, but, a scion of the noblest race and endowed with the greatest fortune in the world (for, a daughter of the Prince de Parme, she had married a cousin of equal princelihood), she sought always, in gratitude to her Creator, to testify to her neighbour, however poor or lowly he might be, that she did not look down upon him. Really, I might have guessed this from her smile. I had seen the Princesse de Luxembourg buy little rye-cakes on the beach at Balbec to give to my grandmother, as though to a caged deer in the zoological garden. But this was only the second Princess of the Blood Royal to whom I had been presented, and I might be excused my failure to discern in her the common factors of the friendliness of the great. Besides, had not they themselves gone out of their way to warn me not to count too much on this friendliness, since the Duchesse de Guermantes, who had waved me so effusive a greeting with her gloved hand at the Opéra-Comique, had appeared furious when I bowed to her in the street, like people who, having once given somebody a sovereign, feel that this has set them free from any further obligation toward him. As for M. de Charlus, his ups and downs were even more sharply contrasted. While in the sequel I have known, as the reader will learn, Highnesses and Majesties of another sort altogether, Queens who play the Queen and speak not after the conventions of their kind but like the Queens in Sardou's plays.

If M. de Guermantes had been in such haste to present me, it was because the presence at a party of anyone not personally known to a Royal Personage is an intolerable state of things which must not be prolonged for a single instant. It was similar to the haste which Saint-Loup had shewn in making me introduce him to my grandmother. By the same token, by a fragmentary survival of the old life of the court which is called social courtesy and is not superficial, in which, rather, by a centripetal reversion, it is the surface that becomes essential and profound, the Duc and Duchesse de Guermantes regarded as a duty more essential than those (which one at least of the pair neglected often enough) of charity, chastity, pity and justice, as a more unalterable law that of never addressing the Princesse de Parme save in the third person.

Having never yet in my life been to Parma (a pilgrimage I had been anxious to make ever since certain Easter holidays long ago), to meet its Princess, who, I knew, owned the finest palace in that matchless city, where, moreover, everything must be in keeping, isolated as it was from the rest of the world, within the polished walls, in the atmosphere, stifling as a breathless summer evening on the Piazza of a small town in Italy, of its compact and almost cloying name, would surely have substituted in a flash for what I had so often tried to imagine all that did really exist at Parma in a sort of partial arrival there, without my having to stir from Paris, of myself; it was in the algebraical expression of a journey to the city of Correggio a simple equation, so to speak, of that unknown quantity. But if I had for many years past—like a perfumer impregnating a solid mass of grease with scent—made this name, Princesse de Parme, absorb the fragrance of thousands of violets, in return, when I set eyes on the Princess, who, until then I should have sworn, must be the Sanseverina herself, a second process began which was not, I may say, completed until several months had passed, and consisted in expelling, by means of fresh chemical combinations, all the essential oil of violets and all the Stendhalian fragrance from the name of the Princess, and in implanting there, in their place, the image of a little dark woman, taken up with good works, of a friendliness so humble that one felt at once in how exalted a pride that friendliness had its roots. Moreover, while, barring a few points of difference, she was exactly like any other great lady, she was as little Stendhalian as is, for example, in Paris, in the Europe quarter, the Rue de Parme, which bears far less resemblance to the name of Parma than to any or all of the neighbouring streets, and reminds one not nearly so much of the Charterhouse in which Fabrice ends his days as of the waiting room in the Saint-Lazare station.

Her friendliness sprang from two causes. The first and more general was the education which this daughter of Kings had received. Her mother (not merely allied by blood to all the royal families of Europe but further-more—in contrast to the Ducal House of Parma—richer than any reigning Princess) had instilled into her from her earliest childhood the arrogantly humble precepts of an evangelical snobbery; and to-day every line of the daughter's face, the curve of her shoulders, the movements of her arms seemed to repeat the lesson: "Remember that if God has caused you to be born on the steps of a throne you ought not to make that a reason for looking down upon those to whom Divine Providence has willed (where-fore His Name be praised) that you should be superior by birth and for-tune. On the contrary, you must suffer the little ones. Your ancestors were Princes of Treves and Juliers from the year 647: God has decreed in His bounty that you should hold practically all the shares in the Suez Canal and three times as many Royal Dutch as Edmond de Rothschild; your pedigree in a direct line has been established by genealogists from the year 63 of the Christian Era; you have as sisters-in-law two Empresses. Therefore never seem, in your speech, to be recalling these great privileges, not that they are precarious (for nothing can alter antiquity of race, while the world will always need petrol), but because it is useless to point out that you are better born than other people or that your investments are all gilt-edged, since everyone knows these facts already. Be helpful to the needy. Furnish to all those whom the bounty of Heaven has done you the favour of placing beneath you as much as you can give them without forfeiture of your rank, that is to say help in the form of money, even your personal service by their sickbeds, but never (bear well in mind) invite them to your parties, which would do them no possible good and, by weakening your own position, would diminish the efficacy of your benevolent activities."

And so even at the moments when she could not do good the Princess endeavoured to shew, or rather to let it be thought, by all the external signs of dumb language, that she did not consider herself superior to the people among whom she found herself thrown. She treated each of them with that charming courtesy with which well-bred people treat their inferiors and was continually, to make herself useful, pushing back her chair so as to leave more room, holding my gloves, offering me all those services which would demean the proud spirit of a commoner but are very willingly rendered by sovereign ladies or, instinctively and by force of professional habit, by retired servants.

But already the Duke, who seemed in a hurry to complete the round of introduction, had led me off to another of the flower-maidens. On hearing her name I told her that I had passed by her country house, not far from Balbec. "Oh, I should have been so pleased to take you over it," she informed me, almost in a whisper, to enhance her modesty, but in a tone of deep feeling, steeped in regret for the loss of an opportunity to enjoy a quite exceptional pleasure; and went on, with a meaning glance: "I do hope you will come again some day. But I must say that what would interest you more still would be my aunt Brancas's place. It was built by Mansard; it is the jewel of the province." It was not only she herself who would have been glad to shew me over her house, but her aunt Brancas would have been no less delighted to do me the honours of hers, or so I was assured by this lady who thought evidently that, especially at a time when the land shewed a tendency to pass into the hands of financiers who had no knowledge of the world, it was important that the great should keep up the exalted traditions of lordly hospitality, by speeches which involved them in nothing. It was also because she sought, like everyone in her world, to say the things which would give most pleasure to the person she was addressing, to give him the highest idea of himself, to make him think that he flattered people by writing to them, that he honoured those who entertained him, that everyone was burning to know him. The desire to give other people this comforting idea of themselves does, it must be admitted, exist even among the middle classes. We find there that kindly disposition, in the form of an individual merit compensating for some other defect, not alas among the most trusty male friends but at any rate among the most agreeable female companions. But there anyhow it blooms only in isolated patches. In an important section of the aristocracy, on the other hand, this characteristic has ceased to be individual; cultivated by education, sustained by the idea of a personal greatness which can fear no humiliation, which knows no rival, is aware that by being pleasant it can make people happy and delights in doing so, it has become the generic feature of a class. And even those whom personal defects of too incompatible a kind prevent from keeping it in their hearts bear the unconscious trace of it in their vocabulary or their gesticulation.

"She is a very good creature," said the Duc de Guermantes, of the Princesse de Parme, "and she can play the 'great lady' when she likes, better than anyone."

While I was being introduced to the ladies, one of the gentlemen of the party had been shewing various signs of agitation: this was Comte Hannibal de Bréauté-Consalvi. Arriving late, he had not had time to investigate the composition of the party, and when I entered the room, seeing in me a guest who was not one of the Duchess's regular circle and must therefore have some quite extraordinary claim to admission, installed his monocle beneath the groined arch of his eyebrow, thinking that this would be a great help to him in discovering what manner of man I was. He knew that Mme. de Guermantes possessed (the priceless appanage of truly superior women) what was called a 'salon,' that is to say added occasionally to the people of her own set some celebrity who had recently come into prominence by the discovery of a new cure for something or the production of a masterpiece. The Faubourg Saint-Germain had not yet recovered from the shock of learning that, to the reception which she had given to meet the King and Queen of England, the Duchess had not been afraid to invite M. Detaille. The clever women of the Faubourg who had not been invited were inconsolable, so deliciously thrilling would it have been to come into contact with that strange genius. Mme. de Courvoisier made out that M. Ribot had been there as well, but this was a pure invention, designed to make people believe that Oriane was aiming at an Embassy for her husband. Finally, a last straw of scandal, M. de Guermantes, with a gallantry that would have done credit to Marshal Saxe, had repaired to the green-room of the Comédie Française, and had begged Mlle. Reichemberg to come and recite before the King, which having come to pass constituted an event without precedent in the annals of routs. Remembering all these surprises, which, moreover, had his entire approval, his own presence being not merely an ornament but, in the same way as that of the Duchesse de Guermantes, a consecration to any drawing-room, M. de Bréauté, when he asked himself who I could be, felt that the field of exploration was very wide. For a moment the name of M. Widor flashed before his mind, but he decided that I was not old enough to be an organist, and M. Widor not striking enough to be 'asked out.' It seemed on the whole more plausible to regard me simply as the new Attaché at the Swedish Legation of whom he

had heard, and he was preparing to ask me for the latest news of King
Oscar, by whom he had several times been very hospitably received; but
when the Duke, in introducing me, had mentioned my name to M. de
Bréauté, the latter, finding that name to be completely unknown to him,
had no longer any doubt that, being where I was, I must be a celebrity of
some sort. Oriane would certainly never invite anyone who was not, and
had the art of attracting men who were in the public eye to her house, in a
ratio that of course never exceeded one per cent, otherwise she would have
lowered its tone. M. de Bréauté began, therefore, to lick his chops and to
sniff the air greedily, his appetite whetted not only by the good dinner upon
which he could count, but by the character of the party, which my presence
could not fail to make interesting, and which would furnish him with a
topic for brilliant conversation next day at the Duc de Chartres's luncheon-
table. He had not yet settled in his own mind whether I was the man who
had just been making those experiments with a serum to cure cancer, or
the author of the new 'curtain-raiser' then in rehearsal at the Théâtre
Français; but, a great intellectual, a great collector of 'travellers' tales,'
he continued an ever increasing display of reverences, signs of mutual
understanding, smiles filtered through the glass of his monocle; either in
the mistaken idea that a man of my standing would esteem him more
highly if he could manage to instil into me the illusion that for him, the
Comte de Bréauté-Consalvi, the privileges of the mind were no less deserv-
ing of respect than those of birth; or simply from the need to express and
difficulty of expressing his satisfaction, in his ignorance of the language in
which he ought to address me, just as if, in fact, he had found himself face
to face with one of the 'natives' of an undiscovered country on which his
keel had grounded, natives from whom, in the hope of ultimate profit, he
would endeavour, observing with interest the while their quaint customs
and without interrupting his demonstrations of friendship, or like them
uttering loud cries, to obtain ostrich eggs and spices in exchange for his
glass beads. Having responded as best I could to his joy, I shook hands
next with the Duc de Châtellerault, whom I had already met at Mme. de
Villeparisis's, who, he informed me, was as 'cunning as they made 'em.' He
was typically Guermantes in the fairness of his hair, his arched profile, the
points where the skin of his cheeks lost colour, all of which may be seen in
the portraits of that family which have come down to us from the sixteenth
and seventeenth centuries. But, as I was no longer in love with the Duchess,
her reincarnation in the person of a young man offered me no attraction.
I interpreted the hook made by the Duc de Châtellerault's nose, as if it
had been the signature of a painter whose work I had long studied but who
no longer interested me in the least. Next, I said good evening also to the
Prince de Foix, and to the detriment of my knuckles, which emerged crushed
and mangled, let them be caught in a vice which was the German handclasp,
accompanied by an ironical or good-natured smile, of the Prince von Faffenheim, M. de Norpois's friend, who, by virtue of the mania for nicknames
which prevailed in this set, was known so universally as Prince Von that he
himself used to sign his letters 'Prince Von,' or, when he wrote to his intimates, 'Von.' And yet this abbreviation was understandable, in view of his

triple-barrelled name. It was less easy to grasp the reasons which made 'Elizabeth' be replaced, now by 'Lili,' now by 'Bebeth,' just as another world swarmed with 'Kikis.' One can realise that these people, albeit in most respects idle and light-minded enough, might have come to adopt 'Quiou' in order not to waste the precious time that it would have taken them to pronounce 'Montesquiou.' But it is not so easy to see what they saved by naming one of their cousins 'Dinand' instead of 'Ferdinand.' It must not be thought, however, that in the invention of nicknames the Guermantes invariably proceed to curtail or reduplicate syllables. Thus two sisters, the Comtesse de Montpeyroux and the Vicomtesse de Vélude, who were both of them enormously stout, invariably heard themselves addressed, without the least trace of annoyance on their part or of amusement on other people's, so long established was the custom, as 'Petite' and 'Mignonne.' Mme. de Guermantes, who adored Mme. de Montpeyroux, would, if her friend had been seriously ill, have flown to the sister with tears in her eyes and exclaimed: "I hear Petite is dreadfully bad!" Mme. de l'Eclin, who wore her hair in bands that entirely hid her ears, was never called anything but 'The Empty Stomach'; in some cases people simply added an 'a' to the last or first name of the husband to indicate the wife. The most miserly, most sordid, most inhuman man in the Faubourg having been christened Raphael, his charmer, his flower springing also from the rock always signed herself 'Raphaela'—but these are merely a few specimens taken from innumerable rules, to which we can always return later on, if the occasion offers, and explain some of them. I then asked the Duke to present me to the Prince d'Agrigente. "What! Do you mean to say you don't know our excellent Gri-gri!" cried M. de Guermantes, and gave M. d'Agrigente my name. His own, so often quoted by Françoise, had always appeared to me like a transparent sheet of coloured glass through which I beheld, struck, on the shore of the violet sea, by the slanting rays of a golden sun, the rosy marble cubes of an ancient city of which I had not the least doubt that the Prince—happening for a miraculous moment to be passing through Paris—was himself, as luminously Sicilian and gloriously mellowed, the absolute sovereign. Alas, the vulgar drone to whom I was introduced, and who wheeled round to bid me good evening with a ponderous ease which he considered elegant, was as independent of his name as of any work of art that he might have owned without bearing upon his person any trace of its beauty, without, perhaps, ever having stopped to examine it. The Prince d'Agrigente was so entirely devoid of anything princely, anything that might make one think of Girgenti that one was led to suppose that his name, entirely distinct from himself, bound by no ties to his person, had had the power of attracting to itself the whole of whatever vague poetical element there might have been in this man as in any other, and isolating it, after the operation, in the enchanted syllables. If any such operation had been performed, it had certainly been done most efficiently, for there remained not an atom of charm to be drawn from this kinsman of Guermantes. With the result that he found himself at one and the same time the only man in the world who was Prince d'Agrigente and the man who, of all the men in the world was, perhaps, least so. He was, for all that, very glad to be what he was, but as a banker is glad to hold a number of shares in a mine without caring whether the said mine answers to the charming name of Ivanhoe or Primrose, or is called merely the Premier. Meanwhile, as these introductions, which it has taken me so long to recount but which, beginning as I entered the room, had lasted only a few seconds, were coming to an end, and Mme. de Guermantes, in an almost suppliant tone, was saying to me: "I am sure Basin is tiring you, dragging you round like that; we are anxious for you to know our friends, but we are a great deal more anxious not to tire you, so that you may come again often," the Duke, with a somewhat awkward and timid wave of the hand, gave (as he would gladly have given it at any time during the last hour, filled for me by the contemplation of his Elstirs) the signal that dinner might now be served.

I should add that one of the guests was still missing, M. de Grouchy, whose wife, a Guermantes by birth, had arrived by herself, her husband being due to come straight from the country, where he had been shooting all day. This M. de Grouchy, a descendant of his namesake of the First Empire, of whom it has been said, quite wrongly, that his absence at the start of the Battle of Waterloo was the principal cause of Napoleon's defeat, came of an excellent family which, however, was not good enough in the eyes of certain fanatics for blue blood. Thus the Prince de Guermantes, whose own tastes, in later life, were to prove more easily satisfied, had been in the habit of saying to his nieces: "What a misfortune for that poor Mme. de Guermantes" (the Vicomtesse de Guermantes, Mme. de Grouchy's mother) "that she has never succeeded in marrying any of her children." "But, uncle, the eldest girl married M. de Grouchy." "I do not call that a husband! However, they say that your uncle François has proposed for the youngest one, so perhaps they won't all die old maids." No sooner was the order to serve dinner given than with a vast gyratory whirr, multiple and simultaneous, the double doors of the dining-room swung apart; a chamberlain with the air of a Lord Chamberlain bowed before the Princesse de Parme and announced the tidings "Madame is served," in a tone such as he would have employed to say "Madame is dead," which, however, cast no gloom over the assembly for it was with an air of unrestrained gaiety and as, in summer, at 'Robinson' that the couples moved forward one behind another to the dining-room, separating when they had reached their places where footmen thrust their chairs in behind them; last of all, Mme. de Guermantes advanced upon me, that I might lead her to the table, and without my feeling the least shadow of the timidity that I might have feared, for, like a huntress to whom her great muscular prowess has made graceful motion an easy thing, observing no doubt that I had placed myself on the wrong side of her, she pivoted with such accuracy round me that I found her arm resting on mine and attuned in the most natural way to a rhythm of precise and noble movements. I yielded to these with all the more readiness in that the Guermantes attached no more importance to them than does to learning a truly learned man in whose company one is less alarmed than in that of a dunce; other doors opened through which there entered the steaming soup, as though the dinner were being held in a puppet-theatre of skilful mechanism where the belated arrival of the young guest set, on a signal from the puppet-master, all the machinery in motion.

Timid and not majestically sovereign had been this signal from the Duke, to which had responded the unlocking of that vast, ingenious, subservient and sumptuous clockwork, mechanical and human. The indecision of his gesture did not spoil for me the effect of the spectacle that was attendant upon it. For I could feel that what had made it hesitating and embarrassed was the fear of letting me see that they were waiting only for myself to begin dinner and that they had been waiting for some time, just as Mme. de Guermantes was afraid that after looking at so many pictures I would find it tiring and would be hindered from taking my ease among them if her husband engaged me in a continuous flow of introductions. So that it was the absence of grandeur in this gesture that disclosed its true grandeur. As, also, did that indifference shewn by the Duke to the splendour of his surroundings, in contrast to his deference towards a guest, however insignificant, whom he desired to honour.

Not that M. de Guermantes was not in certain respects thoroughly commonplace, shewing indeed some of the absurd weaknesses of a man with too much money, the arrogance of an upstart, which he certainly was not. But just as a public official or a priest sees his own humble talents multiplied to infinity (as a wave is by the whole mass of the sea which presses behind it) by those forces on which they can rely, the Government of France and the Catholic Church, so M. de Guermantes was borne on by that other force, aristocratic courtesy in its truest form. This courtesy drew the line at any number of people. Mme. de Guermantes would not have asked to her house Mme. de Cambremer, or M. de Forcheville. But the moment that anyone (as was the case with me) appeared eligible for admission into the Guermantes world, this courtesy revealed treasures of hospitable simplicity more splendid still, were that possible, than those historic rooms, or the marvellous furniture that had remained in them.

When he wished to give pleasure to anyone, M. de Guermantes possessed, in this way, for making his guest for the moment the principal person present, an art which made the most of the circumstances and the place. No doubt at Guermantes his 'distinctions' and 'favours' would have assumed another form. He would have ordered his carriage to take me for a drive, alone with himself, before dinner. Such as they were, one could not help feeling touched by his manners as one is in reading memoirs of the period by those of Louis XIV when he replies good-naturedly, smiling and almost with a bow, to some one who has come to solicit his favour. It must however in both instances be borne in mind that this 'politeness' did not go beyond the strict meaning of the word.

Louis XIV (with whom the sticklers for pure nobility of his day find fault, nevertheless, for his scant regard for etiquette, so much so that, according to Saint-Simon, he was only a very minor king, as kings go, when compared with such monarchs as Philippe de Valois or Charles V), has the most minute instructions drawn up so that Princes of the Blood and Ambassadors may know to what sovereigns they ought to give precedence. In certain cases, in view of the impossibility of arriving at a decision, a compromise is arranged by which the son of Louis XIV, Monseigneur, shall entertain certain foreign sovereigns only out of doors, in the open air, so that it may not be said that in entering the house one has preceded the other; and the Elector Palatine, entertaining the Duc de Chevreuse at dinner, pretends, so as not to have to make way for his guest, to be taken ill, and dines with him indeed, but dines lying down, thus avoiding the difficulty. M. le Duc evading opportunities of paying his duty to Monsieur, the latter, on the advice of the King, his brother, who is moreover extremely attached to him, seizes an excuse for making his cousin attend his levee and forcing him to pass him his shirt. But as soon as the feeling is deep, when the heart is involved, this rule of duty, so inflexible when politeness only is at stake, changes entirely. A few hours after the death of his brother, one of the people whom he most dearly loved, when Monsieur, in the words of the Duc de Montfort, is 'still warm,' we find Louis XIV singing snatches from operas, astonished that the Duchesse de Bourgogne, who has difficulty in concealing her grief, should be looking so woe-begone, and, desiring that the gaiety of the court shall be at once resumed, so that his courtiers may be encouraged to sit down to the tables, ordering the Duc de Bourgogne to start a game of *brelan*. Well, not only in his social and concentrated activities, but in the most spontaneous utterances, the ordinary preoccupations of M. de Guermantes, the use he made of his time, one found a similar contrast; the Guermantes were no more susceptible than other mortals to grief; one might indeed say that their actual sensibility was lower; on the other hand one saw their names every day in the social columns of the *Gaulois* on account of the prodigious number of funerals at which they would have felt it a neglect of duty not to have their presence recorded. As the traveller discovers, almost unaltered, the houses roofed with turf, the terraces which may have met the eyes of Xenophon or Saint Paul, so in the manners of M. de Guermantes, a man who melted one's heart by his courtesy and revolted it by his harshness, I found still intact after the lapse of more than two centuries that deviation typical of court life under Louis XIV which transfers all scruples of conscience from matters of the affections and morality and applies them to purely formal questions.

The other reason for the friendliness shewn me by the Princesse de Parme was of a more personal kind. It was that she was convinced beforehand that everything that she saw at the Duchesse de Guermantes's, people and things alike, was of a quality superior to that of anything that she had at home. It is true that in all the other houses of her acquaintance she behaved as if this had been the case; over the simplest dish, the most ordinary flowers, she was not satisfied with going into ecstasies, she would ask leave to send round next morning, to copy the recipe or to examine the variety of blossom, her head cook or head gardener, gentlemen with large salaries who kept their own carriages and were deeply humiliated at having to come to inquire after a dish they despised or to take notes of a kind of carnation that was not half so fine, had not such ornamental streaks, did not produce so large a blossom as those which they had long been growing for her at home. But if in the Princess, wherever she went, this astonishment at the sight of the most commonplace things was assumed, and intended to shew that she did not derive from the superiority of her rank and riches a pride forbidden by her early instructors, habitually dissembled by her mother and intolerable in the sight of her Creator, it was, on the other hand, in all sincerity that she regarded the drawing-room of the Duchesse de Guermantes as a privileged place in which she could pass only from surprise to delight. To a certain extent, for that matter, though not nearly enough to justify this state of mind, the Guermantes were different from the rest of noble society, they were rarer and more refined. They had given me at first sight the opposite impression; I had found them vulgar, similar to all other men and women, but because before meeting them I had seen in them, as in Balbec, in Florence, in Parma, only names. Evidently, in this drawing-room, all the women whom I had imagined as being like porcelain figures were even more like the great majority of women. But, in the same way as Balbec or Florence, the Guermantes, after first disappointing the imagination because they resembled their fellow-creatures rather than their name, could subsequently, though to a less degree, appeal to the intellect by certain distinctive characteristics. Their bodily structure, the colour—a peculiar pink that merged at times into violet—of their skins, a certain almost flashing fairness of the finely spun hair, even in the men, on whom it was massed in soft golden tufts, half a wall-growing lichen, half a catlike fur (a luminous sparkle to which corresponded a certain brilliance of intellect, for if people spoke of the Guermantes complexion, the Guermantes hair, they spoke also of the wit of the Guermantes, as of the wit of the Mortemarts—a certain social quality whose superior fineness was famed even before the days of Louis XIV and all the more universally recognised since they published the fame of it themselves), all this meant that in the material itself, precious as that might be, in which one found them embedded here and there, the Guermantes remained recognisable, easy to detect and to follow, like the veins whose paleness streaks a block of jasper or onyx, or, better still, like the pliant waving of those tresses of light whose loosened hairs run like flexible rays along the sides of a moss-agate.

The Guermantes—those at least who were worthy of the name—were not only of a quality of flesh, of hair, of transparency of gaze that was exquisite, but had a way of holding themselves, of walking, of bowing, of looking at one before they shook one's hand, of shaking hands, which made them as different in all these respects from an ordinary person in society as he in turn was from a peasant in a smock. And despite their friendliness one asked oneself: "Have they not indeed the right, though they waive it, when they see us walk, bow, leave a room, do any of those things which when performed by them become as graceful as the flight of a swallow or the bending of a rose on its stem, to think: 'These people are of another race than ours, and we are, we, the true lords of creation.'?" Later on, I realised that the Guermantes did indeed regard me as being of another race, but one that aroused their envy because I possessed merits of which I knew nothing and which they professed to regard as alone important. Later still I came to feel that this profession of faith was only half sincere and that in them scorn or surprise could be coexistent with admiration and envy. The physical flexibility essential to the Guermantes was twofold; thanks to one of its forms, constantly in action, at any moment and if, for example, a male Guermantes were about to salute a lady, he produced a silhouette of himself made from the unstable equilibrium of a series of asymmetrical movements with nervous compensations, one leg dragging a little, either on purpose or because, having been broken so often in the hunting-field, it imparted to his trunk in its effort to keep pace with the other a deviation to which the upward thrust of one shoulder gave a counterpoise, while the monocle settled itself before his eye, raising an eyebrow just as the tuft of hair on the forehead was lowered in the formal bow; the other flexibility, like the form of the wave, the wind or the ocean track which is preserved on the shell or the vessel, was so to speak stereotyped in a sort of fixed mobility, curving the arched nose which, beneath the blue, protruding eyes, above the over-thin lips, from which, in the women, there emerged a raucous voice, recalled the fabulous origin attributed in the sixteenth century by the complaisance of parasitic and Hellenising genealogists to his race, ancient beyond dispute, but not to the degree of antiquity which they claimed when they gave as its source the mythological impregnation of a nymph by a divine Bird.

The Guermantes were just as idiomatic from the intellectual as from the physical point of view. With the exception of Prince Gilbert (the husband with antiquated ideas of 'Marie-Gilbert,' who made his wife sit on his left when they drove out together because her blood, though royal, was inferior to his own)—but he was an exception and furnished, behind his back, a perpetual laughing-stock to the rest of the family, who had always fresh anecdotes to tell of him—the Guermantes, while living in the pure cream of aristocracy, affected to take no account of nobility. The theories of the Duchesse de Guermantes, who, to tell the truth, by dint of being a Guermantes, became to a certain extent something different and more attractive, subordinated everything else so completely to intellect, and were in politics so socialistic that one asked oneself where in her mansion could be hiding the familiar spirit whose duty it was to ensure the maintenance of the aristocratic standard of living, and which, always invisible but evidently crouching at one moment in the entrance hall, at another in the drawing-room, at a third in her dressing-room, reminded the servants of this woman who did not believe in titles to address her as Mme. la Duchesse, reminding also herself who cared only for reading and had no respect for persons to go out to dinner with her sister-in-law when eight o'clock struck, and to put on a low gown.

The same familiar spirit represented to Mme. de Guermantes the social duties of duchesses, of the foremost among them, that was, who like herself were multi-millionaires, the sacrifice to boring tea, dinner and evening parties of hours in which she might have read interesting books, as unpleasant necessities like rain, which Mme. de Guermantes accepted, letting play on them her biting humour, but without seeking in any way to justify her acceptance of them. The curious accident by which the butler of Mme. de Guermantes invariably said "Madame la Duchesse" to this woman who believed only in the intellect did not however appear to shock her. Never had it entered her head to request him to address her simply as 'Madame.' Giving her the utmost benefit of the doubt one might have supposed that, thinking of something else at the time, she had heard only the word 'Madame' and that the suffix appended to it had not caught her attention. Only, though she might feign deafness, she was not dumb. In fact, whenever she had a message to give to her husband she would say to the butler: "Remind Monsieur le Duc—"

The familiar spirit had other occupations as well, one of which was to inspire them to talk morality. It is true that there were Guermantes who went in for intellect and Guermantes who went in for morals, and that these two classes did not as a rule coincide. But the former kind—including a Guermantes who had forged cheques, who cheated at cards and was the most delightful of them all, with a mind open to every new and sound idea—spoke even more eloquently upon morals than the others, and in the same strain as Mme. de Villeparisis, at the moments in which the familiar spirit expressed itself through the lips of the old lady. At corresponding moments one saw the Guermantes adopt suddenly a tone almost as old-ladylike, as genial and (as they themselves had more charm) more touching than that of the Marquise, to say of a servant: "One feels that she has a thoroughly sound nature, she's not at all a common girl, she must come of decent parents, she is certainly a girl who has never gone astray." At such moments the familiar spirit took the form of an intonation. But at times it could be bearing also, the expression on a face, the same in the Duchess as in her grandfather the Marshal, a sort of undefinable convulsion (like that of the Serpent, the genius of the Carthaginian family of Barca) by which my heart had more than once been set throbbing, on my morning walks, when before I had recognised Mme. de Guermantes I felt her eyes fastened upon me from the inside of a little dairy. This familiar spirit had intervened in a situation which was far from immaterial not merely to the Guermantes but to the Courvoisiers, the rival faction of the family and, though of as good blood as the Guermantes (it was, indeed, through his Courvoisier grandmother that the Guermantes explained the obsession which led the Prince de Guermantes always to speak of birth and titles as though those were the only things that mattered), their opposite in every respect. Not only did the Courvoisiers not assign to intelligence the same importance as the Guermantes, they had not the same idea of it. For a Guermantes (even were he a fool) to be intelligent meant to have a sharp tongue, to be capable of saying cutting things, to 'get away with it'; but it meant also the capacity to hold one's own equally in painting, music, architecture, to speak English. The Courvoisiers had formed a less favourable impression of intelligence, and unless one were actually of their world being intelligent was almost tantamount to 'having probably murdered one's father and mother.' For them intelligence was the sort of burglar's jemmy by means of which people one did not know from Adam forced the doors of the most reputable drawing-rooms, and it was common knowledge among the Courvoisiers that you always had to pay in the long run for having 'those sort' of people in your house. To the

most trivial statements made by intelligent people who were not 'in society'
the Courvoisiers opposed a systematic distrust. Some one having on one
occasion remarked: "But Swann is younger than Palamède,"—"He says
so, at any rate, and if he says it you may be sure it's because he thinks it
is to his interest!" had been Mme. de Gallardon's retort. Better still, when
some one said of two highly distinguished foreigners whom the Guermantes had entertained that one of them had been sent in first because
she was the elder: "But is she really the elder?" Mme. de Gallardon had
inquired, not positively as though that sort of person did not have any age,
but as if presumably devoid of civil or religious status, of definite traditions, they were both more or less young, like two kittens of the same litter
between which only a veterinary surgeon was competent to decide. The
Courvoisiers, more than the Guermantes, maintained also in a certain
sense the integrity of the titled class thanks at once to the narrowness of
their minds and the bitterness of their hearts. Just as the Guermantes (for
whom, below the royal families and a few others like the Lignes, the La
Trémoïlles and so forth, all the rest were lost in a common rubbish-heap)
were insolent towards various people of long descent who lived round Guermantes, simply because they paid no attention to those secondary distinctions by which the Courvoisiers were enormously impressed, so the
absence of such distinctions affected them little. Certain women who did
not hold any specially exalted rank in their native provinces but, brilliantly married, rich, good-looking, beloved of Duchesses, were for Paris,
where people are never very well up in who one's 'father and mother'
were, an excellent and exclusive piece of 'imported goods.' It might happen, though not commonly, that such women were, through the channel
of the Princesse de Parme or by virtue of their own attractions, received
by certain Guermantes. But with regard to these the indignation of the
Courvoisiers knew no bounds. Having to meet, between five and six in the
afternoon, at their cousin's, people with whose relatives their own relatives
did not care to be seen mixing down in the Perche became for them an
ever-increasing source of rage and an inexhaustible fount of rhetoric. The
moment, for instance, when the charming Comtesse G—— entered the
Guermantes drawing-room, the face of Mme. de Villebon assumed exactly
the expression that would have befitted it had she been called to recite
the line:

And should but one stand fast, that one were surely I,

a line which for that matter was unknown to her. This Courvoisier had
consumed almost every Monday an *éclair* stuffed with cream within a few
feet of the Comtesse G——, but to no consequence. And Mme. de Villebon
confessed in secret that she could not conceive how her cousin Guermantes
could allow a woman into her house who was not even in the second-best
society of Châteaudun. "I really fail to see why my cousin should make
such a fuss about whom she knows; it's making a perfect farce of society!"
concluded Mme. de Villebon with a change of facial expression, this time
a sly smile of despair, which, in a charade, would have been interpreted

rather as indicating another line of poetry, though one with which she was no more familiar than with the first:

Grâce aux Dieux mon malheur passe mon espérance.

We may here anticipate events to explain that the *persévérance* (which rhymes, in the following line with *espérance*) shewn by Mme. de Villebon in snubbing Mme. G—— was not entirely wasted. In the eyes of Mme. G—— it invested Mme. de Villebon with a distinction so supreme, though purely imaginary, that when the time came for Mme. G——'s daughter, who was the prettiest girl and the greatest heiress in the ballrooms of that season, to marry, people were astonished to see her refuse all the Dukes in succession. The fact was that her mother, remembering the weekly humiliations she had had to endure in the Rue de Grenelle on account of Châteaudun could think of only one possible husband for her daughter—a Villebon son.

A single point at which Guermantes and Courvoisiers converged was the art (one, for that matter, of infinite variety) of marking distances. The Guermantes manners were not absolutely uniform towards everyone. And yet, to take an example, all the Guermantes, all those who really were Guermantes, when you were introduced to them proceeded to perform a sort of ceremony almost as though the fact that they held out their hands to you had been as important as the conferring of an order of knighthood. At the moment when a Guermantes, were he no more than twenty, but treading already in the footsteps of his ancestors, heard your name uttered by the person who introduced you, he let fall on you as though he had by no means made up his mind to say "How d'ye do?" a gaze generally blue, always of the coldness of a steel blade which he seemed ready to plunge into the deepest recesses of your heart. Which was a matter of fact what the Guermantes imagined themselves to be doing, each of them regarding himself as a psychologist of the highest order. They thought moreover that they increased by this inspection the affability of the salute which was to follow it, and would not be rendered you without full knowledge of your deserts. All this occurred at a distance from yourself which, little enough had it been a question of a passage of arms, seemed immense for a handclasp, and had as chilling an effect in this connexion as in the other, so that when the Guermantes, after a rapid twisting thrust that explored the most intimate secrets of your soul and laid bare your title to honour, had deemed you worthy to associate with him thereafter, his hand, directed towards you at the end of an arm stretched out to its fullest extent, appeared to be presenting a rapier at you for a single combat, and that hand was in fact placed so far in advance of the Guermantes himself at that moment that when he afterwards bowed his head it was difficult to distinguish whether it was yourself or his own hand that he was saluting. Certain Guermantes, lacking the sense of proportion, or being incapable of refraining from repeating themselves incessantly, went further and repeated this ceremony afresh every time that they met you. Seeing that they had no longer any need to conduct the preliminary psychological investigation for which the 'familiar spirit' had delegated its powers to them and the result of which they had presumably kept in mind, the insistence of the perforating gaze preceding the handclasp could be explained only by the automatism which their gaze had acquired or by some power of fascination which they believed themselves to possess. The Courvoisiers, whose physique was different, had tried in vain to assimilate that searching gaze and had had to fall back upon a lordly stiffness or a rapid indifference. On the other hand, it was from the Courvoisiers that certain very exceptional Guermantes of the gentler sex seemed to have borrowed the feminine form of greeting. At the moment when you were presented to one of these, she made you a sweeping bow in which she carried towards you, almost to an angle of forty-five degrees, her head and bust, the rest of her body (which came very high, up to the belt which formed a pivot) remaining stationary. But no sooner had she projected thus towards you the upper part of her person than she flung it backwards beyond the vertical line by a sudden retirement through almost the same angle. This subsequent withdrawal neutralised what appeared to have been conceded to you; the ground which you believed yourself to have gained did not even remain a conquest, as in a duel; the original positions were retained. This same annulment of affability by the resumption of distance (which was Courvoisier in origin and intended to shew that the advances made in the first movement were no more than a momentary feint) displayed itself equally clearly, in the Courvoisier ladies as in the Guermantes, in the letters which you received from them, at any rate in the first period of your acquaintance. The 'body' of the letter might contain sentences such as one writes only (you would suppose) to a friend, but in vain might you have thought yourself entitled to boast of being in that relation to the lady, since the letter began with *'Monsieur,'* and ended with *'Croyez monsieur à mes sentiments distingués.'* After which, between this cold opening and frigid conclusion which altered the meaning of all the rest, there might come in succession (were it a reply to a letter of condolence from yourself) the most touching pictures of the grief which the Guermantes lady had felt on losing her sister, of the intimacy that had existed between them, of the beauty of the place in which she was staying, of the consolation that she found in the charm of her young children, all this amounted to no more than a letter such as one finds in printed collections, the intimate character of which implied, however, no more intimacy between yourself and the writer than if she had been the Younger Pliny or Mme. de Simiane.

It is true that certain Guermantes ladies wrote to you from the first as 'My dear friend,' or 'My friends'; these were not always the most simple natured among them, but rather those who, living only in the society of kings and being at the same time 'light,' assumed in their pride the certainty that everything which came from themselves gave pleasure and in their corruption the habit of setting no price upon any of the satisfactions that they had to offer. However, since to have had a common ancestor in the reign of Louis XIII was enough to make a young Guermantes say, in speaking of the Marquise de Guermantes: "My aunt Adam," the Guermantes were so numerous a clan that, even among these simple rites, that for example of the bow upon introduction to a stranger, there existed a wide divergence. Each subsection of any refinement had its own, which was handed down from parents to children like the prescription for a liniment or a special way of making jam. Thus it was that we saw Saint-Loup's handclasp thrust out as though involuntarily at the moment of his hearing one's name, without any participation by his eyes, without the addition of a bow. Any unfortunate commoner who for a particular reason—which, for that matter, very rarely occurred—was presented to anyone of the Saint-Loup subsection racked his brains over this abrupt minimum of a greeting, which deliberately assumed the appearance of non-recognition, to discover what in the world the Guermantes—male or female—could have against him. And he was highly surprised to learn that the said Guermantes had thought fit to write specially to the introducer to tell him how delighted he or she had been with the stranger, whom he or she looked forward to meeting again. As specialised as the mechanical gestures of Saint-Loup were the complicated and rapid capers (which M. de Charlus condemned as ridiculous) of the Marquis de Fierbois, the grave and measured paces of the Prince de Guermantes. But it is impossible to describe here the richness of the choreography of the Guermantes ballet owing to the sheer length of the cast.

To return to the antipathy which animated the Courvoisiers against the Duchesse de Guermantes, they might have had the consolation of feeling sorry for her so long as she was still unmarried, for she was then comparatively poor. Unfortunately, at all times and seasons, a sort of fuliginous emanation, quite *sui generis,* enveloped, hid from the eye the wealth of the Courvoisiers which, however great it might be, remained obscure. In vain might a young Courvoisier with an ample dowry find a most eligible bridegroom; it invariably happened that the young couple had no house of their own in Paris, 'came up to stay' in the season with his parents, and for the rest of the year lived down in the country in the thick of a society that may have been unadulterated but was also quite undistinguished. Whereas a Saint-Loup who was up to the eyes in debt dazzled Doncières with his carriage-horses, a Courvoisier who was extremely rich always went in the tram. Similarly (though of course many years earlier) Mlle. de Guermantes (Oriane), who had scarcely a penny to her name, created more stir with her clothes than all the Courvoisiers put together. The really scandalous things she said gave a sort of advertisement to her style of dressing and doing her hair. She had had the audacity to say to the Russian Grand Duke: "Well, Sir, I hear you would like to have Tolstoy murdered?" at a dinner-party to which none of the Courvoisiers, not that any of them knew very much about Tolstoy, had been asked. They knew little more about Greek writers, if we may judge by the Dowager Duchesse de Gallardon (mother-in-law of the Princesse de Gallardon who at that time was still a girl) who, not having been honoured by Oriane with a single visit in five years, replied to some one who asked her the reason for this abstention: "It seems she recites Aristotle" (meaning Aristophanes) "in society. I cannot allow that sort of thing in my house!"

One can imagine how greatly this 'sally' by Mlle. de Guermantes upon

Tolstoy, if it enraged the Courvoisiers, delighted the Guermantes, and by derivation everyone who was not merely closely but even remotely attached to them. The Dowager Comtesse d'Argencourt (*née* Seineport), who entertained a little of everything, because she was a blue-stocking and in spite of her son's being a terrible snob, repeated the saying before her literary friends with the comment: "Oriane de Guermantes, you know; she's as fine as amber, as mischievous as a monkey, there's nothing she couldn't do if she chose, her water-colours are worthy of a great painter and she writes better verses than most of the great poets, and as for family, don't you know, you couldn't imagine anything better, her grandmother was Mlle. de Montpensier, and she is the eighteenth Oriane de Guermantes in succession, without a single misalliance; it's the purest blood, the oldest in the whole of France." And so the sham men of letters, those demi-intellectuals who went to Mme. d'Argencourt's, forming a mental picture of Oriane de Guermantes, whom they would never have an opportunity to know personally, as something more wonderful and more extraordinary than Princess Badroulbadour, not only felt themselves ready to die for her on learning that so noble a person glorified Tolstoy above all others, but felt also quickening with a fresh strength in their minds their own love of Tolstoy, their longing to fight against Tsarism. These liberal ideas might have grown faint in them, they might have begun to doubt their importance, no longer venturing to confess to holding them, when suddenly from Mlle. de Guermantes herself, that is to say from a girl so indisputably cultured and authorised to speak, who wore her hair flat on her brow (a thing that no Courvoisier would ever have consented to do), came this vehement support. A certain number of realities, good or bad in themselves, gain enormously in this way by receiving the adhesion of people who are in authority over us. For instance among the Courvoisiers the rites of affability in a public thoroughfare consisted in a certain bow, very ugly and far from affable in itself but which people knew to be the distinguished way of bidding a person good day, with the result that everyone else, suppressing the instinctive smile of welcome on his own face, endeavoured to imitate these frigid gymnastics. But the Guermantes in general and Oriane in particular, while better conversant than anyone with these rites, did not hesitate, if they caught sight of you from a carriage, to greet you with a sprightly wave of the hand, and in a drawing-room, leaving the Courvoisiers to make their stiff and imitative bows, sketched charming reverences in the air, held out their hands as though to a comrade with a smile from their blue eyes, so that suddenly, thanks to the Guermantes, there entered into the substance of smartness, until then a little hollow and dry, everything that you would naturally have liked and had compelled yourself to forego, a genuine welcome, the effusion of a true friendliness, spontaneity. It is in a similar fashion (but by a rehabilitation which this time is scarcely justified) that people who carry in themselves an instinctive taste for bad music and for melodies, however commonplace, which have in them something easy and caressing, succeed, by dint of education in symphonic culture, in mortifying that appetite. But once they have arrived at this point, when, dazzled—and rightly so—by the brilliant orchestral colouring of Richard Strauss, they see that musician adopt with an indulgence worthy of Auber the most vulgar motifs, what those people originally admired finds suddenly in so high an authority a justification which delights them, and they let themselves be enchanted without scruple and with a twofold gratitude, when they listen to *Salomé*, by what it would have been impossible for them to admire in *Les Diamants de la Couronne*.

Authentic or not, the retort made by Mlle. de Guermantes to the Grand Duke, retailed from house to house, furnished an opportunity to relate the excessive smartness with which Oriane had been turned out at the dinner-party in question. But if such splendour (and this is precisely what rendered it unattainable by the Courvoisiers) springs not from wealth but from prodigality, the latter does nevertheless last longer if it enjoys the constant support of the former, which allows it to spend all its fire. Given the principles openly advertised not only by Oriane but by Mlle. de Villeparisis, namely that nobility does not count, that it is ridiculous to bother one's head about rank, that wealth does not necessarily mean happiness, that intellect, heart, talent are alone of importance, the Courvoisiers were justified in hoping that, as a result of the training she had received from the Marquise, Oriane would marry some one who was not in society, an artist, a fugitive from justice, a scallawag, a free-thinker, that she would pass definitely into the category of what the Courvoisiers called 'detrimentals.' They were all the more justified in this hope since, inasmuch as Mme. de Villeparisis was at this very moment, from the social point of view, passing through an awkward crisis (none of the few bright stars whom I was to meet in her drawing-room had as yet reappeared there), she professed an intense horror of the society which was thus holding her aloof. Even when she referred to her nephew the Prince de Guermantes, whom she did still see, she could never make an end of mocking at him because he was so infatuated about his pedigree. But the moment it became a question of finding a husband for Oriane, it had been no longer the principles publicly advertised by aunt and niece that had controlled the operations, it had been the mysterious 'familiar spirit' of their race. As unerringly as if Mme. de Villeparisis and Oriane had never spoken of anything but rent-rolls and pedigrees in place of literary merit and depth of character, and as if the Marquise, for the space of a few days, had been—as she would ultimately be—dead and on her bier, in the church of Combray, where each member of the family would be reduced to a mere Guermantes, with a forfeiture of individuality and baptismal names to which there testified on the voluminous black drapery of the pall the single 'G' in purple surmounted by the ducal coronet, it was on the wealthiest man and the most nobly born, on the most eligible bachelor of the Faubourg Saint-Germain, on the eldest son of the Duc de Guermantes, the Prince des Laumes, that the familiar spirit had let fall the choice of the intellectual, the critical, the evangelical Mme. de Villeparisis. And for a couple of hours, on the day of the wedding, Mme. de Villeparisis received in her drawing-room all the noble persons at whom she had been in the habit of sneering, at whom she indeed sneered still to the various plebeian intimates whom she had invited and on whom the Prince des Laumes promptly left cards, preparatory to 'cutting the

cable' in the following year. And then, making the Courvoisiers' cup of bitterness overflow, the same old maxims, which made out intellect and talent
to be the sole claims to social pre-eminence, resumed their doctrinal force
in the household of the Princesse des Laumes immediately after her marriage. And in this respect, be it said in passing, the point of view which
Saint-Loup upheld when he lived with Rachel, frequented the friends of
Rachel, would have liked to marry Rachel, implied—whatever the horror
that it inspired in the family—less falsehood than that of the Guermantes
young ladies in general, preaching the virtues of intellect, barely admitting
the possibility of anyone's questioning the equality of mankind, all of
which ended at a given point in the same result as if they had professed the
opposite principles, that is to say in marriage to an extremely wealthy
duke. Saint-Loup did, on the contrary, act in conformity with his theories,
which led people to say that he was treading in evil ways. Certainly from
the moral standpoint Rachel was not altogether satisfactory. But it is by
no means certain whether, if she had been some person no more worthy but
a duchess or the heiress to many millions, Mme. de Marsantes would not
have been in favour of the match.

Well, to return to Mme. des Laumes (shortly afterwards Duchesse de
Guermantes, on the death of her father-in-law), it was the last agonising
straw upon the backs of the Courvoisiers that the theories of the young
Princess, remaining thus lodged in her speech, should not in any sense be
guiding her conduct; with the result that this philosophy (if one may so
call it) in no way impaired the aristocratic smartness of the Guermantes
drawing-room. No doubt all the people whom Mme. de Guermantes did
not invite imagined that it was because they were not clever enough, and
some rich American lady who had never had any book in her possession
except a little old copy, never opened, of Parny's poems, arranged because
it was of the 'period' upon one of the tables in her inner room, shewed how
much importance she attached to the things of the mind by the devouring
gaze which she fastened on the Duchesse de Guermantes when that lady
made her appearance at the Opera. No doubt, also, Mme. de Guermantes
was sincere when she selected a person on account of his or her intellect.
When she said of a woman: "It appears, she's quite charming!" or of a man
that he was the "cleverest person in the world," she imagined herself to
have no other reason for consenting to receive them than this charm or
cleverness, the familiar spirit not interposing itself at this last moment;
more deeply rooted, stationed at the obscure entry of the region in which
the Guermantes exercised their judgment, this vigilant spirit precluded
them from finding the man clever or the woman charming if they had no
social value, actual or potential. The man was pronounced learned, but
like a dictionary, or, on the contrary, common, with the mind of a com-
mercial traveller, the woman pretty, but with a terribly bad style, or too
talkative. As for the people who had no definite position, they were simply
dreadful—such snobs! M. de Bréauté, whose country house was quite
close to Guermantes, mixed with no one below the rank of Highness. But
he laughed at them in his heart and longed only to spend his days in
museums. Accordingly Mme. de Guermantes was indignant when anyone

spoke of M. de Bréauté as a snob. "A snob! Babal! But, my poor friend, you must be mad, it's just the opposite. He loathes smart people; he won't let himself be introduced to anyone. Even in my house! If I ask him to meet some one he doesn't know, he swears at me all the time." This was not to say that, even in practice, the Guermantes did not adopt an entirely different attitude towards cleverness from the Courvoisiers. In a positive sense, this difference between the Guermantes and the Courvoisiers had begun already to bear very promising fruit. Thus the Duchesse de Guermantes, enveloped moreover in a mystery which had set so many poets dreaming of her at a respectful distance, had given that party to which I have already referred, at which the King of England had enjoyed himself more thoroughly than anywhere else, for she had had the idea, which would never have occurred to a Courvoisier mind, of inviting, and the audacity, from which a Courvoisier courage would have recoiled, to invite, apart from the personages already mentioned, the musician Gaston Lemaire and the dramatist Grandmougin. But it was pre-eminently from the negative point of view that intellectuality made itself felt. If the necessary coefficient of cleverness and charm declined steadily as the rank of the person who sought an invitation from the Princesse des Laumes became more exalted, vanishing into zero when he or she was one of the principal Crowned Heads of Europe, conversely the farther they fell below this royal level the higher the coefficient rose. For instance at the Princesse de Parme's parties there were a number of people whom her Royal Highness invited because she had known them as children, or because they were related to some duchess, or attached to the person of some Sovereign, they themselves being quite possibly ugly, boring or stupid; well, with a Courvoisier any of the reasons: "a favourite of the Princesse de Parme," "a niece on the mother's side of the Duchesse d'Arpajon," "spends three months every year with the Queen of Spain," would have been sufficient to make her invite such people to her house, but Mme. de Guermantes, who had politely acknowledged their bows for ten years at the Princesse de Parme's, had never once allowed them to cross her threshold, considering that the same rule applied to a drawing-room in a social as in a material sense, where it only needed a few pieces of furniture which had no particular beauty but were left there to fill the room and as a sign of the owner's wealth, to render it hideous. Such a drawing-room resembled a book in which the author could not refrain from the use of language advertising his own learning, brilliance, fluency. Like a book, like a house, the quality of a 'salon,' thought Mme. de Guermantes—and rightly—is based on the corner-stone of sacrifice.

Many of the friends of the Princesse de Parme, with whom the Duchesse de Guermantes had confined herself for years past to the same conventional greeting, or to returning their cards, without ever inviting them to her parties or going to theirs, complained discreetly of these omissions to her Highness who, on days when M. de Guermantes came by himself to see her, passed on a hint to him. But the wily nobleman, a bad husband to the Duchess in so far as he kept mistresses, but her most tried and trusty friend in everything that concerned the good order of her drawing-room (and her own wit, which formed its chief attraction), replied: "But does my wife know her? Indeed! Oh, well, I daresay she does. But the truth is, Ma'am, that Oriane does not care for women's conversation. She lives surrounded by a court of superior minds—I am not her husband, I am only the first footman. Except for quite a small number, who are all of them very clever indeed, women bore her. Surely, Ma'am, your Highness with all her fine judgment is not going to tell me that the Marquise de Souvré has any brains. Yes, I quite understand, the Princess receives her out of kindness. Besides, your Highness knows her. You tell me that Oriane has met her; it is quite possible, but once or twice at the most, I assure you. And then, I must explain to your Highness, it is really a little my fault as well. My wife is very easily tired, and she is so anxious to be friendly always that if I allowed her she would never stop going to see people. Only yesterday evening she had a temperature, she was afraid of hurting the Duchesse de Bourbon's feelings by not going to see her. I had to shew my teeth, I assure you; I positively forbade them to bring the carriage round. Do you know, Ma'am, I should really prefer not to mention to Oriane that you have spoken to me about Mme. de Souvré. My wife is so devoted to your Highness, she will go round at once to invite Mme. de Souvré to the house; that will mean another call to be paid, it will oblige us to make friends with the sister, whose husband I know quite well. I think I shall say nothing at all about it to Oriane, if the Princess has no objection. That will save her a great deal of strain and excitement. And I assure you that it will be no loss to Mme. de Souvré. She goes everywhere, moves in the most brilliant circles. You know, we don't entertain at all, really, just a few little friendly dinners, Mme. de Souvré would be bored to death." The Princesse de Parme, innocently convinced that the Duc de Guermantes would not transmit her request to his Duchess, and dismayed by her failure to procure the invitation that Mme. de Souvré sought, was all the more flattered to think that she herself was one of the regular frequenters of so exclusive a household. No doubt this satisfaction had its drawbacks also. Thus whenever the Princesse de Parme invited Mme. de Guermantes to her own parties she had to rack her brains to be sure that there was no one else on her list whose presence might offend the Duchess and make her refuse to come again.

On ordinary evenings (after dinner, at which she invariably entertained at a very early hour, for she clung to old customs, a small party) the drawing-room of the Princesse de Parme was thrown open to her regular guests, and, generally speaking, to all the higher ranks of the aristocracy, French and foreign. The order of her receptions was as follows: on issuing from the dining-room the Princess sat down on a sofa before a large round table and chatted with the two most important of the ladies who had dined with her, or else cast her eyes over a magazine, or sometimes played cards (or pretended to play, adopting a German court custom), either a game of patience by herself or selecting as her real or pretended partner some prominent personage. By nine o'clock the double doors of the big drawing-room were in a state of perpetual agitation, opening and shutting and opening again to admit the visitors who had dined quietly at home (or if they had dined in town hurried from their café promising to return later, since they intended only to go in at one door and out at the other) in order to conform with the Princess's time-table. She, meanwhile, her mind fixed on her game or conversation, made a show of not seeing the new arrivals, and it was not until they were actually within reach of her that she rose graciously from her seat, with a friendly smile for the women. The latter thereupon sank before the upright Presence in a courtesy which was tantamount to a genuflexion, so as to bring their lips down to the level of the beautiful hand which hung very low, and to kiss it. But at that moment the Princess, just as if she had been every time surprised by a formality with which nevertheless she was perfectly familiar, raised the kneeling figure as though by main force, and with incomparable grace and sweetness, and kissed her on both cheeks. A grace and sweetness that were conditional, you may say, upon the meekness with which the arriving guest inclined her knee. Very likely; and it seems that in a society without distinctions of rank politeness would vanish, not, as is generally supposed, from want of breeding, but because from one class would have vanished the deference due to a distinction which must be imaginary to be effective, and, more completely still, from the other class the affability in the distribution of which one is prodigal so long as one knows it to be, to the recipient, of an untold value which, in a world based on equality, would at once fall to nothing like everything that has only a promissory worth. But this disappearance of politeness in a reconstructed society is by no means certain, and we are at times too ready to believe that the present is the only possible state of things. People of first-rate intelligence have held the opinion that a Republic could not have any diplomacy or foreign alliances, and, more recently, that the peasant class would not tolerate the separation of Church and State. After all, the survival of politeness in a society levelled to uniformity would be no more miraculous than the practical success of the railway or the use of the aeroplane in war. Besides, even if politeness were to vanish, there is nothing to shew that this would be a misfortune. Lastly, would not society become secretly more hierarchical as it became outwardly more democratic? This seems highly probable. The political power of the Popes has grown enormously since they ceased to possess either States or an Army; our cathedrals meant far less to a devout Catholic of the seventeenth century than they mean to an atheist of the twentieth, and if the Princesse de Parme had been the sovereign ruler of a State, no doubt I should have felt myself impelled to speak of her almost as I should speak of a President of the Republic, that is to say not at all.

As soon as the postulant had been raised from the ground and embraced by the Princess, the latter resumed her seat and returned to her game of patience, but first of all, if the newcomer were of any importance, held her for a moment in conversation, making her sit down in an armchair.

When the room became too crowded the lady in waiting who had to control the traffic cleared the floor by leading the regular guests into an immense hall on to which the drawing-room opened, a hall filled with portraits and minor trophies of the House of Bourbon. The intimate friends of the Princess would then volunteer for the part of guide and would repeat interesting anecdotes, to which the young people had not the patience to listen, more interested in the spectacle of living Royalties (with the possibility of having themselves presented to them by the lady in waiting and the maids of honour) than in examining the relics of dead Sovereigns. Too much occupied with the acquaintances which they would be able to form and the invitations it might perhaps be possible to secure, they knew absolutely nothing, even in after-years, of what there was in this priceless museum of the archives of the Monarchy, and could only recall confusedly that it was decorated with cacti and giant palms which gave this centre of social elegance a look of the palmarium in the Jardin d'Acclimatation.

Naturally the Duchesse de Guermantes, by way of self-mortification, did occasionally appear on these evenings to pay an 'after dinner' call on the Princess, who kept her all the time by her side, while she rallied the Duke. But on evenings when the Duchess came to dine, the Princess took care not to invite her regular party, and closed her doors to the world on rising from table, for fear lest a too liberal selection of guests might offend the exacting Duchess. On such evenings, were any of the faithful who had not received warning to present themselves on the royal doorstep, they would be informed by the porter: "Her Royal Highness is not at home this evening," and would turn away. But, long before this, many of the Princess's friends had known that, on the day in question, they would not be asked to her house. These were a special set of parties, a privilege barred to so many who must have longed for admission. The excluded could, with a practical certainty, enumerate the roll of the elect, and would say irritably among themselves: "You know, of course, that Oriane de Guermantes never goes anywhere without her entire staff." With the help of this body the Princesse de Parme sought to surround the Duchess as with a protecting rampart against those persons the chance of whose making a good impression on her was at all doubtful. But with several of the Duchess's favourites, with several members of this glittering 'staff,' the Princesse de Parme resented having to go out of her way to shew them attentions, seeing that they paid little or no attention to herself. No doubt the Princess was fully prepared to admit that it was possible to derive more enjoyment in the company of the Duchesse de Guermantes than in her own. She could not deny that there was always a 'crush' on the Duchess's at-home days, or that she herself often met there three or four royal personages who thought it sufficient to leave their cards upon her. And in vain might she commit to memory Oriane's witty sayings, copy her gowns, serve at her own tea-parties the same strawberry tarts, there were occasions on which she was left by herself all afternoon with a lady in waiting and some foreign Counsellor of Legation. And so whenever (as had been the case with Swann, for instance, at an earlier period) there was anyone who never let a day pass without going to spend an hour or two at the Duchess's and paid a call once in two years on the Princesse de Parme, the latter felt no great desire, even for the sake of amusing Oriane, to make to this Swann or whoever he was the 'advances' of an invitation to dinner. In a word, having the Duchess in her house was for the Princess a source of endless perplexity, so haunted was she by the fear that Oriane would find fault with everything. But in return, and for the same reason, when the Princesse de Parme came to dine with Mme. de Guermantes she could be certain beforehand that everything would be perfect, delightful, she had only one fear which was that of her own inability to understand, remember, give satisfaction, her inability to assimilate new ideas and people. On this account my presence aroused her attention and excited her cupidity, just as might a new way of decorating the dinner-table with festoons of fruit, uncertain as she was which of the two it might be—the table decorations or my presence—that was the more distinctively one of those charms, the secret of the success of Oriane's parties, and in her uncertainty firmly resolved to try at her own next dinner-party to introduce them both. What for that matter fully justified the enraptured curiosity which the Princesse de Parme brought to the Duchess's house was that element—amusing, dangerous, exciting—into which the Princess used to plunge with a combination of anxiety, shock and delight (as at the seaside on one of those days of 'big waves' of the danger of which the bathing-masters warn us, simply and solely because none of them knows how to swim), from which she used to emerge terrified, happy, rejuvenated, and which was known as the wit of the Guermantes. The wit of the Guermantes—a thing as non-existent as the squared circle, according to the Duchess who regarded herself as the sole Guermantes to possess it—was a family reputation like that of the pork pies of Tours or the biscuits of Rheims. No doubt (since an intellectual peculiarity does not employ for its perpetuation the same channels as a shade of hair or complexion) certain intimate friends of the Duchess who were not of her blood were nevertheless endowed with this wit, which on the other hand had failed to permeate the minds of various Guermantes, too refractory to assimilate wit of any kind. The holders, not related to the Duchess, of this Guermantes wit had generally the characteristic feature of having been brilliant men, fitted for a career to which, whether it were in the arts, diplomacy, parliamentary eloquence or the army, they had preferred the life of a small and intimate group. Possibly this preference could be explained by a certain want of originality, of initiative, of will power, of health or of luck, or possibly by snobbishness.

With certain people (though these, it must be admitted, were the exception) if the Guermantes drawing-room had been the stumbling-block in their careers, it had been without their knowledge. Thus a doctor, a painter and a diplomat of great promise had failed to achieve success in the careers for which they were nevertheless more brilliantly endowed than most of their competitors because their friendship with the Guermantes had the result that the two former were regarded as men of fashion and the third as a reactionary, which had prevented each of the three from winning the recognition of his colleagues. The mediaeval gown and red cap which are still donned by the electoral colleges of the Faculties are (or were at least, not so long since) something more than a purely outward survival from a narrow-minded past, from a rigid sectarianism. Under the cap with its golden tassels, like the High Priest in the conical mitre of the Jews, the 'Professors' were still, in the years that preceded the Dreyfus case, fast rooted in rigorously pharisaical ideas. Du Boulbon was at heart an artist, but was safe because he did not care for society. Cottard was always at the Verdurins'. But Mme. Verdurin was a patient; besides, he was protected by his vulgarity; finally, at his own house he entertained no one outside the Faculty, at banquets over which there floated an aroma of carbolic. But in powerful corporations, where moreover the rigidity of their prejudices is but the price that must be paid for the noblest integrity, the most lofty conceptions of morality, which weaken in an atmosphere that, more tolerant, freer at first, becomes very soon dissolute, a Professor in his gown of scarlet satin faced with ermine, like that of a Doge (which is to say a Duke) of Venice enshrined in the Ducal Palace, was as virtuous, as deeply attached to noble principles, but as unsparing of any alien element as that other Duke, excellent but terrible, whom we know as M. de Saint-Simon. The alien, here, was the wordly doctor, with other manners, other social relations. To make good, the unfortunate of whom we are now speaking, so as not to be accused by his colleagues of looking down on them (the strange ideas of a man of fashion!) if he concealed from them his Duchesse de Guermantes, hoped to disarm them by giving mixed dinner-parties in which the medical element was merged in the fashionable. He was unaware that in so doing he signed his own death-warrant, or rather he discovered this later, when the Council of Ten had to fill a vacant chair, and it was invariably the name of another doctor, more normal, it might be obviously inferior, that leaped from the fatal urn, when their 'Veto' thundered from the ancient Faculty, as solemn, as absurd and as terrible as the 'Juro' that spelled the death of Molière. So too with the painter permanently labelled man of fashion, when fashionable people who dabbled in art had succeeded in making themselves be labelled artists; so with the diplomat who had too many reactionary associations.

But this case was the rarest of all. The type of distinguished man who formed the main substance of the Guermantes drawing-room was that of people who had voluntarily (or so at least they supposed) renounced all else, everything that was incompatible with the wit of the Guermantes, with the courtesy of the Guermantes, with that indefinable charm odious to any 'Corporation' however little centralised.

And the people who were aware that in days gone by one of these frequenters of the Duchess's drawing-room had been awarded the gold medal of the Salon, that another, Secretary to the Bar Council, had made a brilliant start in the Chamber, that a third had ably served France as Chargé d'Affaires, might have been led to regard as 'failures' people who had done nothing more now for twenty years. But there were few who were thus 'well-informed,' and the parties concerned would themselves have been the last to remind people, finding these old distinctions to be now valueless, in the light of this very Guermantes spirit of wit: for did not this condemn respectively as a bore or an usher, and as a counter-jumper a pair of eminent Ministers, one a trifle solemn, the other addicted to puns, of whose praises the newspapers were always full but in whose company Mme. de Guermantes would begin to yawn and shew signs of impatience if the imprudence of a hostess had placed either of them next to her at the dinner-table. Since being a statesman of the first rank was in no sense a recommendation to the Duchess's favour, those of her friends who had definitely abandoned the 'Career' or the 'Service,' who had never stood for the Chamber, felt, as they came day after day to have luncheon and talk with their great friend, or when they met her in the houses of Royal Personages, of whom for that matter they thought very little (or at least they said so), that they themselves had chosen the better part, albeit their melancholy air, even in the midst of the gaiety, seemed somehow to challenge the soundness of this opinion.

It must be recognised also that the refinement of social life, the subtlety of conversation at the Guermantes' did also contain, exiguous as it may have been, an element of reality. No official title was equivalent to the approval of certain chosen friends of Mme. de Guermantes, whom the most powerful Ministers had been unable to attract to their houses. If in this drawing-room so many intellectual ambitions, such noble efforts even had been for ever buried, still at least from their dust the rarest blossoms of civilised society had taken life. Certainly men of wit, Swann for instance, regarded themselves as superior to men of genuine worth, whom they despised, but that was because what the Duchesse de Guermantes valued above everything else was not intellect; it was, according to her, that superior, more exquisite form of the human intellect exalted to a verbal variety of talent—wit. And long ago at the Verdurins' when Swann condemned Brichot and Elstir, one as a pedant and the other as a clown, despite all the learning of one and the other's genius, it was the infiltration of the Guermantes spirit that had led him to classify them so. Never would he have dared to present either of them to the Duchess, conscious instinctively of the air with which she would have listened to Brichot's monologues and Elstir's hair-splittings, the Guermantes spirit regarding pretentious and prolix speech, whether in a serious or a farcical vein, as alike of the most intolerable imbecility.

As for the Guermantes of the true flesh and blood, if the Guermantes spirit had not absorbed them as completely as we see occur in, to take an example, those literary circles in which everyone shares a common way of pronouncing his words, of expressing his thoughts, and consequently of thinking, it was certainly not because originality is stronger in purely social groups or presents any obstacle there to imitation. But imitation depends not merely upon the absence of any unconquerable originality but also demands a relative fineness of ear which enables one first of all to discern what one is afterwards to imitate. Whereas there were several Guermantes in whom this musical sense was as entirely lacking as in the Courvoisiers.

To take as an instance what is called, in another sense of the word imitation, 'giving imitations' (or among the Guermantes was called 'taking off'), Mme. de Guermantes might succeed in this to perfection, the Courvoisiers were as incapable of appreciating her as if they had been a tribe of rabbits instead of men and women, because they had never had the sense to observe the particular defect or accent that the Duchess was endeavouring to copy. When she 'gave an imitation' of the Duc de Limoges, the Courvoisiers would protest: "Oh, no, he doesn't really speak like that! I met him again only yesterday at dinner at Bebeth's; he talked to me all evening and he didn't speak like that at all!" whereas the Guermantes of any degree of culture exclaimed: "Gad, what fun Oriane is! The odd part of it is that when she is copying him she looks exactly like him! I feel I'm listening to him. Oriane, do give us a little more Limoges!" Now these Guermantes (and not necessarily the few really outstanding members of the clan who, when the Duchess imitated the Duc de Limoges, would say admiringly: "Oh, you really have got him," or "You do get him,") might indeed be devoid of wit according to Mme. de Guermantes (and in this respect she was right); yet, by dint of hearing and repeating her sayings they had come to imitate more or less her way of expressing herself, of criticising people, of what Swann, like the Duke himself, used to call her 'phrasing' of things, so that they presented in their conversation something which to the Courvoisiers appeared 'fearfully like' Oriane's wit and was treated by them collectively as the 'wit of the Guermantes.' As these Guermantes were to her not merely kinsfolk but admirers, Oriane (who kept the rest of the family rigorously at arm's-length and now avenged by her disdain the insults that they had heaped upon her in her girlhood) went to call on them now and then, generally in company with the Duke, in the season, when she drove out with him. These visits were historic events. The heart began to beat more rapidly in the bosom of the Princesse d'Epinay, who was 'at home' in her big drawing-room on the ground floor, when she perceived afar off, like the first glow of an innocuous fire, or the 'reconnaissances' of an unexpected invasion, making her way across the courtyard slowly, in a diagonal course, the Duchess crowned with a ravishing hat and holding atilt a sunshade from which there rained down a summer fragrance. "Why, here comes Oriane," she would say, like an 'On guard!' intended to convey a prudent warning to her visitors, so that they should have time to beat an orderly retreat, to clear the rooms without panic. Half of those present dared not remain, and rose at once to go. "But no, why? Sit down again, I insist on keeping you a little longer," said the Princess in a careless tone and seemingly at her ease (to shew herself the great lady) but in a voice that suddenly rang false. "But you may want to talk to each other." "Really, you're in a hurry? Oh, very well, I shall come and see you," replied the lady of the house to those whom she was just as well pleased to see depart. The Duke and Duchess gave a very civil greeting to people whom they had seen there regularly for years, without for that reason coming to know them any better, while these in return barely said good day to them, thinking this more discreet. Scarcely had they left the room before the Duke began asking good-naturedly who they were, so as to appear to be taking an interest in the intrinsic quality of people whom he himself, owing to the cross-purposes of fate or the wretched state of Oriane's nerves, never saw in his own house. "Tell me, who was that little woman in the pink hat?" "Why, my dear cousin, you have seen her hundreds of times, she's the Vicomtesse de Tours, who was a Lamarzelle." "But, do you know, she's quite good-looking; she seems clever too; if it weren't for a little flaw in her upper lip she'd be a regular charmer. If there's a Vicomte de Tours, he can't have any too bad a time. Oriane, do you know what those eyebrows and the way her hair grows reminded me of? Your cousin Hedwige de Ligne."

The Duchesse de Guermantes, who languished whenever people spoke of the beauty of any woman other than herself, let the conversation drop. She had reckoned without the weakness her husband had for letting it be seen that he knew all about the people who did not come to his house, whereby he believed that he shewed himself to be more seriously minded than his wife. "But," he resumed suddenly with emphasis, "you mentioned the name Lamarzelle. I remember, when I was in the Chamber, hearing a really remarkable speech made . . ." "That was the uncle of the young woman you saw just now." "Indeed! What talent! No, my dear girl," he assured the Vicomtesse d'Egremont, whom Mme. de Guermantes could not endure, but who, refusing to stir from the Princesse d'Epinay's drawing-room where she willingly humbled herself to play the part of parlour-maid (and was ready to slap her own parlour-maid on returning home), stayed there, confused, tearful, but stayed when the ducal couple were in the room, took their cloaks, tried to make herself useful, offered discreetly to withdraw into the next room, "you are not to make tea for us, let us just sit and talk quietly, we are simple souls, really, honestly. Besides," he went on, turning to the Princesse d'Epinay (leaving the Egremont lady blushing, humble, ambitious and full of zeal), "we can only give you a quarter of an hour." This quarter of an hour was entirely taken up with a sort of exhibition of the witty things which the Duchess had said during the previous week, and to which she herself would certainly not have referred had not her husband, with great adroitness, by appearing to be rebuking her with reference to the incidents that had provoked them, obliged her as though against her will to repeat them.

The Princesse d'Epinay, who was fond of her cousin and knew that she had a weakness for compliments, went into ecstasies over her hat, her sunshade, her wit. "Talk to her as much as you like about her clothes," said the Duke in the sullen tone which he had adopted and now tempered with a sardonic smile so that his resentment should not be taken seriously, "but for heaven's sake don't speak of her wit, I should be only too glad not to have so witty a wife. You are probably alluding to the shocking pun she made about my brother Palamède," he went on, knowing quite well that the Princess and the rest of the family had not yet heard this pun, and delighted to have an opportunity of shewing off his wife. "In the first place I consider it unworthy of a person who has occasionally, I must admit, said some quite good things, to make bad puns, but especially about my brother, who is very susceptible, and if it is going to lead to his quarrelling with me, that would really be too much of a good thing." "But we never heard a word about it! One of Oriane's puns! It's sure to be delicious. Oh, do tell us!" "No, no," the Duke went on, still sulking though with a broader smile, "I'm so glad you haven't heard it. Seriously, I'm very fond of my brother." "Listen, Basin," broke in the Duchess, the moment having come for her to take up her husband's cue, "I can't think why you should say that it might annoy Palamède, you know quite well it would do nothing of the sort. He is far too intelligent to be vexed by a stupid joke which has nothing offensive about it. You are making them think I said something nasty; I simply uttered a remark which was not in the least funny, it is you who make it

seem important by losing your temper over it. I don't understand you."
"You are making us terribly excited, what is it all about?" "Oh, obviously
nothing serious!" cried M. de Guermantes. "You may have heard that my
brother offered to give Brézé, the place he got from his wife, to his sister
Marsantes." "Yes, but we were told that she didn't want it, she didn't care
for that part of the country, the climate didn't suit her." "Very well, some
one had been telling my wife all that and saying that if my brother was
giving this place to our sister it was not so much to please her as to tease
her. 'He's such a teaser, Charlus,' was what they actually said. Well, you
know Brézé, it's a royal domain, I should say it's worth millions, it used
to be part of the crown lands, it includes one of the finest forests in the
whole of France. There are plenty of people who would be only too delighted
to be teased to that tune. And so when she heard the word 'teaser' applied
to Charlus because he was giving away such a magnificent property, Oriane
could not help exclaiming, without meaning anything, I must admit, there
wasn't a trace of ill-nature about it, for it came like a flash of lightning:
'Teaser, teaser? Then he must be Teaser Augustus.' You understand," he
went on, resuming his sulky tone, having first cast a sweeping glance round
the room in order to judge the effect of his wife's witticism—and in some
doubt as to the extent of Mme. d'Epinay's acquaintance with ancient history, "you understand, it's an allusion to Augustus Caesar, the Roman
Emperor; it's too stupid, a bad play on words, quite unworthy of Oriane.
And then, you see, I am more circumspect than my wife, if I haven't her
wit, I think of the consequences; if anyone should be so ill-advised as to
repeat the remark to my brother there'll be the devil to pay. All the more,"
he went on, "because as you know Palamède is very high and mighty, and
very fussy also, given to gossip and all that sort of thing, so that quite apart
from the question of his giving away Brézé you must admit that 'Teaser
Augustus' suits him down to the ground. That is what justifies my wife's
remarks; even when she is inclined to stoop to what is almost vulgar, she
is always witty and does really describe people."

And so, thanks on one occasion to 'Teaser Augustus,' on another to something else, the visits paid by the Duke and Duchess to their kinsfolk replen-
ished the stock of anecdotes, and the emotion which these visits aroused
lasted long after the departure of the sparkling lady and her 'producer.'
Her hostess would begin by going over again with the privileged persons
who had been at the entertainment (those who had remained in the room)
the clever things that Oriane had said. "You hadn't heard 'Teaser
Augustus'?" asked the Princesse d'Epinay. "Yes," replied the Marquise de
Baveno, blushing as she spoke, "the Princesse de Sarsina (the La Rochefoucauld one) mentioned it to me, not quite in the same words. But of
course it was far more interesting to hear it repeated like that with my
cousin in the room," she went on, as though speaking of a song that had
been accompanied by the composer himself. "We were speaking of Oriane's
latest—she was here just now," her hostess greeted a visitor who would be
plunged in despair at not having arrived an hour earlier. "What! Has
Oriane been here?" "Yes, you ought to have come a little sooner," the
Princesse d'Epinay informed her, not in reproach but letting her under-

stand all that her clumsiness had made her miss. It was her fault alone if
she had not been present at the Creation of the World or at Mme. Carval-
ho's last performance. "What do you think of Oriane's latest? I must say, I
do enjoy 'Teaser Augustus'," and the 'saying' would be served up again
cold next day at luncheon before a few intimate friends who were invited
on purpose, and would reappear under various sauces throughout the week.
Indeed the Princess happening in the course of that week to pay her annual
visit to the Princesse de Parme seized the opportunity to ask whether her
Royal Highness had heard the pun, and repeated it to her. "Ah! Teaser
Augustus," said the Princesse de Parme, her eyes bulging with an instinctive
admiration, which begged however for a complementary elucidation which
Mme. d'Epinay was not loath to furnish. "I must say, 'Teaser Augustus'
pleases me enormously as a piece of 'phrasing'," she concluded. As a matter of fact the word 'phrasing' was not in the least applicable to this pun,
but the Princesse d'Epinay, who claimed to have assimilated her share of the
Guermantes spirit, had borrowed from Oriane the expressions 'phrased' and
'phrasing' and employed them without much discrimination. Now the
Princesse de Parme, who was not at all fond of Mme. d'Epinay, whom she
considered plain, knew to be miserly and believed, on the authority of the
Courvoisiers, to be malicious, recognised this word 'phrasing' which she had
heard used by Mme. de Guermantes but would not by herself have known
how or when to apply. She received the impression that it was in fact its
'phrasing' that formed the charm of 'Teaser Augustus' and, without altogether forgetting her antipathy towards the plain and miserly lady, could
not repress a burst of admiration for a person endowed to such a degree
with the Guermantes spirit, so strong that she was on the point of inviting
the Princesse d'Epinay to the Opera. She was held in check only by the
reflexion that it would be wiser perhaps to consult Mme. de Guermantes
first. As for Mme. d'Epinay, who, unlike the Courvoisiers, paid endless
attentions to Oriane and was genuinely fond of her but was jealous of her
exalted friends and slightly irritated by the fun which the Duchess used
to make of her before everyone on account of her meanness, she reported
on her return home what an effort it had required to make the Princesse de
Parme grasp the point of 'Teaser Augustus,' and declared what a snob
Oriane must be to number such a goose among her friends. "I should never
have been able to see much of the Princesse de Parme even if I had cared
to," she informed the friends who were dining with her. "M. d'Epinay would
not have allowed it for a moment, because of her immorality," she explained,
alluding to certain purely imaginary excesses on the part of the Princess.
"But even if I had had a husband less strict in his views, I must say I could
never have made friends with her. I don't know how Oriane can bear to see
her every other day, as she does. I go there once a year, and it's all I can
do to sit out my call." As for those of the Courvoisiers who happened to be
at Victurnienne's on the day of Mme. de Guermantes's visit, the arrival of
the Duchess generally put them to flight owing to the exasperation they
felt at the 'ridiculous salaams' that were made to her there. One alone
remained on the afternoon of 'Teaser Augustus.' He did not entirely see the
point, but he did see part of it, being an educated man. And the Cour-

voisiers went about repeating that Oriane had called uncle Palamède 'Caesar Augustus,' which was, according to them, a good enough description of him, but why all this endless talk about Oriane, they went on. People couldn't make more fuss about a queen. "After all, what is Oriane? I don't say that the Guermantes aren't an old family, but the Courvoisiers are every bit as good in rank, antiquity, marriages. We mustn't forget that on the Field of the Cloth of Gold, when the King of England asked François I who was the noblest of the lords there present, 'Sire,' said the King of France, 'Courvoisier.' " But even if all the Courvoisiers had stayed in the room to hear them, Oriane's sayings would have fallen on deaf ears, since the incidents that usually gave occasion for those sayings would have been regarded by them from a totally different point of view. If, for instance, a Courvoisier found herself running short of chairs, in the middle of a party, or if she used the wrong name in greeting a guest whose face she did not remember, or if one of her servants said something stupid, the Courvoisier, extremely annoyed, flushed, quivering with excitement, would deplore so unfortunate an occurrence. And when she had a visitor in the room and Oriane was expected, she would say in a tone anxiously and imperiously questioning: "Do you know her?", fearing that if the visitor did not know her his presence might make an unfortunate impression on Oriane. But Mme. de Guermantes on the contrary extracted from such incidents opportunities for stories which made the Guermantes laugh until the tears streamed down their cheeks, so that one was obliged to envy her her having run short of chairs, having herself made or having allowed her servant to make a blunder, having had at her party some one whom nobody knew, as one is obliged to be thankful that great writers have been kept at a distance by men and betrayed by women when their humiliations and their sufferings have been if not the direct stimulus of their genius, at any rate the subject matter of their works.

The Courvoisiers were incapable of rising to the level of the spirit of innovation which the Duchesse de Guermantes introduced into the life of society and, by adapting it, following an unerring instinct, to the necessities of the moment, made into something artistic where the purely rational application of cut and dried rules would have given as unfortunate results as would greet a man who, anxious to succeed in love or in politics, was to reproduce in his own daily life the exploits of Bussy d'Amboise. If the Courvoisiers gave a family dinner or a dinner to meet some prince, the addition of a recognised wit, of some friend of their son seemed to them an anomaly capable of producing the direst consequences. A Courvoisier whose father had been a Minister of the Empire having to give an afternoon party to meet Princesse Mathilde deduced by a geometrical formula that she could invite no one but Bonapartists. Of whom she knew practically none. All the smart women of her acquaintance, all the amusing men were ruthlessly barred because, from their Legitimist views or connexions, they might easily, according to Courvoisier logic, give offence to the Imperial Highness. The latter, who in her own house entertained the flower of the Faubourg Saint-Germain, was quite surprised when she found at Mme. de Courvoisier's only a notorious old sponger whose husband had been an Imperial Prefect, the widow of the Director of Posts and sundry others known for their loyalty to Napoleon, their stupidity and their dullness. Princesse Mathilde, however, in no way stinted the generous and refreshing shower of her sovereign grace over these miserable scarecrows whom the Duchesse de Guermantes, for her part, took good care not to invite when it was her turn to entertain the Princess, but substituted for them without any abstract reasoning about Bonapartism the most brilliant coruscation of all the beauties, all the talents, all the celebrities, who, the exercise of some subtle sixth sense made her feel, would be acceptable to the niece of the Emperor even when they belonged actually to the Royal House. There was not lacking indeed the Duc d'Aumale, and when on withdrawing the Princess, raising Mme. de Guermantes from the ground where she had sunk in a curtsey and was trying to kiss the august hand, embraced her on both cheeks, it was from the bottom of her heart that she was able to assure the Duchess that never had she spent a happier afternoon nor seen so delightful a party. The Princesse de Parme was Courvoisier in her incapacity for innovation in social matters, but unlike the Courvoisiers the surprise that was perpetually caused her by the Duchesse de Guermantes engendered in her not, as in them, antipathy but admiration. This astonishment was still farther enhanced by the infinitely backward state of the Princess's education. Mme. de Guermantes was herself a great deal less advanced than she supposed. But it was enough for her to have gone a little beyond Mme. de Parme to stupefy that lady, and, as the critics of each generation confine themselves to maintaining the direct opposite of the truths admitted by their predecessors, she had only to say that Flaubert, that archenemy of the bourgeois, had been bourgeois through and through, or that there was a great deal of Italian music in Wagner, to open before the Princess, at the cost of a nervous exhaustion which recurred every time, as before the eyes of a swimmer in a stormy sea, horizons that seemed to her unimaginable and remained for ever vague. A stupefaction caused also by the paradoxes uttered with relation not only to works of art but to persons of their acquaintance and to current social events. No doubt the incapacity that prevented Mme. de Parme from distinguishing the true wit of the Guermantes from certain rudimentarily acquired forms of that wit (which made her believe in the high intellectual worth of certain, especially certain female Guermantes, of whom she was bewildered on hearing the Duchess confide to her with a smile that they were mere blockheads) was one of the causes of the astonishment which the Princess always felt on hearing Mme. de Guermantes criticise other people. But there was another cause also, one which I, who knew at this time more books than people and literature better than life, explained to myself by thinking that the Duchess, living this wordly life the idleness and sterility of which are to a true social activity what criticism, in art, is to creation, extended to the persons who surrounded her the instability of point of view, the uneasy thirst of the reasoner who to assuage a mind that has grown too dry goes in search of no matter what paradox that is still fairly new, and will make no bones about upholding the refreshing opinion that the really great *Iphigénie* is Piccini's and not Gluck's, at a pinch the true *Phèdre* that of Pradon.

When a woman who was intelligent, educated, witty had married a shy bumpkin whom one saw but seldom and never heard, Mme. de Guermantes one fine day would find a rare intellectual pleasure not only in decrying the wife but in 'discovering' the husband. In the Cambremer household, for example, if she had lived in that section of society at the time, she would have decreed that Mme. de Cambremer was stupid, and that the really interesting person, misunderstood, delightful, condemned to silence by a chattering wife but himself worth a thousand of her, was the Marquis, and the Duchess would have felt on declaring this the same kind of refreshment as the critic who, after people have for seventy years been admiring *Hernani*, confesses to a preference for *Le Lion Amoureux*. And from this same morbid need of arbitrary novelties, if from her girlhood everyone had been pitying a model wife, a true saint, for being married to a scoundrel, one fine day Mme. de Guermantes would assert that this scoundrel was perhaps a frivolous man but one with a heart of gold, whom the implacable harshness of his wife had driven to do the most inconsistent things. I knew that it is not only over different works, in the long course of centuries, but over different parts of the same work that criticism plays, thrusting back into the shadow what for too long has been thought brilliant, and making emerge what has appeared to be doomed to permanent obscurity. I had not only seen Bellini, Winterhalter, the Jesuit architects, a Restoration cabinet-maker come to take the place of men of genius who were called 'worn out,' simply because they had worn out the lazy minds of the intellectuals, as neurasthenics are always worn out and always changing; I had seen preferred in Sainte-Beuve alternately the critic and the poet, Musset rejected so far as his poetry went save for a few quite unimportant little pieces. No doubt certain essayists are mistaken when they set above the most famous scenes in *Le Cid* or *Polyeucte* some speech from *Le Menteur* which, like an old plan, furnishes information about the Paris of the day, but their predilection, justified if not by considerations of beauty at least by a documentary interest, is still too rational for our criticism run mad. It will barter the whole of Molière for a line from *L'Etourdi*, and even when it pronounces Wagner's *Tristan* a bore will except a 'charming note on the horns' at the point where the hunt goes by. This depravation of taste helped me to understand that of which Mme. de Guermantes gave proof when she decided that a man of their world, recognised as a good fellow but a fool, was a monster of egoism, sharper than people thought—that another widely known for his generosity might be the personification of avarice, that a good mother paid no attention to her children, and that a woman generally supposed to be vicious was really actuated by the noblest feelings. As though spoiled by the nullity of life in society, the intelligence and perception of Mme. de Guermantes were too vacillating for disgust not to follow pretty swiftly in the wake of infatuation (leaving her still ready to feel herself attracted afresh by the kind of cleverness which she had in turn sought out and abandoned) and for the charm which she had felt in some warm-hearted man not to change, if he came too often to see her, sought too freely from her directions which she was incapable of giving him, into an irritation which she believed to be produced by her admirer but which was in fact due to the utter impossibility of finding pleasure when one does nothing else than seek it. The variations of the Duchess's judgment spared no one, except her husband. He alone had never been in love with her, in him she had always felt an iron character, indifferent to the caprices that she displayed, contemptuous of her beauty, violent, of a will that would never bend, the sort under which alone nervous people can find tranquillity. M. de Guermantes on the other hand, pursuing a single type of feminine beauty but seeking it in mistresses whom he constantly replaced, had, once he had left them, and to express derision of them, only an associate, permanent and identical, who irritated him often by her chatter but as to whom he knew that everyone regarded her as the most beautiful, the most virtuous, the cleverest, the best-read member of the aristocracy, as a wife whom he, M. de Guermantes, was only too fortunate to have found, who cloaked all his irregularities, entertained like no one else in the world, and upheld for their drawing-room its position as the premier in the Faubourg Saint-Germain. This common opinion he himself shared; often moved to ill-humour against her, he was proud of her. If, being as niggardly as he was fastidious, he refused her the most trifling sums for her charities or for the servants, yet he insisted upon her wearing the most sumptuous clothes and driving behind the best horses in Paris. Whenever Mme. de Guermantes had just perpetrated, with reference to the merits and defects, which she suddenly transposed, of one of their friends, a new and succulent paradox, she burned to make trial of it before people capable of relishing it, to bring out its psychological originality and to set its epigrammatic brilliance sparkling. No doubt these new opinions embodied as a rule no more truth than the old, often less; but this very element, arbitrary and incalculable, of novelty which they contained conferred on them something intellectual which made the communication of them exciting. Only the patient on whom the Duchess was exercising her psychological skill was generally an intimate friend as to whom those people to whom she longed to hand on her discovery were entirely unaware that he was not still at the apex of her favour; thus the reputation that Mme. de Guermantes had of being an incomparable friend, sentimental, tender and devoted, made it difficult for her to launch the attack herself; she could at the most intervene later on, as though under constraint, by uttering a response to appease, to contradict in appearance but actually to support a partner who had taken it on himself to provoke her; this was precisely the part in which M. de Guermantes excelled.

As for social activities, it was yet another form of pleasure, arbitrary and spectacular, that Mme. de Guermantes felt in uttering, with regard to them, those unexpected judgments which pricked with an incessant and exquisite feeling of surprise the Princesse de Parme. But with this one of the Duchess's pleasures it was not so much with the help of literary criticism as by following political life and the reports of parliamentary debates that I tried to understand in what it might consist. The successive and contradictory edicts by which Mme. de Guermantes continually reversed the scale of values among the people of her world no longer sufficing to distract her, she sought also in the manner in which she ordered her own social behaviour, in which she recorded her own most trivial decisions on points of fashion, to taste those artificial emotions, to fulfil those adventitious obligations which stimulate the perceptions of Parliaments and gain hold of the minds of politicians. We know that when a Minister explains to the Chamber that he believed himself to be acting rightly in following a line of conduct which does, as a matter of fact, appear quite straightforward to the commonsense person who next morning in his newspaper reads the report of the sitting, this commonsense reader does nevertheless feel himself suddenly stirred and begins to doubt whether he has been right in approving the Minister's conduct when he sees that the latter's speech was listened to with the accompaniment of a lively agitation and punctuated with expressions of condemnation such as: "It's most serious!" ejaculated by a Deputy whose name and titles are so long, and followed in the report by movements so emphatic that in the whole interruption the words "It's most serious!" occupy less room than a hemistich does in an alexandrine. For instance in the days when M. de Guermantes, Prince des Laumes, sat in the Chamber, one used to read now and then in the Paris newspapers, albeit it was intended primarily for the Méséglise division, to shew the electors there that they had not given their votes to an inactive or voiceless mandatory:

(Monsieur de Guermantes-Bouillon, Prince des Laumes: "This is serious!" "Hear, hear!" from the Centre and some of the Right benches, loud exclamations from the Extreme Left.)

The commonsense reader still retains a gleam of faith in the sage Minister, but his heart is convulsed with a fresh palpitation by the first words of the speaker who rises to reply:

"The astonishment, it is not too much to say the stupor" (keen sensation on the Right side of the House) "that I have felt at the words of one who is still, I presume, a member of the Government" (thunder of applause) . . . Several Under-Secretaries of State for Posts and Telegraphs without Deputies then crowded round the Ministerial bench. Then rising from his seat, nodded his head in the affirmative.

This 'thunder of applause' carries away the last shred of resistance in the mind of the commonsense reader; he discovers to be an insult to the Chamber, monstrous in fact, a course of procedure which in itself is of no importance; it may be some normal action such as arranging that the rich shall pay more than the poor, bringing to light some piece of injustice, preferring peace to war; he will find it scandalous and will see in it an offence to certain principles to which as a matter of fact he had never given a thought, which are not engraved on the human heart, but which move him forcibly by reason of the acclamations which they provoke and the compact majorities which they assemble.

·It must at the same time be recognised that this subtlety of the politician which served to explain to me the Guermantes circle, and other groups in society later on, is nothing more than the perversion of a certain fineness of interpretation often described as 'reading between the lines.' If in representative assemblies there is absurdity owing to perversion of this quality, there is equally stupidity, through the want of it, in the public who take everything 'literally,' who do not suspect a dismissal when a high dignitary is relieved of his office 'at his own request,' and say: "He cannot have been dismissed, since it was he who asked leave to retire,"—a defeat when the Russians by a strategic movement withdraw upon a stronger position that has been prepared beforehand, a refusal when, a Province having demanded its independence from the German Emperor, he grants it religious autonomy. It is possible, moreover (to return to these sittings of the Chamber), that when they open the Deputies themselves are like the commonsense person who will read the published report. Learning that certain workers on strike have sent their delegates to confer with a Minister, they may ask one another innocently: "There now, I wonder what they can have been saying; let's hope it's all settled," at the moment when the Minister himself mounts the tribune in a solemn silence which has already brought artificial emotions into play. The first words of the Minister: "There is no necessity for me to inform the Chamber that I have too high a sense of what is the duty of the Government to have received a deputation of which the authority entrusted to me could take no cognisance," produce a dramatic effect, for this was the one hypothesis which the commonsense of the Deputies had not imagined. But precisely because of its dramatic effect it is greeted with such applause that it is only after several minutes have passed that the Minister can succeed in making himself heard, the Minister who will receive on returning to his place on the bench the congratulations of his colleagues. We are as deeply moved as on the day when the same Minister failed to invite to a big official reception the President of the Municipal Council who was supporting the Opposition, and declare that on this occasion as on the other he has acted with true statesmanship.

M. de Guermantes at this period in his life had, to the great scandal of the Courvoisiers, frequently been among the crowd of Deputies who came forward to congratulate the Minister. I have heard it said afterwards that even at a time when he was playing a fairly important part in the Chamber and was being thought of in connexion with Ministerial office or an Embassy he was, when a friend came to ask a favour of him, infinitely more simple, behaved politically a great deal less like the important political personage than anyone else who did not happen to be Duc de Guermantes. For if he said that nobility made no difference, that he regarded his fellow Deputies as equals, he did not believe it for a moment. He sought, pretended to value but really despised political importance, and as he remained in his own eyes M. de Guermantes it did not envelop his person in that dead weight of high office which makes other politicians unapproachable. And in this way his pride guarded against every assault not only his manners which were of an ostentatious familiarity but also such true simplicity as he might actually have.

To return to those artificial and moving decisions such as are made by politicians, Mme. de Guermantes was no less disconcerting to the Guermantes, the Courvoisiers, the Faubourg in general and, more than anyone, the Princesse de Parme by her habit of issuing unaccountable decrees behind which one could feel to be latent principles which impressed one all the more, the less one expected them. If the new Greek Minister gave a fancy dress ball, everyone chose a costume and asked everyone else what the Duchess would wear. One thought that she would appear as the Duchesse de Bourgogne, another suggested as probable the guise of Princess of Dujabar, a third Psyche. Finally, a Courvoisier having asked her: "What are you going to wear, Oriane?" provoked the one response of which nobody had thought: "Why, nothing at all!" which at once set every tongue wagging, as revealing Oriane's opinion as to the true social position of the new Greek Minister and the proper attitude to adopt towards him, that is to say the opinion which ought to have been foreseen, namely that a duchess 'was not expected' to attend the fancy dress ball given by this new Minister: "I do not see that there is any necessity to go to the Greek Minister's; I do not know him; I am not a Greek; why should I go to these people's house, I have nothing to do with them?" said the Duchess. "But everybody will be there, they say it's going to be charming!" cried Mme. de Gallardon. "Still, it's just as charming sometimes to sit by one's own fireside," replied Mme. de Guermantes. The Courvoisiers could not get over this, but the Guermantes, without copying it, approved of their cousin's attitude. "Naturally, everybody isn't in a position like Oriane to break with all the conventions. But if you look at it in one way you can't say she was actually wrong in wishing to shew that we are going rather far in flinging ourselves at the feet of all these foreigners who appear from heaven knows where." Naturally, knowing the stream of comment which one or other attitude would not fail to provoke, Mme. de Guermantes took as much pleasure in appearing at a party to which her hostess had not dared to count on her coming as in staying at home or spending the evening at the play with her husband on the night of a party to which 'everybody was going,' or, again, when people imagined that she would eclipse the finest diamonds with some historic diadem, by stealing into the room without a single jewel, and in another style of dress than what had been, wrongly, supposed to be essential to the occasion. Albeit she was anti-Dreyfusard (while retaining her belief in the innocence of Dreyfus, just as she spent her life in the social world believing only in abstract ideas) she had created an enormous sensation at a party at the Princesse de Ligne's, first of all by remaining seated after all the ladies had risen to their feet as General Mercier entered the room, and then by getting up and in a loud voice asking for her carriage when a Nationalist orator had begun to address the gathering, thereby shewing that she did not consider that society was meant for talking politics; all heads were turned towards her at a Good Friday concert at which, although a Voltairean, she had not remained because she thought it indecent to bring Christ upon the stage. We know how important, even for the great queens of society, is that moment of the year at which the round of entertainment begins: so much so that the Marquise d'Amoncourt, who, from a need to say something, a form of mania, and also from want of perception, was always making a fool of herself, had actually replied to somebody who had called to condole with her on the death of her father, M. de Montmorency: "What makes it sadder still is that it should come at a time when one's mirror is simply stuffed with cards!" Very well, at this point in the social year, when people invited the Duchesse de Guermantes to dinner, making every effort to see that she was not already engaged, she declined, for the one reason of which nobody in society would ever have thought; she was just starting on a cruise among the Norwegian fjords, which were so interesting. People in society were stupefied, and, without any thought of following the Duchess's example, derived nevertheless from her action that sense of relief which one has in reading Kant when after the most rigorous demonstration of determinism one finds that above the world of necessity there is the world of freedom. Every invention of which no one has ever thought before excites the interest even of people who can derive no benefit from it. That of steam navigation was a small thing compared with the employment of steam navigation at that sedentary time of year called 'the season.' The idea that anyone could voluntarily renounce a hundred dinners or luncheons, twice as many afternoon teas, three times as many evening parties, the most brilliant Mondays at the Opera and Tuesdays at the Français to visit the Norwegian fjords seemed to the Courvoisiers no more explicable than the idea of *Twenty Thousand Leagues Under the Sea*, but conveyed to them a similar impression of independence and charm. So that not a day passed on which somebody might not be heard to ask, not merely: "You've heard Oriane's latest joke?" but "You know Oriane's latest?" and on 'Oriane's latest' as on 'Oriane's latest joke' would follow the comment: "How typical of Oriane!" "Isn't that pure Oriane?" Oriane's latest might be, for instance, that, having to write on behalf of a patriotic society to Cardinal X——, Bishop of Mâcon (whom M. de Guermantes when he spoke of him invariably called 'Monsieur de Mascon,' thinking this to be 'old French'), when everyone was trying to imagine what form the letter would take, and had no difficulty as to the opening words, the choice lying between 'Eminence,' and 'Monseigneur,' but was puzzled as to the rest, Oriane's letter, to the general astonishment, began: 'Monsieur le Cardinal,' following an old academic form, or: 'My Cousin,' this term being in use among the Princes of the Church, the Guermantes and Crowned Heads, who prayed to God to take each and all of them into 'His fit and holy keeping.' To start people on the topic of an 'Oriane's latest' it was sufficient that at a performance at which all Paris was present and a most charming play was being given, when they looked for Mme. de Guermantes in the boxes of the Princesse de Parme, the Princesse de Guermantes, countless other ladies who had invited her, they discovered her sitting by herself, in black, with a tiny hat on her head, in a stall in which she had arrived before the curtain rose. "You hear better, when it's a play that's worth listening to," she explained, to the scandal of the Courvoisiers and the admiring bewilderment of the Guermantes and the Princesse de Parme, who suddenly discovered that the 'fashion' of hearing the beginning of a play was more up to date, was a proof of greater originality and intelligence (which need not astonish them, coming from Oriane) than that of arriving for the last act after a big dinner-party and 'going on' somewhere first. Such were the various kinds of sur-prise for which the Princesse de Parme knew that she ought to be prepared if she put a literary or social question to Mme. de Guermantes, one result of which was that during these dinner-parties at Oriane's her Royal High-ness never ventured upon the slightest topic save with the uneasy and en-raptured prudence of the bather emerging from between two breakers.

Among the elements which, absent from the three or four other more or less equivalent drawing-rooms that set the fashion for the Faubourg Saint-Germain, differentiated from them that of the Duchesse de Guer-mantes, just as Leibniz allows that each monad, while reflecting the entire universe, adds to it something of its own, one of the least attractive was regularly furnished by one or two extremely good-looking women who had no title to be there apart from their beauty and the use that M. de Guermantes had made of them, and whose presence revealed at once, as does in other drawing-rooms that of certain otherwise unaccountable pic-tures, that in this household the husband was an ardent appreciator of feminine graces. They were all more or less alike, for the Duke had a taste for large women, at once statuesque and loose-limbed, of a type half-way between the Venus of Milo and the Samothracian Victory; often fair, rarely dark, sometimes auburn, like the most recent, who was at this dinner, that Vicomtesse d'Arpajon whom he had loved so well that for a long time he had obliged her to send him as many as ten telegrams daily (which slightly annoyed the Duchess), corresponded with her by carrier pigeon when he was at Guermantes, and from whom moreover he had long been so incapable of tearing himself away that, one winter which he had had to spend at Parma, he travelled back regularly every week to Paris, spend-ing two days in the train, in order to see her.

As a rule these handsome 'supers' had been his mistresses but were no longer (as was Mme. d'Arpajon's case) or were on the point of ceasing to be so. It may well have been that the importance which the Duchess en-joyed in their sight and the hope of being invited to her house, though they themselves came of thoroughly aristocratic, but still not quite first-class stock, had prompted them, even more than the good looks and generosity of the Duke, to yield to his desires. Not that the Duchess would have placed any insuperable obstacle in the way of their crossing her threshold: she was aware that in more than one of them she had found an ally, thanks to whom she had obtained a thousand things which she wanted but which M. de Guermantes pitilessly denied his wife so long as he was not in love with some one else. And so the reason why they were not invited by the Duchess until their intimacy with the Duke was already far advanced lay principally in the fact that he, every time that he had embarked on the deep waters of love, had imagined nothing more than a brief flirtation, as a reward for which he considered an invitation from his wife to be more than adequate. And yet he found himself offering this as the price of far less, for a first kiss in fact, because a resistance upon which he had never reckoned had been brought into play or because there had been no resist-ance. In love it often happens that gratitude, the desire to give pleasure, makes us generous beyond the limits of what the other person's expectation and self-interest could have anticipated. But then the realisation of this offer was hindered by conflicting circumstances. In the first place, all the women who had responded to M. de Guermantes's love, and sometimes even when they had not yet surrendered themselves to him, he had, one after another, segregated from the world. He no longer allowed them to see anyone, spent almost all his time in their company, looked after the education of their children to whom now and again, if one was to judge by certain speaking likenesses later on, he had occasion to present a little brother or sister. And so if, at the start of the connexion, the prospect of an introduction to Mme. de Guermantes, which had never crossed the mind of the Duke, had entered considerably into the thoughts of his mistress, their connexion had by itself altered the whole of the lady's point of view; the Duke was no longer for her merely the husband of the smartest woman in Paris, but a man with whom his new mistress was in love, a man moreover who had given her the means and the inclination for a more luxurious style of living and had transposed the relative importance in her mind of questions of social and of material advantage; while now and then a composite jealousy, into which all these factors entered, of Mme. de Guermantes animated the Duke's mistresses. But this case was the rarest of all; besides, when the day appointed for the introduction at length arrived (at a point when as a rule the Duke had lost practically all interest in the matter, his actions, like everyone's else, being generally dictated by previous actions the prime motive of which had already ceased to exist), it frequently happened that it was Mme. de Guermantes who had sought the acquaintance of the mistress in whom she hoped, and so greatly needed, to discover, against her dread husband, a valuable ally. This is not to say that, save at rare moments, in their own house, where, when the Duchess talked too much, he let fall a few words or, more dreadful still, preserved a silence which rendered her speechless, M. de Guermantes failed in his outward relations with his wife to observe what are called the forms. People who did not know them might easily misunderstand. Sometimes between the racing at Deauville, the course of waters and the return to Guermantes for the shooting, in the few weeks which people spend in Paris, since the Duchess had a liking for café-concerts, the Duke would go with her to spend the evening at one of these. The audience remarked at once, in one of those little open boxes in which there is just room for two, this Hercules in his 'smoking' (for in France we give to everything that is more or less British the one name that it happens not to bear in England), his monocle screwed in his eye, in his plump but finely shaped hand, on the ring-finger of which there glowed a sapphire, a plump cigar from which now and then he drew a puff of smoke, keeping his eyes for the most part on the stage but, when he did let them fall upon the audience in which there was absolutely no one whom he knew, softening them with an air of gentleness, reserve, courtesy and consideration. When a verse struck him as amusing and not too indecent, the Duke would turn round with a smile to his wife, letting her share, by a twinkle of good-natured understanding, the innocent merriment which the new song had aroused in himself. And the spectators might believe that there was no better husband in the world than this, nor anyone more enviable than the Duchess—that woman outside whom every interest in the Duke's life lay, that woman with whom he was not in love, to whom he had been consistently unfaithful; when the Duchess felt tired, they saw M. de Guermantes rise, put on her cloak with his own hands, arranging her necklaces so that they did not catch in the lining, and clear a path for her to the street with an assiduous and respectful attention which she received with the coldness of the woman of the world who sees in such behaviour simply conventional politeness, at times even with the slightly ironical bitterness of the disabused spouse who has no illusion left to shatter. But despite these externals (another element of that politeness which has made duty evolve from the depths of our being to the surface, at a period already remote but still continuing for its survivors) the life of the Duchess was by no means easy. M. de Guermantes never became generous or human save for a new mistress who would take, as it generally happened, the Duchess's part; the latter saw becoming possible for her once again generosities towards inferiors, charities to the poor, even for herself, later on, a new and sumptuous motor-car. But from the irritation which developed as a rule pretty rapidly in Mme. de Guermantes at people whom she found too submissive the Duke's mistresses were not exempt. Presently the Duchess grew tired of them. Simultaneously, at this moment, the Duke's intimacy with Mme. d'Arpajon was drawing to an end. Another mistress dawned on the horizon.

No doubt the love which M. de Guermantes had had for each of them in succession would begin one day to make itself felt afresh; in the first place, this love in dying bequeathed them, like beautiful marbles—marbles beautiful to the Duke, become thus in part an artist, because he had loved them and was sensitive now to lines which he would not have appreciated without love—which brought into juxtaposition in the Duchess's drawing-room their forms long inimical, devoured by jealousies and quarrels, and finally reconciled in the peace of friendship; besides, this friendship itself was an effect of the love which had made M. de Guermantes observe in those who were his mistresses virtues which exist in every human being but are perceptible only to the sensual eye, so much so that the ex-mistress, become 'the best of comrades' who would do anything in the world for one, is as recognised a type as the doctor or father who is not a doctor or a father but a friend. But during a period of transition the woman whom M. de Guermantes was preparing to abandon bewailed her lot, made scenes, shewed herself exacting, appeared indiscreet, became a nuisance. The Duke began to take a dislike to her. Then Mme. de Guermantes had an opportunity to bring into prominence the real or imagined defects of a person who annoyed her. Known as a kind woman, Mme. de Guermantes received the telephone messages, the confidences, the tears of the abandoned mistress and made no complaint. She laughed at them, first with her husband, then with a few chosen friends. And imagining that this pity which she shewed for the poor wretch gave her the right to make fun of her, even to her face, whatever the lady might say, provided it could be included among the attributes of the character for absurdity which the Duke and Duchess had recently fabricated for her, Mme. de Guermantes had no hesitation in exchanging with her husband a glance of ironical connivance.

Meanwhile, as she sat down to table, the Princesse de Parme remembered that she had thought of inviting a certain other Princess to the Opera, and, wishing to be assured that this would not in any way offend Mme. de Guermantes, was preparing to sound her. At this moment there entered M. de Grouchy, whose train, owing to some block on the line, had been held up for an hour. He made what excuses he could. His wife, had she been a Courvoisier, would have died of shame. But Mme. de Grouchy was not a Guermantes for nothing. As her husband was apologising for being late:

"I see," she broke in, "that even in little things arriving late is a tradition in your family."

"Sit down, Grouchy, and don't let them pull your leg," said the Duke.

"I hope I move with the times, still I must admit that the Battle of Waterloo had its points, since it brought about the Restoration of the Bourbons, and better still in a way which made them unpopular. But you seem to be a regular Nimrod!"

"Well, as a matter of fact, I have had quite a good bag. I shall take the liberty of sending the Duchess six brace of pheasants to-morrow."

An idea seemed to flicker in the eyes of Mme. de Guermantes. She insisted that M. de Grouchy must not give himself the trouble of sending the pheasants. And making a sign to the betrothed footman with whom I had exchanged a few words on my way from the Elstir room:

"Poullein," she told him, "you will go to-morrow and fetch M. le Comte's pheasants and bring them straight back—you won't mind, will you, Grouchy, if I make a few little presents. Basin and I can't eat a whole dozen by ourselves."

"But the day after to-morrow will be soon enough," said M. de Grouchy.

"No, to-morrow suits me better," the Duchess insisted.

Poullein had turned pale; his appointment with his sweetheart would have to be missed. This was quite enough for the diversion of the Duchess, who liked to appear to be taking a human interest in everyone. "I know it's your day out," she went on to Poullein, "all you've got to do is to change with Georges; he can take to-morrow off and stay in the day after."

But the day after, Poullein's sweetheart would not be free. A holiday then was of no account to him. As soon as he was out of the room, everyone complimented the Duchess on the interest she took in her servants. "But I only behave towards them as I like people to behave to me." "That's just it. They can say they've found a good place with you." "Oh, nothing so very wonderful. But I think they all like me. That one is a little annoying because he's in love. He thinks it incumbent on him to go about with a long face."

At this point Poullein reappeared. "You're quite right," said M. de Grouchy, "he doesn't look much like smiling. With those fellows one has to be good but not too good." "I admit I'm not a very dreadful mistress.

He'll have nothing to do all day but call for your pheasants, sit in the house doing nothing and eat his share of them." "There are plenty of people who would be glad to be in his place," said M. de Grouchy, for envy makes men blind.

"Oriane," began the Princesse de Parme, "I had a visit the other day from your cousin Heudicourt; of course she's a highly intelligent woman; she's a Guermantes, one can say no more, but they tell me she has a spiteful tongue." The Duke fastened on his wife a slow gaze of deliberate stupefaction. Mme. de Guermantes began to smile. Gradually the Princess became aware of their pantomime. "But . . . do you mean to say . . . you don't agree with me?" she stammered with growing uneasiness. "Really, Ma'am, it's too good of you to pay any attention to Basin's faces. Now, Basin, you're not to hint nasty things about our cousins." "He thinks her too wicked?" inquired the Princess briskly. "Oh, dear me, no!" replied the Duchess. "I don't know who told your Highness that she was spiteful. On the contrary, she's an excellent creature who never said any harm of anyone, or did any harm to any one." "Ah!" sighed Mme. de Parme, greatly relieved. "I must say I never noticed anything myself. But I know it's often difficult not to be a little spiteful when one is so full of wit . . ." "Ah! Now that is a quality of which she has even less." "Less wit?" asked the stupefied Princess. "Come now, Oriane," broke in the Duke in a plaintive tone, casting to right and left of him a glance of amusement, "you heard the Princess tell you that she was a superior woman." "But isn't she?" "Superior in chest measurement, at any rate." "Don't listen to him, Ma'am, he's not sincere; she's as stupid as a (h'm) goose," came in a loud and rasping voice from Mme. de Guermantes, who, a great deal more 'old French' even than the Duke when he was not trying, did often deliberately seek to be, but in a manner the opposite of the lace-neckcloth, deliquescent style of her husband and in reality far more subtle, by a sort of almost peasant pronunciation which had a harsh and delicious flavour of the soil. "But she's the best woman in the world. Besides, I don't really know that one can call it stupidity when it's carried to such a point as that. I don't believe I ever met anyone quite like her; she's a case for a specialist, there's something pathological about her, she's a sort of 'innocent' or 'cretin' or an 'arrested development,' like the people you see in melodramas, or in *L'Arlésienne*. I always ask myself, when she comes to see me, whether the moment may not have arrived at which her intelligence is going to dawn, which makes me a little nervous always." The Princess was lost in admiration of these utterances but remained stupefied by the preceding verdict. "She repeated to me—and so did Mme. d'Epinay—what you said about 'Teaser Augustus.' It's delicious," she put in.

M. de Guermantes explained the joke to me. I wanted to tell him that his brother, who pretended not to know me, was expecting me that same evening at eleven o'clock. But I had not asked Robert whether I might mention this engagement, and as the fact that M. de Charlus had practically fixed it with me himself directly contradicted what he had told the Duchess I judged it more tactful to say nothing. " 'Teaser Augustus' was not bad," said M. de Guermantes, "but Mme. d'Heudicourt probably did not tell you a far better thing that Oriane said to her the other day in reply to an invitation to luncheon." "No, indeed! Do tell me!" "Now Basin, you keep quiet; in the first place, it was a stupid remark, and it will make the Princess think me inferior even to my fool of a cousin. Though I don't know why I should call her my cousin. She's one of Basin's cousins. Still, I believe she is related to me in some sort of way." "Oh!" cried the Princesse de Parme, at the idea that she could possibly think Mme. de Guermantes stupid, and protesting helplessly that nothing could ever lower the Duchess from the place she held in her estimation. "Besides we have already subtracted from her the quality of wit; as what I said to her tends to deny her certain other good qualities also, it seems to me inopportune to repeat it." " 'Deny her!' 'Inopportune!' How well she expresses herself!" said the Duke with a pretence of irony, to win admiration for the Duchess. "Now, then, Basin, you're not to make fun of your wife." "I should explain to your Royal Highness," went on the Duke, "that Oriane's cousin may be superior, good, stout, anything you like to mention, but she is not exactly—what shall I say—lavish." "No, I know, she's terribly close-fisted," broke in the Princess. "I should not have ventured to use the expression, but you have hit on exactly the right word. You can see it in her house-keeping, and especially in the cooking, which is excellent, but strictly rationed." "Which leads to some quite amusing scenes," M. de Bréauté interrupted him. "For instance, my dear Basin, I was down at Heudicourt one day when you were expected, Oriane and yourself. They had made the most elaborate preparations when, during the afternoon, a footman brought in a telegram to say that you weren't coming." "That doesn't surprise me!" said the Duchess, who not only was difficult to secure, but liked people to know as much. "Your cousin read the telegram, was duly distressed, then immediately, without losing her head, telling herself that there was no point in going to unnecessary expense for so unimportant a gentleman as myself, called the footman back. 'Tell the cook not to put on the chicken!' she shouted after him. And that evening I heard her asking the butler: 'Well? What about the beef that was left over yesterday? Aren't you going to let us have that?' " "All the same, one must admit that the cheer you get there is of the very best," said the Duke, who fancied that in using this language he shewed himself to belong to the old school. "I don't know any house where one gets better food." "Or less," put in the Duchess. "It is quite wholesome and quite enough for what you would call a vulgar yokel like myself," went on the Duke, "one keeps one's appetite." "Oh, if it's to be taken as a cure, it's certainly more hygienic than sumptuous. Not that it's as good as all that," added Mme. de Guermantes, who was not at all pleased that the title of 'best table in Paris' should be awarded to any but her own. "With my cousin it's just the same as with those costive authors who hatch out every fifteen years a one-act play or a sonnet. The sort of thing people call a little masterpiece, trifles that are perfect gems, in fact the one thing I loathe most in the world. The cooking at Zénaïde's is not bad, but you would think it more ordinary if she was less parsimonious. There are some things her cook does quite well, and others that he spoils. I have had some thoroughly bad dinners there, as in most houses, only they've done me less harm there because the stomach is, after all, more sensitive to quantity than to quality." "Well, to get on with the story," the Duke concluded, "Zénaïde insisted that Oriane should go to luncheon there, and as my wife is not very fond of going out anywhere she resisted, wanted to be sure that under the pretence of a quiet meal she was not being trapped into some great banquet, and tried in vain to find out who else were to be of the party. 'You must come,' Zénaïde insisted, boasting of all the good things there would be to eat. 'You are going to have a *purée* of chestnuts, I need say no more than that, and there will be seven little *bouchées à la reine*.' 'Seven little *bouchées*!' cried Oriane, 'that means that we shall be at least eight!'" There was silence for a few seconds, and then the Princess having seen the point let her laughter explode like a peal of thunder. "Ah! 'Then we shall be eight,'—it's exquisite. How very well phrased!" she said, having by a supreme effort recaptured the expression she had heard used by Mme. d'Epinay, which this time was more appropriate. "Oriane, that was very charming of the Princess, she said your remark was well phrased." "But, my dear, you're telling me nothing new. I know how clever the Princess is," replied Mme. de Guermantes, who readily assimilated a remark when it was uttered at once by a Royal Personage and in praise of her own wit. "I am very proud that Ma'am should appreciate my humble phrasings. I don't remember, though, that I ever did say such a thing, and if I did it must have been to flatter my cousin, for if she had ordered seven 'mouthfuls,' the mouths, if I may so express myself, would have been a round dozen if not more."

"She used to have all M. de Bornier's manuscripts," went on the Princess, still speaking of Mme. d'Heudicourt, and anxious to make the most of the excellent reasons she might have for associating with that lady. "She must have dreamed it, I don't believe she ever even know him," said the Duchess. "What is really interesting about him is that he kept up a correspondence with people of different nationalities at the same time," put in the Vicomtesse d'Arpajon who, allied to the principal ducal and even reigning families of Europe, was always glad that people should be reminded of the fact. "Surely, Oriane," said M. de Guermantes, with ulterior purpose, "you can't have forgotten that dinner-party where you had M. de Bornier sitting next to you!" "But, Basin," the Duchess interrupted him, "if you mean to inform me that I knew M. de Bornier, why of course I did, he even called upon me several times, but I could never bring myself to invite him to the house because I should always have been obliged to have it disinfected afterwards with formol. As for the dinner you mean, I remember it only too well, but it was certainly not at Zénaïde's, who never set eyes on Bornier in her life, and would probably think if you spoke to her of the *Fille de Roland* that you meant a Bonaparte Princess who was said at one time to be engaged to the son of the King of Greece; no, it was at the Austrian Embassy. Dear Hoyos imagined he was giving me a great treat by planting on the chair next to mine that pestiferous academician. I quite thought I had a squadron of mounted police sitting beside me. I was obliged to stop my nose as best I could, all through dinner; until the gruyère came round I didn't dare to breathe." M. de Guermantes, whose secret object was attained, made a furtive examination of his guests' faces to judge the effect of the Duchess's pleasantry. "You were speaking of correspondence; I must say, I thought Gambetta's admirable," she went on, to shew that she was not afraid to be found taking an interest in a proletarian and a radical. M. de Bréauté, who fully appreciated the brilliance of this feat of daring, gazed round him with an eye at once flashing and affectionate, after which he wiped his monocle.

"Gad, it's infernally dull that *Fille de Roland*," said M. de Guermantes, with the satisfaction which he derived from the sense of his own superiority to a work which had bored him so, perhaps also from the *suave mari magno* feeling one has in the middle of a good dinner, when one recalls so terrible an evening in the past. "Still, there were some quite good lines in it, and a patriotic sentiment."

I let it be understood that I had no admiration for M. de Bornier. "Indeed! You have some fault to find with him?" the Duke asked with a note of curiosity, for he always imagined when anyone spoke ill of a man that it must be on account of a personal resentment, just as to speak well of a woman marked the beginning of a love-affair. "I see you've got your knife into him. What did he do to you? You must tell us. Why yes, there must be some skeleton in the cupboard or you wouldn't run him down. It's long-winded, the *Fille de Roland*, but it's quite strong in parts." "Strong is just the right word for an author who smelt like that," Mme. de Guermantes broke in sarcastically. "If this poor boy ever found himself face to face with him, I can quite understand that he carried away an impression in his nostrils!" "I must confess, though, to Ma'am," the Duke went on, addressing the Princesse de Parme, "that quite apart from the *Fille de Roland*, in literature and even in music I am terribly old-fashioned; no old nightingale can be too stale for my taste. You won't believe me, perhaps, but in the evenings, if my wife sits down to the piano, I find myself calling for some old tune by Auber or Boïeldieu, or even Beethoven! That's the sort of thing that appeals to me. As for Wagner, he sends me to sleep at once." "You are wrong there," said Mme. de Guermantes, "in spite of his insufferable long-windedness, Wagner was a genius. *Lohengrin* is a masterpiece. Even in *Tristan* there are some amusing passages scattered about. And the Chorus of Spinners in the *Flying Dutchman* is a perfect marvel." "A'n't I right, Babal," said M. de Guermantes, turning to M. de Bréauté, "what we like is:

Les rendez-vous de noble compagnie
Se donnent tous en ce charmant séjour.

It's delicious. And *Fra Diavolo*, and the *Magic Flute*, and the *Chalet*, and the *Marriage of Figaro*, and the *Diamants de la Couronne*—there's music for you! It's the same thing in literature. For instance, I adore Balzac, the *Bal de Sceaux*, the *Mohicans de Paris*." "Oh, my dear, if you are going to begin about Balzac, we shall never hear the end of it; do wait, keep it for some evening when Mémé's here. He's even better, he knows it all by heart." Irritated by his wife's interruption, the Duke held her for some seconds under the fire of a menacing silence. And his huntsman's eyes reminded me of a brace of loaded pistols. Meanwhile Mme. d'Arpajon had been exchanging with the Princesse de Parme, upon tragic and other kinds of poetry, a series of remarks which did not reach me distinctly until I caught the following from Mme. d'Arpajon: "Oh, Ma'am is sure to be right; I quite admit he makes the world seem ugly, because he's unable to distinguish between ugliness and beauty, or rather because his insufferable vanity makes him believe that everything he says is beautiful; I agree with your Highness that in the piece we are speaking of there are some ridiculous things, quite unintelligible, errors of taste, that it is difficult to understand, that it's as much trouble to read as if it was written in Russian or Chinese, for of course it's anything in the world but French, still when one has taken the trouble, how richly one is rewarded, it's so full of imagination!" Of this little lecture I had missed the opening sentences. I gathered in the end not only that the poet incapable of distinguishing between beauty and ugliness was Victor Hugo, but furthermore that the poem which was as difficult to understand as Chinese or Russian was

> *Lorsque l'enfant paraît, le cercle de famille*
> *Applaudit à grands cris.*

a piece dating from the poet's earliest period, and perhaps even nearer to Mme. Deshoulières than to the Victor Hugo of the *Légende des Siècles*. Far from condemning Mme. d'Arpajon as absurd, I saw her (the only one, at that table so matter-of-fact, so nondescript, at which I had sat down with such keen disappointment), I saw her in my mind's eye crowned with that lace cap, with the long spiral ringlets falling from it on either side, which was worn by Mme. de Rémusat, Mme. de Broglie, Mme. de Saint-Aularie, all those distinguished women who in their fascinating letters quote with so much learning and so aptly passages from Sophocles, Schiller and the *Imitation*, but in whom the earliest poetry of the Romantics induced the alarm and exhaustion inseparable for my grandmother from the latest verses of Stéphane Mallarmé. "Mme. d'Arpajon is very fond of poetry," said the Princesse de Parme to her hostess, impressed by the ardent tone in which the speech had been delivered. "No; she knows absolutely nothing about it," replied Mme. de Guermantes in an undertone, taking advantage of the fact that Mme. d'Arpajon, who was dealing with an objection raised by General de Beautreillis, was too much intent upon what she herself was saying to hear what was being murmured by the Duchess. "She has become literary since she's been forsaken. I can tell your Highness that it is I who have to bear the whole burden of it because it is to me that she comes in floods of tears whenever Basin hasn't been to see her, which is practically every day. And yet it isn't my fault, after all, if she bores him, and I can't force him to go to her, although I would rather he were a little more faithful to her, because then I shouldn't see quite so much of her myself. But she drives him crazy, and there's nothing extraordinary in that. She isn't a bad sort, but she's boring to a degree you can't imagine. And all this because Basin took it into his head for a year or so to play me false with her. And to have in addition a foot-man who has fallen in love with a little street-walker and goes about with a long face if I don't request the young person to leave her profitable pave-ment for half an hour and come to tea with me! Oh! Life really is too tedious!" the Duchess languorously concluded. Mme. d'Arpajon bored M. de Guermantes principally because he had recently fallen in love with another, whom I discovered to be the Marquise de Surgis-le-Duc. At this moment the footman who had been deprived of his holiday was waiting at table. And it struck me that, still disconsolate, he was doing it with a good deal of difficulty, for I noticed that, in handing the dish to M. de Châtellerault, he performed his task so awkwardly that the Duke's elbow came in contact several times with his own. The young Duke was not in the least annoyed with the blushing footman, but looked up at him rather with a smile in his clear blue eyes. This good humour seemed to me on the guest's part to betoken a kindness of heart. But the persistence of his smile led me to think that, aware of the servant's discomfiture, what he felt was perhaps really a malicious joy. "But, my dear, you know you're not revealing any new discovery when you tell us about Victor Hugo," went on the Duchess, this time addressing Mme. d'Arpajon whom she had just seen turn away from the General with a troubled air. "You mustn't expect to launch that young genius. Everybody knows that he has talent. What is utterly detestable is the Victor Hugo of the last stage, the *Légende des Siècles*, I forget all their names. But in the *Feuilles d'Automne,* the *Chants du Crépuscule,* there's a great deal that's the work of a poet, a true poet! Even in the *Contemplations*," went on the Duchess, whom none of her listeners dared to contradict, and with good reason, "there are still some quite pretty things. But I confess that I prefer not to venture farther than the *Crépuscule!* And then in the finer poems of Victor Hugo, and there really are some, one frequently comes across an idea, even a profound idea." And with the right shade of sentiment, bringing out the sorrowful thought with the full strength of her intonation, planting it somewhere beyond the sound of her voice, and fixing straight in front of her a charm-ing, dreamy gaze, the Duchess said slowly: "Take this:

> La douleur est un fruit, Dieu ne le fait pas croître
> Sur la branche trop faible encor pour le porter.

Or, better still:

> Les morts durent bien peu.
> Hélas, dans le cercueil ils tombent en poussière
> Moins vite qu'en nos cœurs!"

And, while a smile of disillusionment contracted with a graceful undula-tion her sorrowing lips, the Duchess fastened on Mme. d'Arpajon the dreaming gaze of her charming, clear blue eyes. I was beginning to know them, as well as her voice, with its heavy drawl, its harsh savour. In those eyes and in that voice, I recognised much of the life of nature round Com-bray. Certainly, in the affectation with which that voice brought into prominence at times a rudeness of the soil there was more than one element: the wholly provincial origin of one branch of the Guermantes family, which had for long remained more localised, more hardy, wilder, more provoking than the rest; and also the usage of really distinguished people, and of witty people who know that distinction does not consist in mincing speech, and the usage of nobles who fraternise more readily with their peasants than with the middle classes; peculiarities all of which the regal position of Mme. de Guermantes enabled her to display more easily, to bring out with every sail spread. It appears that the same voice existed also in certain of her sisters whom she detested, and who, less intelligent than herself and almost plebeianly married, if one may coin this adverb to speak of unions with obscure noblemen, entrenched on their provincial estates, or, in Paris, in a Faubourg Saint-Germain of no brilliance, possessed this voice also but had bridled it, corrected it, softened it so far as lay in their power, just as it is very rarely that any of us presumes on his own originality and does not apply himself diligently to copying the most approved models. But Oriane was so much more intelligent, so much richer, above all, so much more in fashion than her sisters, she had so effectively, when Princesse des Laumes, behaved just as she pleased in the company of the Prince of Wales, that she had realised that this discordant voice was an attraction, and had made of it, in the social order, with the courage of originality rewarded by success, what in the theatrical order a Réjane, a Jeanne Granier (which implies no comparison, naturally, between the respective merits and talents of those two actresses) had made of theirs, something admirable and distinctive which possibly certain Réjane and Granier sisters, whom no one has ever known, strove to conceal as a defect.

To all these reasons for displaying her local originality, the favourite writers of Mme. de Guermantes—Mérimée, Meilhac and Halévy—had brought in addition, with the respect for what was natural, a feeling for the prosaic by which she attained to poetry and a spirit purely of society which called up distant landscapes before my eyes. Besides, the Duchess was fully capable, adding to these influences an artistic research of her own, of having chosen for the majority of her words the pronunciation that seemed to her most 'Ile de France,' most 'Champenoise,' since, if not quite to the same extent as her sister-in-law Marsantes, she rarely used anything but the pure vocabulary that might have been employed by an old French writer. And when one was tired of the composite patchwork of modern speech, it was, albeit one was aware that she expressed far fewer ideas, a thorough relaxation to listen to the talk of Mme. de Guermantes —almost the same feeling, if one was alone with her and she restrained and clarified still further her flow of words, as one has on hearing an old song. Then, as I looked at, as I listened to Mme. de Guermantes, I could see, a prisoner in the perpetual and quiet afternoon of her eyes, a sky of the Ile de France or of Champagne spread itself, grey-blue, oblique, with the same angle of inclination as in the eyes of Saint-Loup.

Thus, by these several formations, Mme. de Guermantes expressed at once the most ancient aristocratic France, then, from a far later source, the manner in which the Duchesse de Broglie might have enjoyed and found fault with Victor Hugo under the July Monarchy, and, finally, a keen taste for the literature that sprang from Mérimée and Meilhac. The first of these formations attracted me more than the second, did more to console me for the disappointments of my pilgrimage to and arrival in the Faubourg Saint-Germain, so different from what I had imagined it to be; but even the second I preferred to the last. For, so long as Mme. de Guermantes was being, almost spontaneously, a Guermantes and nothing more, her Pailleronism, her taste for the younger Dumas were reflected and deliberate. As this taste was the opposite of my own, she was productive, to my mind, of literature when she talked to me of the Faubourg Saint-Germain, and never seemed to me so stupidly Faubourg Saint-Germain as when she was talking literature.

Moved by this last quotation, Mme. d'Arpajon exclaimed: " *'Ces reliques du cœur ont aussi leur poussière!'*—Sir, you must write that down for me on my fan," she said to M. de Guermantes. "Poor woman, I feel sorry for her!" said the Princesse de Parme to Mme. de Guermantes. "No, really, Ma'am, you must not be soft-hearted, she has only got what she deserves." "But—you'll forgive me for saying this to you—she does really love him all the same!" "Oh, not at all; she isn't capable of it; she thinks she loves him just as she thought just now she was quoting Victor Hugo, when she repeated a line from Musset. Listen," the Duchess went on in a tone of melancholy, "nobody would be more touched than myself by any true sentiment. But let me give you an instance. Only yesterday, she made a terrible scene with Basin. Your Highness thinks perhaps that it was because he's in love with other women, because he no longer loves her; not in the least, it was because he won't put her sons down for the Jockey. Does Ma'am call that the behaviour of a woman in love? No; I will go farther;" Mme. de Guermantes added with precision, "she is a person of singular insensibility." Meanwhile it was with an eye sparkling with satisfaction that M. de Guermantes had listened to his wife talking about Victor Hugo 'point-blank' and quoting his poetry. The Duchess might frequently annoy him; at moments like this he was proud of her. "Oriane is really extraordinary. She can talk about anything, she has read everything. She could not possibly have guessed that the conversation this evening would turn on Victor Hugo. Whatever subject you take up, she is ready for you, she can hold her own with the most learned scholars. This young man must be quite captivated."

"Do let us change the conversation," Mme. de Guermantes went on, "because she's dreadfully susceptible. You will think me quite old-fashioned," she began, turning to me. "I know that nowadays it's considered a weakness to care for ideas in poetry, poetry with some thought in it." "Old-fashioned?" asked the Princesse de Parme, quivering with the slight thrill sent through her by this new wave which she had not expected, albeit she knew that the conversation of the Duchesse de Guermantes always held in store for her these continuous and delightful shocks, that breath-catching panic, that wholesome exhaustion after which her thoughts instinctively turned to the necessity of taking a footbath in a dressing cabin and a brisk walk to 'restore her circulation.'

"For my part, no, Oriane," said Mme. de Brissac, "I don't in the least object to Victor Hugo's having ideas, quite the contrary, but I do object to his seeking for them in sheer monstrosities. After all, it was he who accustomed us to ugliness in literature. There are quite enough ugly things already in real life. Why can't we be allowed at least to forget it while we are reading. A distressing spectacle, from which we should turn away in real life, that is what attracts Victor Hugo."

"Victor Hugo is not as realistic as Zola though, surely?" asked the Princesse de Parme. The name of Zola did not stir a muscle on the face of M. de Beautreillis. The General's anti-Dreyfusism was too deep-rooted for him to seek to give expression to it. And his good-natured silence when anyone broached these topics moved the profane heart as a proof of the same delicacy that a priest shews in avoiding any reference to your religious duties, a financier when he takes care not to recommend your investing in the companies which he himself controls, a strong man when he behaves with lamblike gentleness and does not hit you in the jaw. "I know you're related to Admiral Jurien de la Gravière," was murmured to me with an air of connivance by Mme. de Varambon, the lady in waiting to the Princesse de Parme, an excellent but limited woman, procured for the Princess in the past by the Duke's mother. She had not previously uttered a word to me, and I could never afterwards, despite the admonitions of the Princess and my own protestations, get out of her mind the idea that I was in some way connected with the Academician Admiral, who was a complete stranger to me. The obstinate persistence of the Princesse de Parme's lady in waiting in seeing in me a nephew of Admiral Jurien de la Gravière was in itself quite an ordinary form of silliness. But the mistake she made was only a crowning instance of all the other mistakes, less serious, more elaborate, unconscious or deliberate, which accompany one's name on the label which society writes out and attaches to one. I remember that a friend of the Guermantes who had expressed a keen desire to meet me gave me as the reason that I was a great friend of his cousin, Mme. de Chaussegros. "She is a charming person, she's so fond of you." I scrupulously, though quite vainly, insisted on the fact that there must be some mistake, as I did not know Mme. de Chaussegros. "Then it's her sister you know; it comes to the same thing. She met you in Scotland." I had never been in Scotland, and took the futile precaution, in my honesty, of letting my informant know this. It was Mme. de Chaussegros herself who had said that she knew me, and no doubt sincerely believed it, as a result of some initial confusion, for from that time onwards she never failed to hold out her hand to me whenever she saw me. And as, after all, the world in which I moved was precisely that in which Mme. de Chaussegros moved my modesty had neither rhyme nor reason. To say that I was intimate with the Chaussegros was, literally, a mistake, but from the social point of view was to state an equivalent of my position, if one can speak of the social position of so young a man as I then was. It therefore mattered not in the least that this friend of the Guermantes should tell me only things that were false about myself, he neither lowered nor exalted me (from the worldly point of view) in the idea which he continued to hold of me. And when all is said, for those of us who are not professional actors the tedium of living always in the same character is removed for a moment, as if we were to go on the boards, when another person forms a false idea of us, imagines that we are friends with a lady whom we do not know and are reported to have met in the course of a delightful tour of a foreign country which we have never made. Errors that multiply themselves and are harmless when they have not the inflexible rigidity of this one which had been committed, and continued for the rest of her life to be committed, in spite of my denials, by the imbecile lady in waiting to Mme. de Parme, rooted for all time in the belief that I was related to the tiresome Admiral Jurien de la Gravière. "She is not very strong in her head," the Duke confided to me, "and besides, she ought not to indulge in too many libations. I fancy, she's slightly under the influence of Bacchus." As a matter of fact Mme. de Varambon had drunk nothing but water, but the Duke liked to find scope for his favourite figures of speech. "But Zola is not a realist, Ma'am, he's a poet!" said Mme. de Guermantes, drawing inspiration from the critical essays which she had read in recent years and adapting them to her own personal genius. Agreeably buffeted hitherto, in the course of this bath of wit, a bath stirred for herself, which she was taking this evening and which, she considered, must be particularly good for her health, letting herself be swept away by the waves of paradox which curled and broke one after another, before this, the most enormous of them all, the Princesse de Parme jumped for fear of being knocked over. And it was in a choking voice, as though she were quite out of breath, that she now gasped: "Zola a poet!" "Why, yes," answered the Duchess with a laugh, entranced by this display of suffocation. "Your Highness must have remarked how he magnifies everything he touches. You will tell me that he touches just what—perish the thought! But he makes it into something colossal. His is the epic dungheap. He is the Homer of the sewers! He has not enough capitals to print Cambronne's word." Despite the extreme exhaustion which she was beginning to feel, the Princess was enchanted; never had she felt better. She would not have exchanged for an invitation to Schönbrunn, albeit that was the one thing that really flattered her, these divine dinner-parties at Mme. de Guermantes's, made invigorating by so liberal a dose of attic salt. "He writes it with a big C," cried Mme. d'Arpajon. "Surely with a big M, I think, my dear," replied Mme. de Guermantes, exchanging first with her husband a merry glance which implied: "Did you ever hear such an idiot?" "Wait a minute, now." Mme. de Guermantes turned to me, fixing on me a tender, smiling gaze, because, as an accomplished hostess, she was anxious to display her own knowledge of the artist who interested me specially, to give me, if I required it, an opportunity for exhibiting mine. "Wait," she urged me, gently waving her feather fan, so conscious was she at this moment that she was performing in full the duties of hospitality, and, that she might be found wanting in none of them, making a sign also to the servants to help me to more of the asparagus and *mousseline* sauce: "wait, now, I do believe that Zola has actually written an essay on Elstir, the painter whose things you were looking at just now—the only ones of his, really, that I care for," she concluded. As a matter of fact she hated Elstir's work, but found a unique quality in anything that was in her own house. I asked M. de Guermantes if he knew the name of the gentleman in the tall hat who figured in the picture of the crowd and whom I recognised as the same person whose portrait the Guermantes also had and had hung beside the other, both dating more or less from the same early period in which Elstir's personality was not yet completely established and he derived a certain inspiration from Manet. "Good Lord, yes," he replied, "I know it's a fellow who is quite well-known and no fool either, in his own line, but I have no head for names. I have it on the tip of my tongue, Monsieur . . . . Monsieur . . . . oh, well, it doesn't matter, I can't remember it. Swann would be able to tell you, it was he who made Mme. de Guermantes buy all that stuff; she is always too good-natured, afraid of hurting people's feelings if she refuses to do things; between ourselves, I believe he's landed us with a lot of rubbish. What I can tell you is that the gentleman you mean has been a sort of Maecenas to M. Elstir, he started him and has often helped him out of tight places by ordering pictures from him. As a compliment to this man—if you can call that sort of thing a compliment—he has painted him standing about among that crowd, where with his Sunday-go-to-meeting look he creates a distinctly odd effect. He may be a big gun in his own way but he is evidently not aware of the proper time and place for a top hat. With that thing on his head, among all those bare-headed girls, he looks like a little country lawyer on the razzle-dazzle. But tell me, you seem quite gone on his pictures. If I had only known, I should have got up the subject properly. Not that there's any need to rack one's brains over the meaning of M. Elstir's work, as one would for Ingres's *Source* or the *Princes in the Tower* by Paul Delaroche. What one appreciates in his work is that it's shrewdly observed, amusing, Parisian, and then one passes on to the next thing. One doesn't need to be an expert to look at that sort of thing. I know of course that they're merely sketches, still, I don't feel myself that he puts enough work into them. Swann was determined that we should buy a *Bundle of Asparagus*. In fact it was in the house for several days. There was nothing else in the picture, a bundle of asparagus exactly like what you're eating now. But I must say I declined to swallow M. Elstir's asparagus. He asked three hundred francs for them. Three hundred francs for a bundle of asparagus. A louis, that's as much as they're worth, even if they are out of season. I thought it a bit stiff. When he puts real people into his pictures as well, there's something rather caddish, something detrimental about him which does not appeal to me. I am surprised to see a delicate mind, a superior brain like yours admire that sort of thing." "I don't know why you should say that, Basin," interrupted the Duchess, who did not like to hear people run down anything that her rooms contained. "I am by no means prepared to admit that there's nothing distinguished in Elstir's pictures. You have to take it or leave it. But it's not always lacking in talent. And you must admit that the ones I bought are singularly beautiful." "Well, Oriane, in that style of thing I'd a thousand times rather have the little study by M. Vibert we saw at the water-colour exhibition.

There's nothing much in it, if you like, you could take it in the palm of
your hand, but you can see the man's clever through and through: that
unwashed scarecrow of a missionary standing before the sleek prelate
who is making his little dog do tricks, it's a perfect little poem of subtlety,
and in fact goes really deep." "I believe you know M. Elstir," the Duchess went on to me, "as a man, he's quite pleasant." "He is intelligent,"
said the Duke; "one is surprised, when one talks to him, that his painting should be so vulgar." "He is more than intelligent, he is really quite
clever," said the Duchess in the confidently critical tone of a person who
knew what she was talking about. "Didn't he once start a portrait of you,
Oriane?" asked the Princesse de Parme. "Yes, in shrimp pink," replied
Mme. de Guermantes, "but that's not going to hand his name down to
posterity. It's a ghastly thing; Basin wanted to have it destroyed." This
last statement was one which Mme. de Guermantes often made. But at
other times her appreciation of the picture was different: "I do not care
for his painting, but he did once do a good portrait of me." The former
of these judgments was addressed as a rule to people who spoke to the
Duchess of her portrait, the other to those who did not refer to it and whom
therefore she was anxious to inform of its existence. The former was inspired in her by coquetry, the latter by vanity. "Make a portrait of you
look ghastly! Why, then it can't be a portrait, it's a falsehood; I don't
know one end of a brush from the other, but I'm sure if I were to paint
you, merely putting you down as I see you, I should produce a masterpiece," said the Princesse de Parme ingenuously. "He sees me probably
as I see myself, without any allurements," said the Duchesse de Guermantes, with the look, melancholy, modest and coaxing, which seemed
to her best calculated to make her appear different from what Elstir had
portrayed. "That portrait ought to appeal to Mme. de Gallardon," said
the Duke. "Because she knows nothing about pictures?" asked the Princesse de Parme, who knew that Mme. de Guermantes had an infinite contempt for her cousin. "But she's a very good woman, isn't she?" The Duke
assumed an air of profound astonishment. "Why, Basin, don't you see
the Princess is making fun of you?" (The Princess had never dreamed of
doing such a thing.) "She knows as well as you do that Gallardonette is
an old *poison*," went on Mme. de Guermantes, whose vocabulary, limited
as a rule to all these old expressions, was as savoury as those dishes which
it is possible to come across in the delicious books of Pampille, but which
have in real life become so rare, dishes where the jellies, the butter, the
gravy, the quails are all genuine, permit of no alloy, where even the salt
is brought specially from the salt-marshes of Brittany; from her accent,
her choice of words, one felt that the basis of the Duchess's conversation
came directly from Guermantes. In this way the Duchess differed profoundly from her nephew Saint-Loup, the prey of so many new ideas and
expressions; it is difficult, when one's mind is troubled by the ideas of
Kant and the longings of Baudelaire, to write the exquisite French of
Henri IV, which meant that the very purity of the Duchess's language
was a sign of limitation, and that, in her, both her intelligence and her
sensibility had remained proof against all innovation. Here again, Mme.

de Guermantes's mind attracted me just because of what it excluded (which was exactly the content of my own thoughts) and by everything which, by virtue of that exclusion, it had been able to preserve, that seductive vigour of the supple bodies which no exhausting necessity to think, no moral anxiety or nervous trouble has deformed. Her mind, of a formation so anterior to my own, was for me the equivalent of what had been offered me by the procession of the girls of the little band along the seashore. Mme. de Guermantes offered me, domesticated and held in subjection by her natural courtesy, by the respect due to another person's intellectual worth, all the energy and charm of a cruel little girl of one of the noble families round Combray who from her childhood had been brought up in the saddle, tortured cats, gouged out the eyes of rabbits, and, albeit she had remained a pillar of virtue, might equally well have been, a good few years ago now, the most brilliant mistress of the Prince de Sagan. Only she was incapable of realising what I had sought for in her, the charm of her historic name, and the tiny quantity of it that I had found in her, a rustic survival from Guermantes. Were our relations founded upon a misunderstanding which could not fail to become manifest as soon as my homage, instead of being addressed to the relatively superior woman that she believed herself to be, should be diverted to some other woman of equal mediocrity and breathing the same unconscious charm? A misunderstanding so entirely natural, and one that will always exist between a young dreamer like myself and a woman of the world, one however that profoundly disturbs him, so long as he has not yet discovered the nature of his imaginative faculties and has not acquired his share of the inevitable disappointments which he is destined to find in people, as in the theatre, in his travels and indeed in love. M. de Guermantes having declared (following upon Elstir's asparagus and those that were brought round after the *financière* chicken) that green asparagus grown in the open air, which, as has been so quaintly said by the charming writer who signs himself E. de Clermont-Tonnerre, "have not the impressive rigidity of their sisters," ought to be eaten with eggs: "One man's meat is another man's poison, as they say," replied M. de Bréauté. "In the province of Canton, in China, the greatest delicacy that can be set before one is a dish of ortolan's eggs completely rotten." M. de Bréauté, the author of an essay on the Mormons which had appeared in the *Revue des Deux Mondes,* moved in none but the most aristocratic circles, but among these visited only such as had a certain reputation for intellect, with the result that from his presence, were it at all regular, in a woman's house one could tell that she had a 'salon.' He pretended to a loathing of society, and assured each of his duchesses in turn that it was for the sake of her wit and beauty that he came to see her. They all believed him. Whenever, with death in his heart, he resigned himself to attending a big party at the Princesse de Parme's, he summoned them all to accompany him, to keep up his courage, and thus appeared only to be moving in the midst of an intimate group. So that his reputation as an intellectual might survive his worldly success, applying certain maxims of the Guermantes spirit, he would set out with ladies of fashion on long scientific expeditions at the height of the dancing season, and when a woman who was a snob, and consequently still without any definite position, began to go everywhere, he would put a savage obstinacy into his refusal to know her, to allow himself to be introduced to her. His hatred of snobs was a derivative of his snobbishness, but made the simpletons (in other words, everyone) believe that he was immune from snobbishness. "Babal always knows everything," exclaimed the Duchesse de Guermantes. "I think it must be charming, a country where you can be quite sure that your dairyman will supply you with really rotten eggs, eggs of the year of the comet. I can see myself dipping my bread and butter in them. I must say, you get the same thing at aunt Madeleine's" (Mme. de Villeparisis's) "where everything's served in a state of putrefaction, eggs included." Then, as Mme. d'Arpajon protested, "But my dear Phili, you know it as well as I do. You can see the chicken in the egg. What I can't understand is how they manage not to fall out. It's not an omelette you get there, it's a poultry-yard. You were so wise not to come to dinner there yesterday, there was a brill cooked in carbolic! I assure you, it wasn't a dinner-table, it was far more like an operating-table. Really, Norpois carries loyalty to the pitch of heroism. He actually asked for more!" "I believe I saw you at dinner there the time she made that attack on M. Bloch" (M. de Guermantes, perhaps to give to an Israelite name a more foreign sound, pronounced the 'ch' in Bloch not like a 'k' but as in the German 'hoch') "when he said about some poit" (poet) "or other that he was sublime. Châtellerault did his best to break M. Bloch's shins, the fellow didn't understand in the least and thought my nephew's kick was aimed at a young woman sitting opposite him." (At this point, M. de Guermantes coloured slightly.) "He did not realise that he was annoying our aunt by his 'sublimes' chucked about all over the place like that. In short, aunt Madeleine, who doesn't keep her tongue in her pocket, turned on him with: 'Indeed, Sir, and what epithet do you keep for M. de Bousset?'" (M. de Guermantes thought that, when one mentioned a famous name, the use of 'Monsieur' and a particle was eminently 'old school.') "That put him in his place, all right." "And what answer did this M. Bloch make?" came in a careless tone from Mme. de Guermantes, who, running short for the moment of original ideas, felt that she must copy her husband's teutonic pronunciation. "Ah! I can assure you, M. Bloch did not wait for any more, he's still running." "Yes, I remember quite well seeing you there that evening," said Mme. de Guermantes with emphasis as though, coming from her, there must be something in this reminiscence highly flattering to myself. "It is always so interesting at my aunt's. At the last party she gave, which was, of course, when I met you, I meant to ask you whether that old gentleman who went past where we were sitting wasn't François Coppée. You must know who everyone is," she went on, sincerely envious of my relations with poets and poetry, and also out of 'consideration' for myself, the wish to establish in a better position in the eyes of her other guests a young man so well versed in literature. I assured the Duchess that I had not observed any celebrities at Mme. de Villeparisis's party. "What!" she replied with a bewilderment which revealed that her respect for men of letters and her contempt for society were more superficial than she said, perhaps even than she thought, "What! There were no famous authors there! You aston-ish me! Why, I saw all sorts of quite impossible people!" I remembered the evening in question distinctly owing to an entirely trivial incident that had occurred at the party. Mme. de Villeparisis had introduced Bloch to Mme. Alphonse de Rothschild, but my friend had not caught the name and, thinking he was talking to an old English lady who was a trifle mad, had replied only in monosyllables to the garrulous conversation of the historic beauty, when Mme. de Villeparisis in making her known to some one else uttered, quite distinctly this time: "The Baronne Alphonse de Rothschild." Thereupon there had coursed suddenly and simultaneously through Bloch's arteries so many ideas of millions and of social impor-tance, which it would have been more prudent to subdivide and separate, that he had undergone, so to speak, a momentary failure of heart and brain alike, and cried aloud in the dear old lady's presence: "If I'd only known!" an exclamation the silliness of which kept him from sleeping for at least a week afterwards. His remark was of no great interest, but I re-membered it as a proof that sometimes in this life, under the stress of an exceptional emotion, people do say what is in their minds. "I fancy Mme. de Villeparisis is not absolutely . . . moral," said the Princesse de Parme, who knew that the best people did not visit the Duchess's aunt, and, from what the Duchess herself had just been saying, that one might speak freely about her. But, Mme. de Guermantes not seeming to approve of this criti-cism, she hastened to add: "Though, of course, intellect carried to that degree excuses everything." "But you take the same view of my aunt that everyone else does," replied the Duchess, "which is, really, quite mistaken. It's just what Mémé was saying to me only yesterday." She blushed; a reminiscence unknown to me filmed her eyes. I formed the supposition that M. de Charlus had asked her to cancel my invitation, as he had sent Robert to ask me not to go to her house. I had the impression that the blush—equally incomprehensible to me—which had tinged the Duke's cheek when he made some reference to his brother could not be attributed to the same cause. "My poor aunt—she will always have the reputation of being a lady of the old school, of sparkling wit and uncontrolled passions. And really there's no more middle-class, serious, commonplace mind in Paris. She will go down as a patron of the arts, which means to say that she was once the mistress of a great painter, though he was never able to make her understand what a picture was; and as for her private life, so far from being a depraved woman, she was so much made for marriage, so conjugal from her cradle that, not having succeeded in keeping a hus-band, who incidentally was a cad, she has never had a love-affair which she hasn't taken just as seriously as if it were holy matrimony, with the same susceptibilities, the same quarrels, the same fidelity. By which token, those relations are often the most sincere; you'll find, in fact, more inconsolable lovers than husbands." "Yet, Oriane, if you take the case of your brother-in-law Palamède you were speaking about just now; no mistress in the world could ever dream of being mourned as that poor Mme. de Charlus has been." "Ah!" replied the Duchess, "Your Highness must permit me to be not altogether of her opinion. People don't all like to be mourned in the same way, each of us has his preferences." "Still, he did make a regular cult of her after her death. It is true that people sometimes do for the dead what they would not have done for the living." "For one thing," retorted Mme. de Guermantes in a dreamy tone which belied her teasing purpose, "we go to their funerals, which we never do for the living!" M. de Guermantes gave a sly glance at M. de Bréauté as though to provoke him into laughter at the Duchess's wit. "At the same time I frankly admit," went on Mme. de Guermantes, "that the manner in which I should like to be mourned by a man I loved would not be that adopted by my brother-in-law." The Duke's face darkened. He did not like to hear his wife utter rash judgments, especially about M. de Charlus. "You are very particular. His grief set an example to everyone," he reproved her stiffly. But the Duchess had in dealing with her husband that sort of boldness which animal tamers shew, or people who live with a madman and are not afraid of making him angry. "Oh, very well, just as you like—he does set an example, I never said he didn't, he goes every day to the cemetery to tell her how many people he has had to luncheon, he misses her enormously, but—as he'd mourn for a cousin, a grandmother, a sister. It is not the grief of a husband. It is true that they were a pair of saints, which makes it all rather exceptional." M. de Guermantes, infuriated by his wife's chatter, fixed on her with a terrible immobility a pair of eyes already loaded. "I don't wish to say anything against poor Mémé, who, by the way, could not come this evening," went on the Duchess, "I quite admit there's no one like him, he's delightful; he has a delicacy, a warmth of heart that you don't as a rule find in men. He has a woman's heart, Mémé has!" "What you say is absurd," M. de Guermantes broke in sharply. "There's nothing effeminate about Mémé, I know nobody so manly as he is." "But I am not suggesting that he's the least bit in the world effeminate. Do at least take the trouble to understand what I say," retorted the Duchess. "He's always like that the moment anyone mentions his brother," she added, turning to the Princesse de Parme. "It's very charming, it's a pleasure to hear him. There's nothing so nice as two brothers who are fond of each other," replied the Princess, as many a humbler person might have replied, for it is possible to belong to a princely race by birth and at the same time to be mentally affiliated to a race that is thoroughly plebeian.

"As we're discussing your family, Oriane," said the Princess, "I saw your nephew Saint-Loup yesterday; I believe he wants to ask you to do something for him." The Duc de Guermantes bent his Olympian brow. When he did not himself care to do a service, he preferred his wife not to assume the responsibility for it, knowing that it would come to the same thing in the end and that the people to whom the Duchess would be obliged to apply would put this concession down to the common account of the household, just as much as if it had been asked of them by the husband alone. "Why didn't he tell me about it himself?" said the Duchess. "He was here yesterday and stayed a couple of hours, and heaven only knows what a bore he managed to make himself. He would be no stupider than anyone else if he had only the sense, like many people we know, to be content with being a fool. It's his veneer of knowledge that's so terrible. He wants to preserve an open mind—open to all the things he doesn't understand. He talks to you about Morocco. It's appalling."

"He can't go back there, because of Rachel," said the Prince de Foix. "Surely, now that they've broken it off," interrupted M. de Bréauté. "So far from breaking it off, I found her a couple of days ago in Robert's rooms, they didn't look at all like people who'd quarrelled, I can assure you," replied the Prince de Foix, who loved to spread abroad every rumour that could damage Robert's chances of marrying, and might for that matter have been misled by one of the intermittent resumptions of a connexion that was practically at an end.

"That Rachel was speaking to me about you, I see her like that in the mornings, on the way to the Champs-Elysées; she's a kind of head-in-air, as you say, what you call 'unlaced,' a sort of 'Dame aux Camélias,' only figuratively speaking, of course." This speech was addressed to me by Prince Von, who liked always to appear conversant with French literature and Parisian catchwords.

"Why, that's just what it was—Morocco!" exclaimed the Princess, flinging herself into this opening. "What on earth can he want in Morocco?" asked M. de Guermantes sternly; "Oriane can do absolutely nothing for him there, as he knows perfectly well." "He thinks he invented strategy," Mme. de Guermantes pursued the theme, "and then he uses impossible words for the most trivial things, which doesn't prevent him from making blots all over his letters. The other day he announced that he'd been given some *sublime* potatoes, and that he'd taken a *sublime* stage box." "He speaks Latin," the Duke went one better. "What! Latin?" the Princesse gasped. " 'Pon my soul he does! Ma'am can ask Oriane if I'm not telling the truth." "Why, of course, Ma'am; the other day he said to us straight out, without stopping to think: 'I know of no more touching example of *sic transit gloria mundi*.' I can repeat the phrase now to your Highness because, after endless inquiries and by appealing to *linguists*, we succeeded in reconstructing it, but Robert flung it out without pausing for breath, one could hardly make out that there was Latin in it, he was just like a character in the *Malade Imaginaire*. And all this referred simply to the death of the Empress of Austria!" "Poor woman!" cried the Princess, "what a delicious creature she was." "Yes," replied the Duchess, "a trifle mad, a trifle headstrong, but she was a thoroughly good woman, a nice, kind-hearted lunatic; the only thing I could never make out about her was why she had never managed to get her teeth made to fit her; they always came loose half-way through a sentence and she was obliged to stop short or she'd have swallowed them." "That Rachel was speaking to me about you, she told me that young Saint-Loup worshipped you, that he was fonder of you than he was of her," said Prince Von to me, devouring his food like an ogre as he spoke, his face scarlet, his teeth bared by his perpetual grin. "But in that case she must be jealous of me and hate me," said I. "Not at all, she told me all sorts of nice things about you. The Prince de Foix's mistress would perhaps be jealous if he preferred you to her. You don't understand? Come home with me, and I'll explain it all to you." "I'm afraid I can't, I'm going on to M. de Charlus at eleven."

"Why, he sent round to me yesterday to ask me to dine with him this evening, but told me not to come after a quarter to eleven. But if you must go to him, at least come with me as far as the Théâtre Français, you will be in the periphery," said the Prince, who thought doubtless that this last word meant 'proximity' or possibly 'centre.'

But the bulging eyes in his coarse though handsome red face frightened me and I declined, saying that a friend was coming to call for me. This reply seemed to me in no way offensive. The Prince, however, apparently formed a different impression of it for he did not say another word to me.

"I really must go and see the Queen of Naples; what a grief it must be to her," said (or at least appeared to me to have said) the Princesse de Parme. For her words had come to me only indistinctly through the intervening screen of those addressed to me, albeit in an undertone, by Prince Von, who had doubtless been afraid, if he spoke louder, of being overheard by the Prince de Foix. "Oh, dear, no!" replied the Duchess, "I don't believe it has been any grief at all." "None at all! You do always fly to extremes so, Oriane," said M. de Guermantes, resuming his part of the cliff which by standing up to the wave forces it to fling higher its crest of foam. "Basin knows even better than I that I'm telling the truth," replied the Duchess, "but he thinks he's obliged to look severe because you are present, Ma'am, and he's afraid of my shocking you." "Oh, please, no, I beg of you," cried the Princesse de Parme, dreading the slightest alteration on her account of these delicious Fridays at the Duchesse de Guermantes's, this forbidden fruit which the Queen of Sweden herself had not yet acquired the right to taste. "Why, it was Basin himself that she told, when he said to her with a duly sorrowful expression: 'But the Queen is in mourning; for whom, pray, is it a great grief to your Majesty?'—'No, it's not a deep mourning, it's a light mourning, quite a light mourning, it's my sister.' The truth is, she's delighted about it, as Basin knows perfectly well, she invited us to a party that very evening, and gave me two pearls. I wish she could lose a sister every day! So far from weeping for her sister's death, she was in fits of laughter over it. She probably says to herself, like Robert, 'sic transit——' I forget how it goes on," she added modestly, knowing how it went on perfectly well.

In saying all this Mme. de Guermantes was only being witty, and with complete insincerity, for the Queen of Naples, like the Duchesse d'Alençon, also doomed to a tragic fate, had the warmest heart in the world and mourned quite sincerely for her kinsfolk. Mme. de Guermantes knew those noble Bavarian sisters, her cousins, too well not to be aware of this. "He would like not to go back to Morocco," said the Princesse de Parme, alighting hurriedly again upon the perch of Robert's name which had been held out to her, quite unintentionally, by Mme. de Guermantes. "I believe you know General de Monserfeuil." "Very slightly," replied the Duchess, who was an intimate friend of the officer in question. The Princess explained what it was that Saint-Loup wanted. "Good gracious, yes, if I see him—it is possible that I may meet him," the Duchess replied, so as not to appear to be refusing, the occasions of her meeting General de Monserfeuil seeming to extend rapidly farther apart as soon as it became a question of her asking him for anything. This uncertainty did not, however, satisfy the Duke, who interrupted his wife: "You know perfectly well you won't be seeing him, Oriane, and besides you have already asked him for two things which he hasn't done. My wife has a passion for doing good turns to people," he went on, growing more and more furious, in order to force the Princess to withdraw her request, without there being any question made of his wife's good nature and so that Mme. de Parme should throw the blame back upon his own character, which was essentially obstructive. "Robert could get anything he wanted out of Monserfeuil. Only, as he happens not to know himself what he wants, he gets us to ask for it because he knows there's no better way of making the whole thing fall through. Oriane has asked too many favours of Monserfeuil. A request from her now would be a reason for him to refuse." "Oh, in that case, it would be better if the Duchess did nothing," said Mme. de Parme. "Obviously!" the Duke closed the discussion. "Poor General, he's been defeated again at the elections," said the Princess, so as to turn the conversation from Robert. "Oh, it's nothing serious, it's only the seventh time," said the Duke, who, having been obliged himself to retire from politics, quite enjoyed hearing of other people's failures at the polls. "He has consoled himself by giving his wife another baby." "What! Is that poor Mme. de Monserfeuil in an interesting condition again?" cried the Princess. "Why, of course," replied the Duke, "that's the one division where the poor General has never failed to get in."

In the period that followed I was continually to be invited, were it with a small party only, to these repasts at which I had at one time imagined the guests as seated like the Apostles in the Sainte-Chapelle. They did assemble there indeed, like the early Christians, not to partake merely of a material nourishment, which incidentally was exquisite, but in a sort of social Eucharist; so that in the course of a few dinner-parties I assimilated the acquaintance of all the friends of my hosts, friends to whom they presented me with a shade of benevolent patronage so marked (as a person for whom they had always had a sort of parental affection) that there was not one among them who would not have felt himself to be failing in his duty to the Duke and Duchess if he had given a ball without including my name on his list, and at the same time, while I sipped one of those Yquems which lay concealed in the Guermantes cellars, I tasted ortolans dressed according to each of the different recipes which the Duke himself used to elaborate and modified with prudence. However, for one who had already set his knees more than once beneath the mystic board, the consumption of the latter was not indispensable. Old friends of M. and Mme. de Guermantes came in to see them·after dinner, 'with the tooth-picks,' as Mme. Swann would have said, without being expected, and took in winter a cup of *tilleul* in the lighted warmth of the great drawing-room, in summer a glass of orangeade in the darkness of the little rectangular strip of garden outside. There was no record of anything else, among the Guermantes, in these evenings in the garden, but orangeade. It had a sort of ritual meaning. To have added other refreshments would have seemed to be falsifying the tradition, just as a big at-home in the Faubourg Saint-Germain ceases

to be an at-home if there is a play also, or music. You must be supposed
to have come simply—though there be five hundred of you—to pay a call
on, let us say, the Princesse de Guermantes. People marvelled at my influence because I was able to procure the addition to this orangeade of a
jug containing the juice of stewed cherries or stewed pears. I took a dislike
on this account to the Prince d'Agrigente, who was like all the people who,
lacking in imagination but not in covetousness, take a keen interest in
what one is drinking and ask if they may taste a little of it themselves.
Which meant that, every time, M. d'Agrigente, by diminishing my ration,
spoiled my pleasure. For this fruit juice can never be provided in sufficient
quantities to quench one's thirst for it. Nothing is less cloying than these
transpositions into flavour of the colour of a fruit which when cooked
seems to have travelled backwards to the past season of its blossoming.
Blushing like an orchard in spring, or, it may be, colourless and cool like
the zephyr beneath the fruit-trees, the juice lets itself be breathed and
gazed into one drop by drop, and M. d'Agrigente prevented me, regularly,
from taking my fill of it. Despite these distillations the traditional orangeade persisted like the *tilleul*. In these humble kinds, the social communion
was none the less administered. In this respect, doubtless, the friends of M.
and Mme. de Guermantes had, after all, as I had originally imagined,
remained more different from the rest of humanity than their outward
appearance might have misled me into supposing. Numbers of elderly men
came to receive from the Duchess, together with the invariable drink, a
welcome that was often far from cordial. Now this could not have been
due to snobbishness, they themselves being of a rank to which there was
none superior; nor to love of splendour; they did love it perhaps, but on
less stringent social conditions might have been enjoying a glittering example of it, for on these same evenings the charming wife of a colossally
rich financier would have given anything in the world to have them among
the brilliant shooting-party she was giving for a couple of days for the
King of Spain. They had nevertheless declined her invitation, and had
come round without fail to inquire whether Mme. de Guermantes was at
home. They were not even certain of finding there opinions that conformed entirely with their own, or sentiments of any great warmth; Mme.
de Guermantes let fall now and then, on the Dreyfus case, on the Republic, the Laws against Religion, or even in an undertone on themselves, their
weaknesses, the dullness of their conversation, comments which they had
to appear not to notice. No doubt, if they kept up their habit of coming
there, it was owing to their superfine training as epicures in things worldly,
to their clear consciousness of the prime and perfect quality of the social
dish, with its familiar, reassuring, sappy savour, free from blend or taint,
with the origin and history of which they were as well aware as she who
served them with it, remaining more 'noble' in this respect than they themselves imagined. Now, on this occasion, among the visitors to whom I was
introduced after dinner, it so happened that there was that General de
Monserfeuil of whom the Princesse de Parme had been speaking, while
Mme. de Guermantes, of whose drawing-room he was one of the regular
frequenters, had not known that he was going to be there that evening.

He bowed before me, on hearing my name, as though I had been the President of the Supreme War Council. I had supposed it to be simply from some deep-rooted unwillingness to oblige, in which the Duke, as in wit if not in love, was his wife's accomplice, that the Duchess had practically refused to recommend her nephew to M. de Monserfeuil. And I saw in this an indifference all the more blameworthy in that I seemed to have gathered from a few words let fall by the Princess that Robert was in a post of danger from which it would be prudent to have him removed. But it was by the genuine malice of Mme. de Guermantes that I was revolted when, the Princesse de Parme having timidly suggested that she might say something herself and on her own responsibility to the General, the Duchess did everything in her power to dissuade her. "But Ma'am," she cried, "Monserfeuil has no sort of standing or influence whatever with the new Government. You would be wasting your breath." "I think he can hear us," murmured the Princess, as a hint to the Duchess not to speak so loud. Without lowering her voice: "Your Highness need not be afraid, he's as deaf as a post," said the Duchess, every word reaching the General distinctly. "The thing is, I believe M. de Saint-Loup is in a place that is not very safe," said the Princess. "What is one to do?" replied the Duchess. "He's in the same boat as everybody else, the only difference being that it was he who originally asked to be sent there. Besides, no, it's not really dangerous; if it was, you can imagine how anxious I should be to help. I should have spoken to Saint-Joseph about it during dinner. He has far more influence, and he's a real worker. But, as you see, he's gone now. Still, asking him would be less awkward than going to this one, who has three of his sons in Morocco just now and has refused to apply for them to be exchanged; he might raise that as an objection. Since your Highness insists on it, I shall speak to Saint-Joseph—if I see him again, or to Beautreillis. But if I don't see either of them, you mustn't waste your pity on Robert. It was explained to us the other day exactly where he is. I'm sure he couldn't wish for a better place."

"What a pretty flower, I've never seen one like it; there's no one like you, Oriane, for having such marvellous things in your house," said the Princesse de Parme, who, fearing that General de Monserfeuil might have overheard the Duchess, sought now to change the conversation. I looked and recognised a plant of the sort that I had watched Elstir painting. "I am so glad you like them; they are charming, do look at their little purple velvet collars; the only thing against them is—as may happen with people who are very pretty and very nicely dressed—they have a hideous name and a horrid smell. In spite of which I am very fond of them. But what is rather sad is that they are dying." "But they're growing in a pot, they aren't cut flowers," said the Princess. "No," answered the Duchess with a smile, "but it comes to the same thing, as they're all ladies. It's a kind of plant where the ladies and the gentlemen don't both grow on the same stalk. I'm like people who keep a lady dog. I have to find a husband for my flowers. Otherwise I shan't have any young ones!" "How very strange. Do you mean to say that in nature . . . ?" "Yes! There are certain insects whose duty it is to bring about the marriage, as they do with Sovereigns, by proxy, without the bride and bridegroom ever having set eyes on one another. And so, I assure you, I always tell my man to put my plant out in the window as often as possible, on the courtyard side and the garden side turn about, in the hope that the necessary insect will arrive. But the odds are too great. Fancy, he has first to have been seen by a person of the same species and the opposite sex, and he must then have taken it into his head to come and leave cards at the house. He hasn't appeared so far, I believe my plant can still qualify for the white flower of a blameless life, but I must say a little immodesty would please me better. It's just the same with that fine tree we have in the courtyard; he will die childless because he belongs to a kind that's very rare in these latitudes. In his case, it's the wind that's responsible for consummating the marriage, but the wall is a trifle high." "By Jove, yes," said M. de Bréauté, "you ought to take just a couple of inches off the top, that will be quite enough. There are certain operations one ought to know how to perform. The flavour of vanilla we tasted in the excellent ice you gave us this evening, Duchess, comes from a plant called the vanilla tree. This plant produces flowers which are both male and female, but a sort of solid wall set up between them prevents any communication. And so we could never get any fruit from them until a young Negro, a native of Réunion, by the name of Albins, which by the way is rather an odd name for a black man since it means 'white,' had the happy thought of using the point of a needle to bring the separate organs into contact." "Babal, you're divine, you know everything," cried the Duchess. "But you yourself, Oriane, have told me things I had no idea of," the Princesse de Parme assured her. "I must explain to your Highness that it is Swann who has always talked to me all about botany. Sometimes when we were too bored to go to a tea-party or a concert we would set off for the country, and he would shew me extraordinary marriages between flowers, which was far more amusing than going to human marriages—no wedding-breakfast and no crowd in the sacristy. We never had time to go very far. Now that motor-cars have come in, it would be delightful. Unfortunately, in the interval he himself has made an even more astonishing marriage, which makes everything very difficult. Oh, Ma'am, life is a dreadful business, we spend our whole time doing things that bore us, and when by mere chance we come across somebody with whom we could go and look at something really interesting, he has to make a marriage like Swann's. Faced with the alternatives of giving up my botanical expeditions and being obliged to call upon a degrading person, I chose the former calamity. Besides, when it comes to that, there was no need to go quite so far. It seems that here, in my own little bit of garden, more odd things happen in broad daylight than at midnight—in the Bois de Boulogne! Only they attract no attention, because among flowers it's all done quite simply, you see a little orange shower, or else a very dusty fly coming to wipe its feet or take a bath before crawling into a flower. And that does the trick!" "The cabinet the plant is standing on is splendid, too; it's Empire, I think," said the Princess, who, not being familiar with the works of Darwin and his followers, was unable to grasp the point of the Duchess's pleasantries. "It's lovely, isn't it? I'm so glad

Ma'am likes it," replied the Duchess, "it's a magnificent piece. I must tell you that I've always adored the Empire style, even when it wasn't in fashion. I remember at Guermantes I got into terrible disgrace with my mother-in-law because I told them to bring down from the attics all the splendid Empire furniture Basin had inherited from the Montesquious, and used it to furnish the wing we lived in." M. de Guermantes smiled. He must nevertheless have remembered that the course of events had been totally different. But, the witticisms of the Princesse des Laumes at the expense of her mother-in-law's bad taste having been a tradition during the short time in which the Prince was in love with his wife, his love for the latter had been outlasted by a certain contempt for the intellectual inferiority of the former, a contempt which, however, went hand in hand with a considerable attachment and respect. "The Iénas have the same armchair with Wedgwood medallions, it's a lovely thing, but I prefer my own;" said the Duchess, with the same air of impartiality as if she had been the possessor of neither of the articles under discussion. "I know, of course, that they've some marvellous things which I haven't got." The Princesse de Parme remained silent. "But it's quite true; your Highness hasn't seen their collection. Oh, you ought really to come there one day with me, it's one of the most magnificent things in Paris. You'd say it was a museum come to life." And since this suggestion was one of the most 'Guermantes' of the Duchess's audacities, inasmuch as the Iénas were for the Princesse de Parme rank usurpers, their son bearing like her own the title of Duc de Guastalla, Mme. de Guermantes in thus launching it could not refrain (so far did the love that she bore for her own originality prevail over the deference due to the Princesse de Parme) from casting at her other guests a smiling glance of amusement. They too made an effort to smile, at once frightened, bewildered, and above all delighted to think that they were being ear-witnesses of Oriane's very 'latest' and could carry it away with them 'red hot.' They were only half shocked, knowing that the Duchess had the knack of strewing the ground with all the Courvoisier prejudices to achieve a vital success more thrilling and more enjoyable. Had she not, within the last few years, brought together Princesse Mathilde and that Duc d'Aumale who had written to the Princess's own brother the famous letter: "In my family all the men are brave and the women chaste"? And inasmuch as Princes remain princely even at those moments when they appear anxious to forget that they are, the Duc d'Aumale and Princesse Mathilde had enjoyed themselves so greatly at Mme. de Guermantes's that they had thereafter formed a defensive alliance, with that faculty for forgetting the past which Louis XVIII shewed when he took as his Minister Fouché, who had voted the death of his brother. Mme. de Guermantes was now nourishing a similar project of arranging a meeting between Princesse Murat and the Queen of Naples. In the meantime, the Princesse de Parme appeared as embarrassed as might have been the heirs-apparent to the Thrones of the Netherlands and Belgium, styled respectively Prince of Orange and Duke of Brabant, had one offered to present to them M. de Mailly Nesle, Prince d'Orange, and M. de Charlus, Duc de Brabant. But, before anything further could happen, the Duchess, whom Swann and M. de Charlus between them (albeit the latter was resolute in ignoring the Iénas' existence) had with great difficulty succeeded in making admire the Empire style, exclaimed: "Honestly, Ma'am, I can't tell you how beautiful you will think it! I must confess that the Empire style has always had a fascination for me. But at the Iénas' it is really like a hallucination. That sort of—what shall I say—reflux from the Expedition to Egypt, and also the sweep forward into our own times from Antiquity, all those things that invade our houses, the Sphinxes that come to crouch at the feet of the sofas, the serpents coiled round candelabra, a huge Muse who holds out a little torch for you to play at *bouillotte*, or has quietly climbed on to the mantelpiece and is leaning against your clock; and then all the Pompeian lamps, the little boat-shaped beds which look as if they had been found floating on the Nile so that you expect to see Moses climb out of them, the classical chariots galloping along the bed tables. . . ." "They're not very comfortable to sit in, those Empire chairs," the Princess ventured. "No," the Duchess agreed, "but," she at once added, insisting on the point with a smile: "I like being uncomfortable on those mahogany seats covered with ruby velvet or green silk. I like that discomfort of the warrior who understands nothing but the curule chair and in the middle of his principal drawing-room crosses his fasces and piles his laurels. I can assure you that at the Iénas' one doesn't stop to think for a moment of how comfortable one is, when one sees in front of one a great strapping wench of a Victory painted in fresco on the wall. My husband is going to say that I'm a very bad Royalist, but I'm terribly disaffected, as you know, I can assure you that in those people's house one comes to love all the big N's and all the bees. Good gracious, after all for a good many years under our Kings we weren't exactly surfeited with glory, and so these warriors who brought home so many crowns that they stuck them even on the arms of the chairs, I must say I think it's all rather fetching! Your Highness ought really." "Why, my dear, if you think so," said the Princess, "but it seems to me that it won't be easy." "But Ma'am will find that it will all go quite smoothly. They are very good people, and no fools. We took Mme. de Chevreuse there," added the Duchess, knowing the force of this example, "she was enchanted. The son is really very pleasant. I'm going to say something that's not quite proper," she went on, "but he has a bedroom, and more especially a bed in it, in which I should love to sleep—without him! What is even less proper is that I went to see him once when he was ill and lying in it. By his side on the frame of the bed was moulded a long Siren, stretched out at full length, a lovely thing with a mother-of-pearl tail and some sort of lotus flowers in her hand. I assure you," went on Mme. de Guermantes, reducing the speed of her utterances to bring into even bolder relief the words which she had the air of modelling with the pout of her fine lips, drawing them out with her long expressive hands, directing on the Princess as she spoke a gentle, steady and searching gaze, "that with the palms and the golden crown at the side, it was most moving, it was just the arrangement of Gustave Moreau's *Death and the Young Man* (your Highness must know that great work, of course)." The Princesse de Parme, who did not know so much as the painter's name, made violent movements with her head and smiled ardently, in order to manifest her admiration for his picture. But the intensity of her mimicry could not fill the place of that light which is absent from our eyes so long as we do not understand what people are trying to tell us. "A good-looking boy, I believe?" she asked. "No, for he's just like a tapir. The eyes are a little those of a Queen Hortense on a screen. But he has probably come to the conclusion that it is rather absurd for a man to develop such a resemblance, and it is lost in the encaustic surface of his cheeks which give him really rather a Mameluke appearance. You feel that the polisher must call round every morning. Swann," she went on, reverting to the bed of the young Duke, "was struck by the re-semblance between this Siren and Gustave Moreau's *Death*. But apart from that," she added, her speech becoming more rapid though still serious, so as to provoke more laughter, "there was nothing really that could *strike* us, for it was only a cold in the head, and the young man made a marvellous recovery." "They say he's a snob?" put in M. de Bréauté, with a malicious twinkle, expecting to be answered with the same precision as though he had said: "They tell me that he has only four fingers on his right hand; is that so?" "G—ood g—racious, n—o," replied Mme. de Guermantes with a smile of benign indulgence. "Perhaps just the least little bit of a snob in appearance, because he's extremely young, but I should be surprised to hear that he was really, for he's intelligent," she added, as though there were to her mind some absolute incompatibility between snobbishness and intelligence. "He has wit, too, I've known him to be quite amusing," she said again, laughing with the air of an epicure and expert, as though the act of declaring that a person could be amusing demanded a certain ex-pression of merriment from the speaker, or as though the Duc de Guas-talla's sallies were recurring to her mind as she spoke. "Anyway, as he never goes anywhere, he can't have much field for his snobbishness," she wound up, forgetting that this was hardly encouraging the Princesse de Parme to make overtures. "I cannot help wondering what the Prince de Guermantes, who calls her Mme. Iéna, will say if he hears that I've been to see her." "What!" cried the Duchess with extraordinary vivacity. "Don't you know that it was we who gave up to Gilbert" (she bitterly regretted that surrender now) "a complete card-room done in the Empire style which came to us from Quiou-Quiou, and is an absolute marvel! There was no room for it here, though I think it would look better here than it does with him. It's a thing of sheer beauty, half Etruscan, half Egyptian. . . ." "Egyptian?" queried the Princess, to whom the word Etruscan conveyed little. "Well, really, you know, a little of both. Swann told us that, he explained it all to me, only you know I'm such a dunce. But then, Ma'am, what one has to bear in mind is that the Egypt of the Empire cabinet-makers has nothing to do with the historical Egypt, nor their Roman with the Romans nor their Etruria. . . ." "Indeed," said the Princess. "No, it's like what they used to call a Louis XV costume under the Second Em-pire, when Anna de Monchy and dear Brigode's mother were girls. Basin was talking to you just now about Beethoven. We heard a thing of his played the other day which was really quite good, though a little stiff, with a Russian theme in it. It's pathetic to think that he believed it to be Russian. In the same way as the Chinese painters believed they were copying Bellini. Besides, even in the same country, whenever anybody begins to look at things in a way that is slightly novel, nine hundred and ninety-nine people out of a thousand are totally incapable of seeing what he puts before them. It takes at least forty years before they can manage to make it out." "Forty years!" the Princess cried in alarm. "Why, yes," went on the Duchess, adding more and more to her words (which were practically my own, for I had just been expressing a similar idea to her), thanks to her way of pronouncing them, the equivalent of what on the printed page is called italics: "it's like a sort of first isolated individual of a species which does not yet exist but is going to multiply in the future, an individual endowed with a kind of *sense* which the human race of his generation does not possess. I can hardly give myself as an instance because I, on the contrary, have always loved any interesting production from the very start, however novel it might be. But really, the other day I was with the Grand Duchess in the Louvre and we happened to pass before Manet's *Olympia*. Nowadays nobody is in the least surprised by it. It looks just like an Ingres! And yet, heaven only knows how many spears I've had to break for that picture, which I don't altogether like but which is unquestionably the work of *somebody*." "And is the Grand Duchess well?" inquired the Princesse de Parme, to whom the Tsar's aunt was infinitely more familiar than Manet's model. "Yes; we talked about you. After all," she resumed, clinging to her idea, "the fact of the matter is, as my brother-in-law Palamède always says, that one has between oneself and the rest of the world the barrier of a strange language. Though I admit that there's no one it's quite so true of as Gilbert. If it amuses you to go to the Iénas', you have far too much sense to let your actions be governed by what that poor fellow may think, who is a dear, innocent creature, but really lives in a different world. I feel myself nearer, more akin to my coachman, my horses even, than to a man who keeps on harking back to what people would have thought under Philip the Bold or Louis the Fat. Just fancy, when he goes for a walk in the country, he takes a stick to drive the peasants out of his way, quite in a friendly spirit, saying: 'Get on, clowns!' Really, I'm just as much surprised when he speaks to me as if I heard myself addressed by one of the 'recumbents' on the old gothic tombs. It's all very well that animated gravestone's being my cousin; he frightens me, and the only idea that comes into my head is to let him stay in his Middle Ages. Apart from that, I quite admit that he's never assassinated anyone." "I've just been seeing him at dinner at Mme. de Villeparisis's," said the General, but without either smiling at or endorsing the Duchess's pleasantries. "Was M. de Norpois there?" asked Prince Von, whose mind still ran on the Academy of Moral Sciences. "Why, yes;" said the General. "In fact, he was talking about your Emperor." "It seems, the Emperor William is highly intelligent, but he does not care for Elstir's painting. Not that I'm saying this against him," said the Duchess, "I quite share his point of view. Although Elstir has done a fine portrait of me. You don't know it? It's not in the least like me, but it's a remarkable piece of work. He is interesting while one's sitting to him. He has made me like a little old woman. It's after the style of the *Regents of the Hospital*, by Hals. I expect you know those sublimities, to borrow my nephew's favourite expression," the Duchess turned to myself, gently flapping her fan of black feathers. More than erect on her chair, she flung her head nobly backwards, for, while always a great lady, she was a trifle inclined to play the great lady also. I said that I had been once to Amsterdam and The Hague, but that to avoid confusing my mind, as my time was limited, I had left out Haarlem. "Ah! The Hague! What a gallery!" cried M. de Guermantes. I said to him that he had doubtless admired Vermeer's *Street in Delft*. But the Duke was less erudite than arrogant. Accordingly he contented himself with replying in a tone of sufficiency, as was his habit whenever anyone spoke to him of a picture in a gallery, or in the Salon, which he did not remember having seen. "If it's to be seen, I saw it!" "What? You've been to Holland, and you never visited Haarlem!" cried the Duchess. "Why, even if you had only a quarter of an hour to spend in the place, they're an extraordinary thing to have seen, those Halses. I don't mind saying that a person who only caught a passing glimpse of them from the top of a tramway-car without stopping, supposing they were hung out to view in the street, would open his eyes pretty wide." This utterance shocked me as indicating a misconception of the way in which artistic impressions are formed in our minds, and because it seemed to imply that our eye is in that case simply a recording machine which takes instantaneous photographs.

M. de Guermantes, rejoicing that she should be speaking to me with so competent a knowledge of the subjects that interested me, gazed at the illustrious bearing of his wife, listened to what she was saying about Franz Hals, and thought: "She rides rough-shod over everything! Our young friend can go home and say that he's had before his eyes a great lady of the old school, in the full sense of the word, the like of whom couldn't be found anywhere to-day." Thus I beheld the pair of them, withdrawn from that name Guermantes in which long ago I had imagined them leading an unimaginable life, now just like other men and other women, lingering, only, behind their contemporaries a little way, and that not evenly, as in so many households of the Faubourg, where the wife has had the good taste to stop at the golden, the husband the misfortune to come down to the pinchbeck age of history, she remaining still Louis XV while her partner is pompously Louis-Philippe. That Mme. de Guermantes should be like other women had been for me at first a disappointment; it was now, by a natural reaction and with all these good wines to help, almost a miracle. A Don John of Austria, an Isabella d'Este, situated for us in the world of names, have as little communication with the great pages of history as the Méséglise way had with the Guermantes. Isabella d'Este was no doubt in reality a very minor Princess, similar to those who under Louis XIV obtained no special place at Court. But seeming to us to be of a unique and therefore incomparable essence, we cannot conceive of her as being any less in greatness, so that a supper-party with Louis XIV would appear to us only to be rather interesting, whereas with Isabella d'Este we should find ourselves, were we to meet her, gazing with our own eyes on a supernatural heroine of romance. Well, after we have, in study-ing Isabella d'Este, in transplanting her patiently from this world of fairy-land into that of history, established the fact that her life, her thought contained nothing of that mysterious strangeness which had been sug-gested to us by her name, once this disappointment is complete we feel a boundless gratitude to this Princess for having had, of Mantegna's paint-ings, a knowledge almost equal to that, hitherto despised by us and put, as Françoise would have said, lower than the dirt, of M. Lafenestre. After having scaled the inaccessible heights of the name Guermantes, on de-scending the inner slope of the life of the Duchess, I felt on finding there the names, familiar elsewhere, of Victor Hugo, Franz Hals and, I regret to say, Vibert, the same astonishment that an explorer, after having taken into account, to imagine the singularity of the native customs in some wild valley of Central America or Northern Africa, its geographical remoteness, the strangeness of its flora, feels on discovering, once he has made his way through a hedge of giant aloes or manchineels, inhabitants who (some-times indeed among the ruins of a Roman theatre and beneath a column dedicated to Venus) are engaged in reading *Mérope* or *Alzire*. And simi-larly, so remote, so distinct from, so far superior to the educated women of the middle classes whom I had known, the similar culture by which Mme. de Guermantes had made herself, with no ulterior motive, to gratify no ambition, descend to the level of people whom she would never know, had the character—meritorious, almost touching by virtue of being wholly useless—of an erudition in Phoenician antiquities in a politician or a doctor. "I might have shewn you a very fine one," said Mme. de Guer-mantes, still speaking of Hals, "the finest in existence, some people say, which was left to me by a German cousin. Unfortunately, it turned out to be 'enfeoffed' in the castle—you don't know the expression, nor I either," she added, with her fondness for making jokes (which made her, she thought, seem modern) at the expense of the old customs to which never-theless she was unconsciously but keenly attached. "I am glad you have seen my Elstirs, but, I must admit, I should have been a great deal more glad if I could have done you the honours of my Hals, this 'enfeoffed' picture." "I know the one," said Prince Von, "it's the Grand Duke of Hesse's Hals." "Quite so; his brother married my sister," said M. de Guermantes, "and his mother and Oriane's were first cousins as well." "But so far as M. Elstir is concerned," the Prince went on, "I shall take the liberty of saying, without having any opinion of his work, which I do not know, that the hatred with which the Emperor pursues him ought not, it seems to me, to be counted against him. The Emperor is a man of marvellous intelligence." "Yes, I've met him at dinner twice, once at my aunt Sagan's and once at my aunt Radziwill's, and I must say I found him quite unusual. I didn't find him at all simple! But there is something amusing about him, something 'forced,' " she detached the word, "like a green carnation, that is to say a thing that surprises me and does not please me enormously, a thing it is surprising that anyone should have been able to create but which I feel would have been just as well un-created. I trust I'm not shocking you." "The Emperor is a man of astounding intelligence," resumed the Prince, "he is passionately fond of the arts, he has for works of art a taste that is practically infallible, if a thing is good he spots it at once and takes a dislike to it. If he detests anything, there can be no more doubt about it, the thing is excellent." Everyone smiled. "You set my mind at rest," said the Duchess. "I should be inclined to compare the Emperor," went on the Prince, who, not knowing how to pronounce the word archaeologist (that is to say, as though it were spelt 'arkeologist'), never missed an opportunity of using it, "to an old archaeologist" (but the Prince said 'arsheologist') "we have in Berlin. If you put him in front of a genuine Assyrian antique, he weeps. But if it is a modern sham, if it is not really old, he does not weep. And so, when they want to know whether an arsheological piece is really old, they take it to the old arsheologist. If he weeps, they buy the piece for the Museum. If his eyes remain dry, they send it back to the dealer, and prosecute him for fraud. Well, every time I dine at Potsdam, if the Emperor says to me, of a play: 'Prince, you must see that, it's a work of genius,' I make a note not to go to it; and when I hear him fulminating against an exhibition, I rush to see it at the first possible opportunity." "Norpois is in favour of an Anglo-French understanding, isn't he?" said M. de Guermantes. "What use would that be to you?" asked Prince Von, who could not endure the English, in a tone at once of irritation and cunning. "The English are so *schtubid*. I know, of course, that it would not be as soldiers that they would help you. But one can judge them, all the same, by the stupidity of their Generals. A friend of mine was talking the other day to Botha, you know, the Boer leader. He said to my friend: 'It's terrible, an army like that. I rather like the English, as a matter of fact, but just imagine that I, who am only a peasant, have beaten them in every battle. And in the last, when I gave way before a force twenty times the strength of my own, while I myself surrendered, because I had to, I managed to take two thousand prisoners! That was good enough, because I was only commanding an army of farmers, but if those poor fools ever have to stand up against a European army, one trembles to think what may happen to them!' Besides, you have only to see how their King, whom you know as well as I do, passes for a great man in England." I barely listened to these stories, stories of the kind that M. de Norpois used to tell my father; they supplied no food for my favourite train of thought; and besides, even had they possessed the elements which they lacked, they would have had to be of a very exciting quality for my inner life to awaken during those hours in which I dwelt in my skin, my well-brushed hair, my starched shirt-front, in which, that is to say, I could feel nothing of what constituted for me the pleasure of life. "Oh, I don't agree with you at all," said Mme. de Guermantes, who felt that the German Prince was wanting in tact, "I find King Edward charming, so simple, and much cleverer than people think. And the Queen is, even now, the most beautiful thing I've ever seen in the world." "But, Madame la Duchesse," said the Prince, who was losing his temper and did not see that he was giving offence, "you must admit that if the Prince of Wales had been an ordinary person there isn't a club that wouldn't have blackballed him, and nobody would have been

willing to shake hands with him. The Queen is charming, exceedingly
sweet and limited. But after all there is something shocking about a royal
couple who are literally kept by their subjects, who get the big Jewish
financiers to foot all the bills they ought to pay themselves, and create
them Baronets in return. It's like the Prince of Bulgaria . . ." "He's our
cousin," put in the Duchess. "He's a clever fellow." "He's mine, too, but
we don't think him a good fellow on that account. No, it is us you ought
to make friends with, it's the Emperor's dearest wish, but he insists on
its coming from the heart. He says: 'What I want to see is a hand clasped
in mine, not waving a hat in the air.' With that, you would be invincible.
It would be more practical than the Anglo-French friendship M. de Norpois preaches." "You know him, of course," the Duchess said, turning to
me, so as not to leave me out of the conversation. Remembering that M.
de Norpois had said that I had once looked as though I wanted to kiss his
hand, thinking that he had no doubt repeated this story to Mme. de Guermantes, and in any event could have spoken of me to her only with malice,
since in spite of his friendship with my father he had not hesitated to make
me appear so ridiculous, I did not do what a man of the world would have
done. He would have said that he detested M. de Norpois, and had let
him see it; he would have said this so as to give himself the appearance of
being the deliberate cause of the Ambassador's slanders, which would
then have been no more than lying and calculated reprisals. I said, on the
other hand, that, to my great regret, I was afraid that M. de Norpois did
not like me. "You are quite mistaken," replied the Duchess, "he likes you
very much indeed. You can ask Basin, for if people give me the reputation
of only saying nice things, he certainly doesn't. He will tell you that we
have never heard Norpois speak about anyone so kindly as he spoke to us
of you. And only the other day he was wanting to give you a fine post at
the Ministry. As he knew that you were not very strong and couldn't
accept it, he had the delicacy not to speak of his kind thought to your
father, for whom he has an unbounded admiration." M. de Norpois was
quite the last person whom I should have expected to do me any practical
service. The truth was that, his being a mocking and indeed somewhat
malicious spirit, those people who had let themselves be taken in as I had
by his outward appearance of a Saint Louis delivering justice beneath an
oak-tree, by the sounds, easily modulated to pity, that emerged from his
somewhat too tuneful lips, believed in a deliberate betrayal when they
learned of a slander uttered at their expense by a man who had always
seemed to put his whole heart into his speech. These slanders were frequent enough with him. But that did not prevent him from feeling attractions, from praising the people he liked and taking pleasure in shewing
that he could be of use to them. "Not that I'm in the least surprised at his
appreciating you," said Mme. de Guermantes, "he's an intelligent man.
And I can quite understand," she added, for the benefit of the rest of the
party, making allusion to a purpose of marriage of which I had heard nothing, "that my aunt, who has long ceased to amuse him as an old mistress,
may not seem of very much use to him as a young wife. Especially as I
understand that even as a mistress she has ceased for years now to serve

any practical purpose, she is more wrapped up in her devotions than anything else. Boaz-Norpois can say, in the words of Victor Hugo:

Voilà longtemps que celle avec qui j'ai dormi,
O Seigneur, a quitté ma couche pour la vôtre!

Really, my poor aunt is like the artists of the advanced guard who have stood out all their lives against the Academy, and in the end start a little academy of their own, or the unfrocked priests who get up a little private religion. They should either keep their frocks, or not stick to their profession. And who knows," went on the Duchess with a meditative air, "it may be in preparation for her widowhood, there's nothing sadder than the weeds one's not entitled to wear." "Ah! If Mme. de Villeparisis were to become Mme. de Norpois, I really believe our cousin Gilbert would take to his bed," said General de Monserfeuil. "The Prince de Guermantes is a charming man, but he is, really, very much taken up with questions of birth and manners," said the Princesse de Parme. "I went down to spend a few days with them in the country, when the Princess, unfortunately, was ill in bed. I was accompanied by Petite." (This was a nickname that was given to Mme. d'Hunolstein because she was enormously stout.) "The Prince came to meet me at the foot of the steps, and pretended not to see Petite. We went up to the first floor, to the door into the reception rooms, and then, stepping back to make way for me, he said: 'Oh, how d'ye do, Mme. d'Hunolstein?' (he always calls her that now, since her separation) pretending to have caught sight of Petite for the first time, so as to shew her that he had not come down to receive her at the foot of the steps." "That doesn't surprise me in the least. I don't need to tell you," said the Duke, who regarded himself as extremely modern, more contemptuous than anyone in the world of mere birth, and in fact a Republican, "that I have not many ideas in common with my cousin. Ma'am can imagine that we are just about as much agreed on most subjects as day and night. But I must say that if my aunt were to marry Norpois, for once I should be of Gilbert's opinion. To be the daughter of Florimond de Guise, and then to make a marriage like that would be enough, as the saying is, to make a cat laugh; what more can I say?" These last words, which the Duke uttered as a rule in the middle of a sentence, were here quite superfluous. But he felt a perpetual need to be saying them which made him postpone them to the end of a speech if he had found no place for them elsewhere. They were for him, among other things, almost a question of prosody. "Remember, though," he added, "that the Norpois are gallant gentlemen with a good place, of a good stock."

"Listen to me, Basin, it's really not worth your while to poke fun at Gilbert if you're going to speak the same language as he does," said Mme. de Guermantes, for whom the 'goodness' of a family, no less than that of a wine, consisted in its age. But, less frank than her cousin and more subtle than her husband, she made a point of never in her conversation playing false to the Guermantes spirit, and despised rank in her speech while ready to honour it by her actions. "But aren't you some sort of cousins?" asked General de Monserfeuil. "I seem to remember that Norpois married a La Rochefoucauld." "Not in that way at all, she belonged to the branch of the Ducs de La Rochefoucauld, my grandmother came from the Ducs de Doudeauville. She was own grandmother to Edouard Coco, the wisest man in the family," replied the Duke, whose views of wisdom were somewhat superficial, "and the two branches haven't inter-married since Louis XIV's time; the connexion would be rather distant." "I say, that's interesting; I never knew that," said the General. "However," went on M. de Guermantes, "his mother, I believe, was the sister of the Duc de Montmorency, and had originally been married to a La Tour d'Auvergne. But as those Montmorencys are barely Montmorencys, while those La Tour d'Auvergnes are not La Tour d'Auvergnes at all, I cannot see that it gives him any very great position. He says—and this should be more to the point—that he's descended from Saintrailles, and as we our-selves are in a direct line of descent. . . ."

There was at Combray a Rue de Saintrailles, to which I had never given another thought. It led from the Rue de la Bretonnerie to the Rue de l'Oiseau. And as Saintrailles, the companion of Joan of Arc, had, by mar-rying a Guermantes, brought into that family the County of Combray, his arms were quartered with those of Guermantes at the foot of one of the windows in Saint-Hilaire. I saw again a vision of dark sandstone steps, while a modulation of sound brought to my ears that name, Guermantes, in the forgotten tone in which I used to hear it long ago, so different from that in which it was used to signify the genial hosts with whom I was dining this evening. If the name, Duchesse de Guermantes, was for me a collective name, it was so not merely in history, by the accumulation of all the women who had successively borne it, but also in the course of my own short life, which had already seen, in this single Duchesse de Guermantes, so many different women superimpose themselves, each one vanishing as soon as the next had acquired sufficient consistency. Words do not change their meaning as much in centuries as names do for us in the space of a few years. Our memory and our heart are not large enough to be able to remain faithful. We have not room enough, in our mental field, to keep the dead there as well as the living. We are obliged to build over what has gone before and is brought to light only by a chance excavation, such as the name Saintrailles had just wrought in my mind. I felt that it would be useless to explain all this, and indeed a little while earlier I had lied by implication in not answering when M. de Guermantes said to me: "You don't know our old wheedler?" Perhaps he was quite well aware that I did know him, and it was only from good breeding that he did not press the question.

Mme. de Guermantes drew me out of my meditation. "Really, I find all that sort of thing too deadly. Listen, it's not always as boring as this at my parties. I hope that you will soon come and dine again as a compensa-tion, with no pedigrees next time," she murmured, incapable both of appre-ciating the kind of charm which I could find in her house and of having sufficient humility to be content to appeal to me only as a herbarium, filled with plants of another day.

What Mme. de Guermantes believed to be disappointing my expectations was on the contrary what in the end—for the Duke and the General went on to discuss pedigrees now without stopping—saved my evening from becoming a complete disappointment. How could I have felt otherwise until now? Each of my fellow-guests at dinner, smothering the mysterious name under which I had only at a distance known and dreamed of them with a body and with a mind similar or inferior to those of all the people I knew, had given me the impression of flat vulgarity which the view on entering the Danish port of Elsinore would give to any passionate admirer of *Hamlet*. No doubt those geographical regions and that ancient past which put forest glades and gothic belfries into their names had in a certain measure formed their faces, their intellects and their prejudices, but survived in them only as does the cause in the effect, that is to say as a thing possible for the brain to extract but in no way perceptible to the imagination.

And these old-time prejudices restored in a flash to the friends of M. and Mme. de Guermantes their vanished poetry. Assuredly, the motions in the possession of nobles, which make of them the scholars, the etymologists of the language not of words but of names (and this, moreover, relatively only to the ignorant mass of the middle classes, for if at the same level of mediocrity a devout Catholic would be better able to stand questioning upon the details of the Liturgy than a free-thinker, on the other hand an anti-clerical archaeologist can often give points to his parish priest on everything connected even with the latter's own church), those notions, if we are going to confine ourselves to the truth, that is to say to the spirit, had not for these great gentlemen the charm that they would have had for a man of simple birth. They knew perhaps better than myself that the Duchesse de Guise was Princess of Cleves, of Orleans and of Porcien, and all the rest, but they had known, long before they knew all these names, the face of the Duchesse de Guise which thenceforward the names reflected back to them. I had begun with the fairy—were she fated shortly to perish—they with the woman.

In middle-class families one sometimes sees jealousies spring up if the younger sister is married before the elder. So the aristocratic world, Courvoisiers especially but Guermantes also, reduced its ennobled greatness to simple domestic superiorities, by a system of child's-play which I had met originally (and this gave it for me its sole charm) in books. Is it not just as though Tallemant des Réaux were speaking of the Guermantes, and not of the Rohans, when he relates with evident satisfaction how M. de Guéménée cried to his brother: "You can come in here; this is not the Louvre!" and said of the Chevalier de Rohan (because he was a natural son of the Duc de Clermont): "At any rate, he's a Prince." The only thing that distressed me in all this talk was to find that the absurd stories which were being circulated about the charming Hereditary Grand Duke of Luxembourg found as much credence in this drawing-room as they had among Saint-Loup's friends. Plainly it was an epidemic that would not last longer than perhaps a year or two but had meanwhile infected everyone. People repeated the same old stories, or enriched them with others equally untrue. I gathered that the Princesse de Luxembourg herself, while apparently defending her nephew, supplied weapons for the assault. "You are wrong to stand up for him," M. de Guermantes told me, as Saint-Loup had told me before. "Why, without taking into consideration the opinion of our family, who are unanimous about him, you have only to talk to his servants, and they, after all, are the people who know him best. M. de Luxembourg gave his little Negro page to his nephew. The Negro came back in tears: 'Grand Duke beaten me; me no bad boy; Grand Duke naughty man,' it's really too much. And I can speak with some knowledge, he's Oriane's cousin." I cannot, by the way, say how many times in the course of this evening I heard the word 'cousin' used. On the one hand, M. de Guermantes, almost at every name that was mentioned, exclaimed: "But he's Oriane's cousin!" with the sudden joy of a man who, lost in a forest, reads at the ends of a pair of arrows pointing in opposite directions on a metal plate, and followed by quite a low number of kilometres, the words: "Belvédère Casimir-Perier" and "Croix du Grand-Veneur," and gathers from them that he is on the right road. On the other hand the word cousin was employed in a wholly different connexion (which was here the exception to the prevailing rule) by the Turkish Ambassadress, who had come in after dinner. Devoured by social ambition and endowed with a real power of assimilating knowledge, she would pick up with equal facility the story of the Retreat of the Ten Thousand or the details of sexual perversion among birds. It would have been impossible to 'stump' her on any of the most recent German publications, whether they dealt with political economy, mental aberrations, the various forms of onanism, or the philosophy of Epicurus. She was, incidentally, a dangerous person to listen to, for, perpetually in error, she would point out to you as being of the loosest morals women of irreproachable virtue, would put you on your guard against a gentleman whose intentions were perfectly honourable, and would tell you anecdotes of the sort that seem always to have come out of a book, not so much because they are serious as because they are so wildly improbable.

She was at this period little received in society. She had been going for some weeks now to the houses of women of real social brilliance, such as the Duchesse de Guermantes, but as a general rule had confined herself, of necessity, in the noblest families, to obscure scions whom the Guermantes had ceased to know. She hoped to give herself a really fashionable air by quoting the most historic names of the little-known people who were her friends. At once M. de Guermantes, thinking that she was referring to people who frequently dined at his table, quivered with joy at finding himself once more in sight of a landmark and shouted the rallying-cry: "But he's Oriane's cousin! I know him as well as I know my own name. He lives in the Rue Vaneau. His mother was Mlle. d'Uzés." The Ambassadress was obliged to admit that her specimen had been drawn from smaller game. She tried to connect her friends with those of M. de Guermantes by cutting across his track: "I know quite well who' you mean. No, it's not those ones, they're cousins." But this cross-current launched by the unfortunate Ambassadress ran but a little way. For M. de Guermantes, losing interest, answered: "Oh, then I don't know who' you're talking about." The Ambassadress offered no reply, for if she never knew anyone nearer than the 'cousins' of those whom she ought to have known in person, very often these 'cousins' were not even related at all. Then, from the lips of M. de Guermantes, would flow a fresh wave of "But she's Oriane's cousin!" words which seemed to have for the Duke the same practical value as certain epithets, convenient to the Roman poets because they provided them with dactyls or spondees for their hexameters. At least the explosion of: "But she's Oriane's cousin!" appeared to me quite natural when applied to the Princesse de Guermantes, who was indeed very closely related to the Duchess. The Ambassadress did not seem to care for this Princess. She said to me in an undertone: "She is stupid. No, she is not so beautiful as all that. That claim is usurped. Anyhow," she went on, with an air at once reflective, rejecting and decided, "I find her most uncongenial." But often the cousinship extended a great deal further than this, Mme. de Guermantes making it a point of honour to address as 'Aunt' ladies with whom it would have been impossible to find her an ancestress in common without going back at least to Louis XV; just as, whenever the 'hardness' of the times brought it about that a multimillionairess married a prince whose great-great-grandfather had espoused, as had Oriane's also, a daughter of Louvois, one of the chief joys of the fair American was to be able, after a first visit to the Hôtel de Guermantes, where she was, incidentally, more or less coldly received and hotly cross-examined, to say 'Aunt' to Mme. de Guermantes, who allowed her to do so with a maternal smile. But little did it concern me what birth meant for M. de Guermantes and M. de Monserfeuil; in the conversations which they held on the subject I sought only for a poetic pleasure. Without being conscious of it themselves, they procured me this pleasure as might a couple of labourers or sailors speaking of the soil or the tides, realities too little detached from their own lives for them to be capable of enjoying the beauty which personally I proceeded to extract from them.

Sometimes rather than of a race it was of a particular fact, of a date that a name reminded me. Hearing M. de Guermantes recall that M. de Bréauté's mother had been a Choiseul and his grandmother a Lucinge, I fancied I could see beneath the commonplace shirt with its plain pearl studs, bleeding still in two globes of crystal, those august relics, the hearts of Mme. de Praslin and of the Duc de Berri. Others were more voluptuous: the fine and flowing hair of Mme. de Tallien or Mme. de Sabran.

Better informed than his wife as to what their ancestors had been, M. de Guermantes found himself the possessor of memories which gave to his conversation a fine air of an ancient mansion stripped of its real treasures but still full of pictures, authentic, indifferent and majestic, which taken as a whole look remarkably well. The Prince d'Agrigente having asked why Prince Von had said, in speaking of the Duc d'Aumale, 'my uncle,' M. de Guermantes had replied: "Because his mother's brother, the Duke of Württemberg, married a daughter of Louis-Philippe." At once I was lost in contemplation of a casket, such as Carpaccio or Memling used to paint, from its first panel in which the Princess, at the wedding festivities of her brother the Duc d'Orléans, appeared wearing a plain

garden dress to indicate her resentment at having seen the return, empty-
handed, of the ambassadors who had been sent to sue on her behalf for
the hand of the Prince of Syracuse, down to the last, in which she had
just given birth to a son, the Duke of Württemberg (the first cousin of the
Prince whom I had met at dinner), in that castle called Fantaisie, one of
those places which are as aristocratic as certain families. They, moreover,
outlasting a single generation of men, see attached to themselves more
than one historical personage. In this one, especially, survive side by side
memories of the Margravine of Bayreuth, of this other somewhat fantastic
Princess (the Duc d'Orléans's sister), to whom it was said that the name
of her husband's castle made a distinct appeal, of the King of Bavaria,
and finally of Prince Von, to whom it was simply his own postal address,
at which he had just asked the Duc de Guermantes to write to him, for
he had succeeded to it, and let it only during the Wagner festivals, to the
Prince de Polignac, another delightful 'fantasist.' When M. de Guermantes, to explain how he was related to Mme. d'Arpajon, was obliged,
going so far and so simply, to climb the chain formed by the joined hands
of three or five ancestresses back to Marie-Louise or Colbert, it was still
the same thing in each case; a great historical event appeared only in passing, masked, unnatural, reduced, in the name of a property, in the Christian names of a woman, so selected because she was the granddaughter
of Louis-Philippe and Marie-Amélie, considered no longer as King and
Queen of the French, but merely in the extent to which in their capacity
as grandparents they bequeathed a heritage. (We see for other reasons
in a gazetteer of the works of Balzac, where the most illustrious personages
figure only according to their connexion with the *Comédie Humaine,*
Napoleon occupy a space considerably less than that allotted to Ras-
tignac, and occupy that space solely because he once spoke to the young
ladies of Cinq-Cygne.) Similarly the aristocracy, in its heavy structure,
pierced with rare windows, admitting a scanty daylight, shewing the same
incapacity to soar but also the same massive and blind force as the architecture of the romanesque age, embodies all our history, immures it,
beetles over it.

Thus the empty spaces of my memory were covered by degrees with
names which in taking order, in composing themselves with relation to one
another, in linking themselves to one another by an increasingly numerous
connexion, resembled those finished works of art in which there is not one
touch that is isolated, in which every part in turn receives from the rest a
justification which it confers on them.

M. de Luxembourg's name having come up again in the course of the
conversation, the Turkish Ambassadress told us how, the young bride's
grandfather (he who had made that immense fortune out of flour and
cereals) having invited M. de Luxembourg to luncheon, the latter had
written to decline, putting on the envelope: "M. So-and-So, Miller," to
which the grandfather had replied: "I am all the more disappointed that
you were not able to come, my dear friend, because I should have been able
to enjoy your society quite intimately, for we were quite an intimate party,
just ourselves, and there would have been only the Miller, his Son, and

you." This story was not merely utterly distasteful to me, who knew the impossibility of my dear M. de Nassau's writing to the grandfather of his wife (whose fortune, moreover, he was expecting to inherit) and addressing him as 'Miller'; but furthermore its stupidity became glaring from the start, the word 'Miller' having obviously been dragged in only to lead up to the title of La Fontaine's fable. But there is in the Faubourg Saint-Germain a silliness so great, when it is aggravated by malice, that they all decided that the letter had been sent and that the grandfather, as to whom at once everyone confidently declared that he was a remarkable man, had shewn a prettier wit than his grandson-in-law. The Duc de Châtellerault tried to take advantage of this story to tell the one that I had heard in the café: "Everyone had to lie down!"—but scarcely had he begun, or reported M. de Luxembourg's pretension that in his wife's presence M. de Guermantes ought to stand up, when the Duchess stopped him with the protest: "No, he is very absurd, but not as bad as that." I was privately convinced that all these stories at the expense of M. de Luxembourg were equally untrue, and that whenever I found myself face to face with any of the reputed actors or spectators I should hear the same contradiction. I asked myself, nevertheless, whether the contradiction just uttered by Mme. de Guermantes had been inspired by regard for truth or by self-esteem. In either event the latter quality succumbed to malice, for she went on, with a laugh: "Not that I haven't had my little fling at him too, for he invited me to luncheon, wishing to make me know the Grand Duchess of Luxembourg, which is how he has the good taste to describe his wife when he's writing to his aunt. I sent a reply expressing my regret, and adding: As for the 'Grand Duchess of Luxembourg' (in inverted commas), tell her that if she is coming to see me I am at home every Thursday after five. I have even had another little fling. Happening to be at Luxembourg, I telephoned, asking him to ring me up. His Highness was going to luncheon, had just risen from luncheon, two hours went by and nothing happened; so then I employed another method: 'Will you tell the Comte de Nassau to come and speak to me?' Cut to the quick, he was at the instrument that very minute." Everyone laughed at the Duchess's story, and at other analogous, that is to say (I am convinced of it) equally untrue stories, for a man more intelligent, better, more refined, in a word more exquisite than this Luxembourg-Nassau I have never met. The sequel will shew that it was I who was in the right. I must admit that, in the midst of her onslaught, Mme. de Guermantes had still a kind word for him. "He was not always like that," she informed us. "Before he went off his head, like the man in the story-book who thinks he's become king, he was no fool, and indeed in the early days of his engagement he used to speak of it in really quite a nice way, as something he could never have dreamed of: 'It's just like a fairy-tale; I shall have to make my entry into Luxembourg in a fairy coach,' he said to his uncle d'Ornessan, who answered—for you know it's not a very big place, Luxembourg: 'A fairy coach! I'm afraid, my dear fellow, you'd never get it in. I should suggest that you take a goat carriage.' Not only did this not annoy Nassau, but he was the first to tell us the story, and to laugh at it." "Ornessan is a witty fellow, and he's every reason to be; his mother was a Montjeu. He's in a very bad way now, poor Ornessan." This name had the magic virtue of interrupting the flow of stale witticisms which otherwise would have gone on for ever. In fact, M. de Guermantes had to explain that M. d'Ornessan's great-grandmother had been the sister of Marie de Castille Montjeu, the wife of Timoléon de Lorraine, and consequently Oriane's aunt, with the result that the conversation drifted back to genealogies, while the idiot of a Turkish Ambassadress breathed in my ear: "You appear to be very much in the Duke's good books; have a care!" and, on my demanding an explanation: "I mean to say, you understand what I mean, he's a man to whom one could safely entrust one's daughter, but not one's son." Now if ever, on the contrary, a man existed who was passionately and exclusively a lover of women, it was certainly the Duc de Guermantes. The state of error, the falsehood fatuously believed to be the truth, were for the Ambassadress like a vital element out of which she could not move. "His brother Mémé, who is, as it happens, for other reasons altogether" (he did not bow to her) "profoundly uncongenial to me, is genuinely distressed by the Duke's morals. So is their aunt Villeparisis. Ah, now, her I adore! There is a saint of a woman for you, the true type of the great ladies of the past. It's not only her actual virtue that's so wonderful but her restraint. She still says 'Monsieur' to the Ambassador Norpois whom she sees every day, and who, by the way, left an excellent impression behind him in Turkey."

I did not even reply to the Ambassadress, in order to listen to the genealogies. They were not all of them important. There came up indeed in the course of the conversation one of those unexpected alliances, which, M. de Guermantes informed me, was a misalliance, but not without charm, for, uniting under the July Monarchy the Duc de Guermantes and the Duc de Fezensac with the two irresistible daughters of an eminent navigator, it gave the two Duchesses the exciting novelty of a grace exotically middle-class, 'Louisphilippically' Indian. Or else, under Louis XIV, a Norpois had married the daughter of the Duc de Mortemart, whose illustrious title struck, in the remoteness of that epoch, the name—which I had found colourless and might have supposed to be modern—of Norpois, carving deeply upon it the beauty of an old medal. And in these cases, moreover, it was not only the less well-known name that benefited by the association; the other, grown commonplace by the fact of its lustre, struck me more forcibly in this novel and more obscure aspect, just as among the portraits painted by a brilliant colourist the most striking is sometimes one that is all in black. The sudden mobility with which all these names seemed to me to have been endowed, as they sprang to take their places by the side of others from which I should have supposed them to be remote, was due not to my ignorance alone; the country-dances which they were performing in my mind they had carried out no less spontaneously at those epochs in which a title, being always attached to a piece of land, used to follow it from one family to another, so much so that, for example, in the fine feudal structure that is the title of Duc de Nemours or Duc de Chevreuse, I was able to discover successively hidden, as in the hospitable abode of a hermit-crab, a Guise, a Prince of Savoy, an Orléans, a Luynes. Sometimes several remained in competition for a single shell: for the Principality of Orange the Royal House of the Netherlands and MM. de Mailly-Nesle, for the Duchy of Brabant the Baron de Charlus and the Royal House of Belgium, various others for the titles of Prince of Naples, Duke of Parma, Duke of Reggio. Sometimes it was the other way; the shell had been so long uninhabited by proprietors long since dead that it had never occurred to me that this or that name of a country house could have been, at an epoch which after all was comparatively recent, the name of a family. And so, when M. de Guermantes replied to a question put to him by M. de Monserfeuil: "No, my cousin was a fanatical Royalist; she was the daughter of the Marquis de Féterne, who played a certain part in the Chouan rising," on seeing this name Féterne, which had been for me, since my stay at Balbec, the name of a country house, become, what I had never dreamed that it could possibly be, a family name, I felt the same astonishment as in reading a fairy-tale, where turrets and a terrace come to life and turn into men and women. In this sense of the words, we may say that history, even mere family history, gives life to the old stones of a house. There have been in Parisian society men who played as considerable a part in it, who were more sought after for their distinction or for their wit, who were equally well born as the Duc de Guermantes or the Duc de La Trémoïlle. They have now fallen into oblivion because, as they left no descendants, their name which we no longer hear sounds like a name unknown; at most, the name of a thing beneath which we never think to discover the name of any person, it survives in some country house, some remote village. The day is not distant when the traveller who, in the heart of Burgundy, stops in the little village of Charlus to look at its church, if he has not sufficient industry or is in too great a hurry to examine its tombstones, will go away ignorant that this name, Charlus, was that of a man who ranked with the highest in the land. This thought reminded me that it was time to go, and that while I was listening to M. de Guermantes talking pedigrees, the hour was approaching at which I had promised to call upon his brother. "Who knows," I continued to muse, "whether one day Guermantes itself may not appear nothing more than a place-name, save to the archaeologists who, stopping by chance at Combray and standing beneath the window of Gilbert the Bad, have the patience to listen to the account given them by Théodore's successor or to read the Curé's guide?" But so long as a great name is not extinct it keeps in the full light of day those men and women who bear it; and there can be no doubt that, to a certain extent, the interest which the illustriousness of these families gave them in my eyes lay in the fact that one can, starting from to-day, follow their ascending course, step by step, to a point far beyond the fourteenth century, recover the diaries and correspondence of all the forebears of M. de Charlus, of the Prince d'Agrigente, of the Princesse de Parme, in a past in which an impenetrable night would cloak the origins of a middle-class family, and in which we make out, in the luminous backward projection of a name, the origin and persistence of certain nervous characteristics, certain vices, the disorders of one or another Guermantes. Almost identical pathologically with their namesakes of the present day, they excite from century to century the startled interest of their correspondents, whether these be anterior to the Princess Palatine and Mme. de Motteville, or subsequent to the Prince de Ligne.

However, my historical curiosity was faint in comparison with my aesthetic pleasure. The names cited had the effect of disincarnating the Duchess's guests, whom, for all they might call themselves Prince d'Agrigente or de Cystira, their mask of flesh and of a common intelligence or want of intelligence had transformed into ordinary mortals, so much so that I had made my landing on the ducal door-mat not as upon the threshold (as I had supposed) but as at the farthest confines of the enchanted world of names. The Prince d'Agrigente himself, as soon as I heard that his mother had been a Damas, a granddaughter of the Duke of Modena, was delivered, as from an unstable chemical alloy, from the face and speech that prevented one from recognising him, and went to form with Damas and Modena, which themselves were only titles, a combination infinitely more seductive. Each name displaced by the attractions of another, with which I had never suspected it of having any affinity, left the unalterable position which it had occupied in my brain, where familiarity had dulled it, and, speeding to join the Mortemarts, the Stuarts or the Bourbons, traced with them branches of the most graceful design and an ever-changing colour. The name Guermantes itself received from all the beautiful names—extinct, and so all the more glowingly rekindled—with which I learned only now that it was connected, a new sense and purpose, purely poetical. At the most, at the extremity of each spray that burgeoned from the exalted stem, I could see it flower in some face of a wise king or illustrious princess, like the sire of Henri IV or the Duchesse de Longueville. But as these faces, different in this respect from those of the party around me, were not discoloured for me by any trace of physical experience or fashionable mediocrity, they remained, in their handsome outlines and rainbow iridescence, homogeneous with those names which at regular intervals, each of a different hue, detached themselves from the genealogical tree of Guermantes, and disturbed with no foreign or opaque matter the buds—pellucid, alternate, many-coloured—which (like, in the old Jesse windows, the ancestors of Jesus) blossomed on either side of the tree of glass.

Already I had made several attempts to slip away, on account, more than for any other reason, of the triviality which my presence at it imparted to the gathering, albeit it was one of those which I had long imagined as being so beautiful—as it would doubtless have been had there been no inconvenient witness present. At least my departure would permit the other guests, once the profane intruder was no longer among them, to constitute themselves at length into a secret conclave. They would be free to celebrate the mysteries for the celebration of which they had met together, for it could obviously not have been to talk of Franz Hals or of avarice, and to talk of them in the same way as people talk in middle-class society. They uttered nothing but trivialities, doubtless because I was in the room, and I felt with some compunction, on seeing all these pretty women kept apart, that I was preventing them by my presence from carrying on, in the most precious of its drawing-rooms, the mysterious life of the Faubourg Saint-Germain. But this departure which I was trying at every moment to effect, M. and Mme. de Guermantes carried the spirit of self-sacrifice so far as to postpone, by keeping me in the room. A more curious thing still, several of the ladies who had come hurrying, delighted, beautifully dressed, with constellations of jewels, to be present at a party which, through my fault only, differed in no essential point from those that are given elsewhere than in the Faubourg Saint-Germain, any more than one feels oneself at Balbec to be in a town that differs from what one's eyes are accustomed to see—several of these ladies retired not at all disappointed, as they had every reason to be, but thanking Mme. de Guermantes most effusively for the delightful evening which they had spent, as though on the other days, those on which I was not present, nothing more used to occur.

Was it really for the sake of dinners such as this that all these people dressed themselves up and refused to allow the penetration of middle-class women into their so exclusive drawing-rooms—for dinners such as this? The same, had I been absent? The suspicion flashed across my mind for a moment, but it was too absurd. Plain commonsense enabled me to brush it aside. And then, if I had adopted it, what would have been left of the name Guermantes, already so degraded since Combray?

It struck me that these flower-maidens were, to a strange extent, either ready to be pleased with another person or anxious to make that person pleased with them, for more than one of them, to whom I had not uttered, during the whole course of the evening, more than two or three casual remarks, the stupidity of which had left me blushing, made a point, before leaving the drawing-room, of coming to tell me, fastening on me her fine caressing eyes, straightening as she spoke the garland of orchids that followed the curve of her bosom, what an intense pleasure it had been to her to make my acquaintance, and to speak to me—a veiled allusion to an invitation to dinner—of her desire to 'arrange something' after she had 'fixed a day' with Mme. de Guermantes. None of these flower ladies left the room before the Princesse de Parme. The presence of that lady—one must never depart before Royalty—was one of the two reasons, neither of which I had guessed, for which the Duchess had insisted so strongly on my remaining. As soon as Mme. de Parme had risen, it was like a deliverance. Each of the ladies having made a genuflexion before the Princess, who raised her up from the ground, they received from her, in a kiss, and like a benediction which they had craved kneeling, the permission to ask for their cloaks and carriages. With the result that there followed, at the front door, a sort of stentorian recital of great names from the History of France. The Princesse de Parme had forbidden Mme. de Guermantes to accompany her downstairs to the hall for fear of her catching cold, and the Duke had added: "There, Oriane, since Ma'am gives you leave, remember what the doctor told you."

"I am sure the Princesse de Parme was *most pleased* to take dinner with you." I knew the formula. The Duke had come the whole way across the drawing-room in order to utter it before me with an obliging, concerned air, as though he were handing me a diploma or offering me a plateful of biscuits. And I guessed from the pleasure which he appeared to be feeling as he spoke, and which brought so sweet an expression momentarily into his face, that the effort which this represented for him was of the kind which he would continue to make to the very end of his life, like one of those honorific and easy posts which, even when paralytic, one is still allowed to retain.

Just as I was about to leave, the lady in waiting reappeared in the drawing-room, having forgotten to take away some wonderful carnations, sent up from Guermantes, which the Duchess had presented to Mme. de Parme. The lady in waiting was somewhat flushed, one felt that she had just been receiving a scolding, for the Princess, so kind to everyone else, could not contain her impatience at the stupidity of her attendant. And so the latter picked up the flowers and ran quickly, but to preserve her air of ease and independence flung at me as she passed: "The Princess says I'm keeping her waiting; she wants to be gone, and to have the carnations as well. Good lord! I'm not a little bird, I can't be in two places at once."

Alas! the rule of not leaving before Royalty was not the only one. I could not depart at once, for there was another: this was that the famous lavishness, unknown to the Courvoisiers, with which the Guermantes, whether opulent or practically ruined, excelled in entertaining their friends, was not only a material lavishness, of the kind that I had often experienced with Robert de Saint-Loup, but also a lavish display of charming words, of courteous actions, a whole system of verbal elegance supplied from a positive treasure-house within. But as this last, in the inactivity of fashionable existence, must remain unemployed, it expanded at times, sought an outlet in a sort of fugitive effusion, all the more intense, which might, in Mme. de Guermantes, have led one to suppose a genuine affection for oneself. Which she did, for that matter, feel at the moment when she let it overflow, for she found then in the society of the friend, man or woman, with whom she happened to be a sort of intoxication, in no way sensual, similar to that which music produces in certain people; she would suddenly detach a flower from her bodice, or a medallion, and present it to someone with whom she would have liked to prolong the evening, with a melancholy feeling the while that such a prolongation could have led to nothing but idle talk, into which nothing could have passed of the nervous pleasure, the fleeting emotion, similar to the first warm days of spring in the impression they leave behind them of exhaustion and regret. As for the friend, it did not do for him to put too implicit a faith in the promises, more exhilarating than anything he had ever heard, tendered by these women who, because they feel with so much more force the sweetness of a moment, make of it, with a delicacy, a nobility of which normally constituted creatures are incapable, a compelling masterpiece of grace and goodness, and have no longer anything of themselves left to give when the next moment has arrived. Their affection does not outlive the exaltation that has dictated it; and the subtlety of mind which had then led them to divine all the things that you wished to hear and to say them to you will permit them just as easily, a few days later, to seize hold of your absurdities and use them to entertain another of their visitors with whom they will then be in the act of enjoying one of those 'musical moments' which are so brief.

In the hall where I asked a footman for my snowboots which I had brought as a precaution against the snow, several flakes of which had already fallen, to be converted rapidly into slush, not having realised that they were hardly fashionable, I felt, at the contemptuous smile on all sides, a shame which rose to its highest pitch when I saw that Mme. de Parme had not gone and was watching me put on my American 'rubbers.' The Princess came towards me. "Oh! What a good idea," she exclaimed, "it's so practical! There's a sensible man for you. Madame, we shall have to get a pair of those," she went on to her lady in waiting, while the mockery of the footmen turned to respect and the other guests crowded round me to inquire where I had managed to find these marvels. "With those on, you will have nothing to fear even if it starts snowing again and you have a long way to go. You're independent of the weather," said the Princess to me. "Oh! If it comes to that, your Royal Highness can be reassured," broke in the lady in waiting with a knowing air, "it will not snow again." "What do you know about it, Madame?" came witheringly from the excellent Princesse de Parme, who alone could succeed in piercing the thick skin of her lady in waiting. "I can assure your Royal Highness, it cannot snow again. It is a physical impossibility." "But why?" "It cannot snow any more, they have taken the necessary steps to prevent it, they have put down salt in the streets!" The simple-minded lady did not observe either the anger of the Princess or the mirth of the rest of her audience, for instead of remaining silent she said to me with a genial smile, paying no heed to my repeated denials of any connexion with Admiral Jurien de la Gravière: "Not that it matters, after all. This gentleman must have stout sea-legs. What's bred in the bone!"

Then, having escorted the Princesse de Parme to her carriage, M. de Guermantes said to me, taking hold of my greatcoat: "Let me help you into your skin." He had ceased even to smile when he employed this expression, for those that were most vulgar had for that very reason, because of the Guermantes affectation of simplicity, become aristocratic.

An exaltation that sank only into melancholy, because it was artificial, was what I also, although quite differently from Mme. de Guermantes, felt once I had finally left her house, in the carriage that was taking me to that of M. de Charlus. We can at pleasure abandon ourselves to one or other of two forces of which one rises in ourselves, emanates from our deepest impressions, the other comes to us from without. The first carries with it naturally a joy, the joy that springs from the life of the creator. The other current, that which endeavours to introduce into us the movement by which persons external to ourselves are stirred, is not accompanied by pleasure; but we can add a pleasure to it, by the shock of reaction, in an intoxication so feigned that it turns swiftly into boredom, into melancholy, whence the gloomy faces of so many men of fashion, and all those nervous conditions which may make them end in suicide. Well, in the carriage which was taking me to M. de Charlus, I was a prey to this second sort of exaltation, widely different from that which is given us by a personal impression, such as I had received in other carriages, once at Combray, in Dr. Percepied's gig, from which I had seen painted against the setting sun the spires of Martinville, another day at Balbec, in Mme. de Villeparisis's barouche, when I strove to identify the reminiscence that was suggested to me by an avenue of trees. But in this third carriage, what I had before my mind's eye were those conversations that had seemed to me so tedious at Mme. de Guermante's dinner-table, for example Prince Von's stories about the German Emperor, General Botha and the British Army. I had slipped them into the frame of the internal stereoscope through the lenses of which, once we are no longer ourselves, once, endowed with the spirit of society, we no longer wish to receive our life save from other people, we cast into relief what they have said and done. Like a tipsy man filled with tender feeling for the waiter who has been serving him, I marvelled at my good fortune, a good fortune not realised by me, it is true, at the actual moment, in having dined with a person who knew William II so well, and had told stories about him that were—upon my word—really witty. And, as I repeated to myself, with the Prince's German accent, the story of General Botha, I laughed out loud, as though this laugh, like certain kinds of applause which increase one's inward admiration, were necessary to the story as a corroboration of its comic element. Through the magnifying lenses even those of Mme. de Guermantes's pronouncements which had struck me as being stupid (as for example that on the Hals pictures which one ought to see from the top of a tramway-car) took on a life, a depth that were extraordinary. And I must say that, even if this exaltation was quick to subside, it was not altogether unreasonable. Just as there may always come a day when we are glad to know the person whom we despise more than anyone in the world because he happens to be connected with a girl with whom we are in love, to whom he can introduce us, and thus offers us both utility and gratification, attributes in each of which we should have supposed him to be entirely lacking, so there is no conversation, any more than there are personal relations, from which we can be certain that we shall not one day derive some benefit. What Mme. de Guermantes had said to me about the pictures which it would be interesting to see, even from a tramway-car, was untrue, but it contained a germ of truth which was of value to me later on.

Similarly the lines of Victor Hugo which I had heard her quote were, it must be admitted, of a period earlier than that in which he became something more than a new man, in which he brought to light, in the order of evolution, a literary species till then unknown, endowed with more complex organs than any then in existence. In these first poems, Victor Hugo is still a thinker, instead of contenting himself, like Nature, with supplying food for thought. His 'thoughts' he at that time expressed in the most direct form, almost in the sense in which the Duke employed the word when, feeling it to be out of date and a nuisance that the guests at his big parties at Guermantes should, in the visitors' book, append to their signatures a philosophico-poetical reflexion, he used to warn novices in an appealing tone: "Your name, my dear fellow, but no 'thoughts' please!" Well, it was these 'thoughts' of Victor Hugo (almost as entirely absent from the

Légende des Siècles as 'airs,' as 'melodies' are from Wagner's later manner) that Mme. de Guermantes admired in the early Hugo. Nor was she
altogether wrong. They were touching, and already round about them,
without their form's having yet the depth which it was to acquire only in
later years, the rolling tide of words and of richly articulated rhymes put
them beyond comparison with the lines that one might discover in a Corneille, for example, lines in which a Romanticism that is intermittent,
restrained and so all the more moving, nevertheless has not at all penetrated to the physical sources of life, modified the unconscious and general-
isable organism in which the idea is latent. And so I had been wrong in
confining myself, hitherto, to the later volumes of Hugo. Of the earlier, of
course, it was only a fractional part that Mme. de Guermantes used to
embellish her conversation. But simply by quoting in this way an isolated
line one multiplies its power of attraction tenfold. The lines that had entered
or returned to my mind during this dinner magnetised in turn, summoned
to themselves with such force the poems in the heart of which they were
normally embedded, that my magnetised hands could not hold out for
longer than forty-eight hours against the force that drew them towards the
volume in which were bound up the *Orientales* and the *Chants du Crépuscule.* I cursed Françoise's footman for having made a present to his native
village of my copy of the *Feuilles d'Automne,* and sent him off, with not a
moment to be lost, to procure me another. I read these volumes from cover
to cover and found peace of mind only when I suddenly came across, awaiting me in the light in which she had bathed them, the lines that I had heard
Mme. de Guermantes quote. For all these reasons, conversations with the
Duchess resembled the discoveries that we make in the library of a country
house, out of date, incomplete, incapable of forming a mind, lacking in
almost everything that we value, but offering us now and then some curious
scrap of information, for instance the quotation of a fine passage which
we did not know and as to which we are glad to remember in after years
that we owe our knowledge of it to a stately mansion of the great. We are
then, by having found Balzac's preface to the *Chartreuse,* or some unpub-
lished letters of Joubert, tempted to exaggerate the value of the life we led
there, the sterile frivolity of which, for this windfall of a single evening, we
forget.

From this point of view, if the fashionable world had been unable, at
the first moment, to provide what my imagination expected, and must
consequently strike me first of all by what it had in common with all the
other worlds rather than by its difference, still it revealed itself to me by
degrees as something quite distinct. Great noblemen are almost the only
people of whom one learns as much as one does of peasants; their conversation is adorned with everything that concerns the land, houses, as
people used to live in them long ago, old customs, everything of which the
world of money is profoundly ignorant. Even supposing that the aristocrat
most moderate in his aspirations has finally overtaken the period in which
he lives, his mother, his uncles, his great-aunts keep him in touch, when
he recalls his childhood, with the conditions of a life almost unknown to-
day. In the death-chamber of a contemporary corpse Mme. de Guermantes

would not have pointed out, but would immediately have perceived, all the lapses from the traditional customs. She was shocked to see at a funeral women mingling with the men, when there was a particular ceremony which ought to be celebrated for the women. As for the pall, the use of which Bloch would doubtless have believed to be confined to coffins, on account of the pall bearers of whom one reads in the reports of funerals, M. de Guermantes could remember the time when, as a child, he had seen it borne at the wedding of M. de Mailly-Nesle. While Saint-Loup had sold his priceless 'Genealogical Tree,' old portraits of the Bouillons, letters of Louis XIII, in order to buy Carrières and furniture in the modern style, M. and Mme. de Guermantes, moved by a sentiment in which the burning love of art may have played only a minor part, and which left them themselves more insignificant than before, had kept their marvellous Boule furniture, which presented a picture attractive in a different way to an artist. A literary man would similarly have been enchanted by their conversation, which would have been for him—for one hungry man has no need of another to keep him company—a living dictionary of all those expressions which every day are becoming more and more forgotten: Saint-Joseph cravats, children dedicated to the Blue, and so forth, which one finds to-day only among those people who have constituted themselves the friendly and benevolent custodians of the past. The pleasure that a writer, more than among other writers, feels among them is not without danger, for there is a risk of his coming to believe that the things of the past have a charm in themselves, of his transferring them bodily into his work, still-born in that case, exhaling a tedium for which he consoles himself with the reflexion: "It is attractive because it's true; that is how people do talk." These aristocratic conversations had moreover the charm, with Mme. de Guermantes, of being couched in excellent French. For this reason they made permissible on the Duchess's part her hilarity at the words 'viaticum,' 'cosmic,' 'pythian,' 'pre-eminent,' which Saint-Loup used to employ—as, similarly, at his Bing furniture.

When all was said, very different in this respect from what I had been able to feel before the hawthorns, or when I tasted a crumb of *madeleine,* the stories that I had heard at Mme. de Guermantes's remained alien to me. Entering for a moment into me, who was only physically possessed by them, one would have said that, being of a social, not an individual nature, they were impatient to escape. I writhed in my seat in the carriage like the priestess of an oracle. I looked forward to another dinner-party at which I might myself become a sort of Prince Von to Mme. de Guermantes, and repeat them. In the meantime they made my lips quiver as I stammered them to myself, and I tried in vain to bring back and concentrate a mind that was carried away by a centrifugal force. And so it was with a feverish impatience not to have to bear the whole weight of them any longer by myself in a carriage where, for that matter, I atoned for the lack of conversation by soliloquising aloud, that I rang the bell at M. de Charlus's door, and it was in long monologues with myself, in which I rehearsed everything that I was going to tell him and gave scarcely a thought to what he might have to say to me, that I spent the whole of the time during which I was kept waiting in a drawing-room into which a footman shewed me and where I was incidentally too much excited to look at what it contained. I felt so urgent a need that M. de Charlus should listen to the stories which I was burning to tell him that I was bitterly disappointed to think that the master of the house was perhaps in bed, and that I might have to go home to sleep off by myself my drunkenness of words. I had just noticed, in fact, that I had been twenty-five minutes—that they had perhaps forgotten about me —in this room of which, despite this long wait, I could at the most have said that it was very big, greenish in colour, and contained a large number of portraits. The need to speak prevents one not merely from listening but from seeing things, and in this case the absence of any description of my external surroundings is tantamount to a description of my internal state. I was preparing to leave the room to try to get hold of some one, and if I found no one to make my way back to the hall and have myself let out, when, just as I had risen from my chair and taken a few steps across the mosaic parquet of the floor, a manservant came in, with a troubled expression: "Monsieur le Baron has been engaged all evening, Sir," he told me. "There are still several people waiting to see him. I am doing everything I possibly can to get him to receive you, I have already telephoned up twice to the secretary." "No; please don't bother. I had an appointment with M. le Baron, but it is very late already, and if he is busy this evening I can come back another day." "Oh no, Sir, you must not go away," cried the servant. "M. le Baron might be vexed. I will try again." I was reminded of the things I had heard about M. de Charlus's servants and their devotion to their master. One could not quite say of him as of the Prince de Conti that he sought to give pleasure as much to the valet as to the Minister, but he had shewn such skill in making of the least thing that he asked of them a sort of personal favour that at night, when, his body-servants assembled round him at a respectful distance, after running his eye over them he said: "Coignet, the candlestick!" or "Ducret, the nightshirt!" it was with an envious murmur that the rest used to withdraw, jealous of him who had been singled out by his master's favour. Two of them, indeed, who could not abide one another, used to try to snatch the favour each from his rival by going on the most flimsy pretext with a message to the Baron, if he had gone upstairs earlier than usual, in the hope of being invested for the evening with the charge of candlestick or nightshirt. If he addressed a few words directly to one of them on some subject outside the scope of his duty, still more if in winter, in the garden, knowing that one of his coachmen had caught cold, he said to him, after ten minutes: "Put your cap on!" the others would not speak to the fellow again for a fortnight, in their jealousy of the great distinction that had been conferred on him. I waited ten minutes more, and then, after requesting me not to stay too long as M. le Baron was tired and had had to send away several most important people who had made appointments with him many days before, they admitted me to his presence. This setting with which M. de Charlus surrounded himself seemed to me a great deal less impressive than the simplicity of his brother Guermantes, but already the door stood open, I could see the Baron, in a Chinese dressing-gown, with his throat bare, lying upon a sofa. My eye was caught at the same moment by a tall hat, its nap flashing like a mirror, which had been left on a chair with a cape, as though the Baron had but recently come in. The valet withdrew. I supposed that M. de Charlus would rise to greet me. Without moving a muscle he fixed on me a pair of implacable eyes. I went towards him, I said good evening; he did not hold out his hand, made no reply, did not ask me to take a chair. After a moment's silence I asked him, as one would ask an ill-mannered doctor, whether it was necessary for me to remain standing. I said this without any evil intention, but my words seemed only to intensify the cold fury on M. de Charlus's face. I was not aware, as it happened, that at home, in the country, at the Château de Charlus, he was in the habit, after dinner (so much did he love to play the king) of sprawling in an armchair in the smoking-room, letting his guests remain standing round him. He would ask for a light from one, offer a cigar to another and then, after a few minutes' interval, would say: "But Argencourt, why don't you sit down? Take a chair, my dear fellow," and so forth, having made a point of keeping them standing simply to remind them that it was from himself that permission came to them to be seated. "Put yourself in the Louis XIV seat," he answered me with an imperious air, as though rather to force me to move away farther from himself than to invite me to be seated. I took an armchair which was comparatively near. "Ah! so that is what you call a Louis XIV seat, is it? I can see you have been well educated," he cried in derision. I was so much taken aback that I did not move, either to leave the house, as I ought to have done, or to change my seat, as he wished. "Sir," he next said to me, weighing each of his words, to the more impertinent of which he prefixed a double yoke of consonants, "the interview which I have condescended to grant you at the request of a person who desires to be nameless, will mark the final point in our relations. I shall not conceal from you that I had hoped for better things! I should perhaps be forcing the sense of the words a little, which one ought not to do, even with people who are ignorant of their value, simply out of the respect due to oneself, were I to tell you that I had felt a certain *attraction* towards you. I think, however, that *benevolence*, in its most actively protecting sense, would exceed neither what I felt nor what I was proposing to display. I had, immediately on my return to Paris, given you to understand, while you were still at Balbec, that you could count upon me." I who remembered with what a torrent of abuse M. de Charlus had parted from me at Balbec made an instinctive gesture of contradiction. "What!" he cried with fury, and indeed his face, convulsed and white, differed as much from his ordinary face as does the sea when on a morning of storm one finds instead of its customary smiling surface a thousand serpents writhing in spray and foam, "do you mean to pretend that you did not receive my message—almost a declaration—that you were to remember me? What was there in the way of decoration round the cover of the book that I sent you?" "Some very pretty twined garlands with tooled ornaments," I told him. "Ah!" he replied, with an air of scorn, "these young Frenchmen know little of the treasures of our land. What would be said of a young Berliner who had never heard of the *Walküre*? Besides, you must have eyes to see and see not, since you yourself told me that you had stood for two hours in front of that particular treasure. I can see that you know no more about flowers than you do about styles; don't protest that you know about styles," he cried in a shrill scream of rage, "you can't even tell me what you are sitting on. You offer your hindquarters a Directory *chauffeuse* as a Louis XIV *bergère*. One of these days you'll be mistaking Mme. de Villeparisis's knees for the seat of the rear, and a fine mess you'll make of things then. It's precisely the same; you didn't even recognise on the binding of Bergotte's book the lintel of myosotis over the door of Balbec church. Could there be any clearer way of saying to you: 'Forget me not!'?"

I looked at M. de Charlus. Undoubtedly his magnificent head, though repellent, yet far surpassed that of any of his relatives; you would have called him an Apollo grown old; but an olive-hued, bilious juice seemed ready to start from the corners of his evil mouth; as for intellect, one could not deny that his, over a vast compass, had taken in many things which must always remain unknown to his brother Guermantes. But whatever the fine words with which he coloured all his hatreds, one felt that, even if there was now an offended pride, now a disappointment in love, or a rancour, or sadism, a love of teasing, a fixed obsession, this man was capable of doing murder, and of proving by force of logic that he had been right in doing it and was still superior by a hundred cubits in moral stature to his brother, his sister-in-law, or any of the rest. "Just as, in Velazquez's *Lances*," he went on, "the victor advances towards him who is the humbler in rank, as is the duty of every noble nature, since I was everything and you were nothing, it was I who took the first steps towards you. You have made an idiotic reply to what it is not for me to describe as an act of greatness. But I have not allowed myself to be discouraged. Our religion inculcates patience. The patience I have shewn towards you will be counted, I hope, to my credit, and also my having only smiled at what might be denounced as impertinence, were it within your power to offer any impertinence to me who surpass you in stature by so many cubits; but after all, Sir, all this is now neither here nor there. I have subjected you to the test which the one eminent man of our world has ingeniously named the test of excessive friendliness, and which he rightly declares to be the most terrible of all, the only one that can separate the good grain from the tares. I could scarcely reproach you for having undergone it without success, for those who emerge from it triumphant are very few. But at least, and this is the conclusion which I am entitled to draw from the last words that we shall exchange on this earth, at least I intend to hear nothing more of your calumnious fabrications." So far, I had never dreamed that M. de Charlus's rage could have been caused by an unflattering remark which had been repeated to him; I searched my memory; I had not spoken about him to anyone. Some evil-doer had invented the whole thing. I protested to M. de Charlus that I had said absolutely nothing about him. "I don't think I can have annoyed you by saying to Mme. de Guermantes that I was a friend of yours." He gave a disdainful smile, made his voice climb to the supreme pitch of its highest register, and there, without strain, attacking the shrillest and most insolent note: "Oh! Sir," he said, returning by the most gradual stages to a natural intonation, and seeming to revel as he went in

the oddities of this descending scale, "I think that you are doing yourself
an injustice when you accuse yourself of having said that we were *friends*.
I do not look for any great verbal accuracy in anyone who could readily
mistake a piece of Chippendale for a rococo *chaire*, but really I do not
believe," he went on, with vocal caresses that grew more and more winning
and brought to hover over his lips what was actually a charming smile, "I
do not believe that you can ever have said, or thought, that we were *friends*!
As for your having boasted that you had been *presented* to me, had *talked*
to me, *knew* me slightly, had obtained, almost without solicitation, the
prospect of coming one day under my *protection*, I find it on the contrary
very natural and intelligent of you to have done so. The extreme difference
in age that there is between us enables me to recognise without absurdity
that that *presentation*, those *talks*, that vague prospect of future *relations*
were for you, it is not for me to say an honour, but still, when all is said and
done, an advantage as to which I consider that your folly lay not in divulg-
ing it but in not having had the sense to keep it. I will go so far as to say,"
he went on, passing abruptly for a moment from his arrogant wrath to a
gentleness so tinged with melancholy that I expected him to burst into
tears, "that when you left unanswered the proposal I made to you here in
Paris it seemed to me so unheard-of an act on your part, coming from you
who had struck me as well brought up and of a good *bourgeois* family," (on
this adjective alone his voice sounded a little whistle of impertinence) "that
I was foolish enough to imagine all the excuses that never really happen,
letters miscarrying, addresses copied down wrong. I can see that on my part
it was great foolishness, but Saint Bonaventure preferred to believe that an
ox could fly rather than that his brother was capable of lying. Anyhow, that
is all finished now, the idea did not attract you, there is no more to be said.
It seems to me only that you might have brought yourself," (and there was
a genuine sound of weeping in his voice) "were it only out of consideration
for my age, to write to me. I had conceived and planned for you certain
infinitely seductive things, which I had taken good care not to tell you. You
have preferred to refuse without knowing what they were; that is your
affair. But, as I tell you, one can always *write*. In your place, and indeed in
my own, I should have done so. I like my place, for that reason, better than
yours—I say 'for that reason' because I believe that we are all equal, and
I have more fellow-feeling for an intelligent labourer than for many of our
dukes. But I can say that I prefer my place to yours, because what you
have done, in the whole course of my life, which is beginning now to be a
pretty long one, I am conscious that I have never done." His head was
turned away from the light, and I could not see if his eyes were dropping
tears as I might have supposed from his voice. "I told you that I had taken
a hundred steps towards you; the only effect of that has been to make you
retire two hundred from me. Now it is for me to withdraw, and we shall
know one another no longer. I shall retain not your name but your story, so
that at moments when I might be tempted to believe that men have good
hearts, good manners, or simply the intelligence not to allow an unparalleled
opportunity to escape them, I may remember that that is ranking them too
highly. No, that you should have said that you knew me, when it was true

—for henceforward it ceases to be true—I regard that as only natural, and I take it as an act of homage, that is to say something pleasant. Unfortunately, elsewhere and in other circumstances, you have uttered remarks of a very different nature." "Sir, I swear to you that I have said nothing that could insult you." "And who says that I am insulted?" he cried with fury, flinging himself into an erect posture on the seat on which hitherto he had been reclining motionless, while, as the pale frothing serpents stiffened in his face, his voice became alternately shrill and grave, like the deafening onrush of a storm. (The force with which he habitually spoke, which used to make strangers turn round in the street, was multiplied an hundredfold, as is a musical *forte* if, instead of being played on the piano, it is played by an orchestra, and changed into a *fortissimo* as well. M. de Charlus roared.) "Do you suppose that it is within your power to insult me? You evidently are not aware to whom you are speaking? Do you imagine that the envenomed spittle of five hundred little gentlemen of your type, heaped one upon another, would succeed in slobbering so much as the tips of my august toes?" A moment before this my desire to persuade M. de Charlus that I had never said, nor heard anyone else say any evil of him had given place to a mad rage, caused by the words which were dictated to him solely, to my mind, by his colossal pride. Perhaps they were indeed the effect, in part at any rate, of this pride. Almost all the rest sprang from a feeling of which I was then still ignorant, and for which I could not therefore be blamed for not making due allowance. I could at least, failing this unknown element, have mingled with his pride, had I remembered the words of Mme. de Guermantes, a trace of madness. But at that moment the idea of madness never even entered my head. There was in him, according to me, only pride, in me there was only fury. This fury (at the moment when M. de Charlus ceased to shout, in order to refer to his august toes, with a majesty that was accompanied by a grimace, a nausea of disgust at his obscure blasphemers), this fury could contain itself no longer. With an impulsive movement, I wanted to strike something, and, a lingering trace of discernment making me respect the person of a man so much older than myself, and even, in view of their dignity as works of art, the pieces of German porcelain that were grouped around him, I flung myself upon the Baron's new silk hat, dashed it to the ground, trampled upon it, began blindly pulling it to pieces, wrenched off the brim, tore the crown in two, without heeding the vociferations of M. de Charlus, which continued to sound, and, crossing the room to leave it, opened the door. One on either side of it, to my intense stupefaction, stood two footmen, who moved slowly away, so as to appear only to have been casually passing in the course of their duty. (I afterwards learned their names; one was called Burnier, the other Charmel.) I was not taken in for a moment by this explanation which their leisurely gait seemed to offer me. It was highly improbable; three others appeared to me to be less so; one that the Baron sometimes entertained guests against whom, as he might happen to need assistance (but why?), he deemed it necessary to keep reinforcements posted close at hand. The second was that, drawn by curiosity, they had stopped to listen at the keyhole, not thinking that I should come out so quickly. The third, that,

the whole of the scene which M. de Charlus had made with me having
been prepared and acted, he had himself told them to listen, from a love
of the spectacular combined, perhaps, with a '*nunc crudimini*' from which
each would derive a suitable profit.

My anger had not calmed that of M. de Charlus, my departure from
the room seemed to cause him acute distress; he called me back, made his
servants call me back, and finally, forgetting that a moment earlier, when
he spoke of his 'august toes,' he had thought to make me a witness of his
own deification, came running after me at full speed, overtook me in the
hall, and stood barring the door. "There, now," he said, "don't be childish;
come back for a minute; he who loveth well chasteneth well, and if I have
chastened you well it is because I love you well." My anger had subsided;
I let the word 'chasten' pass, and followed the Baron, who, summoning
a footman, ordered him without a trace of self-consciousness to clear away
the remains of the shattered hat, which was replaced by another. "If you
will tell me, Sir, who it is that has treacherously maligned me," I said to
M. de Charlus, "I will stay here to learn his name and to confute the im-
postor." "Who? Do you not know? Do you retain no memory of the things
you say? Do you think that the people who do me the service of informing
me of those things do not begin by demanding secrecy? And do you imagine
that I am going to betray a person to whom I have given my promise?"
"Sir, is it impossible then for you to tell me?" I asked, racking my brains
in a final effort to discover (and discovering no one) to whom I could have
spoken about M. de Charlus. "You did not hear me say that I had given
a promise of secrecy to my informant?" he said in a snapping voice. "I
see that with your fondness for abject utterances you combine one for
futile persistence. You ought to have at least the intelligence to profit by
a final conversation, and so to speak as to say something that does not
mean precisely nothing." "Sir," I replied, moving away from him, "you
insult me; I am unarmed, because you are several times my age, we are
not equally matched; on the other hand, I cannot convince you; I have
already sworn to you that I have said nothing." "I am lying, then, am I?"
he cried in a terrifying tone, and with a bound forwards that brought him
within a yard of myself. "Some one has misinformed you." Then in a gentle, affectionate, melancholy voice, as in those symphonies which are played
without any break between the different movements, in which a graceful
scherzo, amiable and idyllic, follows the thunder-peals of the opening
pages: "It is quite possible," he told me. "Generally speaking, a remark
repeated at second hand is rarely true. It is your fault if, not having profited
by the opportunities of seeing me which I had held out to you, you have
not furnished me, by that open speech of daily intercourse which creates
confidence, with the unique and sovereign remedy against a spoken word
which made you out a traitor. Either way, true or false, the remark has
done its work. I can never again rid myself of the impression it made on
me. I cannot even say that he who chasteneth well loveth well, for I have
chastened you well enough but I no longer love you." While saying this he
had forced me to sit down and had rung the bell. A different footman appeared. "Bring something to drink and order the brougham." I said that

I was not thirsty and besides had a carriage waiting. "They have probably paid him and sent him away," he told me, "you needn't worry about that. I am ordering a carriage to take you home. . . . If you're anxious about the time . . . I could have given you a room here. . . ." I said that my mother would be uneasy. "Ah! Of course, yes. Well, true or false, the remark has done its work. My affection, a trifle premature, had flowered too soon, and, like those apple trees of which you spoke so poetically at Balbec, it has been unable to withstand the first frost." If M. de Charlus's affection for me had not been destroyed, he could hardly have acted differently, since, while assuring me that we were no longer acquainted, he made me sit down, drink, asked me to stay the night, and was going now to send me home. He had indeed an air of dreading the moment at which he must part from me and find himself alone, that sort of slightly anxious fear which his sister-in-law and cousin Guermantes had appeared to me to be feeling when she had tried to force me to stay a little longer, with something of the same momentary fondness for myself, of the same effort to prolong the passing minute. "Unfortunately," he went on, "I have not the power to make blossom again what has once been destroyed. My affection for you is quite dead. Nothing can revive it. I believe that it is not unworthy of me to confess that I regret it. I always feel myself to be a little like Victor Hugo's Boaz: 'I am widowed and alone, and the darkness gathers o'er me.' "

I passed again with him through the big green drawing-room. I told him, speaking quite at random, how beautiful I thought it. "Ain't it?" he replied. "It's a good thing to be fond of something. The woodwork is Bagard. What is rather charming, d'you see, is that it was made to match the Beauvais chairs and the consoles. You observe, it repeats the same decorative design. There used to be only two places where you could see this, the Louvre and M. d'Hinnisdal's house. But naturally, as soon as I had decided to come and live in this street, there cropped up an old family house of the Chimays which nobody had ever seen before because it came here expressly for *me*. On the whole, it's good. It might perhaps be better, but after all it's not bad. Some pretty things, ain't there? These are portraits of my uncles, the King of Poland and the King of England, by Mignard. But why am I telling you all this? You must know it as well as I do, you were waiting in this room. No? Ah, then they must have put you in the blue drawing-room," he said with an air that might have been either impertinence, on the score of my want of interest, or personal superiority, in not having taken the trouble to ask where I had been kept waiting. "Look now, in this cabinet I have all the hats worn by Mlle. Elisabeth, by the Princesse de Lamballe, and by the Queen. They don't interest you, one would think you couldn't see. Perhaps you are suffering from an affection of the optic nerve. If you like this kind of beauty better, here is a rainbow by Turner beginning to shine out between these two Rembrandts, as a sign of our reconciliation. You hear: Beethoven has come to join him." And indeed one could hear the first chords of the third part of the Pastoral Symphony, 'Joy after the Storm,' performed somewhere not far away, on the first landing no doubt, by a band of musicians. I innocently inquired how they happened to be playing that, and who the musicians were. "Ah, well, one doesn't know. One never does know. They are unseen music. Pretty, ain't it?" he said to me in a slightly impertinent tone, which, nevertheless, suggested somehow the influence and accent of Swann. "But you care about as much for it as a fish does for little apples. You want to go home, regardless of any want of respect for Beethoven or for me. You are uttering your own judgment and condemnation," he added, with an affectionate and mournful air, when the moment had come for me to go. "You will excuse my not accompanying you home, as good manners ordain that I should," he said to me. "Since I have decided not to see you again, spending five minutes more in your company would make very little difference to me. But I am tired, and I have a great deal to do." And then, seeing that it was a fine night: "Very well, yes, I will come in the carriage, there is a superb moon which I shall go on to admire from the Bois after I have taken you home. What, you don't know how to shave; even on a night when you've been dining out, you have still a few hairs here," he said, taking my chin between two fingers, so to speak magnetised, which after a moment's resistance ran up to my ears, like the fingers of a barber. "Ah! It would be pleasant to look at the 'blue light of the moon' in the Bois with some one like yourself," he said to me with a sudden and almost involuntary gentleness, then, in a sadder tone: "For you are nice, all the same; you could be nicer than anyone," he went on, laying his hand in a fatherly way on my shoulder. "Originally, I must say that I found you quite insignificant." I ought to have reflected that he must find me so still. I had only to recall the rage with which he had spoken to me, barely half an hour before. In spite of this I had the impression that he was, for the moment, sincere, that his kindness of heart was prevailing over what I regarded as an almost delirious condition of susceptibility and pride. The carriage was waiting beside us, and still he prolonged the conversation. "Come along," he said abruptly, "jump in, in five minutes we shall be at your door. And I shall bid you a good night which will cut short our relations, and for all time. It is better, since we must part for ever, that we should do so, as in music, on a perfect chord." Despite these solemn affirmations that we should never see one another again, I could have sworn that M. de Charlus, annoyed at having forgotten himself earlier in the evening and afraid of having hurt my feelings, would not have been displeased to see me once again. Nor was I mistaken, for, a moment later: "There, now," he said, "if I hadn't forgotten the most important thing of all. In memory of your grandmother, I have had bound for you a curious edition of Mme. de Sévigné. That is what is going to prevent this from being our last meeting. One must console oneself with the reflexion that complicated affairs are rarely settled in a day. Just look how long they took over the Congress of Vienna." "But I could call for it without disturbing you," I said obligingly. "Will you hold your tongue, you little fool," he replied with anger, "and not give yourself a grotesque appearance of regarding as a small matter the honour of being probably (I do not say certainly, for it will perhaps be one of my servants who hands you the volumes) received by me." Then, regaining possession of himself: "I do not wish to part from you on these words. No dissonance, before the eternal silence of the dominant." It was for his own nerves that he seemed to dread an immediate return home after harsh words of dissension. "You would not care to come to the Bois?" he addressed me in a tone not so much interrogative as affirmative, and that not, as it seemed to me, because he did not wish to make me the offer but because he was afraid that his self-esteem might meet with a refusal. "Oh, very well," he went on, still postponing our separation, "it is the moment when, as Whistler says, the *bourgeois* go to bed" (perhaps he wished now to capture me by my self-esteem) "and the right time to begin to look at things. But you don't even know who Whistler was!" I changed the conversation and asked him whether the Princesse d'Iéna was an intelligent person. M. de Charlus stopped me, and, adopting the most contemptuous tone that I had yet heard him use, "Oh! There, Sir," he informed me, "you are alluding to an order of nomenclature with which I have no concern. There is perhaps an aristocracy among the Tahitians, but I must confess that I know nothing about it. The name which you have just mentioned, strangely enough, did sound in my ears only a few days ago. Some one asked me whether I would condescend to allow them to present to me the young Duc de Guastalla. The request astonished me, for the Duc de Guastalla has no need to get himself presented to me, for the simple reason that he is my cousin, and has known me all his life; he is the son of the Princesse de Parme, and, as a young kinsman of good upbringing, he never fails to come and pay his respects to me on New Year's Day. But, on making inquiries, I discovered that it was not my relative who was meant but the son of the person in whom you are interested. As there exists no Princess of that title, I supposed that my friend was referring to some poor wanton sleeping under the Pont d'Iéna, who had picturesquely assumed the title of Princesse d'Iéna, just as one talks about the Panther of the Batignolles, or the Steel King. But no, the reference was to a rich person who possesses some remarkable furniture which I had seen and admired at an exhibition, and which has this advantage over the name of its owner that it is genuine. As for this self-styled Duc de Guastalla, he, I supposed, must be my secretary's stockbroker; one can procure so many things with money. But no; it was the Emperor, it appears, who amused himself by conferring on these people a title which simply was not his to give. It was perhaps a sign of power, or of ignorance, or of malice; in any case, I consider, it was an exceedingly scurvy trick to play on these unconscious usurpers. But really, I cannot help you by throwing any light on the matter; my knowledge begins and ends with the Faubourg Saint-Germain, where, among all the Courvoisiers and Gallardons, you will find, if you can manage to secure an introduction, plenty of mangy old cats taken straight out of Balzac who will amuse you. Naturally, all that has nothing to do with the position of the Princesse de Guermantes, but without me and my 'Open, Sesame' her portals are unapproachable." "It is really very lovely, isn't it, Sir, the Princesse de Guermantes's mansion?" "Oh, it's not very lovely. It's the loveliest thing in the world. Next to the Princess herself, of course." "The Princesse de Guermantes is better than the Duchesse de Guer-

mantes?" "Oh! There's no comparison." (It is to be observed that, whenever people in society have the least touch of imagination, they will crown
or dethrone, to suit their affections or their quarrels, those whose position
appeared most solid and unalterably fixed.)

"The Duchesse de Guermantes" (possibly, in not calling her 'Oriane,'
he wished to set a greater distance between her and myself) "is delightful,
far superior to anything you can have guessed. But, after all, she is in-
commensurable with her cousin. The Princess is exactly what the people
in the Markets might imagine Princess Metternich to have been, but old
Metternich believed she had started Wagner, because she knew Victor
Maurel. The Princesse de Guermantes, or rather her mother, knew the
man himself. Which is a distinction, not to mention the incredible beauty
of the lady. And the Esther gardens alone!" "One can't see them?" "No,
you would have to be invited, but they never invite *anyone* unless I intervene." But at once withdrawing, after casting it at me, the bait of this
offer, he held out his hand, for we had reached my door. "My part is played,
Sir, I will simply add these few words. Another person will perhaps some
day offer you his affection, as I have done. Let the present example serve
for your instruction. Do not neglect it. Affection is always precious. What
one cannot do by oneself in this life, because there are things which one
cannot ask, nor do, nor wish, nor learn by oneself, one can do in company,
and without needing to be Thirteen, as in Balzac's story, or Four, as in
The Three Musketeers. Good-bye."

He must have been feeling tired and have abandoned the idea of going
to look at the moonlight, for he asked me to tell his coachman to drive
home. At once he made a sharp movement as though he had changed his
mind. But I had already given the order, and, so as not to lose any more
time, went across now to ring the bell, without its entering my head that
I had been meaning to tell M. de Charlus, about the German Emperor
and General Botha, stories which had been an hour ago such an obsession
but which his unexpected and crushing reception had sent flying far out
of my mind.

On entering my room I saw on my desk a letter which Françoise's young
footman had written to one of his friends and had left lying there. Now
that my mother was away, there was no liberty which he had the least
hesitation in taking; I was the more to blame of the two for taking that
of reading the letter which, without an envelope, lay spread out before
me and (which was my sole excuse) seemed to offer itself to my eye.

"Dear Friend and Cousin,

"I hope this finds you in good health, and the same with all the young folk,
particularly my young godson Joseph whom I have not yet had the pleasure of
meeting but whom I prefer to you all as being my godson, these relics of the
heart they have their dust also, upon their blest remains let us not lay our hands.
Besides dear friend and cousin who can say that to-morrow you and your dear
wife my cousin Marie, will not both of you be cast headlong down into the
bottom of the sea, like the sailor clinging to the mast on high, for this life is but
a dark valley. Dear friend I must tell you that my principal occupation, which
will astonish you I am certain, is now poetry which I love passionately, for one

must somehow pass the time away. And so dear friend do not be too surprised
if I have not answered your last letter before now, in place of pardon let oblivion
come. As you are aware, Madame's mother has passed away amid unspeakable
sufferings which fairly exhausted her as she saw as many as three doctors. The
day of her interment was a great day for all Monsieur's relations came in crowds
as well as several Ministers. It took them more than two hours to get to the
cemetery, which will make you all open your eyes pretty wide in your village
for they certainly won't do as much for mother Michu. So all my life to come
can be but one long sob. I am amusing myself enormously with the motorcycle
of which I have recently learned. What would you say, my dear friends, if I
arrived suddenly like that at full speed at Les Ecorces. But on that head I shall
no more keep silence for I feel that the frenzy of grief sweeps its reason away.
I am associating with the Duchesse de Guermantes, people whose very names
you have never heard in our ignorant villages. Therefore it is with pleasure that
I am going to send the works of Racine, of Victor Hugo, of Pages Choisies de
Chenedolle, of Alfred de Musset, for I would cure the land in which I saw the
light of ignorance which leads unerringly to crime. I can think of nothing more
to say to you and send you like the pelican wearied by a long flight my best
regards as well as to your wife my godson and your sister Rose. May it never
be said of her: And Rose she lived only as live the roses, as has been said by
Victor Hugo, the sonnet of Arvers, Alfred de Musset, all those great geniuses
who for that cause have had to die upon the blazing scaffold like Jeanne d'Arc.
Hoping for your next letter soon, receive my kisses like those of a brother.
                                                                    "Périgot (Joseph)."

We are attracted by every form of life which represents to us something
unknown and strange, by a last illusion still unshattered. In spite of this,
the mysterious utterances by means of which M. de Charlus had led me
to imagine the Princesse de Guermantes as an extraordinary creature,
different from anyone that I knew, were not sufficient to account for the
stupefaction in which I was plunged, speedily followed by the fear that
I might be the victim of some bad joke planned by some one who wanted
to send me to the door of a house to which I had not been invited, when,
about two months after my dinner with the Duchess and while she was
at Cannes, having opened an envelope the appearance of which had not
led me to suppose that it contained anything out of the common, I read
the following words engraved on a card: "The Princesse de Guermantes,
née Duchesse en Bavière, At Home, the ——th." No doubt to be invited
to the Princesse de Guermantes's was perhaps not, from the social point
of view, any more difficult than to dine with the Duchess, and my slight
knowledge of heraldry had taught me that the title of Prince is not superior
to that of Duke. Besides, I told myself that the intelligence of a society
woman could not be essentially so heterogeneous to that of her congeners
as M. de Charlus made out, nor so heterogeneous to that of any one other
woman in society. But my imagination, like Elstir engaged upon rendering
some effect of perspective without reference to a knowledge of the laws of
nature which he might quite well possess, depicted for me not what I knew
but what it saw; what it saw, that is to say what the name shewed it. Now,
even before I had met the Duchess, the name Guermantes preceded by

the title of Princess, like a note or a colour or quantity, profoundly modified from the surrounding values by the mathematical or aesthetic sign
that governs it, had already suggested to me something entirely different.
With that title one finds one's thoughts straying instinctively to the memoirs
of the days of Louis XIII and Louis XIV, the English Court, the Queen
of Scots, the Duchesse d'Aumale; and I imagined the town house of the
Princesse de Guermantes as more or less frequented by the Duchesse de
Longueville and the great Condé, whose presence there rendered it highly
improbable that I should ever make my way into it.

Many of the things that M. de Charlus had told me had driven a vigorous spur into my imagination and, making it forget how much the reality
had disappointed me at Mme. de Guermantes's (people's names are in
this respect like the names of places), had swung it towards Oriane's cousin.
For that matter, M. de Charlus misled me at times as to the imaginary
value and variety of people in society only because he was himself at times
misled. And this, perhaps, because he did nothing, did not write, did not
paint, did not even read anything in a serious and thorough manner. But,
superior by several degrees to the people in society, if it was from them
and the spectacle they afforded that he drew the material for his conversation, he was not for that reason understood by them. Speaking as
an artist, he could at the most reveal the fallacious charm of people in
society. But reveal it to artists alone, with relation to whom he might be
said to play the part played by the reindeer among the Esquimaux. This
precious animal plucks for them from the barren rocks lichens and mosses
which they themselves could neither discover nor utilise, but which, once
they have been digested by the reindeer, become for the inhabitants of the
far North a nourishing form of food.

To which I may add that the pictures which M. de Charlus drew of
society were animated with plenty of life by the blend of his ferocious
hatreds and his passionate affections. Hatreds directed mainly against the
young men, adoration aroused principally by certain women.

If among these the Princesse de Guermantes was placed by M. de Charlus
upon the most exalted throne, his mysterious words about the 'unapproachable Aladdin's palace' in which his cousin dwelt were not sufficient to
account for my stupefaction. Apart from whatever may be due to the
divers subjective points of view, of which I shall have to speak later, in
these artificial magnifications, the fact remains that there is a certain objective reality in each of these people, and consequently a difference among
them. And how, when it comes to that, could it be otherwise? The humanity with which we consort and which bears so little resemblance to
our dreams is, for all that, the same that, in the Memoirs, in the Letters
of eminent persons, we have seen described and have felt a desire to know.
The old man of complete insignificance whom we met at dinner is the
same who wrote that proud letter, which (in a book on the War of 1870)
we read with emotion, to Prince Friedrich-Karl. We are bored at a dinner-
table because our imagination is absent, and because it is bearing us company we are interested in a book. But the people in question are the same.
We should like to have known Mme. de Pompadour, who was so valuable

a patron of the arts, and we should have been as much bored in her company as among the modern Egerias, at whose houses we cannot bring ourselves to pay a second call, so uninteresting do we find them. The fact
remains, nevertheless, that these differences do exist. People are never
exactly similar to one another, their mode of behaviour with regard to ourselves, at, one might say, the same level of friendship, reveals differences
which, in the end, offer compensations. When I knew Mme. de Montmorency, she loved to say unpleasant things to me, but if I was in need
of a service she would squander, in the hope of obtaining it for me effectively, all the credit at her disposal, without counting the cost. Whereas
some other woman, Mme. de Guermantes for example, would never have
wished to hurt my feelings, never said anything about me except what
might give me pleasure, showered on me all those tokens of friendship
which formed the rich manner of living, morally, of the Guermantes, but,
had I asked her for the least thing above and beyond that, would not have
moved an inch to procure it for me, as in those country houses where one
has at one's disposal a motor-car and a special footman, but where it is
impossible to obtain a glass of cider, for which no provision has been made
in the arrangements for a party. Which was for me the true friend, Mme.
de Montmorency, so glad always to annoy me and always so ready to
oblige, or Mme. de Guermantes, distressed by the slightest offence that
might have been given me and incapable of the slightest effort to be of
use to me? The types of the human mind are so varied, so opposite, not
only in literature but in society, that Baudelaire and Mérimée are not the
only people who have the right to despise one another mutually. These
peculiarities continue to form in everyone a system of attitudes, of speech,
of actions, so coherent, so despotic, that when we are in the presence of
anyone his or her system seems to us superior to the rest. With Mme. de
Guermantes, her words, deduced like a theorem from her type of mind,
seemed to me the only ones that could possibly be said. And I was, at heart,
of her opinion when she told me that Mme. de Montmorency was stupid
and kept an open mind towards all the things she did not understand, or
when, having heard of some spiteful remark by that lady, she said: "That
is what you call a good woman; it is what I call a monster." But this
tyranny of the reality which confronts us, this preponderance of the lamp-
light which turns the dawn—already distant—as pale as the faintest
memory, disappeared when I was away from Mme. de Guermantes, and
a different lady said to me, putting herself on my level and reckoning the
Duchess as placed far below either of us: "Oriane takes no interest, really,
in anything or anybody," or even (what in the presence of Mme. de Guermantes it would have seemed impossible to believe, so loudly did she herself
proclaim the opposite): "Oriane is a snob." Seeing that no mathematical
process would have enabled one to convert Mme. d'Arpajon and Mme.
de Montpensier into commensurable quantities, it would have been impossible for me to reply, had anyone asked me which of the two seemed to
me superior to the other.

Now, among the peculiar characteristics of the drawing-room of the
Princesse de Guermantes, the one most generally quoted was a certain

exclusiveness, due in part to the royal birth of the Princess, but especially
to the almost fossilised rigidity of the aristocratic prejudices of the Prince,
prejudices which, incidentally, the Duke and Duchess had made no scruple
about deriding in front of me, and which naturally were to make me regard
it as more improbable than ever that I should have been invited to a party
by this man who reckoned only in royalties and dukes, and at every dinner-
party made a scene because he had not been put in the place to which
he would have been entitled under Louis XIV, a place which, thanks to
his immense erudition in matters of history and genealogy, he was the
only person who knew. For this reason, many of the people in society
placed to the credit of the Duke and Duchess the differences which distinguished them from their cousins. "The Duke and Duchess are far more
modern, far more intelligent, they don't think of nothing, like the other
couple, but how many quarterings one has, their house is three hundred
years in advance of their cousins'," were customary remarks, the memory
of which made me tremble as I looked at the card of invitation, to which
they gave a far greater probability of its having been sent me by some
practical joker.

If the Duke and Duchess had not been still at Cannes, I might have
tried to find out from them whether the invitation which I had received
was genuine. This state of doubt in which I was plunged was not due, as
I flattered myself for a time by supposing, to a sentiment which a man of
fashion would not have felt and which, consequently, a writer, even if he
belonged apart from his writership to the fashionable caste, ought to reproduce in order to be thoroughly 'objective' and to depict each class differently. I happened, in fact, only the other day, in a charming volume of
memoirs, to come upon the record of uncertainties analogous to those which
the Princesse de Guermantes's card made me undergo. "Georges and I"
(or "Hély and I," I have not the book at hand to verify the reference)
"were so keen to be asked to Mme. Delessert's that, having received an
invitation from her, we thought it prudent, each of us independently, to
make certain that we were not the victims of an April fool." Now, the
writer is none other than the Comte d'Haussonville (he who married the
Duc de Broglie's daughter) and the other young man who 'independently'
makes sure that he is not having a practical joke played on him is, according to whether he is called Georges or Hély, one or other of the two inseparable friends of M. d'Haussonville, either M. d'Harcourt or the Prince
de Chalais.

The day on which the party was to be given at the Princesse de Guermantes's, I learned that the Duke and Duchess had just returned to Paris.
The Princess's ball would not have brought them back, but one of their
cousins was seriously ill, and moreover the Duke was greatly taken up
with a revel which was to be held the same night, and at which he himself
was to appear as Louis XI and his wife as Isabel of Bavaria. And I determined to go and see her that morning. But, having gone out early, they
had not yet returned; I watched first of all from a little room, which had
seemed to me to be a good look-out post, for the arrival of their carriage.
As a matter of fact I had made a singularly bad choice in my observatory

from which I could barely make out our courtyard, but I did see into several
others, and this, though of no value to me, occupied my mind for a time.
It is not only in Venice that one has those outlooks on to several houses
at once which have proved so tempting to painters; it is just the same in
Paris. Nor do I cite Venice at random. It is of its poorer quarters that
certain poor quarters of Paris make one think, in the morning, with their
tall, wide chimneys to which the sun imparts the most vivid pinks, the
brightest reds; it is a whole garden that flowers above the houses, and
flowers in such a variety of tints that one would call it, planted on top of
the town, the garden of a tulip-fancier of Delft or Haarlem. And then also,
the extreme proximity of the houses, with their windows looking opposite
one another on to a common courtyard, makes of each casement the frame
in which a cook sits dreamily gazing down at the ground below, in which
farther off a girl is having her hair combed by an old woman with the face,
barely distinguishable in the shadow, of a witch: thus each courtyard provides for the adjoining house, by suppressing all sound in its interval, by
leaving visible a series of silent gestures in a series of rectangular frames,
glazed by the closing of the windows, an exhibition of a hundred Dutch
paintings hung in rows. Certainly from the Hôtel de Guermantes one did
not have the same kind of view, but one had curious views also, especially
from the strange trigonometrical point at which I had placed myself and
from which one's gaze was arrested by nothing nearer than the distant
heights formed by the comparatively vague plots of ground which preceded,
on a steep slope, the mansion of the Marquise de Plassac and Mme. de
Tresmes, cousins (of the most noble category) of M. de Guermantes, whom
I did not know. Between me and this house (which was that of their father,
M. de Bréquigny) nothing but blocks of buildings of low elevation, facing·
in every conceivable direction, which, without blocking the view, increased
the distance with their diagonal perspective. The red-tiled turret of the
coach-house in which the Marquis de Frécourt kept his carriages did indeed
end in a spire that rose rather higher, but was so slender that it concealed
nothing, and made one think of those picturesque old buildings in Switzer-
land which spring up in isolation at the foot of a mountain. All these vague
and divergent points on which my eyes rested made more distant apparently than if it had been separated from us by several streets or by a series
of foothills the house of Mme. de Plassac, actually quite near but chimeri-
cally remote as in an Alpine landscape. When its large paned windows,
glittering in the sunlight like flakes of rock crystal, were thrown open so
as to air the rooms, one felt, in following from one floor to the next the
footmen whom it was impossible to see clearly but who were visibly shaking carpets, the same pleasure as when one sees in a landscape by Turner
or Elstir a traveller in a mail-coach, or a guide, at different degrees of
altitude on the Saint-Gothard. But from this point of view in which I had
ensconced myself I should have been in danger of not seeing M. or Mme.
de Guermantes come in, so that when in the afternoon I was free to resume
my survey I simply stood on the staircase, from which the opening of the
carriage-gate could not escape my notice, and it was on this staircase that
I posted myself, albeit there did not appear there, so entrancing with their

footmen rendered minute by distance and busily cleaning, the Alpine beauties of the Bréquigny-Tresmes mansion. Now this wait on the staircase
was to have for me consequences so considerable, and to reveal to me a
picture no longer Turneresque but ethical, of so great importance, that it
is preferable to postpone the account of it for a little while by interposing
first that of my visit to the Guermantes when I knew that they had come
home. It was the Duke alone who received me in the library. As I went
in there came out a little man with snow-white hair, a look of poverty, a
little black neckcloth such as was worn by the lawyer at Combray and
by several of my grandfather's friends, but of a more timid aspect than
they, who, making me a series of profound bows, refused absolutely to go
downstairs until I had passed him. The Duke shouted after him from the
library something which I did not understand, and the other responded
with further bows, addressed to the wall, for the Duke could not see him,
but endlessly repeated nevertheless, like the purposeless smiles on the faces
of people who are talking to one over the telephone; he had a falsetto
voice, and saluted me afresh with the humility of a man of business. And
he might, for that matter, have been a man of business from Combray,
so much was he in the style, provincial, out of date and mild, of the small
folk, the modest elders of those parts. "You shall see Oriane in a minute,"
the Duke told me when I had entered the room. "As Swann is coming in
presently and bringing her the proofs of his book on the coinage of the
Order of Malta, and, what is worse, an immense photograph he has had
taken shewing both sides of each of the coins, Oriane preferred to get
dressed early so that she can stay with him until it's time to go out to
dinner. We have such a heap of things in the house already that we don't
know where to put them all, and I ask myself where on earth we are going
to stick this photograph. But I have too good-natured a wife, who is too
fond of giving people pleasure. She thought it would be polite to ask Swann
to let her see side by side on one sheet the heads of all those Grand Masters
of the Order whose medals he has found at Rhodes. I said Malta, didn't
I, it is Rhodes, but it's all the same Order of Saint John of Jerusalem. As
a matter of fact, she is interested in them only because Swann makes a
hobby of it. Our family is very much mixed up in the whole story; even
at the present day, my brother, whom you know, is one of the highest
dignitaries in the Order of Malta. But I might have told all that to Oriane,
she simply wouldn't have listened to me. On the other hand, it was quite
enough that Swann's researches into the Templars (it's astonishing the
passion that people of one religion have for studying others) should have
led him on to the history of the Knights of Rhodes, who succeeded the
Templars, for Oriane at once to insist on seeing the heads of these Knights.
They were very small fry indeed compared with the Lusignans, Kings of
Cyprus, from whom we descend in a direct line. But so far, as Swann
hasn't taken them up, Oriane doesn't care to hear anything about the
Lusignans." I could not at once explain to the Duke why I had come. What
happened was that several relatives or friends, including Mme. de Silistrie and the Duchesse de Montrose, came to pay a call on the Duchess,
who was often at home before dinner, and not finding her there stayed

for a short while with the Duke. The first of these ladies (the Princesse de Silistrie), simply attired, with a dry but friendly manner, carried a stick in her hand. I was afraid at first that she had injured herself, or was a cripple. She was on the contrary most alert. She spoke regretfully to the Duke of a first cousin of his own—not on the Guermantes side, but more illustrious still, were that possible—whose health, which had been in a grave condition for some time past, had grown suddenly worse. But it was evident that the Duke, while full of pity for his cousin's lot, and repeating "Poor Mama! He's such a good fellow!" had formed a favourable prognosis. The fact was that the dinner at which the Duke was to be present amused him, the big party at the Princesse de Guermantes's did not bore him, but above all he was to go on at one o'clock in the morning with his wife to a great supper and costume ball, with a view to which a costume of Louis XI for himself, and one of Isabel of Bavaria for his wife were waiting in readiness. And the Duke was determined not to be disturbed amid all these gaieties by the sufferings of the worthy Amanien d'Osmond. Two other ladies carrying sticks, Mme. de Plassac and Mme. de Tresmes, both daughters of the Comte de Bréquigny, came in next to pay Basin a visit, and declared that cousin Mama's state left no room now for hope. The Duke shrugged his shoulders, and to change the conversation asked whether they were going that evening to Marie-Gilbert's. They replied that they were not, in view of the state of Amanien who was in his last agony, and indeed they had excused themselves from the dinner to which the Duke was going, the other guests at which they proceeded to enumerate: the brother of King Theodosius, the Infanta Maria Concepcion, and so forth. As the Marquis d'Osmond was less nearly related to them than he was to Basin, their 'defection' appeared to the Duke to be a sort of indirect reproach aimed at his own conduct. And so, albeit they had come down from the heights of the Bréquigny mansion to see the Duchess (or rather to announce to her the alarming character, incompatible for his relatives with attendance at social gatherings, of their cousin's illness) they did not stay long, and, each armed with her alpenstock, Walpurge and Doro-thée (such were the names of the two sisters) retraced the craggy path to their citadel. I never thought of asking the Guermantes what was the meaning of these sticks, so common in a certain part of the Faubourg Saint-Germain. Possibly, looking upon the whole parish as their domain, and not caring to hire cabs, they were in the habit of taking long walks, for which some old fracture, due to immoderate indulgence in the chase, and to the falls from horseback which are often the fruit of that indulgence, or simply rheumatism caused by the dampness of the left bank and of old country houses made a stick necessary. Perhaps they had not set out upon any such long expedition through the quarter, but, having merely come down into their garden (which lay at no distance from that of the Duchess) to pick the fruit required for stewing, had looked in on their way home to bid good evening to Mme. de Guermantes, though without going so far as to bring a pair of shears or a watering-can into her house. The Duke appeared touched that I should have come to see them so soon after their return to Paris. But his face grew dark when I told him that I had come to ask his wife to find out whether her cousin really had invited me. I had touched upon one of those services which M. and Mme. de Guermantes were not fond of rendering. The Duke explained to me that it was too late, that if the Princess had not sent me an invitation it would make him appear to be asking her for one, that his cousins had refused him one once before, and he had no wish to appear either directly or indirectly to be interfering with their visiting list, be 'meddling'; finally, he could not even be sure that he and his wife, who were dining out that evening, would not come straight home afterwards, that in that case their best excuse for not having gone to the Princess's party would be to conceal from her the fact of their return to Paris, instead of hastening to inform her of it, as they must do if they sent her a note, or spoke to her over the telephone about me, and certainly too late to be of any use, since, in all probability, the Princess's list of guests would be closed by now. "You've not fallen foul of her in any way?" he asked in a suspicious tone, the Guermantes living in a constant fear of not being informed of the latest society quarrels, and so of people's trying to climb back into favour on their shoulders. Finally, as the Duke was in the habit of taking upon himself all decisions that might seem not very good-natured: "Listen, my boy," he said to me suddenly, as though the idea had just come into his head, "I would really rather not mention at all to Oriane that you have been speaking to me about it. You know how kind-hearted she is; besides, she has an enormous regard for you, she would insist on sending to ask her cousin, in spite of anything I might say to the contrary, and if she is tired after dinner, there will be no getting out of it, she will be forced to go to the party. No, decidedly, I shall say nothing to her about it. Anyhow, you will see her yourself in a minute. But not a word about that matter, I beg of you. If you decide to go to the party, I have no need to tell you what a pleasure it will be to us to spend the evening there with you." The motives actuating humanity are too sacred for him before whom they are invoked not to bow to them, whether he believes them to be sincere or not; I did not wish to appear to be weighing in the balance for a moment the relative importance of my invitation and the possible tiredness of Mme. de Guermantes, and I promised not to speak to her of the object of my visit, exactly as though I had been taken in by the little farce which M. de Guermantes had performed for my benefit. I asked him if he thought there was any chance of my seeing Mme. de Stermaria at the Princess's. "Why, no," he replied with the air of an expert; "I know the name you mention, from having seen it in lists of club members, it is not at all the type of person who goes to Gilbert's. You will see nobody there who is not excessively proper and intensely boring, duchesses bearing titles which one thought were extinct years ago and which they have revived for the occasion, all the Ambassadors, heaps of Coburgs, foreign royalties, but you mustn't hope for the ghost of a Stermaria. Gilbert would be taken ill at the mere thought of such a thing.

"Wait now, you're fond of painting, I must shew you a superb picture I bought from my cousin, partly in exchange for the Elstirs, which frankly did not appeal to us. It was sold to me as a Philippe de Champaigne, but

I believe myself that it's by some one even greater. Would you like to know my idea? I believe it to be a Velazquez, and of the best period," said the Duke, looking me boldly in the eyes, whether to learn my impression or in the hope of enhancing it. A footman came in. "Mme. la Duchesse has told me to ask M. le Duc if M. le Duc will be so good as to see M. Swann, as Mme.-la Duchesse is not quite ready." "Shew M. Swann in," said the Duke, after looking at his watch and seeing that he had still a few minutes before he need go to dress. "Naturally my wife, who told him to come, is not ready. There's no use saying anything before Swann about Marie-Gilbert's party," said the Duke. "I don't know whether he's been invited. Gilbert likes him immensely, because he believes him to be the natural grandson of the Duc de Berri, but that's a long story. (Otherwise, you can imagine! My cousin, who falls in a fit if he sees a Jew a mile off.) But now, don't you see, the Dreyfus case has made things more serious. Swann ought to have realised that he more than anyone must drop all connexion with those fellows, instead of which he says the most offensive things." The Duke called back the footman to know whether the man who had been sent to inquire at cousin Osmond's had returned. His plan was as follows: as he believed, and rightly, that his cousin was dying, he was anxious to obtain news of him before his death, that is to say before he was obliged to go into mourning. Once covered by the official certainty that Amanien was still alive, he could go without a thought to his dinner, to the Prince's party, to the midnight revel at which he would appear as Louis XI, and had made the most exciting assignation with a new mistress, and would make no more inquiries until the following day, when his pleasures would be at an end. Then one would put on mourning if the cousin had passed away in the night. "No, M. le Duc, he is not back yet." "What in the Name of God! Nothing is ever done in this house till the last minute," cried the Duke, at the thought that Amanien might still be in time to 'croak' for an evening paper, and so make him miss his revel. He sent for the *Temps*, in which there was nothing. I had not seen Swann for a long time, and asked myself at first whether in the old days he used to clip his moustache, or had not his hair brushed up vertically in front, for I found in him something altered; it was simply that he was indeed greatly 'altered' because he was very ill, and illness produces in the face modifications as profound as are created by growing a beard or by changing the line of one's parting. (Swann's illness was the same that had killed his mother, who had been attacked by it at precisely the age which he had now reached. Our existences are in truth, owing to heredity, as full of cabalistic ciphers, of horoscopic castings as if there really were sorcerers in the world. And just as there is a certain duration of life for humanity in general, so there is one for families in particular, that is to say, in any one family, for the members of it who resemble one another.) Swann was dressed with an elegance which, like that of his wife, associated with what he now was what he once had been. Buttoned up in a pearl-grey frockcoat which emphasised the tallness of his figure, slender, his white gloves stitched in black, he carried a grey tall hat of a specially wide shape which Delion had ceased now to make except for

him, the Prince de Sagan, the Marquis de Modène, M. Charles Haas and
Comte Louis de Turenne. I was surprised at the charming smile and
affectionate handclasp with which he replied to my greeting, for I had
imagined that after so long an interval he would not recognise me at once;
I told him of my astonishment; he received it with a shout of laughter, a
trace of indignation and a further grip of my hand, as if it were throwing
doubt on the soundness of his brain or the sincerity of his affection to
suppose that he did not know me. And yet that was what had happened;
he did not identify me, as I learned long afterwards, until several minutes
later when he heard my name mentioned. But no change in his face, in his
speech, in the things he said to me betrayed the discovery which a chance
word from M. de Guermantes had enabled him to make, with such mastery, with such absolute sureness did he play the social game. He brought
to it, moreover, that spontaneity in manners and personal initiative, even
in his style of dress, which characterised the Guermantes type. Thus it
was that the greeting which the old clubman, without recognising me, had
given me was not the cold and stiff greeting of the man of the world who
was a pure formalist, but a greeting full of a real friendliness, of a true
charm, such as the Duchesse de Guermantes, for instance, possessed (carrying it so far as to smile at you first, before you had bowed to her, if
she met you in the street), in contrast to the more mechanical greeting
customary among the ladies of the Faubourg Saint-Germain. In the same
way, again, the hat which, in conformity with a custom that was beginning to disappear, he laid on the floor by his feet, was lined with green
leather, a thing not usually done, because, according to him, this kept
the hat much cleaner, in reality because it was highly becoming. "Now,
Charles, you're a great expert, come and see what I've got to shew you,
after which, my boys, I'm going to ask your permission to leave you together for a moment while I go and change my clothes, besides, I expect
Oriane won't be long now." And he shewed his 'Velazquez' to Swann. "But
it seems to me that I know this," said Swann with the grimace of a sick
man for whom the mere act of speaking requires an effort. "Yes," said
the Duke, turned serious by the time which the expert took in expressing
his admiration. "You have probably seen it at Gilbert's." "Oh, yes, of
course, I remember." "What do you suppose it is?" "Oh, well, if it comes
from Gilbert's, it is probably one of your *ancestors*," said Swann with a
blend of irony and deference towards a form of greatness which he would
have felt it impolite and absurd to despise, but to which for reasons of
good taste he preferred to make only a playful reference.

"To be sure, it is," said the Duke bluntly. "It's Boson, the I forget how
manieth de Guermantes. Not that I care a damn about that. You know
I'm not as feudal as my cousin. I've heard the names mentioned of Rigaud,
Mignard, Velazquez even!" he went on, fastening on Swann the gaze of
an inquisitor and executioner in an attempt at once to read into his mind
and to influence his response. "Well," he concluded, for when he was led
to provoke artificially an opinion which he desired to hear, he had the
faculty, after a few moments, of believing that it had been spontaneously
uttered; "come, now, none of your flattery, do you think it's by one of

those big masters I've mentioned?" "Nnnnno," said Swann. "But after all, I know nothing about these things, it's not for me to decide who daubed the canvas. But you're a dilettante, a master of the subject, to whom do you attribute it? You're enough of an expert to have some idea. What would you put it down as?" Swann hesitated for a moment before the picture, which obviously he thought atrocious. "A bad joke!" he replied, with a smile at the Duke who could not check an impulsive movement of rage. When this had subsided: "Be good fellows, both of you, wait a moment for Oriane, I must go and put on my swallow-tails and then I'll join you. I shall send word to my good woman that you're both waiting for her." I talked for a minute or two with Swann about the Dreyfus case, and asked him how it was that all the Guermantes were anti-Dreyfusards. "In the first place because at heart all these people are anti-Semites," replied Swann, who, all the same, knew very well from experience that certain of them were not, but, like everyone who supports any cause with ardour, preferred, to explain the fact that other people did not share his opinion, to suppose in them a preconceived reason, a prejudice against which there was nothing to be done, rather than reasons which might permit of discussion. Besides, having come to the premature term of his life, like a weary animal that is goaded on, he cried out against these persecutions and was returning to the spiritual fold of his fathers. "Yes, the Prince de Guermantes," I said, "it is true, I've heard that he was anti-semitic." "Oh, that fellow! I wasn't even thinking about him. He carries it to such a point that when he was in the army and had a frightful tooth-ache he preferred to grin and bear it rather than go to the only dentist in the district, who happened to be a Jew, and later on he allowed a wing of his castle which had caught fire to be burned to the ground, because he would have had to send for extinguishers to the place next door, which belongs to the Rothschilds." "Are you going to be there this evening, by any chance?" "Yes," Swann replied, "although I am far too tired. But he sent me a wire to tell me that he has something to say to me. I feel that I shall be too unwell in the next few days to go there or to see him at home; it would upset me, so I prefer to get it over at once." "But the Duc de Guermantes is not anti-semitic?" "You can see quite well that he is, since he's an anti-Dreyfusard," replied Swann, without noticing the logical fallacy. "That doesn't prevent my being very sorry that I disappointed the man—what am I saying? The Duke, I mean—by not admiring his Mignard or whatever he calls it." "But at any rate," I went on, reverting to the Dreyfus case, "the Duchess, she, now, is intelligent." "Yes, she is charming. To my mind, however, she was even more charming when she was still known as the Princesse des Laumes. Her mind has become some-how more angular, it was all much softer in the juvenile great lady, but after all, young or old, men or women, what can you expect, all these peo-ple belong to a different race, one can't have a thousand years of feudalism in one's blood with impunity. Naturally they imagine that it counts for nothing in their opinions." "All the same, Robert de Saint-Loup is a Drey-fusard." "Ah! So much the better, all the more as you know that his mother is extremely 'anti.' I had heard that he was, but I wasn't certain of it. That gives me a great deal of pleasure. It doesn't surprise me, he's highly intelligent. It's a great thing, that is."

Dreyfusism had brought to Swann an extraordinary simplicity of mind and had imparted to his way of looking at things an impulsiveness, an inconsistency more noticeable even than had been the similar effects of his marriage to Odette; this new loss of caste would have been better described as a recasting, and was entirely to his credit, since it made him return to the ways in which his forebears had trodden and from which he had turned aside to mix with the aristocracy. But Swann, just at the very moment when with such lucidity it had been granted to him, thanks to the gifts he had inherited from his race, to perceive a truth that was still hidden from people of fashion, shewed himself nevertheless quite comically blind. He subjected afresh all his admirations and all his contempts to the test of a new criterion, Dreyfusism. That the anti-Dreyfusism of Mme. Bontemps should have made him think her a fool was no more astonishing than that, when he was first married, he should have thought her intelligent. It was not very serious either that the new wave reached also his political judgments and made him lose all memory of having treated as a man with a price, a British spy (this latter was an absurdity of the Guermantes set), Clemenceau, whom he declared now to have always stood up for conscience, to be a man of iron, like Cornély. "No, no, I never told you anything of the sort. You're thinking of some one else." But, sweeping past his political judgments, the wave overthrew in Swann his literary judgments also, and even affected his way of pronouncing them. Barrès had lost all his talent, and even the books of his early days were feeble, one could hardly read them again. "You try, you'll find you can't struggle to the end. What a difference from Clemenceau! Personally, I am not anticlerical, but when you compare them together you must see that Barrès is invertebrate. He's a very great fellow, is old Clemenceau. How he knows the language!" However, the anti-Dreyfusards were in no position to criticise these follies. They explained that one was a Dreyfusard by one's being of Jewish origin. If a practising Catholic like Saniette stood out also for a fresh trial, that was because he was buttonholed by Mme. Verdurin, who behaved like a wild Radical. She was out above all things against the 'frocks.' Saniette was more fool than knave, and had no idea of the harm that the Mistress was doing him. If you pointed out that Brichot was equally a friend of Mme. Verdurin and was a member of the Patrie Française, that was because he was more intelligent. "You see him occasionally?" I asked Swann, referring to Saint-Loup. "No, never. He wrote to me the other day hoping that I would ask the Duc de Mouchy and various other people to vote for him at the Jockey, where for that matter he got through like a letter through the post." "In spite of the Case!" "The question was never raised. However I must tell you that since all this business began I never set foot in the place."

M. de Guermantes returned, and was presently joined by his wife, all ready now for the evening, tall and proud in a gown of red satin the skirt of which was bordered with spangles. She had in her hair a long ostrich feather dyed purple, and over her shoulders a tulle scarf of the same red as her dress. "How nice it is to have one's hat lined with leather," said the Duchess, whom nothing escaped. "However, with you, Charles, everything is always charming, whether it's what you wear or what you say, what you read or what you do." Swann meanwhile, without apparently listening, was considering the Duchess as he would have studied the canvas of a master, and then sought her gaze, making with his lips the grimace which implies: 'The devil!' Mme. de Guermantes rippled with laughter. "So my clothes please you? I'm delighted. But I must say that they don't please me much," she went on with a sulking air. "Good Lord, what a bore it is to have to dress up and go out when one would ever so much rather stay at home!" "What magnificent rubies!" "Ah! my dear Charles, at least one can see that you know what you're talking about, you're not like that brute Monserfeuil who asked me if they were real. I must say that I've never seen anything quite like them. They were a present from the Grand Duchess. They're a little too large for my liking, a little too like claret glasses filled to the brim, but I've put them on because we shall be seeing the Grand Duchess this evening at Marie-Gilbert's," added Mme. de Guermantes, never suspecting that this assertion destroyed the force of those previously made by the Duke. "What's on at the Princess's?" inquired Swann. "Practically nothing," the Duke hastened to reply, the question having made him think that Swann was not invited. "What's that, Basin? When all the highways and hedgerows have been scoured? It will be a deathly crush. What will be pretty, though," she went on, looking wistfully at Swann, "if the storm I can feel in the air now doesn't break, will be those marvellous gardens. You know them, of course. I was there a month ago, at the time when the lilacs were in flower, you can't have any idea how lovely they were. And then the fountain, really, it's Versailles in Paris." "What sort of person is the Princess?" I asked. "Why, you know quite well, you've seen her here, she's as beautiful as the day, also rather an idiot. Very nice, in spite of all her Germanic high-and-mightiness, full of good nature and stupid mistakes." Swann was too subtle not to perceive that the Duchess, in this speech, was trying to shew the 'Guermantes wit,' and at no great cost to herself, for she was only serving up in a less perfect form an old saying of her own. Nevertheless, to prove to the Duchess that he appreciated her intention to be, and as though she had really succeeded in being, funny, he smiled with a slightly forced air, causing me by this particular form of insincerity the same feeling of awkwardness that used to disturb me long ago when I heard my parents discussing with M. Vinteuil the corruption of certain sections of society (when they knew very well that a corruption far greater sat enthroned at Montjouvain), Legrandin colouring his utterances for the benefit of fools, choosing delicate epithets which he knew perfectly well would not be understood by a rich or smart but illiterate public. "Come now, Oriane, what on earth are you saying?" broke in M. de Guermantes. "Marie a fool? Why, she has read everything, she's as musical as a fiddle." "But, my poor little Basin, you're as innocent as a new-born babe. As if one could not be all that, and rather an idiot as well. Idiot is too strong a word; no, she's in the clouds, she's Hesse-Darmstadt, Holy Roman Empire, and

wa-wa-wa. Her pronunciation alone makes me tired. But I quite admit
that she's a charming loony. Simply the idea of stepping down from her
German throne to go and marry, in the most middle-class way, a private
citizen. It is true that she chose him! Yes, it's quite true," she went on,
turning to me, "you don't know Gilbert. Let me give you an idea of him,
he took to his bed once because I had left a card on Mme. Carnot. . . .
But, my little Charles," said the Duchess, changing the conversation
she saw that the story of the card left on the Carnots appeared to irritate
M. de Guermantes, "you know, you've never sent me that photograph of
our Knights of Rhodes, whom I've learned to love through you, and I
am so anxious to make their acquaintance." The Duke meanwhile had not
taken his eyes from his wife's face. "Oriane, you might at least tell the
story properly and not cut out half. I ought to explain," he corrected,
addressing Swann, "that the British Ambassadress at that time, who was
a very worthy woman, but lived rather in the moon and was in the habit
of making up these odd combinations, conceived the distinctly quaint idea
of inviting us with the President and his wife. We were—Oriane herself
was rather surprised, especially as the Ambassadress knew quite enough
of the people we knew not to invite us, of all things, to so ill-assorted a
gathering. There was a Minister there who is a swindler, however I pass
over all that, we had not been warned in time, were caught in the trap,
and, I'm bound to admit, all these people behaved most civilly to us. Only,
once was enough. Mme. de Guermantes, who does not often do me the
honour of consulting me, felt it incumbent upon her to leave a card in the
course of the following week at the Elysée. Gilbert may perhaps have
gone rather far in regarding it as a stain upon our name. But it must not
be forgotten that, politics apart, M. Carnot, who for that matter filled his
post quite adequately, was the grandson of a member of the Revolutionary
Tribunal which caused the death of eleven of our people in a single day."
"In that case, Basin, why did you go every week to dine at Chantilly?
The Duc d'Aumale was just as much the grandson of a member of the
Revolutionary Tribunal, with this difference, that Carnot was a brave man
and Philippe Egalité a wretched scoundrel." "Excuse my interrupting you
to explain that I did send the photograph," said Swann. "I can't understand how it hasn't reached you." "It doesn't altogether surprise me," said
the Duchess, "my servants tell me only what they think fit. They probably
do not approve of the Order of Saint John." And she rang the bell. "You
know, Oriane, that when I used to go to Chantilly it was without enthusiasm." "Without enthusiasm, but with a nightshirt in a bag, in case the
Prince asked you to stay, which for that matter he very rarely did, being
a perfect cad like all the Orléans lot. Do you know who else are to be
dining at Mme. de Saint-Euverte's?" Mme. de Guermantes asked her
husband. "Besides the people you know already, she's asked at the last
moment King Theodosius's brother." At these tidings the Duchess's features breathed contentment and her speech boredom. "Oh, good heavens,
more princes!" "But that one is well-mannered and intelligent," Swann
suggested. "Not altogether, though," replied the Duchess, apparently seeking for words that would give more novelty to the thought expressed.

"Have you ever noticed with princes that the best-mannered among them are not really well-mannered? They must always have an opinion about everything. Then, as they have none of their own, they spend the first half of their lives asking us ours and the other half serving it up to us second-hand. They positively must be able to say that one piece has been well played and the next not so well. When there is no difference. Listen, this little Theodosius junior (I forget his name) asked me what one called an orchestral motif. I replied," said the Duchess, her eyes sparkling while a laugh broke from her beautiful red lips: " 'One calls it an orchestral motif.' I don't think he was any too well pleased, really. Oh, my dear Charles," she went on, "what a bore it can be, dining out. There are evenings when one would sooner die! It is true that dying may be perhaps just as great a bore, because we don't know what it's like." A servant appeared. It was the young lover who used to have trouble with the porter, until the Duchess, in her kindness of heart, brought about an apparent peace between them. "Am I to go up this evening to inquire for M. le Marquis d'Osmond?" he asked. "Most certainly not, nothing before to-morrow morning. In fact I don't want you to remain in the house to-night. The only thing that will happen will be that his footman, who knows you, will come to you with the latest report and send you out after us. Get off, go anywhere you like, have a woman, sleep out, but I don't want to see you here before to-morrow morning." An immense joy overflowed from the footman's face. He would at last be able to spend long hours with his lady-love, whom he had practically ceased to see ever since, after a final scene with the porter, the Duchess had considerately explained to him that it would be better, to avoid further conflicts, if he did not go out at all. He floated, at the thought of having an evening free at last, in a happiness which the Duchess saw and guessed its reason. She felt, so to speak, a tightening of the heart and an itching in all her limbs at the sight of this happiness which an amorous couple were snatching behind her back, concealing themselves from her, which left her irritated and jealous. "No, Basin, let him stay here; I say, he's not to stir out of the house." "But, Oriane, that's absurd, the house is crammed with servants, and you have the costumier's people coming as well at twelve to dress us for this show. There's absolutely nothing for him to do, and he's the only one who's a friend of Mama's footman; I would a thousand times rather get him right away from the house." "Listen, Basin, let me do what I want, I shall have a message for him to take in the evening, as it happens, I can't tell yet at what time. In any case you're not to go out of the house for a single instant, do you hear?" she said to the despairing footman. If there were continual quarrels, and if servants did not stay long with the Duchess, the person to whose charge this guerrilla warfare was to be laid was indeed irremovable, but it was not the porter; no doubt for the rougher tasks, for the martyrdoms that it was more tiring to inflict, for the quarrels which ended in blows, the Duchess entrusted the heavier instruments to him; but even then he played his part without the least suspicion that he had been cast for it. Like the household servants, he admired the Duchess for her kindness of heart; and footmen of little discernment who came back, after leaving her service, to visit Françoise used to say that the Duke's house would have been the finest 'place' in Paris if it had not been for the porter's lodge. The Duchess 'played' the lodge on them, just as at different times clericalism, freemasonry, the Jewish peril have been played on the public. Another footman came into the room. "Why have not they brought up the package that M. Swann sent here? And, by the way (you've heard, Charles, that Mama is seriously ill?), Jules went up to inquire for news of M. le Marquis d'Osmond: has he come back yet?" "He's just come this instant, M. le Duc. They're waiting from one moment to the next for M. le Marquis to pass away." "Ah! He's alive!" exclaimed the Duke with a sigh of relief. "That's all right, that's all right: sold again, Satan! While there's life there's hope," the Duke announced to us with a joyful air. "They've been talking about him as though he were dead and buried. In a week from now he'll be fitter than I am." "It's the Doctors who said that he wouldn't last out the evening. One of them wanted to call again during the night. The head one said it was no use. M. le Marquis would be dead by then; they've only kept him alive by injecting him with camphorated oil." "Hold your tongue, you damned fool," cried the Duke in a paroxysm of rage. "Who the devil asked you to say all that? You haven't understood a word of what they told you." "It wasn't me they told, it was Jules." "Will you hold your tongue!" roared the Duke, and, turning to Swann, "What a blessing he's still alive! He will regain his strength gradually, don't you know. Still alive, after being in such a critical state, that in itself is an excellent sign. One mustn't expect everything at once. It can't be at all unpleasant, a little injection of camphorated oil." He rubbed his hands. "He's alive; what more could anyone want? After going through all that he's gone through, it's a great step forward. Upon my word, I envy him having such a temperament. Ah! these invalids, you know, people do all sorts of little things for them that they don't do for us. Now to-day there was a devil of a cook who sent me up a leg of mutton with *béarnaise* sauce—it was done to a turn, I must admit, but just for that very reason I took so much of it that it's still lying on my stomach. However, that doesn't make people come to inquire for me as they do for dear Amanien. We do too much inquiring. It only tires him. We must let him have room to breathe. They're killing the poor fellow by sending round to him all the time." "Well," said the Duchess to the footman as he was leaving the room, "I gave orders for the envelope containing a photograph which M. Swann sent me to be brought up here." "Madame la Duchesse, it is so large that I didn't know if I could get it through the door. We have left it in the hall. Does Madame la Duchesse wish me to bring it up?" "Oh, in that case, no; they ought to have told me, but if it's so big I shall see it in a moment when I come downstairs." "I forgot to tell Mme. la Duchesse that Mme. la Comtesse Molé left a card this morning for Mme. la Duchesse." "What, this morning?" said the Duchess with an air of disapproval, feeling that so young a woman ought not to take the liberty of leaving cards in the morning. "About ten o'clock, Madame la Duchesse." "Shew me the cards." "In any case, Oriane, when you say that it was a funny idea on Marie's part to marry Gilbert," went on the Duke, reverting to the original topic of conversation, "it is you who have an odd way of writing history. If either of them was a fool, it was Gilbert, for having married of all people a woman so closely related to the King of the Belgians, who has usurped the name of Brabant which belongs to us. To put it briefly, we are of the same blood as the Hesses, and of the elder branch. It is always stupid to talk about oneself," he apologised to me, "but after all, whenever we have been not only at Darmstadt, but even at Cassel and all over Electoral Hesse, the Landgraves have always, all of them, been most courteous in giving us precedence as being of the elder branch." "But really, Basin, you don't mean to tell me that a person who was a Major in every regiment in her country, who had been engaged to the King of Sweden . . ." "Oriane, that is too much; anyone would think that you didn't know that the King of Sweden's grandfather was tilling the soil at Pau when we had been ruling the roost for nine hundred years throughout the whole of Europe." "That doesn't alter the fact that if somebody were to say in the street: 'Hallo, there's the King of Sweden,' everyone would at once rush to see him as far as the Place de la Concorde, and if he said: 'There's M. de Guermantes,' nobody would know who M. de Guermantes was." "What an argument!" "Besides, I never can understand how, once the title of Duke of Brabant has passed to the Belgian Royal Family, you can continue to claim it."

The footman returned with the Comtesse Molé's card, or rather what she had left in place of a card. Alleging that she had none on her, she had taken from her pocket a letter addressed to herself, and keeping the contents had handed in the envelope which bore the inscription: 'La Comtesse Molé.' As the envelope was rather large, following the fashion in notepaper which prevailed that year, this manuscript 'card' was almost twice the size of an ordinary visiting card. "That is what people call Mme. Molé's 'simplicity,' " said the Duchess ironically. "She wants to make us think that she had no cards on her, and to shew her originality. But we know all about that, don't we, my little Charles, we are quite old enough and quite original enough ourselves to see through the tricks of a little lady who has only been going about for four years. She is charming, but she doesn't seem to me, all the same, to be quite 'big' enough to imagine that she can take the world by surprise with so little effort as merely leaving an envelope instead of a card and leaving it at ten o'clock in the morning. Her old mother mouse will shew her that she knows a thing or two about that." Swann could not help smiling at the thought that the Duchess, who was, incidentally, a trifle jealous of Mme. Molé's success, would find it quite in accordance with the 'Guermantes wit' to make some impertinent retort to her visitor. "So far as the title of Duc de Brabant is concerned, I've told you a hundred times, Oriane . . ." the Duke continued, but the Duchess, without listening, cut him short. "But, my little Charles, I'm longing to see your photograph." "Ah! *Extinctor draconis latrator Anubis*," said Swann. "Yes, it was so charming what you said about that when you were comparing the Saint George at Venice. But I don't understand: why Anubis?" "What's the one like who was an ancestor of Babal?" asked M. de Guermantes. "You want to see his bauble?" retorted his wife, dryly, to

shew she herself scorned the pun. "I want to see them all," she added.
"Listen, Charles, let us wait downstairs till the carriage comes," said the
Duke; "you can pay your call on us in the hall, because my wife won't
let us have any peace until she's seen your photograph. I am less impatient, I must say," he added with a satisfied air. "I am not easily moved
myself, but she would see us all dead rather than miss it." "I am entirely
of your opinion, Basin," said the Duchess, "let us go into the hall; we shall
at least know why we have come down from your study, while we shall
never know how we have come down from the Counts of Brabant." "I've
told you a hundred times how the title came into the House of Hesse," said
the Duke (while we were going downstairs to look at the photograph, and I
thought of those that Swann used to bring me at Combray), "through
the marriage of a Brabant in 1241 with the daughter of the last Landgrave
of Thuringia and Hesse, so that really it is the title of Prince of Hesse that
came to the House of Brabant rather than that of Duke of Brabant to
the House of Hesse. You will remember that our battle-cry was that of the
Dukes of Brabant: 'Limbourg to her conqueror!' until we exchanged the
arms of Brabant for those of Guermantes, in which I think myself that we
were wrong, and the example of the Gramonts will not make me change my
opinion." "But," replied Mme. de Guermantes, "as it is the King of the
Belgians who is the conqueror . . . Besides the Belgian Crown Prince
calls himself Duc de Brabant." "But, my dear child, your argument will not
hold water for a moment. You know as well as I do that there are titles of
pretension which can perfectly well exist even if the territory is occupied
by usurpers. For instance, the King of Spain describes himself equally as
Duke of Brabant, claiming in virtue of a possession less ancient than ours,
but more ancient than that of the King of the Belgians. He calls himself
also Duke of Burgundy, King of the Indies Occidental and Oriental, and
Duke of Milan. Well, he is no more in possession of Burgundy, the Indies
or Brabant than I possess Brabant myself, or the Prince of Hesse either,
for that matter. The King of Spain likewise proclaims himself King of
Jerusalem, as does the Austrian Emperor, and Jerusalem belongs to neither
one nor the other." He stopped for a moment with an awkward feeling that
the mention of Jerusalem might have embarrassed Swann, in view of
'current events,' but only went on more rapidly: "What you said just now
might be said of anyone. We were at one time Dukes of Aumale, a duchy
that has passed as regularly to the House of France as Joinville and Chevreuse have to the House of Albert. We make no more claim to those titles
than to that of Marquis de Noirmoutiers, which was at one time ours, and
became perfectly regularly the appanage of the House of La Trémoïlle,
but because certain cessions are valid, it does not follow that they all are.
For instance," he went on, turning to me, "my sister-in-law's son bears the
title of Prince d'Agrigente, which comes to us from Joan the Mad, as that
of Prince de Tarente comes to the La Trémoïlles. Well, Napoleon went
and gave this title of Tarente to a soldier, who may have been admirable
in the ranks, but in doing so the Emperor was disposing of what belonged to him even less than Napoleon III when he created a Duc de
Montmorency, since Périgord had at least a mother who was a Mont-

morency, while the Tarente of Napoleon I had no more Tarente about him than Napoleon's wish that he should become so. That did not prevent Chaix d'Est-Ange, alluding to our uncle Condé, from asking the Procurer Impérial if he had picked up the title of Duc de Montmorency in the moat of Vincennes."

"Listen, Basin, I ask for nothing better than to follow you to the ditches of Vincennes, or even to Taranto. And that reminds me, Charles, of what I was going to say to you when you were telling me about your Saint George at Venice. We have an idea, Basin and I, of spending next spring in Italy and Sicily. If you were to come with us, just think what a difference it would make! I'm not thinking only of the pleasure of seeing you, but imagine, after all you've told me so often about the remains of the Norman Conquest and of ancient history, imagine what a trip like that would become if you came with us! I mean to say that even Basin—what am I saying, Gilbert—would benefit by it, because I feel that even his claims to the throne of Naples and all that sort of thing would interest me if they were explained by you in old romanesque churches in little villages perched on hills like primitive paintings. But now we're going to look at your photograph. Open the envelope," said the Duchess to a footman. "Please, Oriane, not this evening; you can look at it to-morrow," implored the Duke, who had already been making signs of alarm to me on seeing the huge size of the photograph. "But I like to look at it with Charles," said the Duchess, with a smile at once artificially concupiscent and psychologically subtle, for in her desire to be friendly to Swann she spoke of the pleasure which she would have in looking at the photograph as though it were the pleasure an invalid feels he would find in eating an orange, or as though she had managed to combine an escapade with her friends with giving information to a biographer as to some of her favourite pursuits. "All right, he will come again to see you, on purpose," declared the Duke, to whom his wife was obliged to yield. "You can spend three hours in front of it, if that amuses you," he added ironically. "But where are you going to stick a toy of those dimensions?" "Why, in my room, of course. I like to have it before my eyes." "Oh, just as you please; if it's in your room, probably I shall never see it," said the Duke, without thinking of the revelation he was thus blindly making of the negative character of his conjugal relations. "Very well, you will undo it with the greatest care," Mme. de Guermantes told the servant, multiplying her instructions out of politeness to Swann. "And see that you don't crumple the envelope, either." "So even the envelope has got to be respected!" the Duke murmured to me, raising his eyes to the ceiling. "But, Swann," he added, "I, who am only a poor married man and thoroughly prosaic, what I wonder at is how on earth you managed to find an envelope that size. Where did you pick it up?" "Oh, at the photographer's; they're always sending out things like that. But the man is a fool, for I see he's written on it 'The Duchesse de Guermantes,' without putting 'Madame.' " "I'll forgive him for that," said the Duchess carelessly; then, seeming to be struck by a sudden idea which enlivened her, checked a faint smile; but at once returning to Swann: "Well, you don't **say whether** you're coming to Italy with us?" "Madame,

I am really afraid that it will not be possible." "Indeed! Mme. de Montmorency is more fortunate. You went with her to Venice and Vicenza.
She told me that with you one saw things one would never see otherwise,
things no one had ever thought of mentioning before, that you shewed her
things she had never dreamed of, and that even in the well-known things
she had been able to appreciate details which without you she might have
passed by a dozen times without ever noticing. Obviously, she has been
more highly favoured than we are to be. . . . You will take the big envelope from M. Swann's photograph," she said to the servant, "and you
will hand it in, from me, this evening at half past ten at Mme. la Comtesse
Molé's." Swann laughed. "I should like to know, all the same," Mme. de
Guermantes asked him, "how, ten months before the time, you can tell
that a thing will be impossible." "My dear Duchess, I will tell you if you
insist upon it, but, first of all, you can see that I am very ill." "Yes, my
little Charles, I don't think you look at all well. I'm not pleased with your
colour, but I'm not asking you to come with me next week, I ask you to
come in ten months. In ten months one has time to get oneself cured, you
know." At this point a footman came in to say that the carriage was at the
door. "Come, Oriane, to horse," said the Duke, already pawing the ground
with impatience as though he were himself one of the horses that stood
waiting outside. "Very well, give me in one word the reason why you can't
come to Italy," the Duchess put it to Swann as she rose to say good-bye
to us. "But, my dear friend, it's because I shall then have been dead for
several months. According to the doctors I consulted last winter, the thing
I've got—which may, for that matter, carry me off at any moment—won't
in any case leave me more than three or four months to live, and even that
is a generous estimate," replied Swann with a smile, while the footman
opened the glazed door of the hall to let the Duchess out. "What's that
you say?" cried the Duchess, stopping for a moment on her way to the
carriage, and raising her fine eyes, their melancholy blue clouded by uncertainty. Placed for the first time in her life between two duties as incompatible as getting into her carriage to go out to dinner and shewing pity for
a man who was about to die, she could find nothing in the code of conventions that indicated the right line to follow, and, not knowing which to
choose, felt it better to make a show of not believing that the latter alternative need be seriously considered, so as to follow the first, which demanded of her at the moment less effort, and thought that the best way
of settling the conflict would be to deny that any existed. "You're joking,"
she said to Swann. "It would be a joke in charming taste," replied he
ironically. "I don't know why I am telling you this; I have never said a
word to you before about my illness. But as you asked me, and as now I
may die at any moment . . . But whatever I do I mustn't make you late;
you're dining out, remember," he added, because he knew that for other
people their own social obligations took precedence of the death of a
friend, and could put himself in her place by dint of his instinctive politeness. But that of the Duchess enabled her also to perceive in a vague way
that the dinner to which she was going must count for less to Swann than
his own death. And so, while continuing on her way towards the carriage,

she let her shoulders droop, saying: "Don't worry about our dinner. It's not of any importance!" But this put the Duke in a bad humour, who exclaimed: "Come, Oriane, don't stop there chattering like that and exchanging your jeremiads with Swann; you know very well that Mme. de Saint-Euverte insists on sitting down to table at eight o'clock sharp. We must know what you propose to do; the horses have been waiting for a good five minutes. I beg your pardon, Charles," he went on, turning to Swann, "but it's ten minutes to eight already. Oriane is always late, and it will take us more than five minutes to get to old Saint-Euverte's."

Mme. de Guermantes advanced resolutely towards the carriage and uttered a last farewell to Swann. "You know, we can talk about that another time; I don't believe a word you've been saying, but we must discuss it quietly. I expect they gave you a dreadful fright, come to luncheon, whatever day you like" (with Mme. de Guermantes things always resolved themselves into luncheons), "you will let me know your day and time," and, lifting her red skirt, she set her foot on the step. She was just getting into the carriage when, seeing this foot exposed, the Duke cried in a terrifying voice: "Oriane, what have you been thinking of, you wretch? You've kept on your black shoes! With a red dress! Go upstairs quick and put on red shoes, or rather," he said to the footman, "tell the lady's maid at once to bring down a pair of red shoes." "But, my dear," replied the Duchess gently, annoyed to see that Swann, who was leaving the house with me but had stood back to allow the carriage to pass out in front of us, could hear, "since we are late." "No, no, we have plenty of time. It is only ten to; it won't take us ten minutes to get to the Parc Monceau. And, after all, what would it matter? If we turned up at half past eight they'd have to wait for us, but you can't possibly go there in a red dress and black shoes. Besides, we shan't be the last, I can tell you; the Sassenages are coming, and you know they never arrive before twenty to nine." The Duchess went up to her room. "Well," said M. de Guermantes to Swann and myself, "we poor, down-trodden husbands, people laugh at us, but we are of some use all the same. But for me, Oriane would have been going out to dinner in black shoes." "It's not unbecoming," said Swann, "I noticed the black shoes and they didn't offend me in the least." "I don't say you're wrong," replied the Duke, "but it looks better to have them to match the dress. Besides, you needn't worry, she would no sooner have got there than she'd have noticed them, and I should have been obliged to come home and fetch the others. I should have had my dinner at nine o'clock. Good-bye, my children," he said, thrusting us gently from the door, "get away, before Oriane comes down again. It's not that she doesn't like seeing you both. On the contrary, she's too fond of your company. If she finds you still here she will start talking again, she is tired out already, she'll reach the dinner-table quite dead. Besides, I tell you frankly, I'm dying of hunger. I had a wretched luncheon this morning when I came from the train. There was the devil of a *béarnaise* sauce, I admit, but in spite of that I shan't be at all sorry, not at all sorry to sit down to dinner. Five minutes to eight! Oh, women, women! She'll give us both indigestion before to-morrow. She is not nearly as strong as people think." The Duke felt no compunction at speaking thus of his wife's ailments and his own to a dying man, for the former interested him more, appeared to him more important. And so it was simply from good breeding and good fellowship that, after politely shewing us out, he cried 'from off stage,' in a stentorian voice from the porch to Swann, who was already in the courtyard: "You, now, don't let yourself be taken in by the doctors' nonsense, damn them. They're donkeys. You're as strong as the Pont Neuf. You'll live to bury us all!"

MARCEL PROUST (1871–1922) was born and died in Paris. Educated at the Lycée Condorcet, he did one year's military service and briefly studied law and political science. Proust's charm and ambition gained him entrance to the *salons* of Parisian society—the setting that provides the background for *A la recherche du temps perdu*. After his mother's death in 1905 Proust, suffering from asthma, retreated from active social life and secluded himself in a cork-lined room in his Paris apartment. From 1910 on he was at work on *A la recherche du temps perdu*, publishing the first volume at his own expense in 1913. In 1920 the second volume won him the Prix Goncourt. Until his death in 1922 he continued writing and rewriting his monumental work.

VINTAGE BELLES—LETTRES

VINTAGE CRITICISM: LITERATURE, MUSIC, AND ART

VINTAGE FICTION, POETRY, AND PLAYS

VINTAGE POLITICAL SCIENCE AND SOCIAL CRITICISM

VINTAGE HISTORY—WORLD